Surrender

Surrender

Carmen Marcoux

ONE WAY PUBLISHING HOUSE
Saskatoon, Saskatchewan

Surrender
One Way Publishing House

©2006 by Carmen Marcoux

First Printing 2006

Published in Canada. Printed in the United States of America.
ISBN-13: 978-0-9732075-3-8
ISBN-10: 0-9732075-3-1

Cover art & design: Shawna Kunz

Cover painting: Gay Couture

Printing: RR Donnelley, Menasha, WI

All Scripture quotations are taken from
The Catholic Edition of the Revised Standard Version of the Bible,
copyright © 1965, 1966 by the Division of Christian Education
of the National Council of the Churches of Christ
in the United States of America.
Used by permission. All rights reserved.

The setting of this novel is Saskatoon, Saskatchewan. While Saskatoon is
a city located on the prairies in western Canada, the specific locations of
the city and the characters described within this novel are purely fictitious.
The religious order described within this novel is also a fictitious order. Any
similarities to real events or persons, either living or deceased, are entirely
coincidental.

Library and Archives Canada Cataloguing in Publication
Marcoux, Carmen, 1966-
Surrender / Carmen Marcoux.

ISBN-13: 978-0-9732075-3-8
ISBN-10: 0-9732075-3-1

I. Title.

PS8576.A6422S96 2007 C813'.6 C2006-906936-0

ONE WAY PUBLISHING HOUSE
Site 500 Box 17 R.R. #5
Saskatoon, Saskatchewan, S7K 3J8
1-800-705-7396
Website: www.courtshipnow.com

I dedicate this book to Mary,
the Mother of Our Lord and our Mother,
who modelled for all Christians what it means to
fully surrender to God's will when she said,
"Be it done unto me, according to Your Word."

To my husband and best friend, Jim,
and to our eight beautiful children,
Hannah, Rebekah, Mikaelah, Jacinta,
Matthew, Gemma, Benjamin, and Jacob,
thank you for sharing in this work and ministry
with your prayers, your many sacrifices, your love, and your lives.

ಶ್ರೀ

"Blessed are the pure in heart,
for they shall see God."
Matthew 5:8

"I can do all things in him who strengthens me."
Philippians 4: 13

"I came that they may have life,
and have it abundantly."
John 10:10

"Take delight in the Lord,
and he will give you the desires of your heart."
Psalm 37:4

"Behold, I am the handmaid of the Lord;
let it be to me according to your word."
Luke 1:38

"But seek first his kingdom and his righteousness,
and all these things shall be yours as well."
Matthew 6: 33

"Let no one despise your youth, but set the believers an example
in speech and conduct, in love, in faith, in purity."
1 Timothy 4:12

ಶ್ರೀ

ဆာ

"We know that in everything God works for good
with those who love him, who are called according to his purpose."
Romans 8:28

"For I know the plans I have for you, says the Lord,
plans for welfare and not for evil,
to give you a future and a hope."
Jeremiah 29:11

"But the fruit of the Spirit is love, joy, peace, patience, kindness,
goodness, faithfulness, gentleness, self-control;
against such there is no law."
Galatians 5: 22-23

"Do not be conformed to this world
but be transformed by the renewal of your mind
that you may prove what is the will of God,
what is good and acceptable and perfect."
Romans 12:2

"Love is patient and kind;
love is not jealous or boastful; it is not arrogant or rude.
Love does not insist on its own way; it is not irritable or resentful;
it does not rejoice at wrong; but rejoices in the right.
Love bears all things, believes all things,
hopes all things, endures all things.
Love never ends."
1 Corinthians 13: 4-8

ဆာ

Chapter 1

Music played softly in the old green Chevy Caprice, as two boys slouched lazily in the spacious tan-upholstered backseat. Tired from running around in the heat of noonday, they were listening to their mom and dad talking about church service. *Mass,* they called it. Kyle had never before been to Mass, at least as far as he could remember. At almost eight years old, a boy can remember only so much of life's experiences.

Kyle glanced over at his older brother, David. David was Kyle's hero. He was only two years older, but to Kyle, David was the coolest kid on planet earth. He could do anything as far as Kyle was concerned—at least anything that mattered.

He could throw a ball clear across the field in behind their house, past their dad's shop. Not only that, when David climbed the trees in their yard, he could jump from the branch of one tree onto the next all the length of their road. David always said that if there had been one more tree he could have made it into their bedroom window on the second floor of their farm house. And to beat all else, one time David skipped a stone seven times. It would have gone further, if their dugout had not been so small.

Nope, David had no deficiencies. He was Kyle's best friend and they did everything together. Kyle was never afraid to try and do anything when he was with David, at least not until today.

Kyle looked away from David and stared out again through his window. He watched the trees and houses go past—slower, then slower—until finally they came to a stop. He looked forward; there was a red light. As he turned to look back out his window he caught a glimpse of his mom smiling at his dad. He had no idea what they were talking about anymore; he had stopped listening. The little boy paused and fixed his gaze on his mom.

He loved her smile. Her dark eyes seemed to sparkle out past her olive-tanned skin. She had soft skin—the kind that made a seven-year-old just want to sneak a quick kiss after every hug. Kyle hardly even cared if he got caught.

The car pulled ahead slowly from the red light, and Kyle looked out the front window again. He had never been to this part of town before. There were so many trees that they seemed to make a tunnel for the car to drive through.

David kicked out his right foot to nudge Kyle on the leg. "What?" Kyle turned to look at David, who was staring back at him with a curious smile.

David had dark eyes just like their mom, but everything else about him looked like their dad. He was lighter coloured than Kyle. Kyle liked looking like his mom, and it only seemed right that if there were two kids in the family one should look like Dad and the other like Mom. He wondered what would have happened if there had been more kids, but there were just the two of them.

"See where we're going?" David whispered to his brother.

"I don't even know where we are." Kyle craned his head to look out all four directions from the car.

"We're going to *their* house. I heard Mom tell Dad we were invited for lunch." David's eyes sparkled, and his grin reached from one side of his face to the other without showing his teeth at all.

Kyle frantically looked out the car again to try to see where *their* house was. It would have to be a big house—of that he was certain—to hold all those kids. He had never before seen so many kids get into the same vehicle as they were piling into that van after church.

"Are we almost there, Mom?" Kyle asked as he strained his eyes to look for the old white van. He knew it had to be old because it had lots of rust on it. It was the kind of old looking vehicle people always brought to his dad's shop to fix. His dad could fix anything.

"Just about," she answered, without looking back. Then she turned and looked at the boys with a finger pointing from one to the other, as she laid down the law. "And you mind your manners once we get there. No hats on in the house, David. You can wear it outside, but don't forget where you set it down once you get inside."

David pulled his Montreal Canadiens ball cap off his head and examined it. It was getting dirty looking, but he would never get rid of that cap. It had been a gift for his birthday last year from Uncle Darryl who had been to a live Hab's game just that winter. Kyle watched his brother eye over the cap and place it proudly back on top of his mess of light brown curls.

He wished Uncle Darryl had thought to bring him a ball cap, too. Instead, he had received a Habitant T-shirt that was almost too small for him, and he had outgrown it by spring. Uncle Darryl had told him, "I guess I just remembered you to be smaller than you are, sport. But, hey, you're growing! That's a good sign. You've got a long ways to go to catch up to David, mind you. You'll just have to keep eatin' more green beans or somethin' to help you stretch out. They'll do that for you, you know."

Kyle looked down at his legs that just barely reached the floor of the car. He wished they would stretch faster. He ate green beans whenever he could, but he really did not think it was helping much. David just kept getting taller like Dad, and Kyle kept feeling smaller each day. But he had to have grown some—the hockey shirt did not fit him anymore.

"You keep an eye out for Kyle, David. I expect you to watch out for your younger brother and make sure he doesn't get left out again. You understand?" Mom was looking directly at David, who nodded his head as much as to say, "I know, I know!"

Once their mom had turned around, David whispered across the wide seat to Kyle, "If you just stand there with Mom again, I'm takin' off. So if you want to play with me, you'll have to keep up with me, 'cause I'm not waitin' around for you."

Kyle nodded back to David. David was giving him a second chance. Kyle was not sure why he had felt so afraid to go play after church. There had been so many kids taking off to go outside when church was done, and Kyle's feet just froze to the floor as he watched David run off with the rest of them. David had called back to Kyle twice. But in the end, he took off without him. It was Kyle's own fault, and he knew it.

Thankfully two girls came to his rescue—not that a seven-year-old boy wants to be rescued by girls. But with David now out of sight, Kyle realized he had made a big mistake in not following his brother's lead. When their moms introduced them, Kyle was embarrassed to find out the older sister, Maggie, was the same age as he, since he was notably shorter. Amie was two years younger and the same size as Kyle. After a few minutes of persuading, Kyle followed them out to the playground beside the church where the other kids had gone to play. David was way across the field with the other big kids by the time they got out there.

"Come on," Maggie urged him as she began running across the field, auburn pig-tails flying in the wind. Before he had a chance to answer, Amie grabbed his arm and started running. Forced to come along with the blond, curly-haired girl, Kyle gave in to the fun of it all. By the time they were part-way across the field, all three kids were racing. He might have been small for his age, but Kyle was fast. Maggie and Amie came running in behind Kyle, laughing and calling out to the other kids. These two girls had taken it upon themselves to make certain that Kyle was not left out of the play. And so he was not.

Now he was going to their house to play. "I like going to church," Kyle said to his mom.

His mom turned around and smiled at the little boy. "So do I."

"That's it!" Kyle called out, pointing up the street. "That's their van." He leaned forward as far as the seat belt would allow him to stretch, trying to get a better view.

Their dad pulled up and parked in front of the house. It *was* big, just as Kyle had thought it would be.

There on the front steps was Amie. She had been sitting and waiting for their new friends to arrive and was now running across the lawn to meet them. Maggie came running out from the front porch and waited with Amie as the boys got out of the vehicle.

"Sure hope you know how to climb trees," Maggie said, motioning for the boys to follow her. She took off toward the backyard, through the side gate. David followed without even thinking to wait for Kyle.

Amie looked at Kyle and waited a moment. He smiled back shyly at the pretty girl. "Come on," she said, grabbing his hand. "We've got the best tree fort—ever—in our backyard."

Kyle ran along with the little girl, eager to enjoy a day with his new friends from church. He was glad that David was not there to see him holding hands with a girl, or he would have had to let go. This way he could hold Amie's hand all the way there.

As Kyle allowed himself to be led through the side gate by the pretty girl with golden curls, he just knew that life would never be the same again.

✟　　　✟　　　✟

"Remember the first time we ever came here?" Kyle questioned his mother as he turned up the block approaching the Collins family's home.

"June twenty-fourth, 1984," she replied with exactitude.

"Yeah, I guess you do remember," he said, smiling across the front seat at her.

"Feast of St. John the Baptist," she reminded him, "which also happened to be the day our family returned to the Catholic Church. How could I forget that?"

Kyle chuckled. His mom had every feast day firmly fixed in her head. As he was growing up there had always been a reason to attend weekday Mass—it was one feast day or another. They were not quite daily communicants . . . but they certainly qualified for "frequent flyer" status.

"Yeah, I was just remembering driving up this street for the first time," he reminisced, still smiling. "You heard Joanie and Brandon are coming home tomorrow from their honeymoon," he added, matter-of-factly.

"Italy . . . Rome," she softly murmured.

"Apparently. That's what I've heard, anyway."

"I can't believe two weeks have passed since that wedding," she commented, almost to herself. "The most beautiful wedding I've ever attended. It makes a difference when a couple's lived out a chaste relationship."

"I agree . . . and I'm all for it, Mom," Kyle said, stating the obvious to her.

She chuckled at Kyle's assertion. Kathy Bander knew full-well that her sons were leading pure and chaste lives. It was a great consolation to her to never have to worry about their whereabouts, or what they were up to with their friends. They hung around with the nicest group of kids . . . actually, they were pretty well all young adults by now. They had all grown up together, friends from church.

Reaching across the seat, she straightened a piece of Kyle's wavy dark hair that hung loosely around his head in a tidy shag style. He grimaced at her motherly action and looked over at her from the corner of his gentle, dark eyes. She pulled away her hand and smiled meekly back at her twenty-one-year-old boy.

Kyle shook his head with a little laugh as he pulled into the driveway behind the fifteen passenger van, which left just enough room for his black Ford Escort.

Sighing, she asked, "I wonder where your father is?" She looked up and down the street for their old pickup truck. "He was supposed to meet us here for five-thirty." She glanced down at her watch. It was already quarter-to-six. She felt bad for being late and had hoped her husband would have made a better show of it than she had.

"Oh, he'll get here, Mom. Don't worry. The Collins aren't exactly the kind of people to get bent out of shape over being on time," he reminded her as he stepped out of the car to the ambush of two little boys.

"Arghghghghgh!" he bellowed out, suddenly turning on the would-be assassins who nearly jumped out of their skin. It was boy language. No need for words—just a few primordial cries and everyone was good to go. Nine-year-old Zack and six-year-old Aaron took off across the yard, with Kyle close on their heels. As they reached the side gate to the backyard, Kyle veered off toward the front porch and quickly made his way inside. He paused before walking into the old two-storey, turned back and waited for his mother who was coming up the walk. He held the porch door open for her, then knocked on the inside door.

"You know you don't need to knock around here," Amie scolded the young man as she opened the door to greet them. "Everyone just walks in. You're lucky if anyone would hear a knock with all the noise in this house," she added with a laugh.

"Hi, Amie," Kathy warmly greeted the young lady.

"Hi, Mrs. Bander." The friendly girl nodded with a smile. "Mom's in the kitchen—just go on in. Oh, here, I'll take that dessert for you."

"Oh, I'm fine. Thanks anyway, sweetie," she smiled, acknowledging Amie's kind gesture as she walked past and through to the kitchen at the back end of the big old house.

"So, how's it goin'?" Amie asked the young man, still standing in the front entry.

"Good. An' you?" Kyle nodded, making eye-contact with his hostess.

"Awesome!" She grabbed his arm and pulled him in. "You've gotta check out what Isaac's been up to," she enthused as she led him toward the backstairs to the basement.

Kyle just shook his head and chuckled to himself. In thirteen years, Amie had not changed in her approach with him . . . and all these years later, he still did not mind at all.

He looked at the graceful, almost-nineteen-year-old as she paused at the staircase. Her hair still fell over her shoulders in soft blond curls. The years had afforded Kyle a four-inch advantage on Amie for height. It had taken awhile, but the green beans had finally paid off!

"Isaac!" Amie shouted up the stairs. By this time she had let go of Kyle's arm. "Kyle's here. Hurry up and come on down to the music room."

"Okay," a voice faintly sounded from the distance.

Amie and Kyle headed on down ahead of the youth, who soon followed after them—feet pounding all the way down the stairs. By the time Amie and Kyle had reached the bottom step to the basement, Isaac came barrelling in upon them.

The dark-haired, dark-eyed thirteen-year-old pushed past them into the big room that contained a host of instruments, from an electric piano to a full drum set, with a couple violins hanging from hooks on a wall. There was a saggy couch against the back wall with a blanket thrown over the thirty-year outdated upholstery, and there were a few stools strategically located around the room next to guitars left out in their stands. The music room was a favourite spot in their home for the Collins kids to hang out with their friends. Kyle had spent many hours there over the years.

Setting himself up at the drum set, Isaac smiled at Amie with a look that said, "I'm ready."

Amie smiled with much enthusiasm at Kyle and sat down at the keyboard. Her bright blue eyes sparkled with delight as she announced, "We just came up with this today."

The young drummer counted them in and began his sequence. Amie came in at just the right time, and together the brother and sister duo entertained their guest with a jazzed-up rendition of "Oh, When the Saints" that went on for several unsung verses.

Kyle clapped, very impressed with the young drummer. Amie's playing was no surprise to him. Kyle had been playing in a Christian band, *New Spring*, with Amie for over four years now. Isaac was Kyle's aspiring drum student. The kid had talent—no shock there, given his family history. But being the fifth child in a family of eight kids, Kyle imagined that Isaac was not overly doted upon and that the young musician would appreciate the praise.

"Your turn," Isaac stated, tossing the sticks to Kyle.

Kyle dove for the sticks, missing one just before it hit the floor. He recovered it as he moved toward the drum set. His quick movements matched the lithe and athletic build he possessed as a drummer. "You're doing fine," the twenty-one-year-old teacher insisted. "Keep playing."

Isaac had already leapt from the drum stool and was pushing Kyle toward the set. Isaac was a bright student and a quick learner. His talent had come in part from his patient nature that allowed him to sit back quietly and learn, first through observation and then imitation. He took every opportunity he could to study Kyle, a master drummer.

Amie got up to leave the two boys at their "play" when Kyle interrupted her departure from the room. "And just where do you think you're going there, Miss Collins?" he called out playfully.

"I'm going up to help make supper."

"Get back here and sit at that keyboard," he directed her, pointing with his drumstick.

Amie gave in easily to the demand. The girl was passionate for music, and she loved to jam with band members. "Fine . . . but only one piece. I'm really supposed to be upstairs helping."

"Your pick." Kyle motioned to her with his head.

Amie grabbed some music from beside the keyboard. It was a new piece she wanted to have their band do. As she started to play, Kyle nodded and smiled. He could have guessed Amie would have chosen that song. She was completely predictable to him after all these years of friendship.

Waiting for the appropriate cue, Kyle came into the song with the skill of an experienced drummer. The young man simply felt the music. There was nothing calculated or mechanical in his playing. It flowed out of him as easily as his heart kept rhythm within.

Isaac sat back on the old couch, holding another set of sticks. He played along, inadvertently, on his legs.

"I'm out of here," Amie announced, as soon as the song ended. Heading out of the room she paused and looked back at Kyle, who was watching her as she left. "Thanks," she smiled and nodded.

Not quite sure for what she was thanking him, he replied, "You're welcome." He figured it was for taking time with Isaac, but it could have also been for jamming with her. Either way, both were his pleasure.

✠   ✠   ✠

Back in the kitchen Kyle's father, Kevin, had arrived. He was visiting at the big oak dining room table with Amie's dad, John. At six foot two and heavy set, John Collins had a notable presence in any room. His twenty-five years as a high school Phys Ed teacher had earned him the reputation as a tough guy. But among family and friends, he was known to be the friendly jokester that he was.

Kevin Bander was a man of slighter build. Long and thin, with short, wavy hair that was beginning to turn from light brown to silver at the temples, he had a quiet presence about him. He turned his glass around in his oil-stained hands as he listened attentively to John talking about this year's football team at Sacred Heart High School.

The moms were across the room busying themselves with supper preparations as they chatted away. The two dark-haired, dark-eyed women could have passed for sisters, with similar builds, though Kathy Bander had a darker complexion than Judy Collins.

Looking to see what needed to be done, Amie began to set out the plates and cutlery, buffet-style, for supper. Judy smiled at Amie, whose back was now to her. Though mother and daughter did not share any similarities in colouring or complexion, their facial features and warm smiles showed off their family resemblance.

"How many are we?" Amie asked, while counting out names on her fingers.

"We're eight, and the Banders are three," her mom answered, tearing up Romaine lettuce for the Caesar salad.

"Your family numbers are dropping quickly these days," Kathy noted to Judy, as she sliced cucumbers at the island.

"You're telling me!" exclaimed Judy. "First Joanie gets married two weeks ago, and before she can have a chance to get back from her honeymoon, Maggie moves out to live with the Sisters!"

"That caught us all by surprise," John piped in from across the room.

"But it's just Maggie's style." Judy shook her head. "She knew for two months that the Sisters had accepted to take her in this fall, and she didn't say a word to anyone, so as not to take attention away from Joanie and Brandon's wedding."

"She's quite a girl," Kathy chuckled, bringing to mind the twenty-one-year-old with reddish-brown hair. "It's not like anyone was shocked that she was going into religious life, though."

"No, we all saw it coming," John agreed. "But she announces her intentions to move out three days before she leaves. That was a bit hard to handle," he grumbled.

Judy was walking past the dinner table to get a salad bowl out from the buffet and hutch situated on the other side. She stopped behind her husband and wrapped her arms around his neck, giving him a quick hug. "John has a hard time letting his daughters go." She patted him on the shoulder and moved on as he shrugged off her teasing.

"Well, get used to it," Kevin advised. "With a household of beauties like you've got, I'm sure you won't be left with any one of them at home to worry about."

"At home I don't worry about them," John asserted. "It's making sure that they end up with decent guys that keeps me awake at night. I have a mind to pack up the last three girls and send them all off to the convent with Maggie . . . in due time," he added, for just then four-year-old Jessie came bounding into the kitchen and squirmed her way up on Daddy's knee. John snuggled the little auburn-haired, hazel-eyed girl in his big arms and gave her a kiss on the cheek. "At least this one will be sticking around for a while," he consoled himself.

"Oh, Dad." Amie shook her head as she took down a stack of plates from the cupboard, listening to his melodramatics from across the large open room.

"Don't you 'Oh, Dad,' me, little girl. I'm guessing you'll put more grey hairs on my head than all of the others put together," he stated, shaking a finger at her.

"Who, me?" Amie turned around and looked at her father in disbelief. She waved her hand at him and shook her head as she began to leave the room.

"Where're you going?" Judy called after her daughter.

"Upstairs to get Katie. I need some reinforcements down here!" she called back to her mom.

The four adults laughed.

✝   ✝   ✝

Upstairs in their big bedroom, Amie found Katie sitting on the floor, leaning against her bed, drawing. It was a typical pose for Katie, the resident family artist. Katie was musical and sang with the band, but her real passion was for art. The sixteen-year-old always had at least a few projects on the go.

Amie came in, sat on her bed and surveyed the room. Two extra beds, which had belonged to Joanie and Maggie, sat undisturbed in the silence of the room. Amie heaved an audible sigh thinking of her two older sisters so recently moved out.

Katie looked up at Amie. Sensing her sister wanted to talk, she laid down her pencil. "What's up?"

"Nothing, I guess." Amie shrugged off the heaviness of the moment. "What're you drawing?"

Katie turned the drawing board for her sister to see her latest project. "I don't have much time to finish it before they get home tomorrow."

"Katie, that's beautiful!" Amie exclaimed, jumping up from her bed. "It looks just like them!"

Katie handed a photo from Joanie and Brandon's wedding to Amie. "I'm changing the background," she explained, pointing to the shadowed-in image of the Blessed Virgin in her drawing, reaching out with her mantle above the newly weds.

"Ahhhhh! You are *so* talented. They're going to love this!"

"Thanks," the young artist humbly replied. She turned the drawing back around to give it an artist's critical look. Leaning her head to the side, her straight, brown hair hanging loosely over her shoulder, she stated, "I'm happy with it, I think."

"Oh, you make me crazy! What's *not* to be happy about?" Flipping her hands up, Amie's look betrayed her lack of comprehension of artists. "Anyway, I came up here to call you down for supper."

Setting the drawing on a music stand that Katie used as an art easel, the two girls went down to call in all the kids for supper.

✠   ✠   ✠

Isaac and Kyle came up from downstairs while the little boys, Zack and Aaron, ran in from outside and were shooed off to wash their hands in the bathroom. Isaac and Kyle washed up at the kitchen sink. Amie motioned for her friend to come over to where she and Katie were standing. She knew the little boys would have gladly monopolized all of Kyle's time and attention, but she figured he might appreciate a chance for more mature conversation over supper. The young man smiled as he came and took his place between the two young ladies.

After praying grace, the little children were ushered first through the line and set up to eat at the table. Kyle, Amie, Katie, and Isaac filled their plates and headed out on the back patio. It was a beautiful fall day, late in September. Trees were displaying their array of fall colours. The air was still warm from the day, but a light breeze was beginning to cool things off.

"So you've completed a week of classes," commented Amie to Kyle. "How's it going this year?"

"Awesome," he replied. "I'm really enjoying the classes on my schedule this term. We've moved from theory to practical, and that's what I like to do. I like the hands-on stuff—programming and problem solving and all that. It'll be a good term, I think."

"And then you'll be done your course?" Katie asked.

"Not until June. That's when we graduate, and hopefully I can get out there and find a job. I.T. jobs are on the rise right now, but you have to be good at it to get in. There's a lot of competition in the field. I have to keep my grades up, that's for sure."

"Oh, you're so smart," Amie piped in. "You could do well without even trying."

"I don't know about that. It's a lot of work. If I slacked off and got behind, I'd be hooped."

"Good thing you're not a slacker," Amie responded. "And it's great knowing someone who can solve our computer issues. I wish I were more computer literate. Right now I have to call Isaac to help me with everything. He's our computer expert around here."

"Thank you. Thank you," Isaac said, boastfully holding his hands up in the air and bowing forward over his plate of food.

Kyle laughed at the boy.

"Ultimate Frisbee tonight," Amie announced, interrupting her brother's display. "Who all's coming?"

"Which youth group?" Isaac asked, eagerly.

"Both intermediate and senior," she answered.

"Yes!" he exclaimed, pulling down his right fist. "Kyle, are you coming?"

Kyle looked at Amie. "You're the youth group leader. You want me there?"

"Hel-lo!" Amie replied with friendly sarcasm. "You're the one who makes it fun. I'm just there to open up the church and put out snacks at the end. You really should be paid, instead of me. You make it out to most youth groups anyway."

"I don't come for the money," Kyle replied. "I just like to help."

"Eat up," Isaac interjected. "We have to leave here in about twenty minutes to make it on time. Who's driving?"

"I'll drive," Kyle offered. "Mom and Dad have the truck here."

"Do you mind if I drive your car?" Katie asked timidly.

"You just got your licence a few weeks ago, didn't you?"

"Three and a half weeks ago, actually," Katie corrected, her bright blue eyes filled with eager anticipation.

"Yeah." He reached into his pocket and tossed the keys to the hopeful chauffeur.

Katie caught them, almost spilling her plate of food. Recovering from her clumsy moment, Katie smiled meekly and added, "Don't worry, Kyle, I'm a really good driver, even if I look like a total klutz here."

"I'm not worried," the young man replied with a chuckle.

The group ate up and made quick good-byes to the families as they passed through the kitchen and out the front door of the old house. Little ones chased out behind the older kids onto the front lawn to wave good-bye.

Katie ran around to the driver's door. Amie waited by the back door passenger side for the doors to be unlocked. As the locks clicked open, Kyle reached in front of Amie and opened the door for her.

"You're such a gentleman, Kyle," Amie said with a smile. "Why can't there be more guys like you?"

"Yeah," Katie agreed, as they all sat in and buckled up. "Take note, Isaac."

"Yeah, right," Isaac said. "That'll be the day when I open a door for a girl."

"Just you wait," Amie warned him

Kyle looked back at Isaac, seated behind the driver's seat, and offered a sympathetic laugh to the thirteen-year-old as the foursome drove off.

Chapter 2

There was an obvious silence over the room as a young woman quickly and quietly took her place at the dinner table. Fourteen religious Sisters watched the twenty-one-year old pull up her chair. Finally she dared to look up at the others. There was a pause—full of expectation—as Maggie wondered whether or not she should apologize for being late for supper, or if she should wait until she was addressed.

"It would seem prudent," Sr. Charlotte announced, "that when the dinner bell has rung we simply genuflect on our way past the chapel, rather than entering in for a time of prayer. Failing that, perhaps we might look for an alternate—less distracting—route to the dining room."

"I'm really sorry for having made everyone wait for me," Maggie humbly apologized. "I had no idea how long I was there in the chapel until I heard the second bell ring."

There was a snicker from one of the Sisters, then a postulant began to giggle, and soon the entire table of Sisters was in full laughter. Maggie looked around incredulously, and then realized that no one was truly upset with her.

"Let's pray," began Sr. Charlotte with a big smile on her face. "In the name of the Father, and of the Son, and of the Holy Spirit . . ."

A chorus of "Amen" rang out as all the Sisters joined in to pray grace.

It had been a week since Maggie had come to live with the Sisters of the Immaculate Conception. The week of transition had been a wonderful experience for the young woman. She was very at home with these friendly, fun-loving, joy-filled women.

She had felt called to this order from the time she was very young. A number of the Sisters came to their parish of St. James. Maggie had grown up with the Sisters teaching Sunday school classes, leading music ministry, and assisting with sacramental preparations. The fact that this order made an active presence in the community—in a number of parishes, schools, and on campus—is what helped to keep them attracting young women to religious life.

Maggie was one of two aspirants with the order this year. Kyra was a year younger than Maggie, from a small town an hour's drive from Saskatoon, and was much quieter than Maggie. Maggie realized it was going to take a while to get to know her companion. She hoped they would be able to really connect eventually. If they both discerned to continue with their vocations in religious life with this community, they would be spending much of their lives together.

The quiet, sandy-haired Kyra sat across the large oblong table from Maggie. She did not look up as Maggie sat down, nor did she join in with the teasing of the other Sisters as the latecomer continued her apologies after grace. "I really will work on my punctuality for mealtime. It wasn't exactly one of my family's strong points. It usually took several calls to gather us all in—which is a bad habit, I know."

"I remember being totally drawn to the chapel when I first came here," offered Kathleen, a postulant with the order. "It's just so amazing to live under the same roof as Jesus in the Blessed Sacrament."

"It's like a magnetic pull for me to spend every moment in this house with Him," Maggie confessed.

"I imagine growing up in a family of eight kids gets pretty noisy," added Sr. Chelsea, a novice. "I'm sure the chapel is a welcome place of retreat for you."

"I used to be afraid that I'd miss the noise and busyness of my family when I came to the convent. But it hasn't happened yet. I just get lost for hours in the silence," Maggie told them. "Mind you, being in a grade five classroom all day for my internship probably doesn't help. I'm all noised-out by the time I get back here at the end of each day."

"What about you, Kyra?" asked Sr. Charlotte. "Did you come from a noisy household?"

Kyra looked up at Sr. Charlotte and quietly answered, "No." She smiled softly as she looked back down at her plate and took a forkful of mashed potatoes.

"Your sister and you were about five years apart weren't you?" Sr. Charlotte continued to try to invite the quiet girl into their mealtime conversation.

"Mm-hmm," she nodded, glancing briefly at Sr. Charlotte, then across the table at Maggie before she cast her eyes back down to her plate.

Maggie smiled quickly, trying to catch Kyra's eye while she had the chance. Quietly she looked down at her own plate, which she had not yet touched, and began to eat.

Some of the other Sisters began talking about the upcoming day of discernment for college students. Typically they would get about eight girls who would come and spend a day at the house, listen to some of the Sisters' testimonies, and have the opportunity to ask questions about religious life. For most of the girls it would be their first time ever to cross the threshold of a convent. The Sisters of the Immaculate Conception worked hard at attempting to de-mystify the idea of religious life for the average person, and this was one very effective outreach.

In the midst of planning and discussions Kyra looked up and quietly added, "That's what first interested me in religious life, three years ago."

She had finished her meal by now and was sitting quietly with her hands folded on her lap under the table.

The entire table of women looked over as the timid aspirant volunteered into the conversation. She smiled with her lips closed while her eyes quickly glanced at the women seated around the table, letting them all know that's all she had to say for now.

Maggie's face lit up and she looked straight into Kyra's eyes before her comrade had a chance to turn her gaze downward. "I'm glad God called you at the same time as me to be here."

Kyra smiled meekly back at Maggie. "Me, too," she added quietly.

"I think the Lord knew you two needed each other for balance," Sr. Charlotte asserted. The giggles around the table concluded the assertion in the affirmative. "Never before have I seen two aspirants so different in personality at the same time," Sr. Charlotte added with a laugh as she brought her hand to her brow and shook her head almost in disbelief.

"Well, I for one am hoping that Kyra can teach me to like wearing skirts," Maggie added. "This dress code is just about killing me!"

The Sisters laughed heartily, each remembering the transition they had to make when they entered the convent. Though the aspirant does not take the habit when she comes to discern in the Sisters' home, she takes on the dress code of "skirts only". In this way the young woman can grow accustomed to one aspect of wearing a habit, without the visual pressure of already having made a commitment to religious life.

While Kyra seemed very comfortable in her feminine wardrobe, Maggie felt like a fish out of water. She had spent most of her life in blue jeans and sweats. Naturally athletic and very much the tomboy, Maggie would rather climb a tree than sit on a porch swing in a skirt. She would rather work on a car's transmission in her overalls—that she had left back home in her father's workshop—than get dressed up for a party.

What she was coming to realize is that skirts were not just for porch swings and parties. The Sisters did everything in their simple habit which was made up of a navy blue skirt that came down just inches above the ankle, a white blouse with full-length sleeves, and a navy blue vest or sweater to wear over top. Their veils were white and simple, coming about four inches past their shoulders at the back, and allowing their hair to show in front of their ears. They wore a double-sided medallion with the Sacred Heart of Jesus opposite the Immaculate Heart of Mary. The Sisters who were permanently professed in the order wore a plain wedding band on their ring finger, telling the world they were espoused to Christ.

"Don't worry, Maggie," the postulant, Kathleen, assured her. "I've been in skirts now for two years, and it does start to feel normal after a while.

I think the first time I scrubbed the floors in a skirt I realized that this was for real—so I just told myself to accept it and move on."

"That's it," interjected Sr. Charlotte, "Maggie and Kyra, you shall be on floor duty together, tonight after supper."

"Uh," Maggie felt herself wanting to protest but thought better of it. Instead she sat there nodding with her eyebrows raised as if to say, "I guess I asked for this."

Kyra's hint-of-a-smile did not reveal whether or not she was upset with Maggie for having been the cause of floor duty being imposed upon her. Maggie offered her an apologetic look, but refrained from saying a thing. Somehow she felt like a little kid who had just received a consequence for bad behaviour. She realized convent floors needed scrubbing, too, and it was not beneath her to have to do it. She just wished that Sr. Charlotte had not included Kyra in the equation.

Sr. Charlotte nodded to herself and invited the Sisters to move on now from supper. Evening prayers in the chapel would come soon enough, and everyone had plenty to do before then.

Maggie stood up from the table and took her plate, cup, and cutlery to the kitchen. She was on dishes that night. Deciding to make the most of her evening of chores, she began to sing a praise song as she walked back and forth from the kitchen to the dining room, clearing the table. Sr. Becky was also on dishes with her. Sr. Becky, a temporarily professed Sister, had been with the order for about eight years. She was a spunky woman, and Maggie had discovered earlier on that week that Sr. Becky could not resist singing and dancing around the kitchen if she had a partner in praise. Maggie egged on the Sister to move to the beat of the song as they tackled the big job ahead of them. The two women laughed and sang and goofed around for the next forty-five minutes until the last crumb had been swept up off the floor.

Floors, Maggie cringed inside. It was not that she resented doing them; it was just that she now had to go find Kyra to come join her. Kyra was not likely about to party-down while scrubbing floors like Sr. Becky would. Maggie still felt she needed to apologize to her fellow aspirant for having ruined her Saturday night with floor duty. *Maybe I can take her out for an iced cappuccino at Doug's Donuts when we're done,* she thought to herself. She shook her head as she walked up the stairs to the third floor where their rooms were. Kyra was not likely the type to be bought with a cold Italian beverage.

As Maggie reached the top floor of the eighty-year-old house on the narrow, oak staircase, she looked at the three doors before her. Dim evening light from the window over the staircase trickled into the landing, and Maggie reached over to the old-fashioned light switch and pushed the toggle up, throwing a bit more light on the situation. The forty-watt bulb in the antique light fixture that hung above the stairs did not offer much light, but it was enough to allow a person to find her way up the lonely staircase at night.

A small landing opened up at the top of the stairs giving access to the three rooms of the third floor. Kyra's room was on the left, and Maggie's was in the middle. A fairly large bathroom to the right was shared by both girls. Maggie loved the look of the old claw-foot tub that sat prominently in the open space of the bathroom, but she sorely missed taking showers.

Glancing at Kyra's bedroom door, Maggie was glad they did not have to share a room. She had shared a bedroom her whole life with three of her sisters and had completely cherished the memories of that time spent together; however, she knew that personality differences would probably drive both Kyra and her crazy, were they required to share close quarters.

She decided to step into her own room first for a few moments of solitude to collect her thoughts before she faced the task ahead of her. With a room just large enough to house a single bed, a small dresser, a desk with a chair, and a small walk-in closet, Maggie had settled in quite nicely to her new environment.

She lay on her bed and stared at the assortment of pictures she had put up around the room. Two large images, one of Our Lady of Guadalupe and the other of the Divine Mercy, were hung on the wall across from the foot of her bed, where she could easily meditate upon them in prayer. The other walls held a collection of pictures of her favourite saints. On the space above her desk she had a large framed picture of Pope John Paul II holding Mother Teresa's withered face in his fatherly hands as they gazed into each other's eyes. It was her favourite photo of these two great modern saints. She sighed, thinking about the recent death of Mother Teresa just the day before Joanie and Brandon's wedding. *Mother Teresa, pray for us!*

Sitting on her desk was a large framed picture of her family. Her gaze rested there as she lay in the silence and prayed for each of her family members. She missed them in a nostalgic way—but was not at all homesick. She was still revelling in her honeymoon excitement of finally having taken the direction for which she had longed her whole life: to become a Sister of the Immaculate Conception.

She turned to look at the image she had taped up of Mother Marie Angéline. Though Maggie had longed to be a part of this order since childhood, her attachment for the Sisters of the Immaculate Conception came only from her association with this dynamic group of Sisters. She really had known nothing of the order's origins until she arrived.

The order was originally founded in France in the mid-eighteen hundreds by Mother Marie Angéline, a humble woman who had stepped out of her life in an affluent family to serve the poor. The spirituality of this order was built around the Church's teaching of the Immaculate Conception of Mary. Jesus, from all time, had preserved His mother from the stain of original sin so that she could become the perfect vessel for bringing Him—the Word made flesh—into the world. Mary, in all humility, had opened herself to work with God's plan of salvation when she said, "Be it done unto me, according to Thy word." In that moment she had laid aside all her own hopes and dreams as a young girl so that God's will could be accomplished in her life.

The Sisters of the Immaculate Conception, in imitation of Mary, were to detach themselves from the world so that they might humbly open themselves to God's grace and joyfully bring Christ to the world around them.

"Bring Christ to all people, that He may be known and loved throughout the world," Maggie said aloud, as she read the inscription below the picture of Mother Marie Angéline.

As an aspirant in the community, Maggie was being given a time of discernment to see if this was the order and the spirituality to which she was being called in religious life. This time could take half a year or more. No pressure was ever placed on the aspirant to make a decision by a certain deadline. She and the order needed time to mutually discern if they were a good fit for each other. So far Maggie was convinced it was going to be a perfect match.

She glanced at the pile of books she had dropped on her desk when she arrived home from school Friday afternoon. The work of the internship in the grade five classroom at St. Theodore School was beginning to pile up on her. Maggie realized now she should have taken more time throughout the day to go through those intimidating curricula books. She was determined to keep her Sundays free of work, to really enjoy the Lord's Day as a day of rest. But she had not anticipated spending her Saturday evening scrubbing floors.

"Uh . . . floors," she moaned, rolling off her bed to go call Kyra. As she walked to her bedroom door the image of Mother Marie Angéline caught her eye. She could almost hear the old French Sister whispering to her, in an imagined French accent, "Bring Christ to all people, dat He may be known and loved t'roughout da world."

"I guess that means here and now, doesn't it?" she murmured. Suddenly Maggie was determined that if she and Kyra were going to have to tackle this daunting task, she was going to make a memory of it to share with this new companion.

Pulling the cases off her two pillows, she put one over her head to make a veil, like she had done a thousand times growing up with her sisters at home when they would pretend to be the children of Fatima, or Bernadette of Lourdes, or some other favourite peasant saint. Grabbing for a couple of safety pins from her drawer, Maggie pinned together the one pillow case under her hair at the back. She hung the other pillow case over her arm and left the room, quietly closing her door behind her.

She stepped in front of Kyra's bedroom door, knocked on it in a rhythmic manner, and in her best French accent called out, "Kyra, are you in d'ere?"

After a moment, Kyra opened the door and stared blankly at the girl before her wearing a pillow case on her head.

"'Ere you go," Maggie said, lifting the pillow case up to the young woman. "Dis is your veil." Waving her hands with eager invitation, she continued, "Come, we go wash da floors togeder now. It twill be so much fun, j-j-just like Bernadette of Lourdes or Jacinta and Lucia of Fatima. We will crawl about da floors togeder in our beautiful skirts and make dis place look *si beau*." For added effect she kissed her fingers in stereotypical French fashion.

Offering her companion her best smile, Maggie motioned for the dainty girl to turn as she bestowed upon her the veil of peasant Catholic girls. Kyra complied in her quiet way, with a look of disbelief on her face. It was obvious to Maggie that Kyra had never played Our Lady of Fatima or Our Lady of Lourdes growing up.

Maggie realized she had her work cut out for her if she were going to assimilate Kyra into her strange and wonderful outlook on life. With resolve to make this relationship work, on the only terms she knew as the second oldest child of a large family, Maggie took the lead. She grabbed Kyra by the arm and led her co-worker down the stairs to build a memory together.

Chapter 3

John and Judy Collins stood waiting in the Saskatoon airport for the honeymooners to get through customs. John glanced down at his watch. "Two-fifteen a.m.," he announced, somewhat impatiently. "That plane landed almost half an hour ago. What's taking so long? Brandon trying to smuggle drugs in from Italy or somethin'?"

"Just be patient," Judy said, patting him on the arm.

"You weren't up at four-thirty this morning," John reminded her.

"I have no sympathy for golf heroics," she quipped back.

"No, you wouldn't. But when I agreed to pick them up at the airport, their flight was supposed to have arrived at nine-forty-five p.m."

"They couldn't help that there were storms in the east. They had no control on the delay in flight. And I told you, you didn't have to come. I could have come up here with Amie."

"Yeah, nice dad, doesn't even stay awake long enough to come pick up his oldest daughter after her honeymoon. I don't think so, dear," he replied as he began to pace.

After a few more minutes Judy's voice was raised in excitement, "Here they . . . come!" The enthusiasm quickly dropped from her voice.

John turned around to see Joanie, looking as lovely as ever with her long, curly, dark hair pulled up in a ponytail, and a bright smile lighting up her dark eyes. "Hi, Daddy," she called out to him with a wave. "Mom, it's so good to see you," she greeted her mother with a hug.

Judy halfheartedly returned the hug, as both her and John's eyes were fixed on the man standing beside their daughter.

"What the hell happened to you, Brandon?" John asked point-blankly of his son-in-law. "Married life obviously hasn't agreed with you, son!"

There stood Brandon with two weeks of beard growth on his face, his sandy-brown hair was uncharacteristically tussled, and he was leaning on a cane with his right foot wrapped up in a large, black splint.

Joanie stood beside her husband with a sheepish smile on her face. "Apparently Brandon never shaves when he's on holidays," Joanie answered for her husband. "And the sprained ankle just happened two days ago. So up until then he wasn't looking like a broken down, old man."

"How'd it happen?" Judy asked, still looking at Brandon—disbelief now turning into sympathy.

"Go ahead," Brandon said to his wife, knowing she was itching to tell the story from her point-of-view.

"Well," Joanie began, with a curious smile, "we were trying to catch a taxi in Rome on Friday afternoon, to go to the Basilica of St. John Lateran, which we hadn't seen yet. We'd been doing a lot of walking, and we were tired."

Brandon looked at Joanie from the corner of his eye.

"Okay, *I* was tired," she clarified. "And you know how we were just traveling with backpacks so we could get around easily on foot . . . well, I had put my backpack down and was taking a break. Brandon saw a taxi coming, and," she paused and covered her mouth with her hand in an attempt to stifle her urge to laugh, "he tripped over my knapsack and went flying out onto the street." At that point she gave way to full laughter.

Brandon just rolled his eyes. "She's been laughing at me for the past two days now," he informed his in-laws.

"Sorry, dear," she said, wiping away some tears. "I must be tired or something, but that was the funniest thing I've ever seen. I mean in all the time I've known you, Brandon, I've never seen you do anything even remotely clumsy. You're always so suave and debonair, always in control and calm and collected . . ."

As she went on Brandon just stood there, nodding his head and making a talking motion with his free hand. "Yeah, yeah, yeah. Get back to the story."

"Okay, okay. So Brandon landed in front of the taxi. The taxi screeched to a halt. The driver jumped out—I think he thought he had hit Brandon or something. He was speaking about a mile a minute in Italian, and I had no idea what he was saying. Then he realized we spoke English, and his English was really quite good. So he told us, 'I take you to the hospital, no charge. We go now.' He picked up Brandon . . ."

"Hardly," Brandon protested. "The guy was about five-foot-six or something . . . barely as big as you." Brandon, standing at an impressive six-foot-three, was not about to let that one slip by.

"All right, dear," she corrected herself, "he *helped* Brandon up."

"I was sure I had broken my ankle—it hurt so badly. I couldn't put any weight on it at all," he recalled with a wince.

"Oh, and it swelled up like a balloon," Joanie added. "Anyway, we got into the taxi—or should I say, Brandon squeezed into the taxi back seat and hung his leg out through the front window." Again she held back laughter, covering her mouth at the memory of this image.

"You're supposed to elevate an injury like that," he defended himself. "And some of those taxis are so small, there's hardly head-room in them, let alone leg-room."

"Anyway," she went on, "it was amazing. The taxi driver was so nice. Once he found out where we had been trying to go, and he figured out we weren't just tourists but more like pilgrims, he just took us in under his wing."

"Apparently," Brandon interjected, "this guy works two jobs—driving taxis *and* taking pilgrims around to religious sites. He's really knowledgeable about the faith . . . a very devout Catholic himself."

"Mm-hmm," Joanie affirmed. "He has six kids who are now all grown, and his job is more like a vocation to evangelize. He helps teach tourists and pilgrims about the richness of the Church and Her teachings and our Catholic heritage. That's why his English is so good. In fact, I think he told us he speaks five languages."

"Not your typical taxi driver," Brandon added. "So after he took us up to the hospital, he told us he'd come back for us when we were done, and he gave us his name and phone number."

"Paolo," Joanie rolled the Italian name off her tongue. "Is that classic or what? Oh, and tell them about Paolo's gift for us, Brandon"

Brandon laughed. "Yeah, well, when Paolo came back to get us a few hours later from the hospital he handed me a scapular and told me that if I intended to make it a practice of throwing myself out in front of taxis, I should wear one of these."

John and Judy began laughing.

Joanie interjected, "Then Brandon pulled out his own scapular from under his shirt and said, 'I already do. Why do you think you stopped in time?' Well, did Paolo ever get a good laugh over that! He was hilarious, that guy. He gave us a couple of scapulars anyway, as keepsakes of our time in Rome. We just totally hit it off with the guy."

"In fact, he told us to call him on Saturday and that he would take us to *San Giovanni Laterano*," Brandon rolled the Italian name off in his newly acquired accent, glancing down at Joanie. "And then he promised he would get us to Saturday night Mass in time to still catch our plane out of Rome that night."

"Oh, good, you made it to Mass then," Judy remarked.

"Of course, Mom," Joanie laughed, shaking her head. "What do you think? We wouldn't miss Sunday Mass."

"I know," Judy replied. "But it's a mother's responsibility to make sure her children keep practising their faith."

John raised his eyebrows at his wife and then shook his head, winking at Joanie.

"Anyway, it was an awesome day," Joanie exclaimed. "The best tour we'd had of Rome. Paolo was so informative and nice . . ."

"And funny," Brandon added. "The three of us had a great time together."

"It was just a perfect day . . . aside from Brandon with his foot and cane and all."

"Yeah," John jumped in, "so what's with the cane?"

"It was way cheaper than buying crutches, and we decided it would make a better keepsake of our honeymoon," Joanie informed.

"That's right. When we're old and sitting on our porch swing together, I can still use this cane to boss Joanie around with," Brandon said, picking it up and tapping his wife across the back side with it.

"Funny," she said, giving him a gentle backhand to the stomach. "Anyway, we got on our plane Saturday night and had a great flight home, until we reached Toronto. Then the storms held us up there for four hours. And here we are. A little travel-weary, a little broken down," she added, pointing at Brandon with her thumb, "but very happy to be home again."

"Well, it's so good to have you both home, safe and sound," Judy acknowledged, as she gave Brandon a hug now, too, in greeting. "We brought your Pathfinder up, so you can just load your stuff into it and head on home, since it's so late."

"Not much to load," John observed. "Is this *it?*"

"We traveled lightly," Joanie bragged. "You'd have been proud of me, Dad—I hardly bought anything over there. Just a skirt for walking in and a hat . . ."

"And a pair of shoes, and a purse, and some earrings, and a thousand rosaries and medals," Brandon listed off on his fingers.

"All right," the young bride waved at him. "I couldn't resist the Italian leather, and the purse was very practical to hold all those gifts. And how was I supposed to go to Rome and France and Portugal and not come home with souvenirs for my family?"

"The purse weighs about a tonne," Brandon added. "That's why *she's* carrying it."

"My poor injured baby," Joanie teased, rubbing his shoulder with her hand.

"Well, I can see that marriage has settled solidly into your relationship," John observed. "Wife's full of sarcasm and spending all your hard-earned cash before it has a chance to get to know your wallet," he remarked to Brandon. "Did *you* get to buy anything?"

"Just a hat and a rosary," he answered.

"And a cane, and a splint . . ." Joanie recounted back to him on her fingers, while attempting to imitate Brandon's low voice. They all began to laugh.

"Come on," John said. "Let's get you two home before you hurt something else."

"You'll come for supper tomorrow?" Judy asked, in a telling sort of way.

"Sure, Mom, that sounds great. I'm not ready to start cooking for myself yet," Joanie answered. "And I can't wait to see everyone and tell them all about our trip."

The two couples walked out to the parking lot where a well-aged, beat-up, little Toyota Corolla sat next to Brandon and Joanie's unblemished SUV. "Can you tell which couple has been married for twenty-four years and which one is just starting out?" John asked, pointing to the two vehicles.

"Mm-hmm," Judy replied, matter-of-factly. "The old couple drives the old car."

"Someday," John promised his wife, waving a finger in the air, "that'll change."

"I'm not holding my breath," Judy responded. "Besides, I'm just as happy in our little beater. I never worry about whether or not it gets dinged up in the grocery store parking lots."

"I tell ya," John concluded, "poverty is freedom."

Joanie laughed and gave her mom and dad a hug as they said good-night. Brandon followed suit, thanking them for having stayed up so late to come get them from the airport. He carefully manoeuvred his way into the passenger side, as Joanie got into the driver's seat and started up the vehicle.

"All aboard," she called out. She waved one more time to her folks as they got into their own car.

"Home, James," Brandon instructed his chauffeur.

"That's *Madame* James to you, sir," she replied.

"No," he corrected her, "that's Madame Vaughn." He smiled at his beautiful, travel-weary bride, reaching out and holding her hand over the gearshift as she put the vehicle into reverse. He laid his head back against the headrest, closed his eyes, and whispered, "Let's go home."

The next evening, as the newlyweds pulled up in front of the old two-storey family home, half-a-dozen of Joanie's siblings streamed out into the front yard.

"Good to be back," Joanie said to Brandon, smiling at her family waiting to greet them. She hopped out of the driver's side and ran around for hugs. Little Jessie managed to squirm her way to the front of the pack and be the first in line. Joanie picked her up and twirled her around as this littlest sister hung on with great affection. Putting Jessie down, Joanie reached over to hug Aaron and Zack, who then turned to greet Brandon, as he slowly worked his way out of the vehicle with his crutches.

"Where's the cane?" the boys asked, disappointedly.

"Lost that earlier today," Brandon told them. "Canes work all right for traveling where I don't know anyone. But back home, I'll use crutches. Borrowed them from my buddy, Mark—he broke his leg a few years ago."

"That's okay," Zack decided. "Crutches are cool. Can I try them?"

"Wait 'til Brandon has a chance to get into the house," Katie scolded the eager nine-year-old. "And the crutches are going to be way too big for you, Zack."

"I know. I just want to try them."

"You bet, buddy," Brandon said, patting him on the head.

By this time Joanie had made her rounds with all the siblings. "Where's Maggie?"

"She moved out," Jessie said, sadly.

"What?" Joanie asked in disbelief.

"She's living with the Sisters," Aaron informed her.

"When'd this happen?" Joanie asked Amie.

"The weekend before last. She's been gone now for ten days," Amie answered.

"Anything else happen while we were gone?" Joanie asked, looking over at her husband.

"You get married, Amie? Isaac become a priest?" Brandon queried.

"I wish!" Amie replied.

"You want me to become a priest?" Isaac questioned his older sister.

Amie thwacked the back of his head, knocking his ball cap half-off, and rolled her eyes. *Boys!*

The group entered the house, with questions coming at the honeymooners from every direction. Brandon just shook his head and laughed. Somehow the two-week-long honeymoon had dulled his memory to life in the Collins household.

A big "Welcome Home" sign stretched across the frame of the door leading from the front porch to the house. Brandon had to duck to get under it.

He settled himself on a chair at the oak dining room table. Lifting his injured foot up onto another chair, he watched the commotion and hustle and bustle of this busy household that he had come to know and appreciate so much. The evidence that the home-school year had begun was seen in the piles of books and papers on the counters and a few new pictures and charts up on the walls since Brandon had last been in the house.

Joanie went over to the kitchen island to help her mother finish dinner preparations. The smell of barbecued meat came lofting in through the open window from the outside patio. It was late in the fall, and there was no telling how many more barbecue opportunities the season would afford.

John stepped in with a platter full of hamburgers and hotdogs ready to go. Judy pointed to the oven. "We're not ready yet in here—just set them in there to keep warm."

John complied and then turned around to greet his guests. "See you haven't found your razor yet, Brandon. But at least you found a comb today. That's an improvement."

Brandon smiled as Jessie climbed up on his knee to play with his beard. "I like your beard, Brandon," she stated in her little voice. "Don't shave it."

"I'll be shaving it before I go back to work on Wednesday," he told the little girl.

She stuck out her bottom lip and shook her head in disapproval as she continued to pull at the whiskers.

John walked over to the fridge patting Joanie on the shoulder on the way by, snagged two beers, and brought one over for Brandon. "No one offer our guest a drink, yet?"

"Neither him nor *I*," Joanie spoke up.

"Help yourself, dear, there're some cold ones in the fridge," her father answered.

"Hmph," Joanie responded, "I'm your guest now, *too*, Dad."

"You'll always be my daughter first," John protested. "Everything I have is yours—help yourself, Sweet Pea!"

"Fine," she retorted, "I just might take you up on that—then you'll be sorry." She walked over to the fridge and pulled out the juice jug. It was empty. Her point fell mute as she proceeded to replenish the juice supply for the family for supper. "Daughter first and *first* daughter . . . which means—not afraid to help out with the work," she grumbled, looking at her father.

John walked back across the room to kiss his eldest daughter on the cheek; it was his way of saying, "Thank you."

She kissed him back; it was her way of saying, "You're welcome."

He chuckled and changed the topic. "So, kids, tell us about Europe. What was it like?"

Brandon shook his head gently back and forth. "It was incredible. I mean, Europe was beautiful and all . . ."

"It was," Joanie jumped in. "The sights, the sounds . . . *the food!* And just to spend that time leisurely doing whatever we pleased every day, with no agenda, not having to answer to anyone else . . . it was *amazing!*" A dreamy look came over her eyes. "I'd go back in a heartbeat. There was so much to take in; we just barely touched the surface."

"You could spend a year there and never take it all in," Brandon pointed out. "So, we decided to focus mostly on some of the holy shrines. Let me tell you—we have so many riches in our Catholic faith. It just hits you right here," he said as he touched his chest.

"Where all did you go?" Judy inquired. "We just got one postcard from you, today. That one came from Lourdes."

"Postcards never come in order," Joanie said, finally having poured herself some juice. She walked over and sat beside Brandon at the table.

Brandon rearranged his seating position so Joanie could snuggle up close beside him. John watched with amusement as the newly weds cozied up together; he smiled at his daughter. Joanie lifted her glass of juice toward her father, and he saluted her back with his beer and a wink.

Brandon chuckled and continued to answer Judy's question. "We flew into Paris and took it nice and slow for the first few days, taking in some of the regular tourist sights."

"We stayed at a great bed and breakfast there," Joanie jumped in again. "Probably the nicest place we stayed the whole trip. It was very picturesque, with a beautiful view of the Seine River, which was just a block away. We went on a river cruise and strolled the beautiful cobblestone streets. . . . And even though there were people everywhere, we were just in our own little world." Joanie smiled as she held Brandon's hand, playing with his wedding band.

"The whole trip was like that," Brandon added. "Mind you, it's not hard to be in your own little world when you don't speak the language of the people. We discovered that my twelve years of Core French really paid off, though."

"I was useless with the little French I knew. You really should have taught us more French, Mom," the daughter said, looking across the room at her mother.

Judy smiled back and shrugged her shoulders. "Sorry, honey."

Joanie laughed. "That's okay. It gave Brandon a chance to impress me."

Brandon chuckled. "Well, getting back to Paris . . . while we were there the most impressive thing we saw was going to Rue de Bac to see the incorrupt body of St. Catherine Labouré." Brandon paused, his eyes searching in the distance. "I had read about it—even seen pictures—but it's something else when you're standing there looking down at the body of a woman who died in 1876."

"She's so beautiful," Joanie remarked. "Her body's just as fresh as the day she died. Her eyes are still so blue. She's encased now in glass, but they say her arms and legs are supple—just as if she were lying there asleep. And to think, this is the woman that Mary gave the miraculous medal to."

"Wow," Judy said, full of wonder. "I would just love to have the chance to go there and see her."

"Oh," Joanie remembered, "I brought back miraculous medals for everyone from there. Had them blessed, too." She hurried off to the front room to get her purse where she had kept all the little treasures from her trip.

"Nice purse," commented Katie. She left her post of slicing tomatoes for supper, wiped her hands on a hand towel, and walked up to Joanie. "Just feel that leather," she said, running her fingers over the smooth leather bag.

"I know." Joanie smiled, confessing, "This was my one major indulgence on our trip. I bought it at a little street shop in Florence."

"Oh, I'm so jealous," the younger sister—the artist of the family— whined. "I'd love to go to Florence, home of Michelangelo."

"*You'd* have loved it for all the art . . . and the food," Joanie emphasized, holding two thumbs up at her sister and smiling. "But to be honest with you—I was overwhelmed by the crowdedness there. I think you'd have to plan a longer visit, just to Florence, to be able to take it in nice and slowly. We only stayed there two days and one night and then moved on to Perugia, and then to Assisi."

"You two really got around, didn't you? I don't remember wanting to be that busy on our honeymoon," John teased, with a wink at his wife across the room.

Joanie rolled her eyes at her father and chose not to respond. Brandon chuckled and let it go by as well.

"So from there, where'd you go?" Amie jumped in, not at all anxious for anyone to take up her father's direction of conversation.

"From Assisi we worked our way to Lanciano," Brandon replied.

"What's special about Lanciano?" Amie inquired.

"The Miracle of the Eucharist at Lanciano?" Joanie tried to trigger her sister's memory. Amie looked blankly at her. "You remember—the one where the host turned to real flesh, and the wine turned to real blood."

"Hey, that happens at every Mass," their father corrected Joanie.

"I know, Daddy," she said, sounding slightly exasperated. "But don't you remember the story. Back in the eighth century this Basilian monk had doubted in the real presence of Jesus in the Eucharist. He had just finished the prayers of consecration when he discovered the host had been changed into real flesh and the wine into blood."

"Yeah," her dad said with a quiet laugh. "I was just teasing you, Sweet Pea."

"So, did you actually get to see the Miracle?" Judy asked.

"When you go into the Eucharistic sanctuary there are two tabernacles above the altar. The first is to serve the daily needs of the faithful. The one above is for the Eucharistic Miracle, and you can get to it by a staircase at the back of the altar," Joanie began to explain.

"But I agree with you," Brandon spoke up, looking at John.

"You agree with *what?*" Joanie asked, confused by her husband who apparently had fallen out of touch with the conversation.

"About the daily miracle of the Eucharist," Brandon answered. "How often do Catholics just take for granted that the Eucharist is really the body and blood of Jesus—*truly* present?"

"Yup," John nodded.

"I mean there we stood, gazing at this miracle in Lanciano. It was something to see. The flesh and blood have remained intact for *twelve hundred years*. That in itself is a marvel to science. But in the seventies and eighties when they allowed scientists to take samples of the flesh from the host and the blood, which had coagulated into five globules in the chalice, they discovered . . ." Brandon held out his hand and began listing off the scientific evidence of this great Eucharistic Miracle. "The flesh is real flesh. The blood is real blood and is blood-type AB. . . ."

"Which is the same blood-type uncovered in the Shroud of Turin," Joanie interjected.

"Uh-huh," Brandon nodded, continuing with his litany of scientific proof with mounting enthusiasm. "Plus, both the flesh and blood belong to the human species. The flesh is actually heart tissue, and the blood held the same proportions of protein as fresh blood." He paused to give his listeners a chance to absorb it all. "I mean, here's God giving us this miracle to point us toward the reality of each Mass, and yet, how many people have never even heard of this? How many Catholics have no idea?" He shook his head in bewilderment. "I've only been a Catholic now for about six months, and I keep running into Catholics who don't believe in the real presence of Christ in the Eucharist, or they just don't seem to care or be moved by it. Why doesn't anyone ever tell them about this stuff?"

"Why don't you?" Judy suggested.

"Why don't I *what?*" Brandon asked, somewhat cautiously. He could see the dark eyes of his mother-in-law sparkling with that same look his wife's own dark eyes would get when she thought she had a good idea.

"Why don't you start sharing your testimony of faith, your conversion, your experiences? You'd be surprised how many people would be moved by your story," she threw the idea out at him.

"She's got a point, Brandon," Joanie concurred.

"You've got one of those 'from playboy to choirboy' backgrounds that everyone loves to hear about," Judy added.

Brandon winced slightly and looked up at his mother-in-law through his clear blue eyes.

She walked up beside the young man, set her hand on his shoulder and smiled gently down at him. She would never hold his past against him, but she was not likely to pretend it did not exist. "Make the most of it, Brandon. Let God use your past to bring souls to Him." She patted his shoulder gently and then announced, "Supper's been ready for a long time now. Anyone hungry?"

"Starved," said Brandon.

"Me, too," piped in Isaac, who had been sitting across from Brandon, with his head lying on his folded arms on the table. He lifted his head and looked around to the island, all set out with food in buffet style. The sight of the food was beginning to animate his teenage body. He sat up straight and looked around to see if anyone else was going to make a move toward supper.

"Katie, go call the little kids," Judy instructed the sixteen-year-old. "I think they're upstairs. We lost them sometime after Lourdes," she said with a little laugh.

As the family gathered around to say grace, John thanked God for the safe return of the travelers and prayed for blessings on their marriage and on all the family, remembering Maggie in a special way.

Joanie sighed at the thought of her sister no longer being at home. Change can sometimes come swiftly in a family. The unfolding of dreams was exciting . . . but it always involved letting go of something else.

Chapter 4

"We missed you at supper the other night," Amie said to David as she entered the basement of the Bander's house for band practice. *New Spring* had been holding rehearsals down there for a few years. It was the best location they could find. Being situated out of town, there were no neighbours to complain about the noise. Mrs. Bander was never bothered by it. She would often come down and listen to the group. And Mr. Bander usually headed out to the shop to work on vehicles, as he was the type to enjoy silence. A purring motor was music to his ears.

Almost everyone had arrived, and people were still tuning up instruments in the large open room. David was lying back on one of the blue leather sofas of the corner sectional at the far end of the room with his bass guitar lying across his body. He sat up as he replied to Amie, "Missed me for what?"

"We had supper at the Collins' on Saturday night, Mom, Dad, and I," Kyle answered his brother.

"Oh, sorry about that," David replied to Amie who had sat down at the electric keyboard set up in the middle of the room. The other band members sat around on stools and benches, and the drum set was situated behind the keyboard. "I was . . . at Leanne's house for supper that night." David had a shy smile on his face as he looked down at his instrument.

"I know you were," said Amie. "I was just teasing you, David."

"Soooo," Katie piped in, "how long have you been seeing her?" The girls of the band, by this point had all tuned in to the conversation. Ann and Jocelyn Ledoux, cousins of the Collins, had just walked in and were keenly interested in the burgeoning romance in their midst. The other guys from the band, Daniel Schultz, a friend who played guitar, John Delainey, a friend who ran their sound system for them, and Caleb Ledoux, a red-headed cousin from another Ledoux family, stopped their own conversation to catch the latest.

David sat up and looked around, realizing he was now centre-stage. "I met her when I started work at the engineering firm two months ago, but . . . I just finally got up the nerve to ask her out last week."

"What does she look like?" asked Ann, eighteen years old and eager to get all the details.

"Dark hair, green eyes. I don't know how to describe her. She's . . . she's really pretty." David nodded his head as he thought about her.

"Catholic?" Caleb asked, each person trying to pull out whatever information they could get.

"Actually," David answered, "she *is*. She goes to St. Mary Magdalene's."

"How old is she?" John Delainey asked.

"She's twenty-four," David answered, anticipating the reaction.

"Oooooooo," the guys jumped in right away. "An older woman!"

"You are the man!" stated Daniel with an approving nod.

"Is she an engineer, too?" Katie inquired. No one really knew how much information they would get out of David.

"Nope," David replied. "She's a receptionist at the office, and she's really sweet, and there's no way I'm bringing her around here to meet the lot of you . . . so don't even ask!"

"Ahhh. Come on, David, we'll be good," pleaded Amie. "We wouldn't do anything to embarrass you."

"Yeah, right!" he exclaimed. "Nope. If it lasts long enough to amount to anything, and I'm sure she's interested in me enough to not be scared off by this crowd, I'll bring her around. Otherwise, if it's not going to go anywhere, there's no point. And I'd like to give it a fair chance, if you people don't mind."

Amie made a tsking sound with her tongue against the roof of her mouth and shook her head with an impish smile. "Oh, David, I just think it's so sweet to see you all twitter-pated."

He smiled at the girl seated at the electric keyboard.

"Oh, yeah," agreed Kyle, finally joining in the conversation, sounding a little disgruntled, "just like Bambi."

"I'm surprised," stated Ann, turning to David. "You seem more like the Thumper-type," she assessed the almost twenty-three-year-old, light-haired, engineer-by-day, bass-player-by-night.

"Bambi, Thumper," Kyle shrugged it off. "All I know is that a girl can come in and ruin a perfectly good brother!"

"Ahhh," Amie sighed with mock-sympathy for the younger brother. "Maybe it's time for you, Kyle, to find yourself a girl. Then you'll be even, and it won't bother you so much."

"Not ready," he replied, point-blankly, "and not interested right now either."

"You always say that," the pianist retorted, "but you're twenty-one years old. I think you're old enough to be dating by now. I mean . . . I'm warning you, Kyle—you're gonna miss the boat."

"Not worried about that at all. Besides, I thought your family was all about courtship, Amie Collins," Kyle reminded the young lady. "And you were always so big on courtship yourself . . . so why are you so keen on me dating?"

"I'm not keen on you dating. When I say 'dating', I don't mean *'dating'* dating. I just mean, going out with a girl from time to time. You're certainly old enough to start looking around at your options," she pointed out to him.

"I've still got a year to finish at school, and I don't need any girl distracting me. And I'm not ready to get married right now, anyway, so why would I start looking?"

"Because I've got all these girlfriends just dying to go out with you, but by the time you're ready to start courting, they'll all be taken or will have completely lost interest!"

"I don't need a bunch of girls interested in me," he returned. "I'll only need one, when the time is right. When I'm ready to get married I trust God will send the right girl at the right time. And if all goes well, we'll court and get married, and that'll be the end of it. Until then, I'll take my chances on missing out. Who knows, maybe I'm not even called to marriage. I'd never have a chance to find out what God's calling me to, if I kept up with all the dating you had in mind for me."

"You're so exasperating. Such a good catch and so doggone stubborn. And all these friends bugging me because they know you're like a brother to me. But I tell you, Kyle," she warned with a finger waving at the drummer, "I've got a mind to just let you get stuck in your singleness. Then you'll come crying to me someday, begging for help!"

"Please! I give you complete permission to leave me to my own miserable fate." He took up his drum sticks and played a quick drumbeat to punctuate his request.

Amie placed her hands on the keyboard and, without taking her eyes off Kyle, played a quick cadence in reply to the drummer, sticking her nose up in the air in her own friendly way.

"Oh, you two!" Ann scolded. She was a few months younger than Amie and had been a close friend as well as a cousin. They had both home-schooled and had been involved together in music through church choir and *New Spring* for years. She was a few inches shorter than Amie, with very soft facial features that made her seem younger than her age. They did not look much alike, but as far as cousins went, they were inseparable. "Anyway, this is a good chance for me to remind everyone . . ." Ann paused and looked over at Amie.

Amie tilted her head and threw a look at her cousin, anticipating what was coming next. Ann smiled back and began singing "Happy Birthday". The other band members suddenly sat up and joined in with the song. Amie smiled at everyone and thanked them.

"Nineteen today," Katie announced. "And don't worry, Amie, we hadn't all forgotten your birthday. We even have a cake for you upstairs for after practice."

"Thanks," Amie said again to the group.

"But Kyle made it—so don't expect it to be any good," David warned.

"Very funny," Kyle replied.

Amie turned and looked at the drummer. "Thanks, Kyle. I guess I should apologize for being so rough on you, after you've been so nice to me."

"I wouldn't expect you to be anything but you, Amie," he told her, "teasing and all. No apology needed."

The birthday girl smiled back at her friend with a little laugh.

"I guess we'll have to worry about you hanging out at bars from now on," teased the tall and lanky Daniel Schultz.

"Yeah, right!" retorted Amie. "That'll be the day."

"So, any words of wisdom for us?" Jocelyn asked her older cousin.

"Yeah, we'd better start practice now, before someone takes off on another tangent," stated Amie.

Everyone laughed. They all knew they were bad for getting distracted at practices and wasting their time talking.

Ann took the cue and looked around, her short auburn hair flipping from side to side. "Aren't the honeymooners coming?"

"Not likely," said Amie, "they're still suffering from jet lag and Brandon can't move around very well yet on that sprained ankle."

"So, naturally Caleb's going to play lead guitar for now then . . . right?" questioned twenty-year-old Daniel Schultz. He had begun playing acoustic guitar with the band partway through last year—mentored by Brandon. He was a shy performer, happy enough to have the chance to play as long as someone else took lead. His real contribution to the band had always been his ease at harmonizing and his great personality. They all loved having Daniel around, and he loved hanging out with these friends, but he certainly had no intention of playing lead.

"Why should I?" asked Caleb. "You're a great guitar player, Daniel. I can't believe how much you've learned in just a year. I thought I was going to play electric guitar for some of the songs and play the djembe on others," the sixteen-year-old versatile musician responded. Caleb had a natural gift for music. Rather than mastering any one instrument, he dabbled on many; however, Caleb's ability to dabble always seemed to produce a high level of proficiency. "Anyway, Brandon'll be back eventually, and I only brought my electric guitar and djembe for tonight. So, you're on, Daniel—like it or not."

Daniel made a face that showed he was not at all thrilled with the sudden promotion. He did not grumble, though. He simply took his place and shook his head as if to warn the rest of them to keep their expectations low.

Ann watched Daniel move over to Brandon's stool and laughed at his awkwardness. Continuing down the roster of band members, she mentioned, "You all know Leah isn't coming back either. She's gone now for a year with Youth Ministry Network. She left the day after Joanie and Brandon's wedding."

"And I see we've lost Maggie now, too," John Delainey remarked. Seventeen years old, with light brown hair and glasses, John was a friend from church who had joined the group last year as a singer and was now taking over as soundman. John was more into electronics than music anyway. He looked around the group, concluding his observation. "That means both our violinists are gone—Maggie and Leah."

"That's a big loss," Amie commented. "But Maggie's decided that she needs to focus her attention on her internship and discerning her call to religious life at the Sisters. . . . I can't believe how much our group has shrunk in size over just one summer. Even Mike's gone now, too," she remarked sadly, looking at his sisters, Ann and Jocelyn.

"Yup," spoke out sixteen-year-old Jocelyn. "Mike got a job in Calgary, and he moved out just last week. It's going to seem so weird to have him gone from the group. It's really lonely without him at home, too."

"And Ben's gone into the seminary," Caleb added, with regards to his older brother who had made room in the band for Brandon when he had left it temporarily a year ago. "So he won't be coming back now for sure."

"After he left the band last year to go be in a movie, we didn't expect he'd ever be back," commented David. "But none of us expected him to go into the sem." He sat, nodding his head approvingly. "He'll make an awesome priest, though. I can just see him up there giving homilies with his guitar in one hand and a Bible in the other. What a guy." They all laughed, thinking about the crazy antics of Ben Ledoux.

There was a silence in the group as everyone looked around. They had gone from fifteen members in the spring, to nine now at their first band practice of the new season.

"Well," David took the lead, as the oldest band member present, "let's start with a prayer and get this show on the road. We've got a praise night to play at in two weeks, and who knows what we sound like now."

"We'll sound amazing," threw in Amie, full of optimism. "We're here to serve the Lord with our talents, and He's not going to abandon us to failure. Let's just give it our best."

There was mutual agreement with the birthday girl's assertion. A great deal of musical talent was still standing in that room. *New Spring* had gone through several changes of band members over the years, but when drawing its members primarily from large families, there was always a younger sibling to take the place of an older one who had moved on.

As a praise and worship band, their repertoire grew from an ever-growing collection of songs they all loved by contemporary Christian bands. Over the past few years they had also begun writing their own music. They were all committed to the ministry and to the friendships and bonds they had formed over the years of working closely together.

After a few minutes of prayer, they settled down to work for another year of fun and faithful service—two key ingredients to making any youth ministry a success.

Joanie and Brandon walked into their apartment Friday evening after work. The young bride carried a couple bags of groceries into the kitchen while Brandon made his way to an easy chair and kicked up the footrest to elevate his foot. He laid the crutches down beside the chair and reached for the remote control on the stand to turn on the stereo system across the tidy little living room. A Christian CD came on, and Brandon closed his eyes to listen. The throbbing pain in his foot, from overusing it the past few days at work, was quite fatiguing.

Joanie bustled around the kitchen putting away groceries and beginning supper preparations. She sang along with the music coming in from the living room. She loved being married. She loved taking care of her own little home and her injured husband. She loved the serenity of her new life with Brandon.

It had not been easy getting back into the routines of work at the newsroom. Shelly Lesichyn, her senior producer, had allowed Joanie a few days grace before she had to produce a report. Having been out of the country for over two weeks, Joanie felt too out-of-touch to report on any of the local news, so she had spent the last three days getting caught up. Monday morning, though, would find her back in full journalistic mode for the station.

She liked working at the local branch of CNB, Canadian Network Broadcasting, in Saskatoon. If it had not been for taking that job she would never have met Brandon—the over-confident commercial producer that he was. Her mind drifted back to their first meetings at the station, her anxiety over this womanizer who had been making moves on her, and her eventual confusion over her growing attraction to this totally unsuitable man. She now found it hard to remember just what kind of man he had been when they first met.

She glanced out through the kitchen doorway to the living room. She could see Brandon lying back in the chair; it looked as though he had fallen asleep. She smiled at this wonderful man that God had blessed her to marry. Sighing, as she turned to chop onions for supper, she thanked God for having formed Brandon into the devout Christian man that he was today.

You do amazing work, Jesus! Mind you, if You can make everything out of nothing, You certainly are capable of making a real man out of an arrogant, womanizing hedonist. She laughed over her description of the man who had existed before Brandon's conversion. *Thanks, Lord, You really did outdo Yourself—for me!* She peeked out again at Brandon as she carried the onions to the frying pan to sauté them. *Yup,* he definitely was asleep. She could see his stomach rising and falling at a slow rhythmic pace. *Thanks, again!* She said, casting her eyes heavenward.

She began singing out loud, her clear voice filling the kitchen with praise. Life was good, indeed.

Brandon woke up about half an hour later to the movement of his chair, as Joanie came and cuddled up on his knee. She tucked one arm in behind the small of his back, and with the other hand she reached up around his neck and ran her fingers through his hair. His eyes remained closed, but a smile snuck up on his lips. Joanie pulled her head up closer to his face and kissed him softly. Pulling her in even closer with his strong arms, Brandon opened his eyes, smiled, and then closed them again as he proceeded to kiss his bride.

"You can wake me up like this anytime," he advised her after a minute or so had passed.

"Supper's ready," she said, sitting back up on his lap.

"I can smell it. What'd you make?"

"Fried perogies and left-over broccoli soup," she told him as she started to get out of the chair.

He pulled her back and shook his head. "I'm sure it can wait a few more minutes. Soup's probably too hot anyway."

The young bride complied as the couple lost themselves in their own little world of wedded bliss. After more than a year of waiting through a courtship and engagement, this couple had certainly discovered that they were compatible. In a world that insists "you cannot buy a car without test driving it first", it had not always been easy to make the radical decision to court and to set boundaries on physical affection—including no kissing. But it had been worth the wait. They both had agreed on their honeymoon that they would not have changed their course of romance one little bit.

They sat down to eat at the little dining room set in the apartment and said grace. There was a crisp fall breeze blowing in from the patio door to the balcony. The music continued to play from the stereo, and the young couple talked about plans for their life together.

Brandon figured they should start to look for a house soon and had spent some time at work surfing the local real estate sites to assess the market. He had also checked out with the bank what their housing budget would be. He and Joanie had decided before they got married, following the advice of Joanie's folks, to live off of Brandon's wage alone. Whatever money Joanie made could be set aside as a down payment on a house or tucked away into a savings plan for future needs, but they would set their living budget according to Brandon's income. That way, when children came along, Joanie would be free to choose to stay home and not feel trapped to have to continue working to support their standard of living.

They decided to go out driving after supper and look around at some of the neighbourhoods in town, to get a feel for where they would like to live. Motivated by the fun of dreaming together about their future, they ate quickly and got ready to go.

✟   ✟   ✟

"There're some people here to see you, Maggie," called Sr. Becky through the aspirant's bedroom door. Maggie stepped out of the room and thanked Sr. Becky as they walked down the two flights of stairs together. Maggie entered the front waiting room, and there stood Joanie with Brandon.

"Oh!" Maggie screamed and went running to hug her older sister. She greeted her brother-in-law with a big hug as well, trying not to throw off his balance on the crutches. "It's so wonderful to see you—why didn't you call to say you were coming over?"

"A surprise is always better," Joanie said. "We were just out driving around looking at houses, and suddenly I got homesick to see you again."

"Oh, I've been so homesick the last couple of days, myself," confessed Maggie. "I've just been so busy with my internship and getting adjusted to community life, that I haven't taken the time to get home for a visit. Sorry I couldn't make it to your welcome home party at Mom and Dad's the other night, but that was the night of our community meeting, and I couldn't miss it." Maggie was talking a mile a minute. There was just so much catching up to do with her big sister since she had last seen her taking off on an airplane for her European honeymoon.

"Can we stay for a visit, or is tonight a bad night for you?" Joanie asked.

"Oh, no, it's great. Come on, I'll take you up and show you my room. It's in the loft up on the third floor." Maggie grabbed Joanie by the hand.

"Um, I'll just stay down here if that's all right with you," Brandon suggested.

"I'm sorry, Brandon," Maggie apologized. "I completely forgot about your foot. How's it doing?"

"Painful, but . . ."

"Nothing a tough guy like you can't handle," Maggie teased. "Come on, we'll go by the chapel on the way. You can visit with Jesus, while I monopolize your wife for a while."

"Perfect," Brandon agreed.

They left Brandon in the chapel, and Maggie led Joanie up the stairs, running.

"Slow down, Maggie," Joanie complained. "I can't keep up to you."

"Oh, I've gotten used to the stairs," Maggie said. "I decided that would be my exercise program, running up the steps two at a time."

"Somehow I have a hard time picturing Nuns running around their convent. Do they allow you to do that around here?" Joanie queried as they walked up the last flight of steps to the loft.

"First of all, Joanie, they're not 'Nuns', they're Sisters. And yes, they do allow it. I only got in trouble for it once, from Sr. Pauline."

"I can see that," Joanie stated, remembering the elderly Sr. Pauline. She was a lovely woman, but definitely old-school when it came to formalities.

"Mind you, it was kind of late at night, and I had woken her up with my pounding. I've learned to be much more stealthy about it now," Maggie explained, demonstrating her stealthy movement on the last four steps of the staircase.

Joanie laughed and tried to imitate her sister.

"You need practice, Joanie," Maggie advised. "And besides I've found that wearing these skirts all the time has made me much more graceful."

Joanie burst out laughing and then pulled up her hand quickly to cover her mouth. There was nothing graceful about Maggie at all. Skirt and all, she still moved like a tomboy—her stealthy moves were total evidence of that.

"No, I'm totally serious," Maggie explained, standing in front of her bedroom door. "Check it out." The young aspirant strolled back and forth across the landing of the third floor doing her best imitation of a model coming up and down the runway.

Joanie had tears in her eyes from laughing so hard. "Maggie," she called out through her laughter, "stop! You're hurting my stomach."

Joanie held her arms tightly over her stomach as she kept laughing at the incorrigibly free-spirited Maggie, who had never given a hoot what anyone thought of her. She just pressed on through life doing what she felt called to do, never conforming to the crowd, unless of course she agreed with the crowd and then that was not conforming as far as Maggie was concerned. She had always been obedient to her parents and had no problem fully embracing the Church's teachings. It was her way of revolting against peer and secular pressures. Maggie found that being fully Catholic was so totally counter-cultural that it made for a great way to fulfill her need to be her own person, marching to her own beat. It was freedom—especially in the area of fashion, which had always left Maggie unimpressed. So adopting a habit was really no biggie to her, and it did not surprise Joanie at all that Maggie would find her own way to make the most out of the skirt-thing.

Maggie strolled, in her totally unnatural and not-really-so-graceful step, to her bedroom door and opened it up, bowing to her sister to invite her to enter.

Joanie took a deep breath, trying to control her giggles. "Oh, Maggie, you're hopeless. I don't see how the Sisters are ever going to get you whipped into shape."

"No worries there, Joanie. I'm getting *them* whipped into shape. Sr. Becky, Sr. Chelsea, and Kathleen, one of the postulants, have all started to take advantage of our exercise equipment here," Maggie boasted.

"What exercise equipment?"

"The stairs," Maggie stated, as if it had been totally obvious. "This place is loaded with them, and they've all discovered what a good cardiovascular workout it is to take them two at a time—and running, when possible. Carrying books up and down them also adds to good weight-bearing exercise, which is highly recommended for prevention of osteoporosis." Maggie looked at Joanie so matter-of-factly that Joanie started laughing again.

"Oh, Maggie, you do beat all!" Joanie exclaimed.

"Well, I'm having a harder time working on Kyra, though," she admitted, oblivious to how absurd the whole thing really was. It was just so Maggie.

"Who's Kyra?" Joanie asked, sitting down on Maggie's bed, cradling her legs with her arms, resting her chin on her knees. Maggie sat on her pillow with her legs stretched out on the bed.

"She's my companion aspirant."

"Don't you get along?"

"Oh, yeah. Well enough, I guess. I think she thinks I'm a little crazy."

"Shocker," stated Joanie, lifting her head up and raising her eyebrows above wide-open eyes.

"Funny. . . . It's just Kyra is such a lady. She's so refined and so quiet and so well-mannered," Maggie complained.

"The perfect match for you," Joanie blurted out with a clap. "I love God's sense of humour!"

"Anyway, I'm working on her," stated Maggie, with the authority of an older sibling. "I even got her to dress up like the children of Fatima last week to wash floors."

"Maggie, you're so weird!" Joanie exclaimed, rubbing her forehead with her hand and shaking her head. "Doesn't it ever occur to you that you've grown up?"

"Nope," Maggie said bluntly, with a quick turn of her head. "And I don't intend to either. Growing up is for old people, and I plan to stay eternally youthful in Christ. That's why I came here to become a Sister."

Joanie made a little noise under her breath and gave up the cause.

The two sisters sat and talked for almost an hour. It was just like old times at home in their bedroom: so many conversations over the years, so much laughter, so many tears. It had been a privilege to have grown up close. It felt like a lifetime ago, and yet it really had only been a matter of weeks since Joanie got married and moved away from home.

Suddenly Joanie sat up. "Oh my gosh!" she exclaimed. "I'm married!"

"Brandon!" Maggie gasped.

The two girls jumped off the bed and ran down the steps as fast as they could. When they reached the main floor, Maggie went whipping around the corner and did a full body slam against Brandon, who was coming down the hall from the chapel. Crutches went flying, and Brandon landed on his back. Maggie had bounced off Brandon and went slamming back against the wall and fell to the floor. Joanie, who had been on Maggie's heels, came tripping over her sister and did an amazing job of recovering her balance without falling.

Sr. Charlotte and Sr. Becky came running out from the study when they heard the crash. Sr. Charlotte stopped just in time so as not to trip over Brandon, whose large body was blocking the narrow hallway.

Maggie looked up at Sr. Charlotte and said with a sheepish smile, "Sr. Charlotte, you remember my sister, Joanie, and her husband, Brandon?"

Sr. Becky burst out laughing—only Maggie could have orchestrated such a disaster.

"Are you okay, Brandon?" Sr. Charlotte asked with concern, observing the man's splinted foot and the crutches lying on the hallway floor.

"Excellent," Brandon said shaking his head with a laugh. "Although I have to admit that married life has brought out the real klutz in me—first in Rome, now here."

"Oh, I doubt that this was your fault," Sr. Charlotte ascertained, shaking her head hopelessly at Maggie. She chuckled as she picked up the crutches, while Joanie and Maggie struggled to help up Brandon. Sr. Charlotte had a real soft spot for Maggie, but as Director of Novices she really would have to start working on some etiquette with that girl.

"I'm so sorry, Brandon," Maggie genuinely apologized. Then with a quick change of tone, she added, "I never realized how much you're built like a brick wall!"

"I think the expression is, 'Built like a . . .'" Sr. Charlotte began, but taking into account Maggie's naiveté and innocence, she decided to leave well enough alone. "Ah, never mind."

Brandon looked at Sr. Charlotte and laughed. Turning to his sister-in-law, he asked, "Are *you* okay?"

"Pride aside, I'm just fine," she stated. She offered another sheepish smile at Sr. Charlotte whose severe look could not hide her real affection for the young aspirant.

Sr. Becky, having established that everyone was fine, excused herself and went back to the study, still laughing. Life at the convent would never be the same now that Maggie had arrived.

Chapter 5

As Amie walked through the kitchen on a quiet Thursday afternoon, she noticed a pile of mail sitting on the kitchen counter. She rifled through it out of habit, and suddenly her name caught her eye. She turned her gaze to the return address: Stettler College. She tore open the envelope, took out the letter, and skimmed through it until her eyes rested on the word for which she was looking.

"Yes!" she squealed with delight. She went back to the top of the letter and slowly read it in its entirety. When she was finished, she looked around and noted the time on the clock. Her mom would not be back with the little ones for another hour or so, but her dad was out in the garage.

She ran out through the back door and across the yard to her father's workshop in the garage. She opened the door and stepped in, waiting for him to notice her. He looked up from his work after a moment and saw his daughter standing there, with a big smile illuminating her face.

She waved the letter at him and burst out, "I got in! I got accepted into Stettler."

He set down the cloth he had been using to stain wood and nodded his head with an approving smile. "I knew you would," he said, reaching for a rag to wipe his hands with.

"Oh, Daddy, I'm so happy I could just dance," she exclaimed.

"So when do you start?"

"In four weeks."

"That's a strange time to start classes . . . in November?"

"They start up courses each month of the year, as long as they have a big enough class to make it work," she stated.

Her father's mouth took a twisted downward turn and his eyebrows lifted. "And what about your music theory exam in December and your piano exam in January? How are you going to manage that?"

"I'm almost ready for it, Dad. And classes are only six hours a day. That gives me plenty of time to work on my music."

"And what about youth group?"

"Katie will take it over for me for a few months, until I'm done my music, I'm sure."

"That works for the younger youth groups, but what about seniors? She can't very well run the youth group she's a member of," he pointed out.

Amie thought for a second. She lit up as the thought occurred to her. "Kyle can run it. He's awesome with the youth group."

"He's in school, too," her dad reminded her.

"He already comes to just about every youth group. The kids all love him. Now he can get paid for it," she said with a twist of her shoulders and a little smile. She was sure to have an answer for every one of her father's objections. She was not going to let him talk her out of this.

He heaved a sigh. "You really want to do this, do you?"

"Dad," she complained, "what do you have against hairdressing school?"

"Ah, Amie, you have so many talents. You're such a bright girl academically. Why would you want to waste all of that becoming a hairdresser?" he asked with a growing look of disappointment on his face. "You should be going into music studies at university and getting a degree in performance or something like that."

"I'm not wasting any of my talents, Dad. I love my music, but I hate to break it to you . . . I'm not really *that* good." Before he had a chance to argue, she put up her hand to stop him so she could go on. "There are lots of other pianists out there better than I. I mean, I love to play for band and at church. I don't even mind accompanying people. But I really don't like teaching music. That's why I dropped all my students this year. Well, everyone but Zack and Aaron—but they're my brothers, and they don't count. The point is, Dad, I don't want to make music my career." She looked at her dad with pleading eyes. "I really want to do this, Daddy. And I want you to be happy for me."

John Collins could not resist the look in his little girl's eyes. As strict a man as he could be at times, his daughters all had a way of melting him. "Come here." He opened his arms for his daughter to come for a hug.

She stepped forward, looking up at her dad in a manner to size him up. He motioned again for her to come give him a hug, and she stepped into his big arms.

"I'm happy for you, Scuttle-Butt," he said softly.

Amie heaved a sigh and said in a disgruntled tone, "I'm getting a little old for that name, Dad."

"You'll never be too old to be my Scuttle-Butt," he disagreed. "Can I help it that you never bothered to learn how to crawl as a baby?" With a laugh he quickly reminisced how Amie would sit on her bum and push herself around the room. "You didn't want to miss out on a thing going on around you. And you still don't."

"Are you really happy for me, Dad?" the young lady questioned, her head tilted in suspicion.

"Yes, I am. If this is really what you want, I'm happy for you."

"Just think about how I'll be able to evangelize people while cutting hair," she said, trying to get him excited for her. "And the course is only ten months long. So I can start earning money in less than a year . . ."

"To pay off your debt for going to school," he reminded her.

"It's not that bad," she assured him. "I've put away money these past few years. But the point is, once I get married and start having kids, I can work my own hours from the home if we need any extra money. And I can work it around my husband's schedule and my children. It's perfect!"

"Fine," he resigned himself. "You have my blessing."

Satisfied that he really meant it, Amie nodded her head and looked down to see what her father had been working on. "What are these?"

"Baseboards for the upstairs rooms."

"Oh, Mom's going to be thrilled," Amie exclaimed. "How long have we been in this house?"

"Over ten years," her father stated.

"Actually, thirteen," she pointed out. "I was almost six when we moved here." Seeing the raised eyebrows on her father's face, Amie smiled apologetically. She was not really trying to pour salt over an open wound. "I'll go get supper started."

"Your mother's not home yet?"

"She won't be home for a little while," Amie said. "She usually stops to get groceries on her way home from swimming lessons with the kids."

"Well, she'll be excited about your news. She always took your side on this issue." One thing he had learned over the years, raising a houseful of girls: women stick together. Thank goodness the Lord had sent him a few sons for moral support.

Amie patted her dad on the shoulder and then turned to leave.

"Hey, Amie?" her father called out after her. She stopped at the door and turned her head to see what he wanted.

"What's it like for you to be the oldest kid around here now?"

"Not bad," she shrugged her shoulders.

"You miss your sisters?"

"Uh-huh," she nodded. "But life goes on." She waved bye from the door with her acceptance letter in hand and stepped out of the garage.

She paused on the other side for a moment, thinking about her dad. He was a hard-working man. Both he and her mother had made many sacrifices to have a large family, and for that she was grateful. In fact, every one of the kids had made sacrifices, living in a large family, but she could not have imagined life without each and every one of her siblings. It was worth everything she had ever had to do without. And it was exactly what she wanted for herself someday.

She walked into the kitchen and looked into the fridge to see if her mom had set anything out for supper. There was some hamburger meat, so Amie decided to start making a spaghetti sauce with it. She got out a large saucepan, began to brown the meat, and then went back into the fridge to get some onions.

As she moved around the kitchen all alone in the quiet house, she imagined herself someday making supper for her own family—waiting for her husband to come home from work. She sighed as she indulged in her daydreaming.

The fact was, she had always promised herself she would not start seeing anyone until she knew for sure that she would be ready to marry within a year's time. Now that she had been accepted into this course, which was only ten months long, she could see the end in sight. *Okay, Lord, anytime now, I'm ready. Just send him along so we can get this show on the road.*

Amie had longed for years to get married and start a large family right away. All she needed now was the perfect match. As she began thinking through her long inventory of what she wanted in a husband, she got dreamier and dreamier about the whole idea. Soon she found herself singing *Matchmaker* from one of their favourite family movies, *Fiddler on the Roof.*

Getting into character, she began dancing around the kitchen, singing out in full voice, "For papa, make him a scholar. For mamma, make him rich as a king. For me, well, I wouldn't holler if he were as handsome as an-y-thing!" She threw her arms out as she twirled around with a head of celery.

Katie stood in the doorway between the kitchen and living room, watching the show. When Amie caught her sister's eye, she motioned for her to come join in the fun. Without missing a beat, Amie grabbed a couple of tea-towels off the handle of the oven. She tossed one to Katie who tied it peasant style over her head of dark, straight, shoulder-length hair. Amie covered the top of her head, with her long curly, blond locks trailing out beneath the veil.

Together the two girls danced and sang like they had done so many times before. They would have died if anyone else had walked in on them, other than family, but in the privacy of their own kitchen they were free to be stars on Broadway.

When the song ended, Amie tossed Katie the celery to chop up for the sauce. She ran over to the cupboard and picked up her acceptance letter. Waving it in the air, she announced, "I'm in. November third, classes begin."

"Awesome!" enthused Katie. "Free haircuts for the rest of my life!"

"Not only that," Amie smiled, "I'll be all done school and ready to start out on my own in less than a year from now!"

"That's true," Katie said.

"Don't you get it, Katie?" the older sister asked. "I could start courting with a guy any time now."

"You got someone in mind?" Katie questioned cautiously.

"No. But I'm ready whenever he comes along . . . whoever he is."

"Well, I hope you intend to be a little choosey," Katie stated with concern. "Don't just go off and marry the first guy to come around and ask you out."

Amie rolled her eyes and put her hands on her hips. "Do I look that stupid to you, Katie? I have better sense than that."

"I'd hope so. But you can tend to be a little impulsive, Amie."

Amie hated when Katie flipped roles on her and started acting like the older sister. There were three years between them, but Katie just had a more serious nature that made her seem well beyond her years. "I know exactly what I'm looking for in a guy," Amie defended herself.

"Oh?" Katie asked, barely impressed.

"He *has* to be Catholic. He's gotta be musical," the aspiring hairdresser began listing off her criteria. "He's definitely got to be cute. I don't care much about handsome. But definitely cute!"

Katie stood there waiting for Amie to demonstrate a little more depth in thought.

"He has to be taller than me," she continued. "He has to live around here, because I don't want to move away from Saskatoon. He's gotta love children and want to have lots of them. And he absolutely has to be patient, because I know my personality could drive anyone nuts."

Katie chuckled and nodded as she chopped celery.

Amie pulled her lip in on one side, unimpressed with her sister's smugness; after all, she was being openly honest in assessing herself. She thought for a moment and then went on, "I want to marry a guy who's gentle, but not a wimp. He's got to be a real man—not afraid of hard work and not afraid to make sacrifices. And not one of these boys full of modern attitude. I want an old-fashioned guy, with old-fashioned values, who treats me with respect and really knows how to cherish me."

Amie paused with a dreamy look in her eyes, as she mentally searched through her list to see if she had covered it all. Satisfied that she had, she nodded and said, "That's what I'm looking for . . . and I don't intend to settle for anything less."

"Good for you. I hope God sends him around sooner than later. Then I'll get the bedroom all to myself," stated Katie, now finished chopping the celery.

"Oh, by the way, Katie," Amie remembered, "once I get started at Stettler, would you mind taking over the two younger youth groups until I'm done my piano exam in January?"

"No problem," Katie agreed. "You goin' to continue doing seniors?"

"No, I'm goin' to ask Kyle at band practice tonight," she said, looking up at the clock. "Holy smokes! Look at the time. I've gotta shower before we go. Do you mind finishing the spaghetti sauce? Mom should be home anytime now."

"That's fine. . . . Oh, just wait." Katie walked across the room and picked up a package off the dining room table. She opened the brown paper wrap on it to reveal the drawing she had done for Joanie and Brandon's wedding gift.

"You had it framed?" Amie said, duly impressed with the finished work.

"Actually Grandpa paid for the framing. He insisted it needed to be framed, and since I didn't have the money to do it, he had it done. I just picked it up this afternoon," Katie explained.

"It's kickin'," Amie said whole-heartedly, with two thumbs up, as she headed out of the room and upstairs to get ready for band practice.

Katie stood and assessed her work for a few minutes. Suddenly the sound of meat popping on the stove reminded her of the sauce. She ran over to find the hamburger meat a very dark shade of brown with very well fried onions in the saucepan.

The sixteen-year-old shook her head at the thought of her air-headed older sister, as she turned down the heat on the burner. She opened two cans of pasta sauce and stirred them in, in a last-ditch effort to save the meat. Adding the chopped celery and a few spices, she decided she had not done such a bad job in salvaging supper for the family. *It pays to have someone around here grounded in reality,* she thought to herself as she cast her eyes in the direction of her sister in the shower upstairs.

She turned the burner down to simmer and went to package up her artwork so she could get it out of the kitchen before the little kids got home and damaged it. Just then she heard a commotion at the door, announcing the family's return. She hurriedly snatched up her things and headed up to her room before they had a chance to find her.

✟   ✟   ✟

Kathy Bander sat at the square chrome kitchen table with a pen in hand and stationery spread out before her. Her dark hair hung loosely in soft curls just barely reaching her shoulder, as she sat with her head tilted over the letter she was writing to a friend. A cool fall breeze was playing with floral-printed curtains that hung from a café rod over the wooden double-hung window behind her. There was a quaint light fixture hanging over the old table in its out-of-the-way placement in the country kitchen. The only other light on in the room was over the sink, where the other window's curtains and valence were also dancing softly in the breeze. The air was fresh, and the room was cozy and pleasant on this fall evening at the Bander's home.

The entire house had just acquired a peaceful silence as the last carload of young people pulled away following band practice. Kyle entered the kitchen from the back landing, walked over to the fridge, opened the door, and stared inside.

"Looking for the second coming?" his mother asked from across the room, watching the young man do what she had come to witness her sons do routinely so many times a day.

Kyle chuckled and closed the refrigerator door. "I guess it won't be tonight."

"Try beside the microwave," she suggested, pointing with her pen. Her eyes followed her son as he walked across to the counter opposite the kitchen sink. His posture straightened, and a sly smile came over his face as he reached for the freshly baked apple pie.

"When'd you make this?" He lifted the tea towel which had been covering the pie.

"During practice."

"You'd think I would have smelled it?"

"Windows have been open for quite a while," his mother pointed out. "And band practice went long tonight. But you all sounded really good."

"Thanks," he said, taking a slice of pie. He filled a tall glass with milk and came over to sit at the table across from his mother.

Kathy's eyes widened as she looked at the piece of pie that almost filled the plate it was on. "Hungry?"

"Yeah." Then, stopping before he took the first bite, he looked at his mother and offered, "I'm sorry. Did you want any? I can go get you some." He started to get up but she put up her hand to stop him.

"Sit," she said. "Relax and enjoy."

"Where's David?" Kyle asked, looking around. There was no competition for the prized dish.

"He dashed through here after practice so fast I hardly recognized him," she chuckled.

"Talking to Leanne, no doubt," Kyle commented as he took a huge forkful of mouth-watering, warm apple pie. He closed his eyes—David just did not know what he was missing!

Kyle opened his eyes again and looked across the table at his mom who was watching him intently. Raising his eyebrows to question her pensive look, he proceeded to take another bite of pie.

"Good news about Amie," Kathy commented. "She was all lit up like a firefly tonight—even more than usual."

"Oh, she's all set and ready to go," Kyle agreed, nodding his head at his quickly disappearing dessert.

"Oh?" his mother questioned, noting a change in her son's demeanour.

Kyle continued to eat up until his last bite of pie. He slouched back in his chair and pushed the plate forward on the table. Picking up the glass of milk with his left hand, he downed the beverage in a few continuous gulps and set the empty glass beside the empty dish as he proceeded to wipe his mouth with the back of his hand. Still holding the fork, which he had licked clean, he began to lightly tap it against the edge of the chrome table looking up at his mom.

Kathy watched her son. She had set down her pen and was now resting her chin on her open palm, her elbow propped up on the table. Over the years she had become so accustomed to his persistent percussion that she never became annoyed with the constant rhythms coming from the boy.

After a few moments of silence between them, the mother finally asked, "So what's bugging you, son?"

Kyle lifted his eyes almost in surprise. Had he said anything about being bugged? He quickly examined his behaviour to determine what might be giving himself away. "Nothing." He shrugged, without a great deal of conviction.

"Mm-hmm." The astute woman nodded. "It has to do with Amie," she said, taking the lead. "So what's up?"

Kyle stopped tapping the fork and tossed it on the table by the plate and glass. He hesitated a moment, trying to decide for himself what was really bugging him. It was not like he was trying to keep anything from his mom. She had been well aware of her son's feelings for Amie for many years now. It was just that he had not had a chance, since practice, to sort things out in his own mind. Giving way to the opportunity, he decided that talking things out with his mom was probably the best way he would sort things out for himself.

"It's just that Amie's all excited about the fact that she got into her program at Stettler. And that's great and all," he added enthusiastically. "I know how much she's been wanting to do this. It's just . . ." his voice trailed off as he searched for words.

"Just what?" prompted his mom.

"It's just that . . . for *her* . . . well, that means she's available . . . you know," he motioned with his hand to fill in for his stumbling speech, ". . . to begin courting." He paused, still searching for an explanation. "As far as Amie's concerned, she could get married within a year . . . and so she's all pumped and waiting for Mr. Right to show up." He shook his head again, somewhat in disbelief at how predictable Amie was to him, while at the same time so confounding.

"Is that a problem for you?" his mother questioned.

Kyle moved his hands around impatiently and then grabbed again for the fork and resumed tapping. "I-I-I . . . I don't know," he drawled out, sitting forward and resting his chin on his open palm, elbow propped up on the table. Again he dropped the fork down beside the plate and glass, and now with both hands he rubbed his forehead. He then sat back up again in his chair and began tapping his hands on his legs.

"You'll be done school in less than a year from now, too, Kyle," his mom reminded him.

"Yeah, I know," he said with annoyance, getting up from the table and carrying his dishes to the sink. Turning back to his mom, he asked, "Am I crazy that I don't feel ready to do anything about this?" He tossed his hands up in the air and looked to his mother for advice. "I mean, she's all I've ever wanted, for as long as I can remember. But for so long I just kept everything as friends between us, so I wouldn't compromise any chance I'd have later on to win her over. And now that *later on* has arrived, I just don't feel like the time is right. And if I tried to make any move towards courtship with her now, I'm sure she'd kill me!"

Kathy burst out laughing at her son's assertion. "Oh, Kyle, I hardly think she'd kill you!"

"Oh, yes . . . she would," he nodded emphatically. "Amie sees me as a brother—not as a prospect—and I know she'd be turned right off if I tried to imply anything romantic with her right now. She'd get so mad at me . . . she'd kill me," he reasserted.

Still laughing at her son's dramatic assessment, Kathy asked, "So what do you intend to do?"

He paused momentarily. "Wait and pray," he replied, crossing his arms over his chest and leaning against the sink. "And hope like hell *Mr. Right* doesn't show up and steal her away in the meantime."

Kathy shook her head and laughed all the harder. It was difficult to feel her son's stress when he was so down-right comical about the whole thing—not that he was trying to be. It was only from the outside vantage point, she was fully aware, that the humour of the entire situation was apparent.

Getting up and walking over to her son, Kathy put her hand on his shoulder and looked into his dark, gentle eyes. "It'll work out, son," she assured him. "But in the meantime I suggest you start to consider how you are going to tactfully and successfully transition your relationship with Amie."

"It'll happen when the time is right," Kyle stated with confidence. "And as long as I've got my school work and band . . . and now Amie's asked me to take over youth group for her until she finishes her piano exam in January . . . I've got my hands full. I couldn't possibly do justice to a courtship relationship right now. And I know that. That's why I've been waiting until I was ready to move on—be finished with school and have a job in my back pocket." Kyle looked at his mother, still standing there with her hand on his shoulder. "And I'm just trying to trust that if I'm faithful to what I believe God is asking of me, things are going to work out for the best." Then quietly he confessed, "I just hope I haven't deceived myself. And I hope I'll be prepared to accept whatever is really best for both Amie and me."

Kathy Bander put her arms around her son and gave him a warm, motherly embrace. Patting him on the back she whispered, "I'm proud of you, Kyle. Just hang in there and be faithful to what you know God has placed in your heart."

"I will."

"And I'll do my best to keep you in good supply of apple pie while you ride out the storms ahead."

"Thanks, Mom," he said with a smile. "Good night." He bent forward to kiss her on the cheek. She returned a kiss on his cheek and patted him on the shoulder as he turned to go upstairs to his room.

"Good night, son," she called out after him. She was about to go pick up her pen and resume her writing when she decided to call it a night, herself. Gathering her stuff together, she piled it on the counter by the phone for the morning. She left on the light over the sink for when her husband would come in from the shop. As she walked out of the kitchen to get ready for bed, Kathy took her rosary off its special hook on the wall and went to pray for her family's needs.

Chapter 6

Maggie hesitated outside Sr. Charlotte's office before she knocked. She was not late—but by no means early—for her biweekly spiritual direction with the Director of Novices. Sr. Charlotte had not yet brought up the incident with Joanie and Brandon that had taken place over a week ago. Maggie wished that Sr. Charlotte had just come out and dealt with it immediately, rather than allowing her agony to be prolonged, wondering what repercussions there would be for her less-than-Sisterly behaviours. No such luck.

Maggie wondered if Sr. Charlotte secretly enjoyed watching the young aspirant sweat it out. No doubt she was fully aware that Maggie was tormenting over the situation, even though Maggie had tried to offer an apology the night it happened on their way into vespers. Sr. Charlotte had simply nodded her acceptance of the apology and stated that they would discuss it during their next time of spiritual direction.

That time had come. Maggie lifted her hand to knock on the old oak door. No. She could not bring herself to do it just yet. Turning quickly in the direction of the chapel, where she knew Jesus was residing in the Tabernacle, Maggie quickly made the sign of the cross and prayed.

Oh, Jesus, it would be so much easier to just be normal than to be me. Why did You make me to be so impulsive and free-spirited, if You had planned for me to follow a religious vocation? You're goin' to have to help me grow up here if You really intend for me to become a Sister. I promise to be good and follow the rules and settle down and do what's expected of me. Please don't let Sr. Charlotte send me away from here. Help her to see how much I really want to be here. Oh, Jesus . . . I'm just too scared to knock right now . . . so I'm going to let You do the knocking for me.

The young woman lifted her hand to the door to knock and then stood there, as if she were waiting for something to happen. After a few moments she realized how ridiculous she must have looked standing there like a statue. If someone were to come by and see her there . . . *Oh, why do I have to be so different from everyone else? That's it. I'm going to pretend I'm Sr. Becky. She's cool. She's got her act together. She'd just walk right up to this door and . . .*

The sound of her own knocking startled Maggie as she realized she had actually followed through with it this time. She stopped and listened.

"Come in," came a quiet voice from the other side of the door.

Maggie took a deep breath and entered Sr. Charlotte's office. She held her shoulders back straight and took her seat at the big wooden desk as the Director had gestured for the aspirant to do. Maggie tucked her shoulder length hair back behind her ears and sat with her knees together, placing her hands elegantly on her lap, sitting as tall as she could.

A soft smile lifted from the sides of Sr. Charlotte's closed mouth. Her motherly eyes looked tenderly on the young woman before her. She brought her hands together and moved them toward her visitor. "So how's Maggie this evening?"

Sr. Charlotte's voice revealed that she was genuinely enthusiastic to have the opportunity to meet again with her spunky new aspirant. Everything about this woman set Maggie at ease, and the young girl wondered why she had ever been nervous.

"I'm doing well, Sister. How are you?"

"Oh, my back is giving me a little more grief these days than normal, but apart from that, I'm doing marvellously!" the Director returned. Keeping the conversation focused, she directed another question across the desk. "So tell me, how is your internship going so far? You're four weeks into it now. You must be having the opportunity to do more teaching in the classroom."

"Oh, it's going fine," Maggie said, less than enthusiastically. "I'm... I'm... I'm not sure if teaching is really for me," she confessed.

"Oh?" Sr. Charlotte was surprised.

"I mean, I love children, and I love learning, and I love teaching. It's just that I'm not sure about being in a school all day. I thought having a dad as a teacher gave me enough insight as to the goings-on of a school day. But I can see now that having been home-schooled has skewed my view of education completely," the girl explained.

"How so?"

"I just can't get into all the rules and regulations. Kids having to raise their hands to go to the bathroom—in grade five!" The shock of it seemed beyond the young intern's imaginings. "We line them up. They walk down the hallways in a group. They take out their books at the same time. They put them away at the same time—whether they're done their work or not. I sit and listen to Mrs. Nichols explain everything about four times before the kids are ever allowed to get to work. And I can't imagine how bored they are... because I'm just about falling asleep in my corner of the room myself." The young woman stopped and looked up at the Sister, suddenly aware she had been rambling on. She offered a meek, apologetic smile.

Sr. Charlotte began laughing, her white veil moving back and forth as she shook her head. "Oh, Maggie, you are a prize, aren't you?"

Maggie turned her head sheepishly to one side, averting her look for just a moment. When she looked back at Sr. Charlotte, the Director was still chuckling away with delight.

"Tell me," Sr. Charlotte questioned, "what did you expect school to be like?"

"I'm not sure," Maggie confessed. "I just always imagined myself being one of those teachers that you hear of who just connects with the students . . . you know, really meets them where they're at . . . allows them to work at their own pace and inspires them to strive for higher levels of learning."

"Sounds like a wonderful ideal, Maggie," Sr. Charlotte agreed. "So what's stopping you from achieving it?"

"Well, Mrs. Nichols is a lot more . . . institutional, shall we say, than I am by nature. I mean, I can't very well walk into her classroom, take control, and expect her to do things my way. She has her own way of doing things, and to be honest, the kids respect her, and she does have good classroom management. I just think they don't really know to expect more than what they've ever had. And for me to come in and upset the system with my wild and fandangled ideas isn't exactly fair or right of me, is it?"

As the aspirant finished her little speech, she sat back in her chair and stared at the Director of Novices. A look of realization came over Maggie's face as all at once she recognized that she had just described exactly what she had been doing in community life ever since she had come to live with the Sisters. Sr. Charlotte had not had to say a thing.

"Ummm," Maggie wanted to say something, but she did not know where to begin.

Sr. Charlotte's warm smile reached across the desk to the young woman and assured her that she was not there to place judgment on the girl. She was there to help direct her spiritually and to give guidance during her time of discernment as an aspirant with their community.

"Maggie," Sr. Charlotte began, full of energy, "I love your *joie de vivre*. Your enthusiasm for life can fill any room you enter. I don't know how you'd sit on all that joy and energy, even if you tried. It's *who* you are. But what I really want to know from you is . . . are you truly happy being here at the convent?"

Maggie sat up eagerly to answer, but Sr. Charlotte put up her hand to stop her.

"I know you love the idea of religious life, because your devotion to Jesus in the Blessed Sacrament is so very strong. It's plainly obvious that Jesus is your first love—and that you're seeking out a way of living your life fully for Him." Sr. Charlotte stood up from her desk, walked toward the window of her office, and stared out as she continued. "But do you think you are going to find happiness as you begin to rein in some of that wonderful, free-spirited nature of yours in order to accommodate the regulations and routines of religious life?"

"I haven't done very well so far, have I?" queried the aspirant, staring at the back of Sr. Charlotte's white veil.

Sr. Charlotte shrugged her shoulders and turned away from the window to look at the girl who had sunk deeper into her chair. "I wouldn't say that. I love the energy you bring to each task you undertake. Your youthful zeal is so . . . well, it's rather impulsive, but apart from that it's got a wonderfully delightful side to it. I'm afraid though that perhaps I've allowed you a little too much free rein, if you are going to find your way into the routines of religious life."

"I'm really capable of routine," Maggie stated, sitting up straight again in her chair. "We had routine growing up—even if it was a relaxed home environment. We had our school work to get done each day and chores . . . lots of chores, especially for Joanie, Amie, and myself. But I didn't mind. Once our work was done we were free to spend our days as we saw fit—reading and playing together all sorts of fun things. I mean that's the kind of environment I wish I could bring to a classroom. Let students realize that if they get their work done right away, they can be free to do whatever they wanted."

Sr. Charlotte gave a startled look. "Whatever they wanted?"

"I mean, within reason. Like reading, or learning about something that really interested them, or inventing something cool."

"You have to remember, Maggie, that not every child comes from a home environment where they've been raised to be responsible and accountable. There are many children coming into our schools from broken, challenging home lives," Sr. Charlotte reminded her in a sobering manner, indulging the sudden turn in conversation. "Some of them are just there at school to escape the reality of home. Others are there just putting in time, because no one has ever inspired them to give and get more out of life than what's been fed to them. I think kids are naturally wonderful and have an innate desire to learn. But the reality of their environments—between home and media influences, and spending way too much time in front of video games and television—has left a lot of people empty, searching for wholeness and truth, yet not knowing where to turn for answers."

"But that's why I want to be there for them to help show them—*Jesus* is where they need to turn to discover truth and wholeness, to bring meaning into their lives," Maggie jumped in again, full of vision. "I want to bring Jesus to them in meaningful ways and inspire them to dig deeply within themselves so that they can 'give and get' more out of life, just like you said."

Sr. Charlotte smiled.

"Oh, I'm sorry for rambling on again," Maggie apologized. "It's a bad habit of mine, I'm afraid."

Sr. Charlotte nodded her acceptance of the apology, smiling all the while.

"We were talking about routine around here and me fitting into the rules and regulations and all," Maggie refocused the discussion.

"So, how do you feel about that aspect of religious life?" Sr. Charlotte asked.

"I'm fine with it," Maggie stated. "I'll be the first to admit that I need to rein in my impulsive nature and start practising better self-discipline."

"That's fine," Sr. Charlotte agreed, "if you are doing it for the right motives. However, you should also consider that there are other ways for you to live out your desire to be completely devoted to Christ and to serve Him and the Church, other than in religious life."

Maggie's heart began to sink. This was it. Sr. Charlotte was about to show her out the door. "Like married life," Maggie said with dismay.

Sr. Charlotte broke out into laughter, while shaking her head sympathetically. "Sure, married life is one way. And you needn't sound so depressed about the prospect. Honestly, Maggie, most girls who come here to discern have to really struggle with letting go of the dream of getting married and having a family."

"Not me," stated Maggie. "I'm completely certain I am not called to marriage. Not because I don't think it's beautiful. My parents had a great marriage, and my family life was awesome! And I'm happy for all those who are called to that vocation—like Joanie and Brandon. I think their relationship is totally inspiring. But I know it is not for me. I just know that I need to be free to dedicate myself completely to Christ. I know that."

"But there are ways for you to totally dedicate yourself to Christ apart from religious life. There's also the vocation of singleness, Maggie," Sr. Charlotte reminded the young woman. "I know a great many holy people who have dedicated their entire lives to Christ in their singleness. They frequent daily Mass and Eucharistic adoration. They devote their time and talents and energy into the community. They serve their families and their parishes and whomever the Lord places in their lives with a real *singular* devotion—pardon the pun." Smiling at Maggie, who was obviously ill-at-ease with the proposition, the Director continued. "The fact that a single person is not tied down to a family of their own, or a religious community with all its responsibilities, they are free to serve the Lord each day in a way that is so needed in our world."

Maggie listened, but did not really want to be open to what Sr. Charlotte was suggesting. All she could consider, as she sat there with a far-away look in her eyes, was the fact that she had failed miserably at the one thing she had always wanted for herself—the only thing she had ever desired to do with her life—to become a religious Sister.

Sr. Charlotte observed the sunken posture of the young woman and waited for a response, but nothing was forthcoming. "Single Christian men and women do more for our Church than they are ever given credit for, Maggie. And in that simple, humble and hidden way, they are capable of great holiness. What you have to discern, my dear, is which path God is calling you down, in order for you to be truly happy and for you to be able to live out holiness in the life He intends for you."

Maggie sighed and nodded, shifting uncomfortably in her chair.

"Once you've discovered that, it won't really matter which vocation you follow. You'll gladly undertake all the sacrifices of that particular vocation. And you'll be fulfilled, because you're following God's will for your life." Sr. Charlotte leaned forward to catch Maggie's eyes with hers. "What do you think, Maggie?"

"I think . . . I wish I could start over and try again here, and prove myself to you that I *am* capable of being exactly what you expect of me as a Sister of the Immaculate Conception."

"Maggie, my dear . . ." Sr. Charlotte said, walking around to the girl seated on the chair. She took Maggie's hands in hers and quietly assured her, ". . . I expect you to be *you*. And I don't want to see you lose any of your enthusiasm for life trying to make yourself into something or someone you aren't. If you are called to religious life, with the Sisters of the Immaculate Conception, we'll accept you as you are. And you'll find your way in religious life—reining in some of that impulsiveness—in such a way that it won't stifle the woman you were created to be. And," she added with a note of finality, "we will all get into better shape for having discovered the wealth of exercise equipment lying right here beneath our feet."

Maggie started to laugh and reached up to wipe her teary eyes. "So you're not asking me to leave?"

"Heavens, no!" Sr. Charlotte exclaimed. "I'm just trying to help you through your discernment process. You have to consider everything, Maggie. And you are *welcome* to stay here and discern as long as you need. Just . . . maybe slow down coming down the stairs and around corners. Some of the Sisters around here are getting older, you know, and I'd hate to see you take one of them out before her time."

Maggie laughed through her tears and jumped up from the chair, giving Sr. Charlotte a hug. Sr. Charlotte was not asking her to leave. Maggie had not blown her shot at religious life after all. "I promise to leave running to the outdoors."

Sr. Charlotte put her arm over Maggie's shoulder as she walked her to the office door. "I don't know about you, Maggie, but I can't wait to see what the Lord has in store for you. I'm just glad I get to have a front row seat for this show. It really is quite a privilege for me, you know."

"Lucky you," Maggie said with mild sarcasm. "I hope roller coasters don't make you sick."

"No, I love the thrill of them," the older Sister confessed. "It's those spinny rides that make me want to throw up," she said, making a spinning motion with her hand, as an uncharacteristic grimace crept across her kindly face.

"Well, I'll try to get my act together quickly so I don't leave your head spinning," Maggie assured the Director with a hopeful smile, as she took her leave.

Chapter 7

"Look who's finally decided to show up for band practice," announced Annie Ledoux, as the newlyweds stepped into the basement of the Bander's home, fashionably late.

Amie ceremoniously played out the first few familiar bars of "The Wedding March" from *A Midsummer Night's Dream* by Mendelssohn. Joanie smiled coyly at the group while Brandon raised his hands to settle the applause. He was walking with a limp, but no longer needed the crutches to get around.

"Where's your guitar, Brandon?" David noted as the newlyweds took a seat on the corner sectional.

"Left it at home tonight," Brandon replied.

"Why?" asked Amie.

"Don't need it. We just came to listen."

"What do you mean? You're not going to perform with us tomorrow night at the *Praise Event*?" Katie inquired.

"Nope," Brandon replied casually. "Haven't been able to make it to a practice yet, and I'm sure you're getting along just fine without us."

There was a general response of disagreement from the band, particularly from Daniel Schultz who had been filling in lead guitar in Brandon's absence. "Look I wasn't planning on doing this on my own," he protested.

"You're a good guitarist, Daniel," Brandon responded. "You just need the chance to prove it to yourself. Everyone else can see it."

Joanie and Brandon sat back comfortably on the sofa, determined to hold their ground on the issue.

"We're just here for moral support," Joanie explained. "And we'll be there tomorrow night as well. So just go ahead and play. We want to hear how you sound."

After a few more minutes of unsuccessful convincing the group resigned themselves to the decision of the young couple, chose a song, and began to play.

Joanie and Brandon took in the group: their presence, their sound. It was all very impressive. Joanie noted what a beautiful job her sixteen-year-old cousin, Jocelyn, was doing as lead female. It took the young bride back several years to when *New Spring* had just begun—Joanie had been about Jocelyn's age. The resemblances between them were remarkable; with the same colouring of dark hair and eyes, they looked more like sisters than Joanie and Amie did. Jocelyn was a sweet girl. Joanie had done some singing training with Jocelyn over the years. The girl could sing beautifully and had the heart for ministry to pull it off with real humility.

There was a kind of sinking feeling inside as Joanie felt herself letting go of something that had been such a big part of her life, including her relationship with Brandon. But she sensed, as she sat there, that for her and Brandon to come back into the band would squelch the rising talents of the younger members who had stepped up to the plate in their absence.

When the song ended Joanie and Brandon clapped enthusiastically. Truly impressed with the good things happening with the band, they offered their words of encouragement. Band practice unfolded with the couple remaining off to the side throughout. They gave their advice when asked on specific pieces, but otherwise they stuck to the role of audience.

As the newlyweds drove home that night, Joanie was silent. Brandon opened the conversation partway home.

"What do you think of *New Spring's* new sound?" he asked his bride.

"They sound wonderful." After a moment of silence she confessed, "I think I'm kind of feeling jealous."

"Jealous of what?" Brandon asked.

"Jealous of their opportunity to continue to do that kind of ministry work. There's no way that we can go back now, is there?"

"I don't think so. That Jocelyn has an incredible voice. She reminds me of you. But no one would ever hear her if you were there. I mean, I remember noticing before that she could sing, but she was always in the background."

"And she deserves her chance, just like I had, to use that talent the way God intended it to be used—for His glory. I'm really happy to let her have that chance. I'm not at all jealous of *her*," Joanie explained. "I just wish I had a format to keep using my talents for ministry. *New Spring* was my platform—my opportunity. I just feel nostalgic at the idea of letting that go. After all, that's how God brought us together."

"That fateful night I came to hear you sing—if I had only seen what was coming down the pike . . ." Brandon began to tease.

"Would you have run?"

Brandon raised one eyebrow, in his characteristic way, as he pondered the situation. A furrow grew on Joanie's brow as she waited for his reply; finally, she smacked him on the arm with the back of her hand. "That's too long to think about it," she scolded.

Brandon laughed and grabbed her hand as she pulled it away. Pulling it up to his lips, he kissed the back of her hand and offered a quick glance toward her. Turning his eyes back to the road he replied, "I shouldn't have to answer that question at all. You already know I'm happier now than I've ever been in my life."

"That might be so, but it's your duty to tell me often. Everyday, in fact!"

"Really? Don't tell me you're that insecure about our relationship, dear."

"Not insecure at all," she defended. "I just want to be able to bask in it."

"Very well," he nodded. "I can certainly accommodate you. In fact," he added with a boyish grin, "it would be my pleasure to show you just how much I love you as often as you desire." He said as he turned the vehicle into their condo parking lot.

"Oh, you don't miss a beat, do you?" she said with a laugh.

"I don't intend to."

As the couple walked into their apartment, Joanie was quiet. Why did a new beginning have to mean an end to something else? It was an end to something that meant a great deal to her. Still, the gracious thing to do was to step down and let the younger set take over. Joanie knew that. She was convinced it was God's will for her, but she was not finding the process of letting go very easy.

She hung her jacket over the back of the chair as she walked into the kitchen to get a drink of water. "Do you want anything?" she called out to her husband.

"No thanks," Brandon called back from the living room, as he picked up Joanie's jacket and carried it to the front closet to hang it up. Moving around as well as he could on his sore foot, he tidied up the shoes at the front door and then went to sit down at the couch, picking up his twelve string guitar from its stand along the way.

He began fooling around on the guitar, his fingers moving over the strings with familiarity. He hummed quietly as he played.

Joanie walked in from the kitchen and looked over at her husband sitting on the couch. On the wall above him was the beautiful framed drawing that Katie had given them as a wedding gift. *Keep us under your mantle of love and protection,* Joanie prayed silently to the Blessed Mother, gazing at the detail of every fold in Mary's mantle stretched out above the couple. She smiled and sat in the big armchair across the room from Brandon so she could hold him in view with the treasured portrait. "What's that you're playing?" she asked after a moment, returning her attention to him.

"Something I wrote," he replied, looking up at his wife.

Joanie's mouth formed a smile, with her lips still closed. She loved to watch Brandon play guitar. She loved to listen to him sing. His talents never ceased to impress her. Songwriting was a talent that he had just begun exploring over the past few weeks, since their honeymoon—being laid up with his sprained foot. This was a new song that Joanie had not yet heard. It was good. But then, that was not surprising in the least.

"Start over," she said, imploring him with her eyes. "And sing louder so I can hear it all."

Brandon returned the song back to the beginning and began to sing it for his wife. It was a gentle, worship song—beautifully melodic. As Brandon sang, Joanie hummed along in harmony. Catching on to the words of the chorus, she joined in with the simple refrain. She closed her eyes and allowed the melody and words to wash over her.

When the song ended, she asked her husband, "Why did you never compose music before now?"

"I don't know," he shrugged his shoulders. "I guess I never thought I could. Or maybe there were no songs inside of me to write. All I know is that I *have* to do it now because I feel the songs so strongly within me. I can't *not* do it."

"I wish I could write songs," Joanie said.

"You can help me with this one," Brandon suggested. He began strumming an upbeat rhythm. It was a praise song Joanie had heard him working on earlier that week—but all he had ever done was the chorus. She joined in with the singing.

"So what do want help with?"

"There's a verse in there. I can hear the melody for it—I just can't seem to come up with the words. I must just need you to help me," he stated, motioning with his head for Joanie to come sit with him.

She got up from the chair and moved beside him on the couch. As she sat beside him, Brandon used the neck of the guitar to gently pull her to sit further back. Moving the guitar out of his way, he leaned over to give his wife a kiss. "That's better," he stated, bringing his guitar back into position to play. "I'm already feeling inspired."

Joanie shook her head at his playfulness.

For over an hour the couple sat at the couch working on that and several other songs. Brandon would teach Joanie the lyrics, and being the natural performer that she was, the lyrics just stuck. She took the lead in several of the songs, with Brandon singing harmony. Occasionally they would change parts.

Finally they decided to call it a night. They both had to get up for work the next day. Joanie picked up her glass and went into the kitchen. She took another drink of water and then set her glass beside the sink. She turned out the light and headed to the bedroom.

Brandon put away his guitar and went into the kitchen. He turned on the light and got a drink of water for himself. Finishing that, he washed his and Joanie's glasses and put them away in the cupboard. Wiping the counter dry, he hung the tea towel neatly on the handle of the oven, turned off the kitchen light, and left the room. He checked the patio and front doors on his way to bed.

When he got to the bedroom, Joanie had already slipped into her T-shirt nightie. Her clothes were hung out over the chair beside the closet. He picked up her shoes on his way past the closet to get changed into his pyjama bottoms. Putting his pants away in the closet and his shirt into the laundry hamper, he walked into the bathroom en suite where Joanie had just finished getting herself ready for bed. She gave him a quick kiss on the cheek on the way by and went to crawl into bed.

Brandon straightened out the toothpaste tube, then flossed and brushed his teeth. He washed his face and dried off the counter with the towel before turning off the bathroom light to go to bed. He turned off the bedside light as he crawled into bed and snuggled up to his wife.

"We still have to say the rosary," she reminded him.

"I know," he said, reaching back over his shoulder to produce a rosary from his bedside table.

"Just nudge me if I fall asleep while we're praying," Joanie said with a yawn.

"*If?*" Brandon responded with amusement. "You haven't stayed awake once through a rosary that we've tried to say together in bed."

"I can't help it. I grew up Catholic. I used to use the rosary to put myself to sleep at night when I couldn't sleep. If you want me to stay awake through the rosary, we have to say it earlier—not in bed. It's just like a sleeping pill for me."

"I don't really mind you not finishing it with me. It's just that once you fall asleep, I don't get my good-night kiss," he whispered in her ear.

"Well, kiss me now," she suggested.

He leaned over her and kissed her tenderly. After a few moments she interrupted the kiss and said, "That's enough. We still have a rosary to pray."

"We're *definitely* going to have to pray this together earlier in the day," he remarked with feigned dismay, rolling back onto his pillow.

Joanie giggled. With her rosary she made the sign of the cross, kissing the crucifix to venerate the Lord. Brandon followed suit with his own rosary and began to lead, "I believe in God, the Father almighty . . ."

Chapter 8

The next night found Joanie and Brandon at St. James Church basement, sitting in chairs and waiting for the *Praise Event* to begin. This was a ministry that *New Spring* had begun a few years earlier, every second Friday of the month. Their band opened and closed, with other groups getting up to perform throughout the evening. A praise leader kept things moving along, with prayer time between sets as bands changed. Often individuals would come forward and share their testimony of faith. It was always followed by a time of fellowship.

It was to a *Praise Event* that Joanie had invited Brandon to come, just a year and a half earlier. And it was that very event that had set into motion his entire conversion. Sitting together in the audience now, holding hands, took Joanie back to that amazing night—filled with confusion and wonder as Brandon held her hand for the first time.

Joanie smiled down at their hands, with fingers locked together, her engagement and wedding rings sparkling back up at her. She did not say a thing. Brandon caught her expression and whispered into her ear, "No, I haven't forgotten."

"You better not," she threatened, squeezing his hand.

The evening was a completely new experience for Joanie. Never before had she sat out and participated entirely from the audience. *New Spring* and all the other bands had done a wonderful job. But she missed being on the stage. She realized how much of her identity had been wrapped up in her being a performer. She knew that God was asking her to sit back and just be part of the crowd—anonymous and unseen. Certainly she was still fully capable of offering her praise from there.

She resented the pride that she was uncovering dwelling within her heart. Obviously she needed purifying. *I think I'm supposed to thank You, Jesus, for this opportunity to grow in humility. But honestly, I'm having a hard time letting go. I know You have a plan for me—and for all the gifts You've given me. So why am I not trusting You? Help me to trust You, Jesus. Help me not to crave worldly praise and attention, Jesus. Help me to hide my heart in Yours. Purify my heart to serve You faithfully . . . and humbly.*

Brandon looked over at his wife, whose eyes were closed in prayer, but the expression on her face was not at peace. He knew what was going on inside of her, but he was not sure how he could ease her struggle. He just held onto her hand and offered his own prayers for her. He trusted God had a plan. There was no doubt that God intended for Joanie to use her gifts of music to glorify Him. In fact, Brandon was welcoming the opportunity for them, as a couple, to find their own way to serve the Lord together. Joanie just needed to get over this hump: let go before she could move on.

That night back at their condo as Joanie was getting ready for bed, she was obviously agitated. Brandon observed her irritation, but did not say a word. He kept to himself as he got ready for bed.

Taking the tube of toothpaste out from the shelf, he smoothed it out before he used it and then placed it back. Joanie looked at him out of the corner of her eye, but he took no note as he continued his routine of wiping down the countertop.

Joanie did not crawl under the covers as she got into bed that night. She sat up, leaning on her pillow, with her legs pulled up and her arms wrapped around them. Brandon climbed into his side of the bed, but did not turn off the bedside light. He leaned up against the headboard with his head propped up by his pillow and asked, "So, what's up, dear?"

Joanie took a deep breath and pushed it out, blowing some of her long curls off her face in the process.

"Is there something bugging you, Joanie, more than just the band?" Brandon asked, somewhat cautiously.

"You know," she began, "now that you're moving around better, you've begun to fall into some annoying behaviours."

Brandon shook his head in bewilderment. "What are you talking about?"

"It's little things, Brandon. And I'm sure you're not even aware that you're doing them. But it's the way you rearrange everything in a room after I've gone through it—from wiping down the counters, to tidying up my shoes, to picking up my things. . . . And if you smooth out that tube of toothpaste one more time after I use it, I swear, I'm going to hit you over the head with it!"

"Wow," he said, dumbfounded. "I don't know what to say, Joanie." He ran his fingers through his hair and shook his head.

"Just say you'll stop being so . . . so anal-retentive," she blurted out.

"Joanie!" Brandon laughed. "I have two choices right about now. I can pull out my gloves and take you on here, dear. Or I can overlook your harsh criticism of my personality."

"Orrrr," she added a third option, "you can admit you're being a control-freak and say you'll stop following behind me like an over-obsessed maid."

Brandon just started laughing and shook his head slowly back and forth. *"Orrrr,"* he imitated her tone back to her. He was prepared to offer a fourth option. "I could just start kissing you until you snap out of your little tirade. I mean," he added with boyish delight, "that sounds like the option that would present the most fun—and probably produce the best results for conflict-resolution."

Joanie grunted at him and kept a scowl firmly planted on her face. "I'm not ready to be brushed off, Brandon," she stated, soberly.

Brandon scratched his chin and sat up. "Okay, dear. We can talk about this, if you want."

"I wouldn't have brought it up, if I hadn't intended for us to discuss it," she retorted.

"Okay," he responded with growing annoyance. "You know, dear," he began calculating his words, "you come from a large family and you've carried over with you certain large-family habits into marriage that I thought better to just overlook, rather than to quibble about."

"Certain *large-family habits?"* she repeated, punctuating each word.

"You know, like leaving things lying around. You sort of put things away, but not completely where they go. You clean up after yourself, but you never quite finish the task," he explained.

"I do so finish the task," she cut in, defensively. "The problem is, you've lived for so long as a spoiled only-child and then a self-absorbed bachelor, you don't know how to give and take in a relationship," she accused.

Brandon shook his head in disbelief. "Joanie, do you really mean what you're saying?"

"Absolutely," she replied adamantly. "I mean, you criticize me for coming from a large family, Brandon. But I thought you wanted to have a large family of your own. How do you expect to get along, following after me and eight children, picking up behind us everywhere we go? I mean, really, you're going to have to learn to relax your standards a bit."

"I'm not criticizing you coming from a large family," Brandon defended himself. "I'm just pointing out that I understand where some of your habits come from. And I know I've been spoiled my whole life, never having to share my space with anyone else. But that wasn't my fault, you know. I couldn't help it that I was an only-child. But I don't at all agree with your assessment that I don't know how to give and take in a relationship." By this point, Brandon's tone of voice had taken on a certain coolness.

Joanie did not respond immediately. Something in that cool tone of voice broke through her self-absorbed mentality of the moment. She did not want her husband speaking so coolly toward her. Then again, he probably did not want her to be so bitingly critical toward him.

She gave a small heave, reached out, and put her hand on Brandon's arm. "I'm sorry," she said, simply.

"I'm sorry, too," he replied. The coolness was gone, but the hurt was still there in his voice.

"I just feel like I've been living like a guest in *your* home, Brandon. And I don't want to be a guest in your home. I want to be your wife, in *our* home," Joanie explained, openly and honestly.

"Ah, Joanie," Brandon sighed, "I don't mean to make you feel that way. I'm sorry."

"I know you don't," Joanie replied. "I think it's just me going through some sort of identity crisis right now—what with *New Spring* and all. I just feel upset and disoriented, and don't know where to strike out. I'm sorry for striking out at you."

"Hey, what are husbands for?" Brandon responded lightly.

Joanie smiled and leaned her head on Brandon's shoulder. He put his arm around her and gave her shoulder a little squeeze. "You know, we really should lay out some ground rules for fighting."

"For fighting?" Joanie sat up and looked at him. "I don't want to fight with you."

"I'm sure you don't. But I'm sure we will. Little things come up, you know . . . like tonight."

Joanie made a grimacing face. "I suppose. . . . So, what kind of rules are you proposing?"

"Well, first I think we need to curtail the name-calling," he suggested.

"Sorry about that, Brandon." Joanie winced and shrugged her shoulders apologetically.

Brandon chuckled. "And I think we need to be careful not to make accusations at each other. I think we'll do much better if we stick to the *'I feel'* statements," he said, making quotation marks around "I feel" with his fingers in the air. "For example, it might have gone a lot smoother had you just said to me, 'Brandon, I feel hurt when you walk around behind me picking things up,' instead of calling me a spoiled, self-absorbed, anal-retentive, control-freak. Not to say that I'm not all those things, it's just . . . well, a guy kind of likes to hear his wife describe him in gentler, more endearing terms than that."

Joanie's hands were covering her mouth, her eyes wide opened. "Did I really call you all that?" she asked humbly and apologetically.

"Yeah, you did," he answered with a chuckle. "But I'm willing to forgive and forget."

"Please," she beseeched him. "Could you just strike it from the record?"

"Done." He smiled at his wife through piercing blue eyes, with that smile that had first caught Joanie's attention and which eventually had helped to capture her heart.

"Is it too late to go with that kissing option?" she asked, nudging Brandon with her shoulder.

"Oh, never too late for that," he replied with eagerness.

"I love you," she said, as he took her into his arms.

"I love you, too," he replied, his hand playing with her long locks of curly hair. "And you're right," he admitted, stopping himself before kissing his bride. "I'm going to have to learn how to relax my obsessive standards, if I'm going to survive with a large family."

Joanie giggled and nodded. "Thank you for being so wonderful and so patient with me, Brandon. I think *you* are going to be an awesome father for as large a family as the Lord sees fit to bless us with. I wouldn't have married you, if I hadn't thought so in the first place."

"Thanks," he said, accepting the compliment. "You know . . . I love your big family, Joanie. I want to have a family just like that with you."

"Well, we *could* get to work on that right now, sir, if you wanted," Joanie suggested with a coy smile.

"Now, that's the best suggestion I've heard all evening," Brandon replied, with a twinkle in his eye. "I'd be more than happy to comply, my lady."

Joanie laughed at his playfulness as Brandon reached behind his back and turned off the bedside light.

✝   ✝   ✝

Joanie came into the apartment from running errands the next morning; her hands were clutching several bags of groceries. Brandon jumped up from the couch where he had been playing guitar, laid his guitar down on the couch, and hobbled quickly across the room to help his bride.

"Relax," Joanie said. "I can handle these. And you still have a foot to baby, there, sir."

"Why didn't you tell me you were getting groceries?" he scolded. "I would have gone to help."

"You have a sore foot, Mr. Vaughn. And you should be taking better care of it, or I'll be stuck with a crippled husband for the rest of my life," she scolded back with a smile. "And I'm a big girl; I can make my way through a grocery store just fine."

"I know you can. I just like going with you. I like playing house with you," he said, smiling.

"Well, if you're that determined to stand on your foot, you can help me put away the groceries. I'll take these things to our bathroom."

By the time she had returned to the kitchen, Brandon had just about everything put away. She picked up the empty plastic grocery bags and tucked them into their holder on the inside of the pantry door. "I was thinking we could make French onion soup for lunch," she said, kissing Brandon on the cheek as she walked passed him to get the onions from the pantry.

"Sounds good," Brandon replied, then looking at his wife curiously he added, "What's up with you, today?"

"Oh," she began, while getting out a cutting board and knife, "I've been thinking about your songwriting."

"Yeah?" He took the knife from her hand in an effort to offer to cut the onions. She relinquished the knife and turned to take out a pot and the other ingredients.

"Maybe we should be looking at recording music, ourselves," Joanie suggested. "I mean we've always talked about it, and I've been thinking now that we're free of the band commitment, maybe it's the right time."

Brandon nodded with a smile. "I was thinking about the same thing, myself. But I wanted to wait until you were ready to move on from *New Spring*."

"I'm ready," she stated with finality. "One door closes; another one opens. And I was thinking, we can bring Amie in to do the keyboarding, and Kyle to do the drumming. We can pull in other instruments and voices from the other members of the band as we need."

"And I've got top rate, professional equipment at the studio—free for our use during off-hours. We could stay after work and begin laying tracks any time we're ready," he suggested.

"It's exciting, isn't it?" She stepped up beside him and wrapped her hands around his arm, laying her head against his shoulder. "The kind of stuff dreams are made of . . . don't you think?"

"It definitely has got potential," Brandon agreed, gazing down at his wife. After a few moments, he began to shake his head. "Nah, there's something else about you today."

"What d'you mean?" she replied, looking up at him mysteriously.

"You've got something up your sleeve." He set down the knife and pointed at her.

Joanie bit down on her lip, smiling. "Come with me," she said, taking him by the hand and leading him to their room.

Chapter 9

In Canada, Thanksgiving is celebrated the second Monday of October. All day long the Collins household had been buzzing with the excitement of cleaning up and getting the big meal prepared for that evening. This was the first opportunity for all their family to be together again since Joanie and Brandon's wedding. Even Maggie was coming home for the first time from the Sisters of the Immaculate Conception for the day. And Grandma and Grandpa Ledoux were coming over as well.

Jessie ran out to greet Joanie and Brandon as they pulled into the driveway.

"Where's everyone else?" Brandon asked, picking up the little girl and carrying her up to the house.

"Brandon, let me carry her," Joanie said.

"Relax, honey. My foot is just fine," Brandon called over his shoulder, shaking his head back and forth. "I think I can handle carrying this little bundle," he stated, looking into Jessie's big hazel eyes.

Jessie wrapped her arms tightly around Brandon's neck and gave him a big hug.

"So where is everyone?" Joanie repeated the question.

"They're in the house with Grandma and Grandpa," Jessie called out over Brandon's shoulder.

When the three walked into the house, they found Grandpa Ledoux sitting in the living room, telling a story with all the children gathered around him. He was a robust, bald man, with the charm of age written all over him. Joanie and Brandon slipped in quietly and took a seat at the couch next to Grandma Ledoux. Grandma was a slight woman, much smaller than Joanie, and spry as could be. Grandma reached over and took Joanie's hand in hers and held it. Joanie leaned over and gave her Grandma a kiss on the cheek.

Grandpa was telling a story about riding the rails during the Dirty Thirties. He talked about how he and his brother had made their way to Alberta to look for work. "I remember going one time for a whole week without having eaten a thing," he told the children. "You kids don't know what it's like to be hungry. But my brother, Bernard, and I, we were truly hungry." He paused for effect. "Can you imagine what it'd be like to go without food for a whole week?" he asked the children.

A near-dozen pairs of eyes looked back at the old man, mesmerized by their grandpa's commanding presence. A few of the little children shook their heads in response to his question, but they did not dare say a word to interrupt the expert story-teller.

"Well, as luck would have it, one day we spotted a potato patch behind a farmer's yard. And you have to remember, back in those years of drought not every farmer had a garden. Food was just plain scarce. We waited until nightfall and then we snuck into the garden." Grandpa made a crawling motion with his hands and legs. "In the dark we crawled through the potato plants and felt under each one—not wanting to disturb them so they could keep growing and provide food for the farmer and his family. We dug around carefully and pulled a potato out from about a dozen plants or so. We carried the potatoes out in our shirts and went back to where we had left our little packs. We had an old tin can that we had found, about yay big," he said, motioning with his big hands. "We poured in some water that we had gotten from a well the day before, knocked off the dirt from the potatoes, and cooked them up. Let me tell you," he said, nodding to each of the children, "no potato—before or since—has ever tasted better to me than the potatoes Bernard and I shared together that night.

"Now I suppose it was wrong for us to have stolen those potatoes. I don't want to go on the record as condoning stealing or nothing . . . I wouldn't wanna lead you kids down the garden path." He shook a finger in the air at the grandchildren in warning, while chuckling at his play on words. A few confused faces stared back at him, not at all seeking an explanation as to why they should not become gardeners. Grandpa went on to make his point.

"We were starving, and we weren't thinking about right from wrong. I suppose we should have gone back the next day and confessed to the farmer. But those were tough times. A boy could've gotten shot by an angry farmer for stealing potatoes. So we just said a prayer for him and his family and moved on our way the next day."

"Did you ever get caught?" asked a wide-eyed Aaron.

"No, Aaron, we didn't," Grandpa replied.

"Grandpa?" Aaron asked again, confused and fascinated over the story. "Did you ever go to confession?"

"For stealing?" Grandpa asked the lad.

"Yeah," Aaron said, nodding his head.

"As a matter of fact, I did, Aaron, a little later on," Grandpa answered, smiling as he patted the blond-haired boy on the head.

"The whole story is a good reminder," interjected Grandma from across the room. "We have so much in our world now—we forget what it's like to go without. In fact, you children have *never* had to go without. You don't know what it's like to go all day without eating and finally get a slice of dried out, flat bread at the end of the day to hold your belly while you sleep."

"I'll tell you this much," stated Grandpa, "when you've done without, you learn all about gratitude for what you finally do get. For example, if you're grateful for that piece of bread you have to eat, you won't be complaining about the steak you wanted to have instead."

"That's for sure," agreed Grandma. "For as certain as you have it given to you, it can all be taken away as well."

"So, that's your Thanksgiving lesson," Grandpa said, brushing his hands together in finality. "Let's just be thankful to God for everything we have. I know I'm sure thankful to be sitting here smelling that turkey in the other room."

He turned his head toward the doorway between the kitchen and living room where Judy had been standing, listening to her father talk. John stood just behind her with his hand resting on her shoulder.

"Supper's all ready to go," she announced. "So you don't need to just sit there and smell it, Dad. You can come an' get it."

As everyone began to get up to move to the kitchen, John put up his hand to stop them. "Why don't we just pray our grace here," he suggested. "And before we do that, let's all take a turn saying one thing that we're thankful to God for today. I'll begin. I'm thankful to enjoy a day with my entire family gathered together."

Judy took her turn thanking God for the gift of her parents. Maggie was thankful that the Sisters of the Immaculate Conception had not yet kicked her out. Everyone laughed. "Seriously, though, I'm thankful that the Lord has blessed me with the opportunity to serve Him through a religious vocation." Amie was thankful for getting accepted into Stettler College. Isaac was thankful for his new guitar. Grandpa was thankful for his grandchildren. Aaron was thankful that Grandpa had not been shot for stealing potatoes. Zack was thankful that his grandpa was no longer a thief. Grandpa's deep rumbling laugh echoed in the background as the boys took their turns. Katie was thankful that she had a place to keep her artwork and supplies safe in her bedroom, now that Joanie and Maggie had moved out. Amie leaned over to Maggie and whispered, "You should see how she's taken over the room with her easels." Maggie giggled. Jessie was thankful for her mommy and daddy. Grandma was thankful for living in a free country.

Finally it came around for Joanie to take her turn. She paused for a moment, turned to Brandon with a curious smile on her face, and announced, "I'm thankful that mom and dad are going to become grandparents."

There was a moment of silence in the room and then Katie screamed out, "Joanie's pregnant!" Suddenly there was a great commotion surrounding Joanie and Brandon.

"When'd you find out?" asked Amie.

"Yesterday," Joanie said. "I went out to get groceries—and pick up a pregnancy test—and then gave Brandon a really good surprise when I got home."

"I don't know why I wasn't expecting it," he said. "I guess when we decided to just leave it all in God's hands I wasn't paying very good attention to how much time had passed. And you know how time flies when you're having a good time," he added with a wink—to the amusement of Grandpa Ledoux, whose husky laugh rose up from across the room.

"It just made it all the more fun for me to be able to surprise you, dear," Joanie said, giving her husband a kiss.

"Well, in keeping with the momentum of grace, here, I'm really thankful that I'm going to be a dad," Brandon announced, turning his attention back to the family sitting around the room.

Everyone laughed.

"On that happy note, I think we should finish grace," John stated. He offered up a prayer of thanksgiving and then led the family in their traditional grace and the Angelus.

When the prayers concluded, Judy invited everyone to the table where the Thanksgiving feast would be served. She asked her older girls to step into the kitchen to help her bring over the food.

When Joanie approached to get the cooked veggies, her mother tugged her on the arm and turned her daughter toward her to give her a big hug. Suddenly both Joanie and her mother had tears in their eyes. They began to laugh at themselves, but before they could dry their eyes, Maggie, Amie, and Katie had joined in a group hug.

"You spend twenty-some years raising a family," Judy stated, wiping her eyes with a napkin, "and all of a sudden everything seems to happen at once. When are you due?"

"The beginning of June," Joanie answered, smiling at her mom. "June sixth, to be exact." There was a moment's pause and then Joanie hugged her mom again. "I'm so happy, Mom," she whispered. "I always wanted to be just like you when I grew up."

Judy laughed and then began crying all over again. Not knowing what to say, she hugged her eldest daughter again. "I love you, sweetheart."

"If you ladies in the kitchen would stop crying," John called out from the table, "you might notice the rest of us starving over here."

"Yeah, come on," Zack called out impatiently. "I'm totally starving."

Maggie carried the platter of turkey over to her dad and quickly kissed him on the cheek before going back to get more food from the island in the kitchen. John smiled at his daughter. How he missed having her around.

Conversation over dinner was in typical Collins style—completely random. They talked about all kinds of things, with all sorts of speculations about the newest member of the family hidden in their midst. Over dessert, the children managed to beg another couple of stories from Grandpa about the good ol' days. Then Maggie shared about her experiences over at the Sisters' house. She kept everyone in stitches, as she recounted one misadventure after another. They all knew Maggie and wondered how the Sisters would ever survive her presence.

Finally the little children, from Zack down, begged to be excused. As they left the table there was a lull in the conversation.

After a few moments of silence, Katie casually commented, "Well, I'm impressed about one thing. I never thought I'd see the day when Maggie would be wearing a skirt. But here she is."

"I wear these crazy things every day—day in, day out," Maggie bragged to her younger, more fashionable and more femininely-inclined sister.

"So do you like it?" Katie asked.

"Ah, it's growing on me," Maggie admitted. "When I first started, I didn't think I'd survive. But after washing the floors in them, I decided to resign myself to my fate. However, I have decided that I won't let skirts change me. I still climb trees. There's a great tree in the backyard at the Sisters for climbing. I just tie my skirt together between my legs. Since I wear long, loose ones anyway, it works perfectly. I climb the tree, untie my skirt, and sit there for as long as I want, reading and praying."

"Only you," Katie responded to her older sister.

"I'm not like you, Katie," Maggie replied. "You wear skirts for no reason at all; in fact, you probably actually *like* wearing skirts."

"That's because I'm a girl, Maggie," Katie whispered back, as though letting her sister in on a secret.

Judy laughed. Her daughters were all so very different.

"I have to admit," Joanie interjected. "I've been wearing skirts more often lately, too, at work. And I find that I feel different when I'm in a skirt."

"Of course you do," Grandma Ledoux spoke up. "When a girl wears a skirt she remembers *who* she is. It helps you to be in touch with your feminine virtues, dear. You walk differently. You act differently. You carry yourself differently."

"I bet that sounds too old-fashioned for this younger generation," Grandpa piped in. "But I can tell you this much. When a man sees a woman in a skirt, *he* remembers who she is, too. And he's much more likely to be a gentleman toward her."

"I agree," stated John.

"Well, why'd you never say anything about it before now?" Judy asked her husband. "We've been married twenty-four years, and you've never once mentioned to me you'd rather see me in a skirt."

"I don't know," John replied with a shrug. "It's just that men and women—all of us—have become so accustomed to women in pants, we just don't even question it anymore. But I think women look . . . well, more feminine . . . in a skirt." Hesitating to go on, John threw a look at his son-in-law and asked, "What do you think about it, Brandon?"

"Oh, I'm just still thinking about fatherhood these days," Brandon responded, to which everyone laughed.

"Come on, son, you don't get off that easy," John coaxed him. "What would you prefer to see your wife in, pants or a skirt?"

"Well, probably a skirt," Brandon replied, not really thinking about it.

"Really?" asked Joanie. "We've been married five weeks, and you've never once mentioned this to me before now?"

Everyone laughed, as the young wife imitated her mother.

"I don't know," Brandon added with reflection, "skirt or pants . . . I think what's most important is that a woman dresses modestly. And I have to tell you just how much I appreciate the fact that the women in this family do dress modestly. It's something I noticed right away when I first started coming around here. And it shows that you all have self-respect."

"Thank you," said Judy in response to her son-in-law's observation.

"As you remember—all too well—I wouldn't have *always* said that. But at the time in my life when I didn't value modesty in women, I also had no use for a girl's self-respect. The two kind of play hand in hand. How a girl dresses certainly implies to the guys around her what her morals are."

"And I don't think that girls have half-a-clue what dressing immodestly does to men," added Grandma Ledoux. "Here we've got such a sophisticated generation, with all their technologies and highfalutin education, and yet they still don't grasp the simplest things about human nature. And we wonder why there's so much sin in the world," she said shaking her head.

"Why does all the responsibility fall on girls?" Maggie complained. "Why can't boys learn to just keep their eyes in their head?"

"Some of us do try," replied Brandon. "But then again, I didn't always. You have to remember, Maggie, there are good guys out there, and there are bad guys."

"Yes," agreed John, "and you want to make it easy for the good guys to stay good and hard for the bad guys to be bad . . . just remember that." He playfully shook a scolding finger at his daughters.

Again, laughter rose around the table.

"And it's a lot harder on guys than you would ever realize," said Grandpa. "A man—right from the time he's a boy—needs to learn to take custody of his eyes. He needs to learn to look at a woman—or a girl—as a person, not an object for his pleasure. Well, it's a whole lot easier on the guy when the girl is dressed modestly. When a girl is dressed immodestly, it takes a lot more effort for the guy to keep his attention on her and not her body. It takes real self-discipline."

"And unfortunately, not every guy out there is willing to be disciplined in that manner," Brandon added.

"They sure aren't," agreed John. "And our society is just training guys to view women as objects."

"And it reduces women to value themselves only for their appearance," added Judy. "Body image issues are taking their toll on girls. I just wish every girl could see herself as that unrepeatable, irreplaceable, unique, and beautiful child of God that she is—no matter what her size or shape."

"Truly, I've never seen a girl that did not possess physical beauty," stated Grandpa.

"But I've met a whole lot of girls and women who are unhappy with how they look," said Joanie. "There's just so much pressure to be picture-perfect. And we all feel that to some degree. It's easy to see why so many girls give into the latest fashions—immodest and all."

"A girl just naturally wants to receive attention from men," said Grandma. "It's just unfortunate that so many are willing to accept dressing immodestly to receive it. In the end, it's not the kind of attention that helps her to value herself as a person."

"No, it ends up having the opposite effect," agreed Judy. "But when a guy makes the effort to treat a girl with respect, to look at her as a person—and take his eyes off her body—it goes a long way to reinforcing her sense of self-worth."

"But a girl has to have that sense of self-worth, regardless," objected Maggie. "She shouldn't base her worth on how others see her. What matters is how Jesus sees us."

"True," Grandma responded. "But we're not islands, my dear—we *are* influenced by the way others treat us. And that's why dressing modestly not only communicates to the world about a girl's morals, but it also helps her to value herself all the more by the way others respond to her."

"And I have to say," Judy interjected, "having five daughters of my own, it's hard for a girl now-a-days to shop for modest clothes. It's hard to make good modest choices. There's a lot of pressure on them to fit in and to be fashionable. I think *any* effort they make needs to be applauded and

Surrender

supported. Let's face it, they could all be running around out there with low-cut shirts and skimpy nothings, and it would never be questioned by our society. I see a lot of these girls really trying hard to be modest with what they have to work with. What we need are good, moral, fashion designers to start making a difference in the industry so that our girls have some real options for modest fashions. After all, who wants to run around in a potato sack?"

"I'm trying to design modest clothes," jumped in Katie. "I just need a chance to get my designs out there."

"You do lovely work designing clothes, my dear," Grandma Ledoux complimented the sixteen-year-old. "And you just keep it up, because you *are* making a difference around you. And God's going to put those talents to use—you bet."

"Hear! Hear!" saluted Grandpa Ledoux with his glass toward his granddaughter. He winked at her and she returned his look with a shy but big, beautiful smile. Katie was not immune to praise and appreciation, especially when it came from her grandpa.

"Well, that was a lovely meal, daughter," Grandpa Ledoux concluded. "But it's Thanksgiving Day, and we're not leaving here until we've had a family sing-song. I've got a fiddle out there in the front room that's begging to be played. And I noticed young Brandon walked in here today without a guitar, but I'm sure we can scrounge something up for you around this house."

Isaac jumped up at the suggestion and responded to the cause, saying, "I'll go get one for him."

"And get one for yourself, too," called out Grandpa. "We have to keep the music going in the family."

As the men retired to the living room, the women started clearing the table.

"This hardly seems fair," Katie complained. "How come *they* get to go off and play, and we get stuck cleaning up? We were the ones making the meal all day."

"Oh, don't you fret over that," Grandma answered the girl. "Who wants them in here anyway? I mean, far be it from me to say men shouldn't help with housework. It's important for a man to give his wife a hand with clean-up, and boys certainly need to help with dishes on a regular basis. But when there's a group of women to work together, we can enjoy some nice girl-talk without them around putting their two cents in."

The girls laughed at their grandmother, as she brought her finger over her lips to indicate for them to keep the secret.

"That's what I love about you, Grandma," said Amie. "You always find a silver lining to every cloud."

"I've always said—there's nothing all bad, that something good doesn't come of it," she reminded the girls.

As they cleared the table, put away food, loaded a dishwasher, and began scrubbing pots and pans, the ladies indulged in good womanly conversation.

"So how far along are you in your pregnancy, Joanie?" Maggie asked.

Joanie kind of laughed and replied, "*Officially*, I'm six weeks pregnant."

"Six weeks?" Maggie blurted out. "You've only been married five."

Joanie laughed, having anticipated that response. "Maggie, they count pregnancy from the beginning of a woman's last cycle—not from conception. So forty weeks of pregnancy actually accounts for two weeks prior to conception."

"Oh," Maggie nodded. "Not that you had me worried regarding your morals. I was just wondering how you'd become such a yutz at math."

"I just hope I'm not any too early delivering this baby," Joanie added. "I don't want people questioning my math . . . or my morals."

"I didn't have that problem when I got married," Grandma stated. "It was a whole month after we got married before we were able to . . . consummate our union."

The girls giggled, moving in closer to Grandma who was looking around the room cautiously and speaking in lower tones. "You see, Grandpa got good and sick on our wedding night. We had to leave the reception early, because he wasn't feeling well. In sickness and in health," she reminded the girls. "I just didn't expect it to start quite so soon. We went back to our little house that we had rented in town. Grandpa started throwing up and complaining about pain, and by midnight he had a terrible fever. I was just panicking. I didn't know what to do. So I ran over to the rectory, which was the closest place I could think of with a phone. I woke up Fr. Benoit and explained the situation. He had a car and came back with me to take Grandpa up to the hospital in the next town. It was a small hospital, and they had to call in the doctor in the middle of the night. As soon as Dr. McCormick got there he said he'd have to operate. He told me after the surgery that if I had waited until morning, Grandpa would have likely died. His appendix had ruptured. And we didn't have drugs back then like we do now to take care of infections. Grandpa took a good four weeks to recover from surgery. But . . . when all was said n' done, we figured out what comes naturally to young couples . . . and all was well. Your Uncle Joe was born nine months later."

The girls laughed over their grandmother's quaint and discreet story.

"And people are quite capable of figuring out what comes naturally," she stated emphatically. "All this," she paused and turned to make sure there were no children in the room, "all this *sex* education in schools is ridiculous," she admonished. "You don't need to teach a cat how to catch a mouse, and you don't need to teach a man and a woman how to be married. They figure it out just fine. I knew next to nothing about men when I got married and I still managed to have twelve children."

"Oh, Grandma," Amie said, giving the smaller, spry woman a hug, "you are so much fun to be around."

Grandma laughed and patted Amie on the back. "I like being around you kids, too," she replied. "I have wonderful grandchildren, and I'm proud of all of them. And whether their parents have home-schooled them or sent them to school, I'm happy to see that you've all been kept out of those shameless," she paused again to check out the vicinity, lowering her voice, "those shameless sex education programs in school. Good grief, you teach driver's education so that a kid can drive a car. You teach a kid how to swing a bat so he can play baseball. So what? You teach," she hushed her voice again, "you teach sex education to these kids so they can do what? *I'll* tell you what they're doing," she stood there waving a scolding finger in the air and raising her voice. "I may be old, but I'm not blind. And I didn't get all these white hairs on my head without having learned a thing or two about life."

By this time, Joanie, Maggie, Amie, and Katie were laughing so hard at their grandmother's speech that they could not keep working on the dishes. Judy finally called out through her laughter, "Oh, Mom, stop. You're killing us."

Grandma chuckled with the rest of them. "Well, you get my meaning," she said, nodding. "It's a mother's job to teach her daughters, and a father's job to teach his sons. I've heard some people say, 'We have to have those programs in schools because our kids are exposed to so much.' Bahh," she said, waving her hand in disgust. "Stop exposing your kids to it! If people would keep those filthy TV shows and movies out of their homes, and learn how to control those crazy computers, they would have fewer problems with their children."

"Amen!" exclaimed Maggie.

Grandma chuckled again, at herself. "Oh, I should stop going on. I think we've covered it all, anyway. So, now that we've solved half the world's problems and we've finished the dishes, why don't we go join the men?"

The women all followed their grandmother's lead and headed into the living room. The singing and playing and laughing carried on until about ten o'clock. Being a work night, the family reluctantly packed it in and said good-night to their guests as Grandma and Grandpa, Joanie and Brandon, and Maggie all left.

✝   ✝   ✝

When Judy was finally able to crawl into bed that night, she snuggled up to John, gave him a kiss on the cheek, and whispered, "Good-night, Grandpa."

"Good-night, Grandma," he whispered back over his shoulder.

"I was thinking," she said.

"Oh, oh," he replied. "Those are always dangerous words coming from a woman."

She smacked him on the shoulder. "Cut it out," she scolded. "I was just wondering, do you think we'll be grandparents like my mom and dad?"

"What do you mean?" John returned, rolling onto his back to turn toward his wife.

"Able to pull off everything with such humour and fun," Judy answered. "Even when those two are serious, they keep us laughing. I don't remember them being like that when I was growing up. I mean, they were always fun and spunky. But they've acquired a certain gracefulness with age that I admire so much in them now."

"It could be that you've just grown up enough to appreciate them," John teased.

Judy chuckled in agreement.

"But I really think that it's because your mom and dad will always be young at heart, no matter how old they get," John commented. "And I don't see any reason for us to get old, just because we're starting to go grey, and we're now being promoted up a generation to grandparenthood."

"Well, as much as I like being young at heart and plan to stay that way," Judy stated, wrapping her arms around her husband, "I'm glad that I get to grow old with you."

Chapter 10

Brandon was in the kitchen preparing supper for their guests, Mark and Justine Jacobs. As he stood there, browning strips of meat for beef stroganoff, his thoughts were focused on Mark, his best friend from childhood. They had grown up together like brothers. By the time they were teens, Brandon had managed to influence Mark to leave his Evangelical Church and become an atheist. Freed from the burdens of religious constraints, the two boys pursued lives of hedonistic pleasure together, until one day Brandon met a girl who changed everything. . . .

"And here she is," Brandon announced, his thoughts interrupted as Joanie walked into the kitchen to get plates to set the table for supper.

"And here *who* is?" she inquired, looking around playfully.

"Here's the girl who changed it all," he said, giving Joanie a quick kiss on his way to the fridge to get the cream for the white sauce.

"Don't know what you're talking about, and I'm not sure if I want to."

"I was just thinking about me and Mark, growing up," Brandon said, as he worked over the hot stove. "I'm sure glad you came along and saved me from myself when you did."

"You're welcome," she said, taking down the dishes from the cupboard. "It was a soul well-worth saving," she quipped. "Though, I just pointed you in the right direction—Jesus is the One who does the saving."

"Well, I'm grateful He used you as the road sign for me."

"And then He used you for Mark and Justine. Faith—the gift that just keeps giving." She smiled and winked at her husband.

"I'm sure grateful to be such close friends with them still," Brandon reflected as he added pepper to his culinary creation. "In fact, sharing faith together has made my friendship with Mark much closer than it ever was—or could have been—before."

"They're a blessing in our life, that's for sure. . . . I've been thinking about them all day, myself." Joanie sat at their little kitchen island on a counter stool. "I was wondering how they'll take the news of our baby."

"I know," Brandon said, soberly. "I'm kind of apprehensive about that myself. When we saw them right after our honeymoon, Mark was telling me that things weren't going so well in that department for them."

"I know how much Justine wants to start a family," Joanie added. "I just feel guilty that they were married a few months before us, and now we're expecting before them. Yet I want to be happy about our baby. I *am* happy. I just don't want to rub salt into an open wound."

Brandon was finishing up the last touches for the meal. He poured the meat and sauce into a serving dish with a lid and set it in the oven to keep warm until supper. "Come on," he said, carrying the dishes for his wife. "I'll help set the table and then we can sit and pray until they get here, okay?"

Joanie followed him out into the dining area of their little apartment, and together they quickly got the table set for the meal. Once the job was done they sat down on the couch, held hands, and prayed. Brandon led them in offering up some petitions and spontaneous prayers; they then prayed the Lord's Prayer and a Hail Mary. That was as far as they got before the buzzer rang. Brandon jumped up to buzz their guests into the building and wait for them at the door. Joanie stood beside him.

Mark and Justine entered the apartment, with Mark's typical exuberant energy filling the place as he came in. Joanie immediately felt better seeing them. Justine was as beautiful as ever: her layers of blond hair hung elegantly over her shoulders. She had a regal presence to her, always carrying herself gracefully. Her bright blue eyes sparkled over a warm, friendly smile. She held onto Mark's hand as they came in and sat down on the couch. Mark's boyish grin shone out through his green eyes, under a head of wavy, brown hair.

The two couples chitchatted casually, catching up on the two weeks since they had last seen each other. Finally, Brandon decided that sooner was better than later, and they would do best to just make the announcement rather than prolong the situation.

"So . . . we have some news for you," he said, with a glint in his eyes.

Joanie noticed Justine's manner change, ever-so-slightly. She held Brandon's hand and waited for him to go on.

"We're expecting a baby," he announced.

There was a brief pause as Mark shook off the surprise. Evidently he had not anticipated such immediate results. He jumped up and reached out his hand toward Brandon. Brandon stood up to receive the handshake and Mark pulled him in for a hug.

"That's amazing!" Mark said, full of enthusiasm. "Mommy!" he exclaimed, with a big smile as Joanie stood up beside Brandon. Mark stepped over to hug her as well.

Justine got up to join the group, and she, too, gave a hug to the newly expectant parents. She was smiling as she said, "Congratulations," but her voice was quiet and controlled.

"So tell me," Mark chided, "how'd you do it? We're still trying to figure out how to make things work." He put his arm around Justine's shoulder.

Justine shook her head and tapped her husband on the belly. She was still smiling, but still quiet.

"Well, that's not all," Brandon stated, holding up his hands, not wanting to divert the conversation just yet. "We also want to ask the two of you if you would do us the honour of being godparents for this baby."

Justine's eyes opened wide, "Oh, I'd be so honoured," she said with a great deal of emotion. That was all she said. Joanie could see how her friend was struggling with the weight of everything on her heart.

"Actually," Brandon clarified, "Justine would be godmother and you, Mark, would technically *not* be 'godfather' . . . since we haven't managed to get you converted quite yet," he added with a wink.

Mark chuckled at Brandon's friendly teasing.

"As I understand it, Church regulations require at least one Catholic godparent, and the other can be a practising Christian, but then he or she is called a 'Christian Witness', not godparent," Brandon finished explaining.

"But to be honest," added Joanie, "we can't imagine a better Christian Witness for our child than what you would be, Mark."

Justine smiled up at her husband who still had his arm over her shoulder.

"Well, I have a solution for that," Mark said in return. "I've already talked to Fr. Steve about it, and I'll be coming into the Church next Easter. So if you wait to have this baby until after Easter, I'll be able to be the godfather, after all."

Brandon and Joanie laughed. "Sounds perfect, buddy," Brandon threw back to his friend.

"And while we're on the topic, I'm counting on you to be my sponsor through the R.C.I.A. program, Brandon."

Brandon grabbed Mark into another hug. "It's a deal, buddy. Come on—let's go celebrate with a drink." The men headed toward the kitchen. "Can I get anything for you ladies?" Brandon called back.

"A cooler would be great," replied Justine. "Any flavour will do. Thanks."

"One cooler coming up. And you, dear?"

"Just some pop, honey," Joanie called back.

"Oh, yeah," he corrected himself, "what was I thinking?"

Joanie laughed at him as he disappeared into the kitchen. He came trotting back out a few moments later with drinks for the girls, handed them over, and returned to the kitchen as quickly as he had come out.

"I guess they want some boys' time," Joanie remarked. She lifted her drink toward Justine's and toasted, "Here's to friendship."

Justine lifted her bottle to clank it lightly against Joanie's can, as the two ladies sat back down on the couch and loveseat across from each other.

"So tell me, honestly, Justine," Joanie began, now that it was just the two of them, "how do feel about all this? I mean, how are you doing . . . ?" Her voice trailed off, not knowing how to form the question and wondering whether or not she should be asking it at all.

Justine smiled through closed lips and thought for a moment. "I'm fine. I . . . I'm very happy for you, Joanie. And I'd be lying if I didn't say I was feeling a little jealous, but that's not because I'm not happy for you. . . . I just want to be able to have a baby, too." Determined not to let herself cry, Justine managed to choke back the tears that were filling her eyes.

"I know," Joanie responded, filled with compassion, and fighting back tears now herself. "I want you and Mark to have a baby as well. And I can't imagine how hard it is for you to not have that happen right away, when you want it so much."

"When I saw a doctor last month he told me that we'd have to try for a whole year before they would even look at doing tests or anything. Apparently, we're trying *too* hard," Justine said with sarcasm as she wiped her eyes dry.

Joanie scoffed in disbelief, "What does *that* mean?"

"He suggested that if we don't think about it too much, it might reduce the stress associated with it and then things can happen," she explained. "But I don't know how to *not* be stressed about it. I mean, I'm stressed because I *can't* get pregnant. . . . I wasn't stressed before we started to try."

"Ah, Justine." Joanie hesitated. She really did not know what to say. "I'm struggling inside with knowing how best to be a supportive friend for you through this. And at the same time, I want to be free to share with you and Mark about our baby. We want so much for you to be the godparents—because you're so important to us."

"Look, Joanie," Justine said, sitting up tall again. Joanie had not even noticed that Justine had sunken in her posture, but there was a visible change now in her resolve. "I'm happy for you and Brandon, and I don't intend to steal one moment of your joy from you." She put up her hand to show she wanted to say something more. "It would be easy for me to fall into self-pity. And being jealous is just plain . . . well, it's wrong. I love you and Brandon and want what's best for you. I have to accept that God has a plan for Mark and me, and that it's going to be perfect—because that's the way God is. And it doesn't mean that it won't be painful. I just know that in the end, if we just trust God to lead us through this, we'll be able to see that His hand was guiding and protecting us. And I have to hold onto that—because it's the only thing that can make sense out of this for me right now."

"Justine, *you* are an amazing woman. I'd like to think I would be as gracious as you, if I were in the same position."

"I'm sure you would be," Justine returned. "I learned half of what I'm saying from you, you know." She smiled sincerely at her friend.

Joanie shook her head. "I don't know about that. I've learned a lot from you, and I'm grateful to have you as a friend. . . . Come on," she said, beginning to get up from the loveseat, "let's go round up those guys for supper."

Chapter 11

Paul Petros poked his head into Brandon's office Monday morning. "I just heard the news."

Brandon swirled his chair around to the sound of the thirty-four-year-old cameraman's voice. "Hey," he said, with a big smile.

A broad smile showed off Paul's white teeth against his dark complexion. "You two sure didn't waste any time figuring out how things work."

"We couldn't see any good reason why we should wait to start a family," Brandon replied.

"Not if you're going to fit in those dozen kids that I'm sure you and Joanie are planning to have." Over the time that Paul had watched the relationship between Joanie and Brandon blossom, from its secretive beginnings at the station until their engagement and wedding, he had grown to have a real appreciation for the Christian convictions of this young couple.

"God-willing," Brandon answered. "We'll take as many as He'll send. . . . So, how was your holiday?"

"Great. Left the kids with Grandma and Grandpa, and Camille and I took off for eight days together on a Caribbean cruise. Now that's living!" he exclaimed. "Hard to come back to reality. And I love my two kids, but it was still hard to come home."

"Has Joanie seen you yet?" asked Brandon. "She sure missed you while you were gone. There's no cameraman she'd rather work with than you, Paul. You've spoiled her."

"We go out on a shoot later this morning," Paul told him. "That is if she can pull herself away from the toilet."

Brandon looked at his friend curiously. "What are you talking about?"

"When I met with her just twenty minutes ago, she was sicker than a dog. Reminded me of Camille when she was pregnant. Makes me appreciate I'm a man," he stated.

Brandon got up in a hurry from his chair. "I'll just go check on her," he said, moving past Paul.

Paul patted his friend on the back as he left the office.

✠   ✠   ✠

Brandon found Joanie at her cubicle in the newsroom. Her head was resting in the crook of her arms on her desktop. "Hey," he said, softly. "What's up?"

"Breakfast was up a few minutes ago," she mumbled, not lifting her head.

"You gonna be okay? You look awful," he said, crouching down beside her chair and rubbing her back.

She moaned and pulled away slightly from his hand. "Don't shake me, please," she whispered.

"Do you need to go home?"

"I don't think I can make it through the day. I thought if I let myself throw up I'd feel better. And I did for about fifteen minutes. But it's all coming back," she answered, without opening her eyes.

"I'm going to go talk to Shelly," he told her. "I'll be back right away to take you home."

Shelly Lesichyn was in a meeting with Mr. Lemay, the station manager, when Brandon located her. Getting permission to interrupt the meeting, the commercial producer stepped in. Explaining Joanie's situation, he asked to be able to take her home. He would return to work later that day. Shelly had to make alternate arrangements to fill in for Joanie's spot on the news that night. She left the meeting with Mr. Lemay and walked out with Brandon.

"You take good care of that wife of yours," she said to Brandon.

"I'll do my best."

✠   ✠   ✠

Joanie's "morning sickness" turned into an "all day and even throughout the night" sickness. She quickly found herself bedridden. After missing two days of work Brandon took her in to see the doctor who prescribed a medication to help control nausea.

"It's a combination of vitamin B6 and an antihistamine," Dr. Wilson informed her. "It's been on the market for almost twenty years in Canada, and it's considered safe for both mom and baby," she assured Joanie.

"I just feel awful about taking any medication during pregnancy," Joanie stated.

"Joanie, you haven't held down anything for a few days, now. Becoming dehydrated, not to mention malnourished, will have worse effects on you and the baby. And if this continues, we'll be hospitalizing you," Dr. Wilson warned the newly expectant mother.

"I am tired of being sick around the clock," Joanie agreed. "Who ever came up with the term 'morning sickness'?"

Dr. Wilson laughed. Her smile was warm and motherly. "And I want you off work until you're feeling better," she added, still with a maternal tone.

Joanie took the medication and stayed off work until the following Monday. By then, though still very much nauseated, she at least was not constantly throwing up. Though she knew she needed to eat, the thought and smells of most foods made her feel sick. She ate small amounts at a time and managed her best to keep it down. Every waking moment was an effort. Brandon was concerned that she was not ready to go back to work, but Joanie insisted that she had a responsibility to her employer.

"You're still looking green around the gills," Shelly told her on Monday morning when Joanie showed up for the morning conference.

Joanie made an attempt at pitching a story idea for that day. Shelly told her they would talk after the conference. Once everyone else had their assignments set out for the day, Joanie and Shelly were left alone in the conference room.

"I don't think this is going to work, Joanie," Shelly began, taking off her glasses and leaving them to hang on a chain around her neck. "There's no way you're up to doing an assignment in this condition. Don't get me wrong. I want to have you here working. I love the work you do. But you can't get on the air each night looking like this. It wouldn't be fair to you to put you through all the work you have to do each day to bring a story to air, either. I think you should take a sick leave, until you get over this. And I'm saying this to you as a woman who has a great deal of respect and admiration for you. I don't want you to take it the wrong way."

Joanie looked at Shelly with tears in her eyes. At first Shelly thought that Joanie might be upset with her. Finally, with a rather weak voice, Joanie said, "Thank you." She was much too sick to force the issue and was more than happy to relinquish her position at the station until she got back to normal. She had only been sick for a week and already she really could not quite remember what normal felt like. She gave Shelly a hug and went back to her work station to pack up things. From there she called Brandon to take her home.

"You going to be fine here?" he asked Joanie as he was getting ready to head back to work. Joanie was lying in bed, curled up in a ball, hugging a pillow.

"I'll be fine," she assured him.

He gave her a kiss on the cheek and with some holy water he traced a cross on her forehead in blessing. "I'll come home right after work," he promised her. "Call me if you need anything. I have my cell on me."

Brandon left, and Joanie lay in bed saying some prayers. She was relieved to be free of the responsibility of work. She felt for women who had no choice but to work through the sickness of pregnancy. What a blessing it was to have a husband with a good-paying job, and to not have to worry about the finances. She soon fell asleep and stayed asleep until Brandon came home after work.

✝   ✝   ✝

"Hey, girl," came a soft voice in Joanie's ear as she lay in bed somewhere between sleeping and waking. Her eyes gradually flickered open and there, sitting at her bedside, was Maggie.

"Hey, girl," Joanie answered weakly, with a feeble smile.

"What'chya doing getting so sick on us?" Maggie asked, lightly running her fingers through her sister's hair.

Joanie heaved an almost imperceptible sigh. Everything was an effort. "I wasn't planning on this," she told her sister.

"We never do," came a familiar voice from at the foot of her bed.

Joanie's eyes opened wider to see her mother standing in the room. "Mom," she said, with a sense of peace and comfort coming over her.

"Do you remember me being laid up in bed, and you two taking care of me?" Judy asked her girls. "Just part of the privilege you both had, being the eldest daughters."

"How did you ever go through this eight times?" Joanie asked weakly.

"I went through this more than eight times. I had three miscarriages along the way," Judy reminded her daughter. "But I got through it each time because the Lord gave me the most incredible husband and daughters to help me get through it, not to mention the help I got from Grandma Ledoux and Grandma Collins—God bless her soul. And it was worth every moment of suffering, for the joy that each of you children has brought me."

Joanie smiled. She remembered getting meals for her mother in bed, tending to younger siblings, answering phone calls, and whatever else needed to be done while her mom was nauseated during the first few months of each pregnancy—at least the ones that she was old enough to remember. No matter how much work it meant for her, nor how much sacrifice was involved, after each baby was born she and her siblings begged her mom and dad to have more children.

"I know it's hard to even remember what normal feels like," her mother said gently, "but I promise you, Joanie . . . this, too, will pass."

"I know it will, Mom," she whispered.

"And we're here," Maggie said, "to let you know that we haven't forgotten you, out in the real world. Since you can't come to us, we came to you."

"How's it going for you?" Joanie asked her sister, tugging on her skirt.

"Much better than it's going for you," Maggie answered.

Joanie smiled again and sat up in bed.

"Don't get up now. We're going to get going," her mother said. "And since I know how awful it is to cook when you're sick, I brought you some meals. A taste of my mother's cooking always made me feel better." She gave her daughter a kiss and told her to call if she needed anything.

Judy and Maggie stepped out of the bedroom and closed the door quietly behind them.

"Were you ever this sick?" Brandon asked Judy.

"Never," Judy answered. "Oh, I was sick. And I spent a lot of time in bed when I was nauseated. But I think Joanie is worse than I ever was. Then again, the years could have faded my memory. I was sick enough that if it hadn't been for Joanie, Maggie, and Amie helping me out, and my mother and mother-in-law, I don't know how I would have ever managed to have kept my family alive."

"You were blessed to have had such support," Brandon remarked.

"I sure was," Judy agreed.

"Just talking about it sure makes me miss Grandma Collins," Maggie commented.

"Me, too," Judy said, looking at her daughter.

"What was John's mother like?" Brandon asked.

"A real go-getter," Judy told him. "At seventy-eight, she was still running circles around us, getting things done. She was an incredible woman. And I missed her terribly when she died—which is already eight years ago. My how the years roll by."

Brandon gave Judy a hug. "Well, I'm sure grateful that we've been blessed with such support as well," he commented to his mother-in-law. "Thanks for coming and bringing the care-package of meals."

"No problem at all, Brandon. It was my pleasure. You take good care of her, son," she instructed him with a smile. "And I want to remind you of what I just reminded Joanie—this, too, shall pass. But in the meantime, call if you need anything."

After they left Brandon went back to his guitar on the couch. With Joanie so sick it was certainly affording him time to work on their songs. He wondered if they would ever get to realize the dream of recording music together or not. "This, too, shall pass," rang through his thoughts loud and clear. Before he knew it, a new song was being born in his heart. He picked up a pen and began to write.

Chapter 12

"Are you ready to take things over from here?" Amie asked Kyle one Sunday evening after youth group. "You remember, I start classes tomorrow."

"Yes, I am, and yes, I remembered," he replied. "I just hope they don't expect me to be as creative as you when planning activities. We're going to be doing a lot of sports for the next couple of months," he warned.

"Go ahead and do whatever you want," Amie granted her permission. "Just don't do anything scandalous with them," she advised with a laugh. What a joke that was—Kyle was as clean-cut and decent a guy as she had ever known.

"I'll keep that in mind," he acknowledged.

"Are you coming out now to *Doug's Donuts*? There's a whole group of us meeting there in about ten, fifteen minutes," Amie said, looking at her watch.

"Sure, I'll come along," he answered, as he continued to pack the equipment into the storage room at the end of the church hall.

Katie came walking out of the kitchen, having finished the dishes from youth group. "Thanks for helping with clean-up, Kyle," she called out. Turning to her older sister, she asked, "So are we ready to go to *Doug's Donuts?*"

"I think so," Amie replied.

"Great, can I drive?" the novice driver asked.

"As you wish," Amie complied. She never minded letting someone else take the driver's seat.

"Ready to lock up," Kyle announced, approaching the two young ladies as he looked over the room. The three of them walked to the door, and he turned out the lights and locked up the hall. They went upstairs and stopped in the church before leaving. One at a time they blessed themselves with holy water and genuflected toward the little red light, shining out in the dark church from the front, beside the Tabernacle.

Kyle locked the front doors to the church as they left the building. "Meet you over there," he called out as they parted ways to go to their vehicles.

Arriving at *Doug's Donuts* at the same time, Kyle held the door open for Amie and Katie as they stepped inside. There were two tables pulled together at the far side of the establishment, with four of their band members sitting around laughing. They got themselves each a drink at the counter and went to sit down.

"So, you start tomorrow, Amie," Ann Ledoux stated. She, herself, was in her second year of university in the college of nursing. It was exciting for her to see her cousin moving on with her dream of hair design—it just suited Amie. "Are you excited?"

"I am. . . . Well, actually I'm quite nervous," Amie confessed, as she sat and twirled one of her long curls in her fingers.

"What's to be nervous about?" Daniel Schultz piped in. "I mean you're learning how to cut hair, and you already know how to do that. You've been cutting hair for most of us for years now." He ran his hands back and forth through his light brown hair. "You give the best haircuts I've ever had."

"That's because all you ever had were buzz cuts from your dad until I started cutting your hair," Amie responded.

"Number two setting on the razor," Daniel said, nodding his head.

"That was cool," Kyle added. "I liked getting buzz cuts."

"You would," Amie retorted, shaking her head and rolling her eyes at the guys. "Anyway, that's what I'm worried about—that I've been doing it for so long now. I'm sure I've developed all kinds of bad habits that they're going to discover. And I just hate being criticized, especially in public. I just don't want to embarrass myself."

"So what do you think about the news in the family?" Katie asked, changing the topic.

"It's awesome!" Kyle answered. "Brandon and Joanie having a baby— that rocks."

"It does," said Amie. "Although right now Joanie's sicker than a dog. She's off work until she starts to feel better."

"Wow," Daniel commented. "Did I ever mention how glad I am that I'm a guy?"

The group laughed.

"That's too bad," Kyle said. "But if anyone can pull it off with grace—it'll be Joanie. She won't waste one ounce of that suffering. I'm sure she'll be offering it up for all kinds of good intentions—that's just her style."

"That's for sure," Ann agreed. "She's such an inspiring person."

"I know I was impressed by her and Brandon's courtship," Kyle stated. Then for emphasis, he added, "And Joanie's perseverance to wait until she was ready to get married before she ever seriously dated a guy was downright inspiring."

"No kidding," agreed Daniel. "That girl sure gets what she wants out of life, doesn't she?"

"She sticks to her principles," Kyle commented. "You can't go wrong when you do that."

"I thought it was cool at their wedding to see their first kiss," Ann added. "But I don't know if I could do that, myself."

"How come?" asked Katie. "What's so hard about that?" the idealistic teenager questioned.

"It's not so much about how hard it would be; although, I'm sure it was quite a challenge for Joanie and Brandon to not kiss at all while courting. I mean, think about it—it's gotta take a lot of self-control," Ann responded. "But for me, I just think that I would be way too self-conscious kissing in front of a crowd of people for the first time. What if I blew it, or something? What if I looked like an idiot?"

"How can you blow a kiss, Annie?" jumped in Jocelyn, Ann's younger sister.

"Like this," Amie replied, blowing a kiss across the table to her younger cousin.

"You know what I mean," returned Jocelyn. "I mean, a kiss is a kiss. Not that I've ever kissed a guy before, but I can't imagine messing it up. Unless of course you both closed your eyes and then missed."

The group of friends began laughing and speculating over the ways they could mess up kissing.

"Well, I think I agree with Annie," Amie cut in. "I think I'd want to kiss my husband, even just once, before our wedding day."

"Not me," said Kyle. "At the altar suits me fine. I can't see the point in striking the match long before you ever plan to light the fire."

"You have so many standards," Amie scolded Kyle, "you'll be lucky to find a girl that not only meets your qualifications, but that can live with all your demands."

"I'm not that demanding," Kyle retorted. "I'm picky—yes. I have high standards—yes. I intend to stick to my principles—yes. But I'm not demanding. And whatever girl I marry is going to have to have the same standards as me. Why else would I want to marry her?"

"I think any girl who gets you for a husband is going to be very lucky," Ann stated, in her sincere manner, looking across the table at Kyle.

"Thanks, Ann," Kyle said, accepting the compliment, with a sideways glance toward Amie as if to say, "So there."

"Oh, she'll be lucky all right," Amie agreed. "She'll be lucky if Kyle marries her while they're still young enough to have children."

"I never said that I was planning on waiting forever until I get married," defended the young man. "You sure are a stubborn girl, aren't you?"

Katie began laughing. "You should try living with her, Kyle."

"Now *that* would go completely against *all* my principles," Kyle replied. The girls giggled around the table.

"I'm not that bad," Amie stated in her own defence, ignoring the implied joke.

"No, you're not," agreed Katie. "You're actually a wonderful sister, and I wouldn't trade you for anyone."

"Thanks," stated Amie, making a sideways glance toward Kyle as if to say, "So there."

"I didn't say anything about it," Kyle said, putting up his hands in his defence. "I think you'll make a great wife, Amie, for some lucky guy some day. Honestly."

"Well," Amie said, considering the compliment, "thanks."

The group visited for a while longer. They sat around and were entertained by Caleb Ledoux and John Delainey. These two younger band members had sat quietly throughout the exchange. They were not much for jumping into conversation—especially when it was about girls, kissing, and marriage—but they were quite the entertainers when they had the chance. They demonstrated twenty ways one could use a straw to save his life, until Amie and Ann made them stop—afraid they would all get kicked out of the doughnut shop for making too much noise with their laughter.

Stettler College was in the downtown of Saskatoon. The bus took Amie all the way to within half a block from the building. It was a brisk, fall day with a real chill in the air. The leaves had all fallen from the trees, no longer displaying their array of fall colours. The sky was gloomy, and the forecast was for snow by the end of the day.

Amie pulled up the collar of her jacket as she stepped off the bus. *Ready or not,* she thought to herself, *here I come.* As she approached the building she decided she had better say a quick prayer. *There's got to be a patron saint for hairdressers,* she thought to herself. Her mind raced through a dozen or more saints before she finally decided to pray to St. Rose of Lima. After all, Amie's middle name was Rose. She recalled reading the story of how St. Rose of Lima had cut off her long beautiful hair so as not to allow that worldly charm to cause her vanity and distract her from Christ. Amie thought about her own lovely locks of golden curls.

Oh, Lord, please don't expect me to do that. I don't think I'm quite cut out for this saint business. I just want to be holy in little ways—nothing too dramatic. . . . Anyway, here goes. St. Rose, I'm not sure if you're the patroness of hairdressers or not, but you're my patron saint anyway. First of all, please help me not to be vain about my hair—so I don't have to cut it off. Secondly, please help me to have the right heart in becoming a hairdresser. Help me to be a strong witness for Christ in this environment. And help me to do well so that I can use my talent to give glory to God someday in my work. Oh, yes, and help me to not make a fool of myself here—at least not on the first day.

By the time she had finished her prayer, she was standing in front of the door to enter the building. She would have hesitated, but two other girls came walking up just at that time, so Amie opened the door for the group of them.

When they got inside, they all looked a little lost. Amie asked if they knew where to go for the hair design college. They had no idea themselves, but they were on their way there as well. The three new students stood looking at the display board in the entry, and finally one of the girls announced, "Oh, there it is, on the third floor."

"Here goes nothing," Amie suggested. "Stairs or elevator?"

"Stairs," the other two agreed. "We need to work off a bit of this nervousness."

"I'm with you," Amie stated.

As the three girls walked up to the third floor they introduced themselves to each other. The other two girls were friends from a small town and had just moved to the city that past weekend. They were renting a small apartment together. It was the first time living away from home for both of them.

Amie liked them right away. The one girl, Samantha, was shorter and a little stockier than the other girl, Krystal. They both were very pretty girls, with their make-up done up just so. Samantha had dark, shoulder-length hair. Krystal's hair was light brown and cut short and stylishly. They were both very outgoing, and Amie had a feeling they would all get along great. She was so glad not to have to walk in alone.

The old building had that old-building smell to it. But as they turned to go up the last flight of stairs, the odour of hair products came wafting down to greet them. Samantha breathed in, "Ah, that's a smell I can relate to," she said. "My mom's a hairdresser in our hometown. I spent half my life in her salon watching her cut hair. *Now* I feel at home."

Reaching the top, Amie opened the door again for the three of them to enter. Krystal walked in first, then Samantha, followed by Amie. There was a little front reception area with a desk and an older woman sitting at it. Behind that, the room extended into a large open space that seemed to go on forever. There were all kinds of stations set up: row upon row of them. There were hardly any windows at all, just a little one over the chairs in the waiting area and a couple of small windows on the far side of the room. It seemed dark and dreary and not at all a welcoming environment.

"I change my mind," Samantha whispered. "I no longer feel at home."

Amie and Krystal smiled at each other and gave a little chuckle at the shorter girl standing between them.

Mustering up the courage to step forward, Amie approached the woman at the desk. At first glance, the woman gave the impression of an army captain. But as she looked up from her papers and smiled, Amie felt herself relaxing immediately.

"We're here, all three of us, to begin classes today for hair design," Amie stated. Looking around and noticing no one else in the waiting area she asked, "Are we late or something?"

"No, not at all," the woman answered. "Classes don't start until nine a.m., and you three are a bit early. Come, I'll introduce you to a senior who can show you around quickly before your first class begins. My name is Sherry. I'm one of your instructors."

Sherry led them almost all the way to the back of the room and then turned to go down a little hallway off to the right. There were doors on either side. "These are our classrooms. And back here is our student lounge."

She opened the door and called one of the students over. Introducing her to the three girls, Sherry let them know that they would get their registration papers and schedules at their first class.

Colleen was a senior at the school, which meant she was in her final set of classes. Since classes only ran for ten months, she really had not been there that much longer than these new girls. "I remember what I felt like on my first day," she told them. "And all I can say is—relax. This place is way more friendly than it looks. I know it looks kind of like a dungeon."

The girls nodded in agreement.

"But after a few days you're going to find yourselves so at home here, you won't even notice that about it anymore," she assured them.

It turned out that Colleen was right. Amie and her new friends found themselves very much at home in the relaxed environment of the college. Their class was made up of nineteen students, including three guys. All in all, the group of students formed an amiable lot, which made sense: hairdressers have to have good interpersonal skills.

Of all the students in the class, Amie knew that her first two companions were probably the ones with whom she would most naturally get along. They were down-to-earth and unpretentious. Amie had not yet figured out if they had a Christian background or not, but she hoped they would be able to find that in common as well.

✟   ✟   ✟

Though Amie was thoroughly enjoying her classes at Stettler, her life had begun to pick up pace. She was getting out of bed bright and early each morning to head off to school. When she got home at the end of the day, she dove into her musical studies. She stayed up late each night studying for her upcoming music theory exam or finishing any homework that had been assigned from school.

By Thursday night band practice she was whipped. She sat at the keyboard and played her parts, but she did not have much to contribute to the conversations. Ann noticed how uncharacteristically quiet Amie was, and came to sit down beside her during a break between songs. "Is school going okay for you, Amie? You seem a little down."

"Oh, school's been awesome. I love it, and I know I'm going to love doing hair design. It's just I'm so exhausted from burning my candle at both ends. This piano exam is taking a lot out of me . . . trying to get four hours a day of practice time in."

"Four hours? That would kill me," Ann stated. "I quit piano lessons years ago when I found one hour a day too much. But I could never play the way you do, so it wasn't any great loss."

Amie laughed, remembering how much Ann had hated piano lessons. She was more sports-minded and was a great volleyball and basketball player. She sang really well and loved being in *New Spring*, but music was certainly not her passion.

Ann put her arm over her cousin's shoulder and gave her a little squeeze. "Hang in there, cuz, it'll only be another couple of months and you'll be free from that. And you'll do awesome—at both things—I just know you."

Amie smiled at her cousin, leaned her head on Ann's shoulder, and rubbed her eyes. David called out the next song, and Ann jumped up to go back to her place. Amie stretched out a yawn at the keyboard and turned to Kyle behind her to give him the cue to bring them in. He offered a sympathetic smile at the tired pianist, then counted them all in, tapping his sticks together.

Amie played as well as she could, but band practice could not have ended early enough. She and Katie went home as soon as it was over so that she could finish up an assignment for the next day.

Chapter 13

"You're looking better today," Ann noted to her cousin, following Sunday Mass.

"I'm feeling better," Amie replied, all smiles, her blue eyes beaming. "I went for a nap Friday after class, and I slept until Saturday morning. I couldn't believe I slept straight through supper and everything. I was just out."

"Holy smokes! You really *were* tired." Ann looked at Amie and then, tilting her head to the side, her auburn ponytail hanging almost to her shoulder, she commented, "That's not all. There's something else up. You don't come around looking that bubbly just because you had a good night's sleep."

Amie gave a slight shrug of her shoulders and moved her eyes back and forth to see who was standing nearby.

"Out with it, girl," Ann demanded in a hushed tone, grabbing her cousin by the shoulders and giving her a little shake.

Amie laughed and replied, "I went to a music workshop yesterday, offered by my piano teacher. It was really good. I learned a lot."

"You don't get a look in your eyes like that over a piano workshop, either," Ann retorted, unimpressed. She let go of Amie's shoulders and stood back, waiting.

Amie tossed her head from side to side, playfully. "No, I don't," she agreed. "But if you had met the guy sitting beside me, Annie, you'd understand this look."

Ann leaned toward her cousin and grabbed her arm, pulling her off to the side of the church hall for privacy. "Details, girl. Details."

"Well, at first I just noticed he was really good-looking when he walked in. Then he came and sat beside me—which I thought was kind of cool. We introduced ourselves. I had never met him before. He's from Manitoba and has just moved here to work on a music degree in piano."

"Name . . . details," insisted Ann. "What does he look like?"

"Very cute," Amie replied. "Dark hair and eyes. I think he's probably got a Mediterranean background—you know that really dark complexion. He's tall and kind of thin, but very good-looking. His name is Tyson."

"Mm-hmm," Ann said, rolling her hand in circles, motioning for more details.

"Anyway, we spent the day together at the workshop. We sat together for lunch, and I got to know him a bit. He seems really nice. He's not shy at all . . . and he's definitely confident around girls."

"Is he Catholic?" Ann asked, in a sobering tone.

"No," Amie replied, somewhat defensively. "But then again, neither was Brandon when Joanie met him."

Ann heaved a sigh and squinted her hazel eyes at her cousin. "Amie Collins," she scolded, "for one, Joanie had a better head on her shoulders than you've ever had regarding guys."

"Hey," Amie squawked, taking offence.

"Think about it," Ann went on. "We're as close as sisters, Amie, and I wouldn't say a thing to hurt you—unless I thought it would help you. I just mean that Joanie wasn't looking for something when Brandon came along. It just happened. And she certainly put him through the hoops before she ever allowed a romance to develop."

"I haven't done anything," Amie said, still defensive, "other than giving him my phone number."

"Agh," Ann groaned. "Amie, you should be more careful."

"He asked for my number, and I gave it to him. But," she said, in an attempt to vindicate herself, "I also told him that if he wanted to go out with me, he'd first have to ask my father's permission. So there."

"Well, that's something," Ann concurred. "What did he say to that?"

"He thought it was charming," Amie stated in Tyson's defence. "He said that he'd be in touch."

"So when was this?" Ann asked.

"Yesterday afternoon. The workshop went until suppertime, and I went home. I had lots of work to do for school and practising. And he had lots of work to do, too. He's a hard-working music student," Amie emphasized, to promote his character.

"So what's his last name?"

"Straker."

"Tyson Straker?" Ann repeated. "That doesn't sound Mediterranean to me."

"Well, his mother could be," Amie replied. "You should see him, Annie. He's totally dreamy."

Just then Ann noticed some of their friends looking suspiciously over at the two girls talking off to the side. "We'd better go join the gang, before your cover is blown here."

Amie turned and looked over her shoulder. She smiled and waved coyly at Kyle and Daniel who were talking with some of the girls.

The two girls walked over to join in with the conversation.

"You're a lot perkier today," commented Daniel to Amie. "You looked like you were about to die at band practice the other night."

"I just about did," Amie responded. "I was so exhausted. Honestly, I don't think I'm cut out for this double life. I'll be glad when my theory and piano exams are done."

"You good for a haircut sometime?" Kyle asked. "Or are you too busy, now?"

"I'll cut your hair for you," Amie said. "Someone's got to keep you looking good for when you finally decide to get a girlfriend," she teased.

"When's good for you?" he asked, shaking his head over her comment and smiling.

"I can do it this afternoon. . . . You have youth group tonight. What've you got planned?" she asked.

"Not much," he confessed. "But maybe you can give me some inspiration while you cut my hair."

"How about you come over and have lunch with us today? We'll talk about youth group over lunch; I can cut your hair and then you'll be good to go," she suggested.

Other people set their plans for the day, and the group soon dispersed.

When Isaac, Zack, and Aaron heard that Kyle was coming for lunch, they begged to go with him in his car.

"As long as you ask your folks," Kyle replied.

It was agreed, and they took off, arriving minutes before the Collins in their fifteen-seat van, affectionately referred to as their "Catholic Cadillac".

Amie and Kyle discussed plans for youth group over lunch. She decided, with some persuasion, that she would go; after all, it was Sunday, and she had finished her homework on Saturday night so she would not have to work today.

Kyle helped with dishes and then Amie set up to cut his hair in the kitchen. She got him to wet down his hair in the sink and then tossed him a towel to pat it dry. The family had taken off in separate directions after lunch so it was just the two of them until Katie came in with a sketchbook and sat down at the dining table across the room.

"The usual," Kyle said, taking a seat on a stool.

"Meaning?" Amie asked as she placed her haircutting cloth over his shoulders

"Do whatever you think looks best. I have no opinion, and I hardly care. It's just that my mom's giving me the gears about my hair getting too long, and she's threatening to cut it herself. I figure, I care enough to not have it butchered. So, do whatever you want."

Amie began working on his hair. She was not very talkative today. Kyle just sat and let her work. After a few minutes Katie spoke up from across the room, "So, Kyle, has Amie told you about Tyson yet?"

Amie threw a sharp look at her sister. Katie covered her mouth apologetically, but it was too late.

"Nope," Kyle answered. He waited for someone to go on, but neither girl did. "So who's Tyson?" he asked casually.

"Just a guy I met at a music workshop," Amie answered.

"Hmm," he replied. He was not quite sure what else he should say.

"Oh," Katie piped in. "I just have to comment on this, because I think it's so funny. I haven't met the guy, but if you heard Amie describe him, you'd swear she was describing you, Kyle." Katie started laughing.

Amie looked at her sister curiously from across the room. She pondered a moment and then a look of realization spread across her face, as her eyes widened. "You know, Kyle," she said in amazement, "it's true. He does sort of look like you."

"Tall, dark, and handsome," Katie called out from her perch at the table.

"Thanks," Kyle commented with his chin down, looking at the floor in front of him.

"You're actually more the tall, dark, and cute type," Amie corrected.

"Gee, thanks," Kyle responded. "Guys really like being called cute."

"Like it or not, girls are crazy over cute guys. Handsome guys are sometimes a little too much to handle. Usually too full of themselves—since everyone's told them their whole life how handsome they are. It's the cute guys that are the real catches," she explained.

"Well, thanks again, I guess," he said, as she lifted his chin and came around to the front to assess the situation and decide where to go next with the cut.

Still holding her finger under his chin she looked him straight in the eyes and smiled, "You're welcome."

Kyle smiled back at the unpretentious girl before him. He really enjoyed the fact that Amie was not at all attracted to him, because if she had been, there would be no way for him to resist those sparkling blue eyes. As it was, the simplicity of their friendship allowed him to keep a healthy emotional distance between them so as to guard her heart, as well as his own.

As Amie moved to his right side to cut there next, Kyle commented. "So it sounds like this Tyson doesn't have much chance with the girls then, poor guy—tall, dark, and *handsome*—must be quite a handicap."

"Oh, I don't think he's ever suffered for lack of female attention," Amie commented. "And he's not so handsome that he doesn't qualify as cute."

Just then Zack came running around the corner carrying the cordless phone. "Amie, it's for you," he called out as he tossed the phone on the table.

"Thanks, Zack," she called out after him. She picked up the phone and answered, somewhat apologetically, for the loud thump in whoever's ear was on the other side.

It was Tyson. Amie's manner immediately changed. She stood up straight and tidied up her hair with her free hand. He was calling to speak to her dad, but first he wanted to know if she was free on Friday night. She told him she was playing at a praise night at their church. That suited him fine; he would love to come and hear her play. After agreeing on a time for pick up, Amie ran the phone out to the garage to find her father in his shop. She stood attentively waiting, nervously pacing as she listened to her father give this guy a few turns on the rack. Finally he got off the phone.

"So, how come I never heard about this guy before now?" questioned John, handing the phone back to his daughter.

"I just met him yesterday, Dad. I never had a chance to mention him to you," she replied. "But he's really nice. I know you'll like him."

"Well, he'll come here first before you go to the church for your *Praise Event*," he told her. "And I can't say that I'm all excited about this, Amie."

"Why? What's wrong?"

"I don't know. Just have a funny feeling after talking to the guy, though I can't say why. And it's not fair to judge a man before I've met him. But I have my reservations."

"I don't get it, Dad. Tyson seemed like a really great guy," Amie stated.

"Maybe. But he seems like a bit of a smooth-talker, and I can't say that I like that quality in a man."

"You'll meet him on Friday night and, trust me, you'll be impressed," she told him. She kissed her dad on the cheek, said a quick thank you, and went running back to the house.

She had not noticed on her way out to the garage how cold it was outside, but this was November in Saskatchewan, and there was a light layer of snow on the ground. She shook off the chill as she re-entered the house, ran to the kitchen, and announced to Katie and Kyle, "It's a date! Tyson's coming to the *Praise Event* Friday night. Trust me, you're gonna love him," she assured them.

Katie looked over at Kyle, patiently sitting on a stool with a cape over his shoulders and half a haircut. "That's great, Amie," she replied. "But perhaps you could finish Kyle's haircut before then?"

"Oh, Kyle," Amie apologized, remembering why he was sitting there in the first place. "I completely forgot about you."

"No problem," Kyle answered. "Gave me the opportunity to say some prayers while I was waiting for you."

"Ah, I'm so sorry," she apologized. "You have to be the most patient guy I know, Kyle. I swear you're going to make an amazing husband for some girl someday. I just hope you don't end up with an airhead like me who would constantly push you to the limits of your patience."

"What's the point of having a virtue if you never get to practise it?" he replied.

Amie laughed and picked up her scissors and comb. "I'll get you finished up here in no time," she promised.

The young hairstylist flitted about as she finished the haircut, rambling on and on about how awesome Friday night was going to be. She was nervous that she might not play so well; after all, Tyson was majoring in piano for a performance degree—the guy had to be good. Kyle assured her that she could not possibly play poorly—she was just too fine a musician. "If I hear you screw up, though," he offered, "I'll just do a drum solo or something to cover it up."

"Thanks," Amie said, patting Kyle on the shoulder, "I can always count on you to watch out for me. And look, we're done," she announced, undoing the cape and removing it carefully. "There's a mirror right there," she said, pointing to the counter.

"No need," he replied. "I trust you."

"Oh, you make me crazy sometimes," she said, shaking her fists in front of herself. "I could never go get a haircut and not look to see if it turned out right."

"I told you, I trust you."

"Aghghgh," she replied in frustration. "You just do that to drive me crazy, don't you?"

"Not at all. Here." He picked up the hand mirror and took a quick look from side to side. "Look's great. Are you satisfied?"

"Yes," she said. "Thank you."

"No problem. Can't have you going crazy before your big date on Friday night."

She stuck out her tongue at him playfully, and he smiled and waved at her in reply.

"Look," Katie announced from across the room. She lifted up her sketchbook to reveal a picture of Amie cutting Kyle's hair. "It's not as good as it could be, because Amie was always moving around. But Kyle was sitting there for so long like a statue, I was able to do a good job of him."

Kyle stepped over to examine the sketch. "It's good," he said with a little laugh. "I like the half-done haircut look."

"Since you sat there for so long with it half-done," Katie stated, "I figured it would make for a more realistic study of the subject."

Amie glanced at the sketch. "Good job, Katie," she said without really taking much note of it. She was putting her haircutting things away and was obviously preoccupied by her latest distraction in life.

Kyle picked up the broom which she had left leaning on the counter and finished sweeping up the hair.

"Oh, I'll do that," Amie said.

"It's okay. It's the least I can do. And here," he reached into his pocket to give her some money.

"Kyle, I don't want your money," she scolded him.

"We go through this every time," he said, holding a few bills out before her. "You either take it, or I won't let you cut my hair again."

"Fine," she said, reluctantly taking the money.

"And here," he said, handing her a prayer card.

"What's this?"

"A sort of congratulations for starting your hair design course. It's St. Mary Magdalene. She's one of the patron saints for hairstylists," he told her. "I was in the Catholic bookstore one day after school and noticed a list of patron saints. I looked up the one for hairstylists, and she was listed there. Look," he pointed out, "she washed the Lord's feet with her hair. I thought you'd appreciate it."

"Kyle, that's so beautiful," she said, giving him a hug. "I'll keep this with me everyday when I go to school." She stared at the beautiful image of St. Mary Magdalene. "Thank you," she said again, still looking at the card.

"Well, I should get going," he announced, picking up the hair with the dustpan. He carried it over to the garbage can under the sink and tossed it in. "I want to spend some time with my family before youth group tonight. Will you still come?"

"Oh, sure, I'll tag along with Katie," Amie replied.

"Then I'll see you tonight. Thanks for the haircut. And thanks, Katie, for keeping me company," he called out to the young artist, as he left the room.

"No problem, Kyle," she called back.

Kyle left without the typical Collins family commotion; the little kids were playing downstairs and did not know he was leaving. Amie followed him to the door and waved good-bye as he drove off. She looked down again at the prayer card and ran upstairs to her bedroom to put it in her purse.

Chapter 14

Friday evening could not have rolled around fast enough for Amie. School seemed to drag on forever each day. Piano practice was long and tedious each evening. Band practice had been torturous, as everyone knew she was bringing someone to the *Praise Event,* and they were all poking fun at their love-struck pianist. David Bander reminded her that that was exactly why he had not yet brought Leanne around to meet the group.

By the time Friday night finally did come, Amie could hardly eat supper. She managed to skirt her way out of dishes and ran upstairs to get ready. She chose a brown skirt with small embroidery trim around the bottom hem; it flowed elegantly around her. Under a beige sweater, she wore a light blue top. The colours worked nicely together, accentuating both her blue eyes and her golden hair. She pinned up a few long curls on both sides, leaving the hair at the back to hang loosely, creating a sweet and simple look. She checked herself out in the mirror and decided she was happy with the final results of her efforts and went downstairs to wait for Tyson to arrive.

"He's here," announced Zack, looking through the bay window of their front room.

"You guys behave," Amie warned the three boys as she went to the door. "I'm warning you now," she added with a severe look.

The boys laughed and completely disregarded the threat. They had no intention of being anything other than themselves.

Tyson stepped into the house. He was dressed to the nines, with his label jeans, a charcoal shirt, and a brown, leather jacket done up only half-way. He came in and one by one met the family. Amie's father was the last to come into the room to meet the young man. John was polite, but none-too-friendly with his greeting. He eyed up the musician, taking in his every move and expression, his reaction to the other children, and the manner in which he responded to Amie.

As the couple got ready to leave for the church, John called out, "I want to see you home here by eleven-thirty, Amie."

Amie stopped, embarrassed and stunned by her father. She stayed out later than that on a regular basis with her friends. She did not quite know how to respond. She did not want to make a scene with Tyson there. On the other hand, she could only imagine what was going through his head: a twenty-year-old man with an eleven-thirty curfew. Taking in her father's expression, she knew he would not be bending on the issue. He had that look that said, "Just try me." She knew enough not to go there.

"I'll see you then," she replied quietly as she closed the door behind them.

"That was a little severe," Judy admonished her husband. "You could have tried to be friendlier. And what's with the eleven-thirty curfew? They don't normally get home from the church that early when they have a praise night. You know that."

"I want to see if that man has enough respect for Amie to respect me as her father. I wouldn't even allow them to stay out that late together, if it wasn't for them being at the church tonight, surrounded by family and friends. There's not one of Amie's guy-friends that would let a thing happen to her. I know I can trust them to keep an eye out for her. . . . No, I'm not giving this Tyson any licence with my daughter. If he's got any amount of manhood within him, he'll have recognized that. If not . . ." he paused, "let's just say I'm trying to sift the chaff from the wheat."

✟   ✟   ✟

By the time they arrived, just about all of the band was at the church setting up. Amie made a brief introduction of Tyson to the group. She walked over to the keyboard and set her music in order. Tyson asked for permission to play.

"I'd love to hear you play," Amie replied. "There's plenty of time before we start tonight."

Tyson played a most impressive passage from a concerto. He did not play the entire piece; it would have gone on too long. Amie clapped, and the other band members joined in with her.

Tyson stood up from the keyboard. "It sounds better on a *real* piano. But thanks," he said, looking around the room.

Amie had a proud look on her face. She was enjoying showing off her friend. She took him to find a place to sit and asked him to save her a seat beside him so she could join him after their first set. She sat to talk with him for a few minutes when it suddenly occurred to her that she still did not even know if this guy was a Christian.

"I'm curious," she asked with reservation. "Do you have any church background or is this completely foreign to you?"

"No and no," he replied.

She shook her head, confused.

"No church background, but no, this isn't foreign to me. You see, I've played and accompanied at lots of church concerts and functions over the years. And I've played all kinds of praise music for various events. It's just another application of my music. I usually find the atmosphere dull—it's such an easy crowd to please. They can be blown away by even a mediocre performance—so there's not much challenge in it." He moved his head from side to side. "I could take it or leave it. . . . It's not at all dull here tonight, though," he added with a smile at Amie. "It's always more interesting, coming with a pretty girl."

Amie smiled shyly and said, "Thanks." She excused herself to go pray with the band. She entered the side room to find the group had already started without her. She sat on a chair at the edge of the room, aware that some of the wind had been knocked out of her sails, though she was not quite sure what was really bothering her. She figured she was still just upset with her father. He obviously had misjudged Tyson. Curfew aside, she could tell by his abrupt manner with the young man that he had not been impressed. She decided to pray silently that Tyson would prove her father's judgmental attitude all wrong.

The evening began with *New Spring* leading three songs. Amie was so nervous at the piano that she really was struggling to hold it together. When she turned to Kyle for the pick-up on the third piece, he shot one of his winning smiles toward her, and she suddenly felt totally reassured. The piece went well; her playing was full of life, and she was able to refocus her efforts on the Lord, not on worrying about what Tyson was thinking. As they stepped down off the stage she whispered a thank you to Kyle, and he winked back at her with a quick nod.

She took her place by Tyson and awkwardly tried to participate in the evening of praise, but he was as stiff as a board. He seemed mildly amused by the evening. When the last set finally finished, he stood and waited for Amie to rejoin him. He looked at his watch. It was only ten o'clock. He was not at all interested in sticking around to visit with her family and friends. He finally convinced her to go out with him for a drink so that they could have a chance to get to know each other better, one on one.

Katie was quite perturbed with her sister when Amie told her she would be leaving early.

"I was planning to get a ride home with Tyson anyway," Amie stated. "We came separately, why shouldn't we go home separately?"

"I don't think Mom and Dad would approve of you going off alone," she warned. "But you can take that up with them when you get home."

"Dad never said we couldn't," Amie reminded her sister. "He just said we had to be in by eleven-thirty. And Tyson has every intention of getting me home in time."

Amie and Tyson left. As they approached his brand new, red Mazda Miata, Tyson unlocked the doors with his remote. *Pretty fancy car*, Amie thought, *for a university student.* Tyson ran around to the driver's side and got in. Amie paused before stepping in, aware that guys like Kyle, Daniel, and her cousins had totally spoiled her.

"So where did you want to go?" Amie asked, figuring they'd hit a place like *Doug's Donuts* or one of the burger shops for a pop.

"There's a bar on campus," he suggested. "I've been there a few times. It's not bad."

"A bar?" Amie questioned. "I'm not sure I want to go to a bar."

"Come on. I sat through your concert tonight. And by the way," he remarked, "you're a pretty fair piano player. I was impressed."

He smiled at Amie in a way that she was not used to guys smiling at her. It did not exactly make her feel uncomfortable, just unsure of herself.

"Come on," he said again, motioning with his head for her to go along with his plan. "You'll like it. And if you don't, we can go somewhere else."

"Fine," she said with weak determination.

He put the car in gear and began to drive in the direction of campus.

"So did you get anything out of the evening?" she asked, curiously.

"Not really." He shook his head. "I've heard all that stuff before—it never impresses me. I mean, I believe there's a God. And I believe Jesus was probably what He said He was—the Son of God. I figure if I lead a good enough life, I don't need to bother with religion and religion doesn't need to bother me. And since I've managed to support myself through school largely on the pocketbooks of religious people, I don't intend to offend them by becoming an atheist." He laughed and winked at Amie.

She smiled back at him, less and less convinced that she wanted to be where she was.

He turned on some classical music as they drove. "Ahh," he said raising his hand in the air, "now *this* is good music." They listened for a few minutes, then he turned to her and said, "It's a recording I did last summer for a local station back home. What d'you think?"

"Oh," Amie replied, tuning in to what he had said. "It's good. Very impressive. You must be proud of your accomplishments."

"I've done well," he agreed. "But I intend to keep doing better. Can't stop improving or I'll stagnate. And then I'll have no career, will I? I'll end up stuck teaching a bunch of snotty-nosed little kids piano lessons everyday after school. Wouldn't that just be a total waste of my talents?"

"Don't you like kids?" Amie asked.

"Take 'em or leave 'em—as long as they're someone else's. Can't see myself ever being stuck with them. Maybe one. Two at the most. That'd be a long time down the road, though. I've got a musical career to get established, and I wouldn't want to have that ruined by a family."

Amie was silent. She had no more questions. Suddenly she knew she had made the wrong decision in coming out alone with Tyson.

"We're here," he announced. He turned off the vehicle and jumped out.

Amie waited in the car. He looked back at her and raised his hands, peering down at her through the window. "You coming or what?"

She stepped out of the vehicle and closed the door. Tyson stood waiting for her to catch up to him in front of the vehicle. As she approached he grabbed her hand and started to lead her inside.

Amie felt awkward with Tyson holding her hand. He did not at all seem to notice her walking a step or two behind him. She wondered if she was getting herself into trouble or not. She kept trying to think of a graceful way to get out of the situation.

"You know, Tyson," she said as they approached the bar's entrance. "I feel really awkward about this. I just can't see myself enjoying the atmosphere of a bar."

"Obviously you've never been to one. You won't know until you've tried. And I haven't come this close just to walk away. So let's go," he said, pulling her along. "You're a sweet kid, Amie, but you really need to do some growing up. There's nothing wrong with having a drink at a bar. I'm not asking you to get drunk or anything, unless, of course, you want to. Then you'd see what a good time we could have together." The smile on his face made Amie's skin crawl. She wanted to slap it right off him.

Her head was swimming in frustration and confusion. She was angry that she did not seem to have the ability to state her wishes firmly, and then have them met. Tyson was moving on his own agenda, and she felt completely powerless.

They walked into the noisy, smoky atmosphere of the bar. She rolled her eyes; it was exactly what she had anticipated it to be like. *Now can I go home?* she asked inside her head.

Tyson led her to a small booth. He casually took off his jacket, settling in for the evening. Amie intended to keep hers on, but the crowded room was very warm. After a few minutes, she took off her jacket and held onto it in front of herself. Tyson was not paying attention to her at all; he was too busy looking around. He finally caught the eye of a waitress, and she stepped up to the booth. Tyson ordered a couple of drinks.

"I don't intend to drink that," Amie told him. "I don't even want to be here. *I don't drink*."

"You're kidding?" he asked in amazement. "Girl, you need some schooling in a big, bad way. I thought it was quaint that your father wanted to meet me and that I had to ask his permission. But I really didn't think you bought into that whole routine. I figured you were just going along with him so as not to upset the old man."

"I love my father," she snapped back. "I would never try to be underhanded with him. I respect him." Suddenly she realized that if what she was saying were true, she still would have been back at St. James Church with the rest of her friends, and this whole situation would never have happened. She felt sick.

"Come on," Tyson said, grabbing her hand and pulling her up. "Let's dance."

"Haven't you been listening to me at all? *I don't want to be here*."

Tyson kept pulling on her arm. Amie tucked her purse into her jacket and left them behind on her seat. Once on the dance floor, Tyson pulled her in close to his body, as if he had not heard a word she had said. "You just need to relax," he whispered in her ear, moving to the slow song.

Amie tried to push herself away, but Tyson's grip was tight around her. She was ready to scream, but too awkward in the environment to do so.

"Come on. Relax. I won't bite," he spoke softly in her ear again.

She pulled her head back and away from him. Then realizing he was going to try to kiss her, she averted her head to the side and pulled it in closer so he could not reach her without loosening his grip on her back.

He laughed, "Well, at least I've got you back where I wanted you in the first place."

"Please take me home," she said firmly over his shoulder.

"I'm staying here until I've had my drink. And I'll get you home for your curfew, don't worry. But since the chances of me taking you out again are remote at best, you may as well enjoy the moment. You obviously have been deprived of male attention," he commented. "A little bit of loving would go a long way to soften you up."

Amie did not respond verbally. She pushed herself back from him with as much force as she could.

"You win," he said with a laugh. "Drinks are at the table."

He let go of his hold on her, and she stumbled backwards, almost falling. He laughed again, this time at her, as he walked past the young girl to go get his drink.

Amie stepped over to the booth and grabbed her purse and jacket. "I'm going to the washroom," she told him.

He tipped his glass toward her and watched as she walked through the crowded room to the front entry where the washrooms were.

Once out of sight, Amie slipped on her jacket and ran to a pay phone. She picked it up to dial. She needed a quarter. She rummaged through her purse desperately looking for some change: two dimes and a nickel. She placed them in and dialed home. She kept her eyes on the entrance into the bar in case Tyson came out. Then she decided he probably would not leave his drink behind.

The phone rang: once, twice . . . her dad picked it up.

"Daddy," she cried into the phone.

"Amie?" John's voice boomed into the receiver. "Is that you?"

"Daddy, come get me, please," she cried again, holding tightly to the receiver.

"Where are you?"

"I'm at a bar—on campus," she told him. "I don't even know what the place is called. Just wait." She craned her neck around to read the sign. "Karl's Place," she told him. "Can you come get me?"

"Are you in danger right now?"

"No. I don't think so," she answered.

"How'd you end up at a bar, Amie? Ahh, never mind that," he stopped himself. This was not the time for lectures. "Look, if you're at a bar, there should be a bouncer near the door. Do you see anyone like that, Amie?"

Amie looked over to the entrance. There was a man in a uniform standing with his hands behind his back. "I see someone," she told her father.

"Keep him in your sight," John instructed his daughter. "If you have any troubles, call out to him for help. That's what he's there for, sweetheart."

"Okay," she said. Her voice was much calmer as she kept her eyes focussed on the big man in the uniform.

"I'll be there in about ten minutes," John told her. "Do not step outside alone. I'll come in and get you. Do you understand?"

"I do, Daddy. Just hurry." She hung up and decided the safest place for her would be in the ladies' room until her dad arrived. If Tyson came looking for her, she did not want him to find her.

She walked into the washroom and stepped into a cubicle. She did not have to use the toilet. She did not even think she could if she had wanted to, she was so fearful of Tyson showing up and pulling her out of there. She just stood inside, staring at the door. She was disgusted by all the advertisements. Finally, she closed her eyes and did what she should have done long before this point. She prayed.

Oh, Jesus, get me out of here. I'm so sorry I let myself get so caught up in this guy's attention that I completely lost all my sense of reason. I need you right now to hold me close and protect me until my dad gets here.

Her eyes were filled with tears. She turned around and leaned her back against the stall door, waiting for the longest ten minutes of her life. She prayed one Hail Mary after another. Then she remembered something. She rummaged through her purse and found it: her prayer card of St. Mary Magdalene. She gazed at the image of the beautiful saint who had once known the pain of sin that comes from bad choices—and yet knew so well the love and forgiveness of the Lord. Amie felt a peace inside: Jesus was watching over her and protecting her—in spite of herself. Finally she decided she had better step out and look for her dad.

She opened the bathroom door cautiously and there, across the hall, was Tyson waiting for her.

"What the hell are you doing in there?" he called out to her with a real look of disdain.

Amie could see the man in the uniform standing fifteen feet or so behind Tyson. She stepped out casually, keeping her distance from Tyson. "I'm waiting for my father to come get me," she informed him. "He should be here any moment."

"You're insane!" he threw out at her. "I've never met a more uptight bitch, my whole life." He turned on his heel and walked back into the bar.

Amie noticed the man in the uniform looking at her. He had been watching the interaction. He stood there silently. Amie walked toward the door. As she approached, the guard asked her if she was all right or if she needed any help. She thanked him and told him she was waiting for her ride. Just then she saw her dad running up the walk. She ran out to meet him and threw her arms around him. He held onto his daughter, looking over her shoulder for Tyson.

"Where is that jerk?" he asked.

"He's inside the bar," she told him.

John considered stepping inside and taking the boy out—but remembered that his priority was his daughter at the moment. "Come on, Amie. I'll take you home."

Amie walked sheepishly beside her father. He held the door for her as she got into the small beat-up Toyota. She waited in silence for her father to say something when he got in. He looked over at his daughter as he started up the car. After a moment he asked, "Are you all right? Did that jerk do anything to you . . . try anything with you?"

"I'm fine," she answered. "Other than dancing with me way too close, no, he didn't do anything to me."

"How'd you end up at a bar? You were supposed to be at the church."
He was not impressed.

Amie explained the whole evening to her father. She cried as she
apologized for having made such poor decisions. She rubbed her eyes and
blew her nose with a napkin that had been left lying on the dashboard.

"I'm so sorry, Daddy," she whispered.

"Well, Amie, I'm sorry, too," her dad responded.

"What are you sorry for?" she asked, totally shocked.

"I had a bad feeling about that guy from the word go. I should have
trusted my instincts, but I was afraid that if I interfered too much, you'd
just rebel against me. And I was wrong, Amie. It's my job as your father to
protect you. And sometimes that means I won't be popular with my kids.
That doesn't matter. I should have trusted my instincts and not gambled
with your safety. I'm sorry," he said, slowly and deliberately.

"Daddy, I love you," she said softly, taking his hand in hers. "You're
the most incredible dad I can think of, and I hope I never give you cause
again to think that I would rebel against you. I may make bad decisions
at times, but I would never openly go against you. I respect you, even if I
didn't show it tonight."

"I love you, too, Amie. All the way over here I just kept thinking the worst.
I was so afraid I'd find you beat up or abused or . . . missing completely."

"I'm so naïve, Daddy. I really had no idea how badly a date could get out
of control. I should have used way better judgment from the word go. I'm
such an idiot. . . . I can see now how girls end up in situations of date rape.
If he had driven me to some dark, out-of-the-way place in that car, I wouldn't
have been able to get away. I had just so convinced myself that he was a
nice guy, that even when he was doing his best to show me throughout the
evening that he really was a useless jerk, I couldn't see it. . . . I just thank
God he was more interested in his booze than in me. I couldn't even get
away from his grip while we were dancing—and he's not a big man."

"Guys don't have to be big to be strong, Amie," he warned.

They were silent as they drove the last two blocks home. "You're mother's
going to be worried sick in there. Let's get you inside and set her heart
at ease."

Judy ran out from the front door and down the steps to meet her
daughter. She pulled Amie into her arms and hugged her tightly, crying.
"Oh, you scared the living daylights out of us. Are you okay, Amie?"

Amie held on to her mother tightly. She gave her mom a squeeze, "I'm
all right now, Mom. But I've learned a lot tonight. And I won't be such an
idiot again. I promise."

Judy stood back and took a look at her daughter. She gave her another quick hug and said, "You're home now. That's what counts. Come on inside. I'll fix you a nice cup of tea and we'll talk."

John and Judy took their places on either side of their daughter and walked her into the house. Just then, Katie and Isaac pulled up into the driveway, home early from their evening at the church. John waited at the door for them.

"Was that Amie?" Katie called out, as she came up the walk. "I'm glad she's home," she went on, presuming the answer to her question. "I was really worried about her tonight."

"She's home," John replied, patting Katie on the shoulder as she walked by him. As Katie and Isaac went into the house, John latched the porch door and turned out the outside light. His family was all at home, safe and sound for the night. "Thank you, Jesus," he murmured, looking heavenward.

Chapter 15

Kyle and Daniel joined in with the group who had gathered around to visit after Sunday Mass. Amie had talked with Ann Ledoux over the weekend—so her cousin was aware of the piano player's date fiasco from Friday night, but no one else knew anything about it. Naturally the guys were curious as to how things had gone. Kyle was none too impressed that this guy had run off with Amie without making any effort to meet her friends. He had a bad feeling about the guy—but enough respect for Amie not to say anything in front of her friends.

"So, how was the big date?" Daniel opened the discussion, his brown eyes entreating Amie for news—ready to jump into teasing mode, once she had given the guys fuel for the fire.

Amie rolled her eyes and said, "Don't ask." The tone of her voice did not invite the continuation of any more conversation on the topic.

Daniel looked at her, then around the circle of friends. "That bad?" he asked, in disbelief.

"Let's just say I learned a lot Friday night. And I am never going out again with another guy who isn't Catholic, totally involved in his faith, and willing to show some interest in my family and friends," Amie replied.

"Those sound like good criteria," Kyle agreed, not at all smugly. He looked at Amie with eyes that seemed to be reading her soul.

She stared back at him. He was her friend, and she wanted to tell him what had happened, but something inside stopped her. She was too ashamed of herself. Although she knew Kyle would never judge her, she really did not want him to know just how stupid and naïve she had been. "Yeah," she nodded, "I guess it doesn't hurt to keep your standards too high for some things."

He smiled at her with all the warmth and kindness of a good friend. "So what's on for this afternoon?" he asked, changing the topic as he looked around the group of friends. "We could head over to my place, make up some lunch together, and then play some cards. Who's in?"

"Sounds great," Katie spoke up. "I've gotta get out of my house. I'm starting to get cabin-fever. I love home-schooling and all, but after a while, a girl's gotta see the outside world—even if it's just the inside of your house, Kyle."

The group all agreed it was a good plan. Kyle informed them that they had plenty of ingredients at home to make up a mess of bacon and eggs and toast. His mom loved it when he had his friends over. It was never an issue for her.

"Does anyone want a ride out?" he asked. "I'm coming back in for youth group tonight."

"Can you take us?" Amie asked, still subdued.

"Always," he replied with his friendly smile. "Anyone else?"

Ann and Jocelyn had to go home first anyway—so they said they would just meet up with the group later. Daniel had his own set of wheels and offered to give John Delainey and Caleb Ledoux a ride. Once all was settled, everyone separated to confirm plans with their families. John Collins was more than happy to let Amie go out with her friends, emphasizing how safe he felt when she was with them.

She thanked him with a hug and a forced smile. Walking away, she wondered how long he would keep reminding her about her miserable date, in subtle ways. Deciding he had a right to rub it in—after all he never wanted for it to happen again—she determined for herself to put up with his little remarks without comment.

✟   ✟   ✟

Making lunch together was fun. Amie loved working in the Bander's country kitchen—it was so quaint and cozy. Mr. and Mrs. Bander enjoyed the young people and were right in there working with them. In no time they had a smorgasbord set out on the counter. Everyone gathered in to pray grace and then line up for the bounty prepared by the work of their own hands.

David had been out when they all got there. He showed up with a surprise, just as everyone was filling their plates. Beside him was a lovely young woman with brown hair and green eyes. Coming up to his shoulder in height, she had a sweet and shy smile on her face as she held his hand, walking into the kitchen from the back entry.

"Hello, Leanne," greeted Mrs. Bander warmly. "You two made it just in time for lunch." She stepped back from her place in line to allow the young couple to go before her.

David had an awkward moment, faced with introducing Leanne to everyone. He assessed the room full of friends with his dark brown eyes and then, running his hand through his head of light brown curls, he said, "Leanne, this is everyone from my band. Everyone, this is Leanne. I'm not bothering going through everyone's name right now—so just introduce yourselves later while we're eating."

Everyone smiled and made a quick a greeting to the young lady. Kyle stepped over and said, "Hi, Leanne, nice to see you again."

"Hi, Kyle. Nice to see a familiar face in the crowd," she said back to him in a hushed voice, with a charming smile.

"Just get your food, and we'll introduce you around," he told her. He gave David a slug on the shoulder as he passed him by, and went to the back of the line.

Amie was in front of the young couple in line so she turned around to Leanne and introduced herself. "I'm Amie Collins. It's really nice to meet you."

"Hi, Amie. It's nice to meet you, too," Leanne replied. "You must be Joanie's sister."

"Yeah," she answered. "Do you know Joanie?"

"No," replied Leanne with a little giggle. "It's just David has told me so much about your family and Joanie and Brandon's courtship and wedding that I just recognized your last name."

"Joanie and Brandon are super cool," Amie commented as she filled her plate.

"I had never heard about the idea of courtship before David came along. He was quite insistent that that was the only way to go about things," Leanne stated, filling her plate behind Amie. "And so far, it's been really neat. Mind you, he just about blew my parents away when he phoned them up and asked for their permission to date me on a steady basis, in what he called a courtship relationship. My father thought he was a lunatic at first."

Amie laughed and looked at David in line behind Leanne. "He *is* fairly crazy," Amie stated, with a wink. "But I'm sure you've figured that out by now."

"See why I was afraid to bring you around my friends, Leanne," David said. "If you haven't discovered all my faults on your own by now—they'll be more than happy to point them out to you."

"Oh, I'm just teasing. David's one of the nicest guys I've ever known," Amie told Leanne. "And I'm sure you've figured that out by now, too."

Leanne smiled and looked at David. He held out the jug of juice and offered to pour her a glass. She picked up a glass and held it while he poured. Taking her meal, she followed Amie to the living room, where Amie introduced her to everyone. David came in right behind and sat with them. He was happy to see that Amie had taken Leanne under her wing and decided to just let her continue the introductions.

When they were done eating, everyone pitched in with the clean-up. Eventually there were not enough jobs left to keep them all busy, so most of the group headed down to the basement to set up for cards. Amie was washing dishes, and Kyle was drying and putting them away, so it was just the two of them left in the kitchen.

"So, how's school going?" Amie asked.

"Busy like crazy these days," he answered. "I've got a bunch of assignments coming up over the next few weeks. I've really got to get down to work."

"Maybe you should have taken today to get caught up," she suggested.

"Nah, I try my best to work hard the other six days so that I can keep my Sundays open to spend with my family and friends."

Amie turned her head toward the young man and smiled, a long curl hanging down in front of her face. "You know," she said thoughtfully, "if I could just bottle you and sell you—I'd make a fortune. You know how many girls out there would want a guy just like you?"

"If they were all like me, I'd hardly seem special," he retorted playfully.

"In other words we still need the jerks around to make guys like you stand out?"

"Exactly," he replied, nodding his head in a playfully conceited manner.

"I don't know about that." Amie blew her hair back off her face with a slight toss of her head as she leaned forward over the sink. After a pause she added, "Take Mr. Slimeball from Friday night. I could definitely have lived without that experience."

"You learned something from it at least."

"Yeah, but who's to say I won't be that stupid again? I'd like to think I was a better judge of character than that—but look how far off I was."

"Well, I can't comment exactly, since I don't know all the details, but . . ."

"But what?" Amie asked, as Kyle hesitated over what he was about to say.

"It just seems to me that maybe you're trying too hard," he went on, cautiously.

"In what way trying too hard?" she asked, feeling somewhat exasperated, more with herself than with Kyle.

"I don't know. . . . It just seems to me that you want something to work out for the sake of working out. Maybe you just need to be patient and let God bring the right guy into your life at the right time."

Amie stood there silently, staring at the dish in her hand that she had stopped washing to listen to Kyle.

"I'm not trying to make you feel bad," Kyle went on. "It's just when this guy was so eager to ditch your family and friends Friday night—warning bells should have gone off for you, Amie. What kind of guy manoeuvres a girl to get her all alone like that?"

"I know," Amie agreed, with resignation. "I was trying to make him into something he wasn't, even though he was doing his best to show me what a jerk he really was. I was blind to it because I had convinced myself so much that he was a really nice guy."

"Let a guy prove himself to you," Kyle said. "You're worth too much to settle for anything less than that. I mean, lots of guys are going to find you attractive, Amie. You're a good-looking girl."

"Thanks," Amie replied with a little smile.

"And you're possibly going to be attracted to an awful lot of guys," he went on. "But if you're called to marriage, you're only going to marry one of them. So don't let attraction distract you from what's really important about a guy. Be *so* choosey, it drives the guys nuts."

Amie laughed and nodded in agreement.

"I'm your friend, Amie" Kyle stated plainly. "I don't want to see you get hurt."

She looked at him squarely and then stated, with an impish grin, "On second thought, maybe I should turn you into some sort of powder and just sprinkle you like fairy dust on the next best prospect."

"You ain't turning me into some sort of fairy nothing," Kyle retorted, pointing a finger at Amie. "I'll keep my manhood intact, and you're on your own to find Mr. Right."

Amie laughed at Kyle's defensiveness. "Fine, I'm on my own. But I give you permission to still keep your eye out for me like the big brother I never had."

"I can do that for you," Kyle promised.

Amie stepped aside and pulled the frying pan over to the sink to begin scrubbing it. "You got anything around here to scrub this with?" she asked, looking around the back of the countertop.

"Look under the sink on the left," he answered as he picked up a stack of plates to put away.

"Do you ever miss having a dishwasher?" Amie asked curiously as she bent down to find the scrub pad.

"Small family . . . and mom never wanted one," Kyle answered. "She figured we'd get closer if we had to do dishes together everyday. And it worked. David and I are as close as brothers come."

"You are." She smiled, thinking about David and added, "Leanne's a real sweetheart."

"She sure is," agreed Kyle. "David's pretty taken with her."

"I think the feeling is mutual. Leanne seems to be quite happy with David."

"She fits in well with the family. It'll be interesting to see where this relationship goes."

Amie was quiet for a minute as she finished scrubbing the frying pan and rinsed it off. "Leanne's a lucky girl. I hope someday I find a guy as decent and good as David or you." She nudged him with her shoulder and smiled. "You're both great guys, and I'm sure glad to be your friend."

"The feeling's mutual," Kyle replied, nudging her back. He took the pan out of the sink and dried it. "Come on. We're done. Let's go play cards."

Amie finished rinsing out the sink as Kyle put away the last pan, then the two friends took off downstairs for an afternoon of fun and laughs with everyone else. Amie and Katie stayed and had supper with the Banders and then went in for youth group with Kyle. He took them home straight after youth group.

Another weekend was gone—Amie was glad to put it behind her. She wanted to forget all about Friday, while at the same time never forgetting the lessons she had learned. As she lay in bed she prayed for God to grant her some wisdom and patience. *Even a little bit would go a long way for me, Lord.* She said her evening prayers and soon fell asleep.

Chapter 16

Amie buckled down over the next few weeks. Caught up between school and preparing for her music theory exam, she did not have time to fret over finding Mr. Right for the time being. Finally, at long last, the day of the written exam came and went. Confident that she had passed, and not overly concerned over her final grade, Amie was more than ready to put that stage of her musical education behind her and focus on her work at Stettler College, while still preparing for the piano performance exam coming up in January.

Maggie's internship at school was moving along. She was now into her experience of full-time teaching. To her surprise, her supervising teacher had allowed Maggie the freedom to direct the class in her own style. Though not every one of her ideas had proven successful in the classroom, she was finding that she really did like teaching after all. Taking her internship more seriously had also caused her to settle down more at the Sisters' house and ultimately to slow down. Suddenly she seemed to be getting herself into less trouble and to be adapting to the pace of religious life more naturally.

Joanie eventually got past the first trimester nausea and rediscovered for herself what "normal" felt like—a state of being she thought she would never again experience. Her changing body had pushed her out of her regular clothes, and she desperately needed some maternity outfits, especially now that she was back at work.

With that in mind Joanie arranged for some sister time, and together the four older girls went out shopping for maternity clothes for the expectant mother.

"This is just like old times," Katie remarked as the four sisters stepped out of Joanie's Pathfinder in the underground parking lot of the shopping mall. It was good to be together again. They took off their winter jackets and left them in the vehicle before heading to the mall entrance. "You know, as you all move on in life sometimes it gets really lonesome around home," commented the sixteen-year-old.

Maggie stepped over and threw her arm over Katie's shoulder to walk along with her younger sister. "I miss spending time with you all, too. I love living with the Sisters and all, but it's not the same as my *real* sisters."

Katie laughed and reached her arm up and around Maggie's back, hanging her hand over her sister's shoulder. "So what's the best thing about religious life?"

"Jesus," Maggie said quite simply. "I love being able to spend time alone with Him everyday in the chapel. It makes everyday worth getting out of bed for."

"And what time *do* you get out of bed?" Amie asked, remembering how Maggie loved to sleep in at home.

"Between five-thirty and six, most mornings."

"You're kidding!" Katie exploded. "What time do you go to bed?"

"Most nights, about ten . . . ten-thirty. Sometimes later, if I have a lot of work to do for school."

"Who are you, and what have you done with my sister?" Amie asked rather emphatically, reaching down and grabbing at Maggie's skirt—giving it a little tug.

"Yeah, it's quite amazing," Maggie agreed, grabbing her skirt with her free hand and giving it a little shake. "But deep down, below this feminine exterior and this disciplined life of routine, still lurks the unruly tomboy you all know and love. Really, I'm still just plain ol' Maggie."

"You'll always be our Maggie," Joanie piped in, smiling at her sister. "Brandon still has marks on his body to prove that."

"Are you serious?" Maggie asked incredulously.

"No," Joanie answered with a laugh. "But I'll never forget the sight of the two of you sprawled out on the floor in the convent, with Sr. Charlotte standing there looking down on the both of you. That was total, unadulterated, classic Maggie-ness at its best," she said, motioning with both hands down for emphasis.

The sisters all giggled, recalling the situation.

"But let's get down to business," Joanie got serious. "I need clothes and I need them in a *big* bad way." She placed her hands over her growing tummy. She had a loose T-shirt hanging over a pair of pants which she confessed to her sisters were not even done up all the way. "I'm getting desperate. And I have nothing for work that I can even squeeze into anymore."

"To the maternity shop it is," announced Maggie, sticking her arm forward, like a general leading his troops into battle. The three other girls picked up pace behind Maggie as she forged ahead through the mall.

"Wait," Katie called ahead to their stalwart leader. "You're going the wrong way, Maggie. The maternity shop is back there," she said pointing in the direction opposite from where Maggie was headed.

"Who decided to let her lead, anyway?" Amie piped in. "Maggie couldn't find her way through a shopping mall if her life depended on it."

"See," pointed out Joanie, turning Maggie around in the right direction, with Katie now leading the group. "Once a Maggie, always a Maggie."

✠   ✠   ✠

After six hours spent in various malls around town, the four sisters walked back into their family home, triumphant in their mission accomplished.

"Hey girls, how did it go?" Judy called out from the kitchen as she heard the girls coming in the front entry, all giggles.

"Awesome," called back Katie. "You should see how we've got Joanie decked out now for clothes."

Judy Collins stepped up to the doorway from the kitchen to the living room. She stood there in a skirt and apron, her hair pulled up.

"Mom, you look so good," Joanie commented walking up to give her mom a hug.

"All dressed up to do my housework," Judy replied, pulling at her skirt. "I even washed floors today, Maggie—you'd've been impressed with me."

"That's me—Maggie the trend-setter," the young aspirant boasted.

Her sisters and mother started laughing.

"Now that's a scary thought," responded Katie. "You've got about as much fashion-sense as a . . ." The young girl's mind raced for an appropriate simile.

". . . as a porcupine?" filled in Joanie, with a giggle.

Maggie turned and gave a cross-eyed look to her older sister while pulling her hair up on end.

Joanie burst out laughing. "Sorry, Maggie, I couldn't resist," the older sister stated, recalling a conversation the two of them once had.

"Nah . . . I'd say she has the fashion-sense of a *Nun*," threw in Amie, thoughtfully assessing her older sister.

"I keep telling you folks—I'm not becoming a 'Nun' . . . I'm becoming a religious Sister—we're not cloistered," Maggie corrected. "But I'm just glad our order still wears a habit. It takes all the thinking and worrying about clothes out of the equation, so I can concentrate on . . . on less-worldly things," she stated in a lofty tone, motioning with her hand in a regal gesture. Maggie then laughed at herself, for she knew full-well that she had absolutely no fashion sense at all.

"Well, there's freedom in that, for sure," Joanie agreed. "I work out in the world—on television five nights a week. Believe me, there's pressure to dress well."

"Well, there may not be as much pressure to dress fashionably on a stay-at-home mom like me," Judy said, "but I like to be presentable when I have to go out. Since I've decided to try to wear skirts a little more often,

I'm finding it a challenge to find skirts that are comfortable, modest, *and* in-style, all at the same time."

"You're doing an awesome job, Mom," Katie said, with encouragement. "You look great."

"Thanks. To be honest, I actually do like wearing skirts more than I thought I would. And like grandma said, I do feel more feminine in a skirt. . . . I just don't want to look out-of-touch and give motherhood a bad rap when I'm out in the world," she said self-consciously.

"I'm with Katie. I think you look awesome, Mom," Joanie said with encouragement. "And you've always given motherhood a beautiful face— that's why I've always wanted to be just like you."

Judy smiled and patted Joanie on the shoulder. "So, how did you all make out with your shopping?"

"Actually, I think we did quite well," Joanie replied.

"Oh, yeah," exclaimed Amie.

"We did great, Mom." Katie said, lifting up the bags she was holding. "We even got some of our Christmas shopping done."

"Wow!" Judy exclaimed. "With not even three weeks left to Christmas— I'm impressed. I should have gone with you so I could have done mine."

"You should have!" Katie agreed. "Next time, you're not staying home."

"Well, someone has to look after the little kids," Judy reminded her.

"Dump them off on Brandon next time," Joanie offered. "He needs all the practice he can get."

"Oh, he's fairly handy with kids," Judy remarked. "I don't think you have to worry about him. . . . So, do I get to see the spoils of war or not?"

The group of women moved into the kitchen and opened up their bags of treasures on the dining room table. Katie kept guard to make sure little ones did not come running in to spoil their Christmas surprises. Judy talked Joanie into putting on a fashion show, so the eldest daughter slipped into the corner kitchen pantry to change into her various outfits. Katie ran off to the living room and grabbed a throw cushion to put under Joanie's tops to add to the effect. They all laughed as Joanie strutted around in her newly-acquired wardrobe.

"Honestly," she said, placing her hands over her pillow-belly. "I hope I don't get this big!" she exclaimed.

"You saw me pregnant enough times to remember how big I got," Judy responded. "You'll be lucky if you only get that big."

Joanie stuck out a pouting lip and looked down at her protruding stomach and pulled the pillow out from under her top.

"And you don't have much say in the matter, either," Judy added, soberly. "So just accept whatever the Lord deals out to you and be glad you've been blessed to be able to have children."

Joanie looked up at her mom and nodded, now sober herself. "Yeah. You know Justine and Mark are really struggling with that themselves."

"I know," said Judy. "That reminds me," her voice lifted, and she pointed her index finger up as she went to search through a kitchen drawer. "Someone gave me some information the other day that I thought you should pass on to Justine. It's a Web site for a place in the states called . . ." She hesitated as she grabbed for her reading glasses to make out the small print from the paper she was now holding in her hand. ". . . *Pope Paul VI Institute for the Study of Human Reproduction.* Apparently it was founded in the eighties by a Dr. Hilgers in response to the Church's call for medical support in the area of Natural Family Planning and reproductive technology for women. So everything they do is in line with the Church's moral teachings in those areas. And I understand they have doctors trained in this throughout the United States and even some here in Canada. I thought maybe Justine and Mark could find some help there. I don't know. What do you think?"

"That sounds awesome," Joanie said, taking the slip of paper from her mom. "I'm sure any help they can get would be appreciated. The world's gone crazy out there with all kinds of fertility solutions that are so out of line with Christian morality, I think a lot of couples find it really confusing," Joanie stated, looking down at the paper in her hands. She walked to the front room and tucked it into her purse in the front closet.

"Thanks," she said to her mom, as she stepped back into the kitchen. Joanie went into the pantry to gather up her things. "And you're right, Mom," she said as she stepped out with her arms full. "I am very blessed to have been able to have a baby so easily. Nausea and all—it's worth every bit of suffering, just to be able to bring a new life into the world. It's a real privilege and blessing."

Chapter 17

December's *Praise Event* found two new girls in the audience. Amie had talked her two new friends from hair design school into coming out for the evening. She had found out that they were not Catholic, but both had been baptized in other Christian denominations. Neither had gone to church on a regular basis growing up, but neither of them seemed against religion either. They simply had grown up with very little religious input—neither negative nor positive.

Samantha and Krystal had both come to accept Amie with all her religious convictions, of which she spoke quite freely at school. They were prepared for the *Praise Event* to be religious, but they were not too sure if it would also include any fun or not. Amie had convinced them though that it was a great way to meet kids their age since they were from out of town and had not yet made too many new acquaintances.

Up until now, Amie had been so busy with her music theory exam she had not gone out to do any socializing after school hours with these two girls. One day after class her friends were telling Amie about their previous night out. Krystal was complaining about some jerk who had tried to pick her up at a bar.

"He was a real jerk," Samantha agreed. "Slimy, to say the least. You could tell he was there for one thing and one thing only."

"He asked me to dance," Krystal said, "and then as soon as we got out on the dance floor he had his hands all over me. I mean, I'm no prude or anything, but I'm not about to put up with that kind of behaviour from any guy. And this guy wasn't even that cute. I'm not sure why I even said 'yes' to dancing with him."

"Did you keep dancing with him?" Amie asked, her face contorted with disgust.

"Well, I didn't want to be rude or anything—so I just waited until the dance was over and then grabbed Samantha, and we high-tailed it out of there," she explained.

"You're kidding!" Amie exclaimed, fully shocked. "Why would you have even finished dancing with the jerk?"

"I don't know," Krystal stated. "I just didn't want to make a scene or anything there."

Amie just shook her head in total disbelief. "Krystal, you are such an awesome girl. You don't need to go to bars to pick up guys or to be picked up by them. You, too, Samantha. I just wouldn't put up with that at all," Amie exclaimed. "I mean, there was that one time only—you remember me telling you about that total loser I went out with last month. There was no way he was touching me anywhere I didn't want him to." She paused for a moment. "Mind you, I do appreciate how hard it is to get away from a jerk like that—but at least he knew I wanted to get away. I wasn't concerned about being polite to him."

"We're not exactly like you, Amie," Samantha said, defending her friend. "We didn't grow up with that kind of hands-off attitude. And it's not like we have guys lining up for us. I mean, sometimes a girl takes what she can get. Although, that guy was definitely too much!"

"Who needs guys lining up for you?" burst out Amie. "And I have a hands-off attitude for a good reason. I'm not just an object for some guy's pleasure," she stood there tapping her index finger on her breastbone. "I'm an intelligent, beautiful, made-in-the-image-of-God, one-of-a-kind person, with dignity and worthy of respect. And so are you! Both of you!" She stared at her friends with fire in her eyes. They listened without daring to interrupt Amie's lecture. "And you don't need guys lining up for you, nor do you really want them to. All you need is one good, decent guy . . . not a whole herd of them."

"True," agreed Krystal. "But where are you going to meet him? I don't think good, decent guys even truly exist anymore. They went extinct with the dinosaurs."

"No, they didn't," answered Amie, shaking her head at her friend. "But why would you expect to meet a good and decent guy at a bar? Remember this," she said, shaking her finger at both of her friends, "if you don't want to be treated like a piece of meat, you don't go walking in and putting yourself up for sale in a meat market!"

Samantha chuckled at Amie.

Krystal shrugged. "My parents met at a bar."

"I'm not saying that it's impossible for God to make good come out of anything, but . . . think about it . . . you go digging for gold where there's gold to be found. You want to meet a decent guy—I'll introduce you to a whole bunch of them."

Amie then proceeded to tell her two friends that they were going with her on Friday to her church's praise and worship night. She did not invite them—she informed them they were going. She told them what time to be ready and that she would come pick them up.

"You really are a determined woman, aren't you, Amie?" Samantha observed.

"You better believe it."

"I kind of feel nervous for the guy who marries you," Krystal teased. "You are definitely a force to be reckoned with."

"You're right about that," Amie concurred. "And I feel sorry for him, too—poor soul. But on the bright side, I'm sure God's going to have to instill a lot of virtue in him. Some virtues—to meet my high standards. Other virtues—to be able to put up with my personality."

They all laughed together at Amie's conclusions.

"Either way," she went on, "he'll end up being perfect for me, because if God's calling me to marriage, then He's got the perfect guy in mind for me already. And that goes for both of you as well."

"You really believe that?" Krystal asked. "I mean, that sounds a little simplistic, doesn't it?"

"Maybe," agreed Amie. "But why should we try to complicate it? I don't think God's up there trying to play games with us to make it hard for us to be able to find happiness in this life. I believe He grants us the desires of our heart. But we have to be willing to work with Him and follow His plans. Otherwise, we'll never find happiness. We'll just keep chasing after what we think we want or need—like chickens with our heads cut off—and we'll almost always come up empty or wanting more."

Amie looked at her two friends and smiled. "Relax. You are going to have an awesome time. And . . . I'm bringing you both to church with me on Sunday morning, as well."

"Oh, no." Krystal shook her head. "We don't go to church, and Sunday's our sleep-in day."

"Well, it's time you did, and you can sleep in on Saturday this week. Besides, I want you to come to my house for brunch on Sunday and meet my family. I really want you to meet them, and they'll love you both. And . . . it's a free meal," she added, appealing to their status as students. "Plus, my mom's a great cook." She offered them a friendly, pleading smile. "Please?"

"Fine," Samantha said, turning her eyes toward Krystal. "It won't kill us to go once, and I'm starved for a home-cooked meal."

It was agreed, and Amie was thrilled to have the opportunity to show off to these girls her friends, her family, and her faith. She knew that God could handle it from there.

Amie made sure to introduce Krystal and Samantha to all the guys she knew at the *Praise Event*. There were the guys from the band, Kyle, Daniel, and David, but there was also a whole group of guys that she knew from Catholic Campus Evangelization.

C.C.E. was a group of young Catholics committed to bringing the Gospel to youth on campus. They set up all sorts of Catholic events for university-aged students. Since many Catholic kids would hit university and promptly lose their faith—a group of students years back had started C.C.E. in order to take advantage of the university years as a formative time for young Catholics in their faith. The formula for these events included both faith-formation and fun. That's what had made the ministry such a success.

Amie's family had been connected to the ministry for years, sponsoring young missionaries to go and work with youth on campus. Eventually Amie and her sisters had become involved in the ministry when they were old enough to participate themselves.

There was also a number of girls to whom Amie introduced her new friends. She was excited to be able to put such a positive face on religion for these two girls who had grown up with nothing.

On the way home in the car Krystal commented, "Who's the cute drummer, again?"

"Oh, that's Kyle," Amie replied. "You can forget about him, though. Kyle's not interested in dating."

"He doesn't like girls?" Krystal asked, putting a modern notion behind the question.

"Oh, no—not that," Amie responded, realizing what her friend was implying. "Kyle's totally straight. He's one hundred percent, solid guy. He's just determined to not date or anything until he's completely ready for marriage."

"Well, he's totally hot," Krystal put in. "I'd say he's worth waiting for."

"Yeah, if he wasn't like a brother to me, and if he didn't drive me completely nuts," Amie agreed, "I'd probably think the same thing."

"Personally, I think that guy from C.C.E. in the bright orange shirt was really cute," Samantha put in.

"Josh Forsythe," Amie answered. "Yeah, he's really nice. Small town boy, in agriculture. He'll end up going back to the farm someday, I'm sure, and making some girl a totally awesome husband."

"I have to admit, Amie, you were definitely right about there being lots of really great guys here," Krystal stated. "I didn't think that church events could be that much fun. Can we come again?"

Amie was waiting at a red light. She turned to Krystal, sitting in the passenger seat beside her. "You can come out to as many events as we have on. All the C.C.E. events are open to anyone. And they're so much fun. And I'd love to be able to do more things with the two of you, now that I'm not quite as busy as I was before my music theory exam."

"Speaking of which," Samantha piped in from the back seat. "You are an awesome piano player."

"Thanks," Amie replied. "I have fun. I just hope I can get that good at hair dressing."

"After the perm fiasco you had last week, I think you'd better concentrate a bit more on your classes at Stettler," Krystal teased.

The three girls began laughing, recalling how Amie had totally frizzed out a sixty-year-old woman's hair. "The expression on Sherry's face was worth it all," Samantha said, imitating the look of horror that the instructor had made. "I can't believe she didn't just lose it on you."

"Oh, and I felt so sorry for that old woman. She was so sweet about the whole thing," Amie said penitently. "She even gave me a tip, if you can believe it. I just felt awful for having left the perm in too long. I had set the timer for the wrong time, and it way over-processed."

"Well, hair dressing I can handle," stated Samantha with confidence. "So you just keep us in touch with a social life, and we'll keep you focused on your studies."

"Deal," agreed Amie. She pulled up in front of the girls' apartment building and reminded them that she would be back Sunday morning to pick them up at nine-thirty. They both eagerly looked forward to the opportunity.

"I could really get into this church-thing," Krystal exclaimed, "just as long as there are enough cute guys there to keep it interesting."

Amie laughed and said good-night. She waited until her friends got into the front entrance of their apartment building before she pulled away.

As she drove home she thanked the Lord for having let the evening turn out so successfully for her friends. *And since they're so interested in guys, Lord, why not show off to them just how attractive You really are. I'm sure once they got to know You, they'd fall in love with You—no problem. . . . They're just searching for love like the rest of us.*

She pondered the thought for a moment. *And since You, Yourself, are love, we'd probably all do well to just keep our eyes focused on You, rather than looking for Mr. Right at every corner,* she concluded. *You know, Lord, I must be acquiring some of that wisdom and patience I've been praying for. But You'd better keep it coming—'cause I don't expect that I've exceeded my limits on the virtues by any means.*

✟   ✟   ✟

Amie picked up her friends Sunday morning for Mass. On the way to church she decided she had better address with them the communion issue. She did her best to explain how Catholics believe that the Eucharist really is the body and blood of Christ. "When you receive Holy Communion," she told them, "you are not only receiving Christ's body, but you are affirming that you do in fact believe it *is* His real presence and, that *you* are in union with His body, the Church. And if you are not in union with the Church, through Baptism, and by living according to the Church's teachings, then you shouldn't receive the Eucharist. It kind of becomes a lie. Does that make any sense to you?" she asked, somewhat apologetically. She did not want to offend them by not welcoming them to communion, but she did not want to leave them uninformed of the Church's position on intercommunion.

"Not really," Krystal admitted. "But it's no big deal to me. I don't need to go up. I'm really just coming to meet people—and since this is where you promised us all the good and decent guys hang out, I wanted to come and see if it was true."

"Oh, you two are impossible," Amie said with a laugh. "I thought I was bad about wanting to find a husband, but you two take the cake."

"Full-fledged, certified, guy hunters," Krystal announced. "We won't stop chasing until one finally catches us."

"That's right," agreed Samantha. "I don't intend to go through life single and lonely."

"There are worse things than being single," Amie warned them. "And not all single people are lonely. And there are an awful lot of unhappy married people out there. So, I'd advise that you spend less time hunting and more time praying for the right guy. 'Cause nights can be long when spent alone . . . but I'm sure they're even longer when the man's not right!"

"Don't you sound all full of wisdom?" Krystal remarked.

"Ah, I'm just paraphrasing a line I got from an old musical, *Brigadoon*," Amie confessed with a laugh. "My family's really into old movies. But the point remains true—you'd do best to put your efforts into praying, rather than hunting."

"And *that's* why we're here," exclaimed Krystal as they pulled up into the parking lot of St. James Church. "We're here to pray for a man."

They jumped out of the Collinses's old, beat-up Toyota. Krystal closed the door behind her, rather forcefully, and announced, "Look out, God, here we come!"

Samantha lowered her head and threw a glance around to see if anyone had noticed her friend's loud display. Amie stood on the other side of the vehicle, laughing. *Oh boy, Lord, do You ever have Your work cut out for You, or what? But You heard the lady—they're all Yours from here on in.*

The three young women walked through the deep snow filled with footprints leading up the church's front steps. It had snowed through the night and no one had yet had a chance to shovel the walks.

When they stepped through the doors Amie invited the girls to hang up their coats in the entry. A number of parishioners were gathered around, visiting eagerly before Mass. Amie told her friends to follow her into the church.

The two visitors watched as Amie dipped her hands in the holy water font and then genuflected. Samantha was right behind Amie and decided to do as she saw, but once she got down on her one knee, she realized she had no idea how to make the sign of the cross like Amie had done. How many times had she seen that in movies? It seemed like such a simple manoeuvre, until she actually tried to do it herself. Krystal gave her companion a bit of a shove on the shoulder from behind, and not wanting to look like an idiot herself, decided to take a pass on the curtsy and the wave.

They followed Amie into a pew and sat down, taking in their new environment. St. James Church was not big for size, and it was really quite a plain brick construction, but the stained glass windows on the four wings of the cross-shaped church were breathtaking. The other remarkable feature of this church was the life-size crucifix at the front behind the altar. Krystal stared at it for a few minutes. She was not quite sure if she found it to be scary or not. It was certainly impressive. Even though she tried to look around elsewhere, her eyes kept coming back to Jesus on the cross.

In the car on the way back to Amie's house after Mass, the girls talked over their experience.

"You were definitely right about there being quite a few cute guys our age at your church," Krystal noted. "Is that typical? I didn't think that many young people went to church anymore."

"I don't think it's really typical," Amie admitted. "We just have a really special parish. It's made up of families from all over the city who come because it's such a traditional parish."

Krystal scratched her head and looked inquisitively at Amie. "You're saying that there are so many young people here because your church is so traditional?"

"Definitely," Amie replied. "The younger families like mine, and the youth our age who are coming back to church, are coming because they're hungry for the truth. So, what happens—in a traditional parish like ours—is that really great community forms because these families are all searching for the same thing. They want to keep their kids Catholic, and they want them to grow up with a fighting chance against all the problems in our secular world."

"I don't get it," Krystal said, shaking her head. "I admit the world has lots of problems, but I don't see how going to church is going to solve that."

"I think I see it," Samantha piped up from the back. "I've been to other churches before—all kinds of different faiths. I've even been to a Catholic church once before. But it was nothing like this. Your church really is special, Amie," the girl in the back seat concluded. "I'd come back again, and I'm not at all religious. But I loved the way everyone was so welcoming and," she paused for a moment trying to put her finger on the experience, "and joyful," she finally concluded. "Those people genuinely wanted to be there today. It wasn't like the forced-to-be-at-church kinds of kids we grew up with, Krystal."

"That's true," agreed her friend from the front. "Most of the kids who went to church where we grew up hated it. They were forced to go by their families—but they sure weren't happy about it. These people at your parish seemed really happy to be there. Even the teens. I've never seen that before."

"Like I said, it's a special parish. And I know not all Catholic parishes are like that. I know lots of families living in other places that don't have the luxury of a really dynamic, youth-oriented parish like we have. So I really appreciate what a gift God has given us here. But I think it's also meant to be an example for other parishes, so that they can see that good fellowship and community can all be a part of the Catholic experience. And there doesn't have to be a compromise on the Church's teachings. On the contrary, I think the more founded a parish community is on the Church's teachings, the stronger it'll be. It's the rock!" Amie said, raising a fist in the air to emphasize the strength of the Church's foundation.

"Not to change the subject, but . . ." Krystal began. Amie just knew something had to be coming about boys. "Who was that total hunk-of-a-guy priest you have at your church?"

Amie shook her head, and looked at Krystal with one eyebrow raised.

"Krystal!" Samantha scolded from the back seat. "He's a priest!"

"True, but he's a total hunk as well," Krystal added. "Don't tell me you didn't notice that."

Amie jumped in. "Look, he may be a total hunk, but he's also a totally awesome, rock-solid, priest."

"I've heard lots about priests who fool around on the side," Krystal commented. "I wouldn't be surprised if a good-looking guy like that didn't have a few girls in the wings."

"Krystal!" Samantha scolded again.

"Look, Krystal," Amie began, patiently enduring her friend's lack of tact, without getting defensive. "I'm fully aware that there are some lousy priests out there who have brought terrible scandal to the Church. But first of all, being good-looking does not necessarily make you morally weak. Secondly, there are many husbands and wives out there who are scummy enough to cheat on their spouse, but you can't assume that every husband cheats on his wife or vice versa. And thirdly, if you knew Fr. Steve at all, you would know that he is a very holy man—a real man of integrity. Now I'm not saying that temptation can't come to priests, and a good-looking priest like that might have women who throw themselves at him. But Fr. Steve is not about to betray Christ and His Church, and I know that as surely as I know my name is Amie Rose Collins. I've known Fr. Steve for years. He's a friend of our family. And he's so much more than just a hunk."

Krystal sat there, playing with her short, light brown hair as she listened to Amie. "I was simply making an observation. I wasn't suggesting I'd throw myself at him. And besides, there were enough guys there our age to keep me interested without having to chase after a man of God."

Amie laughed. This girl was incorrigible. "Look, Krystal," Amie began, half-teasing, half-scolding. "You are definitely going to have to get past seeing guys as objects of your pursuit if you ever hope to find a guy who sees you as more than an object of his pleasure."

"Amen, sister!" Samantha called out from the back seat.

Krystal flashed a look in the direction of her friend behind her and then started laughing. "Oh my God, Amie. You've got Samantha turned all religious on me."

Amie laughed with the two girls for a moment, then thought she'd better address a language issue before they got to her house.

"By the way, Krystal, you know how I mentioned to you before about saying 'Oh my God'?" Amie began.

"Oh, jeez, sorry about that, Amie. It just slipped out," Krystal said, covering her mouth, apologetically.

"I know. And you've been really good about it at school, and I really appreciate that," Amie said. "It's hard to break old habits. It's just, I thought I should warn you that in my family we view that as swearing, because it's taking the Lord's name in vain. Even if you don't mean it—or realize it—it does. And my younger brothers and sister are totally scandalized whenever they hear someone say that. So, I just thought I'd remind you now, if you don't mind being extra careful today."

Krystal was nodding the whole time Amie was speaking. "Totally, Amie. I promise to watch what I'm saying. I don't want to upset anyone." She looked out the window as Amie was slowing down in front of a beautiful, old, character home. "Is that your house?" she asked, duly impressed.

"Yeah, I wish," Amie replied. "No, *that's* our home." She pointed across the street to their old, two-storey, not-quite-so-impressive, character home. She turned the car into the driveway and parked behind the Catholic

Cadillac. "In spite of my dad's best efforts to keep up this place and his constant renovations—I'm afraid we help to keep the property values from climbing too high in this neighbourhood."

"Oh, I think it's really quaint," put in Samantha. "I love old houses. And I love the fifteen passenger van. Now *there's* a real status symbol, Amie. You're the only friend I have who not only has a van that size, but whose family can almost fill it," she enthused.

"Samantha, you have to be one of the most positive people I've ever met," replied Amie.

Samantha smiled as she climbed out of the backseat through the front passenger door. "I hope your family likes us. I'm so homesick; I'd really like it if we could just adopt your family for the next nine months."

"Consider yourselves adopted," Amie stated. "My family is really quick to let in anybody—even crazy, small-town girls like you two."

They laughed as they came up the walk to the front porch entry.

"I love glassed-in porches," said Samantha. "My grandma's house had one, and we used to spend hours in it as kids."

"Our porch gets well used," Amie told her. "And you're welcome to come hang out in it anytime."

As Samantha and Krystal walked into the Collins family's front room, they felt as though they were stepping into a whole new world. Both girls had grown up in smaller families. Krystal was the youngest of three girls, and Samantha had one younger brother. They were instantly aware of the Christian presence in this family, from the numerous religious pictures on the walls, to the large crucifix prominently located over the door between the living room and the kitchen area. There was also a different feeling in this family. They could not quite place a finger on it, but it was so real it was almost tangible.

Krystal instantly took to Jessie. She always wished she had had a younger sister to spoil. She offered to do the four-year-old's hair up in pretty braids before brunch. Samantha was completely taken with Amie's younger brothers. Her brother, Brian, was five years younger than she was, and coming here felt like having him around in some sort of triplicate time-warp. Isaac was just one year younger than Brian, but the same size. Zack had the same boyish energy about him that she remembered Brian having had at nine. And Aaron looked just like Brian had looked as a little boy, with his blond hair and brown eyes.

The most notable thing for these girls was to see how this large family interacted: working together to get the meal ready, praying together before their meal, laughing throughout brunch and clean-up. They really seemed genuinely happy to be together.

On the way home that afternoon Amie apologized to her friends. The fact that they were new on the scene had made it impossible for them to have any time alone together, just the three of them. The little ones had been drawn to the new girls like magnets to steel. "But don't worry," she promised them, "the novelty will wear off and eventually you'll be able to come over without being treated like circus attractions."

"I loved it," Samantha said. "I love to be around kids. I always wished my parents had had more children, but they were determined that two was all they could handle. But I've always said when I get married I'm having at least four kids. I loved all the hustle and bustle around your house. I bet you were never bored growing up."

"I didn't dare get bored," Amie told her. "To announce boredom to my mom or dad was a sure way to secure extra chores. So we made sure we had something to do, and if we didn't, we never complained about it. But yes, growing up in a big family is awesome—I can't think of one thing in the world that I would have taken in exchange for it."

"My two older sisters and I never got along. That's why I had always wished for a little sister that I could have spoiled, so that she would have loved and idolized me," stated Krystal.

"Well, feel free to spoil Jessie," Amie told her, "if you can possibly spoil her any more than she already is."

Amie stopped in at Krystal and Samantha's little apartment when she dropped them off. It was sparsely furnished, but whatever they had was in excellent condition, and it all matched. Tastefully decorated and tidy though it was, it still did not feel like a home. Amie decided to be sure to keep the invitation open to her new friends. She could not think of anything better to offer to these girls than that which she cherished most—her family.

Chapter 18

Maggie awkwardly manoeuvred the doorknob to her bedroom from beneath an armload of books and gifts. Turning sideways, she managed to get her shoulder in place to push open the door. She stumbled inside and dropped everything on the bed. It was the last day of her internship, and she was filled with mixed emotions as she walked back to shut the door. What a relief for it to be all done, but oh, how she was going to miss those kids!

Her four weeks of full-time teaching had solidified her love for the profession and had created a bond in her heart with each of the twenty-six grade five students she had come to know so well. The number of Christmas presents they had brought to school that day to give to the young intern was proof that she, too, had worked her way into their hearts. Though she knew she could go back for a visit to the school to see them, it would never be the same. Letting go of persons and experiences she loved had always been a challenge for Maggie.

She glanced down at the opened packages. She picked up the pile of cards that the students had written to her and began to reread them. She was touched by their affection for her, which they so openly displayed in their writing. It stirred up the emotions she had felt as she hugged each one good-bye. Even most of the boys in the class had not been too shy to give her a hug, except for Liam. He had stood there stiffly, with his hand extended forward to show that he was not going to hug a teacher. Maggie returned his gesture with a firm handshake and a warm smile. As she now read his card, she was moved by the fact that he had signed it, "With love and prayers for the best teacher I've ever known." A tear rolled down her cheek; she reached up to wipe it away.

Turning to her dresser to get a tissue, Maggie noticed—for the first time since having entered her room that afternoon—a beautiful bouquet of flowers. It was an arrangement of white carnations with some fern greenery and twigs of red holly berries. She walked to the dresser, drying her teary eyes with the tips of her fingers. Carefully lifting the little card out of the clip holding it in the bouquet, she read aloud, "Congratulations! Kyra."

Maggie's eyes opened wide, and she flipped over the card to see if there was anything else written on it. There was just a stamp on the back with the florist shop name. She looked back at the bouquet and bent over to smell the fragrant carnations. As she breathed in deeply the fresh scent, a smile crept up on her face.

Maggie walked out of her room into the small landing of the third floor and over to Kyra's room. She hesitated a moment before knocking, looking down at the little card still in her hand. Seeing Kyra's name written there brought to mind the dainty, sandy-haired companion aspirant whom Maggie had more or less neglected over the past six weeks, as she had been so caught up in her internship.

She and Kyra had never really connected since both coming to live with the Sisters. Their lives were very busy, with Maggie at school and Kyra working at her secretarial job in a downtown accounting firm. They really only ever saw each other during community prayer and meal time.

Maggie felt bad as she looked down at the card. It was such a kind gesture from Kyra, and Maggie felt undeserving of the honour. She sighed and pondered a moment what she would say to her companion. Funny how she always thought of Kyra as her companion—they had not yet bridged the gap in their relationship to friendship. With new determination, Maggie knocked on the old oak door.

There was a pause. Maggie heard the chair in the room push across the floor. Slowly and quietly the door opened.

Maggie had a big smile on her face to greet Kyra. She held up her hand with the small card and then reaching forward she offered Kyra a warm hug. "Thank you so much," she whispered in Kyra's ear. "That was such a nice surprise for me when I came home today."

"You're welcome," Kyra said with her shy but friendly smile and a slight shrug of her shoulders. "I just wanted to acknowledge your accomplishment in a special way. I hope you don't mind that I just walked into your room like that to put the flowers on your desk."

"Are you kidding? I come from a family of eight kids. We had no locks on our bedroom doors—it was an old house—and everyone just walked in on everyone else. Actually our family could have certainly worked on better manners that way. But anyway," she said, shaking off her tangent, "I don't mind at all. I value friendship way more than my privacy."

Kyra's eyes lit up at the word "friendship". Maggie realized her negligence in this relationship.

"You know, I'm sorry I've been so busy that I haven't made much time for you," Maggie offered.

"I knew you were busy. I'm just looking forward to maybe being able to get to know each other better now. You know . . ." Kyra paused, deciding whether or not she should say what she was about to say. Maggie leaned her head slightly forward, encouraging the timid girl on. "It's just that I've always been a real introvert. And I look at you, and you're so outgoing and friendly with everyone. Everyone loves to be around you, and you never seem to have any difficulty knowing what to say."

Maggie let out a small burst of laughter. "You mean, I never know when or how to shut up."

"No," Kyra said with a laugh. "I wish I could be more like you. But I'm not, and I never will be. I know that. But I just find that I've been so lonely since I came here to live with the Sisters. And the loneliness is really making it hard for me to discern. All the Sisters are so wonderful to me. It's not that I don't feel welcome. I'm just not good at establishing myself in new environments. You seem so at home, and I still feel like a visitor who needs to apologize for every little inconvenience I cause anybody around here."

Maggie reached up and put her hand on Kyra's shoulder. She offered her new friend a big smile, gave her a little tug, and said, "Come on, I'll show you what I brought home today from school."

Maggie took Kyra into her room, and together they reopened each of the presents that Maggie had received from her students. Maggie told Kyra about each of the kids as the gifts were unwrapped. She shared little stories of her internship, and together the two young women laughed as they passed away the hour until the dinner bell rang.

"Quick," Maggie said, jumping up. "I'll show you the fastest way down to the dining room."

She grabbed Kyra by the arm and led her down the flight of steps from the third floor to the second. Rather than continuing down the regular flight that would have brought them to the front entry—by which route they would have had to pass the chapel—Maggie led her friend to the back staircase.

"I think this was a servant's staircase at one time," she explained in a hushed voice as they entered the narrow, dark stairwell. "The steps are steeper, and it's dark, so don't wipe out," Maggie warned. They hurried down the steps which came to an end, abruptly, at a door. Maggie explained to Kyra to watch out for that, as Maggie herself had crashed right into it the first time she had come down the steps in a hurry. It was so dark in the stairwell that she had miscalculated just how close the door was to the steps. "So you have to make sure to run with one arm reaching out in front of you."

She felt around for the handle in the darkness and opened the door which led to the back entry behind the kitchen. "Watch your step here," Maggie warned. There was one last step after the door was opened. Kyra stepped down after Maggie, and Maggie quietly closed the door behind her.

"Now you don't want to just race through the kitchen, because I think somehow the other Sisters would find that rude. So, I go this way," she explained in a whisper as she navigated past the door to the kitchen through a small hallway. From there they went through a little passageway that led into a broom closet just next to the entrance of the dining room.

Once inside the closet, Maggie whispered to Kyra, "I usually just stop and listen here to make sure no one is passing by when I step out of the closet."

Kyra held a hand over her mouth as she fought back the urge to burst out laughing. She had felt the giggles working their way up through her ever since the dark stairwell, but somehow the secrecy of the mission had been able to keep her giddiness contained.

"Shhhh," Maggie said softly. "I hear Sr. Pauline going by with Sr. Thérèse. I think Sr. Thérèse would be fine if we came popping out of the broom closet, but I'm sure Sr. Pauline would die of a heart attack on the spot."

Kyra put her other hand over the hand that was already covering her mouth. Her side was aching from her efforts to suppress her laughter as she pictured the elderly and stately Sr. Pauline's expression if the two aspirants were to have emerged suddenly from the broom closet.

"Coast is clear," Maggie whispered. "Come, quickly."

Maggie carefully opened the closet door and peeked both ways down the hall. The door to the dining room was open, but the closet was tucked behind it, such that no one sitting in the dining room would be able to see them step out. With her best posture and a totally dignified manner, Maggie strolled out through the closet door—with Kyra close on her heels, doing her best to regain her composure. The two young ladies entered the dining room in as natural a manner as they could, given the nature of the circumstances.

"Good evening, girls," came the greeting from Sr. Pauline. "I must say, you do look fresh and bright this evening. I trust you had a good day."

"Oh, yes, we did indeed, Sr. Pauline." Kyra was the model of elegance and etiquette.

Kyra smiled at Maggie as they took their places across the table from each other. Maggie was truly impressed with Kyra's ability to rise to the occasion and not let on to any of the Sisters of their secret entry. The fact that Kyra was capable of getting the giggles was a very encouraging sign in her character; however, Maggie had been nervous that her comrade's sudden giddiness was going to blow their cover. Not at all—Kyra had reined it all in with the skill of an experienced actress, politely carrying on conversation with the other Sisters at the table in total nonchalance.

Maggie sat and listened, realizing that perhaps she may have just found for herself a truly "kindred spirit", as Anne of Green Gables—one of Maggie's childhood heroes—would have put it.

Chapter 19

It was December twelfth, the feast of Our Lady of Guadalupe, and Catholic Campus Evangelization was hosting a Mexican feast at St. James parish hall in the church basement. It was a popular feast day on account of the great Patroness of the Americas, and it was a popular event for C.C.E. on account of the great atmosphere of a Mexican fiesta.

Amie was there early, along with a whole crew of "C.C.E.-ers", decorating the hall in Mexican fair and creating a feast of tacos in the kitchen. The organizers of the event had picked up the ingredients, with the parish of St. James having paid for the hamburger meat, cheese, and tortillas for the meal. They were expecting about a hundred students. That was always the hard thing about planning such an event. They never pre-sold tickets, so as not to discourage anyone from just showing up at the door. On the other hand, they never knew the numbers for which to prepare. Their motto was, "Too much was better than running short." However, in the event that they would not have enough to feed the multitudes, it would be up to the Lord to multiply the loaves and the fishes, such as they were.

The crew of students and C.C.E. staff were in great form as they bustled around the hall and the kitchen. Streamers were strung across from the lights, gracefully swooping down over the tables. Paper was being rolled out on the tables to create the table cloths, with a flower centerpiece set out on each. Mexican blankets, sombreros, and anything remotely Mexican and colourful were being hung around on the walls. Finally, there was a big piñata to be hung in the centre of the room. The first time C.C.E. had put on the event someone suggested that university students would find the idea of a piñata too juvenile, but that theory was quickly proved wrong. The breaking of the piñata became a highlight of the annual event.

Amie Collins and Annie Ledoux were coordinating the decorating of the hall. They were putting things up themselves, but also calling out orders to the handful of guys assigned to help out. Connor Easton, a fourth year engineering student, waited hand and foot on the young ladies as they oversaw the transformation of the hall. They laughed and joked around with the pleasant, blond-haired, blue-eyed man. He was of stocky build, not much taller than Amie, and the broadness of his shoulders showed off his athletic physique. He had competed on the university wrestling team, very successfully, but an injury earlier in the fall had ended his season. His dislocated shoulder was healing well, but he decided to let his wrestling career come to an end as he was preparing for his last term of engineering after Christmas.

"Over this way a bit more," Ann called up to Connor as he stood on a ladder to hang the piñata.

"I'd do better if I could stop this crazy thing from waving everywhere," he called down, while trying to direct the rope from which the festive piece hung.

"Here, let me help you," Amie said. She came across the room and climbed up on a table to hold onto the piñata in order to stop it from waving around.

"Thanks," he said, looking at the young girl, with a tender smile.

She smiled back up at him and, for the first time ever, something in his smile stopped her. Was it her imagination or was there something there? The look in his eyes was communicating something more than she felt for Connor or than she thought he felt for her. She did her best to dismiss the distracting thought and return her focus to the piñata.

"Can you lean any further this way?" Ann called up to Connor, still directing from the floor.

"Not without moving the ladder," he called down.

"Don't worry about it. It's perfect where it is," the red-headed girl concluded. "Now can you get it secured to that beam?" The ceiling was created with open beams, much like a gymnasium ceiling. It provided for great decorating possibilities as it was strong enough to hang just about anything from it yet not as high as a gymnasium.

"What d'you put in this thing?" Connor asked, looking at Amie as he tightened the rope. "It's darn heavy."

"You'll find out later. I don't want to spoil your fun."

"You couldn't possibly spoil my fun," he answered her, as he began to step down the ladder. Stopping at her height on the table he looked right into her eyes. "You can let go now; it's good and secure—my guarantee."

Amie got a funny feeling as he reached forward to pull her hand away from the piñata. He gently held her hand in his, for just a moment. Amie was now ninety-nine percent sure there was something there with Connor that had not been there before. *Okay, Lord, maybe ninety-five percent. I don't know. I just know that this guy has got that look, and I'm not sure what to do about it.*

Getting down from the table, she pulled her skirt close to her legs and stepped onto the chair she had used to climb up. Connor reached out his hand, offering her some help.

Do I take it? Don't I? What will he think if I don't? What will he think if I do? Randomly she searched her thoughts and decided it would be rude for her to turn down his gentlemanly gesture.

"Thanks," she said with a quick smile. She turned quickly to Ann. Slipping her arm around her cousin's waist, she asked, "So what do you think? Did we do good?"

"The room looks awesome," concluded Ann. "And that piñata is the best one ever."

"It's definitely the biggest one," Connor agreed, stepping back to assess it, beside Amie and Ann. He looked over at the blond girl, with her hair pulled up in a bright clip and long curls cascading down at the back. There were a few kiss curls lying loosely around her face and neck.

"Well, our job's done here. Let's go see what we can do in the kitchen, Annie," Amie said, hooking her right arm through the red-head's left and pulling her in the direction of the kitchen.

Connor stepped back out of the way to let the two ladies pass. He turned to the ladder, closed it up, and carried it to the storage room at the far end of the hall.

"Did you see that?" Amie asked Ann in a hushed tone as they walked toward the kitchen. She slowed down her pace and looked back over her shoulder. Connor was heading the other direction.

Ann craned her head to look back over her shoulder as well. Not quite sure what she should be looking for, her eyes quickly searched the room.

Amie gave her cousin's arm a little jerk, turning her back to face forward. "Don't stare," she scolded. "He might notice."

"*Who* might notice what?" Ann returned, in a hushed tone. "What are you talking about Amie?"

"Connor," Amie mouthed.

"What about him?" Ann asked, totally bewildered.

Amie widened her eyes and heaved an irritated sigh. "Connor's got something for me all of a sudden. Didn't you see the way he was looking at me and the way he reached out his hand to help me?"

"Connor's a really nice guy, Amie. He always treats the girls like ladies. I wouldn't read too much into it," Ann advised.

"It wasn't just that," Amie explained. By this time the two girls had stopped off to the side of the kitchen entry. Amie kept looking around to be sure no one was within earshot and that they were not drawing Connor's attention. He was talking to some of the other guys across the room. "It was the way he looked at me—right in the eyes, as though . . ."

"As though *what?*" Ann asked, looking straight into Amie's eyes.

"Oh, Ann Louise Ledoux, don't be so dense. A girl knows when a guy gives her that kind of look."

"Really?" Ann returned. "I guess maybe no guy has ever looked at me that way, because I think you're being a little daffy about this. Do you like Connor or something? Like is there something you're not telling me?"

"Ohhh! You're driving me nuts. No, I don't have anything for Connor.

But I can guarantee you that he suddenly has something for me. Just keep your eyes open this evening. You'll see it. And if you don't, and I'm totally off on this, that'll be fine with me." Amie stood up straight again and gave her cousin a little tug on the arm.

Ann looked over to see Connor walking toward them. She smiled pleasantly at him. "Hey, Connor, looks great! Thanks for the help," she called out.

"No problem," he answered. He stopped beside the two girls. "Is there anything else I can do?"

"I think we're good to go," Ann replied.

Amie smiled and shrugged her shoulders.

"I'll go see if they need some help upstairs in the church foyer. People are going to start showing up anytime now," he said.

As the young man walked toward the stairs, his back turned to the girls, Ann watched him carefully. Turning to her cousin with a disapproving look in her eyes she whispered, "I think you're crazy. *If* Connor has something for you, you should be honoured. He's one of the nicest guys around. What's wrong with you all of a sudden? Only jerks attract your attention or something?"

Amie cocked her head to the side and her mouth opened, but nothing came out at first. Finally she said, "Annie?"

"Sorry," Ann replied. "That probably wasn't very fair. But when I think of that jerk, Tyson, and compare him to a man of character like Connor, I really have to wonder about you, Amie."

Amie shrugged her shoulders. "I guess I've just never seen Connor in that way before. Maybe I just have to get used to the idea. Maybe God's trying to point me in the right direction."

Ann looked at her cousin, with apologetic eyes. "I shouldn't have made that comment, Amie. I'm really sorry."

"Forgotten," Amie said with a smile. "Besides, you were right. I'll give Connor a fair chance, *if* I'm not totally mistaken here."

The girls stepped into the kitchen. There stood Kyle Bander, Daniel Schultz, Josh Forsythe, and Ben Ledoux, all with white puffy chef's hats, working over the hot stoves. The smell of ground beef, seasoned with Mexican spices, filled the room.

Amie walked over and slipped her arm around her cousin Ben's waist. Ann came up on the other side of their cousin and put her arm around his waist as well.

"Hey, it's 'Double-A Battery' trouble," he greeted the girls. He had always referred to the Amie-Annie cousin combo in this way. The two girls had spent so much time together growing up, and with names that matched so closely, all the cousins were forever mixing them up, even though they did not look at all alike.

"Nice to have you back," Amie said giving him a hug in the form of a squeeze from the side. Ann matched the hug from her side, pulling him slightly off balance.

"It's awesome to be back, and just in time for Our Lady of Guadalupe," Ben responded. "Doesn't get any better than this."

"How's it going in the sem?" Ann asked.

"Awesome. I totally love it. I'm not sure why it took me this long to decide God might be calling me to the priesthood, but I'm just loving it—big time."

Ben was the same height as Amie, with auburn hair and a personality that could fill any room. It had been awhile since he had left Saskatoon, first to go to Calgary to play back-up guitar in a movie being filmed there. He had come home for just a few months through the summer before taking off again to enter a seminary in the States. The last time any of them had seen him was at Joanie and Brandon's wedding at the beginning of September.

"It's good to be home and with everyone again. . . . Gangway!" he called out to his two younger cousins, lifting the pan of meat off the stove and taking it to the long island in the middle of the big kitchen.

Amie and Ann jumped out of the way and laughed as they watched their twenty-two-year-old cousin perform his typical antics. Ben was a favourite in any crowd. He was pure entertainer at all times.

"Hey, boys," Amie called out to the other guys, still busy at their posts. "Y'all almost done?"

"Coming right up," announced Daniel.

Josh turned and brought over his pan of meat. Kyle turned off the stove and waited until there was enough room on the island for him to bring over his pan as well. Amie walked up beside her friend and looked over his shoulder at the pan of meat.

"Smells good," she said with a smile.

"*Good?*" called out Ben from across the room. "This is going to be the *best* taco meat you've ever tasted or my name isn't Benjamin Joseph Ledoux. I took the liberty of spicing it myself, with a recipe I picked up from a Mexican buddy in the sem. Believe me, this stuff is going to knock your socks off, Double-A."

The girls laughed. Ann walked over to help some of the other girls grating cheese at the far counter. Amie decided she had better go up to the church entry to keep an eye out for Krystal and Samantha who had promised to come to the fiesta.

Chapter 20

Earlier that week Krystal and Samantha had been confused over the particular feast they were going to be celebrating with Amie, but as Krystal put it, "Any excuse is good enough for a party—especially if those cute Catholic boys are going to be there!" She was starting to become convinced that there might just be something different about these religious boys.

Amie was excited about the opportunity that Our Lady of Guadalupe was providing for her to witness to her friends. She picked up prayer cards to give to her friends one day at school, but the day had just been too busy, so Amie invited herself over to the girls' apartment after classes. She caught a ride with them to their place in Krystal's little Honda Civic.

While the three girls were sitting at the kitchen table enjoying a glass of juice, Amie pulled out the cards to show her friends just whose feast they would be celebrating that Friday night at her church. She did her best to explain to them the story of Our Lady of Guadalupe and how Mary had appeared to Blessed Juan Diego in the year 1531 at Tepeyac Hill just outside of Mexico City.

"Our Lady asked Juan Diego, who was just a poor native Mexican, to speak to the Bishop about building a church on the site where she had appeared to him." Amie stood up to show the girls how Mary had arranged roses inside Juan's cloak to take to the Bishop. "The roses themselves were a miracle because it was wintertime, and not only that, these were roses from Spain."

"What, they have special roses in Spain?" Krystal asked.

"Well, these in particular the Bishop would have recognized as native from his homeland of Castile. There was no way for them to be there in Mexico—and in the wintertime. But that was just part of the miracle. When Juan Diego went to speak to the Bishop, he opened his cloak and the roses fell out onto the floor and suddenly, before everyone's eyes, this image appeared on Juan Diego's garment." Amie's voice was fully animated as she told the story to her friends. Sitting back down at the table, she pointed to the image of Our Lady of Guadalupe on one of the prayer cards.

"Cool," said Krystal, looking at the image on the holy card.

"Oh, it gets really interesting," Amie went on. "You see, the garment he wore was called a 'tilma', made out of cactus-cloth, and should have deteriorated within twenty years. But still, over four hundred and fifty years later, the material remains in perfect condition. Not only that, scientists have tried to determine what the pigment is on the cloth, and it's not plant, animal, or mineral in origin."

"Meaning?" Krystal prompted her friend for more explanation.

"Meaning, there's *no way* for scientists to identify the source of the pigment or how to explain it. It's literally from out of this world. And the list goes on. I mean, this image has so many amazing details within it . . . like the eyes."

Samantha leaned over, her shoulder-length, dark brown hair framing her round face, as she stared intently at the image to see what was so special about the eyes.

"On a small replica like this you can't see it," Amie went on to explain, "but if you were to magnify the eyes on the original, you could actually see the people who were standing in the Bishop's office that day with Juan Diego."

"What do you mean?" Krystal asked.

"You know how eyes will reflect things? Here, look at my eyes." She leaned forward for Krystal to look into her eyes. "Can you see your reflection in my eyes?"

Krystal stared into Amie's eyes until finally she could focus in on her own reflection. "Yeah, okay. I see what you mean."

"Well, in this image of Our Lady, you can see the reflection of the other people who were there in the room. It was as if a camera snapped a picture of Mary right at the moment when the roses fell from Juan's tilma."

"Maybe somebody did," Krystal said. "Maybe it's just a big hoax."

"Well, that *might* be a reasonable explanation nowadays, Krystal. But this was back in the sixteenth century. They didn't have that kind of technology back then."

"I guess," Krystal conceded, shrugging it off.

"I mean, every last detail of this image is completely miraculous."

"So what's become of it?" Samantha asked. "I've never even heard of it."

"It still exists," Amie told them. "It's kept at the church that was built on the spot where Mary had appeared to Juan Diego, and pilgrims and tourists can go and see it there . . . in Mexico."

"Maybe we should go check it out," Krystal said, looking playfully back and forth between her two friends.

"I'd be game to go," Amie returned enthusiastically. "I'd just have to find someone willing to pay for it, 'cause there's no way I could afford it."

"Nah, me neither," said Samantha.

"That's okay. I was just looking for an excuse for a holiday—and maybe check out the Catholic boys in Latin America," Krystal confessed.

"Now why am I not surprised?" Amie asked, rolling her eyes. "But I'd take you anyway if I could. It'd be good for you. . . . You know that Our Lady of Guadalupe was responsible for the conversion of over nine million native Americans in the sixteenth century?"

"No kidding!" Krystal replied. "And, I suppose you want to take me to see if you can make it nine million and one."

Amie laughed. "Well, I don't need to take you to Mexico for Our Lady to work her miracles. And really, Krystal, whether or not you convert is God's business, not mine. I'm just hear to tell you what I know. I mean, this is really cool stuff. It's kept scientists baffled for over four centuries now, and yet, it's like Sam said, you never hear about it."

"Well, I agree. I think it's really cool," Samantha said, looking at the card with the simplicity of a child holding something truly precious in her hands. "I'm glad you told us about it."

"A painting from the hand of God," Amie said, smiling at her friend. "Anyway, that's why I got you each a card. And there's a prayer on the back of it that you can say to Our Lady, if you're comfortable."

Samantha thanked Amie for the gift and promised to say the prayer.

Krystal was a little hesitant. "Not that I hold any religious convictions of my own," she explained, tucking her short, light-brown hair behind her ears. "But it just seems weird that you would pray to a piece of paper."

"No, no," Amie said with a laugh. She pointed down to the card she had set on the table before Krystal. "You don't pray to a card. You pray to the woman who is represented on the card, Mary—the Mother of God, Queen of Heaven."

"Aren't you just supposed to pray to God?" Krystal challenged her. "Isn't that somewhat sacrilegious or something to pray to other people?"

"Praying just means speaking to someone earnestly. Of course we pray to God—and we should every day, all the time. We should just talk to Him out of habit as we do things throughout the day. We should take special time in prayer with Him, to build our relationship . . . all that stuff," she explained. "But I can speak with you or anyone else in an earnest way as well. When we pray to the saints, we're doing just that—talking to them, like we would talk to our friends here."

"Yeah, but that's just the thing," Krystal pointed out. "Your friends *are* here. Right here," she said holding her hands out to gesture their real presence. "How do you go about talking to dead people?"

"The saints aren't dead, Krystal," Amie told her. "In fact, *they* are more alive than we are, because they live in the presence of God, Himself. Life just doesn't get any more *real* than that. And we can talk to them because the Lord allows us to be connected to the Communion of Saints in heaven so that they can pray for us."

Krystal looked genuinely unimpressed, but Samantha was listening attentively to Amie.

Amie went on, "Look, it's just like me coming and asking you two to pray for me if I had a really big problem. You're not praying people, true. But you probably wouldn't find it weird for me to ask you to pray for me. So why not also ask the people who are now the closest to the Lord in heaven?"

Samantha nodded her head, looking at the card. Truly the image of Our Lady of Guadalupe was filled with breathtaking beauty. Amie pointed to the card that Samantha was holding. "She's beautiful isn't she?"

Samantha nodded. "She is."

"You know," Amie went on, "the mystery of that simple tilma, along with the gentleness of Our Lady herself, is why she remains one of the greatest treasures of *all* Christians, even those who are not Catholic. She's for you as much as she's for me."

Samantha looked up at Amie and nodded.

"I know some Christians—who are not Catholic—think that we worship Mary. But first of all, we don't *worship* her. We honour her, in keeping with the fourth commandment—Thou shalt honour thy father and mother. And no other person in history would be better at keeping the commandments than the One who made them—Jesus. So we honour His mother, because *He* honours her. And we simply try to imitate Him in all things.

"Secondly, there is no denying the special dignity and specific role that Mary played in salvation history. As Mother Theresa, who just died here this past fall, so often would say, 'No Mary, No Jesus.' Mary was the one through whom Jesus Himself chose to become man for our salvation. No other person has ever been closer to Our Lord than Our Lady. Much like no one likely knows you better than your mother."

"That makes sense," Samantha agreed. "I've never thought about it that way. But then again, I've never really thought about it at all."

Krystal laughed. "And Amie shouldn't be trying to get you thinking about it now. You've lived all your life just fine without it. So why would you want to get religious now at your age?" Krystal turned to Amie and lifted her glass of juice toward her friend saying, "No offence."

"No offence taken," Amie replied with a little laugh. "But let me tell you, Krystal, people get religious at all ages and stages in life. And I've never heard of one person who, upon finding God and faith, ever said, 'I wish I hadn't discovered this—my life was good enough without it.' In fact, they usually say something quite opposite, like they regret that they had gone so long in life without knowing Our Lord."

"That's true," Samantha agreed. "I mean I don't know that many religious people, but the ones I do are fairly happy to be able to know God, I think." She shrugged her shoulders slightly and then lifted her glass of juice toward Amie. "I don't know many people as happy as you are with your life. And you totally love what you believe in—that's fairly obvious. I mean, it's kind of contagious to see how excited you get about your faith. It makes me wish I had something in my life that I was that excited about . . . that I was that confident in . . . that I really believed in."

"Faith is a gift from God," Amie told her. "Just keep praying to Him and asking Him to bless you with that gift. And," she added, pointing to the card in Samantha's hand, "ask *her* to help you to get to know her Son. I've never known a mother more eager to show off her Son to the world than Mary!"

Samantha laughed. "You sure have a way of stating it simply. It just makes sense. Nothing ever really seems that complicated the way you explain it."

"God's not complicated," Amie assured her. "We're the ones who try to complicate the matter. But He's pretty good at breaking through even the most hardened of hearts," she said, turning her glance toward Krystal.

"What?" Krystal said defensively. "Do you really think I've got a cold, hard heart? I promise you, this heart is ready for love—I just have to find it now."

"I keep telling you, Krystal. You're looking for love in all the wrong places," Amie warned her.

"What? I'm going to a religious fiesta with you on Friday night, am I not? I thought you said that's the place to find the right sort of guys," Krystal returned.

"True," Amie agreed. "But you still need to find Love. And Love is not a thing, it's a person—it's Jesus. Until you find Him, you won't ever really find love—just cheap imitations, counterfeits of the original."

"Well, we'll see about that," Krystal replied. "I'm not worried. I'll just wait for some hot Catholic boy to come into my life and convert me—that'll be the test of true love."

Samantha and Amie laughed. Krystal was a completely hopeless cause. *Well, not completely,* Amie reminded herself. *You're her hope, Jesus.* She glanced at the stubborn girl taking a sip of her orange juice across the table. *Make that—her only hope, Lord.*

Chapter 21

Amie walked out of the basement kitchen of the church and up the stairs to the front foyer, keeping her eye out for Samantha and Krystal to arrive. Suddenly she realized that she was looking for Connor. She found him helping a friend, Cheri Tulsend, putting up the welcome sign for the *Our Lady of Guadalupe Fiesta*. It kept falling, due to the wind rushing in each time the front doors of the church entry were opened. It was a cold December night.

Offering her assistance, Amie went and stood between Connor and Cheri, who were holding the poster up at each end trying to re-tape it.

"Thanks, Amie," said Cheri with a bright smile. Her dark complexion was set off beautifully by the bold, festive colours she was wearing for the occasion. Her shoulder-length hair was pulled up stylishly with bright flowers pinned around in it.

"You look awesome tonight, Cheri," Amie remarked. "You look great in those colours."

"Thanks," Cheri answered, with a piece of tape held between her teeth.

"You're looking great tonight, yourself," commented Connor. "Nothing wrong with those bright colours on you."

"Thanks," Amie said, feeling the warmth of the compliment. "I don't normally wear colours like these—I tend to be more of a spring complexion on the colour chart."

"Don't know anything about colour charts," stated Connor. "Just know a pretty girl when I see one. And right now I happen to see two of them."

Cheri giggled as she stepped back to assess the security of the poster. "It'll have to do. Next time it comes down, it stays down."

"Sounds good to me," Amie agreed.

"Coming back downstairs, Amie?" Connor asked, as he turned to follow Cheri back to the basement.

"I'm just waiting for a couple of friends from my hair design school to show up," Amie answered. "They don't really know anyone else here, so I want to be sure to make them feel welcome."

"I'll hang out with you," Connor offered. He casually stood beside her, facing the door, his big arms crossed over his chest.

Amie smiled politely. "How's the shoulder doing?" she asked, after a moment of awkward silence.

"Great." He rolled his shoulders back and stretched his neck to the side, opposite the injured shoulder. "Still hurts a bit at times, but it'll heal completely if I give it enough rest. That's why I've decided to quit the wrestling team for good."

"That must be a real disappointment. You were hoping for a medal this year, weren't you?"

"Hoping is one thing," he said. "I'm not sure if it was really within my reach, but the Lord sure took care of that worry for me. Now I'm able to just concentrate on finishing school."

"That's true," Amie said, putting her hands together.

"Plus, it's time I begin thinking more seriously about getting a good paying job to be able to support myself, rather than playing sports," he commented.

"That's true, too," Amie agreed. "Can't play your life away."

"For everything there is a season," he said, "to quote Ecclesiastes."

"That's true," Amie repeated. She was beginning to feel nervous, wondering if Connor was planning to take this conversation in another direction. She rubbed her hands together in front of herself and commented, "What a cold night this is."

"Minus thirty-five," he informed her. "Sure hope everyone's vehicle starts up at the end of the evening."

"Mm-hmm," she said through closed lips, nodding her head slowly.

Suddenly the door pushed open, and a few students came running in, shivering and brushing off snow.

"When did it start snowing?" Connor inquired.

"Just a few minutes ago," one young man replied. "But I think we're in for a good storm tonight. You two the welcoming committee?" he asked, pointing to the pair standing at the door.

"Just waiting for some friends," Amie answered.

Just then the door opened again. Another group of C.C.E. regulars stepped in, carrying some desserts with them. "Just run those down to the kitchen," Amie instructed them. "They were filling out dessert trays to put out for later."

Again the door opened to some young people whom Amie did not recognize. Connor knew them from campus. He welcomed them and pointed them toward the basement.

After about thirty people had stepped through the doors, Amie was beginning to wonder if her friends were going to make it out or if the weather was going to stop them. Finally Krystal came in through the doors, with Samantha close behind her.

"It's colder than hell out there," Krystal announced.

"You know, some people do maintain that hell's actually cold, not hot," Connor commented, greeting the young ladies with a smile as they stepped up to Amie. "They claim it's due to the absence of God's love—which is a burning fire. In God's complete absence, which is what hell is, there's no warmth of His love to be felt—so it's cold—damn cold," he said with a laugh.

"Who's the cute philosopher, Amie?" Krystal asked, smiling coyly at the young man.

Amie made the introduction. "Connor Easton, this is Krystal Burgess and Samantha Roark, both from the town of Kentfield. We go to Stettler College together."

"Pleased to meet you ladies," Connor said with such sincerity that Amie felt a fluttering feeling inside.

Krystal and Samantha said something in return, but Amie missed it completely as she tried to understand the meaning of this unexpected reaction.

"Oh," she awkwardly jumped back into the conversation, "come on down, girls." Amie looked around at her three friends standing there, hoping no one had noticed her attention had slipped away. If they had, she wondered if they would have suspected why.

They walked down to the basement with several other C.C.E.-ers who had come in just after Krystal and Samantha. The two hair dressing students were greatly impressed by the decorated hall.

"Amie deserves the credit for all this," Connor boasted, stepping away from the group toward the kitchen. He had noticed someone needing a hand carrying trays out for the buffet tables.

"What a sweetie that one is," Krystal whispered to Amie. "And I think he's got something for you—the way he looked at you as he talked."

Thank you, Amie said to herself. *Someone else has noticed—so it's not just me. But is that a sign for me, Lord? Am I supposed to be taking special note of Connor? I mean, he's not that bad, now that I think about it.*

"Don't you think so, Samantha?" Krystal asked, turning to the shorter, dark-haired girl.

"I'm just thinking we should have dressed up," Samantha commented, looking around at the number of people who had decked themselves out as festively as possible.

"I told you to," Amie said. "But don't worry—there are lots of people dressed in their regular blue jeans and all. You'll fit in just fine," she assured the quieter of her companions. "Come on, I'll introduce you around again to some people."

It did not take long before dinner was announced and grace was being led by Fr. Steve, the spiritual director of C.C.E. There were four buffet lines set up to best serve the crowd of hungry university students, a good eighty of whom had shown up so far. The weather may have held some back—but chances were there would be stragglers coming in all throughout the evening. The main thing was, there was plenty of food for all, much to the organizers' relief.

Amie sat down with Krystal, Samantha, and Ann, across the table from Ben, Kyle, Daniel, and Josh. Samantha was happy to have the opportunity to get to talk with Josh Forsythe, the tall, lanky, brown-haired farm boy who had caught her eye at the praise and worship night. Though she was a quiet girl, she was not too shy to stir up conversation.

"This idea of Our Lady of Guada-lu-pe," she stumbled over the title, "is all new to me. But what a lot of fun. It never occurred to me how much fun you Catholics might be having."

"Not every Catholic makes the most of our feast days," Josh told her. "I never really paid much attention to my faith until I came to school in Saskatoon and got involved with C.C.E. I had no idea that faith could be so much fun."

"It sure makes a person think twice about religious stereotypes," Samantha commented. She glanced around the room, taking in the festive atmosphere. As she did so, she reached her right hand up to her shoulder and began rubbing it.

"Your shoulder bothering you?" Amie asked her friend.

Samantha realized what she was doing and stopped. "Oh," she said with a smile, "I guess it is. I think the fact that I'm so short is starting to take its toll with full days of haircutting. I'm always having to reach up." She demonstrated by putting her arms out in front of herself.

"That's right!" Josh interjected. "You're all going to . . ." he paused trying to remember the name of the hair design school.

"Stettler College," Samantha filled in, "downtown. It's just a ten month program, and we're six weeks into it."

"So you'll be done . . ." he began to do the calculation in his head.

"September, ninety-eight," Amie announced. "In some ways it seems like such a long way off, and in other ways it seems like it's going to be here before we know it."

"Well, if you need any practice," Josh offered, looking at Samantha, "you can cut my hair for me. I'll sit on a really short stool, though, for you." He slumped down in his chair, making the girls laughed.

"Just how tall are you?" Krystal inquired.

"Six-foot-three," he answered. "I think I look taller 'cause I'm so thin. But can't do much about that. My family seems to have been born with tape worms. We all eat like crazy, but just can't seem to bulk up."

"I wish my family suffered that problem," Samantha commented. "I just look at food and it jumps on my hips. And the fact that I'm only five-foot-three doesn't really help the situation."

"Oh my ... *gosh*," Krystal fumbled, glancing at Amie as she remembered not to use the Lord's name in vain, "you two are exactly twelve inches apart in height. Stand up. I want to see where Samantha comes on you," Krystal said, pushing her friend half out of her chair.

Samantha hesitated to stand up, but Josh willingly complied and walked around the table to stand next to the short hair dresser.

"That's hilarious," Krystal burst out. "You two would make quite the couple."

Samantha threw a look at her friend as Josh stepped back around the table. Maybe Krystal was okay with being so forward, but that was definitely not Samantha's style.

Josh just nodded and smiled as he walked back to his seat. "We'd look like the Jolly Green Giant and the Little Green Sprout together. Hope you like the colour green," he added, looking at Samantha with a friendly smile.

She felt relieved that he had not been taken aback by Krystal's comment. On the other hand, she was not sure if he was just trying to be polite and friendly with her or if he was implying a real interest. She definitely was attracted to him, and obviously he was not completely turned off by her size and shape. Why would he be still smiling at her that way? Suddenly she remembered he had just asked her a question. "Oh, yeah," she replied. "I like green."

His smile turned into a little chuckle, and he announced he was going back for a second helping to feed his tape worm. Daniel Schultz and Ben Ledoux jumped in right behind him.

"You're not going back for seconds?" Amie asked Kyle, noticing his empty plate.

"I'm not feeling that great tonight," he commented. "I think I'd better stop there."

"You seem awfully quiet," she commented. "You all right?"

"Yeah, I'll be fine."

"School going okay for you?" she queried.

"Busy. I still have three exams next week," he told her. "I'll probably be cutting out before the evening's done here."

"That's too bad," Krystal jumped in. "I was looking forward to seeing this piñata competition."

"That'll still be going on," he informed the girl, sitting across the table from him. "I'm sure they'll manage to smash it without me."

"I was just hoping to cheer you on," Krystal said, leaning forward.

Amie looked across the table at Kyle and stifled a laugh as she picked up her napkin to wipe her mouth. Kyle caught Amie's expression and politely responded to Krystal, "There are plenty of guys around here to cheer for."

Krystal accepted her defeat. Amie had warned her about Kyle. Hot as he was, she realized that she would not get very far with him.

"Anyway," he said, looking again at Amie, "I think I'll be going home now."

"You sure you're okay?" Amie asked. "You don't look well to me—you're just not yourself tonight."

"I'll be fine. Hope you ladies have a good evening." He turned and nodded to Amie's two friends as he stood up to take his leave from the party.

Amie watched her friend as he left the room, saying a few good-nights on his way out. Connor walked up to Kyle as he left. The two spoke casually at the foot of the stairs, and then Kyle headed out.

Connor walked over to Amie's table and asked if he could join them. Amie invited him to sit down and take Kyle's spot. Krystal nudged Amie on the leg with her knee. Amie threw a quick prayer out, *Oh, Lord, don't let her start in on me and Connor now like she did to poor Samantha and Josh.* She knew that her friend really did have good intentions, she just did not seem to realize that not everyone shared her "here I am, world" style. Amie turned to Krystal and asked her if she wanted any dessert.

Connor jumped up, "I'd be happy to get something for you girls. What'll it be?"

"Let's go look together," Krystal suggested, dragging Amie up by the arm.

Amie set down the napkin she had been holding and allowed herself to be dragged to the dessert table. Ann got up to join them.

"Come on, Samantha," Krystal called back. "You joining us, too?"

"Oh, what the heck," Samantha said, with resignation. "Yeah, I'll come. The diet can wait another day."

Amie looked at her friend and paused to be able to walk beside her. "You don't need to diet, Samantha. You're gorgeous the way you are. I wouldn't change a thing about you—I really mean that."

Samantha smiled at Amie. She figured Amie had never really suffered the body-image challenge of modern society. Amie was taller and thinner, and what would she have known about what it felt like to be short and fat? Not that Samantha was fat; she just could not appreciate her shape and was so fearful of gaining weight that she perceived herself to be fat.

"Thanks," she said meekly to Amie.

"No, really," Amie insisted, realizing that Samantha was probably self-conscious of her size. "You are beautiful. And not only do I think so, but I'm guessing that a certain Jolly Green Giant has noticed that for himself." Amie offered her friend an encouraging smile.

A smile spread across Samantha's lovely face. Amie motioned her eyes off to the left of Samantha. Josh was walking toward them with his plateful of food.

"You ladies are coming back right away, aren't you?" he asked, looking at Samantha.

"We're just getting dessert," she told him. "Can I get you anything?"

"Lots of anything, or some of everything would be great," he answered with a laugh, moving on toward their table.

Connor and the girls brought back a few plates of desserts to share. While everyone enjoyed their food, a short program began. Students got up and entertained with jokes and led games that involved individuals getting up and running around doing certain crazy tasks. And of course, there was music; there were always at least a few musicians lurking about in this crowd. There was even a castanet playing competition. Ben Ledoux came in a close second to Cheri Tulsend—but since Cheri's mom was from South America, she definitely had the cultural advantage over the crazy seminarian.

Clean-up in the kitchen after the meal was as much a part of the fun of the event as anything. Guys and girls worked alongside each other in an atmosphere of teasing and fun to get the job done.

Krystal actually found herself enjoying the evening so much for the fun of it all that she became less and less obsessed with checking out the guys. This was obviously a different atmosphere than the bar scene to which she had accustomed herself over the past year. These guys genuinely seemed to enjoy her company, her outgoing personality, and her off-the-wall at times sense of humour, without making her feel like she needed to give them anything in return.

By the time the piñata competition began, Krystal was right in there. It brought back memories of childhood parties. In the end, Daniel Schultz brought the piñata down, and it burst open with a mixture of candies and rosaries.

Each rosary had attached to it a small piece of paper explaining how to pray the rosary. Every person was challenged to take a rosary, which had been blessed by Fr. Steve, and pass it along to someone else. "Share Mary, so that she can share her Son," Fr. Steve told them as he explained to the students what to do with their treasures. "But go ahead and eat the candies here tonight, if you want."

Krystal was not quite sure what to do with a rosary, so at first she did not pick one up, but then Annie Ledoux came along and insisted she have one. Krystal picked out a red one and tucked it into the side pocket of her purse—she would decide what to do with it later.

Samantha was thrilled to receive the rosary. She picked out a white one and carefully put it away in her purse for when she got home. "Thank you," she mouthed to Amie.

Connor had hung out with Amie and her friends for most of the evening. He did not say anything unusual, but Amie was sure—by the way he was paying so much attention to her—that something was definitely up. She avoided being alone with him during clean-up at the end of the evening, but he managed to catch up with her while getting something from the storage room.

"Here, I'll do that for you," he offered, taking the big dust broom from her hand.

"Thanks," she said, looking around to see what else she could do. They were alone, and she was aware that he was aware of that, too.

"You know, Amie, I'd like to get together with you sometime soon," he mentioned.

"Oh? What for?"

"I'd just like to talk to you about some things." He paused and then obviously decided not to get into it there at that moment, standing in a storage closet with a broom in hand. "I'd rather wait until we can have a chance to really talk."

"Well," she replied somewhat hesitantly. She did not exactly want to brush him off. And actually, she was glad to have a few days ahead of time to contemplate what she thought might be coming down the pike, before it actually arrived. "How about Sunday afternoon? I'm just too busy during the week to get together with friends these days."

"Sunday sounds great," he said enthusiastically. "Could I take you out for lunch after Mass?"

"Oh?" she replied, a little surprised. That actually sounded like a date. She had not really considered going out with him alone. "I suppose it'll be fine. I'll talk to my folks about it and get back to you—just in case the family has anything planned for Sunday."

"That'd be great," he said with a big smile. "And I don't mind phoning your father and asking his permission to take you out."

"Oh?" Amie replied, again. This was really starting to sound like a date.

She smiled back. Connor was such a nice guy, and really she could see no good reason not to want to go out with him. What was she so worried about? This just might be Mr. Right. "Well, go ahead. Do you have my number?"

"I can get it from the phone book," he told her.

"Good. . . . So, as long as there's no problem, I guess I'll be seeing you Sunday after Mass," she said to him as he began to leave the storage room with the broom.

He stopped and turned back to her, his smile as big as ever. "Great!"

Amie stood alone for a moment in the storage room. She was trying to assess her feelings, but for the most part she could not even really find one to try to identify. She just felt plain and natural. Maybe that was a good sign—from God. *Maybe I don't need to feel all twitter-pated to fall in love,* she reasoned. *Maybe that'll come if I give it a chance. So God, I'm giving it a chance—just in case You are the one pointing me in this direction.*

Her thoughts were interrupted as Ann stepped into the storage room. "What are you doing in here all alone, Amie?" her cousin asked.

"Oh, I was getting something, but I guess I don't need it now. Why?"

"I was looking for you to see if you wanted to get going soon," Ann returned. "We're just about done the clean-up and Connor, Josh, and Daniel said they would close up the place. Everyone else is leaving."

Amie stepped out and noticed that the job was almost done. Connor, Josh, and Daniel were racing back and forth across the length of the hall—tag teaming the sweeping in high-speed fashion; the job would be done in no time. The kitchen was closed up, and Krystal and Samantha were waiting by the stairs to head out, as others were already leaving.

Amie ran across the room to say good-night to her friends. They had both had an awesome time.

"Is it all right if we come to Mass again this Sunday?" Samantha asked.

"Of course it is," Amie answered. "Mass is open to anyone. And I'd love to see you there." The girls were just about to walk away when Amie suddenly remembered something. "Oh, but I won't be able to do anything after Mass. I have plans for Sunday this week."

"That's okay." Samantha smiled. "I just want to come because I like it here. You don't have to baby-sit us," she teased.

"We made some friends here tonight," Krystal added. "It was a lot of fun. Thanks."

"Don't thank me," Amie said, in fun. "Thank Our Lady of Guadalupe."

Krystal laughed. "Oh, right. I'll be sure to do that the next time I run into her."

Amie laughed, as Krystal and Samantha began walking up the stairs to leave. Ann hooked her arm through Amie's, and the two cousins followed. Amie turned back, calling out her thanks to the guys. They waved good-bye and kept on working.

✟   ✟   ✟

At home that night in bed, Amie asked Katie what she thought about Connor. She explained the impending situation and wanted Katie's honest opinion.

"I like Connor," Katie replied. "Everyone does. But is he really what you're looking for in a husband?"

"Well, he's cute enough," Amie answered, thoughtfully.

Katie just rolled her eyes—that was *so* Amie.

"He's Catholic. He's hard-working. He's going to be employable soon, and I'm sure he'll get a good-paying job. He's a really nice guy—so easy to get along with and so nice to everyone," she said as she listed his qualities out loud. "I can't see any reason for not wanting a guy like Connor."

"But are you interested in him, in that way?" Katie probed.

"I'm not sure, yet. I guess that's what I'll find out."

"I'm not sure if it works that way," Katie stated. She rolled over in bed, pulling the covers up around her shoulder. "I think you'd better do some serious praying about this, Amie," she warned. "I'd hate to see you hurt Connor just because you don't know what you really want."

Amie took offence to the comment. She had no intention of hurting Connor. And she *did* know what she wanted—sort of. She fully intended to prove Katie wrong. *If it's meant to be, Lord, well then, just let it happen.*

Chapter 22

The following Sunday was the Third Sunday of Advent. Amie found herself hanging around after Mass with Connor which, given the circumstances, felt rather awkward for her. She managed to quietly suggest to Connor that they stall off leaving until most of their other friends had left. Ann Ledoux knew what was going on, so she willingly helped divert the conversations so as not to draw attention to the situation.

Connor himself was nervous about the date, and was not at all anxious for their friends to know—just in case it did not go as he hoped. He happily followed Amie's lead and patiently stood around waiting for the right moment. Finally when Amie's family was leaving anyway, she and Connor decided to use that as the opportune time of departure.

Amie waited outside near their family van, and Connor pulled up in his two-door Cavalier to pick her up. Amie called out good-bye to her family and hopped into the little white vehicle with Connor.

He had made reservations at a small restaurant in an out-of-the-way location in town. They did not say much to each other during the drive in the car. Amie felt totally awkward. It was not like she had ever found it difficult to carry on a conversation with Connor. But she was not about to open the conversation herself today, and he was so nervous and awkward himself, he seemed to be all tongue-tied. She felt bad for him. She really hoped Katie had not been prophetic at all in implying that Amie might hurt him. Connor was a great guy and deserved to be treated well.

Finally, Amie could not take it anymore. "You have any CD's in here?" she asked, pointing to the CD player.

"Yeah, I've got some really good music. I don't know why I didn't put it on." He seemed relieved to fill the silence with some Christian tunes.

Amie kept beat to the music with her hands on her legs. Connor drove on intently to the restaurant.

They arrived at *The Country Corner Café* and were seated in a quiet booth. It was a pretty little restaurant, and the quaint café curtains in the windows reminded her of the Bander's little country kitchen. She loved that look; it felt so homey.

"Nice restaurant," she commented, taking off her winter jacket and setting it on the bench beside her, along with her mitts and purse. "I've never been here."

"I asked around to find out what was a nice place. I've never been here before either," he confessed as he pulled off his winter jacket.

"Well, someone's got good taste," she stated, looking around at the quaint light fixtures that hung in each booth and the pretty decorations on the walls.

"Actually, it was Kyle," he told her.

"Kyle?" Amie returned. "When has he ever been here?"

"Apparently his family comes here often enough. His mom is friends with the owner's wife."

"That would explain the decor. I guess I'll have to thank Kyle next time I see him," she said flippantly.

Connor smiled and turned to his menu to order. Amie wondered if this guy was ever going to get around to stating his intentions or not. It was probably well enough to let it wait a little while longer. She looked through her menu and chose the chicken *cordon bleu*. Connor chose a steak sandwich, and they waited for the waitress. When she came around, Connor gave her their orders and asked Amie what she wanted to drink. She ordered some pop, and so did he.

Amie was impressed with Connor's good manners and attentiveness. She liked a guy who knew how to act like a man and take on the man's role. He opened doors for her and waited on her, like a real gentleman. It was definitely working in his favour.

They ate and made small talk—very small talk. Amie kept wondering when this guy was ever going to get to the point. Then all of a sudden the realization struck her: maybe there was no point. Maybe she had been reading into this more than what was really there. Maybe he really had just wanted to get together to have lunch and nothing else.

Suddenly Amie had a sense of disappointment come over her. Here she had built herself up for two days, praying and discerning, wondering and worrying, anxiously anticipating some big question to come from this guy. Maybe there was not going to be one. Amie felt her heart sink a little as they waited for their desserts to come.

Connor asked her about Christmas plans for her family and told her that he would be going back home to Regina, a city just a few hours from Saskatoon. He would not be leaving until the twenty-third, because of his part-time job. Amie's family would be staying around home as usual. Maggie would be coming home for Christmas Eve, but spending Christmas Day with the Sisters of the Immaculate Conception. Joanie and Brandon would be home for Christmas, too, but then off to visit his mother in Calgary.

Their desserts came, and Amie took a taste of the chocolate amaretto cheesecake. It was incredible!

"Kyle told me to be sure to order the cheesecake here," Connor told her. "I guess he knew what he was talking about," he said as he took a second bite.

As Amie savoured each bite she found the disappointment was wearing off, and she resigned herself to just enjoying the pleasantness of the moment. The waitress came and refilled their coffees. Amie began doctoring hers up with cream and sugar.

"So how would you feel about courting with me?" Connor finally came out with it. He sat across the table from Amie with his blue eyes looking so intently at her, she felt trapped to look away.

Her mouth fell partway open, as Amie realized that after two days of preparing for this moment, she had been caught completely off-guard.

"I've already spoken with your father about it," he informed her. "I know how your family feels about courtship, and I think it's a wonderful idea."

Amie closed her mouth, swallowed, and then opened it again to say something—but nothing came out.

"I know this is probably all rather sudden," Connor told her. "But I've been thinking about this for a long time and praying about it. I really think that you are exactly the kind of girl I'd like to marry. But I know we've been friends for a few years now and maybe you're not at all interested in pursuing a romantic relationship with me," he explained, without even fumbling over the words.

Amie was still quiet, trying to dig back to the feelings she had just covered over with chocolate amaretto cheesecake. Where were they? They had to still be in there somewhere. Just minutes before she had been enjoying Connor's attentiveness . . . and his gentlemanliness. There they were. She suddenly found herself smiling and then she began laughing.

His eyes began to question her reaction, and Amie caught herself in time so as not to give the wrong impression. She was not laughing at him at all.

"Oh, Connor," she began, trying to hold back her laughter. "I've been expecting you to ask me the entire meal and when I finally gave up on you—thinking you probably had no intention of asking me—you finally decided to ask. I'm just . . . I'm just trying to remember how I was planning to answer you in the first place."

"So, you've been thinking about this as well?" he asked, rather hopefully.

"Well, no," she answered. Then, realizing that probably sounded insulting, she added, "I mean, I just had a feeling the other night when we were standing together in the storage room that that's what you were wanting to meet me about." She searched quickly for something to say that would sound sincere. "I've just had the last couple of days to consider it, and I'm not sure, yet. What did my father say? And when did you talk to him about this?"

"I actually went and met him after school one day about a week ago, which is why I knew I should phone him about taking you out today. He explained to me what his expectations would be for us to go out. And he said he was comfortable with a man like me courting his daughter, but it would obviously be up to you as to whether or not you were interested. . . . So, what do you say? Would you like to enter into a courtship relationship to see if God might be calling us to marriage?"

Wow! Am I really ready for this? Amie closed her eyes and searched inside her heart for a moment. "Connor, I have to be honest with you. I think you're an awesome guy, and I think you'll make some girl an amazing husband some day, but . . ." She could see the disappointment growing in his eyes. "I've never really thought of us in that way before, so I'm not sure if I'm ready for that kind of commitment. But I have to say," she added, in a tone of encouragement, "I really enjoyed being with you today, and it made me realize that maybe there is a possibility here between us. I just want a little time to think about it. I'm not saying 'no' to you," she assured him. "I just want a bit of time to be sure that it's a good decision right now."

Connor nodded his head and looked down at his coffee. "I can respect that. I just wanted you to know how I felt about you. But I don't need an answer today."

Amie smiled affectionately at the young man. "Connor, you are so amazing! You really do deserve a wonderful girl to fall in love with you. I hope that if that girl is meant to be me, you'll be satisfied with what you get."

"Oh, I know I'd be satisfied," he assured her. "You're exactly the kind of girl I've always hoped to find someday."

"Well, how about we do something together this afternoon," she offered. "I think I just need to have a chance to spend some time alone with you—I mean without our whole group of friends around—so that I can think about this."

"Do you like bowling?"

"Love it. But I'm not really any good at it," she warned. "Is your shoulder really up to that?"

"Shoulder's great. And both shoulders are feeling a whole lot lighter now that I've had a chance to tell you how I feel," he added, lifting his hands in a way to show the weight was gone.

Amie laughed. "I'm ready to go when you are."

They left the restaurant and drove to a bowling ally. They played three games, and Amie improved constantly as Connor patiently taught her some technique. It was fun, and there could not have been a nicer guy with whom she would have wanted to spend the afternoon. As he drove her home, she decided to bring up the subject again.

"You know, Connor," Amie began, wringing her mittens between her hands as she spoke, "I've been thinking about your proposal, and I think I'd like to give it a try."

Connor looked over at the girl beside him. "Are you serious? Are you sure you don't want more time to think about this?"

Amie shook her head and answered, "No. I think I'm ready to give it a go. In fact, I'd like you to stay and have supper with my family tonight. You might have second thoughts after you get to know that loony crew."

"I don't think so. And I'd love to come have supper with your family."

"I guess it can be official, then. We're courting, which . . . would make you my boyfriend," she mused.

"And that makes you my girlfriend," he concluded enthusiastically. He reached over and took her hand in his.

Amie felt a slight surge of panic run through her as she let him take her hand. She looked over at Connor who had a smile from ear to ear as he looked straight ahead out the windshield. Her heart softened at the sight of his pleasure. He was so sweet and unpretentious. And he was . . . her boyfriend! *And I'm his girlfriend! Oh, Lord, don't let me blow it. Connor deserves not to get hurt. So just help me to guard his heart while I guard my own.*

✟   ✟   ✟

John Collins crawled into bed that night next to his wife. He was chuckling away to himself.

"What are you laughing about?" Judy asked, rolling over to look at her husband.

"I give it two weeks," he told her, chuckling all the harder.

"John, why in the world did you agree to let Amie court this guy?" Judy asked, full of confusion. "You can see as plain as day that she's not attracted to him."

"I can see that, dear. You can see that, too. But Amie will have to see it for herself," he explained. "And Connor is a great guy. I trust him to treat Amie with total respect. I'm not at all worried about her spending time with him."

"But are you being fair to Connor?" Judy asked, sitting up in bed, looking sternly at her husband. "Connor is a nice young man. I don't want to see him get hurt, just because you think Amie needs to learn a lesson."

John stopped and thought about that for a moment. "Well, Connor's a big boy. I didn't ask him to ask her out. And I warned him that Amie doesn't always know her own mind—and she can change it quite easily. So, at least I tried to prepare him for that," he pondered out loud.

"John, are you being fair?" Judy insisted.

"What was I supposed to say to him? 'No, you can't court my daughter because'. . . because, why? There was no reason for me to say 'no' to his request. I had no idea whether or not Amie was attracted to him. She's a big girl—she should have said 'no' if she had no interest. But she didn't." His tone was serious at first, but as he reflected on Amie he began chuckling all over again.

"Amie's not that good at saying 'no'," Judy pointed out.

"She's going to have to learn. It's not up to me to play cupid with our children. My job is to protect them from the jerks and creeps and to make sure the good guys that come around stay in line. Now," he added, "admittedly, I failed at my duty with that smooth-talking music boy, Tyler."

"Tyson," Judy corrected, in a tone of annoyance.

"Tyson, Tyler . . . tomato, tomata," he said, throwing out the names. "The point is I've learned to trust my own instincts better. If Connor had been a jerk, I would have sent him packing in no uncertain terms. On the contrary, Connor is a fine young man—strong in his faith, dedicated to his studies, committed to his friends, from a close-knit family . . . on what basis did I have to say 'no' to him?" John was lying back on his pillow, his hands raised up above him in question. He looked at his wife who was sitting up in bed with her arms wrapped around her legs, her chin cushioned by the soft feather duvet covering her.

"I don't know," she murmured. "I just feel bad for Connor because I can see this is not going to turn out the way he wants it to. I mean, did you see the way he was looking at Amie throughout supper? And how totally unnatural it was for Amie to hold his hand?"

"Maybe you need to have a talk with Amie," John suggested.

"I tried, just before I came to bed. She's convinced that she just needs a little time to get used to the idea of thinking of Connor in romantic terms. So I told her, that's fine—but then don't begin a courtship until you have the feelings to match. But she's so determined that she needs to give it a chance in this way. And I just can't get her to hear what I'm saying." Judy stretched her arms upward to heaven. "I'm not sure what else to say to her, short of telling her she can't."

"Then tell her that," John stated.

"If I tell her that she can't court with Connor, she'll be all the more determined to do it—just to prove me wrong. It's not like she's trying to be stubborn or rebellious—she just wants to prove that she's grown up and can make adult decisions" Judy reflected for a moment. "She's the same age, I guess, as I was when we started going out."

"And so she is," remarked John. "And, both she and Connor can deal with the consequences of their adult decisions. It's not like they're proposing anything immoral. They're not asking to live together—nor do I expect they will. They're both strong enough in their moral convictions that they're not going to get themselves into trouble. And who knows," he added, with a chuckle, "maybe Amie will suddenly find herself falling in love with the guy. He's a good looking fellow—strong, athletic, blond hair, blue eyes . . . kind of reminds me of someone else I know."

"Someone else you once *knew*," she returned, "some twenty-five years ago!"

"I might not be as athletic as I once was, and my hair might not be so blond . . ." he began.

"I'd say it's turned to more of a metallic blond, from the silvering happening there at the temples," she said with a laugh, turning around to face her husband. She reached over and ran her fingers through his hair. "But still good looking," she concurred, upon assessment. She gave him a little smile and winked. "Oh, I guess you're right," she said, her thoughts having moved back to the subject at hand. "There's not much to do but sit back and watch this whole thing unfold."

"Exactly," he agreed. He reached up and pulled his wife gently by the shoulders to come lie down beside him. "So let's enjoy the ride," he suggested, the humour of the situation returning to him. "I can guarantee you that we'll get our money's worth in entertainment value, watching Amie sort this all out."

Judy smacked her husband on the belly, half-playfully and sat up, leaning back on her elbow. "John, you shouldn't be enjoying other people's potential misery so much," she scolded. "You should be praying that they don't get hurt along the way."

"You're right, dear," he replied, attempting to take on a tone of contrition, without much success.

She looked at him with one eyebrow raised, her lips pursed to scold.

"All right," he said with a renewed tone of sincerity. "Let's say some prayers together here and set your mind at ease."

Judy huffed, trying to decide whether or not her husband was still just humouring her. Nevertheless, she realized that this might be as close as she would get tonight to him being serious about the subject, so she followed his lead and reached for her rosary on the bedside table. John reached for his and turned out the bedside light. Together they offered up the intentions and needs of their family, asking the Mother of God to take them to her Son.

Chapter 23

"Something bothering you, son?" Kevin Bander asked Kyle as they worked together in his shop. The bright trouble light shone down into the open engine as the two men stood in their shop coveralls on opposite sides of the vehicle's front end.

"No," Kyle answered, nonchalantly. "Why?"

"Well, I just asked for a seven-sixteenths socket, and you passed me a seven-sixteenths wrench. So I'm thinking, maybe you've got something else on your mind this evening other than this radiator shroud," his father commented, pointing down into the engine with the wrench.

Kyle looked down at the tool in his father's hand. "Sorry, Dad." The twenty-one-year-old quickly took it out of his father's possession and turned to get the correct tool.

"Don't worry about it," his father answered.

Kyle passed the socket to his father and stood watching as he removed the radiator shroud. After a few moments of silence the boy spoke up. "Actually, Dad, something is on my mind."

"Go ahead," his father replied, not bothering to look up.

"How'd you know Mom was the right one for you?"

Kevin paused and stood up to look at his son. "I don't think I really did."

"What d'you mean?"

"You remember, son, your mother and I did not exactly go about life and love the right way," his father answered cautiously. "We were caught up in the ways of the world. I met her, and within a month we were living together. But she wasn't the first woman I had ever been with . . . that I had even lived with. She was there, and it just seemed like the thing to do. Now don't get me wrong. I was awfully attracted to your mother—but not for any noble reason. She was, and still is, a good-looking woman. And she was not naïve to the ways of the world, herself."

Kyle looked at his father, nodding slowly. He knew all of this. His parents had shared their story with Kyle and David before. Not proud of their past, they knew it was important for their sons to know the truth of their relationship—but more importantly how God's love and mercy could come in and redeem anyone of any sins.

"I suppose it wasn't until quite a while after you were born that I realized that she was truly the one for me." Kevin stepped around to Kyle's side of the vehicle and leaned against the car. Kyle turned around so that he, too, was now leaning on the car, shoulder to shoulder with his father.

"As you know, we got married while your mom was pregnant with David. Then you came along almost two years after your brother. And that was it. I went out and made sure we'd never have children again." He shook his head shamefully. "That's a decision I've had to live with and regret all these years."

Kyle stood there listening. He did not comment, nor did he ask any questions.

"We never had the best of marriages, and although I never cheated on your mother, I was always looking around—aware I had options. She was not fully satisfied at home. Though she had never been a career woman, there was a restlessness about her as you boys began to grow up. I realize now that that was due to the sinfulness of our lives—both before and during marriage. You see, you can't live in a sterilized marriage and not suffer the effects of the lie that it is. On one hand you're saying, 'I'm giving myself to you completely,' and on the other hand you're saying, 'but you can't have this part of me—my fertility.' And before you know it," he continued, "you're holding back all kinds of things from each other—not just your fertility. It's your thoughts, your desires, your dreams, your affection. You begin to allow yourself to let those things go in any direction you want.

"And the fact that we hadn't waited for marriage in the first place always created a certain amount of tension between us. Sex outside of marriage does that—it plants seeds of insecurity and distrust in a relationship. I think your mother was really just afraid that one day I'd pack up and leave. I found her insecurities annoying and grating—she was so dependent on me for everything. I couldn't understand that the more I pushed her away, the more she clung. And she couldn't understand that the more she clung, the more I wanted to push her away. It was a vicious cycle, rooted in sin. And to be honest, I was tempted to run away from my responsibilities a number of times. But deep down inside I really did love your mother . . . and you boys. I was just too lacking in manhood to know what that really meant."

Kyle glanced momentarily at his father, and then looked back down at the floor in front of him. His eyes were fixed on an oil stain in the cement. He waited for his father to continue.

"So by the time you were seven years old our marriage was really just hanging by a thread. But then something happened." Kevin elbowed his son lightly in the ribs. "You got sick. Struck with meningitis, we didn't know if you were going to live or die. And if you survived, there was a good chance of brain damage. So, for the first time in our married life your mother began to pray. Now remember, she had grown up Catholic.

So had I. We were even married in a Catholic church—not that we had a sniff of what that meant. You boys had been baptized, just to satisfy your grandmothers. And that was it. We were done with church and with God. But now, faced with the possible death of her child, your mother began to pray—and pray hard."

Kyle smiled, without parting his lips. He thought of his mother now and how fervently she prayed every day. It was almost impossible for him to imagine her not as a praying woman.

"I was too angry with God and unable to cope with the potential loss of a child to pray. I figured if God existed at all He was a fairly arbitrary guy, doing as He pleased—when and how. He certainly wasn't too interested in this ol' mechanic," Kevin said, pointing to himself, "nor in what happened to my kids. I could see no point in praying.

"But your mom threw herself into prayer like only a mother can, and she begged God for your life. She promised Him that no matter what happened, if you were spared to live, even if you had brain damage, she would begin taking her boys to church. Well, son . . ." Kevin placed his arm over Kyle's shoulder, ". . . you lived!" A broad smile stretched across the father's face.

Kyle chuckled and nodded, looking into his father's moist eyes.

"I never really accepted that it was a miracle. After all, kids recover from illnesses all the time. We live in Canada. I figured that we had the best of health care in the world here—not that you'd ever hear me say that these days," he said with a laugh. "But I credited the doctors for doing a fine job and was just happy to be taking you home.

"Your mother informed me, though, that once you were well enough to go, she'd be taking you two boys to church." Kevin paused and tilted his head, reflecting on it all. "I didn't take her that seriously. I figured she'd get over the feeling, once things settled back to normal. But what I didn't realize was that by this point in time she had already connected with a woman from St. James parish.

"They had met in a grocery line, of all places, while you were sick in the hospital. Your mother was beside herself with worry, and there was a woman standing in line in front of her with all these children. Judy Collins turned to your mother and asked if she was all right. Of course your mother was not. And women just have a way of being able to reach out to each other. They ended up standing and talking in the parking lot for almost an hour. Judy gave your mother her phone number and assured her that she and her family would pray for you."

Kevin nodded with a chuckle and looked at his son. "God had a plan and nothing happens by accident. Sure enough, as soon as your mother brought you home, there was Judy Collins showing up with casseroles from almost a dozen women from St. James parish, all with cards saying they were praying for us. So when the time came, a few weeks later, your mother knew where she would be going to church. And of course, by this time, I had been so beaten down by the stress of it all and was so relieved that it was over that I agreed to go with her. I guess you can say I had made a sort of resolution to try all over again and begin working on our marriage. I finally began appreciating all I had, because I had come so close to losing it. And so off to St. James Catholic parish we went one Sunday in June."

"June twenty-fourth," Kyle said, under his breath.

"That's right," said Kevin. "Your mother won't let any one of us forget that, now will she?" They laughed together. The spiritual fortitude of that woman was something her family had all come to admire.

"So when did you decide that Mom was the right girl for you?" Kyle reiterated the original question.

"When I saw her sitting by your bedside in the hospital, praying, I realized she was the most beautiful woman in the world I had ever known. There was just something about her at that time—a strength in her that I had never before seen. It was God's grace moving through her! I promised myself never to look at another woman lustfully again. All I wanted was for a chance to start over. And I got that chance," Kevin stated.

"So when did you begin to believe in God?" Kyle asked. "'Cause I don't ever remember a time when you weren't strong in your faith."

"My conversion of heart came shortly after we started going back to church. There was something about that community that really touched me. We began to get involved with the other families . . . and those other dads were real leaders in their homes. I admired their spiritual strength, their devotion to their families and to God. And eventually I went to confession with Fr. Joe. . . . Remember good ol' Fr. Joe?" he asked with a smile.

Kyle nodded, smiling as well.

"It had been almost twenty years since I had been to confession. And you know what happened?"

Kyle shook his head.

"I was set free of all those sins from my past. Just something inside of me said, 'You're free!' And I knew it was true." Kevin Bander stood there silent for a moment. "Now I'm not saying that I was never bothered again from my sinful life. On the contrary, I was haunted by certain things for a long time. It took a lot of self-discipline to un-train myself from looking at women as objects for my pleasure. Lust is a hard sin to uproot—and it doesn't happen without effort. . . . It takes lots of prayer and fasting, and thank goodness for the sacrament of confession.

"Another was the fact that now that I had discovered the true joy and meaning of fatherhood, I had ruined our chances to ever have any more kids. I had a reversal of the vasectomy, but we never did conceive another child."

Kyle was silent. How he had longed for more siblings his whole life. He was close to David, and he was grateful for that. But there had always been a longing to have come from a larger family, especially when he had grown up knowing several from their parish. He could see what a blessing it was for a family to have many children—even when they struggled financially. The Collins family had been the greatest inspiration to him in that matter.

"It was hardest on your mother," Kevin went on. "I know that there was a longing inside of her to share the gift of her motherhood with many children, and it just would never be—because of a selfish decision we had made when we were younger. We pay the price of our decisions. Though our sins can be forgiven, we still live with the consequences. . . . Anyway, your mother's faith was stronger than her suffering. She began volunteering at the crisis pregnancy centre. She's helped thousands of women and girls over the years through her prayers and support."

Kyle smiled again, broadly. "She's quite a woman."

"That she is," Kevin agreed. "I just wished I had had the eyes to have seen that years earlier, and the faith to have been a real man of integrity when we had first met. No," he stated firmly, "your mother is definitely the right woman for me, and the only woman I'll ever want to be with. But it took you almost dying to make me see that. So thanks, son," he said with a nudge.

Kyle looked at his father and laughed as he replied, "No problem. Don't mention it."

"So," Kevin asked, stepping forward to pick up an oil rag. He began to wipe his hands. "What's this all about, Kyle?"

Kyle shrugged his shoulders and sighed. "I'm not sure. It's just that . . . I just heard that Amie Collins has begun courting a friend of mine from C.C.E., Connor Easton. He's a really great guy. I'm happy for him, except . . ."

Kevin jumped in, "Except that he's got your girl."

"I can't exactly call Amie *my* girl," Kyle responded. "We've never gone out, and she has no notion of my feelings for her beyond friendship. I'm just like a big brother to her, and that's it."

"So what are you going to do about it?" his father asked.

"Nothing, I suppose," Kyle replied. "What can I do? If I step forward and say something, Amie will totally reject me—I know her. She's not ready for that. And I can hardly tell Connor to back off, he's got my girl. She's *not* my girl. So what do I do?"

"To start with, you pray," Kevin said.

"Been doing lots of that," Kyle returned.

"And you trust God that if Amie really is meant for you, she'll be there. And if she's not, then you know God has a better plan for you—better than you can imagine," advised the father.

"I know. . . . I know it in my head. I just wish I could make that twelve inch drop now to my heart," Kyle said lightly, thinking of how his mother always said a person needs to take their intellectual faith and do the twelve inch drop to the heart so that their relationship with Christ could become real. "I guess if I keep Christ there," Kyle said, pointing to his heart, "then He'll take care of the rest, won't He?"

"I believe that's how it goes," Kevin answered. "But that doesn't make it any easier when you're going through the trials. There's always the temptation to despair. And the will has to assert itself over that temptation. Believe me, it takes strength to be man-enough to surrender yourself humbly to God's will."

"I know it does. That's why I'm glad I have you to look up to," Kyle said, patting his dad on the shoulder.

"Thanks, son. But Christ's the real model of manhood. We're all just cheap imitations—doing our best in spite of our weaknesses and human frailty."

"I know. But He's supplied me with some pretty awesome examples to look up to as well, not the least of which is him." Kyle pointed up to a picture of St. Joseph on the wall of the shop. His father had put it there years ago. Not framed, it was tattered on the edges, and the colour was somewhat faded.

"St. Joseph's the man," Kevin agreed. "I don't think I could have made it all these years without St. Joseph's prayers for me and my family. I was too weak on my own. I needed his help in order to be the husband and father I was called to be. Relying on myself, without God and without the help of the saints, I had screwed up big time. But the point to all this, son, is just what St. Paul says, 'I can do all things in Him who strengthens me.'"

"Philippians," Kyle said.

"Chapter four, verse thirteen. There are few passages from scripture that I know by heart, but that's one of them. And here's the other one that comes to mind for what you're dealing with right now, son." The mechanic straightened up, searching his mind to remember the correct wording of the passage. "I'm not that great on quoting things verbatim, but Romans eight, twenty-eight basically says this—we know that God works everything for good, for those who love the Lord."

"You're on a real roll here tonight, Dad," Kyle said with a laugh.

"Well, all this time spent out here in a shop by myself gives me the opportunity to contemplate life."

"And memorize scripture?"

"That comes from listening to all those tapes your mother buys," Kevin said with a laugh. "Let me tell you, Kyle, I keep company with some of the finest Catholic theologians in the world out here in my little shop."

"You're a great man, Dad," Kyle said, placing his hand on his father's shoulder as he stepped away from the car. "Thanks for taking time for me. But I'd better go get ready for band practice tonight." He began to walk away.

"I hope it goes well," Kevin called out to his son by the door.

"Thanks." Kyle looked back at his dad as he opened the shop door to the cold, wintry night. Kevin waved his hand at his son, and Kyle left, sticking his hands into his overall pockets to keep them warm as he walked across the yard to the house.

He needed some time to go pray before everyone arrived. He was bracing himself for Amie. Although he had heard about her courtship, he had not yet had a chance to see her, nor to hear it from her lips. He smiled, thinking about the spunky girl with the long blond curls and bright blue eyes who had caught his eye and his heart so many years before. *She's Yours, God. Not that You didn't already know that, but I just wanted to let You know that I know it, too.*

Chapter 24

Band members filtered down to the basement of the Bander's home for their regular practice time. With less than a week to Christmas they had much to work through to get ready for their New Year's Eve gig.

David came down with Leanne. The short, dark-haired girl had been coming out to the last few band practices, singing back-up. Everyone had taken to her gentle personality, and she felt most welcomed in the group. With each practice her fun-loving nature was more and more revealed. David was looking happier than ever these days, with a smile that rarely left his face.

Kyle was quiet as the group set up and tuned their instruments. He sat patiently at his drum set, behind the keyboard, tapping his sticks on his legs.

Amie was quiet this evening as well. She came in with Katie and took her place at the keyboard.

"Do you have anything to share with the class, Amie?" asked Daniel Schultz as he sat at a stool, tuning his acoustic guitar. All one could see was his head of light brown hair bent over his instrument. The lanky guitar player looked up at the pianist with a broad smile that said, "We're waiting."

"What's the point?" she asked, pulling back her hair over her shoulders, smiling at the guitarist. "You obviously know my news."

"Oh, but it'll be so much better coming from you," he teased.

Kyle sat and watched the young girl as she fussed to get comfortable at the keyboard. She straightened her bunnyhug, pulling at the bottom edge of the hooded-sweatshirt. She stopped and looked around at everyone, only to realize the whole group was waiting for this big announcement.

"Okay," she said. "Connor and I are going out." She shrugged her shoulders. "But you all knew that, so I don't know what else to say."

"Well, Connor sure has a lot to say these days," returned Daniel. "You can't wipe the smile from his face. When he told me he was courting the prettiest girl in the world, I just knew he had to mean you." Daniel's brown eyes were full of fun.

"Oh, shut-up!" Amie returned playfully. "He didn't say that, and even if he had you would never have concluded it was me, Daniel."

Daniel shrugged his shoulders and lifted his hands up. "I'm just telling you what I know."

"I think we should get at practice," Amie suggested. "We've got a lot to cover if we're going to be ready for New Year's Eve."

"I thought you'd be a lot more fun to tease than that," Daniel said with disappointment.

"I didn't agree to a courtship with Connor just to give you fuel for teasing me," she retorted.

"So why did you?" came Kyle's voice from behind her.

Amie turned and looked at the drummer. She had not even said 'hi' to him yet this evening. He had been so quiet that she had almost forgotten he was there. "Why did I what?"

"Why did you agree to court with him?" Kyle asked plainly.

Amie hesitated. "That's kind of a personal question, don't you think?"

"I don't think so," piped in Jocelyn, her younger cousin, now lead singer for the group. "I want to hear details." Her dark eyes were all lit up, waiting to get the latest on the newest romance in their midst.

"Well, he asked me on Sunday," Amie began, her mind racing, "so we haven't exactly been at this very long. I've hardly had a chance to see him since then. But . . . well, you know Connor. He's a great guy—Catholic, hard-working . . . cute," she added with a little smile. "I don't know. We'll see where it goes. I just don't have much to say about it yet."

Jocelyn smiled back at her older cousin.

The room was silent for a moment. Suddenly Kyle called out the title of a song and counted in, "One, two, three, four . . ." and began the drum intro.

Daniel quickly sat up at attention with his guitar and found his way into the piece, just in time. Caleb grabbed for his electric guitar and, in spite of coming in a few measures late, managed to make a smooth entry into the piece. David casually brought in the bass, and Amie started playing the keyboard part, relieved to have the practice begin. *Thank you, Kyle.* The singers all took their places and joined in with the song.

Practice was intense. They went for two hours straight, from one piece into the next. Finally Jocelyn called out, "I can't take it anymore. Even at gigs we take breaks. What's with you people tonight? You're driving the music like there's no tomorrow?"

Amie looked over at the young lead singer. "Sorry, Jocelyn. I guess we could take a break here."

"Even I'm having a hard time keeping up with you all tonight," admitted John Delainey, running the sound system. "I don't think you've ever pushed through that many songs in one practice."

"Why don't we call it a night," suggested David. "Let's shut it down and just relax for a while. Maybe we could play some cards. I'm getting tired, too."

There was a general consensus in favour of David's suggestion. A group of tired singers stepped back from their microphones with relief, and then suddenly perked up as they realized that they were done for the night.

Ann came and sat down beside Amie. "You okay?" she asked her cousin.

"Sure. Why d'you ask?"

"I don't know. You just seem to be so intent on the music tonight, like you're trying to get your mind off something else," Ann observed.

"Nah, I'm fine." Amie put her arm around her cousin's shoulder. "Couldn't be better. Got myself a good man," she said with a little smile, as she tilted her head toward her cousin.

"No kidding!" Ann exclaimed. "Connor's awesome! If I were you, I'd be jumping out of my skin with excitement. . . . That's what I don't get. You seem so subdued for you, Amie—even under normal circumstances. But now that you've got a boyfriend, I'd have figured you'd be bouncing off the ceiling here."

"I guess I'm just tired with everything on my plate. School's been busy. Last day tomorrow before Christmas break—thank goodness! And I've been practising for my piano exam four hours a day. Plus, I am *so* not ready for Christmas. I'll perk up, once I have a chance for it all to sink in."

Ann nodded. "Come on. Let's go relax with everyone else."

The group had dispersed. Kyle had run upstairs to get some food, and David was pulling out the card tables. The room was filled with the laughter and goofiness typical of this crowd. Amie looked around, not quite in the mood to celebrate. She decided to run upstairs to see if she could offer Kyle a hand.

"Can I help with that?" she asked, as Kyle stood waiting for the corn to pop.

"Sure," he said, his voice revealing his surprise at the offer. "I'm just melting some butter here." He stepped up to the stove and stirred the contents of the little saucepan. "This is ready," he stated, turning off the gas element. He brought the little pot to the counter and threw a potholder under it, leaving it for Amie to fix up the popcorn when it was done popping. Kyle went to the freezer and pulled out some cans of juice, took out a couple of jugs, and began making them up.

"You okay, this evening? You seem awfully quiet," Amie observed.

"Lots on my mind these days, I guess," he said with a little shrug. "But I'm fine."

"Yeah, me too," Amie replied. "It must be the season or something."

"Yeah, something like that," the young man replied. He stepped up to the counter beside Amie as she was mixing up the popcorn and handed her the salt shaker.

"Thanks," she said, with a smile. "You were reading my mind."

"Amie, I don't think I could ever even come close to knowing what goes on up there," he returned playfully, tapping her lightly on the temple.

She nudged her shoulder into his body and giggled. "You're probably safer not even trying to figure me out."

"That's what I figure, too." He patted her gently on the shoulder as he went back to the juice jugs.

"Oh, by the way," she turned to Kyle, her voice revealing she had just remembered something important to say. "Thanks for the tip to Connor about *The Country Corner Café*. It was beautiful. It reminded me of your house," she said with a smile, looking around. "And I love your house," she added with a nod, as she put some popcorn into her mouth.

"It belongs to friends of ours. My mom helped decorate it, actually."

"I can tell. It's great. And the cheesecake was awesome!"

"Well, when Connor asked me for a suggestion, there was only one to make. And you can't go to *The Country Corner Café* and not eat cheesecake. I'm glad you liked it."

"Loved it," she enthused. "You definitely have great taste . . . a man after my own heart," she added with a big smile.

Kyle offered her a warm smile in return as he picked up the two jugs of juice to carry downstairs. He did not mind at all that the irony of what Amie had just said was completely lost on her. In fact, he was grateful that she had absolutely no inkling as to his feelings. Some things are best left unspoken.

Amie picked up the bowl of popcorn and followed him to the top of the stairs.

"Ladies first," he said, motioning with his head to allow Amie to step in front of him.

"Thank you, kind sir," she returned, taking the lead down to the rest of the group. For some reason she felt all perked up again, ready now for the party to begin.

Chapter 25

The Fourth Sunday of Advent found Connor spending the day with the Collins family. It was a beautiful winter day: cold, but enough snow on the ground to make it fun if a person bundled up. Connor and Amie took the kids, from Isaac down, to the big tobogganing hill in town.

It was great fun as they teamed up and raced down the long slope. Connor would load Jessie back onto the toboggan at the bottom of the hill and run her up. The four-year-old was in seventh heaven. "I'm on Connor's team," she would call out at the top of the hill every time.

Connor was genuinely wonderful with the kids. He had grown up the second youngest of a family of five children. He understood the dynamics of a larger family. He loved the commotion and all the teasing. He enjoyed wrestling with the boys. Connor was a regular hero among them with his years of wrestling in high school and at university.

Amie enjoyed the fact that Connor had been so well-received in her family. She took extra delight in seeing how much he loved children and willingly played with them. *Yup, God. He's definitely a good catch!*

They came back to the house for hot chocolate and cookies. Katie was there with Jocelyn Ledoux working together on a home-schooling project. They had decided to sew some clothes together to give as Christmas gifts for children through the local "Secret Santa" initiative. They had sewing machines, sergers, patterns, material, and notions spread out all over the rumpus room floor. When they heard the troop come in, they decided to take a break and go join them up in the kitchen.

"No one goes down into the rumpus room without Jocelyn or me," Katie announced, as they came into the kitchen.

"I want to see the pretty dresses," Jessie said. "Take me down."

"Later, Jessie," Katie answered the little girl. "You can go down with us when we're ready to go back. I'm exhausted and I want to take a break."

"Too bad we put this off so late," Jocelyn commented. "We only have four days until Christmas now, and we have to drop this off by Christmas Eve."

"You staying for a sleepover for a few nights?" Amie asked her younger cousin.

"She's staying until we're done," replied Katie, reaching for a chocolate chip cookie. "So how was the tobogganing?" she asked Connor, who was standing in the kitchen next to Amie, stirring cups of hot chocolate for the kids.

"Excellent," he replied.

"We had *so* much fun!" exclaimed Zack. "Connor taught us these great wrestling moves . . ."

"And he showed us how to go super fast down the hill," boasted Aaron. He reached up and offered Connor a high-five, which Connor returned.

"It was a lot of fun," agreed Amie. She smiled and patted Connor on the shoulder.

Connor smiled. He enjoyed the sense of acceptance he had in Amie's family.

After their snack they got the kids set up to watch an old Christmas movie, *It's a Wonderful Life*. Amie sat beside Connor on the couch, and he took her hand in his. Life was definitely wonderful.

Following supper Connor and Amie went out for a walk. The little kids begged and pleaded to join them but Judy stepped in and put a kibosh on their intrusion. "Let Connor and Amie have some time alone," she scolded the little ones, shooing them off to go play somewhere else. The kids reluctantly decided to take out a board game.

Connor and Amie strolled down the street. Falling snow glimmered in the streetlights. The Christmas decorations and lights on the houses emitted a lovely glow through the snow piling softly on them. The Collinses lived on a street which had beautiful elm trees stretching over the road. Even in the winter, without their cloak of green, the trees were beautiful.

It was cold; Amie wrapped her arms in front of herself to keep warm. Connor would have liked to have held her hand, but he did not press the point. He walked alongside her, wistfully talking about plans for the holidays.

"I'd really like for you to come down to Regina to meet my family," he told her.

"That'd be nice."

"When would be good? I could even drive back to Saskatoon to pick you up," he offered.

"Oh, don't be silly. I can take the bus down. Maybe I could go on the twenty-seventh, that's a Saturday. I'll have to be back in Saskatoon by the twenty-ninth for band practice. We have a big gig on the thirty-first—the C.C.E. New Year's Eve Party—and we desperately need the time to prepare."

"Well, if you come down by bus, that'll be fine. But I'm definitely driving you back up. I'm planning to go to that party anyway, and I'd like to hear your band play, and . . . I'd like to bring in the New Year together with you." His voice was gentle and entreating.

"That'd be great," Amie replied, overlooking the tenderness of the man next to her. "I could stay with my Auntie Céline and Uncle Martin in Regina. I don't get to see them that often, and I know they wouldn't mind. I'll just check it out with my parents to be sure it's all right with them. Unless, of course, you already have," she added with mild sarcasm.

"No, I haven't," he said with a laugh. "But now I wish I had, just to have stayed one step ahead of you."

"Oh, I feel like you're about ten steps ahead of me," she said flippantly.

"What d'you mean?"

"Oh, just that I have so many other things on my mind these days, what with school, piano practising, band, Christmas. I have a hard time remembering that we're even courting." She laughed and looked up at Connor.

He smiled back, but somehow she detected a bit of hurt. She turned her head back down and shut her eyes tightly for a moment. *Oops! Okay, Lord, I can see I need to have an attitude adjustment to this whole courtship thing. Connor and I are on two different pages entirely, and I can't seem to get where he is.*

They walked on for a few minutes in silence. Amie prayed to be able to find the affection in her heart for Connor that he seemed to have for her. She liked him. She really did. But she still was not sure if she could bring herself to like him in the way that he wanted her to like him. She looked back up at him. Deciding it would help if she just demonstrated a bit more affection, she reached over and tucked her arm in around his. Connor smiled and placed his hand across hers as it rested on his arm.

Amie looked down at their hands in mitts. Somehow she did not mind the extra layer between them—giving her time to sort out her feelings. She wondered if this was the way it was for other women, falling in love gradually. She wondered if she would ever actually fall in love with Connor or not. She wondered if it was even fair for them to be courting when she was still so unsure of her own feelings.

They eventually came back to her house, and he walked her up to the door. She invited him to come in but he declined, having to get up early for work the next morning. She thanked him for the great day they had spent together.

"Thank you," he returned. "If it's all right, I'd like to come by and see you on Tuesday before I leave for Regina."

"That'd be great," Amie answered. "I should be home all day. I'm not in school this week."

"Great. So, I'll see you then."

"Sounds good." She waved to him from the doorstep as he turned to walk to his vehicle. She watched as he started it and then brushed the snow off while the car warmed up. She leaned against the doorframe and looked up and down the street at the Christmas lights on the neighbours' homes. She loved the Christmas season, but somehow this year she was not quite into it. She looked back at Connor as he got into his vehicle and waved good-bye. Amie waved back and then stepped into the house as he drove away.

Chapter 26

"What are you doing there?" Brandon asked his bride as she carried in an armload of presents to put under their tree.

"Wrapping presents for our families and for the baby." She crawled about arranging them one at a time into just the right place. She would sit back on her heels and look, and then move forward and rearrange them until she was satisfied.

"There are an awful lot of presents there," he commented, setting aside the book he had been reading. "How many of those are for the baby?"

"The ones wrapped in this pretty baby Jesus paper," she pointed out.

"All those? There have to be about twenty presents under the tree in that wrapping paper."

"It's stuff we had to buy for the baby anyway."

"Seems like a lot of wrapping and unwrapping to do for a baby who isn't even born yet," he commented with a laugh.

"Look, Mr. Vaughn, if you insist on being a Mr. Scrooge, you are just going to have to leave," she informed him, as she came and sat on his knee.

"And how am I going to leave with you planted here on my knee?"

"You can't—so you'll just have to stop being a Mr. Scrooge," she said, kissing him lightly on the cheek.

He placed his hand on her growing tummy and tapped a few times gently. "Hey, baby, better close your eyes. Mommy's making the moves on me here," he uttered to the unseen child.

"Brandon!" Joanie said, smacking him on the shoulder. "Just for that, I'm not going to make any more moves."

"Too late, dear," he said, picking her up and carrying her to the bedroom.

"Brandon, put me down!" she called out, laughing.

He stepped over the threshold to their room and stopped, looked at his wife and said, "I guess you win." The bed was covered with wrapping paper, scissors, tape, ribbons, bows, packaging, and bags. Every square inch was covered.

"Hah!" she said, as he gently set her down. "But you can help me clean up this mess."

"I'm going into the kitchen to make supper," he announced. "I'll catch up with you later, Mrs. Vaughn."

Joanie laughed as Brandon stepped out of the room. She whisked about collecting the garbage and putting all the wrapping paraphernalia into a box. Satisfied that the job was done, she went into the kitchen. She quietly stepped up behind Brandon and wrapped her arms around him as he stood at the stove, browning some meat.

"Smells good," she said, breathing deeply.

"Just hamburger meat," he stated.

"Not the meat, silly," she said, giving him a little squeeze. "You!"

He chuckled. "Do you mind giving me some room here, Missus? That is if you're done smelling my back. I need to get some things for the sauce."

Reluctantly she let go. "Fine. I'll just sit back and watch you work," she said, climbing up onto the counter stool at the small island. "I like to see you in action. It's that Ephesians-five thing."

"Yeah, yeah. Husbands lay down your life for your wife, just as Christ laid down His life for His Bride, the Church," Brandon quoted. "You women really like that don't you?"

"Sure we do," Joanie responded. "Every woman wants her man to save her. It does something for us to see you living out your manhood to the fullest. Protect. Provide. Be the warrior in battle." She lowered her voice to imitate a manly man and held her arms out in militant fashion.

"And me making spaghetti sauce does that for you?" he questioned as he cracked open a jar of pasta sauce to add to the meat. He pulled up the sleeve of his shirt and flexed his brawny arm at her.

"Very impressive, dear," she remarked. "It's not *what* you do that impresses me, Brandon. It's the fact that you *want* to do it for me that gets me excited. It makes it much easier for me to let you be the head of our home—the fact that you're so willing to serve. I think if more men understood that, women would find it so much easier to be submissive."

"Mm-hmm," he agreed.

"It's all those radical feminists out there who have the world up in arms over that word—submission," she went on, getting somewhat heated up over the topic. "If they just understood that St. Paul was asking us to place ourselves under our husband's mission—and that his mission is to serve his wife and lay down his life for her—it would be much better received, I'm sure. But no one ever focuses on that. They just look for the negative and call St. Paul a male chauvinist so that they can discount him, along with the rest of the Bible."

"Well, I'm just glad I got me a wife who's not a radical feminist," Brandon commented as he brought his wife a drink of water.

"Thanks, honey," she said with a smile, lifting the glass up toward him. "Like you would have ever attracted one of those," she added with a laugh.

"You'd be surprised how many women living loosely out there are propelled by the feminist movement," he remarked. "As much as I was out to use them, they were out to use me, too. They've got a whole society buying into the lie that it's *your* body and you can do with it what you want—but no one ever stops to think about the consequences. The whole contraception-abortion attitude of our society just trains men and women to act like animals and to use each other for pleasure. It's all about "freedom"—no commitment and no responsibilities. And you better believe that those radical feminists are all about that."

"But that's not what *real* freedom is.... Ohhhhh, I just get so tired—as a woman—of having our society shove that pro-choice feminist agenda down our throats," Joanie said, through clenched teeth. It didn't take much to get her heated up over that issue. She was good and ready to take on the whole culture of death. Resigned to the fact that they would never solve all the world's problems—discussing them around their little kitchen island—she still found it satisfying to be able to hash it out with her like-minded husband, who at the moment was busy chopping vegetables for their supper.

"Feminism doesn't represent women *or* their best interests at all," she asserted, sneaking a piece of celery. "And it's just so hard for me to relate to all that hogwash—because my parents raised us to see that men and women, while equal in dignity, have very different roles to play in our world. And it only makes sense. If we were meant to do the same things and to be the same, why would God have created us distinctly different—male and female? It's written into our very nature to take on different roles, but you try to tell that to the feminists."

"They won't have anything to do with that," he said. "I tell you, I find those women scary. You try to open a door for them, and they'd just as soon kick you in the shins as to walk through that door. It makes it hard for a guy to be a gentleman."

"I'm sure it does. Our whole culture has been working hard to strip men of their manhood for a few generations now. And look at the results—men are unsure of how to be men anymore, if they even dare, lest they get kicked or chastised by women. They're told to get in touch with their feminine side and to throw away all their manly virtues, like providing and protecting—and we wonder why so many men skip off and abandon their responsibilities."

"Well, don't worry, dear," Brandon assured her. "I won't go skipping out on you and our children. And I'll just keep being a gentleman and running the risk of bruised shins—lest those radical feminists think they've won the war. If enough of us men would just press on, regardless, things would soon turn around. I'm convinced of that. We men just have to start acting like *real* men, for a change."

"And there's hope for your shins, Brandon," Joanie remarked in an upbeat tone, pointing at him with her celery stick. "There's a whole new generation of women coming along, like the one you got for a wife. And we like being women—*real* women. And we like it when men open up doors for us."

He winked at his wife as he picked up the chopping board full of vegetables to go add to the sauce simmering on the stove.

"I really believe that women are tired of being duped—being told to abandon feminine virtues and turn themselves into pseudo-men," she went on. "What's wrong with accepting the way God created us? There's the world screaming at us to practise contraception, to deny our femininity, to act like men—as if it's a disgrace to be a woman. Thank goodness the Catholic Church doesn't draw its wisdom from the world, and that we have a pope like John Paul II who's willing to uphold the long-standing teachings of our Church. Just look at his writings—where else do you see women held with such high regard and respect?"

"Now that's something I just don't get," he interjected.

"What, John Paul's writings?" she asked, confused.

"No," he said with a chuckle, shaking his head. "It just totally amazed me, when I came into the Church, to see so many people attacking the Church, not just from the outside, but from *within*," Brandon commented in disbelief.

"Oh, that," she said in acknowledgement. "Yeah, you hear it all the time. For example, the Catholic Church is oppressing women. Give me a break," she said in exasperation, crunching down on her celery.

Brandon looked at his wife, as he wiped down the counter with a dishrag. "I'm glad to know you're not feeling oppressed," he said with a laugh.

"On the contrary . . . I feel very liberated as I watch you make our meal here tonight." She took a sip of water and smiled as she watched her husband walk between the counter and the sink. "Seriously, though, I do feel liberated by the truth—free to be all God created me to be. I don't need to subject myself to the pain and suffering that comes from the world's empty promises. I'd rather listen to a Church that loves me enough to *dare* suggest a standard for sex that's different from the world's. Why do people want to listen to the culture of death when they can have life-giving love?"

"Because it seems easy," Brandon said. "Look at what the world teaches us about sex. If it feels good—do it. No accountability. No responsibility. It's all about pleasure."

"But it's so empty."

"Tell me about it," he responded. "But it's blinding as well. I couldn't see it until I received the grace through Jesus to see it. And then, when I finally was introduced to what the Catholic Church teaches, it just blew me away. How the Church holds the gift of human sexuality in such high regard . . . well, as you know, dear, it completely rocked my world."

"Which I am happy it did," Joanie said with a big smile. She lifted her empty glass toward Brandon, hinting for more.

"And I'll never understand why Catholics want to compromise that?" Brandon stated, reaching out to get the empty glass. He walked over to the fridge, took out a jug of juice and offered it to his wife. She nodded and gave him a thumbs-up, so as not to interrupt. "There's the Church teaching us to guard sex and protect it within the boundaries of marriage. She calls it holy and sacred, and elevates marriage to a sacrament. I don't know about you, but I've never heard the world describe sex that way."

Joanie laughed, "Now there's an understatement!"

"You know, when I lived according to the world, I behaved just like the world wanted me to—like an animal, driven by instincts and desires. But I was never satisfied, nor could I ever have been. The desires just grew bigger, and the instincts harder to control."

"And that's the point!" Joanie exclaimed, tapping her finger on the counter. "There's the Catholic Church acknowledging our ability to reason and to exert our will over our instincts and desires. On the other hand, the wisdom of the world tells us to use birth-control, in other words—forget all about self-control. Well, I don't want to be reduced to an animal that has no control over my instincts and no ability to discern right from wrong. Why would I want to buy into that line of crap?"

"Now don't hold back, dear," Brandon teased. "Let me know how you *really* feel about this."

Joanie laughed. It was not that often she spoke in such earthy terms. "Well, why would anyone want to buy into those lies?" she reasserted.

"Because they've never really heard the truth," he said, handing her back the glass now filled with juice. "But I'll tell you this much, and I know it from experience, the men and women out there in the world who buy into those lies are hurting and empty."

"They are. . . ." Joanie's voice was now softened. "And so is our whole society. Where do you see that more evident than in the whole abortion issue?" She set down her glass, placed her hands over her tummy, and looked down. "I will never understand how the Pro-Choice movement has managed to dupe so many men and women into accepting abortion as something good. Now that I have a child growing within me, I can't imagine what kind of brainwashing it must take to convince a woman to detach herself from the natural bonds of motherhood."

"All I know is that I had no problem with accepting abortion when my life revolved completely around me," Brandon responded, going back to stir his sauce on the stove. "That's what our society is all about. Me! Now! And I was totally caught up in that. I was the jerk who fathered how many children who ended up aborted, either surgically or by chemical abortion from women on the pill? I had no idea what it meant to really be a man—to love and to protect and to provide for a woman. I was just there to use them for my own selfish pleasure, and then move on. . . . And that lifestyle still haunts me, Joanie. It always will." His voice had grown quiet as he looked down at the sauce simmering away.

He put the lid back on the pot and looked seriously at his wife. "Don't think that every time I see you standing there, glowing in your maternity clothes, your body full of life, that I don't feel the pangs of guilt for those other babies who came into the world because of my selfishness, and yet were sentenced to death before they ever had a chance to see the light of day. . . . And what about all the suffering that those women have experienced, because of me?" He walked over to his wife and put his hand on her shoulder. "I don't mean to take away from the excitement of our baby, Joanie. But the joy is mixed with pain at times."

"I know it is, Brandon," she replied, slipping her arms around his waist and hugging him. "I feel it, too. And my heart aches for those women who get conned by the lies of the culture of death, and take the *'easy way out'*," she said, sitting back and making quotation marks with her fingers. "There's nothing *easy* about it. I used to judge women before, who had had abortions. But I don't now."

"No, neither do I," said Brandon. "They've all be lied to . . . by some guy, by some doctor, by this whole culture of death. And they're just as much a victim of abortion as the baby is."

"And they say abortion is about women's health and women's rights. It's the greatest tragedy that could ever be inflicted upon a woman—a complete crime against her mind, her heart, her body, and her soul. I maybe have never suffered that tragedy myself, but I know this much—*every* woman who's had an abortion is paying for that mistake over and over again," Joanie stated. "I remember sitting around once talking about abortion with a group of friends at university. After the conversation this girl came up to me; she was a friend I had known for a few years, and she wanted to thank me for telling the others not to judge. As it turned out, she had had an abortion when she was seventeen. I was the *only* person she had ever told!"

"It's sad, isn't it?" Brandon commented.

"They're around us, everywhere. They're sitting beside us on the bus. They're standing in front of us at the grocery store line. They're sitting beside us in the church pews. They're suffering . . . alone and in silence. And we have to be compassionate to them. Post-abortion syndrome is real. It's hurting women . . . some it's even killing." Joanie sat there shaking her head.

"Women *and* men, Joanie," Brandon whispered.

Joanie looked up at her husband; she could see the pain in his eyes. "I know, honey." After a moment she whispered, "I'm just so glad you came to know God's mercy and forgiveness, Brandon. . . . I'm glad you were set free to love me."

"So am I," he murmured softly.

"All we can do now for those women is to pray for them to discover God's love and mercy in their lives. They have to come to know that He's forgiven them, so that they can forgive themselves and move on with their lives. . . . Only His love can restore them to wholeness again. . . . And I guess the other thing we can do is try our best to give witness to the culture of life."

"Which, I must say," Brandon replied with great tenderness, placing his hand over his wife's tummy, "that you do so beautifully!" He smiled and gave her a kiss on the forehead.

Joanie reached out and wrapped her arms around him again, resting her head against his chest.

After a few moments of hugging his wife, Brandon looked over at the pot on the stove. "Well, sorry to change the topic, but I've got to get back to work serving my family here, Mrs. Vaughn, if we're ever going to eat supper tonight."

Joanie giggled softly and held on.

"Which means, you're going to have to let me go, dear, so I can get the spaghetti going."

"If I have to," she replied, with reluctance, "I will. But I've got a date with you for later, Mister . . . and don't you think that I intend to play second fiddle to noodles and ground beef for the rest of my life."

"Oh, I can assure you, you won't, Mrs. Vaughn. And about that date later—you're on," he replied, giving her a quick kiss on the lips before he got back to work.

Chapter 27

The newlyweds settled down for a quiet evening of making music together after cleaning up their spaghetti dishes from supper. They had not worked much on their songs while Joanie had been sick. It seemed that pregnancy had put several things on hold in their life. There had been less contact with friends, simply because Joanie had been too sick and exhausted for socializing. They had decided to leave house shopping until spring. And their plans for recording music would now have to wait until Joanie was on maternity leave.

Joanie had already decided that she would not be going back to work at the television station after the baby was born. Her dream of being a stay-at-home mom was much greater than any career aspirations. Though she loved her job as a research-reporter, she knew that her chance as a mother to stay at home with her children was a once-in-a-lifetime opportunity. She was not going to miss out on it.

The couple sat side-by-side on the couch as they looked through the songs they had been writing together. Joanie held the song-binder on her lap as she leafed through the few pages, clicking a pen in her left hand.

"We need a Christmas song in here," Joanie suggested, setting the pen on top of a blank page.

"You'd put a Christmas song in the middle of a praise album?" Brandon asked, strumming quietly on his twelve string guitar.

"Sure. Or maybe an advent song—something that talks about the sanctity of life, something that points to Christ sharing in our humanity so that we can someday share in His divinity."

"So just like that you want us to write a song?" Brandon questioned, looking at his wife. "It's a great topic and all, but I'm feeling a little shy on inspiration at the moment."

"Let's just pray about it for a few minutes." She took his hand in hers. "We'll see what God does to inspire us."

She closed her eyes to pray. Brandon kept looking at her, not quite sure about the whole thing. He had never approached songwriting from that point-of-view. He had always worked from inspiration to song, not from song request to inspiration. Joanie opened one eye and peeked at her husband.

"Come on, Brandon. Close your eyes and lead us in prayer," she said, tugging on his hand.

Brandon chuckled at her persistence and complied. He closed his eyes and began praying, asking the Lord to inspire them to write a song that would glorify Him in His nativity. They had only just begun to pray when their apartment buzzer rang.

Brandon stood up and carried his guitar across the room with him to answer the door. It was Mark and Justine. He buzzed them in.

"I guess that's as far as we go tonight with our songwriting," Brandon said, putting away his guitar.

Joanie clipped the pen onto the binder and tucked it under the couch. "That's okay. I haven't seen Justine in a while. You and Mark get to see each other every week for R.C.I.A., but I miss seeing Justine." She walked over to the door to wait for them.

"Hey, let's have some fun with them," Brandon suggested, with childish glee.

"What are you doing?" Joanie asked as she watched Brandon slip in behind the door.

"Just open it for them," Brandon whispered to her, holding a finger over his lips.

Joanie raised an eyebrow at her husband as she stood by the door waiting for their friends to arrive. The knock came at the door, and she threw another glance at Brandon, who just kept his finger over his lips and waited in silence. Joanie opened the door.

"Merry Christmas!" called out Mark from behind a box that was about four feet high and two feet across, all wrapped up in shiny Christmas foil and ribbons. He waited to let Justine step in ahead of him.

"Merry Christmas, Joanie!" Justine said, giving her friend a hug.

"Merry Christmas. What are you two up to?" Joanie had become so distracted by the big package Mark was carrying that she forgot about her husband, hiding behind the door.

Suddenly, Brandon jumped out. Mark started and jumped forward. The large parcel began to fall out of his grip. Joanie, standing in front of Mark, backed up to get out of the way, but the parcel was coming down too fast. She put out her arms to catch it. Justine jumped in behind Joanie to stop her from falling over the loveseat behind her. Joanie tripped backwards over Justine, who ended up pinned between the pregnant mom and the loveseat. Somehow Joanie managed to balance the parcel in her arms. Mark and Brandon stood frozen in front of the girls, watching the disaster unfold.

There was a brief moment of silence. Everyone stood motionless, wondering if the dominoes would keep falling or not. Suddenly Justine started laughing from behind Joanie. Mark stepped forward and took the parcel from Joanie, who was now laughing on top of Justine. Mark turned around to face Brandon. He handed him the parcel and said, "Merry Christmas. This is for you and our godchild."

The girls stood back up, each making sure the other was fine. By this point everyone was staring at Brandon. "Merry Christmas," Brandon said, rather sheepishly. "I'll just go put this under the tree." He kicked the door closed behind him and carried the large gift across the room.

"Are you girls all right?" Mark asked.

The two ladies resumed laughing and concluded they were no worse for the wear.

"Well, now might be a good time to offer you all a drink," Brandon said. "We're freshly stocked with eggnog. And I've got rum.... And I'm sorry about all that... I couldn't tell, from behind the door, that Mark was packing such a big gift for his godchild. I would have waited to scare the living daylights out of him until after he had put the package down. But," Brandon pointed at Mark, with a big smile on his face, "I got ya good."

Mark nodded and admitted that Brandon had gotten him. "Your sense of timing could use some work, though, Big Guy," he chided. "But I'll take you up on that drink. Come on." He followed his friend into the kitchen.

The girls went to sit down in the living room. Justine admired the Christmas tree and decorations around the apartment.

"We have a gift for you as well," Joanie told her friend. "Do you want to open gifts together tonight, or wait until Christmas?"

"Let's wait," Justine suggested.

Joanie got up and brought the gift from under the tree over to her friend. Sitting beside Justine, she handed her the package, saying, "Well, let's not forget to send it home with you at the end of the evening." It was a much smaller package than the one Mark had carried in, but it weighed just about as much.

"What is it? It feels like it's made out of gold," Justine said, balancing the weight of the parcel in her hands.

"Its contents are worth much more than gold," Brandon assured her, coming back into the room with the drinks. "But you have to wait until Christmas, and we're not telling."

Justine set the package down, thanking their friends for the gift in advance, and took her drink from Mark.

Brandon handed Joanie her drink. "Rum eggnog . . . hold the rum," he told her.

"Thanks," she said with a smile.

"Well, well . . . haven't we come full circle?" Mark observed, as Brandon sat beside him. "The girls sit together on the loveseat, and you and I are left to sit together over here on the couch."

Justine laughed and waved her fingers at her husband. "You two do look cute together over there."

Mark waggled his eyebrows at his wife and took a sip from his drink.

"Well, let's make a toast and get on with the evening," Brandon suggested. "To friendship."

They all chimed in, "To friendship."

After raising their glasses and taking a drink, Brandon suggested they play cards. "Anyone up for Canasta? The night's young. We could still get in a game before midnight," he noted, looking at his watch.

"I'm in," said Mark, rubbing his hands together as he stood up. "I've got a feeling the guys are going to win tonight."

"Well, wouldn't that be a change?" Justine quipped.

"I'm sorry, Mark, but I'm afraid we're just going to have to prove you wrong there," Joanie contended, walking over to the dining table with Justine.

"There's only one way to find out," Brandon said, dropping four Canasta decks onto the table. "Let the games begin."

The first wild card fell to Mark. "What'd I tell ya, girls? It's boy's night all the way," he declared. The girls just rolled their eyes and laughed as the confident young man picked up the cards and began to deal.

Settling into the game, the two couples soon began catching up with one another. Justine asked Joanie how she was feeling. Joanie was relieved to have Justine bring up the whole topic of pregnancy. It was an awkward subject for her, as she never knew if she should ask Justine how she was coping with waiting. Justine jumped into the topic herself. She thanked Joanie for the information on *Pope Paul VI Institute*. She had been spending quite a bit of time reading and had actually made some investigations. Though her family doctor was not at all interested in Natural Family Planning, Justine had managed to get some training through the institute and had begun charting her cycles.

"You know what I've learned?" she put forth the rhetorical question and proceeded to answer it herself as she organized her hand of cards. "When I was fourteen years old my family doctor put me on the pill because I was having irregular cycles. I spent ten years of my life on the pill. Of course, by the time I was sixteen and my boyfriend found out I was on birth control, he really pressured me into having sex. Since I had no reason to say 'no'—not having any value for chastity in my life or any real self-esteem—I gave in. That relationship only lasted about a month longer, maybe not even that. After that I moved from one boyfriend to the next, and they always wanted the same thing. I never knew how to say 'no'."

"Until you finally did with me," Mark pointed out.

"And aren't you glad I did?" she returned, her blue eyes meeting her husband's green eyes playfully.

"It was the best thing that you ever could have done, dear," he agreed.

"Otherwise I'd probably still be living a life confined to the chains of selfishness and lust." He held his card hand face down in front of him, waiting for his play.

"Exactly," she agreed. "And I would never have discovered the freedom of living with the self-respect and dignity that come from chastity."

"Hear! Hear!" Brandon said, picking up his drink to toast. "To chastity." They all chimed in, took a sip from their drinks, and laughed.

"But anyway," Justine went on, playing out her cards on her turn, "I discovered two things. First of all, I spent all those years treating my fertility as though it was a disease—some unwanted condition that needed to be cured. I had no appreciation for what a gift fertility is—a very fragile gift—one that needs to be protected and cared for, and saved for marriage."

"It's crazy," Mark jumped in. "The reproductive system is the only system in the body that medicine treats because it's functioning properly. It's absurd, really. It completely goes against 'good medicine'," he said, making quotation marks with his fingers. "A doctor would never prescribe me a pill to stop my pancreas or liver from functioning. Yet they put women on the pill all the time to stop their reproductive system from functioning properly. They don't care about the dangers to women or the side-effects. . . . Really, they should all be put in jail for malpractice," he stated, pounding his fist down on the table for emphasis, making the cards jump up.

Brandon looked at his friend and laughed. "I vote Mark for Prime Minister," he said, raising his hand.

"Hear, hear," Joanie agreed.

Justine shook her head. "I don't want to live with a politician. Sorry, folks, you'll have to find someone else."

"Ahhh," Brandon said, waving a finger at the young lady off to the side of the table, "if God calls Mark to politics, you'll have to let him go."

Justine frowned. "Well, I trust He won't call him until I'm ready to let him go—and that's no time soon."

They all laughed. Mark looked at his wife and prompted her. "And what's the other thing you were going to say, honey?"

"Yeah," she said, returning to the subject at hand. "The other thing I discovered about oral contraceptives—which they put me on to regulate my cycles as a teenager—is that coming off the pill ten years later, I was still left with an immature, undeveloped reproductive system. Going on the pill does not regulate your periods—it suppresses your reproductive system. So the problems I'm having now are the same as the ones I was having ten years ago. Once I began charting, I began seeing patterns that reflect low progesterone levels in my cycle. I've only gone through two cycles so far, but I'm really hoping that once I can get in with an ob-gyn, I can talk to her about starting me on progesterone therapy."

"That's really exciting, Justine," Joanie said. She looked across the table at her friend. "We're really praying that it'll work out for you two to be able to have children—soon!"

"I know you are," Justine said. "And I've heard about a really good Pro-Life ob-gyn; I'm just waiting to get in with my family doctor to get him to make a referral. In the meantime, I'll just keep charting so I have good documentation to take in to her when I finally do get in."

"Let's hope it all works out," Brandon said, picking up two cards on his turn.

"Actually," Justine went on, a little less enthusiastically, "as I've read and researched, I've also discovered that the fact that I've picked up a few STDs over the years with multiple partners—and Mark having had multiple partners and a few STDs himself that he passed on to me—that there's actually a fairly good chance that I've suffered scarring and damage to my reproductive system. I might not ever be able to get pregnant," she stated. She shrugged and flipped her shoulder-length blond hair to the side.

"How are you with that?" Joanie asked, cautiously.

"I've come to accept it," Justine stated. "I can't spend the rest of my life depressed or obsessed with getting pregnant. I know I just have to surrender that all to Jesus. I really trust that—even if we didn't follow His original plan for our lives—that He's still got a perfect plan for us now." She looked over at Mark.

Mark winked back at his wife and played out his cards. "Hey, look at that, Brandon. I'm opening our sevens."

Brandon nodded and smiled. He was unsure how to respond to his friends. They seemed so casual about the whole thing.

"I'm really impressed, Justine," Joanie finally said. "I don't know how you can be so at peace with all of this. I mean, I think it's beautiful. I'd like to think I had that kind of faith. But if push came to shove, I'm not sure if I'd be able to be so . . . so peaceful."

Justine smiled. She was a beautiful woman—with striking good looks—but at the moment what really stood out for all to see was the light of Christ, transforming her beauty into something absolutely radiant.

"You know, I don't think I could be so at peace if it weren't for the grace of the Holy Spirit . . . and the sacraments. Mark and I've been managing to get to daily Mass—and believe me, that is my *absolute* source of grace," Justine responded. "And something else . . . you know what First Thessalonians five, verses sixteen to eighteen says?" she asked.

Joanie and Brandon shook their heads and waited for her to tell them.

"Rejoice always, pray constantly, give thanks in *all* circumstances; for this is the will of God in Christ Jesus for you." She paused and there was silence in the room.

Brandon nodded. He understood where Justine was going with this.

"We have a choice in this time of trial in our life," she said, glancing over at Mark.

He smiled back at his wife, delighting in her strength of character.

"We can give in to despair and frustration," she explained, "or we can praise God and give thanks to Him—even for this suffering."

Joanie shook her head, in awe and respect for their friends' deep convictions.

Justine sighed heavily, looking around the room. A big smile spread across her face. She had a mysterious look. "And I just think Jesus wants to make good come out of all this, for His glory."

Joanie looked at her friend curiously. "Like what?" She could tell there was something more that Justine was not yet saying.

"Well, starting in the New Year, I'll be working for the Teen-Chastity program full-time," Justine announced. Her smile grew even bigger.

"Seriously?" Joanie asked. She was shocked. "What about your work at the nursing home?"

"I've given them my notice," Justine said. "I love working with the older people, and I know I'm going to miss it. But I've already made arrangements to do some volunteer work there—just visiting. That's the part I love the most. Some of those people are so dear to me now, after having been there for over six years. But I really need to do this. I just happened to notice an ad in the newspaper one day—advertising a position for a Teen-Chastity teacher to go into the high schools, beginning in January. I called them up . . . had an interview . . . and I got the job." Justine's face was all lit up. "They normally only hire people with an education degree—but after talking for over an hour, they offered me the job. I guess they decided that life experience and conviction were even greater qualifications for the work."

"That's got to be the hardest work I can imagine," Joanie commented. "It's not like young people are really receptive to the chastity message. And there's so much peer pressure."

"Uh-hmm," Justine agreed, nodding. "But they need to hear it. Sexual promiscuity is destroying kids' lives, and there are very few people out there trying to point them in the right direction. If I can save *one* girl from going through the heart-break, the pain, the confusion, and now the possible infertility that I'm going through," Justine stated, "it'll be worth all the challenges I face going in there."

"Good for you," Joanie said, with total admiration for her friend.

"I have no intention of letting these kids—with all their teen-age attitude—scare me off. I've been there. I've done it. I've seen the hurt, and I've lived through the pain of it all. I'm not easily pushed around—anymore." She smiled and looked around the table. "That's the gift of confidence that chastity gave to me."

Joanie shook her head, smiling at her friend. She had tears in her eyes. "I'm so proud of you, Justine," she said quietly. Tears began rolling down her cheeks. "I totally support you . . . and I'll do anything I can to help you out."

"Thanks," Justine said, smiling back, with tears in her own eyes. "For right now I'm just reading up on all the information they've given me for training. Let me tell you—it's an eye-opener. I just wish everyone knew this stuff. If parents really knew what was going on out there—what their kids are up to—and the consequences of what they're doing . . . they'd be standing up for their kids and putting a stop to it. But so many parents are sleeping at the switch. They've bought into the lies that their kids have the right to do whatever they want, which is hogwash—why did God give kids parents anyway? And they're too insecure to say 'no' to their kids because so many of them lived impure lives themselves. They think they'd be hypocrites if they said 'no' to their children because they, themselves, never practised chastity. But you know what?" she asked, looking around the room.

Everyone looked back at her, waiting for her to go on with her point.

"What makes them hypocrites is when they tell their children they love them, but then sit back and watch while their kids make the same mistakes they made—without trying to stop them." Justine paused. She was all fired up and ready to take on the world in the battle for purity.

"I know everyone has free will. But parents need to accept the responsibility of forming and shaping their kids' consciences. It's not enough to say they have free will and then let them grow up in a vacuum," she stated.

"Nature abhors a vacuum," Brandon remarked.

"Exactly," Justine said. "And in the absence of moral formation, who do you think is going to jump in and try to snatch away the souls of these kids?"

"Satan's been after souls for a long time," Brandon stated. "He knows all the tricks, all the lies that seduce. And his best trick of all is that he's got a whole world thinking he doesn't even exist. They're all sleeping with their doors unlocked, while the enemy lurks about."

"It's true," Mark agreed. "It was bad enough when we were kids making a mess of our lives. How many of us got sucked in? But these kids nowadays are getting in way deeper than we ever did, way earlier. They're children playing with matches, and no one's even trying anymore to stop them. . . . Hell, they're giving them lighter fluid and kindling for the fire."

Brandon laughed at his friend's assertion. "And then when they get burned, no one wants to accept the responsibility for it."

"Well, I intend to do my part to save as many as I can reach," Justine stated.

"You go, girl," Brandon said, reaching over to pat Justine on the back.

"Thanks," she said. Her head was held up with confidence. "And you know—it's not just the negative message of what happens when young people don't live out a pure life—I want to inspire them with the message of purity."

"You know, sorry to interrupt you, Justine, but I think we're going to have to break our agreement here," Brandon said, getting up from their card game to go over to the coffee table. He picked up the gift they had bought for Justine and Mark and brought it back to the table. "You need to open this now," he said, handing the package to Justine.

She looked up at Brandon curiously and then across at Mark who just shrugged his shoulders and told her, "Go ahead, honey."

Justine carefully removed the ribbon, undid the tape, and unfolded the wrapping paper to uncover a book. "John Paul II's *Theology of the Body!*" she said with enthusiasm. "This is *perfect*—and perfect timing, too."

Mark got up, walked over to where Justine was sitting, and looked over her shoulder as she leafed through the book. "That's awesome," he said to his friends. *"Theology of the Body,"* he read aloud. "I've been looking for this."

"I know," said Brandon. "That's why I ordered in a copy for you and one for us."

"I love what this pope has to say about sex," Mark went on. "You know, I think most people would think that to study God through the body—especially with regards to sex and all—would be sacrilegious or something. But JP II has got it all together, doesn't he? Just think about it—the Church's teachings on human sexuality and its real meaning is the very thing that brought three of the people in this room to God."

"Like you said, Brandon, this gift is worth way more than gold," Justine affirmed. "Thank you so much!"

"If any couple would appreciate a gift like that, we knew it would be you two," Joanie said. "We just didn't realize how timely it would be in your life to have a resource like that on hand."

"No kidding," Mark stated. "But, hey . . . since we've opened our gift, you two are going to have to open yours now, too." He went over and brought back the large package, passing it to Brandon.

Brandon tore open the wrapping paper, while Joanie laughed and teased at the contrast between his and Justine's styles of gift-opening.

"Come on . . . it's more fun this way," Brandon responded, finally pulling off the last pieces of paper.

"A car seat for baby," Joanie called out. "That's perfect."

"Yeah, thanks, you guys," Brandon added, turning it around to get a look at the picture on the box.

"Well, we wanted to be sure our godchild was safe. But apparently it also doubles as a lethal weapon," Mark warned, "so use it carefully."

They all laughed.

"Well, we really should get back to our card game here," Justine suggested. "That is if you two men aren't afraid of getting beaten by a couple of girls. After all, we're almost booked, and you haven't even opened your sevens," she pointed out.

"We're doing just fine, here," returned Mark. "It's all part of our strategy to let you ladies think you have the advantage over us. We're just about ready to move in for the kill."

Brandon raised his eyebrows at his partner's optimism. "Yeah, something like that," he added.

As the two couples got back into their game Justine thanked their friends again for the gift. "You know, it's just what I was saying before—I want to inspire young people with a message of purity and hope, and that's what this is all about," she asserted, setting her hand on the treasured book beside her on the table. "And it's not just head knowledge that counts. A person has to live it to really know it and then to be able to share it with others."

Looking across the table at Joanie, Justine went on to say, "You know, when I first met you, Joanie, I was so inspired by your hold on life. You had such confidence and self-respect. You were so joy-filled and ready to live life to the fullest. It was absolutely contagious."

Joanie smiled humbly at her friend. "Well, that was the gift of my faith and my upbringing, Justine. I can't very well take credit for that."

"I know it was," Justine said. "But I want young people to know that they can have that, too. No matter what their story, their life, their background . . . they can choose right now to start living their lives for Christ. I turned my life around. I believe that everyone is capable of being set free in Christ. They just have to choose it—each and every day—even when it's not easy. And believe me . . . it wasn't easy to start with."

"No, it sure wasn't," Mark agreed.

Everyone looked over at Mark. He smiled back at the group of them. "But it was worth every bit of suffering I went through, which in hindsight now doesn't even seem like suffering at all. But at the time . . . I thought my world had come to an end."

"You were quite a baby about it as I recall," Brandon chided his friend.

Mark scoffed at Brandon's remark. "Like you handed over your hedonistic life with such ease."

Brandon looked over at Joanie. "The prize was worth the fight. And I've never looked back."

"Neither have I," Mark agreed. He smiled at his wife. "In spite of myself, I ended up with the most beautiful wife I could ever have wanted. I'll be coming into the Church at Easter time. I'll be able to receive Jesus in the Blessed Sacrament. I mean, what more can a guy ask for than that? I've got heaven here on earth *and* the hope of eternal life. I'm a happy man."

Justine smiled back at Mark. She knew that his joy was sincere, but she could only imagine what joy they would share if they could have children. She appreciated how supportive he was as they carried the cross of infertility. They had no way of knowing if this would be a temporary cross in their lives, or a life-long cross to bear. Either way, they had no control over the cross itself, just how they would choose to carry it together. Thank God He had opened their eyes to the freedom that comes from embracing joy, even in adversity.

Their time of praying, studying, researching, and charting had brought them so much closer to each other than they had been before this all began to unfold in their lives. Justine knew that through this suffering God would be glorified, and they would be given the graces they needed to grow in holiness. That was enough for her for the moment.

Still looking at her husband, Justine said, "I'm glad to know you're so happy about life, Mark," as she began playing out her cards, ". . . because I am about to go out." She laid out her cards one by one until she set down her final discard with great ceremony.

"Whew-hew!" Joanie called out from across the table. She reached over and gave Justine a high-five. "You *are* the woman!"

"Yes, you are," Mark agreed.

They counted up their hands and went on to the next round. The four friends spent a wonderful evening of visiting, card playing, teasing, laughing, and sharing dreams.

By midnight they wrapped up the last Canasta hand. Though they had gone into the last round with the girls behind in points, Joanie and Justine managed to book out before the guys could even open, and thus the girls established a solid victory over their rivals.

Brandon and Mark had no intention of contesting. These two women were living out their lives with heroic virtue, and somehow it just seemed right tonight that they would take the victory at cards.

✝   ✝   ✝

After Mark and Justine left, Brandon went and picked up his guitar. Joanie asked him what he was up to. It was late and they had to get up for work the next day.

"I think the inspiration for that song came to me tonight, while I was listening to Mark and Justine. It's all about trusting in God's plan for our lives. That's what Mary and Joseph did, even when they didn't understand. That's what we all have to do. 'Be it done unto me, according to Thy Word,'" he said, quoting the Blessed Virgin Mary. "How can we know what crosses will lie ahead of us? We can't. We just have to trust that God has a perfect plan for us. I think that's how we uncover joy—when we realize He's in control and we completely surrender to His will."

Joanie was leaning against the loveseat. She smiled at her husband. "Sounds like you've got an inspiration, honey. I'll just go to bed and sleep for the both of us."

"You mean all three of us?" he corrected her, pointing to the baby held safely within her womb.

"All three of us," she repeated after her husband. "Good-night, sweetheart." She stepped up to the couch where he was sitting with his guitar and softly kissed him on the lips. "I love you. And I'm glad that you were part of God's perfect plan for my life."

"Even though I didn't always live according to His plan, somehow He still made it all work out."

"Praise God," she said.

Brandon reached up and gently pulled Joanie forward for another kiss. "You know, maybe this inspiration can wait until tomorrow," he suggested, waggling his eyebrows at his wife.

"No, it can't," she disagreed. "Because I have to sleep for at least two of us—even if you can get by with no sleep, Mister. So you just do your thing out here, and I'll go do my thing in there."

Brandon laughed as Joanie headed off to bed. He sat back into the couch and began to strum his guitar, trying to find a melody to put to the words that were forming in his heart. *Be it done unto me, according to Thy Word.*

Chapter 28

Fr. Steve entered the rectory, following an hour of adoration spent before the Tabernacle at St. James Parish. He tried to be faithful in getting an hour alone with the Lord each day. Most days he was able to meet the personal commitment, while at the same time fulfilling his obligation in doing his daily office of prayer. But the demands of being a parish priest sometimes interfered with his getting in a full holy hour.

The front room of the rectory was an inviting sight to the tired man. There was a wood-burning fireplace at the far end of the room, begging to be lit. Beside it stood a scraggly Christmas tree, twinkling soft, coloured lights into the darkness. Opposite the Christmas tree, by the fireplace, was Fr. Steve's reading chair. Sitting on an end table, by the cozy rocker-recliner, were his Bible and a few other books he had on the go. But what was calling to him most was the old couch which had been donated by a parishioner to the church eighteen years earlier. Though outdated in appearance, the tan upholstered cushions of both the couch and matching loveseat were still in good condition, offering him a comfortable place to rest. An afghan which his grandmother had made for him lay over the back of the couch enticingly. He resisted, knowing that if he were to lie down there, he would never find his way back up again tonight.

The young priest stepped into the kitchen from the front hall and put on a kettle of water for tea. He looked up at the clock; it was twelve minutes past eight. The Fourth Sunday of Advent had come and gone, and he was tired and ready for bed. Having said four Masses over the weekend, attended a parish seniors' Christmas supper and committee meeting, heard first confessions for twenty-three grade two children and their family members on Saturday, and visited a sick parishioner that evening, had all added up to another exhausting weekend.

He sat at the small kitchen table on a vinyl-covered, chrome chair and watched the teakettle. He was too tired to endeavour to clean up the dishes he had left in the sink after supper. Fr. Steve leaned his elbow on the table and propped his face up with his fist. His dark eyes stared blankly at the dirty frying pan, plate, cup, and utensils sitting on the counter. They could wait until morning's dishes. He ran his other hand over his jaw, rubbing at his five o'clock shadow. The dark whiskers scraped against his open palm. He closed his eyes and waited for the kettle, since water always boils faster when one is not looking.

Fr. Steve started at the sound of the doorbell. He looked up at the clock: eight-forty-two. The kettle had been boiling for some time. He jumped up and unplugged it, realizing he had actually fallen asleep sitting up. He shook the kettle; it had almost boiled dry. The doorbell rang a second time. Fr. Steve set the kettle down and ran to the front door. He paused momentarily to run his fingers through his thick, dark hair and to rub his eyes awake, before opening the door.

There standing on his doorstep was Kyle Bander. Fr. Steve greeted the young man with a big smile. He knew Kyle very well from his years as pastor at St. James. "Come in, Kyle," he said, forgetting his fatigue. "What brings you here on a cold, winter night like this?"

"Did you forget about our appointment?" Kyle asked with a laugh.

Fr. Steve tapped himself lightly on the forehead. "Eight-forty-five," he recalled out loud. Looking at this watch, he added, "You're three minutes early, but come on in anyway."

Kyle laughed and stepped into the rectory.

"Would you like tea or something to drink?" Fr. Steve asked as he motioned for Kyle to follow him into the kitchen.

"No, I'm fine," called out Kyle as he removed his boots at the front door and took off his winter jacket and mitts.

"D'you mind if I have some?" the young priest called back.

"Well, if you're making it anyway, I'll have some with you," Kyle answered, stepping into the kitchen and taking a seat at the old, chrome table.

"I'm glad I set up this meeting with you," Fr. Steve confessed. "I would have burned down my house if that doorbell hadn't woken me up. I fell asleep with the teakettle boiling." He refilled the kettle at the sink and plugged it in again.

"You know, you can buy those things with automatic shut-offs now," Kyle informed the cleric.

"That sounds way too modern for this old kitchen," the priest returned—holding out his arms. "There's not one appliance in this room younger than I am . . . and I'm thirty-four years old."

Kyle chuckled.

"You take anything in your tea?" Fr. Steve asked.

"Straight up," the young man replied.

Fr. Steve took down a teapot from a cupboard and a couple of mugs. "Nothing fancy around here. And I hope you don't mind lemon-chamomile. It's my night-time routine. Helps me to sleep better—though I probably don't need it tonight. I was falling asleep just fine without it."

"Good enough for me," Kyle said, "as long as it doesn't put me to sleep before I get home."

Fr. Steve pulled a chair out from the table and sat down across from the young man. "So what's on your mind these days, Kyle?"

"Vocations. Discernment. The usual stuff," he said with a smile.

"What's up?" the priest asked with curiosity.

Kyle explained to Fr. Steve, with some embarrassment, about his life-long attraction to Amie Collins. "You probably think I'm pretty weird."

"Not at all," Fr. Steve replied. "I've known the Collins family for almost ten years now, and I can't see why you wouldn't be attracted to Amie."

Kyle smiled and nodded.

"She's a great girl, Kyle. And there's no shame in having good taste in women," he pointed out. "But I'm still not sure what the problem is for you."

"You haven't heard then that Amie and Connor Easton are courting now?"

"No. Had not heard that," Fr. Steve said, rubbing his face pensively. He got up and stood beside the kettle, waiting for it to boil. "So, Amie and Connor?" he pondered aloud.

Kyle nodded. "Connor's a great guy and a good friend, too. I'm not about to step in. On the other hand, I'm not sure how good I'll feel if all works out for them, and I'm sitting at their wedding some day. I'm wondering if I won't regret that I didn't state my case earlier. But I know I'm not ready to get married yet, or to get involved in a courtship right now . . . and I can guarantee you that Amie sees me too much as a brother to ever seriously consider courting with me right now anyway."

Fr. Steve came back to the table with the teapot and mugs. He set them down between himself and Kyle and looked at the young man. "I'm not sure what to say to you, Kyle," Fr. Steve said, sitting down again. "I want to direct you to trust God's will for your life. If you, Amie, and Connor are all faithfully seeking His will—it'll all work out for the best. If she's meant for you, it'll happen. If she's not, you're better off without her—'cause God'll have something better in the works for both of you. It's all about trusting in God's will. But . . . it's a whole lot easier to talk about it than it is to live it out."

Kyle raised his eyebrows and nodded. "Way easier."

"And I don't want to sound unsympathetic," Fr. Steve went on, "but you've really got to wait this one out and trust God has your happiness in mind. 'For I know the plans I have for you, says the Lord, plans for your good and not for evil, to give you a future and a hope.' You remember that passage from Jeremiah."

Kyle knew it well. "Jeremiah twenty-nine, eleven," he stated. Fr. Steve had made all the kids memorize that in youth group a few years back. "I know . . . and I trust it, too."

The kettle began to boil. Fr. Steve got up, unplugged it, and brought it over to fill the teapot at the table. "So what did you need to see me about?" he asked, with a smile. "There's more, isn't there?"

"Actually, yes," admitted the young man. "I've been wondering if now wouldn't be a good time for me to seriously discern religious life."

Fr. Steve's smile broadened. "Ahhhhh . . . let God catch you on the rebound?"

"If He wants me, now's about as good a time for Him to get me as ever," Kyle said with a chuckle.

Fr. Steve looked intently at the young man. "You know, God caught me on the rebound about thirteen years ago."

"I remember you sharing your conversion story with us and your call to the priesthood. I've been thinking about that lately. I'm just wondering, how does a guy know when God is really calling him or when he's just running away from his problems?"

"Good question," the priest replied. "I think sometimes it can be a bit of both, like for me when I broke up with that girl and was left totally confused about life and love and all the rest. My mother kept telling me she thought I'd make a good priest. Having come out of a very intense physical relationship with a girl, believe me, that was the last thing I was interested in. But I was lonely and hurting and empty. My mom kept telling me to just start praying—one Hail Mary a day at first. Before long I was praying a rosary a day, and at some point I found my way back to confession. I started attending Mass, not just on Sundays, but throughout the week. As time went on I was no longer running away from the pain—I was finding meaning in it. As I started to offer up my suffering to God, uniting it to Christ's suffering on the cross, a hunger began to grow inside of me. I wanted to offer up more than just my broken heart to Christ. I wanted to offer up my very life to Him."

Kyle listened and watched as Fr. Steve poured out their tea. Fr. Steve sat back quietly as he remembered back to the experience of feeling called to the priesthood.

"I started discovering that leading a celibate life was not a calling for men who couldn't cut it in romance . . . it was a calling for real men—men strong enough to lay down their own desires. I remember hearing one priest say that all men are searching for three things to give meaning to their life—a faith worth living for, a trophy worth fighting for, and a woman worth dying for." Fr. Steve counted out all three on his fingers as he spoke. "As a man called to priesthood, I found all three. I had certainly come to find the faith that was worth living for. I had felt the emptiness and pain in my own life that comes from listening to the world. People need to be set free from their selfishness and have their eyes opened to the truth. I found myself wanting to bring the Gospel to a world that was dying to hear it. I had a hunger for saving souls—and suddenly I realized—that was the trophy, the prize worth fighting for." Fr. Steve held onto his second finger as he spoke.

"And the woman worth dying for?" Kyle asked.

"Holy Mother Church—the Bride of Christ," Fr. Steve replied, moving along to his third finger. "Once I fell in love with her, I couldn't imagine another woman in my life. Well," he corrected himself, "I quickly became aware of three women in my life—Mary, who had led me to her Son . . . Holy Mother Church, for whom I would gladly lay down my life . . . and my mom. I would never have found my way without all her prayers and sacrifice."

Kyle nodded. He knew well the power of a mother's prayers and sacrifices.

"And you know, Kyle," Fr. Steve went on, taking a sip of his tea, "once you commit yourself to your bride, you become a warrior—a man willing to lay down his life for his bride. Priesthood is not for cowards and weaklings. It's for real men who aren't afraid of anything."

Kyle knew that what Fr. Steve was saying was not just words for him. This priest lived out his priesthood, day by day, blow by blow. There was no doubt that he had purpose and meaning in his life. There was no questioning his courage and strength as a man. Hearing Fr. Steve talk about it all in these terms certainly increased the appeal to the priesthood for Kyle. It spoke to the deepest instincts of a young man.

Kyle looked Fr. Steve in the eye. "Have you ever missed giving up the chance to get married and have a family?" He could not help but wonder if he could ever let go of that dream for himself.

Fr. Steve smiled. "I am married, and I do have a family—a very large, demanding family at times."

"Fair enough," Kyle said with a chuckle. "But . . ." he hesitated over how to ask.

"As for romance, marriage, sex? A real man can set those things aside once he discovers the rest. I've been living a chaste life for over thirteen years now, and it hasn't killed me. In fact, I just grow stronger as a man each day. Doesn't mean I don't suffer temptation. And believe me, there are women out there who have no qualms about trying to seduce a priest. But a man learns to flee immorality—just like St. Paul tells us in First Corinthians, six."

Fr. Steve motioned with his hands the speed at which a man should flee. Kyle smiled and nodded, picked up his mug, and took a sip of his tea.

"You see, Kyle, a real priest is a man who embraces everything it is to be a man and directs all that energy to a spiritual marriage and to spiritual fatherhood. He doesn't give it all up—he just redirects that energy. It's fulfilling, Kyle. As men we are capable of rising above our instincts and living for a higher purpose. Married men have to learn that as well. They can't just go running around ruled by passions and desires of the flesh. They have to live chastely, according to their state in life. They have to be self-disciplined and live out times of abstinence. They have to," he paused as he recounted the three things on his fingers. "They have to have a faith worth living for, a trophy worth fighting for, and a woman worth dying for."

"I can see how the two parallel," Kyle said. "So how does a man know which calling is for him?"

"As I said earlier," Fr. Steve pointed out, "for me I stopped running from the pain of life and started embracing it. Once I joined myself to Christ on the cross, I didn't want down. I just wanted to stay there with Him—for all those reasons."

"So you just came to realize it in your own life," Kyle concluded. "It wasn't like there was an obvious sign to you?"

"For me it was gradual . . . it happened over a period of about six months. But for some priests it just hits them—BAM!" Fr. Steve clapped his hands together, and Kyle started.

They both began to laugh. "Have you ever felt anything hit you like that?" Fr. Steve asked, still laughing at the young man's reaction.

"Not yet," Kyle answered, with both hands up. He was quiet for a moment. "I guess I'm just trying to make sense out of what the outcome might be with Amie."

"I think it's a very good thing that Amie's taken for now, Kyle. That's all part of God's plan—for both of you. He's in control; He knows what He's doing. He's giving you a chance to discern things in life on an even scale—you no longer have one side weighted down over the other." Fr. Steve motioned with his hands, imitating a scale as he brought them back into balance. "You have to offer her back up to the Lord. Allow Him to bring her back into your life *if* it's meant to be, *when* it's meant to be and *how* it's meant to be. This is a grace-filled time, giving you a good opportunity to seek His will for you, without distraction. And if things don't work out with her and Connor, well you just might get a second chance with her. But by then, you might not want it anymore."

Kyle's eyes opened wide, the possibility of not wanting Amie—were she to become available again—had never occurred to him. He chuckled at himself. "What you're saying is learn to love with no strings attached."

"Something like that," the priest replied, pointing at Kyle to show that the young man was on the right track. "You've got the idea. Love is all about giving of yourself." Fr. Steve gestured in a giving motion, away from himself. "It's not about taking. You just have to look at the cross, Kyle." The priest pointed above the kitchen table where a beautiful crucifix hung.

Kyle looked at it as Fr. Steve went on. "It's about self-denial, sacrifice, making a gift of yourself, endurance, patience, strength, courage, and hope. They're all virtues that are part of what it means to really love . . . and they're all the marks of a real man. Whatever love Jesus calls you to in your life, has to be measured up to *that* standard." He pointed again to the crucifix. "And you can start living that right now—you don't have to wait until you know your vocation, Kyle. Get ready now, while you're still single, to live out that call to the fullest."

"I'll work on it," Kyle said.

Fr. Steve chuckled, picking up his mug and looking at it. "You're eons ahead of where I was when I started, Kyle." The priest set his empty mug back down. "You've lived a pure life, committed to your faith, willing to sacrifice. You're a real man of integrity—that's plain to see. Just keep living that way, each day. Take it all in stride and persevere with patience."

Kyle nodded. He looked down at his empty mug. "Had enough tea to get back to sleep yet, Fr. Steve?"

"Like a baby," the priest replied.

"Well, I'll get out of here so you can get back to sawing those logs," Kyle said, getting up.

"They'll be Yuletide Logs," Fr. Steve replied, walking Kyle to the front door. "Christmas Eve is in three days. I've got a busy week ahead of me."

"Four Masses over Christmas?" Kyle asked.

"Yup," the priest answered, stretching his arms out with a yawn. "And two more penitential services yet to go."

"You'd better get a good night's sleep," the young man stated, "so that you're in good form to celebrate. After all, you want to make your Bride look Her best for Christmas."

Fr. Steve chuckled as he brought his arms back down and crossed them over his chest.

"Thanks, Fr. Steve," Kyle said, extending his hand.

The pastor leaned forward, took the young man's hand in a firm grip, and shook it. "I'll be offering up some prayers for your intentions there, Kyle. I expect great things will come of it all."

"Thanks," Kyle repeated as he stepped out into the night.

Kyle listened to Christmas music as he drove home, tapping along on the steering wheel of his Escort. He sang along with *Silent Night,* his tenor voice harmonizing to the familiar melody being sung against the plucking of a guitar. It was such a simple song, yet so powerful and rich in significance. He pictured Mary, the Virgin Mother, holding the infant Jesus in her arms that first Christmas night. She and Joseph had no idea what plan God had in store for them. Still, they trusted and followed—without knowing, without being able to fully understand.

I guess that's what faith's all about—trusting, even when we can't see, believing You've got a greater plan for us than what we could ever imagine for ourselves. I can rest my hope in that, Jesus. I'm not sure what You're calling me to do with my life. Just help me to be open to whatever it is—no strings attached.

Chapter 29

With Christmas fast approaching, the Collins home was full of energy and excitement. The children had set aside their school books for the holidays. The kitchen was in constant baking production of cookies, cakes, tarts, and other treats, and of course, tourtières. These were the traditional French Canadian meat pies that they would eat during *Réveillon*, their celebration following Christmas Eve Mass.

The house was being transformed one decoration at a time. Christmas carols carried throughout the home from the old Heintzman piano. When the piano was quiet, the Christmas albums sang out from the CD player. It was a joyous time of preparation.

In the midst of all the hustle and bustle a nineteen-year-old girl wandered aimlessly, from one chore to the next, seemingly lost in another world. Eventually she found her way to her bedroom and flopped down on her bed. . . .

"Honestly, Amie," her mother scolded, standing in Amie's bedroom doorway with her hands on her hips, having startled Amie back to reality. "I can't get through to you at all these days. I've been calling you for the last ten minutes. What are you doing up here?"

"Oh, I was just . . . cleaning my room," Amie replied, sitting up and grabbing for a shirt to fold that had been lying across the foot of her bed.

Judy threw a quick glance around the tidy bedroom. "It's clean. Compared to the rest of the house, this looks like Shangri-La! Now if you don't mind, I could use your help in the kitchen."

"Sorry, Mom," Amie replied. She pulled her hair back in a ponytail. Looking in the mirror, she noticed her sweatpants and sweatshirt did not match at all. *Oh, who cares? It's good enough for housework,* she thought to herself as she headed down to the kitchen.

She was not five minutes into her work, mixing pie dough, when the doorbell rang. Within moments Zack came bursting into the room. "Amie, Connor's here," he announced in full voice.

Amie quickly looked down at her sweatshirt, now covered in flour. *Oh well,* she thought to herself. She grabbed for a towel and wiped off her hands. She stepped into the front room, where Connor stood in the doorway, with his winter jacket open over his casual shirt and pants. He looked good; she felt somewhat embarrassed that she was so frumpy.

"Hey, Connor. I completely forgot you said you'd be coming by today," she said, apologetically.

Connor just smiled, but Amie could have kicked herself for having said that. How many times was she going to send him the message that this courtship was not her first priority?

Little ones were jumping at Connor by now. Jessie wanted to give him a hug, and Aaron and Zack were begging for Connor to come wrestle with them.

"Guys, stop it," Amie scolded the boys, as she took Jessie from Connor's arms. "Come on, Connor, let's step into the front porch," she suggested pointing to the door behind him.

"Sure," he replied with a laugh.

"You kids go play," she said to Jessie.

"Bye, Connor," the little girl said, waving her fingers by her sad eyes.

"Bye, Jessie," he said, waving back with a smile. "See you boys," he called out to the guys. "You all have a good Christmas."

"You too, Connor," Aaron called out.

"Come back and wrestle with us after Christmas," Zack yelled, as the door shut him out.

"Sorry about that," Amie apologized again.

"No problem. . . . I'm just heading out of town now, and I wanted to drop off this little gift for you for Christmas."

"Oh?" Amie was stunned. She had not bought Connor anything for Christmas. How could she have been so dumb? What an oversight that was. "Connor, I wasn't expecting you to get me anything for Christmas. I mean," she fumbled to say this tactfully, "I just thought since we were so new into this courtship, we'd maybe wait for a while to exchange gifts." *Okay, that was totally lame. But it's all I can come up with on the spot.*

"That's fine. It's not a big gift at all," he assured her, holding out the rectangular package, neatly wrapped with a blue ribbon and bow.

"It's heavy," she commented, as she took the gift, feeling its weight compared to its size.

"It's not much, really. I just wanted to let you know I was thinking about you—and will be looking forward to seeing you on the twenty-seventh . . . if that's all right with your folks?"

"Yes!" she responded rather triumphantly, raising her finger in the air, indicating she had remembered. That would prove he had been on her mind, at least in that matter. He *was* on her mind lots—just not in the same way she seemed to have been on his.

"It's fine with them?" he asked, waiting for her to say something more about it.

She smiled and refocused. "It's perfect. I'll be coming down on the two o'clock bus—so you can pick me up at four-forty-five at the bus depot. Unless, of course, weather conditions slow up the bus."

"I'll call and check with the bus depot to be sure."

"And my aunt and uncle are looking forward to having me stay with them. As long as you don't mind dropping me off and picking me up at their house. My parents are just more comfortable with me staying with relatives, so that it doesn't give the wrong impression about us to your family and neighbours."

"That's perfectly fine," he agreed. "I'd be more than happy to chauffeur you around Regina."

"So," she said, looking down at the gift. "Do you want me to open this now? Or should I wait until Christmas?"

"Go ahead and open it now," he suggested.

Amie bit down on her lip and looked at the gift. She carefully undid the tape on the ends and lifted the paper. Inside there was a picture in an ornately decorated pewter frame. "St. Cecilia," she said with a smile, recognizing the familiar saint.

"Patron Saint of music. I figured you would appreciate that, especially with your piano exam coming up in a month's time."

"Yeah," she said, rolling her eyes at the reminder of the work ahead of her. She looked at the picture. "What a beautiful image of her. Where did you get it?"

"At the Catholic bookstore downtown. I wanted to give you a gift that would mean something to you—without strings attached."

"Connor, you are so thoughtful. I feel really bad that I did nothing for you. I just haven't really thought about it. I'm more of a last minute person and . . ."

"Don't sweat it. Really! I just wanted to give you something—no strings attached—just to show my appreciation. I wasn't looking for anything in return."

"I know," she said. "You're too nice to expect anything in return. But I still wish I had done something."

Connor looked at his watch. "I actually have to get on the road here right away. I promised my younger sister, Abby, I'd be there for a concert she's in tonight—and I don't want to disappoint her."

"I'm looking forward to meeting your family," Amie told him.

"They're dying to meet you," Connor assured her, zipping up his jacket. "I'll see you on Saturday, then?"

"Saturday," she agreed.

"Merry Christmas, Amie," he said, somewhat awkwardly.

Amie reached up and gave Connor a friendly hug. "Merry Christmas, Connor," she said softly.

He returned the hug, gently, and stepped away. Amie smiled at him, as she stood there, hugging the picture in front of her. Connor opened the door and left. Amie watched as he got into his car and drove away.

She looked back down at the picture of the noble saint, dressed in a flowing gown, seated at a harp. "Pray for me, St. Cecilia," the young musician murmured. "And pray for me to not end up breaking Connor's heart."

Chapter 30

"Ho, ho, ho! Merry Christmas," called out James Vaughn in full baritone voice as he entered Joanie and Brandon's apartment two nights before Christmas, his arms loaded down with presents.

Brandon was still looking at Joanie in disbelief. He had not quite recovered from the shock of two minutes earlier when his father had buzzed their apartment to see if they were home. They had not seen James since their wedding, though they had spoken to him several times over the phone. Usually he announced when he was coming to town on business and would set up a dinner date at a restaurant with the young couple. This was so uncharacteristic of him.

"Come in, Santa," Brandon said with a laugh. "Can I help you with your load?"

"Just point me to the tree and I'll drop it down there," his father replied.

Brandon pointed him toward the Christmas tree beside the fireplace and watched as his father unloaded ten parcels. James stood up again and turned around to face the young couple with a smile that looked so much like his son's that it still struck Joanie each time she saw Brandon's dad. His blond hair, with just a bit of greying at the temples, his striking blue eyes, the shape of his face, his build: everything about this man resembled a twenty-some-year older version of her husband.

"It's wonderful to see you again, James," Joanie said, walking across the room to give him a hug.

"Hey, little mama," he said, opening wide his arms to greet her. "You look more beautiful each time I see you. So how's my grandchild doing?"

"Wonderfully," she answered, laying her hands on her rounded tummy.

"And how's baby's mama? You all better now?"

"I am," she answered with a smile. "And how about grandpa?"

"*Grandpa?*" he repeated the word. "Hmm. I have a ways to go to get used to that title. I could have sworn I was too young to be a grandpa."

"Have you eaten?" Brandon asked his dad. "We just finished supper, but we can pull out some leftovers for you."

"No, thanks, I'm good. I'm not planning to stay long, anyway. I just wanted to drop off these things for you two and the baby and Joanie's family," he said, motioning to the pile of gifts he had left in front of the tree.

"You didn't need to do that, James," Joanie said, walking over to the tree to look at the packages.

"Where else am I going to spend my money?" he asked.

"Well, it's just nice to see you, Dad. I hope you intend on staying now and spending Christmas with us," Brandon said.

The last time Brandon had spent Christmas with his father was when he was eight years old, just before his parents had separated and divorced. So many years had passed by—so many Christmases that they had missed out on together. Their reconciliation with each other had come out of Brandon's discovery of Christianity. Though James himself was not at all a religious man, he had welcomed the opportunity that Brandon's conversion had given him to get to know his son as an adult.

Brandon looked intently at his father, hoping his father would say 'yes'.

"No," James said, shaking his head. "I'm catching a plane back to Toronto tomorrow morning."

Joanie put her hands on her hips and stared down her father-in-law.

"And nothing you can say is going to change my mind," he added, his hands held up in protest.

"Dad, we haven't seen you since our wedding, and we've hardly heard from you," Brandon said. "You think you're going to get away that easily?"

"I've got plans back in Toronto," the older man said. "I sure do appreciate that you asked, though. Maybe next year."

"Sit down and at least have a drink with us." Brandon looked at his dad. The two men stood almost eye-to-eye, Brandon having a one inch height advantage over his father. The father looked back at his son, calculating a decision. He wanted to stay; he just did not want to impose.

Joanie stood back and waited, hoping James would stay. Suddenly she had a thought. "You haven't even seen our wedding pictures. Not to mention pictures from our honeymoon in Europe—the tickets for which you paid, thank you very much," she added, bowing her head in a gesture of gratitude. "So . . . you *have* to stay and I'm not going to hear any more about it." She walked up beside James, slipped her arm through his and walked him over to the dining table. "Here, I'll take your coat and you sit down," she told him. She waited as he unzipped his leather jacket so she could go hang it up for him. "I'll be right back with the albums, and Brandon'll get you a drink. You can pour me some juice, honey," she called back over her shoulder as she hurried off.

"Hard for a man to say 'no' to that woman, isn't it?" James commented to his son.

"How'd you think I ended up here today?" Brandon asked, motioning both hands toward himself.

James smiled. "Better you than me, son."

"I heard that," Joanie called out from the bedroom.

James laughed as he made himself comfortable at the table.

Joanie returned with a box filled with albums and other treasures. "Just for that last comment, I'm going to make you sit through the entire six-album collection," she informed him.

James raised an eyebrow in the same manner that Brandon always did.

"And don't think that little irresistible eyebrow manoeuvre is going to work any better for you than it does for my husband. I still always get my way," she informed her father-in-law.

James smiled and patted Joanie's hand. "Just between the two of us, I'm glad you got your way with him. You rescued him from ending up a miserable, lonely man like me," he said in a low voice just above a whisper.

Joanie tilted her head, her long dark curls falling to the side. Never before had she heard James make any such confession. She knew his swinging bachelor life had to be empty and unfulfilling—but she never expected him to admit that. She smiled and quickly leaned forward to kiss her father-in-law on the cheek. "I'm glad I did too. He saved me from becoming an old maid," she whispered to him with a giggle.

James put his head down and laughed just as Brandon came back into the room with their drinks.

"Stealing kisses from my wife?" Brandon asked his father. He looked over at his wife, an eyebrow raised in his characteristic way.

"Just you never mind," Joanie said. "You sit there on the other side of your dad so he can't escape," she instructed her husband. She nudged her father-in-law and whispered, "You see, I've become immune to that disarming look of you Vaughn men."

James winked at the girl beside him, with a smile that warmed her heart. She really was not immune to the debonair qualities of these men—she was just good at making them think she was.

Brandon did as he was told, putting their drinks down on the table. The newlyweds went through albums and shared stories with Brandon's father. It ended up being the most enjoyable evening the three of them had ever shared. James especially enjoyed the pictures of Brandon, post-honeymoon.

"That was a fairly rocky start to married life, son," the older man chided. "I sure hope it has improved since then."

Joanie smiled. "I think he's managing to survive."

"I'm more than surviving, dear," Brandon returned. "I've never been happier in my life."

"Good for you, son," James said. "I'm happy for both of you. If I wasn't so set in my ways, I'd actually think there was something to this whole Christianity-thing." He motioned his hand toward the albums, filled with pictures of Holy Shrines and religious places. "But I guess I enjoy being a sinner too much to want to change."

"Be careful there, Dad," Brandon warned. "I lived that life for a number of years myself, and I know how empty it is. When the kick's all gone, what then?"

"Don't know," James replied. "Life hasn't lost its kick, yet."

"That's too bad," Joanie said, looking at James.

James chuckled. "Oh, you'd just love to see me converted, wouldn't you?"

"Of course I would," Joanie replied. "Sometimes you can't know what kind of prison cell you're living in until you've been set free. And I just want to see you free."

"I'm not in any prison," James informed her. "I'm free to come and go as I please. I answer to no one. And I like it that way."

"Sure you do, Dad," Brandon said. "I remember what it was like. I also remember that I was constantly going from one experience to the next trying to satisfy my emptiness inside. I was always looking for a bigger and better kick."

"But as long as I can still find one, why should I complain?" James returned.

"So, what plans *do* you have for Christmas?" Brandon asked, pointedly.

James looked at his son. He knew that Brandon knew he had no plans. He knew that Brandon could see he would be going back to Toronto to spend another Christmas all alone. Maybe he would pick up some lonely girl at a bar, but that would just make Christmas day like any other lonely day of the year.

"You know," he told Brandon, "Christmas is a special day for some folks. But for guys like me, it's just one in three hundred and sixty-five. It comes and it goes. I enjoy the hoopla of parties beforehand. I don't get worked up over the day itself. There's no Christmas tree in my apartment—no decorations. I endure the day and then life gets back to normal."

"So you *don't* have plans?" Joanie said, in an accusing tone of voice.

"Not really. Same old, same old," James replied, turning his hands upward.

"So why not spend it with us?" Joanie begged. "It'd be so wonderful to share our first Christmas with you. You could come over and party with my family—we really have a great time together."

James shook a finger at his daughter-in-law. "Joanie, I think the world of you and your family. But I'm not sticking around for Christmas. And," he looked down at his watch, "I have a plane to catch in seven hours, so I'd better get back to my hotel." He stood up and stretched out his arms. "I really enjoyed my evening with you two. I don't even mind your feeble attempts to convert me. I know you mean well by it. Makes me feel like you care."

"We do care, James," Joanie said. She stood up and gave him a big hug. "And I don't intend to ever stop caring about you and your soul . . . so, as long as we both understand each other, I think we'll get along just fine."

James chuckled and gave his daughter-in-law an extra squeeze before he let go of the hug.

Brandon gave his dad a hug as well. "Merry Christmas, Dad. I hope you come back to visit us real soon."

"Oh, and we sent a package out to you for Christmas," Joanie said. "I didn't think we'd get to see you beforehand. So, hopefully you'll get it soon. It's not much—just our way of saying that we love you, and we miss you." She shrugged her shoulders. The smile on her face was sincere.

James smiled back at the girl. "I appreciate that. I'll be watching for it." He slipped on his jacket, pulled the keys for his rental car out of the pocket, and flipped them around in his hand as he stood at the door. After a moment he said, "Well, I'd better get going. Thanks again for tonight. I had a great time."

Joanie patted him on the back as he turned to walk out the apartment door. She and Brandon watched from their doorway as James made his way down the hall. He turned and waved back to them as he exited at the stairwell.

Brandon sent Joanie off to bed while he cleaned up. They both had to work the next day, and he was concerned she would never make it with only a few hours of rest. It had been two late nights in a row: first Justine and Mark's unexpected visit, then his father's. Brandon flirted with the idea of not answering the buzzer again until after Christmas, just so Joanie would not get worn out. But who was he to thwart God's timing? They had both been grace-filled evenings. Holidays would be coming in a few more days for them—she could catch up on her rest then.

Joanie was fast asleep by the time Brandon climbed into bed fifteen minutes later. He gently kissed her on the forehead and blessed her before lying down on his pillow. Sleep did not come quickly for him though he, too, was exhausted.

He thought about his father's life. Brandon remembered the loneliness of his own life before Joanie . . . before Jesus. Brandon knew that the grace of conversion was just that: a grace. No one can talk another person into truly accepting Christ. That faith comes as pure gift. So why were some people able to receive that gift and others not? Surely God would want everyone to have it. Brandon pondered that for a while.

He knew that a person must be open to that grace. God will not force His way into anyone's life. Brandon remembered Joanie sharing with him about God for the first time—sitting at *Doug's Donuts*. He smiled, picturing the feisty girl boldly explaining how Christ would spend the rest of Brandon's life trying to seek him out. If Brandon had not already known such loneliness—in spite of all the distractions of a hedonistic lifestyle—he would never have listened to her. But her words had fallen on his heart that night like rain on a desert plain. He had been ready to accept Christ, though he could not see it or identify it for himself.

Brandon hoped that, through the witness of their lives, Joanie and he could somehow help his father see what was lacking in his own life. He wanted so much to be able to enjoy someday the fullness of a relationship with his dad that can only come when two persons share a common faith. He wanted his father to know the freedom that could only come from embracing God's laws: the Truth—which is Jesus Christ Himself.

As much as Brandon wanted that gift for his father, he knew that Jesus wanted it for his father even more. For that reason alone, Brandon knew that someday, somehow, it would happen . . . all in God's time.

The young man lay in bed and prayed for his dad's conversion. Finally, without warning, sleep stole upon him.

Chapter 31

"What a cold Christmas Eve," announced John Collins, as he closed the door behind him. He took off his winter coat and hung it in the front closet. The family had just come home following Christmas Eve Mass, and they were now scattered, getting ready for all the company to arrive for *Réveillon*.

It was a French Catholic tradition to celebrate late into the night—following Midnight Mass—with food, song, and whatever family and friends were able to gather together. Though John himself was not of French origin, his wife, née Judith Ledoux, was. He found his fondest traditions raising their children were borrowed from his wife's rich French Catholic heritage. Though she had been the generation to have lost the language, the richness of her French heritage was to be found in the Catholic traditions that had shaped this culture over the centuries.

This year the Collins family would be hosting all the Ledoux cousins who lived in Saskatoon. This made Christmas even more exciting than normal for the children. The house would soon be filled with "cousins by the dozens", ready to celebrate the birth of their Saviour.

Maggie came into the front room. Seeing her father, a smile lit up her face as she watched him picking up the kids' boots that had been left scattered by the door. "I'm so happy to be home for this," Maggie said, stepping up to give her dad a hand. "*Réveillon* just would not be the same anywhere else."

"It's good to have my Schnooks home for Christmas," John said, calling her by the pet name he had given her as a child. He stood up and gave her a big hug, picking her up and twirling her around.

Her skirt puffed up at the bottom as he set her down. She looked down and laughed at her feet with Christmas socks that totally did not match what she was wearing. "Is this a fashion statement or what?"

"And I thought Katie was the fashionable one around here. . . . You look great kid," he said, squeezing Maggie's cheek, "and so relaxed. Religious life is treating you well."

"It is, Daddy. I'm just as happy as could be. I am so certain this is what God wants of me, and it just feels good to be moving in that direction. Plus, my internship is behind me. I have only four classes left next term, and I'll have my teacher's degree. So, life is simply *fantabulous!*" she exclaimed with typical Maggie exuberance, her arms stretched wide.

"That's what I miss around here," John said, putting his arm over

Maggie's shoulder and walking toward the kitchen. "Maggie energy! No one has quite the same *joie de vivre* as you do."

Just then Jessie came running around the corner in her Christmas dress, all ribbons and bows, and crashed into her father's legs. The four-year-old bounced off him, giggling with excitement.

"On second thought, there might be another one with that kind of energy to replace you," he commented to his second eldest daughter, swooping the fallen child up in his arms. "Jessie, Jessie," he said, shaking his head and smiling, "what's the hurry?"

The auburn-haired child wiggled to get free of her father's hold. "Grandma and Grandpa are here," she whined, as he put her down. "I want to go see them at the door," she called back, running off toward the front porch.

"I'm not sure how you'd possibly find time to miss me," Maggie commented. "I'm so accustomed to the quiet at the Sisters' house now that I've forgotten just how noisy and wild this place gets."

"It gets even noisier and wilder when you show up," he noted, standing and waiting for his in-laws to come in.

"So does the Sisters' house," she said with a laugh.

Grandma and Grandpa Ledoux entered to the hugs and kisses of their grandchildren. The robust man opened up his accordion case right away and called out, "Where are the others? I thought we were going full-out *Réveillon* this year—pull out all the stops?"

"Why don't you start the music and see if that brings them in any faster?" Maggie suggested. She gave her grandpa a quick kiss on the cheek before she headed off to the kitchen to help her mother.

Grandpa's smile followed the young girl out of the room. "Well, if someone gets me some wine to keep my throat wet, I'll be able to sing songs all night long," the old man suggested, ready to oblige as he slipped his arms into the accordion straps.

"I'll get you some wine," Zack yelled out, running to the kitchen.

"Hey, Isaac, get out something to play," Grandpa instructed the nearly-fourteen-year-old. "Guitar, drums . . . anything."

"Got my guitar right here," answered the dark-haired boy with eager eyes.

"Good," stated Grandpa. "Let's see if we can get Grandma up jigging again this year."

"Not on your life," declared the feisty, curly-haired woman. "I'm keeping my feet firmly planted, and all the coaxing in the world is not going to get them lifted off the ground tonight."

"Please, Grandma," came the little voice of Jessie, pulling on her grandmother's skirt. "I can dance with you."

Grandma looked at the little girl, whose hazel eyes had just grown two sizes bigger, and said, "Tell you what, Jessie. You get Grandpa to play you some jigging music, and you show me how you can dance now in that pretty Christmas dress."

"Okay, Grandpa?" Jessie asked eagerly as she turned to the man behind the accordion.

"You get that sister Maggie of yours back out here with her fiddle. Jigging's just not the same without a fiddle playing," he told the little girl.

Jessie ran off to find Maggie in the kitchen. She grabbed her big sister by the hand and started to pull. "Come on, Maggie. Grandpa needs your fiddle or I can't dance!"

Maggie picked up her fiddle case on her way into the living room and opened it up. She quickly tuned with Grandpa and began to play some old time fiddle music. Grandpa joined in, and Isaac soon followed with the guitar. Jessie lifted the sides of her skirt and began to twirl. Amie came into the room at the sound of the music. She stopped to do a quick jig with Jessie on her way by, lifting the sides of her skirt to match her little sister. Jessie giggled and danced on as Amie found her way to the piano. Katie came and joined in the dance, trying her best to recall the jig steps that her grandmother had once taught her. Zack and Aaron got up and started to do some goofy moves to the music—hardly a jigging style, but at least they were having fun.

They were not long into the music before the door burst open to the energetic entrance of the first Ledoux clan to arrive. The music paused only momentarily: long enough for Grandpa to call out to Leah to get that fiddle tuned up quickly. Leah had been away for the past four months serving with the Youth Ministry Network. Everyone was excited to see her again. Mike, who was home from Calgary for Christmas, was not getting off the hook either. Amie got up from the piano and pushed her older cousin over to the piano bench. She sat down beside him, looking forward to the chance to improvise along with him, duet style. Jocelyn quickly took her place with Katie, leading the children in dance, and Ann went and sat beside their grandma on the couch.

The music had just nicely gotten underway again, when Ben and Caleb Ledoux came barrelling into the house with a chorus of "Ho, ho, ho's". Both were sporting a Santa's cap atop a mop of red hair; they had also made themselves beards and moustaches out of white cotton balls. The little children ran eagerly to their two big boy cousins to see what they had in the big sacks they were carrying over their shoulders. To their delight, Ben and Caleb produced tins of poppycock and Christmas baking, boxes of candy canes and Christmas oranges, and a wonderful assortment of noise-making party favours for the children.

"We really are pulling out all the stops this year," Grandpa called out above all the commotion.

The two Santas were not to be left out of the music making. Isaac pointed Caleb to the djembe. He loved to have the opportunity to jam with this cousin who was only a few years older than he. Ben ran back out to their car to bring in his guitar.

Aunts and Uncles found their way to sit on the couch and chairs, as John shooed the little children off the furniture to make room for the adults. Judy had set out food on the dining room table and invited everyone to help themselves.

"Not before we all pray," John said.

"But we're not all here," protested Katie.

"Who's missing?" asked the father.

"Uncle Jack and Auntie Karen aren't here yet," piped in Jessie, who was eagerly awaiting the arrival of the cousins her age.

"And what about us?" John turned around to see Joanie standing with her hands on her hips, staring at her father with a scolding expression.

"How could I forget my Sweet Pea?" He walked over and gave his daughter a hug.

"With all the noise in here, I'm surprised you can think at all," commented Brandon, carrying his guitar into the living room. "You sure you want me to bother with this?"

"Are you kidding?" Ben Ledoux yelled out from across the room. "When's the last time we had a chance to really jam together?"

"Hey, hey!" Brandon called out in greeting to Ben and Mike. "I'm in!" Brandon took his guitar and set himself up between the two young men. They had become good friends over the past couple of years, and Brandon welcomed the chance to spend time with the guys.

"I think we now have more musicians than singers," Grandma called out over the noise.

"But not enough dancers," Jessie complained, pulling at Grandma's hands.

"Oh, no, sweetie," Grandma said gently to the little girl. "I already told you I won't be jigging this year. I'm just too . . ."

Grandma looked up, interrupted by a steady beating of hands and a chorus of "Grandma, Grandma, Grandma . . ." being raised around the room. All the grandchildren were urging her on to dance. Grandpa was smiling at his wife, nodding—in his own way of prodding her on. Jessie kept pulling on Grandma's hands. Suddenly, Jessie had a helper. Her four-year-old cousin, Gianna, had finally arrived with Uncle Jack and Auntie Karen.

Grandma turned to greet her youngest son, Jacques, who had just walked in with his family of six children: ages ten down to a baby in arms. He waved at his mother from across the room. Seeing the struggle the children were having in getting her up to dance, Jack passed baby Max over to his wife and strode over to his mother. A sea of children parted as the tall, red-headed man moved through the crowd. Jack extended his hand forward to his mother, inviting her to dance. Cheers rose up throughout the room as Grandma Ledoux gave in to her son.

He led his mother to the middle of the room, while a ring of children of all ages formed around them. Grandpa began the jigging music, calling out the key in which he was playing, and the instruments all joined in. Jack began to jig with his mother in the French Canadian style of jigging that she had taught him as a child. He was a good dancer and, paired up with the white-haired, tiny woman, they were quite a sight.

After about three minutes of heavy-duty dancing, Grandma Ledoux stepped into her son's arms and sighed. "I'm giving up the jig!"

Jack laughed, hugging his mother. He walked her back to her seat, to the applause of all the family gathered in the room.

When the applause settled enough for John to make himself heard over the noise, he began in his deep, low, voice, "In the name of the Father . . ."

Quickly the entire crew fell into silence and joined in with "Uncle John" to say grace, to bless the bounteous feast they were about to eat, and to bless their time of celebration as a family. Then John invited Grandpa to add to the prayers for their family. Grandpa prayed for all the members of the family who were too far away to be with them that night. He prayed for all their relatives who had died and gone before them. He prayed for the grace for their families to always live in the fullness of their faith. And he prayed for peace on earth, on this the birth of the Prince of Peace.

Following their time of prayer, Judy invited everyone to help themselves to all the food set out in the dining room. John served drinks to the adults. He remarked that the number of adults was dramatically increasing each year, as the children were growing up. "I'll have to start buying more wine to keep up with this crew."

"Either that, or you'll have to get the Lord to teach you how to turn water into wine," chided his brother-in-law, Frank Ledoux.

With the noise level of the gathering now somewhat subdued, Grandpa began leading the singing of Christmas carols. His rich baritone voice carried out across the room, over the children's smaller voices. Harmonies began to ring out from every corner. The other instruments softly played along where they could, without any music to follow. Learning to play by ear was a definite asset in this family.

Children filed back into the living room from the dining room with their plates filled with food, and sat around on the floor in front of their grandpa. Aaron jumped up and ran over to the light switch, turning off the big light that hung in the middle of the room, so that the atmosphere would be just right. The lights of the Christmas tree in the corner by the piano flickered on and off. With table lamps on in a couple of corners of the room and a half-dozen candles burning, there was just enough lighting for everyone to see.

Grandpa smiled, gazing out across the room, as he led the singing. This was what Christmas Eve was all about for him: to be surrounded by his family and singing songs of praise to God for the gift of His Son. In the seventy-seven Christmases he had lived through over the years, this recipe had never once grown old.

Chapter 32

Boxing Day found Joanie and Brandon all packed up in their SUV, traveling down a highway through a quiet winter prairie, as they headed to Calgary to visit his mom and step-father. This was Caroline's first Christmas celebrated back in the Church. She had spent thirty-two years away from God, following the untimely deaths of her parents when she was just twelve years old. Through Brandon's conversion, she had found the courage to reach out to God again in her life. It had only been a year since that had all taken place.

She and her husband, Dan Taylor, had become quite active in their parish of St. Philomena's in the time since then. Though Dan himself was not yet Catholic, he was preparing to enter the Church at Easter.

"Joanie!" called out Caroline, standing in the doorway of their split-level home as she anxiously waited for the young couple to get into the house. "You look beautiful," exclaimed the mother-in-law.

"Doesn't she, though?" called back Brandon, as he took an armful of things from the back of the Pathfinder.

"Merry Christmas, Caroline," Joanie said, hugging the auburn-haired woman who stood just a few inches shorter than she. "It's so good to see you again."

Caroline's green eyes sparkled with delight. Her smile showed off the fine features of her face, with all the warmth and love that she possessed.

"Hey, gorgeous," Brandon said, dropping his armload in the front entry and picking up his mother in a big bear hug. "How's my favourite mother?"

Caroline hugged her son tightly. They were close; they always had been. Caroline had raised Brandon as a single mom after his father had walked out on them when Brandon was a boy. They had survived many struggles and hardships, but the hard years eventually passed, and the bond between them had only been strengthened by the adversities. Now that they shared a common faith in Jesus, they were closer than ever.

"Look at you, son," she said, proudly. "Married life is treating you well."

The handsome young man winked at his mother. "You better believe it is. So where's Dan?" he asked, looking into the house behind his mother.

"He'll be back right away. He just slipped out to pick up some things for me for supper. I told him to wait, but he insisted it would be easier to get away before you arrived than afterward. But come in; sit down. I'll get you something to eat. Are you hungry?"

"Oh, that would be great," Joanie jumped in, before Brandon could decline the offer. "I'm just famished."

"You don't feed your wife?" Caroline questioned her son.

"We just stopped for lunch a few hours ago. She was so full, she couldn't eat another bite. Now she's famished. How do I keep up with her?"

"Well, there's a competition in here for space between the baby and my stomach. I can't help it if I get hungry so often."

"We'll get you something, sweetheart," Caroline said, taking Joanie by the hand, leading her to the kitchen. "I want to be sure that grandchild of mine is well taken care of."

Joanie smiled as she followed Caroline.

"And you carry your bags upstairs, Brandon," Caroline called out. "I set you up in the room on the right-hand side of the hall up there."

"Yes, mother," he replied, obediently.

"He's a good boy," Joanie reported to her mother-in-law. "He does what he's told without complaining."

"That's good. But I want to hear if he starts slacking off," Caroline added in a motherly tone. She chuckled and added, "You look lovely, Joanie. Motherhood looks good on you."

"Thanks," Joanie replied, straightening out her maternity top over her skirt. "I'm getting used to this changing body of mine, I think."

"Women who are pregnant are just radiant. I often wished I could have had more children. But life is what it is."

"I'm just glad you had the one you did," Joanie said.

Caroline set out a snack for the travelers, and before long Dan arrived. The foursome talked and caught up on life. They had supper and then played Canasta into the wee hours of the morning.

"Great game," stated Dan, stretching as he stood up from the table. He was a heavy set man with round, jovial features and a thick silver head of hair. "I'm bushed, though. Can't keep hours like this anymore," he said, looking at his watch. "It's almost three a.m."

"We should all call it a night," Brandon agreed. "I can't believe you stayed awake this late, Joanie."

"I slept in the car on the way out here," she reminded her husband. "And after all, it was Canasta! I could have gone another game."

"You have to understand the Collins family and Canasta," Brandon explained, putting his arm around his wife, as he started to pull her toward the stairs. "It's like a religion or something. They're all driven Canasta freaks. I've never seen anything like it."

"Oh, cut it out," Joanie said, backhanding Brandon on the stomach. "You like it just as much as I do."

"What can I say?" he defended himself. "I was desperate to fit into your family. I knew I had to get good at Canasta if I was going to win your hand in marriage."

Joanie shook her head, closing her eyes momentarily. "Good-night, Caroline and Dan. Thanks for the fun game."

✝   ✝   ✝

The following few days were spent mostly with Caroline and Dan, shopping, visiting, catching daily Mass, and touring around Calgary. Monday night, though, they had set aside for Joanie's cousin, Mike Ledoux. He had taken an engineering job in Calgary that fall and they had seen him only briefly over Christmas back in Saskatoon.

Mike had played keyboard for *New Spring* for years and was a close friend, as well as cousin, to Joanie. When Brandon came on the scene, Mike, being a faithful young Catholic, took the recent convert to Christianity and mentored him in the faith. He had been Brandon's sponsor in the R.C.I.A. program and also one of Brandon's groomsmen at his wedding.

"I'm glad your work brought you back to Calgary before we had to leave," Brandon said to Mike, shaking his hand in greeting. Mike was a few inches shorter than Brandon, but still a fairly tall guy. "We didn't get much of a visit together Christmas Eve—with the Collinses' house packed full for *Réveillon*. It would have been a shame to have missed out on a real visit here, since we don't get out this way too often."

"No, you sure don't," Mike agreed. "And I was ready for a good dose of Joanie and Brandon, to be honest." He turned to Joanie and gave her a big hug. "You look wonderful, cuz. And I still can't get over that there's a baby on the way," he said, tapping her lightly on her rounded tummy. "That's so awesome." He had a grin from ear to ear.

"Mike, you're the same as ever," Joanie said, mussing up his thick, dark, wavy hair. "I've sure missed having you around." She gave him another hug and then kept her arm around him as they walked into his apartment. "Nice place you have here."

"It's small. It's poorly furnished. But it'll do. I've only had a few pay-cheques to start to build my mansion with," he reminded them. "And student loans suck up a good portion of that."

"No kidding," Joanie said. "But it's quaint . . . and Catholic," she said, pointing to the crucifix and the pictures of the Sacred Heart of Jesus and the Immaculate Heart of Mary. "What else do you need?"

Mike laughed and shrugged his shoulders. "I guess."

Joanie and Brandon sat down on the somewhat worn, second-hand couch, while Mike sat across from them on the loveseat. "I've got a friend coming over in a little while, but I wanted to have a chance to visit with you two, first," he informed them. "Can I get you anything?"

"No, we're great," Joanie answered. "So . . . *who's* the friend?" she asked in that female way of knowing that he meant a girl.

"Ashleen Cole. She's a girl I met here a month or so ago. We've been seeing each other now for a little while, and I wanted her to meet you two."

"Ashleen's a pretty name," Joanie remarked.

"Irish background," Mike noted.

"Catholic girl?" Joanie asked, her eyes widened with curiosity.

Mike hesitated. "No. Which is why I wanted to talk to you."

"So what's the deal?" Brandon asked. "How d'you meet?"

"We met at a party through work. Ashleen had come with another guy, actually," he said with a laugh. "But the guy was a jerk and got drinking too much. When I saw them getting ready to leave together I stepped in. I didn't think it was right for him to drive home drunk. Ashleen was quite relieved. I drove them home. The guy was right out of it. I dropped him off at his house and then took Ashleen home. Calgary's a big city. It was a long car ride, and we had a chance to talk. Since neither of us were drunk, we had quite a good conversation. And a week or so later I called her up. She wasn't seeing that guy anymore, and so . . ."

"So you stepped in," Joanie said with a smile. "Mike, you are a smooth-mover," she said accusingly to the good-looking young man. "I've never known you to have a girlfriend."

"Ashleen's the first girl I've dated steadily. And she was totally freaked out about the idea of courtship, so I just suggested to her that we go out together for a while, spend some time together getting to know each other as friends, and then see what happens from there."

"And so, what's happening?" Brandon asked.

"Well, we're more than friends, I guess. We're not exactly courting. . . . I have to admit, I'm feeling quite isolated in my faith-walk out here in Calgary. I just don't know anyone else who's Catholic. I mean, yes, we have a few cousins out here, but I'm older than all of them. It's not the same kind of support we had back in Saskatoon. And I'm just feeling a little too awkward to push the point with Ashleen."

"Is she not Christian at all?" Joanie asked, cautiously.

"Actually, she's quite anti-Christian," Mike answered, somewhat shamefully. "She's a self-proclaimed atheist. And I keep wondering to myself, 'Why am I going out with this girl?' I really like her. Yet I know the relationship can't go any further unless something changes. Then I think about you two, and what a heathen *he* was when you met him, Joanie," Mike said, pointing a finger toward Brandon with a laugh.

Brandon nodded his head, raising his hands up in front of him, "No argument here."

"But that was different," Joanie said. "I didn't start going out with Brandon until he had accepted Christ into his life. And he was never hostile—I mean after that point—to the Catholic faith. By the time we were courting, he was eager to learn about God, and that gave us something to build our relationship on as we studied our faith together," she reminded Mike.

"I know," Mike said. "But I'm not sure how to break things off with Ashleen now. I just feel like I need to give it a chance—long enough for her to see what it means to be Christian. She's a really nice girl, Joanie. Smart, talented . . . good-looking," he added with a smile. "She's got a lot of great qualities about her. But . . ."

"But she's not Catholic," Joanie cut in. "She's not even Christian, Mike. I just think you should be careful."

"You know after Joanie and I began courting, which I did because her father insisted on it, and it seemed to make good sense to me," Brandon added, "I went out and started reading more on the topic. One thing that really struck me, Mike, was one of the differences between dating and courtship. You might date someone whom you would not consider marrying, but you would never begin courting someone whom you didn't think was a suitable choice for marriage."

"It's just that when you begin a courtship the stakes are higher," Joanie jumped in. "It's pointing toward marriage the whole time—so you're always aware of it."

"And boy, are your ever aware of it!" Brandon added.

Joanie threw a sideways glance at Brandon, and he winked back at her in his disarming way. Mike laughed at the young couple. "Yeah, I hear what you're saying, Brandon."

"The thing about dating is that you just go out for fun, or for companionship, or for whatever reason . . . and so you might find yourself going out with just anybody," Brandon pointed out. "But after a while the relationship can just become a habit, and you maybe end up even getting married—but to someone whom you would've never considered for marriage. It's just a habit you couldn't break."

Mike sat there nodding. "That's pretty much what's happening here. And to be honest, I've really compromised my standards with this girl. I mean, I never even intended to kiss her, but she's fairly experienced with guys and was putting a lot of pressure on me for a physical relationship, which I've kept really limited. But even at kissing, I know I've compromised with her, and that frustrates me. It's just so hard—without a courtship framework or mentality—to even talk about boundaries, let alone establish them. Ashleen just keeps trying to push the line with me, and I keep wondering where the line really is—if it's there at all! I just feel like I need a good kick in the pants. And I was kind of hoping the two of you would be the ones to do it for me!"

Joanie laughed and kicked her foot up toward Mike from where she was sitting. "Mike I'd be more than happy to kick you. I love you enough to want what's best for you. And I can't say that what you're telling us sounds that great."

"I think you need to break things off with this girl for a while," Brandon stated. "I think you need to lay it on the line with her. State your expectations, in terms of faith. You want to marry a church-going, practising-Catholic girl, Mike. If she's interested in coming along for the ride, then you can begin to introduce her to the faith so she can see it for herself. And I know you're a good teacher when it comes to the faith there, buddy."

"And you said you wanted to stick with her long enough to show her what it means to be a Christian—but are you showing her what a Christian really is, or is she just dragging you down with secular living?" Joanie threw out at her cousin.

Mike stretched his arms up and heaved a sigh, bringing them back down again. "No, I'm not living up to it, Joanie. And yes, Brandon, I know you're right. I would have been disappointed if you hadn't said that to me. But somehow I thought that hearing it from you would boost my motivation to actually act on it."

"And it doesn't?" Joanie asked.

Mike shook his head. "Nope. I'm still feeling like a coward."

Brandon reached up and scratched the back of his neck. Raising an eyebrow, he posed the question. "Mike, how's your own faith life these days? You going to church regularly and praying daily?"

Mike looked down at the floor in front of him and thought for a moment. "Not so good. When I first came out here I was pumped and ready to go. I church hopped for a while—trying to find a community of faith like I had had back home, but I didn't connect with anyone anywhere. I didn't miss Mass on Sunday at all. But after a while, week after week went by and Sunday Mass just became a matter of obligation, not choice. I still hop around from parish to parish. Haven't made any Catholic friends yet. And as for praying, well, I'm sorry to say that my prayer life has really gone down hill."

"So what do you do everyday after work?" Joanie asked.

"Go out with Ashleen. We go to bars. She likes dancing. We take in movies."

Joanie hung her head, disappointment apparent in her eyes. "Mike, there's so much more to you than that!" she scolded, waving her hand in the air at the man seated across the room from her. "I grew up with you. You're way more fun and dynamic and talented a person than that. To think of you hanging out at bars and wasting your time on movies just kills me!"

"I agree, Joanie," Mike said humbly. "And I know it's killing me, too, at least spiritually it is."

"You know I don't know about the scene here in Calgary. It's a big city, and I'm sure you could connect with some Catholics who are really solid in their faith. But it's finding them that's the challenge," Brandon remarked. "And I've seen it in Saskatoon. Kids come in from the towns around the province. So often they've had no Catholic community to speak of to grow up with. C.C.E. picks up the slack at university and propels some of them along in their faith. But how many kids never hear about C.C.E., or never have an opportunity to connect with a vibrant faith community? How many good kids grow up and lose their faith for lack of community?"

"The lack of youth ministry in our Church is deplorable," Joanie stated. "It's always been something that has irked my parents, which is why they pushed so hard to have a good youth group at our parish."

"And it's one reason we started up *New Spring*," Mike added.

"Exactly!" Joanie exclaimed, pointing at Mike. "So where's your evangelical drive there, boy? You used to lead our praise and worship nights! Why'd you let it all go?"

"'Cause he needs community, Joanie," Brandon answered. "And he's going to get off his butt and find one," he added, looking straight at Mike. "And you're going to find a place where you can get to weekday Mass on a regular basis, and you're going to start spending some time in prayer before the Blessed Sacrament."

Mike sat and nodded.

"I mean it, Mike," Brandon stated authoritatively. "I didn't journey in my faith with you as far as I did to see my guide fall off the path. You're getting back up on your feet, starting right now tonight, and you're going to find your way back into the heart of your faith where you belong."

Mike was still nodding, listening.

"Here," Brandon called out, tossing a rosary across the room to his friend—he always carried one in his pocket. "You remember how to use one of those things?"

Mike laughed and nodded again, looking Brandon in the eye.

"Well, go find yours and let's pray together, before Ashleen shows up," he said.

Mike stood up and went to his bedroom. It took a few minutes but he came back with the sought-after item.

"I was beginning to think you were going to come back empty-handed," Brandon remarked.

"I was beginning to wonder in there, myself," Mike stated. "It was buried deep—but not lost."

"Buried treasure is always worth the effort it takes to uncover it," Brandon said. "Let's begin."

The couple and the cousin prayed the joyful mysteries of the rosary, reflecting on Christ's life through the eyes of His mother: the one who knew Him best here on earth, and who remains the closest to her Son and the Blessed Trinity in heaven, and the one who desires most for us to know Him and to love Him.

Following the rosary, Brandon said, "I'll be calling you once a week, Mike, and we're going to do some Scripture study together over the phone. We'll get this turned around in no time."

"Thanks, guys," Mike said. "I needed you to do exactly what I knew you would do. And I'm feeling better. Actually, I'm feeling a lot better. It reminded me of old times and whetted my appetite for more. I can't believe how far away I had let myself get. But I'm good to go now." Then he looked at Brandon and said, "And I think I need to do some butt-kicking myself."

"Oh?" Brandon asked. "Whose butt?"

"Yours," Mike replied. "You know as we were praying the rosary I was thinking about what you were telling me, in terms of the lack of community for so many Catholic kids, especially in the rural parts of the province. I know that's true. I remember those kids coming in from small towns when we were in C.C.E. So often they came from towns where there were no other young families going to church. They were so isolated."

Brandon nodded in agreement, waiting for Mike to make his point.

"*You* should start up a ministry, Brandon," Mike said, as if he was stating the obvious. "You and Joanie," he added, looking at his cousin.

"That might be a little challenging now," she said, pulling at the hem of her maternity top to remind her cousin of her condition.

"True, but I still think there's a calling for you there. I mean you two are the perfect combination—a powerhouse of faith, loaded with talent, a great conversion testimony, a great courtship story, wonderful role models, jam-packed with knowledge of the Church and Her teachings. You should be organizing retreats and inviting kids out from wherever you can find them. Draw them in out of the woodwork and get them pumped about their faith," Mike suggested, his voice ringing with enthusiasm.

"It's something that's run through my mind a few times," Brandon admitted.

"It has?" Joanie asked. "Why haven't you said anything to me?"

"You were so sick. I missed the ministry work we did in *New Spring*, and yet I felt called to do something other than just the band. Then we talked about recording music together, but still that didn't seem like enough—by itself," Brandon explained. "Now as Mike's talking, I think he's on to something here. I can't say I had exactly considered that idea. But it's speaking to my heart, that's for sure."

"Brandon, you can reach the kids where they're at because you lived the secular life. You know how empty it is. You know the joy you experienced when you found Christ. And you've got the desire to bring souls to Christ, like I've hardly ever seen in anyone before," Mike said, assessing the candidate for the job.

"We'll pray about it," Brandon answered, looking at Joanie beside him.

"I guess I know what we'll be talking about, all the way back to Saskatoon," she stated with mild sarcasm. "Thanks, Mike, for getting Brandon all primed up for me to deal with now."

"No problem," he said with a laugh. "Thank *you* for getting me all primed up, too."

They visited some more as they waited for Ashleen. Finally the phone rang. It was Ashleen calling to cancel.

"Must not have been meant to be," Mike stated, after getting off the phone. "She knew that you two were the ones I had mentioned when I tried to tell her about courtship. I think she was a bit intimidated to meet you."

"That's okay," Joanie said. "I'm glad we have more time alone with you, Mike."

They ordered some Chinese food for supper and kept on visiting, catching up on life, reminiscing about old times. The evening passed way too quickly, and before they realized it, it was after midnight. Mike had to get up early for work, and Joanie and Brandon had to leave the next day for Saskatoon since they both had to work on Wednesday. They said their good-byes and Brandon reminded Mike about their telephone Scripture studies. Mike laughed and assured Brandon that he would be holding him to that. Joanie gave her cousin one last hug, then she and Brandon left.

✟   ✟   ✟

The young couple arrived at their apartment late Tuesday evening, tired out from the late nights they had spent in Calgary. Despite his fatigue, Brandon could not hold back his enthusiasm over the idea of beginning a youth ministry. Joanie shared his excitement, but was concerned at how they could possibly work it out between work and the family life that would soon be upon them.

"We'll just keep praying about it, dear," Brandon told her. "I'm not going to start up anything without some serious discernment. And a few signs from heaven pointing us in this direction would be helpful," he added, looking upward.

Joanie laughed, yawning and stretching as she walked to the bedroom. "I'm wasted," she told Brandon. "So if you want to sit up and pray for a while, that's fine with me, but I'm going to bed or I'll never make it to work in the morning."

"Good-night, honey," Brandon called out after her. "I'll get these things unpacked, and I'll be coming to bed soon."

She waved over her shoulder, without turning around.

Brandon got to work putting away things from their trip. Being the neat-freak that he was, he could not stand to leave the place in disarray at night. There was nothing worse than waking up to a mess.

Finally, he was done. He sat in his big, black leather chair and picked up his Bible. Searching for a sign from heaven, he hoped he might find something there. After reading different passages for about half-an-hour he realized he was either trying too hard, or God was telling him to be patient. Either way, he did not get the satisfaction he was seeking in his discernment process. Resolving to let the issue rest for a while, until the Lord brought it up again, Brandon went to bed.

He crawled into bed beside his wife, who was sound asleep. Admiring her beauty as she lay peacefully on the pillow next to him, he carefully pulled back a long curl that was lying over her face. Then kissing her gently on the forehead, Brandon lightly made the sign of the cross there with his thumb, and whispered good-night to his bride.

Chapter 33

Connor was waiting at the depot when Amie's bus arrived Saturday afternoon. He jumped up and ran over to the door as she stepped down off the bus. "Hi, Amie," he said, full of enthusiasm. "You made it."

"I did," she replied.

There was an awkward moment where she knew he probably wanted to hug her, but she just did not feel right about it. The whole bus trip down to Regina she questioned herself about this courtship. What was she doing? She kept waiting for a sign to prove to her that Connor was *the one*. Maybe a few days with his family would set it straight for her. She was nervous, though. Somehow she felt she was coming under false pretences.

She had talked to her mother and father quite at length the night before. They had encouraged her to call things off until she found the appropriate feelings to go with the status of their relationship. That made sense to her. But how could she break up with Connor over the phone, two days after Christmas? And how could she travel to Regina to spend two days with his family, just to dump him?

No. She was determined this was it. *Lord, if You want me to fall in love with this boy, it's now or never. I'm leaving it completely up to You.*

Connor picked up her bags from the bag check and carried them to his car parked out in front of the depot. Amie walked beside him and they made small talk about Christmas.

Connor's family had all been home for Christmas, but his oldest sister and brother had left with their families on Friday. There was just his brother, Craig, who was two years older than Connor, and his fifteen-year-old sister, Abby, at home now. Craig was going out for the evening, so Amie would meet him tomorrow. Abby had wanted to come with Connor to the station to get Amie, but he wanted a chance to spend some time alone with her before he brought her to the house.

"Where would you like to go for supper?" he asked. "Any preferences?"

"It's your hometown. Whatever you choose will be fine with me."

"You like pasta?"

"Love it," she said.

He decided to take her to an Italian restaurant not far from his parents' house. It had wonderful Italian décor, but was crowded and noisy, with light classical music being piped in over the chatter at every little table and booth. They managed to get a little table off to the side, not quite as private as a booth, but tucked in out of the way enough that they could enjoy some conversation all to themselves.

About half-way through the meal Connor asked Amie a question for which she was not entirely prepared. He set aside his fork and, with his blue eyes looking into her own, asked, "Amie, are you happy that you're courting with me?"

Amie had just taken a mouthful of pasta. She set down her fork and covered her mouth awkwardly while she chewed her food. She was grateful to have an excuse not to deliver an answer immediately to the question. What would she say? How was she to answer this sensitively?

She swallowed with great effort and took a sip of water from her glass. Looking back up at Connor, who had not taken his eyes off her since he had thrown the question out in the air, she confessed, "I don't know what to say, Connor."

"It's a straightforward question, Amie," he said with a little chuckle, bringing some levity to a very charged moment. "Are you happy or not?"

"I am, and I'm not," she told him, plainly.

"Can you explain that to me?"

"I'm happy that you're such a great guy and that I can feel so completely safe with you. You're so honourable and respectful. And I keep telling myself I should be thrilled that I have such a great guy interested in me."

"But you're not," he said.

"No," she answered softly. "I'm not. There's something missing inside of me and no matter how I try to muster up the feelings, they don't come. And I keep wondering what's wrong with me. I must be crazy, because I can feel this opportunity slipping out of my grasp. But my grasp just keeps loosening," she said, holding her hands open in front of her.

"I thought as much," he told her. "But I just needed to see you one more time to be sure, before I brought it up."

"Connor, I don't want to hurt you," Amie stated. "I really like you and respect you, and I'm so mad at myself that I wasn't honest enough—with myself—when this whole thing began. I just wanted so much to have it work out. I want to court a wonderful guy—just like you—and get married and start a family right away. But . . . obviously, it mustn't be you, or I'd be feeling differently inside. Wouldn't I?"

"Well, personally, I'd kind of like the girl that I marry to actually fall in love with *me*, not just the *idea* of me." He winked at her playfully.

"You're not angry with me?" she asked, almost in amazement.

"How could I be angry with you? Amie, a courtship is all about discerning whether or not God's calling us to marriage or not. I think we've discerned that quite plainly. So, I'd say the courtship was a success."

"Do you really feel okay with all this?" she asked again.

"I'd feel worse if we had kept it going on longer, and it had ended up like this. But I knew when I asked you that you were unsure of your feelings. And I was okay with that. I figured if we gave it a go those feelings would either come or they wouldn't. And they didn't. So, it must not be meant to be."

"I don't think it is," she told him.

"I'm fairly sure God's calling me to marriage," he told Amie. "And I'm placing my bet that that's your vocation as well. So I'm just glad that we were able to walk into this relationship with pure intentions, and walk out of it with our purity still intact."

Amie smiled. "Oh, Connor. I just hope the Lord finds me a man as good as you! I really mean that! I just wish I could fall in love with you and get it over with. But I know you're right. I've given it every chance I could, and those feelings just aren't there. And in my heart, I know it wasn't meant to be. But I still feel bad that I didn't have the courage to just come out and be honest with you about that."

"I don't feel bad at all," he assured her. "Amie, *you* are an awesome girl—just the kind I hope to marry someday. And it has been an honour having spent time with you these past few weeks. I've learned a lot."

"Yeah? Like what?"

"Like the fact that I'm not going to ask a girl to court again, unless I'm first convinced that she's interested in me."

Amie laughed. "Tough lesson to learn."

"It was mixed with pleasure," he assured her. "I had a lot of fun with you and your family."

"Oh! My family! My brothers and little sister are going to be *so* upset with me. They just loved you, Connor!"

"There you go . . . at least someone had feelings for me," he said with a laugh. "So it wasn't all for naught. Maybe I could just wait for Jessie to grow up—give her fifteen years or so."

Amie laughed. "You really are something special, aren't you, Connor?"

"Oh, I don't know about that. I've had a few days back home with my family to think about it. And I talked it over with my mom and dad. Really, my mother's insights were the most helpful to me. She told me that when she and Dad started going steady, she could hardly contain all her excitement. She was just floating on air. She couldn't wait to see Dad between dates. And she was so happy—the whole world knew it. So then I compared that to my impression of your feelings regarding our relationship. . . ."

Amie put a hand to her forehead, covering her eyes, and peeked between her fingers at Connor. "I'm so embarrassed, Connor."

"Don't be. You were just being who you were—true to your feelings, or lack thereof. But it was better that way. It kept me on guard. I kept hoping for more, but when it didn't come, my expectations lessened all the time."

Amie heaved a sigh and smiled apologetically at the young man sitting across the table from her.

"So, I decided that when I came to pick you up this evening, I was going to lay all the cards on the table. My family knows that we might not still be courting by the time we get to our house. And they're all okay with that. Really, they are," he assured Amie.

"What did you tell them?"

"I just said that I had a feeling that our courtship was not going to last and that I wanted to give you a chance . . . for us to end it before you came to meet my family. I just didn't want you meeting them under false pretences or anything. I thought it'd be easier on everyone if the expectations were lessened all 'round."

"Connor," Amie said. "Thank you. I don't think I deserved to have been treated as well as you've treated me, but you are such a gentleman. And I want you to know that I have fond memories of our time together—but I'm very glad, too, that neither of us compromised ourselves in any way for our future spouses." She smiled at Connor and reached across the table to put her hand on his. "Thank you."

"You're welcome, Amie," he said sincerely.

They finished their meal, and Connor drove Amie to his house to meet his family before he took her to her aunt and uncle's place to sleep. They enjoyed two days of family fun together. The Eastons were so similar to the Collins family. They loved to play board games and cards, and the two days went by faster than Amie could have expected. When it finally came time to leave, Amie made her good-byes to the family, giving them each a big hug. She really felt she had made good friends and was honoured that they had welcomed her into their home with such hospitality.

The car ride back to Saskatoon was totally pleasant and fun. In fact, Amie confessed that she had never enjoyed her time with Connor more than after they had broken up.

"You definitely are way more relaxed," he told her. "Just like the Amie I had known before all this began."

"Are you still okay with everything?" she asked him.

"Perfect," he told her. "I'm more than ready to move on to whatever God has for me next. And I don't regret a thing."

They arrived back to the city by mid-afternoon, and Connor carried

Amie's things up to the door. "If you don't mind, I don't think I'll come in right now. I'd rather let you tell your family in your own way, and I'm sure I'll see them around again."

"You better. You promised to teach my brothers how to wrestle," she reminded him.

She asked if he was still planning to come out to their New Year's Eve gig. He was. After all, there would be plenty of other friends there to visit with—and he and Amie were still friends.

She gave him a big hug. Somehow it was so much easier to do that now that they were not going out. *No strings attached,* she told herself, remembering the gift Connor had given her. *Thank you, St. Cecilia. You helped to guard our hearts well.*

Chapter 34

Kathy Bander stood on the steps listening to her son drumming. His back was to her, and he was not aware that he had an audience. She waited until there was a break and then she spoke. "You coming up for lunch, son?"

Kyle turned and looked at his mother. "I don't feel much like eating right now. Do you mind if I pass?"

"That's fine," she answered. "It's just you and me for lunch today. David's at work, and your father's delivering some things to some customers. He won't be back until later this afternoon."

Kyle sat at his drum set silently.

"Something on your mind, Kyle, that you'd like to talk to me about?"

He cast his eyes down thoughtfully and then looked back up at his mother. "I've just been thinking lately that maybe I should have contemplated the call to the priesthood a little more seriously."

"That's a sudden change for you, Kyle," his mother commented. "I've never heard you mention any desire to become a priest before."

"That's because I didn't have any," he informed her.

"And so . . . you do now?" she questioned, walking over to sit on the piano bench at the keyboard in front of the drums.

"I'm not sure. I had a good talk with Fr. Steve just before Christmas. Just listening to him talk about priesthood really makes me think about it more. But I'm still not sure if it's for me."

"I'm glad to hear you're keeping yourself open to the option," she affirmed. "But I think this has more to do with Amie's courtship with Connor than it does with God calling you to the priesthood, doesn't it?"

Kyle shrugged and nodded in agreement. "I guess it does."

"And it seems to me that God is no more interested in being picked up on the rebound, than any girl or guy would be," she suggested.

Kyle smiled and raised a finger in the air. "On the contrary, Fr. Steve claims that's where God caught him."

"I guess he knows what he's talking about," she said, willing to be corrected. "But I'm sure that by the time Fr. Steve made that decision, he was no longer rebounding."

"No," agreed Kyle. "He was fairly solid in his calling by that point. It's just that it took that circumstance to get his attention in the first place. I'm just wondering if that's what God's doing with me right now. I guess I just want to make sense of it all, and use this time to make myself a better man for whatever God is calling me to do with my life." Kyle looked at his mom. Was she convinced of his sincerity?

"Well, it's all right for you to discern your vocation, Kyle. And I certainly appreciate you wanting to make yourself a better man." She leaned forward and looked intently at her son. "Just don't go jumping off the deep end . . . just because all your childhood dreams seem to be shattering before your very eyes." She punctuated her advice with a smile and a wink.

"Very funny, Mom. I'll remember how compassionate you were someday when I'm a priest, and you come to me for confession." He pointed at her with his drumsticks.

Kathy laughed at her son. "Come on, Kyle," she said, standing up. "Come upstairs with me to eat. You have to get ready to go for your gig tonight, and I want to enjoy some last bit of time with you this year. I won't be seeing you again until next year," she reminded him.

Kyle put down his sticks and walked upstairs with his mom to have a bite of lunch.

✝   ✝   ✝

New Year's Eve found Amie flying high as she was getting ready to go out for their gig. She had a new lease on life.

"That's it," she told her mom and dad. "I'm sworn off from guys for a good long while. I've bungled up the only two attempts I've had since I decided I was ready to court, and I'm done with it. I'm not going looking anymore."

"I'll believe that when I see it, Scuttle-Butt," her dad replied.

"Seriously, Daddy, I'm done. The only guy I need in my life right now is Jesus. And it'll be up to Him to find me the right guy when the time is right. I'm officially off the market."

"Well, I'm glad to see you've come to your senses," her mother said. "I was starting to worry that you just might be headstrong enough to have talked yourself into marrying Connor. And I just knew he wasn't the right one for you. Don't get me wrong. I like Connor and all. But I think I had more feelings for the poor boy than you did."

Amie laughed. Her mom was right—as usual. "I should learn to listen better, Mom. And I will. I am learning . . . even if my lessons seem to always come the hard way."

"I'm just glad you don't need to learn about drugs," John stated. "If you have to learn your lessons the hard way, let's keep them to simple subject matter."

Amie gave her dad a light tap on the front of his shoulder. "You enjoyed every minute of that courtship, didn't you?" she threw out in accusation.

"Maybe I did," he said with a laugh. "I gave your relationship with Connor two weeks, and it was two weeks later that you broke up with him," he informed his daughter, with pride.

"Dad!" Amie exclaimed. "That's so mean."

"Not at all, Scuttle-Butt," he returned. "I'm just keeping my father-antennae tuned in to my children. And I was bang on with you."

"Humph," she exclaimed, muffled under her breath, but soon she found herself laughing. "Exactly two weeks?"

"Less a day," he confirmed.

"Well . . . you just keep those antennae screwed in the right way," she advised him, as she approached and began playfully pulling at his hair to make antennae.

He took his daughter in his arms and gave her a hug. "I'm glad my Amie's back," he whispered in her ear.

"Thanks, Dad. . . . Well, I'd better get myself ready to go out, or we'll be late," she told her parents.

Amie and Katie finished getting dressed up for the evening, each in their formal attire. Amie's dress was deep blue, with a light, long-sleeve cover over top—as most dresses in the stores came strapless, even in the winter. Katie had designed her own outfit with a skirt to mid-calf, out of a black, elegant material. It had a matching black camisole, over which she wore a dark green, three-quarter-length sleeve sweater.

While it was their priority to dress modestly, Amie and Katie worked hard to demonstrate their ability to stay in-touch with current styles to the best of their abilities—given a limited budget. It was not always easy, but both girls were stubborn enough to make it work.

Finally ready to go, they said good-night and "Happy New Year" to everyone as they left. As the two sisters drove off for their gig, they laughed with each other at Amie's "air-headedness" over the past few months. Katie told Amie it felt good to have her sister back to normal. "Whatever normal really is, when you're referring to Amie," Katie added.

Amie laughed. It was all very true. She did not mind being the topic of humour for her family. She was running on renewed convictions, and no one was about to bring her down.

✟   ✟   ✟

They arrived and began helping to set up equipment in the hall where the dance was being held. It was a C.C.E. event, and it was a fairly big one at that. There would be about two hundred in attendance, all having just participated in a New Year's retreat for the past three days. These youth were pumped and ready to praise God into the New Year.

Kyle took note of Amie's happy demeanour. He had not seen her looking like that for a while. She was bubbly, with enough energy to fill the hall. She joked around as she set up equipment. It was the old Amie back in full form.

Courtship must really be agreeing with her, he figured. She had spent a few days down with Connor's family. The time must have confirmed her decision—Amie certainly had that glow about her that a girl would have when she was in love.

She was beautiful. She was everything she had ever been to Kyle and then some. And . . . she was someone else's girl, not his, he reminded himself, so it was not for him to be admiring her like some school boy in love. *Detach,* he warned himself.

Connor came into the hall with some other friends. When Amie saw him she went up to greet him with a hug. He just laughed and teased her that had she been this free with her hugs while they were courting, they would probably still be together. She laughed and told him she had to get back to setting up. She just wanted to be sure he was still okay with everything . . . and he was.

Kyle watched the young couple at the door. Amie was all decked out in her formal dress; Connor, in a suit. They looked good together. Really, he should have been happy to see Amie so happy. Connor was certainly looking happy. Why should he not? He had the best girl in his arms.

Detach, man. You're going to be a wreck if you don't just let this whole thing go! Okay, Jesus. I'm not doing this very well on my own strength. So, I'm asking You to help me be the friend I'm meant to be to Amie and Connor and be happy for them. In Your Name, Lord, please give me some peace.

Amie walked back up on the stage and sat at the keyboard in front of the drum set. "You need any help with that?" she asked Kyle, as she watched him set his cymbals.

"I'm doing fine," he answered, a little abruptly for Kyle.

"You okay tonight?"

"Perfect."

"You don't seem to be yourself," she pressed the point. "Come on, Kyle. It's Amie. You can talk to me."

He looked up at the beautiful girl sitting before him, her curly hair hanging loosely around her face and neck. He shook his head to himself and went back to work on his set of drums.

"Come on, Kyle!" Amie said, walking over to him. "What's bugging you?"

"Amie, it's . . ." he fumbled for words. "I'm just having to deal with some personal stuff right now, and I'm sorry if I was abrupt with you."

"Kyle," she said softly, placing her hand on his arm. "I'm okay. I just want *you* to be okay, 'cause you're my friend."

The warmth of her touch matched that of her statement. She was completely being sincere with him in her friendship, and he scolded himself for failing to be the friend for her that he knew he should be.

"I'm okay," he told her with a smile. "Thanks."

She smiled and patted his arm. "I'm here if you need a friend," she said, turning back to take her place

"Hey, Amie," he called to her.

She turned and looked back at him.

"You look great tonight, like you're ready to party . . . so let's get on with it!" His smile was somewhat forced, but she appreciated his effort to get into the groove of the evening.

"You look awesome there yourself, sir. But then you always did look good in a suit! Who knows? Maybe I can even find you a girl here tonight," she said with a wink and a sly smile.

The humour was not lost on Kyle. The old Amie was back—the one he had not seen for a few weeks, but definitely the one he had come to know and love.

New Year's was a special celebration with C.C.E. It was a time for partying and praising to maximum capacity. The excitement built throughout the evening until the countdown to midnight. Finally the New Year was brought in with all the cheers, whistles, hooting, and hollering that a group of two hundred plus university students can create.

The band went around, greeting each other with a New Year's hug. When Amie met up with Kyle she gave him an extra big hug—because he was such a good friend, and because she knew he needed it tonight.

He held her in his arms and hugged her back, almost afraid to let go—lest she see the pain in his heart through his eyes. He turned away, before she had the chance.

She continued greeting friends with her new-lease-on-life enthusiasm. When she met up with Connor he laughed and warned her not to look so happy—it was giving him a bad reputation, since others had heard the news of their break-up. She apologized, and he laughed with her, giving her a big hug. "I'm just teasing. You're radiant tonight, Amie. And I'm happy to see that."

With a group like C.C.E., New Year's hugging took quite a while for everyone to work their way through the crowd. Finally the band reassembled and began playing *Auld Lang Syne*, the traditional song of the New Year. Amie played away, her hands floating over the keyboard with a truly graceful touch. Indeed, she had been touched by grace that night: the grace of reclaiming her first love in life—Jesus.

As the band disassembled at the end of the night, Kyle quickly worked at taking down his set. Amie stepped over to help, as she could not carry her keyboard out by herself anyway. She usually got Kyle to give her a hand in exchange for her helping him with his drums.

"I can manage. Why not go visit with some friends," he suggested.

"I am. You're my friend, Kyle. Even if you're not that interested in my friendship this evening," she said in a slightly disgruntled tone—for added effect.

"I am so," he said. "I just thought that you'd want to say good-night to Connor."

Amie turned and saw him walking out the door with some friends. She waved enthusiastically from the stage, and he waved back.

Ann Ledoux came over to offer a hand. It was late and they had to be out of the hall at a certain time. "You sure missed the boat on that one," Ann scolded Amie as she looked at the doorway through which Connor had just left.

"Why?" Amie asked.

"Connor's such a great guy," she said. "I can't believe you let him go."

"He's all yours if you want him, Annie," Amie teased her cousin.

"Like I'd take your leftovers on the rebound! I have more self-respect than that."

"Oh, he's not rebounding," Amie assured her. "He was quite okay with our break-up."

Kyle listened as he packed equipment. He did not say a thing—not sure if he was hearing what he thought he had heard, or if he was hearing what he had hoped to hear.

"What d'you think about it?" Ann asked the drummer.

"About what?" Kyle asked, not looking up.

"Amie and Connor's courtship has come to an end—after only two weeks," she informed him. "Doesn't that surprise you?"

"Why should it?" he asked.

"Because Amie's the one who's been mooning over getting married for so long now," Ann threw out, "I just figured she'd marry the first guy who came around, and she wouldn't look back. But I was wrong."

"I keep telling you, Annie," Amie said to her cousin, "I've got room right now in my heart for Jesus, and Jesus alone. I'm done with romance for the time being." She looked down at Kyle who was bent over as he worked. "Now aren't you impressed that I've learned something from you after all these years?"

"From me?" he questioned. "How so?"

"You're always so cool about not dating, not getting involved with a romantic relationship until the time is right. And I've always given you such a hard time about that."

"Yeah," he agreed.

"But now I think that I'm ready to take your advice and just lay low and let Jesus really be my number one," she stated.

"Amie," Kyle said, looking up at the girl, "I can't tell you how glad I am to hear you say something like that."

"Thanks," she said with a big smile. "You know, you can be pretty smart about some things. I should listen to you more often."

"Don't get carried away," he warned her. "I'm just as apt to make a fool out of myself as the next guy. Just keep your eyes focused on Jesus and follow His example, not mine."

Amie patted Kyle on the back. "Well, if you really don't need my help here tonight, Annie and I'll start loading equipment into our van."

Kyle nodded to let the girls move on. He watched Amie as she bounced around the room, laughing with friends and sparkling with that "Amie" passion for life.

No wonder she's more beautiful tonight than usual, Lord—she's got her heart all wrapped up in You, like it should be. I just want to say thanks for giving me a second chance. And since she's going to keep her eyes on You for a while, help me to do the same—just in case You are calling me to something else, other than her.

He paused for a moment and then went on with his conversation with Jesus. *Would You consider me shallow if I admit I hope You don't have something else in store for me?* He shook his head at himself. He was supposed to be learning to love without strings attached. *Man, this whole concept of surrendering never gets easy, does it?*

He smiled at the thought of Amie being free again. *You won't really mind if I just savour the opportunity to hope again that she might be for me—just for a few moments before I let the strings go? Thanks, I was hoping You'd understand.*

Chapter 35

January held a certain excitement for the Collins family—it marked John and Judy's twenty-fifth anniversary. Everyone was involved in the preparations for a celebration at their parish near the end of the month that would involve Mass, supper, and a dance. John wanted to be sure they marked the occasion well. "With all the attacks on marriage in our society," he told his kids, "I want to be sure that you see just how much it means to us."

Amie was in the final stages of preparation for her piano music degree exam. She cut herself off all extra activities for the first two weeks of January, including anniversary preparations and band practice, and buried herself in their family music room when she was not at school. The Sisters of the Immaculate Conception invited her to come and practise on their grand piano whenever she wanted, so Amie took advantage of that offer a few times on her way home from school.

Maggie was thrilled to have Amie there. The aspirant would curl up with a book in one of the armchairs in the corner of the room by the big fireplace. Across the room, the grand piano sat in front of a bay window where one could see the branches of the big willow tree in the yard swaying gracefully in the winter breeze, as if it they dancing to the music coming forth from the young musician's hands.

Amie would practise for an hour straight and then take a fifteen minute break. Maggie attended her sister, as though serving royalty. It was fun. It reminded them of having tea parties together when they were children, only this time they did not have to imagine that they were in a grand old home—they were. They sat together at the two big chairs by the fire, sipped tea, ate cookies or cake, or whatever Maggie could find in the kitchen for them to enjoy together, and they would talk.

"So is religious life all you ever hoped it would be, Maggie?" the younger sister asked.

"I love it! I love it so much, I hardly feel worthy of it. And when I talk to the other Sisters and listen to the struggles that so many of them had to overcome to embrace this life—I feel so spoiled by God, that He's made my path so easy."

"You always were extra special, Maggie. Even we other kids could see God had something special in mind for you. And it suits you. You just seem perfectly at home in this setting," Amie said, motioning with her hand toward the rest of the house that lay beyond the closed French doors.

"Where I feel most at home," Maggie told her, "is in the chapel. I could just spend hours there before the Blessed Sacrament. And now that my internship is done, and I'm just taking classes again, I can go in there and study and pray for hours. I'm home all day Tuesdays and Thursdays—and that's perfect. This time in my life is just pure gift, and I know it's going to come to an end all too quickly and then I'll begin working full-time. So I really appreciate what a luxury it is for now."

Amie was happy for her sister. She shared with Maggie how she too was feeling a particular grace of satisfaction in her own life. "It's like now that I've taken all that pressure off myself about worrying who Mr. Right might be, I'm feeling so completely free. I don't care now how long it takes until I get married—well, within reason," she clarified. "But I'm just enjoying this me-and-Jesus time in my life. And I suddenly appreciate the gift of my singleness in a way I never have before. It's limited time. And it's a gift—because I really have no responsibilities that tie me down, so I can dedicate myself to my studies, and developing my music, and doing youth and music ministry . . . when else am I ever going to be so free?"

"It's true," Maggie agreed. "Even for me, I have to participate in community life—which I love, don't get me wrong. But I'm not free to just do whatever I want all day. I have a responsibility to this community. It's part of religious life, and I gladly choose it. But being single has its own . . . benefits, I guess—for lack of a better word."

"I can see how it's a real vocation," Amie stated. "I guess it's not entirely chosen by some. I know some people fall into it because marriage doesn't work out for them. But I think of Auntie Yvette, and how she gives so much of her time freely to serving others in a way that a married woman couldn't."

"And she's kept herself pure for Christ in the process," Maggie added. "She's not out there living a worldly lifestyle, which so many men and women do."

"She's a great lady," Amie agreed. "I don't know. I guess I'm school-girlish enough to want my prince charming to come and take me away to his castle where we can live happily-ever-after."

Maggie laughed as Amie dramatically waved her arms about.

"It must be hard for women who are getting older, and they still haven't found prince charming. But lately, it occurs to me that Prince Charming *has* swept me off to His Kingdom," Amie said. "And I just want to hold myself in His heart, until some other man proves himself worthy of my love. You know what I mean?"

"I do," Maggie said. "For me, I know I'm going to stay with the Prince. But I think He has a special place for those who live in waiting—hoping to discover whatever He has planned for them."

"I just hope that if the wait is long, I won't lose heart," Amie stated. "Right now, I'm just high on Jesus. And my prayer life has never been more focused. But I think of how Auntie Céline waited until she was past forty before she met and married Uncle Martin."

"And they were never able to have children," Maggie said, "which must have been hard on her—to never have been able to live out that dream."

"You know, I talked to Auntie Céline about it when I was in Regina over Christmas, since I was staying with her and Uncle Martin. Connor and I had just broken up, and even though I wasn't upset, I was just wondering how long I would have to wait for the right guy to come along. She told me that all those long years of waiting for the right man had been worth it all. She's so happy with Uncle Martin now. And to have married the wrong man and to have been miserable all those years would have been much worse than the time spent waiting for what God had in store for her."

"And she didn't exactly waste those years, either," Maggie said.

"No, she didn't," Amie agreed.

"Remember how she would take us out and spoil us when we were little. She was always helping others, and she still is. I've never met a more generous woman with her time and money," Maggie stated. "I actually thought about her a lot a while ago, because Sr. Charlotte was challenging me to consider whether or not God was calling me to single life. I know He's not. But thinking of Auntie Céline and Auntie Yvette just opened my eyes to how noble and self-sacrificing the call to singleness really can be!"

"I have to admit, though, as much as I admire it, I really hope God doesn't call me to it," Amie confessed. "I know it's probably shallow, but I really do want my dreams of my *other* prince charming to come true!"

Maggie laughed at her sister. "I think that's normal, Amie. And I don't think you're alone in that. But I know God's going to grant you the desires of your heart. It just might be in a way you wouldn't ever expect. But if you place your trust in Him, that's where you'll find happiness."

Amie nodded.

Maggie looked up at the clock sitting on the mantle. "Amie! Your fifteen minute break just turned into thirty-five minutes with us yapping." Assuming the tone of a schoolmarm, she said, "You get back to work or you can't come back here to practise anymore."

Amie chuckled at the demand and, with a bit of reluctance, pulled herself out of the cozy armchair. Her passion for playing returned at the sight of the grand and beautiful instrument. Its rich, ringing tone was such a treat—appreciated all the more by a student of such accomplished talents.

✝   ✝   ✝

Finally the day of Amie's piano exam came. She was nervous, as most students are before a performance—especially one that is being evaluated for accreditation. But as she and her mom prayed a rosary together on the way to the exam, she realized that all she needed to do was play for Jesus. She would simply imagine the examiner to be Jesus, if it were a man, or Mary, if it were a woman. One way or the other, her music was going to be played for the King or Queen of Heaven, neither of whom would ever reject her gift to them. She was set and ready to go.

Her confidence was shaken somewhat when the examiner stepped in: a woman of rather stern and impersonal demeanour—not at all Amie's image of the Queen of Heaven. She smiled at the woman, who lifted her eyebrows at Amie and asked if she had chosen to begin with her pieces or technical work. It was right down to business, Amie realized. No time for small formalities like, "Hi, my name is . . ." or anything like that. In all her years of doing exams, she had never come across a more severe-looking examiner.

Amie closed her eyes quickly and searched inside her mind for the most gentle, maternal image of Mary that she could muster up on the spot. She breathed a sigh and looked back up at the examiner. Somewhere, under all that cold, hard façade, was a woman endowed with all the feminine virtues that women possess. That was the place, in her mind, where Amie could find an image of Mary in this woman—and it was for that gentle and maternal woman that Amie was going to perform her exam.

The exam went well. It was long and hard—and the coldness of the examiner never did melt away. But Amie did not care. She kept her focus as she recalled the words of one of her favourite composers, J.S. Bach: "The aim and final end of all music should be none other than for the glory of God and the refreshment of the soul." For this noble purpose alone did Amie play. The results of the exam, grade-wise, were in God's hands.

"How did it go?" her mother asked, as Amie stepped out of the examining room.

"It went. How it went, is up to God," she said with a laugh. "But I'm done, Mom!"

Judy hooked her arm around her daughter's and said, "Let me take you out for lunch, kiddo. It's time to celebrate."

Amie requested that they go to *The Country Corner Café*.

Judy was very impressed with the little restaurant. Together the mother and daughter leisurely spent half the afternoon visiting over fine food, cheesecake, and gourmet coffee. The Collins family did not splurge like that on a regular basis—not with eight children to feed. But occasionally either John or Judy would take out one of their children on a date and lavish their time and attention on that particular child.

Amie had grown up so much—especially over the past few months. Judy realized it would not be long before Amie, too, would be moving on with life. She savoured every moment they spent together that afternoon, as much as she had the cheesecake.

Judy and John stood at the altar at St. James Church and renewed the vows that they had made to each other and to God twenty-five years earlier. Standing behind them, in a line, were their eight children and Brandon. It was the beginning of their celebration. Gathered together for the Holy Sacrifice of the Mass, they received Christ in the Eucharist, from Whom came the graces they all needed to live out their Christian faith.

The party to follow was a typical Collins-style event: much food, much music, and much laughter. The parish hall was packed with relatives and friends. Being part of a large Christian community, as they were, there was no way not to include everyone in their celebration.

The dance went well into the night with everyone involved, from the littlest ones who needed to be carried around on the dance floor, to the grandmas and grandpas who modelled graceful dance movements that harkened back to a time when life was filled with the simple pleasures that were so satisfying.

Amie watched her grandparents dancing a waltz. Her parents, though they looked lovely together, were no match for Grandma and Grandpa Ledoux. Amie longed to learn how to move that gracefully across the dance floor with a man.

That was it! She was signing up for ballroom dancing. She talked to Annie Ledoux about it, and together they decided that they would do their best to organize a group of friends—including the guys—to sign up for the second term dance classes that would soon start up on campus.

As Amie bustled around, talking with friends about their plans, she finally caught up with Kyle. "I'm not much of a dancer," he warned her. "But I'm willing to try. Sounds like fun."

Amie grabbed him by the arm, "Let's give it a whirl here now. This is a two-step, and anyone can dance to that beat—especially a drummer."

"You know, you might give a guy a chance to ask you," he scolded her.

"Well, ask me then," she returned, pausing in her step and letting go of his arm.

He laughed and with grand gesture said, "May I have the honour of this dance, Miss Collins?"

"By all means, kind sir," she replied in feigned southern accent.

The handsome young gentleman, in his black suit, took the elegant girl, in her formal blue attire, on his arm and led her to the dance floor. As he slipped his hand behind her back, and she placed her hand on his shoulder, Amie began to giggle—the formality was broken. Kyle laughed with her, and they began to dance the two-step.

"I definitely could improve on my dancing skills," Kyle commented.

"Actually, you're better than most of the guys. At least you keep the beat."

"And at least you follow my lead. It's hard enough to dance without competing with the girl for the lead."

Amie laughed. She knew it was true. It was hard to fight off the temptation to lead when she was dancing, especially if the guy had a weak lead. Dance classes would definitely help everyone in their group of friends.

"How's life treating you lately?" he asked. "Now that your exam is done and all."

"I'm so relaxed. I just feel so free."

"School's going good?"

"Excellent. I'm actually getting quite good at this hair dressing stuff. There was way more to learn—like get down and study work—than I ever anticipated. But I love it."

"You're good at it."

"Thanks. So how's school going for you?"

"Five months left, and I'm a free man," he announced. "That's going to be a great feeling—although, it's still somewhat intimidating. Then I have to find a job and begin working in the real world. But I'll be glad to be done with the studies. I've got so many assignments constantly on the go, and I'm always feeling bogged down."

"Well, I'm ready to take over youth group again. Thanks for filling in for me."

"My pleasure. What are friends for? But I'm more than ready to give it back to you," he admitted.

They danced through two dances, then Amie thanked Kyle and moved on, flitting about the room like the social butterfly she was. Kyle was glad to have had that much time alone with her on such a busy day and in such a crowded setting. Having held her in his arms to dance only confirmed for him that no other woman would ever fill that place.

Five more months, he reminded himself. *And then I have to figure out how to get Amie to see me for more than just a friend. That part, Lord, is in Your hands. If it's meant to be—which I hope with everything that's in me that it is—You'll have to make it happen.*

✟   ✟   ✟

Mike Ledoux came in from Calgary for the anniversary celebration, bringing with him a lovely young woman with dark hair, hazel eyes, and a complexion like cream.

Joanie and Brandon were happy that things were going well again for Mike. He had broken up with Ashleen, when she refused to have anything to do with religion. Mike spent the following few weeks diving back into his faith with renewed fervour. After two weeks without him in her life, Ashleen had called up Mike again, and they met for coffee to talk.

"I'm not going to pretend," she told him. "I have absolutely no interest in religion at all. But I'm willing to let you *try* to convince me that God exists and that He can make a difference in my life, because I've never known another guy like you, Mike. And I'm not willing to let you walk out of my life without even trying."

Mike was thrilled to have a second chance, only this time he was doing things the right way. "If we get back together then it's going to be a courtship or nothing," he informed her. "And by that I mean that we are setting boundaries to our physical relationship, which will amount to us holding hands and hugging—chastely—for now."

"Doesn't sound like much fun. Wouldn't you rather take me back in your arms and kiss me again?" she offered, enticingly.

"Of course I would," he said with a laugh. "But since I have no idea right now whether or not we'll someday marry, I'm not running the risk anymore of kissing another man's wife. And I plan to save all my kisses, from here on in, for my future wife someday . . . and for her alone."

"What if I am going to be your wife?"

"Then I'll kiss you like nobody's business when you are," he assured her.

"Humph," she grumbled. "So far you haven't convinced me that this whole religion thing is going to be any fun at all."

"No? Well, I'm not worried about that. You either want to get back together with me because of who I am—a devout Catholic man—or you don't, Ashleen. And I'm okay with either. But what I'm not okay with is compromising my morals any longer. I intend to treat you like a lady, with more respect than any man has probably ever given you. And if you don't enjoy that—well, then there's nothing I can do about it. But if you just give me a chance," he said, with a twinkle in his eyes that she found absolutely irresistible, "I'll show you a whole new world."

"Got a magic carpet to go with that offer?" she asked, enchantingly.

"I just might," he said mysteriously. "But you'll have to find that out for yourself."

She heaved a sigh and stared at the tall, dark, and handsome man. "You are so different from any other guy I've ever known," she stated with resignation. "And I have to admit to being completely curious as to what makes you so different. But I'm not promising anything about buying into your faith, Mike."

"Deal. You keep your integrity, and so will I. I won't ask you to compromise your beliefs, and you don't ask me to either. And if along the way Christ gets to you—it'll be all His fault, and not mine. So you'll have to take it up with Him then."

"And you think this two-thousand-year-old dead guy can do that?"

"Absolutely," Mike said, nodding. "But I'll let Him prove that to you in His own way."

So they agreed to set up a courtship relationship, which meant they would discern whether or not they were to get married. For Mike that meant through prayer. For Ashleen that meant through reasoning and assessing her feelings about the relationship. Mike was okay with the difference in their interpretation of discernment for now, as long as she understood that he would never be able to make the step toward marriage unless she had accepted his faith.

Courting also meant that they would observe all kinds of physical boundaries in their relationship, and they would stop spending time in isolation together. Mike had chosen to belong to St. Philomena's Parish in Calgary, because that's where Brandon's mom and step-father went. He had asked them if they would be a mentoring couple for him and Ashleen. Caroline and Dan were more than happy to assist this young couple in their courtship.

And finally, Ashleen agreed to study the faith—purely from an academic point-of-view. Mike was satisfied with that because he knew that the

Catholic faith made perfect sense for those who took off the blinders set up by secular culture. He just prayed that God would remove the blinders from Ashleen's eyes.

Brandon and Joanie went out of their way to spend time together with Mike and Ashleen at the anniversary celebration. Mark and Justine were also there, and that made for a perfect mix. Mark was more than eager to talk about his faith and his excitement at coming into the Church at Easter. Ashleen found him to be quite a curiosity as he insisted he had spent almost ten years of his life as an atheist. He knew the arguments. He knew the stumbling blocks. As the two engaged in conversation, one by one Mark shot down Ashleen's various objections to faith with all the eloquence of natural law to defend his newly-prized belief system.

The entire feeling of the day's celebration impressed Ashleen. Never before had she experienced such closeness in a family or an entire community. Mike had boasted about his family and friends back home, but she always figured that he was exaggerating due to being homesick. Now she realized that perhaps he had understated the case.

By the end of the night Ashleen was sparkling with real enthusiasm. She held onto Mike's hand as though she had found a real treasure with which she would not part. Mike was calm and cool. He obviously was taken with Ashleen's natural charm and beauty, but he was not losing his head over this girl. He was like a rock in his faith these days, and he vowed that he would never step off the *Rock* again!

Chapter 36

"The plumbing in this old house is going to be the death of me yet," declared Sr. Charlotte as she came up from the basement early one cold Tuesday morning in February.

"What's the problem now?" Sr. Thérèse asked.

"There's a leak in the basement. I mopped up the mess, and I've got a pail catching water from the pipe—but someone's going to have to dump the pail every hour or so until Charles can get here," she stated.

"I'm home all day," Maggie mentioned. "Do you want me to take care of that?"

"Would you, dear?" Sr. Charlotte asked. "My brother, Charles, is coming over to fix it. He does all our repair work around here. I can't afford to pay what it would cost to hire all the repairmen needed to keep this old house standing, so I always call upon poor Charles. He's taking over the family farm and is a real Mr. Fix-it. I called him this morning, and he said he could be here shortly after lunch."

"I don't mind," Maggie said. "I'm here anyway. And I can give him a hand, too. I used to help my dad with all kinds of mechanical, electrical, and plumbing things at our old house. I know what you mean about *all* the repairs. My dad swore he would never buy an old house again. But thank goodness, he's a jack-of-all-trades himself."

"I'd appreciate that, Maggie," Sr. Charlotte stated. "I've got to run, I'm late for a meeting at the chancery office this morning and then I'm off to give some talks in a grade three classroom this afternoon."

"And I'm going to be late, too," Sr. Thérèse said, looking at the clock on the wall. "I've got pastoral duty at the hospital this morning." She quickly excused herself as well and left.

Maggie stood in the kitchen of the old house doing breakfast dishes. She had offered to take on extra duties on Tuesdays and Thursdays, since she was home all day from her studies. She loved the time alone in the quiet, old house. Most of the Sisters carried on apostolic work outside of the house throughout the day, or they worked at jobs. There was always someone coming or going, but in general their community life ran in separate directions all day long during the week. The evenings and weekends were when they spent their time together in prayer, common studies, and meetings. And then, of course, it all started over early each morning with prayers and Mass, until the activities of the day pulled them apart once again.

Maggie quickly finished the dishes and decided to get some school work done early so she would be free to help out with the plumbing. She ran down and checked the pail which was half-full. She poked around to assess the leak, while switching the pail and dumping the water. The water was not dripping as fast as Sr. Charlotte had first thought. At the rate it was leaking, she would have a good hour or more before she would have to change it again.

She ran back up to the third floor, taking her back staircase from the kitchen. Two steps at a time was a harder feat to accomplish on the dark, steep staircase, but she loved the extra challenge. By the time she reached the third floor she was completely exhausted—but energized all the same from her morning workout.

Maggie picked up a few text books and went down to the chapel to study and pray. She figured that with Christ watching over her, she could double the effectiveness of her time spent studying.

She had a small lunch; just she and Sr. Pauline were there. Maggie happily offered to clean up the kitchen when they were done so that the older Sister could be off to one of the nursing homes. Sr. Pauline, who was in her late seventies, was retired from nursing but not from life. Many hours of service were still given freely in the community for elderly and shut-in persons.

The older Sister chuckled on her way by the kitchen, seeing Maggie dancing about while doing the dishes. She had come to quite enjoy the energetic company of the young aspirant. Maggie had worked her way into the hearts of all the community, and they into hers.

As she was finishing up, putting away the dishes, the doorbell rang. Maggie ran to the door and opened it. There stood a young man in a winter coat, holding a pail full of tools in one hand and empty water containers in the other. He quickly stepped in out of the cold and stomped his feet on the mat in front of the door.

"You must be Charles," Maggie said, as he set down the pail and two empty five gallon camping jugs. He began to take off his coat.

"Guilty as charged," he replied with a big, friendly smile that showed off his slightly overcrowded white teeth. He pulled off a toque, uncovering his thick, brown, messed-up hair.

"Here, let me take that for you," Maggie offered, reaching for his coat.

"Thanks," he said, passing it to the young lady. As she turned to hang up the jacket, he straightened his hair, instinctively knowing that it would be messy.

"I'm Maggie Collins," she introduced herself, talking over her shoulder to Charles. "I'm one of the two new aspirants here at the Sisters' house this year." She turned back to the young man offering her hand to him.

By this time he had slipped off his boots, and she noticed he was not very tall—maybe three inches taller than she, and she was only five foot five.

He took her hand and shook it, nodding his head in greeting. "Nice to meet you, Maggie," he said, somewhat awkwardly.

"Are you planning on going camping anytime soon?" quipped Maggie, pointing to the large containers.

Charles grinned. "No, but you might be if I can't get the leak fixed today." He reached down to grab his tools and said, "Sr. Charlotte told me I'd find the leaky pipe in the basement."

"You bet; just follow me," Maggie said, as she led the way to the back staircase. "I offered to Sr. Charlotte that I could give you a hand, if you want. I used to help my dad with all the repairs back home—I really love that kind of stuff."

"That's cool," he said with a chuckle. "I don't meet too many girls who like to get messy."

"This girl doesn't care much about whether she's messy or not," Maggie admitted. "I'm from a family of eight kids, second oldest—four girls at the top. By the time my first brother arrived, I had long-since filled in the role as daddy's little helper. It kind of stuck with me. What about you? I didn't expect Sr. Charlotte's brother to be so young. How old are you, anyway?"

"I'm twenty-eight," he told her, "the youngest of the family. There're ten of us kids, and Sr. Charlotte's the oldest. She had actually moved out to the convent by the time I was born, so I've only ever known her as Sr. Charlotte."

"Serious?"

"Yup. She's actually my godmother, which is why I was named Charles."

"That's really cool," Maggie stated. "That must have been weird being her brother and not growing up with her at all, though."

"Actually, I used to see lots of Sr. Charlotte when I was little. I remember coming here as a little boy and playing in all the secret hiding places in this old house. Bet you I could show you some cool stuff around here," he added, with boyish delight.

"I've done my own share of exploring these past few months," she confessed. "This place is great. It'd make for some awesome games of hide and seek."

"And murder in the dark," he told her. "But our screaming kind of freaked out some of the older Sisters, so we had to put the kibosh on that game."

"Yeah," Maggie nodded, "I've given a few of the women around here some good starts. I don't think they were quite prepared for me when I arrived. I've had to tone it down."

He laughed. "Well, I was younger than you when I used to run around this place, but we sure did have fun," he told her in a reminiscing tone, "me and my sister and brother—that is. We were the three youngest kids in my family. Used to get into all kinds of mischief around here." He stopped to look around as they reached the bottom of the stairs.

"I bet you could have," Maggie said. She, too, looked about from the landing of the basement which opened up to rooms in every direction.

"I'm sure you've found the old stairwell that leads from the basement to the second floor?" he asked.

"I use it just about everyday. I like that old staircase."

"Did you ever find the secret passageway through the broom closet beside the dining room?" he asked.

Maggie contemplated whether she should admit to Charles that she regularly employed that route to the dining room. "I stumbled across it one day in my explorations," she said, cautiously.

"Ahhh," he said, figuring he had one up on her, "but did you ever find the secret passageway that connects these two old houses?"

"No," she stated with disappointment. "Where is it?"

"You get to it from the third floor," he said, pointing upward. By this time they had stepped over to where the pail was collecting the leaky water. He looked up at the pipes, craning his head around to assess the situation.

"That's where my bedroom is," she told him. "I've never seen anything that looked like a passageway up there."

"That's what makes it a *secret* passageway," he whispered, his hazel eyes lit up playfully, looking back at the girl.

"Well, now you had better tell me," she warned him, enjoying the intrigue of the conversation. "You can't just come in here and say something like that and leave me hanging."

"It'd be more fun for you to find it yourself," he told her, wiggling the leaky pipe, as he looked back up. "Wouldn't want to ruin the fun for you."

"Charles," she scolded, slapping her hands on her legs, "that's not fair!"

"Tell you what," he said, looking Maggie in the eye. "I'll let you look for it yourself tonight, and if you don't find it, I promise to tell you where it is tomorrow."

"Tomorrow?" she questioned.

"Looking at this mess of pipes, I'll be here a few days, I'm sure. Which is fine," he said with resolution. "Things are slow at the farm these days. It's a better time for a leak than during seeding or harvest."

"I have classes tomorrow morning at campus. I won't get back until two-thirty," she said with disappointment.

"I'm sure I'll still be around when you get home," he assured her.

"You better," she said, waving a finger at him. "You promised."

"And I always keep my promises," he told her.

She smiled back at him, resolved to wait. Actually the fun of exploring the third floor for herself did have a definite appeal. She determined then and there that she was going to find the secret passageway herself, just to prove that she could.

Charles smiled back at the adventurous young woman. In all his years of knowing the Sisters, never before had he met one that was quite as spunky as this Maggie.

"So, what do we need to do?" she asked, turning her attention to the job.

"First I'm going to have to shut the water off to the house to get at this. Can you find some pails to take to each of the bathrooms and fill them with water? I'll go fill those camping jugs for the kitchen, just in case I can't get the water on before I have to leave tonight."

"I can do that," she replied, ready to take on any task. "I guess it's a-camping-we-will-go, after all," she chimed, as she scooted out of the utility room to search for some pails. She was sure she had come across a room with stuff like that before; it was just a matter of remembering which one it was, as there were so many doors to check. At last she came to a room full of all kinds of pails, jars, and boxes. She snooped around until she found a stack of one-gallon pails. That would do the trick.

She went about to the three bathrooms on that side of the house, getting the job done as quickly as she could. She filled four pails for each. With the job accomplished, she ran back down the stairs to report back for duty.

"Done so quickly?" Charles asked.

"Yup, what's next?"

"Oh, I'm just trying to get some of this area cleared away so that I can work in here. For a house this size, you'd think they'd have had the room to make it easier to get in around these pipes and this old boiler. But everything's just so crammed in together," he said, as he worked at squeezing his lithe body into the tight corner. "Good thing I'm a little guy."

Maggie laughed.

"How 'bout once I get into this corner to work, you pass me my tools," he suggested.

"That's a familiar job," she told him.

"Ah, yes. Daddy's little helper. So you should know the names of those tools in there," he pointed to the pail.

"I'll do my best to make my daddy proud," she answered.

He laughed and asked her to pass him a pipe wrench, which she promptly pulled out of the pail and passed to him.

"Scoring one for one," he commented, taking the tool from his assistant.

Over the next few hours, the pair of plumbers worked at their job. They chatted a bit, but for the most part they concentrated on the work they had to do. Maggie had learned over the years to allow her father to work in silence, without her bothering him with constant chatter. Whenever he took a break, was when she could ask questions. Charles was impressed that Maggie really knew what she was doing. Not only did she know the names of the tools, but she knew how to use them. She was a rare girl, indeed.

Finally they came to a standstill in the job. "We can't go on," Charles told her, "until I go pick up parts from the hardware store." He set his tools aside, piled neatly in the corner.

"Do you want to come and have a snack before you take off? I can put on a pot of tea, and we can have crumpets and tea together," she offered as they began walking up the stairs.

"Sounds good," he said. "What are crumpets?"

"I have no idea," Maggie stated. "When I was a kid my sisters and I would have tea parties, with 'crumpets and tea'. We would drink with our pinkies sticking up." She demonstrated, holding up her hands as if drinking tea, and speaking in a lofty tone. "And anything we could find to go with the tea became crumpets—crackers, bread, cookies, cake . . . but the best was when Mom made fresh biscuits, because we always figured that was probably the closest thing to crumpets. But to be honest, I still haven't the faintest idea what a crumpet is." She laughed as she entered the kitchen and stepped over to the stove to put on a kettle of water to boil. "I love this old kettle. We have an electric kettle at home, but it's not the same thing."

Charles sat back and chuckled as Maggie rambled on. She was obviously making up for the past two hours of curbing her inclination to talk.

"Any preference for tea?" she asked, as she looked into the cupboard with all the varieties of tea lined up in boxes.

"I'm easy to please. Go ahead and pick your favourite," he suggested.

"I like spicy teas." She looked until she found a flavour that appealed to her. She turned and showed him the box. "How's Apple Spice?"

"Perfect." He smiled and sat at the island in the big kitchen of the old house. "Cold day out there," he commented, looking out the window into the Sisters' backyard.

"It sure is. I'm glad I got to stay home today. 'Sides, I would never have met you and had all that fun working in the basement," she said with a big smile. "I just love working with tools."

"You're good at it," he said. "Maybe you'll take over my position around here."

"Oh, no. I'm only good as an assistant. I don't have the head to think through the job. So, you're not off the hook that easily."

"That's okay," he said. "I like coming around here. You just feel like you're on holy ground when you walk into this house."

"You sure do," agreed Maggie. "I love it here."

"So what are you studying at university?"

"Education. I'll be finished my teacher's degree in a few months," she said, getting cups and saucers down from the cupboard for their tea.

"You'd make a good teacher—lots of fun for the students."

"I hope so. . . . Now, what kind of crumpets can I scrounge up around here?" She walked through the big kitchen, opening and closing cupboard doors in her search for just the right crumpets for the occasion.

He chuckled and shook his head. "We're having a full-fledged tea party, are we?"

"Crumpets and all," she told him. "Ah-hah!" she announced, triumphantly. "Check this out." She produced a bag of chocolate chip oatmeal cookies. "These dunk really well in tea."

"I'm not sure if they permit dunking at high tea," he cautioned the girl.

"Collins family rules," she told him. "Dunking is always permitted, as long as you hold up your pinkie when you drink."

"I'll remember that," he said with a laugh, as he practised lifting the empty cup off the saucer with his pinkie extended.

"Not bad for a farmer."

"Thanks," he returned with a chuckle, accepting the compliment. "Living out on a farm all alone a guy can forget all about etiquette, you know."

"You're all alone on the farm?" Maggie asked. "I just figured you would be married or something."

"Or something," he answered. "My parents just moved off the farm this past fall—took a small house in town. My dad comes out often to supervise—make sure I'm doing the job right and all."

"That must be lonely for you. I can't imagine being all alone."

"I guess I'm a bit of a loner," Charles admitted. "I don't mind. I figure if God wants me to get married He'll send along the right girl sooner or later—but so far He seems to be quite satisfied to see me a poor, single farmer."

"Ahhh," Maggie said, with a smile. "I'll have to keep my eyes open for you."

"Thanks, but no," he told her. "I've got four sisters trying to matchmake for me on a regular basis. And I frustrate the heck out of them all with my inability to attract women. I just find it too hard to talk to girls."

"You're talking to me."

"You're different than most girls—you like to get messy and play with tools," he reminded her.

"That's true. But I'm sure the right girl's out there somewhere for you."

"I'm not worried," he told her. "Really, I'm quite happy with my life. I have seventeen nieces and nephews that keep me hopping all year round. They love to come out to the farm and play on the big toys."

"Big toys?" Maggie asked.

"Snowmobiles in the winter, and quads and dirt bikes in the summer," he told her. "I have a few nephews who love to drive the tractors and farm trucks—so I get help when I need it. In fact, two nephews have come out to live with me on the farm the past couple of summers—and we just have a blast. Figured I might just turn it into a discernment house for young men."

"Sounds like a glorified bachelor pad," she told him. "My brothers would definitely die for a place like that."

"Actually, I get to daily Mass," he corrected her assumption that he was all about play. "And I never miss saying my prayers. And when the nieces and nephews come to visit, they have to come with me to church. Just the way it is."

"Good for you," she said with a laugh. "You're just about as rare a guy as I am a girl."

"Probably," he agreed.

Maggie poured the tea into their cups, and they enjoyed another twenty minutes or so of visiting. Charles looked at his watch and decided he had better head out to the hardware store for parts if he were going to get the job done before nightfall.

"Thanks for the crumpets and tea," he told the young lady. "I'll keep working on that pinkie."

Maggie laughed. "You did great. Just as much fun as I ever had with my sisters and brothers back home."

She walked Charles to the door and saw him out. Once he was gone she went back to the kitchen to clean up from their tea party. Suddenly she remembered the secret passageway on the third floor. Finishing her work in the kitchen, and leaving a note for the Sisters that the water was turned off in the house, Maggie ran up the back stairwell to her room.

Chapter 37

Maggie stood in the landing on the third floor, staring at every wall, every door, looking at the ceiling trying to see any evidence of a secret passageway in the open area. Nothing caught her eye. She figured it was probably tucked away in one of the three rooms. She hoped it would not be Kyra's room. She would have to search out her own room and the bathroom first, and if all else failed, she would have to draw Kyra into her little adventure. *Might make for a good bonding experience,* she thought.

Okay, St. Anthony, she prayed to the patron saint of lost things, *I figure you're the saint for this job. Help me find that secret passageway.*

She searched throughout her room, behind the bed and dresser, in the closet. She tapped on the walls, wondering if she could find a spot in the lath and plaster that would show where an old doorway had been sealed over. She loved feeling like Sherlock Holmes. It did not really disappoint her when she found nothing in her room—that just made the mystery even more intense.

She went into the bathroom, and as soon as she stepped in she figured she was getting warmer in her search. She rubbed her hands together and looked around. "Secret passageway," she whispered, with a grin on her face as she bit down on her lip and began her search. She looked behind the door, behind the radiator, behind the bathtub, even behind the toilet.

Finally she turned to the linen closet. It was about four feet wide and stretched up to the ceiling, made up of built-in shelves on the top and four drawers on the bottom. She opened the doors to the upper shelving part. She tried to look to the very back of it to see if she could detect a door. It was too dark. The shelves were about three feet deep so she could hardly reach to the back when standing on the floor. She would have to climb in part way to feel around the back wall of the cupboards.

She pulled out the towels from the bottom shelf and stacked them neatly on the floor. Looking around for something to use to step up on, she spotted the garbage can and decided it would be strong enough, turned upside down, to hold her weight. She dumped the garbage into a plastic bag, tied it up, and tossed it by the door to take down with her when she went down for supper. She flipped the garbage can over in front of the closet, stepped up on it with her left foot, and hoisted herself up onto the bottom shelf.

She felt around the entire wall with her right hand and to her disappointment found nothing. She tried with her left arm, and still she came up empty handed. She lay on her side inside the closet and heaved a sigh. She was so sure she had been on the right trail.

All that effort for nothing. Now she was going to have to go back to Charles and admit defeat, which was fine—it was not like he had bet against her finding it. In fact, he seemed to be so sure she could find it on her own. No. It had to be in here somewhere: perhaps on one of the other shelves. She rolled onto her back, staring up in the darkness of the closet, contemplating how she would get onto the upper shelves to check them out.

Looking up, she noticed something on the bottom of the shelf directly above her head against the right hand wall. It looked like a latch of some kind. She reached up, with a resurgence of her sense of adventure, and felt the latch. With a bit of a tug, the latch pulled and slid all along a groove on the shelf. As she pulled the latch across, the back wall of the closet came forward. It was not a wall at all—it was a board. She realized she would have to get out of the closet to let it fall all the way down.

She jumped off the shelf and stood balancing with one foot on the upside down garbage can and pulled the latch. The back panel lay down and opened up to a room on the other side of the house. It was a storage room that she had never before seen. She rarely went to the third floor on the other side of the house. She climbed back into the closet to take a closer look.

The storage room on the other side was not much for size. She figured it was maybe eight by ten feet, at best. It was filled with all kinds of boxes, books, a couple of suitcases, and other miscellaneous items hanging from the wall. There was a small window with a little lace curtain over it, allowing light into the storage area. She debated stepping down into it, but decided against it. It was enough that she had found the secret passageway. She really did not feel right about exploring a room that was not intended for her to enter. Still, she was curious as to what the opening looked like from that side.

She rolled over on the shelf, lay on her back, stuck her neck out into the room, and looked up. There was a wooden casement around the opening, which the little wooden panel that she was lying on filled in when it was closed. It did not seem much like a secret passage from that side. After all, anyone in the storage room could plainly see that there was something there on the wall. She decided that there must have been a latch with which to open the panel from that side. She looked around and discovered that the wooden casement slid over on the left side of the opening. There, hidden underneath it, was a latch that slid from top to bottom. It was obviously connected to the mechanism that she had pulled from her side to open the panel.

It was all too cool. "Thanks, St. Anthony," she whispered.

Maggie climbed back out of her side of the closet and pushed on the latch.

It stuck for a moment, and her heart skipped a beat, thinking that perhaps she was going to have to fess up with her adventure to the Sisters. All at once she realized that her hand was still leaning on the panel, holding it down. She heaved a sigh of relief and lifted her hand. The latch slid smoothly back, pulling the panel up with it.

Maggie put all the towels back in their place and returned the garbage can to its spot. "Great adventure," she said with a smile. "Thanks, Charles."

Maggie left the bathroom and went to her room. She glanced at her alarm clock; it was almost suppertime. She walked down the regular staircase, taking the garbage down with her. She carried herself as tall and as gracefully as possible—making her best effort to return to proper decorum for a Sister.

"Where have you been, Maggie?" asked Sr. Pauline.

"I was upstairs, just . . . being me," she said with a smile. "Is Charles back yet with the stuff to fix the plumbing?"

"No, he called and said he would have to come back first thing in the morning. He went to three hardware stores and couldn't find the part he was looking for. But one store told him they could have it in by tomorrow morning. So," she said with a sigh, "I guess we go without water until then. Thanks for filling these pails. I hope we don't have to go much longer than one night, though, without water."

Maggie threw out the garbage and then helped with supper. She was disappointed not to be able to see Charles again that night. She wanted to boast over her accomplishment—and he was the only one with whom she could share her little secret. Maybe she would tell Kyra about it, too. On second thought, she just could not picture dainty, refined Kyra crawling up onto that closet shelf. She would have to wait until she saw Charles the next day after her classes.

✞   ✞   ✞

Maggie raced home from campus following her last class on Wednesday. She could not wait to talk to Charles, telling him all about her adventure. She was also looking forward to helping him with the plumbing—hopefully he had not finished the job without her. He had promised to still be there, anyway, to tell her about the secret passageway. And he had assured her that he always kept his promises.

The ten minute walk home from campus seemed to take longer than usual, even though she ran most of the way. She reached the gate of the little fence around their house property, opened it quickly, ran up the walk, and bounded in through the front door. Quickly hanging up her things, she ran upstairs to put away her books. She stopped and looked in the mirror before heading down. A little disgruntled with her appearance, Maggie decided to take a few moments to tidy herself up. After a few unsuccessful attempts to do something stylish with her hair, she finally just pulled it back in a ponytail, and left it at that.

She hurried down the back staircase to the basement. When she emerged into the boiler room where Charles was working, he called out, without taking his eyes away from his work, "At last, my helper has arrived."

"How'd you know it was me?"

"In twenty-eight years of visiting at this house, Maggie, I've never heard anyone else come down those back stairs like that. It had to be you."

Maggie laughed. "I guess you've got me all figured out after one day, haven't you?"

"Oh, I'm sure there's a lot of mystery to a girl like you," he stated, looking at the girl from the step ladder. "And I'm not one for figuring out women."

"Well, I did some figuring last night," Maggie told him, her voice raised with excitement.

His face lit up with a big, friendly smile. He stopped his work for a moment and looked down from the top of the ladder at the girl who was just bursting to tell all. "You must have found it."

"I sure did. It took me almost half-an-hour, and I had almost given up, when I lay on my back in that silly little closet, and there it was—the latch."

"I can't believe you actually crawled up into that little closet," he said, duly impressed. "I haven't been in there for years—but it wasn't that big."

"I'm not that big, either," she said. "I just barely fit—but I did. It was so cool. What do you suppose they had that there for?"

"I asked Sr. Charlotte about it once, and she had no idea herself. The Sisters of the Immaculate Conception bought the house as it is now from some really rich family who had the two properties joined back in the forties. So that's when that storage room and bathroom were connected," he informed her.

"When did the Sisters buy this house?"

"In the fifties sometime. Cool, old place, isn't it?"

"It is," she said with a smile.

"And I'm very impressed that you were able to find that. I'll have to keep you in mind if I ever need a private detective for anything."

"I'm always ready for an adventure," she told him. "So what's up with this mess?"

"I'd have been done long ago if I had had my faithful assistant by my side, passing me tools," he commented, looking at the job. "As it was, I got a lot of exercise going up and down this ladder this afternoon."

"I'm here now, sir," she told him. "So put me to work."

The plumbing twosome worked on the job for over two hours. It was getting close to suppertime, and Charles had promised his sister he would have the water back on for supper—and he always kept his promises. Maggie was careful not to distract him from his goal. Finally at almost a quarter-to-six, Charles announced that they could put the water back on.

"You're sure we're okay?" Maggie asked, cautiously.

"We'll soon find out," he said, raising his eyebrows playfully at the girl.

She followed him to the side of the room where the main water line valve was situated. "Go ahead, Maggie," he said, giving her the honours. "Turn it all the way on."

They listened as the water rushed to fill all the pipes in the house.

"Quick," he told her, "go stand over there and watch to see if there's any leak."

Maggie skipped across the room and stood there staring up at the pipes where the leak had once been. "We're looking dry," she called out.

Charles stepped up beside the young lady and looked up at his handiwork. "I think we have a winner," he announced.

"Good work, partner," she said, turning to Charles and extending her hand for him to shake.

He took Maggie's hand and shook it as he looked into her soft hazel, eyes, dancing with delight. "It was a lot of fun working with you, Maggie. Thanks."

"So, when will I see you again?" she asked, still shaking his hand with Maggie-exuberance. "I'm going to miss working with you."

"Tell you what . . . " He stepped back from her and turned to clean up the mess. "You're so clever about these things—if you want to see me again, just go jimmy up some plumbing or something electrical, and Sr. Charlotte will give me a call to come back."

"Sounds like an idea," Maggie said. "Although, I'm not sure if I could do that without having to go to confession."

"True. I guess then we can just pray for something to break down on its own so that I can come back again real soon," he said with a gentle smile.

"*That* I can do in good conscience," Maggie told him.

"Oh, by the way," he said, pulling a folded paper out of his pocket, "I have something for you."

"You do?" Filled with curiosity, Maggie took the paper from his hand and unfolded it. "A recipe for crumpets," she said with a laugh. "That's awesome! Where d'you find it?"

"I looked through some of my mom's old cookbooks. It wasn't easy—but I finally found it in one that had been published back in the forties. I thought you'd appreciate it," he said, reaching down to pick up his pail.

"I love it," she said, turning over the paper with the handwritten recipe on it to see if anything else was on it. "You've got nice printing."

"My best subject in school," he informed her.

"Funny," she said with a chuckle. "Come on, I'll help you with this stuff."

The young man and woman walked up the stairs carrying tools and plumbing supplies to the kitchen.

"You two all done?" Sr. Charlotte asked, hopefully. "I just heard the pipes begin to creak again and thought I'd come check on your progress, but I got distracted here in the kitchen on my way down."

"Water's back on," announced the young aspirant. She walked over to the sink to demonstrate.

"Praise the Lord!" exclaimed Sr. Charlotte. "Oh, Charles, you are a gem," she said, giving her younger brother a hug.

Charles returned the hug to his older sister. "It was my pleasure. And say thanks to that little lady." He pointed his thumb toward Maggie who had stepped back beside him. "She's quite handy to have around. I'd say you'd do well to hang on to her," he advised his sister.

"Oh, we all love Maggie," Sr. Charlotte assured him. "But it's up to the good Lord as to whether or not we get to keep her."

Maggie smiled at Sr. Charlotte.

"Stay for supper with us, Charles," Sr. Charlotte said.

"Oh, no. I don't want to be a bother here."

"Charles, you just fixed our plumbing for nothing," she reminded him. "It's the least we can do for you. Besides, we've got fried chicken, which I know you love. I special-requested it just for you."

"Twist my rubber arm," he said with a smile. "I'll just put these things away and get cleaned up in the washroom."

"I'll help you," Maggie said, picking up the supplies she had carried up the stairs. "That is with putting things away. You're on your own for clean up," she clarified, somewhat embarrassed.

Charles and Sr. Charlotte laughed at the sweet innocence of this simple girl.

The fried chicken was excellent, and Charles was a welcome guest at the Sisters' table. All the Sisters had adopted him as their "younger" brother over the years, even those who were a few years younger than Charles. He enjoyed the heroic status he held at the Sisters' house—as plumber, electrician, mechanic, carpenter, or whatever title the job demanded.

"It's an honour to serve the Brides of Christ," he told them. "And if that doesn't merit me any grace, I don't know what will."

"Speaking of serving the Brides of Christ," Sr. Charlotte began with a suspicious smile on her face.

"Oh-oh," Charles said. "I recognize that tone of voice. You've got another job for me, don't you?"

"As a matter of fact we do. And I thought that this might be the best time of year for you to undertake a longer project for us—before spring," she said, her eyes appealing to her brother's sense of honour.

"Okay, let's have it," he said, setting his napkin beside his plate.

"We need to do a minor kitchen renovation," she explained. "We've bought a new refrigerator, but it doesn't fit in the old space, and the old one is on its last legs. The freezer compartment doesn't work at all, and it's really too small. So we want to have you come in and take out some cupboards, put in a walk-in pantry, and make room for the new fridge."

All the other Sisters, as if on cue, turned and smiled at Charles with an encouraging nod.

"Did you ladies rehearse this or something?" he asked with a laugh. "You know I can't turn down your requests at the best of times, but least of all when you're all looking so eager and being so doggone appreciative."

Sr. Pauline spoke up, "Charles, we would do anything in return for all you do around here for us."

"Really, just keep praying for me. That's all I ever ask for. Money can't replace the grace I get by helping you out."

"So when could you start?" Sr. Charlotte asked.

"I'll take a look at it tonight and assess how much work is involved in this *minor* reno. It all depends on whether or not I have to do some construction back home in my shop first for the job. But I'm free to begin anytime now," he assured them.

"Wonderful!" said Sr. Pauline. The older Sister clapped her hands together with delight. "I've been waiting almost twenty years now for that fridge to finally die so we could get a new one."

Everyone around the table laughed at Sr. Pauline's exclamation.

"I know I should have just been grateful for having a fridge at all—but I never did like that pathetic little thing," she confessed.

"I'll get it out of there, Sr. Pauline, just as fast as I can," promised Charles. "After all, a man could get spoiled by all this good food and hospitality—I certainly don't eat like this when I cook for myself on the farm."

"And you're welcome to stay in our guest room rather than drive back and forth to the farm," Sr. Charlotte told him.

"We'll see," Charles answered. "Someone still has to be there to take care of the livestock," he reminded his older sister.

After the meal, Charles, Sr. Charlotte, Sr. Thérèse, and Sr. Becky went into the kitchen to assess the job. Sr. Charlotte invited Maggie to join them as she figured they could make use of the young aspirant's experience in renovating and construction.

It was decided that Charles could probably begin work the following Tuesday—which worked well for his assistant, as she had the day off classes anyway.

Chapter 38

The following Sunday the Collins family gathered together to celebrate Joanie's birthday. They had come to the stage in family life when they truly appreciated the special occasions which drew them together. John and Judy marvelled at how quickly their life had changed in one year—while the family was getting smaller at home, it was still growing larger.

Since Joanie's birthday fell directly after St. Valentine's Day, there was always a heart-shaped cake for her birthday. Katie and Jessie had made it and decorated it together this year. Jessie was very excited to have everyone admire her handiwork.

As the family sat around after brunch, eating cake and sipping coffee, they caught up on all that was happening in each other's lives. Maggie excitedly shared about the repair and renovation work going on at the Sisters' house. "And Dad, you would love Charles. He's just like you—a real jack-of-all-trades. It's so much fun to work with him—it reminds me of old times with you."

"Those times aren't so old," he reminded her. "You were helping me repair the water heater just last summer."

"I guess," she said. "It just feels like I've been away for five years, not five months."

"I haven't seen Charles in a while," John commented, thinking of the brown-haired, shy boy he once knew. "But he always was handy with the tools—even from a young age. We've worked together on projects at the Sisters' house over the years, like the time we rebuilt their fence in the backyard. Don't you remember coming and helping me with that?" he asked his daughter.

"I do," she answered. "But I don't remember Charles."

"That's because you were too young to notice a good-looking young guy like that," John teased.

"Daddy!" Maggie responded, defensively. "I'm still too young to notice a good-looking guy like that."

Everyone around the table laughed.

"How old is Charles now, anyway?" asked Judy.

"Twenty-eight," Maggie answered.

"And still single?" Judy inquired.

"Apparently," Maggie said. "He's taking over the family farm—and since he's not married he jokes about turning it into a discernment house for young men." She took a mouthful of the birthday cake, savouring its richness and moistness. Katie always did make the best chocolate cakes.

"Cool!" exclaimed Isaac. "I'd go live there when I finish school."

"You would," said Katie, shaking her head. "I'm just not sure how much discerning you'd do around all those big farm tractors."

"And all the small farm toys," Maggie added. "It sounds like Charles has every motorized toy that they've come up with for boys to play with."

"I wonder if I could go check it out sometime," queried Isaac. "Bet he's got skidoos."

"I think he's got about four snowmobiles," she told him. "He buys them cheap and then repairs them and sells them. Not to mention dirt bikes and quads."

Isaac turned straight on to face Maggie and pleaded, "You've got to take us out there sometime." Zack and Aaron sat nodding their heads in enthusiastic agreement.

"I wouldn't know where it is," she told Isaac. "But if you want, I can ask Charles if he's open to hosting retreats for home-schooled brats like you, Zack, and Aaron."

"Don't forget me," said Jessie with a big pout. "I want to go, too."

"You're not a brat," Maggie corrected the four-year-old, "so I'm sure he'd let you come, too, no problem."

Jessie's smile came back over her face as she turned up her little nose at her older brothers.

Zack and Aaron were definitely in on the deal and begged Maggie to talk to Charles next time she saw him. Maggie promised she would ask, but was not guaranteeing any results.

"I don't home-school," said Brandon, "but I sure wouldn't mind being the one to take the boys out sometime."

"Oh, I bet you wouldn't mind," added Joanie. "You guys are all the same, aren't you? Play, play, play. Would you even think of taking me along?"

"In your delicate condition, dear?" Brandon asked, covering up his oversight.

"I'll give you delicate," Joanie said, shaking a fist at her husband with a laugh.

"You can come; I want you to come," he told her, holding back her hand. "I've learned not to mess with that hand—so by all means, if you're interested, you just come right along with us. It just wouldn't be the same without you there, dear."

"Well, even though I doubt your sincerity, *dear*," Joanie responded, "I'll accept your invitation, anyway."

"Hey, while I'm thinking of it, Brandon, how's Mike doing?" Judy interrupted, changing the topic.

"Really well," Brandon answered. "It doesn't hurt that Ashleen's been going to church with him every Sunday, and she's actually starting to sound interested in learning about the faith. For a while, she was digging in her atheistic heels fairly deep."

"I just think she's so taken with Mike that she can't help wanting to figure out what makes him tick," Joanie said.

"I wouldn't be surprised," Brandon added. "That's how I felt about you once upon a time."

"And now?" Joanie asked, a slight edge to her voice. She held a forkful of cake in front of her mouth, waiting for her husband's reply.

"And now we're living happily ever after, dear," he said, smoothly removing his foot from his mouth.

Joanie proceeded to put the bite of cake into her mouth, as she smiled through closed lips at Brandon.

"Well, I'm neither once upon a time nor happily ever after, these days," Amie threw out. "But let me tell you—I've never enjoyed being single so much as I do now."

"Really?" said John. "That totally surprises me, Scuttle-Butt. You've always been such a starry-eyed romantic."

"I think I'm cured for a while. I just don't feel anxious about it anymore. And I'm just loving ballroom dance classes, and school's fun, and *New Spring's* been a blast lately, and I'm all done music studies—forever!" she added emphatically.

"You've just got the world by the tail and a downward pull, don't you?" John remarked, smiling at his daughter.

"I sure do. Which reminds me," she said, looking over at Katie. "Dance class starts in twenty-five minutes. We've gotta get going."

Katie looked at the clock and jumped up, beginning to stack dishes.

"Maggie and I'll do dishes," Joanie offered to her sisters. "Go have fun."

"Are you sure?" Katie asked. "It's your birthday."

"We're going to have so much fun," Maggie promised Katie, "you'll be jealous you had to leave."

"Probably," Katie agreed, looking melancholy. "I miss those days."

"Hurry up," Amie said, taking Katie's arm to lead her out of the dining room. "I don't want to be late."

They hurried to get their winter jackets on, and just as they were leaving Amie called back, "We've got youth group tonight, so we won't be home for supper."

Judy smiled and raised her coffee cup toward her husband. John picked up his coffee cup and returned the salute to his wife. "They come; they go; and life moves on," he soliloquized.

Chapter 39

Sunday afternoon dance classes turned out to be a great opportunity for their whole group of friends to get together and have fun, not just hanging out wasting time. Learning to dance was a life-skill they had all come to appreciate, especially upon discovering just how challenging it was to get good at it. There were so many things to think about all at once. Some in their group were more natural at it than others, but they all encouraged each other along.

Even Krystal and Samantha were coming out to classes. Krystal had toned down her man-hunting inclinations, realizing that in this group of young men there was much more choice than she had ever expected. Though she had not given herself over to any religious affiliations, she could see that religion did seem to make a difference in a man's character—at least these men. She definitely was hoping to eventually snag for herself a good Catholic boy who would make a good husband and know how to raise good kids. But what was the hurry? She was going to take her time and be choosey about it.

Week after week, Samantha and Josh were showing signs of a real interest in each other. Though not officially a couple "to speak of", they definitely found each other several times at each dance class. Samantha was going out for Bible studies through C.C.E. and meeting with Josh to talk about faith issues. She had told Amie she wanted to become Catholic, but not just because of Josh—though that certainly did not hurt her interest in any way. Mostly though, she had begun praying the rosary daily, and she was beginning to feel a real longing and hunger for Christ in the Eucharist.

Amie was not surprised. "Mary has a way of bringing souls to her Son, like no one's business," she told Samantha one day as the girls were eating lunch. "You just have to give her a chance."

"I'm also not wanting to get serious with Josh until I know for certain that I'm going to become Catholic. I don't want to convert just because of a guy. I think there'd be too much pressure on our relationship," she told Amie.

"I think you're wise to wait, Sam. It's so important to build a foundation of friendship first anyway. And I don't think Josh is going anywhere in the meantime," she added with a smile.

"I hope not," Samantha stated. "I'm just hoping and praying that God will take care of that for me."

"Aghghghghghgh!" grumbled Krystal, stamping her feet childishly. "I can't believe you're praying. I've known you practically your whole life. It just blows me away to watch you polish those beads each night." She made a rubbing motion, imitating a rosary flying through her fingertips, and began laughing. With all her antics, her lunch bag slipped off her lap.

"Laugh, whine, pout all you want," Samantha told her friend, as she leaned forward to save her friend's lunch. "But if you think you're going to catch one of these guys without learning how to polish beads, you're crazy."

"Perhaps," Krystal said. "But I'm not polishing any beads just to get me a guy. If God's really up there—and you can really get to know Him by saying all those prayers—then He'll just have to make me really want to do it. And so far, He doesn't seem too interested in talking to me at all."

"How would you know?" Samantha asked. "You've never given Him a chance to hang up on you—since you've never bothered to call."

"I was raised to wait for the guy to call first," Krystal said, sarcastically.

"Like hell you were," Samantha said with a laugh.

"But that's okay," Amie jumped in, laughing with her friends. "God's a real gentleman. You just wait and see how He finally decides to court you for His own," she said, pointing a miniature carrot at Krystal and throwing a wink her way.

"Sounds romantic," Krystal admitted. "And I'm all about romance."

"Then get ready to be blown away by God's love," Amie told her. "I don't know when or how . . . but He's going to get you good. And you'll be worse than Sam." Amie popped the tiny carrot into her mouth.

"Hah!" Krystal exploded.

Samantha sat there with her sandwich, nodding knowingly. She had already felt enough of God's work in her life to know what Amie was saying was true. The shorter, dark-haired girl could not wait to see the day when her proud friend would finally cave.

Amie and Katie had picked up their cousins, Ann and Jocelyn, on their way to dance class. They met up with Samantha and Krystal, walking in to the building. The six girls came in to the big hall where the classes were held. It was the top floor of an old school, used now for community activities and events. There were big columns supporting the roof structure over this wide-open space. Large windows along the two ends of the room brightened the hall enough that lights were not needed during the day.

The young ladies looked around to assess the situation with their friends: some had already arrived. The girls walked over to join the group.

David Bander was holding hands with Leanne. They looked good together; everyone thought so. Leanne was always so happy when she came around. It was understandable—David treated her like gold.

The dark-haired, green-eyed girl seemed even more cheerful than usual this sunny winter afternoon. Suddenly Amie thought to look down at Leanne's left hand which was swallowed up inside of David's larger right hand.

David winked at Amie and lifted his hand to the side just slightly. A diamond sparkled back up at Amie's eyes. Katie caught sight of it as well.

"Ohhh!" Amie screamed. "David, you popped the question!"

"Uh-huh! Valentine's Day," Leanne told the group, pulling her hand free to show off her new jewel.

"I'm not sure what's sparkling more, the diamond or you," Amie said, giving Leanne a hug. "I'm so happy for you both." She turned and gave David a big hug, saying, "Congratulations!"

"Thanks," he said, hugging her back.

By this time everyone in the group was extending their best wishes for the couple. A few more friends from C.C.E. walked in and joined in on the excitement. The hullabaloo from their side of the room eventually got the attention of the other students and class instructors.

Amie lifted up Leanne's hand and called out, "They just got engaged!"

Everyone in the room clapped for the young couple. Amie stood there with her hands held over her mouth, holding back her excitement. Kyle was standing off to the side behind David. She walked over to her friend and grabbed his hands. "Aren't you thrilled for them?"

Kyle laughed. "I'm really happy about it. David's got himself a wonderful girl."

Amie shook his hands and bit down on her lip. "Just you wait, Kyle. You'll be the next one to make off with some wonderful girl."

"We'll see," he said, with a chuckle. He motioned with his head for Amie to turn around as the class was beginning. She gave his hands a little squeeze and let them go as she moved beside him to face the instructors.

After a few announcements, the men and women were divided into their usual line-ups for instruction. The class was reviewing steps from the cha-cha which they had learned the week before. The lead male instructor had the men lined up along one side as he and his assistant demonstrated the steps. The lead female instructor was doing the same for the women on the opposite side of the hall with her assistant teacher.

Once the group had reviewed the step, they were to find a partner and practise. As Kyle began to walk across the room to ask one of the girls to dance, another student intercepted him and asked him to dance with her. The young woman appeared to be in her early twenties. He smiled politely and agreed—as it was expected that students would mix and dance with everyone.

She was a fairly tall woman, and with her dance shoes on she looked Kyle eye-to-eye. She wore skin-tight dress pants that revealed her shapely figure. Her low-cut sweater exposed plenty of cleavage. Her low-rise pants came an inch or so below her top, leaving an obvious midriff. Kyle stood straight, uncomfortably trying to remember how to hold his dance frame.

"I picked you," the girl informed him, looking at him with enticing blue eyes, "because you're such a good dancer. I've kept my eye on you at other classes. My name's Dana."

"I'm Kyle. And I'm not *that* good at dancing—so don't mind me if I just concentrate on my part."

"Don't worry," she assured him. "I'll make you look good. But feel free to look down whenever you want."

"It's not good dance-training for me to watch my feet. So, I'll just keep my head up." He concentrated on the dance move, looking around at the other partners, trying to remember what he was supposed to be doing in the lead part. He was not used to being around forward, immodestly dressed girls, and his awkwardness just spurred on this girl's nerve.

She waited for him to look back at her, then said, "I didn't really mean for you to look at your feet." Her manner was alluring which only served to solidify Kyle's resolve.

"Actually, I prefer to look a girl in the eyes," he told her. "I'm all about respecting girls for who they are."

She laughed at him. "As you wish . . . but it's all the same to me."

"Maybe it wouldn't be if you were used to guys treating you with respect," he said, gaining confidence by the moment.

"I'm not sure what you mean," she replied. "But if that's an invitation to spend more time with you, I accept."

"No, it wasn't," he told her plainly.

"So, what if I make the invitation to you," she offered.

"I'd have to decline." He looked around the room. He could feel himself fumbling to follow the proper steps and his annoyance with Dana was becoming apparent.

"Got a girlfriend?"

"Nope," he replied, doing his best to remain polite. "Just happy being single and concentrating on my studies . . . and on this dance step, at the moment."

"I'm not suggesting you stop being single," she said, with an obvious attempt to entice. "We could just hook up for an evening—say, tonight. See what comes of it."

"That's not my style." He looked around the room. Thankfully, the instructors had begun teaching again. He looked back at Dana and smiled courteously as he stepped away. "Thanks for the dance, Dana."

Dana opened her mouth to say something, but he had already turned his back to walk away. She watched him move across the floor. Finally she turned to seek out another good-looking guy. There had to be someone there who was not so uptight about girls.

Kyle quickly found his friends and went and took his place by Amie. She looked at him and commented, "That girl's got something for you."

"Well, it's not mutual, and I certainly don't want to encourage anything," he whispered back. "Dance with me next?"

"Yeah, I'll bail you out of this one, since she's obviously not your type," Amie said with a little laugh.

"Not in the least," he replied. "And thanks."

They danced together and Kyle fell back into form. He was a good dancer, with a strong lead. With Amie or any of his other girl-friends, he was completely comfortable to be himself. The fact that none of them dressed immodestly went a long way to adding to that relaxed feeling. He did not have to work at looking away from them—or feel nervous that they were trying to lure him with their "charms".

"Thanks," he said, looking Amie in the eye.

"For what?" she asked with a laugh. "For stepping on your toes just now, like a total klutz?"

"No. For being the girl you are. I can't tell you how grateful I am to have you for a friend."

He was so serious; Amie tilted her head sideways, with a funny look, trying to figure him out. "Ohhh," she said, her eyes widening, as she began laughing. "Little Miss 'Come-and-Get-Me' was a bit much for you?"

Kyle just shook his head and closed his eyes. "Just a bit," he said sarcastically. "And if I ever thought you would make moves on a guy like that, I'd haul you out of here and back to your parents' home so fast, it'd make your head spin."

Amie laughed. "That's what I love about you, Kyle—just like the big brother I never had."

"That's right. And I'm happy to take out any guy that ever treats you like trash. I just can't stand seeing those attitudes."

"Don't worry," she assured him. "The girls and I will protect you while we're here at dance classes—keep you good and occupied. And you can protect us when we go out into the world."

"Deal," he said. They finished their dance and Amie led Kyle right into Ann's arms for the next dance.

There were certainly enough in their group of friends to keep themselves busy dancing with each other. Though they did not want to be rude to other students, Kyle made sure to avoid the brazen, immodest types again.

As he noticed Dana working on other guys around the room, he offered up silent prayers for her.

She's Your daughter, God. If it bothers me this much, I can't imagine how much it must bother You. So I'm just praying that You find a way for her to see her true dignity and worth. I'm sure that deep down she's just hungering and thirsting for Your love. Don't let her settle for cheap imitations. Don't let her sell herself for the empty promises of worldly pleasure and attention from guys. The guys who want what she's offering are just going to use her and treat her like dirt. But You created her for so much more than that. Mother Mary, intercede for her to find the way to Your Son so that she can discover what real love is all about. In Your Name, Lord Jesus. Amen.

Chapter 40

Tuesday could not come soon enough for Maggie—she was so excited about starting in on the renovations in the kitchen. When the front doorbell rang, she jumped up from the island in the kitchen where she had been visiting with Sr. Charlotte, waiting for Charles' arrival.

"I'll get it," she called out to her superior.

Maggie ran to the front entry and opened up the large oak door to greet Charles, who was standing there in his winter coat, toque, and mitts, with his pail of tools in his right hand. She gave him a big smile and grabbed his left arm to pull him in out of the cold. "Come in, it's freezing out there."

"Don't mind if I do. What took you so long to answer the door?" he asked with a laugh, noticing that Maggie was somewhat out of breath.

She laughed back. "I guess I am a little excited about getting to work. I just live for stuff like this. It takes me back to working with my dad on our old house." She took his coat from him and stuffed his mitts and toque into the sleeves before she hung it up.

Sr. Charlotte came to the entry and gave her brother a hug. "Hello, Charles," she greeted him with a smile. "Our knight in shining armour."

"Scrubby, old overalls is more like it," he corrected her.

"Armour takes many forms," Sr. Charlotte told him. "We can't thank you enough for taking on this project. And as you can see, you won't be working alone." Sr. Charlotte turned to Maggie, who was eagerly standing off to the side, ready to get to work.

"I appreciate the help," Charles told his sister. "Come on," he said to his assistant. "Let's get at it."

They went into the kitchen and Charles immediately started directing Maggie as to what they would do first. Sr. Charlotte took her leave of them and told Maggie to come get her if they needed anything—she would be in her office for the day.

The cupboards that would be ripped out had already been emptied by the Sisters, with the contents loaded into boxes that were lining the hallway outside the kitchen to keep them out of the way. Charles and Maggie began taking out the cupboards.

"We can't really save these," he told her. "They were built right into the walls—not like the modular units they build now-a-days. But the door fronts can be saved. Make two piles—junk wood over there and door fronts over there. We can load it all up in the back of my truck later."

"No problem," Maggie said.

Charles worked at pulling the wood down. He passed it to Maggie, who then made stacks where he had instructed. Watching her carrying the wood, he paused. "You know, I feel bad making an 'almost-Sister' haul wood."

"Don't worry about it. I love the work. Just think of me as one of the guys."

"That's hard to do with you in a skirt."

"This old thing?" she said, lifting at it with one hand. "This is my work skirt. And you'll just have to get over the fact that I'm a girl. I'm a good, hard worker—so don't take it easy on me, or I'll be insulted."

"Insulting you is the last thing I want to do. But getting over the fact that you're a girl might not be that easy." He turned back to his demolition work.

Maggie laughed. "Well, I'm not a typical girl. So just create a new category in your mind for 'Maggies'."

"You are definitely in a league all your own," he assured her, passing her a door front.

She smiled up at him as she took the wooden door. "So are you, Charles. You're like a younger version of my dad, and that's the best compliment I could ever give a guy."

"I'll take it," he said, with a smile. "I've known your dad since I was a boy, and I have a lot of respect for him."

"Well, it's mutual. Dad certainly had good things to say about you."

"Really? You were talking about me?"

"Yes, I was," she said, mysteriously.

"Hmm," he replied, turning back to his work.

Before long the demolition was done. The two workers brought in the power tools that Charles had in the back of his truck and then hauled out the salvage wood and the scraps.

"You want to come with me? I've got to take this out to the dump, drop the other stuff off at the farm, and then pick up some more supplies." He looked at this watch. It was eleven o'clock. "I'll take you for lunch, too, since it's that time of day."

"Sounds great," Maggie answered. "I'll just let Sr. Charlotte know where we're going, and I'll be out in a minute."

Charles started the truck and let it warm up while he sat waiting for Maggie to return.

"Let's go," the bubbly girl said as she hopped into the vehicle.

"Lunch first or the dump?"

"The dump, definitely," she said. "We'll get that out of the way first."

Charles put the truck into gear and they left.

"Actually, I have to confess," she began, "I really want to see your farm. My brothers made me promise to ask you if they could come out some time and play with some of your toys."

"No problem. Any time they want. Your whole family can come out some Sunday, maybe. We can have a big play day."

"Cool," she said. "I like snowmobiling, too."

He smiled at the girl beside him in the cab of the truck. "I figured you would."

They finished unloading the junk at the city dump and then decided on a place to pick up some fast-food for lunch. "We can eat as we drive," Charles suggested. "It takes about thirty minutes to get to the farm from here."

They visited the whole way out and the time passed by quickly. As Charles pulled up the road lined with large evergreen trees, Maggie turned her attention out the window. "Charles," she whispered in awe, "this place is beautiful!"

The road opened up to a lovely farmyard, with an old two-storey house and a small hip-roofed barn across from it, and three horses standing in the barnyard. A black dog with white and brown markings came bounding up the road to greet them. "That's Kaiser," Charles announced. "Part German shepherd, part Border collie. Name means 'emperor' in German. And believe me, he rules the barnyard around here," he said with a laugh. "Seriously, though, he's five years old and as gentle as the day is long."

Maggie smiled, looking at the dog who happily bounced around the vehicle, running beside it, waiting for his master to get out.

There was a large Quonset out behind the house that was obviously used as a garage and shop. Charles drove around to the Quonset and backed up to the large overhead door which he opened from inside the truck.

They stepped out of the vehicle and began unloading the cupboard doors.

"Here," Charles instructed the girl, "we'll stack them up over along this wall. And come look at this," he said, as they set down their first armload. He walked across the open space of the large shop with Maggie following him.

"Charles, it's breathtaking!" Maggie said, stepping ahead as she saw where he was leading her. "You had time to build this since last week?" she asked, incredulously.

"I have nothing else to do. Remember, I'm just an old bachelor."

"You're not old," she corrected him. "And for the life of me I don't know why you're still a bachelor." She looked at the large oak door and stained glass window he had built for the new walk-in pantry. The door was stained in a cinnamon colour to match the light red wood in the rest of the Sisters' kitchen. The stained glass window was framed in the same cinnamon oak, with an image of a sheaf of wheat and a clump of grapes designed in it. Maggie took her hand out of her mitt and ran her fingers over the smooth finished surface of the large door. Then she gently touched the glass of the window—afraid that she might break it. She turned to Charles who had a satisfied look on his face. "You're amazing," she said, quite simply.

"So are you," he answered, as he stepped away to finish their job.

Maggie slipped her mitt back on and caught up to Charles. They unloaded the wood, and he picked out a few tools that he had forgotten the first time.

"Are we loading those up to take them back today?" she asked, pointing to the door and window.

"Nope. We have to get the walls framed in first and dry-walled. Do you mind helping me load that stuff?" he asked, pointing to the pile of lumber and drywall near the front of the shop.

"Of course I don't mind," she answered, almost defensively. "I told you, Charles, I'm not afraid of hard work."

"I don't want to assume things," he said. "I've also got some paint around here from when I repainted that kitchen four years ago. And we can load the drywall mud and tape while we're at it. We have a bit more work ahead of us."

"Good," she said, clapping her hands together in her mitts. "I wouldn't want the fun to end too soon."

"No danger of that," he assured her.

They loaded the supplies into the back of the truck. It was a cold, winter day, and they could see their breath, but the fresh air felt good and exhilarating—and they both had the personalities to appreciate it.

"You want to see the house?" he asked, when they were done.

"I'd love to," she said, waiting for Charles to close up the Quonset door.

"Come on." He motioned with his hand for her to walk ahead of him.

Maggie stepped forward and followed the well-trodden path to the house, through the trees. "You have so many trees here."

"My grandma planted those years ago. When they first settled this farm there wasn't a tree on this land. Just bald prairie."

"Amazing. . . . You know," she remarked, stopping to look out at the farmyard from the top of the front steps to the house, "if I were ever to have married, this is exactly the kind of place where I would have wanted to live. There's too much farm girl in me—even though I grew up in the city—to have stayed in the city my whole life . . . except at the Sisters' house. I love it there so much that it's easy to overlook the fact that I'm stuck in a city."

"You're welcome to come out to our farm anytime you need to get away," he told her as he opened the door for her to go into the house.

Maggie slipped off her boots and stepped from the entry into the kitchen. It was an old country kitchen, with an old country feel to it. It was charming: tidy and clean. "Charles, you are one neat bachelor," she commented. She walked across the room to look at a family picture on the wall beside the old buffet. "This your family?"

"Yup," he answered, stepping up beside her. He pointed to the picture, "Of course you know who that is."

"Sr. Charlotte," she said. "Where are you?"

"Find me."

Maggie stared at the picture—it was about ten years old. After a few moments of scrutinizing she pointed to a young man in a brush cut and moustache. "Is that you?" she asked hesitantly.

"Yeah," he said with a laugh. "Can you believe it?"

She looked from the picture to Charles and back again. "It's hilarious. You look much better without the moustache," she told him, quite frankly.

"Thanks. But what can I say. It helped to solidify my singleness."

She laughed. "You really like being single?"

"It's where I'm meant to be right now. Otherwise God would have supplied the right girl in my life, and he hasn't yet. And I definitely know I'm not called to be a priest. I could never endure all those years of study—or being off the farm. Too much farm boy in me."

"I say—stay just the way you are," she told him, pointing a finger at him. "Someday some lucky girl is going to hit the jackpot with you."

Charles smiled. He looked down, scratching his temple casually, and stepped back from her side. He invited Maggie to look around the house if she wanted. She took him up on the offer. The house had that wonderful Catholic feel, with images of Jesus and Mary on the walls, and a crucifix prominently hung in every room.

"My grandparents built this home back in the forties. I love it. Wouldn't change it at all."

"No," she agreed. "Keep it just the way it is."

"Can I get you something to drink or eat before we take off?" he offered.

"No, we'd better get going. It's already one-thirty."

As they left the house, Maggie admired the horses in the barnyard.

"Sally, Pete and Moses," he told her, pointing to each horse as he named them.

"Funny names," she said with a laugh, as they walked to the truck.

"What can I say? That's probably why I'm still a bachelor. I'd never be able to name children."

"You'd have a wife to help you," she said looking up at him as he opened the truck door for her to get in.

"That would be a definite asset," he commented, "if I were to have children."

Maggie laughed. She sat in the cab of the truck and looked around the farmyard some more. "You're lucky," she said to Charles as he got into the driver's seat.

"Why?"

"You have all this," she said, dreamily looking around.

"I've been really blessed," he agreed.

They arrived back at the Sisters' house just after two o'clock. Sr. Charlotte met them in the kitchen as they brought in supplies for the job.

"What a beautiful home you grew up in," Maggie commented to Sr. Charlotte as she carried in some lumber.

"You liked it?" Sr. Charlotte asked with a smile.

"Loved it!" Maggie exclaimed. "It was perfect."

"It was a wonderful place to grow up," Sr. Charlotte stated. "So where are we at in the work?"

Charles brought his sister up to date with the status of the job. He figured by suppertime they could have the pantry walls framed in.

Maggie told Sr. Charlotte about the door and window that Charles had built for the new pantry.

"We knew what we were doing when we asked him," she told Maggie.

Charles scratched at his ear, humbly turning away from excessive praise. Sr. Charlotte shook her head with a little laugh. She knew her brother was not the type to stay in the limelight. "I've got to run out for a couple of hours. I'll let you two get back to work, and I'll see you later."

Maggie waved good-bye as she leaned against the counter waiting for instructions from Charles.

Charles was crouched down on the floor, doing some calculations on a paper. He looked up at the young lady whose eyes were on him, patiently waiting. He smiled and looked back at the clipboard in his hand.

Okay God, he began in his head, *I'm having a hard time concentrating on this job. But I'm having an even harder time believing that You're calling her to be a Sister—or that I'm called to be single, for that matter. If she weren't so perfect in every way for me, I'd find this a whole lot easier. Do I run? Emergency bailout procedure? What do You want from me here?*

Maggie waited and watched. She would never have rushed him—she was used to working with her dad, giving him time to think without constant chatter.

This is a good opportunity for me to talk to you, Jesus. I just can't believe what a wonderful man you've made in Charles. Somewhere there's got to be the perfect girl for him. Don't make him wait forever. He'd make such an excellent husband and father. Bless him to always be so wholesome and good, faithful and true.

She smiled as she watched him work. He was obviously deep in thought. "Is there anything I can help you with?" she finally asked.

He looked back up at her. "I'm sorry," he said, standing up again. "Here." He stepped up to the island beside her with the clipboard. "Let's get some measurements down. He pulled out a tape measure from his pocket and walked over to the corner where the pantry was to go.

Maggie took the clipboard and got ready to take notes. Charles called out some numbers and Maggie quickly sketched the pantry, putting the measurements in the right place on the design. Charles walked back to the island to take a look.

"Here," Maggie said, offering the clipboard back to him.

"Hey," he stated. "You're good at this."

"I'm just trying to impress you," she said, simply, with a smile.

"You couldn't possibly impress me any more than you already have," he said, sincerely.

Maggie smiled. "I just want to do my dad proud."

"You do that, and then some," he said, turning around to assess the job. "Let's start cutting that wood."

By the time Sr. Chelsea came in to start supper, the two workers had the walls built and were just securing them in place.

"We can stop to give you more room to work, Sister," Charles told the young novice. "Is there anything I can do to help you with supper?" he offered, as they cleaned up the work area.

"Heavens, no!" exclaimed Sr. Chelsea. "Haven't you done enough for us?"

"I don't like to stand around doing nothing," he told her. "Put me to work for a while."

"You're staying for supper aren't you?" Maggie asked.

"That was the plan," he said.

"Well, then let's go shovel snow until supper," she suggested.

"Maggie!" scolded Sr. Chelsea. "Give the poor man a break."

"He's a farm boy," Maggie answered with a laugh. "He was made for working."

"It's true," Charles told Sr. Chelsea. "She knows what she's talking about."

"Come on," Maggie said. "There's a part in the back that's all iced up that you can help me chip away."

Maggie and Charles got dressed up for going outside again and went out through the back door to the large yard of the Sisters' house.

"See why I find this place adequate compensation for city life?" asked Maggie. "That's the tree I like to climb to read in." She pointed to the large willow in the corner of the yard.

"You climb trees in your skirt?"

"Absolutely. I can't give up being me altogether—at least not just yet. I guess in time if they ask me to start behaving more like a lady, I'll have to. But for now, they don't seem to mind my wild ways entirely. I think they've come to accept I'm not your stereotype for a Sister."

"You certainly are not," Charles agreed. "I'm sure they've created their own 'Maggie category' by now."

Maggie laughed. "How are *you* doing with categorizing me?"

"I'm working on it," he said. By this time he had taken the pick and had begun to work at the large ice patch on the walkway. He looked up at the icicles hanging from the drainpipe and commented, "I can see what job I have to do here next spring."

"You're a good man, Charles," Maggie said, working away at the ice with a spade. "I think I'll have to adopt you as my big brother."

Charles shook his head and smiled with his eyes closed. *I guess that's the answer I was looking for, God. But somehow it's not the one I was hoping for. I can respect it, though. Just be sure to let me know if there's any hope of it changing.*

Chapter 41

Wednesday was another great day. Maggie got home just as quickly as she could from her classes to work with Charles. She ran up to her room to drop off her books, fussed around with her hair in the mirror for a few minutes, and then ran down. He was as happy as ever to greet his co-worker, and was most appreciative of the extra set of hands. The twosome worked well together. Maggie just seemed to know what Charles needed before he even asked.

Thursday was an even better day. Maggie was home all day, and they were able to get at the job right after breakfast. Charles had come in earlier than the day before. They worked all morning and had a quick lunch break around eleven-thirty as they were both really hungry.

They got right back at the project after lunch. The pantry was taking great shape. They were sanding the drywall mud and getting ready to paint. Maggie loved painting. She had been looking forward to that job all along.

By two-thirty in the afternoon Maggie announced it was break time.

"Why? We're on a roll, here," he said, lifting the paint roller up toward his partner.

She laughed at his little pun. "I have a surprise for you," she informed him. "So just close up those cans of paint for a little while, and I'll get it ready."

She went and got the kettle off the stove, filled it with water, and returned it to the burner to heat it up.

"Tea?" he asked, keeping his eyes on the young girl, curious as to what she had up her sleeve.

"Mm-hmm," she answered, evasively.

She got the teapot out from one of the few remaining cupboards in the under-construction kitchen. She then went to the hallway where the boxes were lined up on the floor, and rummaged around until she found some tea. Harvest Spice was a flavour she loved. She set things out on the kitchen island as Charles came over to take a seat at one of the stools.

"So what's the big surprise?" he asked.

She smiled at him in a mysterious way as she set a plate out on the counter before him with a tea towel over it. "Check it out," she said, biting her lip with a big smile.

He lifted the towel, uncovering flat muffin-like pastries on the plate. "What is it?"

"Can't you guess?" she returned, tickled with delight.

Charles' eyes widened, his confused look now replace by a big smile. "Crumpets?" he asked with a laugh.

"I made them last night, just for you," she announced. "Aren't they the most pathetic looking things you've ever seen? And they taste even worse than they look," she warned him. "I'm afraid I'm not a very good cook."

Charles laughed. This girl took such delight in everything, even her failures. "Maggie, you are something else!"

"Try one," she implored him. "Go on. They taste just awful, but I made them for you, and I can't imagine another person on the face of this planet who would be brave enough to eat my lousy crumpets."

He continued to chuckle as he took one. She took one as well as she watched for his expression. He took a small bite and chewed. He shook his head a bit back and forth, as he let the jury of taste buds decide.

"They're not *that* bad," he said. "Kind of tasteless. Definitely chewy. But if you like chewy crumpets they're probably great."

She laughed. "Come on, Charles. They're awful. Just say it! You can't hurt my feelings."

"No, really," he insisted, "they're not that bad. Do you mind if I dunk it?" he said, aiming it toward his cup of tea?

"There are no high tea rules today," Maggie told him. "You don't even have to hold up your pinkie with crumpets such as these."

"Sorry, but the habit is already formed, my lady," he said as he lifted the cup to his mouth with his pinkie raised. He then took the crumpet and dipped it in and took another bite. "Really, they're not that bad," he assured her.

"Watch out or I'll send the whole batch of them home with you," she warned him. "That'll be your punishment for lying."

"Well, you're eating them," he said, pointing to the crumpet in her hand.

"I have to. It's called learning by natural consequence. If you create a baking disaster like this," she said, pointing to the crumpets, "then you won't repeat that mistake again if you have to eat the lousy things. I'm just not sure why you're punishing yourself like this."

"I feel a sense of responsibility, having given you the recipe for them," he confessed.

"Bet you won't do something as foolish as that again," she commented.

"You can't be this bad a cook at everything." He held a crumpet out in front of himself for examination.

"Maybe not *this* bad—but I am a fairly bad cook all 'round," she admitted. "My family didn't allow me too many opportunities in the kitchen. They couldn't stand to eat all my failed experiments. Like egg salad sandwiches. How can you go wrong with that? But they were *so* bad. I hadn't let the eggs cook long enough, and so they were all still runny when I mixed them up." She scrunched up her nose in disgust.

"And then there was the time I made macaroni and cheese," she went on. "I cooked it on low heat for almost an hour, without ever having brought the macaroni to a boil. It was just like a pot of glue ... absolutely disgusting. Need I go on?"

"I'm beginning to get a picture here," he told her.

"What about you? Can you cook at all?"

"I'm surviving as a bachelor," he told her, tapping his belly.

"Not that you have a gut on you or anything, Mr. 'Zero Percent Body Fat'," she returned.

"I don't think I'm quite that thin," he returned. "But I'm not that bad a cook at all, if I do say so myself. Maybe I'll have to have you out sometime so that I can cook for you."

"Show off," Maggie said in reply to his offer.

"How about Sunday? Have you asked your family yet if they're free to come?" he questioned, reminding her of their proposed plans to go snowmobiling on the weekend. "I'll make supper for everyone."

"I'll phone my folks tonight to find out. I mentioned it the other day, but Mom wasn't sure if it would work for them. And you *don't* have to make us all supper."

"Remember, I come from a large family, too. I know how to cook for a crowd."

"Fine. But let me know what we can bring," she said, waving a crumpet at him.

"Anything but crumpets," he said, with a laugh, ducking with his arms up to protect himself as Maggie threw the one at him that she had in her hand.

The crumpet hit him on the shoulder and bounced off onto the floor. "Good bounce to those things," he said, most impressed.

Maggie laughed, and Charles laughed with her.

They finished their tea party—crumpets and all—with more than a dozen left over for her to package up and send home with him, just as she had warned him she would do.

They got back to their painting and laughed their way through another fun afternoon of work together.

✟   ✟   ✟

Amie and Katie climbed into their beds Thursday night following band practice. It was another cold, winter's night. The temperature had taken a steep dive over the course of the week to minus forty. The old, poorly insulated house had a hard time keeping up with the heat under those conditions. The girls wrapped themselves up snugly in their beds with an extra blanket under their covers.

"Katie?" Amie called out quietly in the darkness of their room.

"Mm-hmm?" answered the younger sister.

"Have you ever thought about religious life for yourself?" Amie asked.

"Not really," Katie admitted. "I mean I'm not against it or anything— but deep down inside I'm afraid that if I think about it too much God might call me to it, and I really don't want to give up my dream of getting married someday and having a family."

"I know what you mean," Amie said. "I used to always feel that way, too. But lately I keep thinking how it might be really cool to give my life to Christ the way Maggie has."

"Serious?" asked Katie. "That's so unlike you, Amie."

"I know. Which makes me wonder if I really have a calling to religious life or not. I mean, for the first time in my life, I'm not afraid to think about it."

"Wow," Katie remarked. "I don't think I'm where you're at. I was just as happy to know that God had called Maggie—which somehow sort of meant the rest of us were off the hook."

The two girls started giggling together. They both knew how ridiculous the thought was—but somehow in the desperate attempts of a teenage girl to sort out life, it just made sense.

"Poor Maggie," Amie said, still giggling. "I don't know if she realizes that she's some sort of victim soul for the rest of us. Maybe she wasn't called to religious life at all. Maybe it's supposed to be me, and I've shirked my responsibility, so she's had to pick up the slack for the family and sacrifice her vocation to married life."

"I'm okay with that," Katie stated, "just as long as you don't decide that it really was supposed to be me—and you two run off getting married and stick me with religious life."

The two sisters began laughing harder.

"Aren't we bad?" Amie said, pulling her covers up around her more snugly. "Why do girls always have so many fears about religious life? As if they would somehow be cheated by God if they were called to that instead of marriage?"

"I don't know," Katie answered. "Probably because we don't want to give up our fairy-tale dreams of being carried off by a knight in shining armour to some castle where we can live happily-ever-after."

"But when does that ever happen?" Amie asked.

"Probably never," stated Katie. "But the dream still exists in almost every girl I know."

"I mean every marriage—no matter how good it'll be—will have suffering. And I know Mom's happy to be a mom, but it sure hasn't been easy for her to raise a family. And I love Dad and all—I might even pass him off as a knight in shining armour—but this house is no castle," Amie stated.

"I don't know," Katie remarked. "I understand those old castles get pretty cold at night."

They both laughed. It was freezing in their bedroom.

"Good point. I don't think I have any feeling left in my nose." Amie reached up from under the covers to touch it. "It's still there," she announced, as she quickly pulled her hand back under the covers.

"Are you really thinking about religious life?" Katie asked, more seriously.

"I am," Amie answered. "I really am."

"Well," Katie stated, thoughtfully, "maybe the real prince in our dreams is Jesus, and His Kingdom is much better than any old, cold castle we could dream up here on earth."

"Could be," Amie replied. "I mean, ultimately, even for those called to marriage, the real union we seek is with Christ. So maybe those who are called to religious life just skip that step and go straight for the glory."

"Maybe," Katie commented. "But obviously some are called to marriage for good reason."

"Of course," Amie agreed. "I'm just trying to figure out why religious life suddenly keeps pulling at my heart these days?"

"I'll pray for you—to know God's will," Katie told her sister. "Just don't go trying to loop me into this vocational crisis. I'm happy with my fairy-tale dreams for now."

"I promise," Amie assured her. "Are you too tired to pray a rosary with me now?"

"I'll start it," Katie answered. "But I can't guarantee to stay awake throughout it. Hypothermia might set in before we finish, and I might fall asleep and never wake up."

Amie chuckled. "Well, then you can go be with the real Prince Charming in His Kingdom forever. So, you just can't lose," she said, reaching for her rosary under her pillow. She made the sign of the cross and then quickly rearranged the covers tightly around her as they began to pray.

Chapter 42

Friday morning Maggie was glad to be going off to early classes, even if it was freezing outside. She had not eaten breakfast that morning—she was not at all hungry. As she walked to campus, all bundled up, her thoughts went back to her dream from the night before.

She was standing in a beautiful garden, it was so colourful—whoever said you don't dream in colour? Maggie's dream had been in Technicolor! The plants in the garden were so green, and the soil so rich and dark and fertile. There were pretty flowers all around the edge of the garden. As she looked beyond, she saw children at play. They were so sweet and so happy. Then she realized someone was standing beside her. She looked up, and it was Charles.

Maggie looked into his eyes; he seemed so familiar. Suddenly she realized—they were married. Panic raced through her mind as she tried to remember when this had happened. How had it happened? It felt so natural to be standing there with Charles. She looked over again at the children, two red-headed girls in ponytails, and two dark-haired boys in overalls. They were all so adorable. And those boys—both of them, Charles in miniature—were just too cute for words.

She looked back up at Charles. He was more than cute. He was handsome. His eyes were so gentle, his smile, so warm and welcoming. He was everything she could have ever wanted in a husband—strong, true, devout in his faith, funny. She liked to be with him. He made her laugh. He made her feel so alive and so appreciated—so cherished. He was perfect for her.

She quickly looked back to the children, and they were gone. As she looked around she realized the garden was gone. Charles was gone. Where was she?

She was sitting on the doorstep at the Sisters' house. It was a cool spring day. It was very cool. In fact, it was cold. She tried to pull her sweater tighter around her shoulders, but it kept slipping out of her fingers. The colder she felt, the more she tried, and the more frustrated she became. Suddenly, in frustration, she stood up.

Maggie woke up to find herself standing beside her bed. She was shivering. It was freezing in her room. Her comforter was on the floor. She reached down and grabbed it and jumped back into bed. She pulled the comforter in around her and shivered away in the dark. She looked at her alarm clock—it was five-thirty-three in the morning. It would soon be time for her to get up.

Her mind quickly went back to the garden. It had been so warm and beautiful. The children—she wanted to see her children again. What did they look like? How many had there been? A boy. No, two boys and two girls. They were so sweet, so innocent, so happy. And Charles. She thought about how he looked in the dream. It was how he truly looked— handsome as could be. Why had she never before stopped to consider just how handsome he really was? She wanted to reach out and touch him and remember how real he was: not just a dream, but the man she knew. She wished she had just held his hand, even once, in that dream. She wanted to hold his hand for real. She wanted to be married to him for real. She wanted to have those children for real.

As all the emotions of the dream welled up inside of Maggie, she grabbed her comforter and pulled it overtop of her head. She lay for a moment under the blankets—hoping the feelings would all disappear in the stillness of early morning. She breathed calmly and closed her eyes. She was fine. It had just been a dream. *Oh, but what a dream!* And then . . . her heart betrayed her mind, and Charles was there again—just as he had been in her dream—looking back at her in her mind's eye.

She threw the covers back off of her and sat up in bed. She was so upset that she completely forgot how cold she was. She searched in the dim light of the room to see her pictures of Our Lady of Guadalupe and the Divine Mercy image of Christ, which hung on the wall across from the foot of her bed. As her eyes worked to make out the shapes of Our Lady and Our Lord, they slowly began to take form, and she found the words inside of herself to pray.

I have never before wanted a man in my life for anything other than a friend or a brother, so what are You doing to me, Jesus, sending me a dream like that? What am I supposed to think now? How am I supposed to work with Charles now? How am I supposed to face him—now that I've felt what it would be like to be his wife?

How could You have made him so perfect for me? Why . . . after all these years of me only wanting to be Your bride, are You allowing someone into my life to distract me from You? Don't You want me anymore? Is this what You really want for me? In all these years I've never felt You calling me to marriage. So what? You send me to a convent now, so I could discover my call to married life?

What do You want from me? Why do You have to be so confusing and so evasive? Why can't You just spell out Your will for my life? I've never been angry with You before—but I am so upset over this. I don't know who to be angry with, You or me?

Have I failed You, or have You failed me somehow? Okay, now that I say that, I know it's ridiculous. You could never fail me. So obviously I'm failing You. Unless, of course, I'm not. Unless, of course, this is what You want for me.

Have You ever considered being more direct with Your children? You can do anything—You're God. So why don't You just speak to me right now so that I know what You really want from me? Oh, why does this have to be so hard?

Maggie sunk her head into her hands and began to cry. She cried for herself and her shattered dreams of religious life. She felt like she had somehow betrayed Christ in her weakness, and that even if she were to continue with religious life, she would never be the same again.

Then she began to feel cheated out of her eclipsing dream of married life with Charles. Maybe that was not for her after all, and now she would be stuck forever in religious life, and she would have to allow that beautiful dream to fade from her mind and her heart. How could she let go of that image, now that it had imprinted itself in her mind? How could she forget those children—*her* children—her children with *Charles?* She threw her face down into her pillow and sobbed. Never before in her life had she ever cried like this.

She cried until her head hurt. She cried until the throbbing in her head began to feel so real that she could actually hear it . . . throb . . . throb . . . throb . . .

It was her alarm. She *never* set it to that obnoxious beeping sound—she always had it set to the local Christian radio station. It was as though God was mocking her in her misery. She hit the snooze button on the alarm to shut-up the noise and then she picked it up to turn it off so it would not go off again. She stared at the time: five-fifty a.m.

Wiping her eyes, she got up from her bed. She shivered in the cold of her room as she quickly got dressed for the day. She slipped into the bathroom to get ready to go down for morning prayers—the Sisters would be meeting in just a few minutes. She splashed water over her eyes to try to help the redness go down. Her eyes were puffy and swollen. She looked awful. She looked worse than awful. Someone would be sure to ask. She splashed more water on her face and did her best to pull herself together.

She went down for prayers, avoiding eye contact with everyone. As soon as prayers were done, she bundled up as warmly as she could for the day, grabbed her book bag, and left before anyone could ask her any questions.

As Maggie walked to campus, she knew that today would be a total right-off for classes. She could not concentrate. All she could think about was that dream and Charles. Why had she had a dream like that? Was she really in love with Charles? She thought back over the last few days they had spent together working. She had never had so much fun building—not even with her father. It was different with Charles. His attentiveness to her was so different from what she had ever experienced with any other man.

She thought back to how she had been around him. Was she sending him signals of affection without even being aware that she was? She thought of how she would race to meet him each day. She thought about how she would fuss in the morning to get ready for the day. She had been paying special attention to her appearance all week. She spent every possible moment with him. She had even made him crumpets—lousy, awful-tasting crumpets—that he was polite enough to eat with her. He had even taken the leftovers home with him! Now, if that was not love, what was?

She was beginning to face the fact that she did have feelings for Charles that she had never before considered. And he obviously must have had feelings for her as well. *De-Nile is not just a river in Egypt,* she reminded herself. *How, Lord, could I have possibly been so fooled by myself? Here I was thinking I was so cool with Charles—just like a sister and brother. What a fool I've been. I can't believe I've made such a fool out of myself. How will I face him again, this afternoon? I can't do it, Lord. I'm too afraid of what I'll discover when I look into those hazel eyes of his again in person, not just in a dream.*

As Maggie walked slowly to campus she knew she was in no shape to go to classes. She was early—plenty early—for school. She looked at her watch. She had time to go to the chapel to pray. That's what she would do.

She found her way to the Catholic college and went straight to the chapel, hoping not to run into anyone she knew. Sitting in the back corner of the chapel, she looked up at the little, red light flickering by the tabernacle. Somehow her heart was not stirred by Christ's real presence. That was not a typical experience for Maggie. She was always so spiritually in tune. Today her spirit and mind were just completely out of sync. She sat and stared. Finally when nothing was soothing her soul anyway, she got up and walked to her first class. It was going to be a long day.

Chapter 43

Charles looked up at the clock on the wall as Maggie walked slowly into the kitchen. "What happened to you?" he asked. "I was beginning to worry that something was wrong. I thought maybe I should go looking for you in the cold—but then again, I had no idea where you were."

"No need to fuss over me," she said quietly. "I was just taking my time today."

Charles stopped his work and looked at the young woman. Something was wrong. The skip was gone from her step. The sparkle was missing from her eyes.

"Are you okay? You don't seem to be yourself today."

"I just had a bad sleep last night. I'll be fine. Let's get to work. How can I help you?"

"You sure that's it?"

"Yeah, I ate one too many of those lousy crumpets yesterday," she said, trying to pick up her voice in humour, but not quite succeeding.

"Couldn't be that. I had two before I went to bed last night, and I slept like a baby."

She shrugged her shoulders. "So what can I do for you today, sir?"

"You're really not gonna tell me what's on your mind?"

"Nope," she said, shaking her head with a little smile. "You'll just have to put up with me. Remember, I'm a girl. It's good for you to see this emotionally unstable part of my personality. I wouldn't want you to go away from here thinking I was above such things."

"Well," he said shaking his head slightly, "I grew up with five sisters. I've seen it all when it comes to girls and their ups and downs. Nothing you can do can shock me. And I've also come to the conclusion that God made men fairly emotionally stable," he motioned with his hand as though running it across a straight surface, "to bring balance to this universe with women."

Maggie chuckled at his philosophizing. "Good luck bringing balance to my universe today."

He chuckled with her. "Just remember," he added, looking directly at her, more seriously this time. "If you don't want to talk to me about what's bugging you—no problem. I'm not insulted. But don't expect me to read your mind. If you want to tell me something . . . if I've done something to offend you, Maggie, I want you to tell me straight out. Don't get upset with me for not knowing what you're thinking."

"I'm not upset with you at all, Charles," she said, sincerely. She looked up at him, into his eyes—and that was the mistake she made. *Oh, shoot, Maggie. Why'd you do that? You knew you'd get into trouble for that!* She took a deep breath. Her eyes were locked with his.

He looked down at her, patiently waiting for her to say something else. She just stood there staring back, biting down on her bottom lip. Her eyes began to tear a bit. She closed them, silently working at reining in her emotions.

Charles put his hand on Maggie's shoulder. The touch of his hand was something she had never felt before—warmth ran through her body. She kept her eyes closed and breathed deeply. She was not going to break down here and cry. She was not going to tell him what was going on inside of her. She was going to open her eyes again and get back to work as if everything was fine. She was going to sort this out on her own—or with her parents' advice. But she was not going to impose—or expose—her emotional frailty of the moment on Charles. She took another deep breath, opened her eyes, and smiled back up at him.

Charles was impressed. This girl had fortitude. "You okay?"

She nodded. "Let's get to work."

He could see she needed to keep whatever was upsetting her to herself for the time being, and he more than respected that. He handed her a small paint brush for cutting in. She knew what to do with it, and so she got right to work.

They worked in silence for a long time. Charles plugged away at his tasks, while Maggie did hers. They passed things back and forth to each other as needed, but otherwise, nothing else was said.

By the time Sr. Becky came in to get supper going, things were looking pretty good. The painting was almost done. Charles had brought over the door and window, but these would not be able to be put in until the paint had dried enough. He also had all the hardware sitting in a box ready to go to install shelves. The boards for the shelves had been measured and cut at home before he came—with the edges all finished and ready to be put up.

"Looks like we'll have to work on this tomorrow," he told Maggie. "You free to help?"

"I should be. I don't have anything on Saturdays."

"Great. Well, I'll get going then," he announced as he cleaned up the work area.

"You're not staying for supper?" Sr. Becky asked.

"Not today," he told her. "I fast on Fridays anyway—and I should get back to the farm to do some chores. Thanks anyway."

Maggie was disappointed and relieved all at the same time to see Charles packing up to go. She walked him to the door, carrying a few things for him. As he stopped to get his jacket on, she stood there waiting, wondering if she should say something. Finally, just as he was ready to leave, she spoke. "I'm sorry about today, Charles."

"What are you apologizing for?" he asked, smiling at her. "We all have bad days, Maggie."

She nodded. "But I shouldn't have taken my bad day out on you."

"I don't think you did. I think you were just being comfortable enough to be you. I'll take it as a compliment," he added with another smile.

"You're a really great guy, Charles. I've never known anyone like you."

"Trust me, Maggie. I'm not this candid and comfortable around everyone. You just have a way of making me feel free to be me. So watch out," he warned her, "I might be the one having the bad day next. Then *you'll* have to deal with it."

Maggie laughed. "Thanks, Charles, for being so understanding."

"No problem. You have a good night, Maggie, and I'll see you tomorrow. We started this thing together and we're almost done."

"Oh," she added, perking up as she remembered to tell him something. "My mom called last night and said that Sunday was a go for them . . . that is, if it still works for you."

"Got it marked on my calendar already."

"And I mentioned to her about supper, and she said to tell you that she'll bring dessert."

"Sounds like a deal. I'll go get those snowmobiles tuned up and ready to go. And let's pray that Sunday's not so cold. Snowmobiling is no fun in this kind of weather."

Maggie smiled. "Sounds good." She felt relaxed and free for the first time that day. For a moment, the distraction of Sunday's plans helped her to forget her other worries. "I'll see you tomorrow," she said, waving her hand as Charles turned to leave.

He waved back and headed down the front step, pulling his jacket in snugly around his neck—it was bitingly cold.

✝   ✝   ✝

"Well, what brings us the honour of this visit?" John Collins asked, as Maggie entered the dining room of their house that Friday evening after supper.

"I needed to come home for a visit." She walked over to the big oak table and gave her dad a hug.

"Nice to see you, Schnooks," he said, hugging her back. "Come, sit and visit with us."

Judy walked over to the table from the kitchen and gave Maggie a hug. As Maggie hugged her mom, she began to cry.

"What's up, sweetheart?" Judy asked her daughter, still holding her in a hug.

"Can we go for a drive or something?" Maggie asked. "I'd just like to talk to the two of you in private, if that's okay."

"Better than that," John suggested, "you just come up to our bedroom, and we'll close the door on the rest of the world. It's too cold a night to go driving."

"Sounds good," Maggie said.

Judy led the way with Maggie holding her hand as they walked up to her parents' room.

"Hey, Maggie's home!" exclaimed Zack on his way down the stairs.

"Hi, Zack," Maggie said with a big smile—effectively covering up her state of emotional chaos.

"Maggie's here, but Maggie's going to be busy with us for a little while," Judy told her son. "She can come play cards or something with you kids later."

"Cool," said Zack.

"Oh, and by the way, Zack, Charles said you can all come out snow-mobiling on Sunday. But you'd better pray for warmer weather," she told the red-headed boy.

"Yes!" he exclaimed, pulling his arm down in a fist beside him. He ran off to tell Isaac, Aaron, and Jessie the good news.

"Quick, Schnooks, in here," her dad said, pulling her into the room before anyone else saw her.

Maggie laughed at his playfulness, and ran in quickly as he closed the door behind her and her mother.

"You take the seat of honour," Judy told her, pointing to the rocking chair in the corner of the room.

John picked up the chair and placed it right beside the bed, motioning for Maggie to be seated. He and his wife sat side by side on the bed, facing Maggie, and waited for her to tell them what this was all about.

Maggie looked at them both and suddenly felt completely stupid about the whole thing. She was no longer even sure why she had come home.

"What's up, Maggie?" Judy asked. "Are you going to just look at us all night, or are you going to talk?"

Maggie kind of smiled and then shook her head. "I just feel so silly. Suddenly when I'm sitting here looking at the two of you, it just seems like my problems aren't even real."

"Well, what are your problems?" John asked.

"Can you guess?" Maggie asked, testing her parents' perceptiveness.

Judy looked at John, who just raised his hands toward his daughter. He was completely clueless. Maggie looked at her mom. Judy looked back into her daughter's eyes, knowingly. Maggie just waited for her mom to say something.

"It's Charles, isn't it?" Judy asked.

Maggie started nodding. She closed her eyes and then all the feelings came back at the sound of his name coming from her mother: all the confusion, all the questioning, and the dream from the night before. It was all there, and Maggie began to cry.

"What about Charles?" John asked. "Have I missed something here?"

"Sort of," Judy told him, patting him on the leg. "But you're a guy—you're not expected to pick up on these things."

Maggie started laughing through her tears.

"Would you please fill me in?" John asked, looking at Maggie with anxious eyes.

"Dad, my whole life I thought I knew God was calling me to religious life. I can't ever remember a time when I didn't want to become a Sister—especially a Sister of the Immaculate Conception. And my whole time there at the Sisters' house has been perfect—completely confirming that this is my vocation. And then . . ." she paused, as if she did not need to state the obvious.

"And then Charles came along?" her father asked. "I thought you were still too young to notice a good-looking young man like that," he stated, reminding her of their conversation over last Sunday's supper.

"I thought I was," she told him. "I thought I was above such silliness as 'falling in love' . . . which was completely incomprehensible to me my whole life. I could never relate to other girls' foolishness over boys. But I guess I was wrong—I'm not above it at all. And I feel so confused now and silly and stupid and frustrated and, you name it, I feel it."

"Have you talked to Charles about your feelings?" Judy asked her daughter.

"Not at all," she stated emphatically. "Although, I know he knows something's upsetting me. I was just awful to him today when he came to work at the house. I can't believe how out of control all my emotions are. I'm so embarrassed."

"So he hasn't said anything to you?" John asked. "I mean, in terms of his feelings."

"Not at all," Maggie stated. "He's way too gentlemanly to make a move on an 'almost-Sister', as he puts it."

"So, I'm still confused here," said John. "What exactly has happened between you two?"

Maggie went on to explain her relationship with Charles, the time they had spent together. She even mentioned the crumpets, at which point they all had a good laugh. Then she told her parents about her dream and how she had woken up that morning, suddenly aware that Charles had crept into her heart—in a place that had only ever belonged to Jesus before now.

"I guess I should have been guarding my heart better," she told her parents. "I just didn't think my heart was capable of these feelings—so I never worried about it."

John scratched his head and looked at Maggie. "You know, honey, you keep sounding like falling in love with a man is the worst thing that could ever happen to you. But maybe, just maybe, God placed Charles in your life because He is calling you to marriage—not religious life. And if that were the case, there is absolutely no disgrace in that at all. Personally, I like Charles. I'd have no problem with you marrying a man like Charles . . . if that is indeed what God has planned for you."

Maggie sighed and kept silent.

"Look, honey," her mother said, "the choice between religious life and marriage is not the choice between good versus evil. It's the choice between two goods. They're both beautiful callings in life. But I have to say, I really think it's wonderful that you've finally discovered that you have a woman's heart. You're normal, Maggie." Judy laughed and shook her head, looking straight into Maggie's eyes. "Honestly, sweetheart, I used to worry about you and the way you'd look down at the other girls for being so interested in boys. You need to have the balance of seeing the beauty of both vocations, and the call to single life as well, for that matter."

"So you don't think I'm being silly?" Maggie asked.

"Do you think I was silly for falling in love with your father and marrying him?" Judy returned the question.

Maggie looked over at her dad, who smiled back at her expectantly. "Do you really want me to answer that?" Maggie teased, still looking at her father.

"Be careful there, Schnooks," her father said, raising a finger in warning.

"You're right, Mom," she said, taking a deep breath as she cast her gaze downward. "I just woke up this morning, so afraid of all these new emotions. I didn't know what to do with them at all." Maggie sat silently for a moment. Looking up again at both her parents, she asked. "What do you think I should do? I mean, what do *you* think God's calling me to?"

"Uh-uh," Judy said with a laugh, shaking a finger at Maggie. "This is *your* discernment process, honey. We're not going to sit here and tell you what to do."

"Not at all," her father said in agreement with his wife. "You have to walk through this, Maggie, yourself, in order to come to the place where *you* know in your own heart what God is calling you to."

"Can't you advise me at all?" she asked, disappointment apparent.

"Yeah," John said. "Go talk to Sr. Charlotte."

"Are you *kidding?*" Maggie asked, her voice raised in total disbelief. "I can't go to *her*. Charles is her brother! She'll never forgive me for . . . well, for sort of falling in love with him."

John and Judy started laughing. "Maggie," Judy said, looking directly into her daughter's eyes. "If you and Charles are called to marriage, do you think you're somehow going to pull it off without Sr. Charlotte finding out? Of course you have to go talk to her about this."

"Not only that, sweetie," John added. "Sr. Charlotte is your superior— the Director of Novices for *your* chosen order. If you become a Sister of the Immaculate Conception, you'll be going to her and answering to her for a great many years, my dear. You'd better get used to it now."

Maggie looked down at her feet and anxiously bounced them about on the floor in front of her chair. "I guess you're right," she said with great resignation. "Aghghgh!" she grunted, pounding her feet on the floor. "I wanted to get through this without her finding out. I just wanted to come to you, find out I'm crazy, and just let the whole Charles-thing go, and then move on without ever having to admit to Sr. Charlotte that I had been totally attracted to her younger brother—with whom I've just spent the last week of my life, every day, under her own nose. I just feel so cheap about the whole thing—when I think about it—like I've done something dishonest."

"Maggie! There's that terrible attitude surfacing again. The one that says romance is something cheap and beneath you. And I don't like it," her mother admonished. "I am so happy that the Lord has brought this into your life, because you are going to have to grapple with the fact that the love between a man and a woman—as it was intended to be by God—is a holy, beautiful thing. And then, only then, will you be free to choose between marriage and religious life."

Maggie looked at her mother, like a child who had just been scolded—as she was.

"I want you to pray about this seriously," her mother told her. "I want you to ask Jesus to reveal to you what His will is for you and for Charles and your relationship. And I want you to do it in a way that treats Charles with the respect he deserves. . . . And I don't think you should talk to him about this just yet. I think this is something you have to sort out for yourself in prayer, first."

"I agree," John said. "In fact, I think we should pray about this together right now—the three of us."

Maggie nodded. They each made the sign of the cross and then, holding hands together, began to pray.

"Heavenly Father," began John, "we lift up to You our daughter, Maggie—who is first and foremost Your daughter. We ask You to guide her mind and her heart through this time of discernment so that she will know what Your holy will is for her life. We ask You to pour out the Precious Blood of Your Son, Our Lord Jesus Christ, over Maggie and Charles, protecting them from all deception and all temptations that might present themselves in their relationship. Keep them pure and keep their eyes and hearts focused on You and Your most holy will. We thank You, Lord, for the gift of Your love poured out in our lives, and we ask that You would reveal to Maggie how she is being called to share that love—which is You—in our world. May all we do be for Your love and for Your glory. We pray this all in Jesus' name. Your will be done. Amen."

✟   ✟   ✟

When Charles showed up the next morning at the Sisters' house there was a "renewed" Maggie, greeting him at the door.

"Come on in, Charles," she said, with a bright, happy smile. She reached forward to take his coat for him. "Are you ready to get to work?"

Charles looked at Maggie and laughed. "I'm ready if you are."

"Well, let's get at 'er," she said. "Daylight's wasting."

Maggie and Charles got right at the job before them. The new refrigerator was being delivered that afternoon, and they wanted the pantry shelves, door, and window installed before that so that they could present the order with their new and improved kitchen all at once.

They worked; they talked; they laughed: just like nothing had ever happened differently the day before.

Though Charles was confused over the dramatic change in Maggie, he knew enough not to question it. He had spent much of the night before praying for Maggie and praying for himself. Instinctively he knew that Maggie was struggling over him. He was struggling over her.

He knew he needed to go to Sr. Charlotte and discuss the whole thing with her. He also knew that there was no way he could breach the topic of their relationship with Maggie for the time being. Maggie was discerning her call as a Bride of Christ. Who was he to step in and try to steal her heart away from the Lord?

No. If they were meant to be together, God would reveal it to him in a way that was completely clear. And if they were not meant to be together, God would set him at peace with Maggie becoming a Sister. Of these things Charles was certain.

By three in the afternoon the new fridge was in its place, the pantry was ready to go, and the two renovators called all the Sisters down into the kitchen and told them to keep their eyes closed. Maggie and Charles assisted the women to walk in, while covering their eyes. Once everyone had made it into the room, Maggie called out, "Tah-dah!" with her arms opened wide.

The Sisters opened their eyes, and to their delight the kitchen was not just completed, it was beautiful. Maggie told Kyra to go open the pantry door, which her companion aspirant did. As Kyra opened the door, the light for the pantry came on, shining through the stained glass window. Everyone was awed by the sight of it.

"It was Charles' idea to put in the window and to install the light switch in the door," Maggie boasted of her co-worker's creativity.

"Very impressive, brother," Sr. Charlotte said.

Sr. Pauline went over and checked out the new fridge. She was pleased. They all laughed at how she was especially thrilled with the see-through drawers for produce in the fridge.

All-in-all the renovation had been a great success, met by the approval of the entire order. They celebrated with cookies and juice in the dining room.

Charles did not stay for supper that night. He had things to get done back at the farm, especially with company coming the next day. Maggie helped him clean up his tools and load up the supplies in the back of his truck.

"It's a nicer day today," he commented to the young woman as they walked down the front walk from the Sisters' house together.

"Sorry that yesterday was so awkward," she apologized.

"No, silly," he said with a laugh. "I'm referring to the weather. It's warming up in time for our snowmobile-fest tomorrow."

"Oh, I'm not surprised at all," she informed Charles, with a laugh. "My brothers are all at home praying hard for good weather for tomorrow."

"I'll have to remember them the next time I need something. I can always use a few good prayer warriors," he remarked while loading the last few things into the truck.

"So, we'll see you in the afternoon," she said. "We'll eat lunch in the car as we drive out after morning Mass."

"Sounds good," he said with a smile. He walked around to the driver's side and waved to Maggie as he got into the truck.

She waved back to him enthusiastically, with a smile going from ear to ear, as he drove off.

Charles was relieved to see Maggie back to her old self again. It had been an enjoyable day together, and he was looking forward to the next day with her whole family at the farm. But he was cautious in his anticipation. As he drove home, he prayed.

Lord Jesus, help me to keep this relationship in perspective. Give me the patience I need to allow You to reveal Your will for Maggie and me. I need a sign from You, Jesus—boy, do I ever!

I'm just so confused by my feelings for her. I've never felt like this toward any girl before. But that doesn't mean she's for me. And until You show me that she is for me, Lord ... and I mean, I want You to show me so that there's no mistaking it ... well, until that time, Lord, help me to treat Your daughter with the respect deserving of the daughter of a King. Help me to honour her and to cherish her as my sister in You.

And help me to be grateful, no matter what, for the gift she has been in my life. I thank You for this beautiful woman, Lord. I know I'm a better man for having come to know Maggie as You have allowed me to come to know her.

Fill us both with Your love and a desire to do Your will at all times. And if she's meant to be a Sister, bless her in her vocation ... and give us both Your peace. Amen.

Chapter 44

That Saturday night Amie got ready for bed earlier than usual. She was tired and just wanted to cozy up with a good book. As she was climbing into her bed to get comfortable, she decided she would do better first to have a talk with her parents. There had been something on her mind for several days—persistently nagging at her. Perhaps talking about it with her mom and dad would help her to be able to set it all to rest, or open it up to be dealt with. One way or another she knew it was time.

She slipped a bathrobe on over her pyjamas and sought out her folks for a little talk. She found them in the living room, reading, all alone. That itself felt like a sign from God. When, with all those little kids in the house, did she ever find her parents all alone—unplanned?

"Hey, Mom . . . hey, Dad."

"What's up, Scuttle-Butt?" her father asked, not looking up from his magazine.

"You got a minute?" she asked.

John put the magazine down on his lap and looked up at his daughter. "I think I can spare a minute or two for you. What about you, dear?"

"Well, make it fast," Judy said looking at her watch, as she closed the book she had been reading. "I've got some pies in the oven for tomorrow." Seeing Amie's confused look, Judy laughed and motioned for her daughter to come sit with them. "I'm just joking, honey. Of course I have time for you."

Amie laughed and sat down on the footstool by the couch, facing her parents. "I just wanted to ask you both to pray for me," she said, in quite a serious manner. "You see, lately I've been wondering if God's calling me to religious life or not."

Judy and John's faces fell blank.

"You're kidding," said Judy. "I mean . . ." she shook her head to correct herself for her response and added, with calculation, "I mean . . . that's really something, dear. When did this all come about?"

John just sat there, staring blankly at his daughter—as if he did not even recognize her.

"Come on," Amie said, patting her legs nervously, looking anxiously from her mom to her dad and back again. "Don't make fun of me, guys. I'm serious."

"Honey, I'm not trying to make fun of you," her mother said, sincerely. "I'm just . . . shocked. This is so unexpected from you."

John still said nothing.

"Dad, stop looking at me that way," Amie pleaded. "You're making me nervous." She reached forward, grabbed his leg, and shook it.

"Amie," John began, slowly, "I just am at a total loss for words here. I have no idea what to say to you. I just ... if you had come in here and told me that you had just met some guy and that you were all in love and wanted to get married—now that I'd be prepared for. But ... religious life? That's just so un-Amie-ish."

"So, what you're saying is—you don't think I'd make a very good Sister or Nun?" she asked with accusation ringing in her voice.

"No, Amie, I'm not saying that at all. I'm just saying I wasn't prepared for this. I have to wrap my mind around it a bit," he told her.

"Well, how about I put it this way, then," she proposed. "I just wanted to let you both know that there's some guy in my life right now who's got me totally captivated ... and I think I've fallen in love with Him. Now, how does that sound?"

"Sounds wonderful, sweetheart," said her mom with a chuckle, "And very Amie-ish. And assuming that this captivating guy that you are referring to is Jesus ... well, that just makes it even more wonderful."

"Yeah," the young girl said, looking very much *"in love"*. "It really is. And I just feel so drawn to Jesus these days, in a whole new way. And suddenly I realized—for the first time in my life—that maybe religious life isn't so scary after all. I mean ... well, you know what I mean. You know how the idea of giving up the chance to get married and have children is such a big obstacle for so many girls, when it comes to considering religious life. Now, suddenly for me it just seems that dedicating my life to Christ in that way ... well, maybe I wouldn't miss those other things so much. I mean, maybe what I would get in return from Christ would more than compensate for what I would be giving up to become His bride."

She looked at her parents, trying to figure out if she had lost them in her feeble attempt to express what she was feeling. "I'm just saying that I'm open to religious life ... and that's such a revelation for me that I felt it was worth mentioning to you both, and asking you both to pray for me."

Judy smiled warmly at her daughter. "Oh, my Amie," she said, with all her maternal affection. "I think it's a wonderful revelation, and I would be more than happy to pray for you about it. And ... I'm sorry we didn't give you a better reaction."

Judy looked over at her husband who still had a confused look on his face. She smacked him on the leg and he turned his head to her, trying to bring to mind what she had just said. "Say something, John ... intelligent."

"I'm sorry, but I'm still lost on the idea that this is Amie, and meanwhile . . ." he cut himself off before he revealed anything about Maggie's situation to Amie. "Sorry, Scuttle-Butt," he corrected himself. "I haven't been listening very well. I just had other things on my mind. But I heard enough to say this—I'm proud of you."

Amie smiled at her dad.

"Really, it's showing that you've come to a maturity beyond just, 'I'm ready for marriage, let's get on with it,' " he said, attempting to imitate Amie, rather playfully.

"Dad!" She hit him on the leg. "I don't talk like that!"

"Of course you don't, sweetie," he returned with a big laugh. "I'm just having some fun with you. But seriously, it is nice to see you embracing your relationship with Christ in this way. I'm not sure what will come of it. Maybe you will be called to religious life. I think that'd be really awesome . . . Sister Amie," he added, for emphasis.

Amie shook her head and rolled her eyes at her dad.

"And we'll be happy to say some extra prayers for you, honey," he told her.

"Thanks. That's all I wanted to say." She stood up and adjusted her bathrobe which had started to come open.

"You going to bed this early?" her mom asked, looking at her watch. "It's only ten o'clock on a Saturday night. Really . . . who are you and what have you done with our daughter?"

Amie laughed. "I'm just tired, and I want to go snuggle up with a book in bed until I fall asleep."

"Don't knock it," John said to his wife. "There are other girls her age who go out on Saturday nights looking for a boy to snuggle up with. Let her have the book and don't make a big deal of it."

"Like I'd ever do that, Dad!" Amie returned in a disgruntled tone.

John laughed. "Hey, Scuttle," he began as she turned to leave the room. "How are those two friends of yours doing? Samantha and . . ."

"Krystal," Amie finished for him.

"Yeah, those two," he said. "I sure get a kick out of them whenever they come around, but I haven't seen them for a few weeks."

"Oh, they're doing great. They went home this weekend. But they're doing good."

"Samantha still asking about God?" Judy asked.

"Yeah, she's really interested. She prays all the time now. She's always asking me to give her books and prayer cards and such. It's really cool. Jesus has really touched her life in a big way." She stood leaning against the far end of the piano, facing her parents, her fingers lightly touching the piano keys without making a sound. "I've given her some really great Christian music to listen to as well. She loves it."

"And what about Krystal?" her dad asked. "She's quite the character, that one."

"She sure is," Amie agreed. "No. Krystal's the same as ever. She keeps saying she's not interested in God at all, but then she keeps wanting to come out to C.C.E. events. I know something's going to happen to her eventually. You just can't spend all that time around people who are authentically living out their faith with joy and not be moved by it."

"That's the gift of C.C.E.," Judy said. "It's a great ministry."

"Which is why we keep pouring our money out into it every month," John added with a bit of light sarcasm.

"Not *our* money, dear," Judy corrected him. "It's God's money. It comes from our tithe, and it goes back into the Lord's work. So don't give me that business." She nudged him with her foot.

John winked at Amie across the room. "Good-night, Princess. Happy book-snuggling."

Amie laughed. Just before she left, she realized she had not kissed her folks good-night. She stepped back across the room and gave them each a hug and a kiss. She was nineteen years old, but affection for parents has no age limits. She loved her parents a great deal and was not ashamed to show it to them . . . often.

✞   ✞   ✞

"How's that for life turning on a dime?" John asked Judy as they got ready for bed that night. "Can you get over this? Tell me, what's happening to our family?"

Judy sat on the bed by her pillow, her arms wrapped around her legs pulled up in front of her. She just laughed as John spoke. What could she say?

"It's unbelievable. In a matter of twenty-four hours Maggie's thinking about getting married, and Amie's wanting to become a Nun!" he exclaimed. "Could anything in life have prepared you for this?" he asked his wife, looking straight at her as he stood at the foot of their bed.

"No," she said with a laugh. She shrugged her shoulders and closed her eyes in disbelief.

"Am I off my rocker here, or something?" he asked. "'Cause I could have sworn, their whole lives, that Maggie would enter religious life someday—which she did, quite happily, all on her own. And Amie would fall in love—at a young age, because that's just her impulsive style—and get married. And I was okay with all that. I was mentally prepared to have Sister Maggie in her little category in my brain and Amie the bride and mother in her category. So . . .?" He raised his hands in a question.

"Don't look at me, John," his wife returned, defensively. "I didn't see any of this coming, either."

"Do you think it's for real?"

Judy shrugged her shoulders and raised her eyebrows, while lifting her hands up.

"So, Mrs. Collins," John said, crawling onto the bed from the foot. "Do *you* have any surprises for me? Any secret lovers you've never told me about? Any secret desires to leave married life and go become a cloistered Nun? Anything wild and radical going on with you?" he asked as he approached her.

"Cut it out, John," she said with a laugh, pushing him away.

"I want an answer, Mrs. Collins." He grabbed her by the shoulders and gently pushed her back onto the pillow. "Do you love me?" he sang, in imitation of Tevye, the "Papa" from *Fiddler on the Roof.*

"You're a fool," she returned, quoting Golde, the "Mama", with a laugh. "And yes, after twenty-five years of all that stuff—and don't expect me to remember all the words from that song—I love you, and I'm very happily married . . . with no surprises at this point in time to report."

John laughed and gave his wife a little kiss on the forehead, as he rolled over beside her, lying on his back. He opened his arms wide on the bed, laying his left arm gently across his wife's tummy. She lifted the arm and maneuvered herself around it until the arm was under her, and she was snuggled up to her husband.

"It's Saturday night, and I understand some girls my age snuggle with their husbands in bed on cold, wintry, Saturday nights like this," she said in light humour.

"Not enough of them do," he said, philosophically. "It's part of the problem with our society. More snuggling after marriage and less beforehand would go a long way to solving the world's problems."

"Well," she said with a laugh, "I'm doing my part."

"And so you are, Mrs. Collins," he agreed, reaching over with his right hand to turn off the light.

Chapter 45

"Come in," called Sr. Charlotte, in response to the knock on her office door.

A timid Maggie stepped into the office and carefully closed the door behind her. Sr. Charlotte motioned for the aspirant to sit on the chair across the desk from her, and Maggie complied.

"How can I help you, Maggie?" asked Sr. Charlotte, who had become very curious over the young girl's behaviour. This was not the typically spunky girl who bounced around the convent.

"I need to talk to you, Sr. Charlotte, about something rather important," Maggie stated. She stopped and waited for Sr. Charlotte to prompt her. Interiorly she hoped that the Director of Novices would be able to guess as to her problem so that she would not have to actually verbalize it.

Sr. Charlotte looked at Maggie, leaning her head forward. She waited for the girl to continue.

Maggie sighed. She was going to have to just come out with it. "I need to talk to you about your . . ." Maggie stopped herself. She just could not bring herself to say it.

"About my what, Maggie?" asked the older Sister, with great patience.

Maggie fidgeted in the big armchair, looked out the window—into the dark of the night—and back at Sr. Charlotte. She closed her eyes and quickly searched for the words to express her feelings, without sounding school-girlish and silly. After all, it was probably just a crush—a passing thing. Really, there was no point in even bringing up the whole thing. . . . Having come to her new conclusion, Maggie was ready to get up and leave. She set her hands on the arms of the chair and began to push herself up when Sr. Charlotte's patient gaze caught her eye. *Oops,* she thought to herself, *I guess I don't get off that easy.*

Again the young girl sighed and began over. "I need to talk to you about . . . your brother . . . Charles," Maggie announced with deliberate effort.

Sr. Charlotte's eyes widened. Realization dawned upon her and her entire expression changed. A little smile crept up on the corners of her mouth, but she controlled herself, lest she give Maggie the impression that she was not taking her seriously. "Charles?" she asked.

Maggie sighed again, deeper and heavier than before. She brought her hands up to her mouth and covered it, shaking her head, wishing she had never set foot into Sr. Charlotte's office that evening. She then nodded in reply; no words would come out.

"Is Charles all right?" asked Sr. Charlotte. "Is there something I should know about him?" Her tone was concerned, effectively covering up her comprehension in order to allow Maggie to express her feelings herself, without direction or prompting.

"No!" exclaimed Maggie. "He's just fine. He's perfect. In fact," she paused and closed her eyes, "that's the problem—he's perfect." She looked at Sr. Charlotte hoping the Director would catch her meaning, without her having to be explicit.

"Maggie," Sr. Charlotte responded in a calm, clear voice, "please just tell me what you came in here to talk about. At this rate, we're going to be here all night." The older woman looked at the clock on the wall: it was already twenty to nine.

"Okay," Maggie said with determination. She wiggled around until she was sitting on her hands and took a deep breath and began slowly. "I think I've fallen for Charles . . . as in, I'm totally attracted to your younger brother. And I never meant for any of this to happen," she continued, picking up speed. "I'm not even sure when it happened. It just happened. And then I woke up yesterday morning, and I realized it had happened. And that dream just set me right off. I was so unprepared for it—because I've never had feelings like this before for a guy. I just didn't think it was possible for me to have these feelings. I would have been more guarded and more careful about everything, if I had only even considered it could happen to me. And I just don't know what to do about it." By the end of her explanation, Maggie was talking at record speed and Sr. Charlotte leaned forward in an effort to catch it all as it flew out of the young girl's mouth.

"Whew," Sr. Charlotte said softly, with a smile. "I guess I asked for that. Um, I think we should just take this step by step. You said something about a dream?"

Maggie went on to explain her dream. Though she started off slowly, she soon began again to pick up speed, at which point Sr. Charlotte gently raised her hands to slow Maggie down. This pattern of communication repeated itself until Maggie finally got through the whole explanation: the dream, her realization of her feelings, a reflection on the time she had spent with Charles, her conversation with her parents the night before. The more she talked, the easier it all came out.

Sr. Charlotte shook her head gently. She got up from her chair, walked around the desk, and put her hand on Maggie's shoulder. "Dear, sweet, Maggie. I hardly know what to say to you. I have to confess that I have mixed emotions about this whole thing. On the one hand I want to direct you without bias. On the other hand, I think you and Charles would make a wonderful couple, and I'd hate to be the one to stand in the way of that—if I were to redirect you back to religious life. I guess I'm just a romantic at heart," she said with a laugh.

Maggie turned and looked up at Sr. Charlotte, eyes widening in disbelief at what she was hearing coming from her Director.

Sr. Charlotte stepped away and stood by her window as she continued. "I have such a soft spot in my heart for both you and Charles that it makes it hard to look at this situation without kind of hoping that something can come of this. After all, while I might lose you as a Sister of the Immaculate Conception, I'd still gain you as a sister-in-law."

Maggie's eyes widened even more. "You mean you're not angry with me? You don't think I'm some foolish little girl?"

"Heavens, no!" replied Sr. Charlotte. "On the other hand," she added cautiously, "I probably should not have confessed to you my personal bias. You can't go marrying my brother just to satisfy my desire to see him happy and to have you in my family."

"No," Maggie agreed, shaking her head and nodding it, both at the same time.

Sr. Charlotte laughed, watching the girl's confusion. "Listen, Maggie. There are a few issues here. First of all you must discern God's will for you in terms of your vocation either to religious life or to married life. Then you'll have to sort out the Charles issue, as to whether or not he's the one you're called to marry . . . if, in fact, you discern God calling you to marriage."

Maggie nodded but said nothing. That made sense: take it one step at a time.

Sr. Charlotte continued, "You're really going to have to search your heart about this, Maggie. You can't just go flying off the deep-end because feelings have surfaced in your life. Perhaps this is the first time *you've* experienced these feelings, but there is nothing novel about romance in human nature. And I assure you, becoming a religious Sister will not make you immune to the possibility of feeling attracted toward a man. We are not a cloistered order of Nuns here. And being in an apostolic order like this, which goes out into the world, you will be faced with the potential of meeting men whom you might find attractive. It's what you will do with those feelings that will determine your faithfulness to Christ and to your vocation. And trust me, it can happen to married women, too—to become attracted to another man. What you have to do is learn to guard and protect your heart."

Sr. Charlotte paused for a moment. She turned herself to face Maggie straight on and added, "The first step in that is to avoid the 'near occasion of sin'. Flee temptation. . . . Looking back on this situation, it was an oversight on my part to have allowed you and Charles all that time alone together.

The possibility of this happening never once occurred to me, either." She raised up her hands and lifted her eyes upward. "Believe me!" Her voice was full of exasperation, which quickly changed as she laid her hands over her chest. She then added, most sincerely, "I apologize for not having used better judgment as your superior, Maggie."

Maggie was shocked. "I don't think you need to apologize for anything."

"Oh, but I do," Sr. Charlotte insisted, now holding her hands together. "I should understand human nature better than that. I should never have lulled myself into thinking my brother or one of my aspirants could be beyond the scope of romantic feelings."

"I certainly forgive you," Maggie said, wondering if that was appropriate or not. Growing up she had been taught always to respond to an apology with forgiveness. She felt awkward extending that to her superior for something like this.

Sr. Charlotte nodded and thanked Maggie. "And so we have learned a lesson about the frailty of the human heart," she said to Maggie with a smile and renewed perkiness in her voice. "And all is not lost, for perhaps God wanted it this way—and allowed for my blindness—because He is calling you and Charles to marriage. The Lord moves in mysterious ways."

Maggie chuckled. "And so He does. So what now?"

"I'm jumping ahead of myself," Sr. Charlotte stated, raising a finger in the air. "You still need to determine *if* God's calling you to marriage or religious life. And *if* in fact you discern that it is not religious life . . . well, then you can bring Charles back into the picture."

Maggie heaved a big sigh, blowing her bangs up with her exhaling breath, sensing the weight of the decision upon her.

"Your discovering feelings for Charles might not mean that you are called to marry him—no matter how much that might appeal to *me*," Sr. Charlotte added with a gentle smile.

Maggie smiled in return. Indeed, it was quite a compliment to have Sr. Charlotte approve of her as a suitable wife for her brother.

Sr. Charlotte went on. "It might just be God showing you, Maggie Collins, that you have a heart capable of romance—as do we all—and that you must learn to guard it and keep it from wandering. That skill, that virtue of self-discipline, applies to every person no matter their calling in life. We cannot allow our hearts to rule our life. We have an intellect and a will with which to balance our emotional responses to life around us."

Maggie sat and nodded her head, listening carefully to Sr. Charlotte's every word.

"And I know that whatever the outcome of this situation will be, Maggie, you will become a better religious Sister or wife because of it. In the meantime," Sr. Charlotte said, raising her hands and shrugging her shoulders, "don't expect this to be easy or to be able to discern this overnight. Pray about it each day and ask God to allow your desire for religious life to either grow, if that is where He is calling you, or to diminish, if you are not being called to it. You'll find the answer, Maggie. I know you will. . . . And, I assure you, you would not be the first woman to enter religious life who had to choose between that and a man."

Sr. Charlotte paused and waited with amusement as she watched Maggie's reaction. "*You,* Sr. Charlotte?" the aspirant asked, cautiously.

Sr. Charlotte laughed and nodded. "It was so many years ago that it hardly seems real anymore. But at the time, it was bigger than life, my dear." Sr. Charlotte sat down in her chair across the desk from the aspirant. "His name is of no importance now. He was tall and handsome and everything I ever would have wanted in a husband . . . and I was so in love." Her eyes gazed into the distance, as they wandered back into yesteryear.

"What happened?" Maggie asked. "Or . . . may I ask?" she corrected herself.

Sr. Charlotte laughed as she came back to the present moment. "It just wasn't meant to be. Though I longed for marriage and motherhood, there was still something inside of me feeling restless. As time went on I became terribly fearful that maybe I was being called to religious life. Finally, one day in late spring, I came and spoke with Sr. Monica—you remember meeting her at Christmas, Maggie."

Maggie brought to mind the elderly Sister who had traveled to Saskatoon for a visit over the Christmas holidays, staying at their house for four days. Sr. Monica had moved away from Saskatoon over twenty years earlier to start another house for the Sisters of the Immaculate Conception in Edmonton, but her close ties to Saskatoon brought her back every so often. Maggie had been quite taken with the eighty-three-year-old Sister with so much vitality.

"Sr. Monica," the Director went on, "was so wise. She simply told me to allow the desire for religious life to just sit in my heart and see what God would do with it—either He would make it grow or take it away from me. And so I did. And over the course of that summer something amazing happened, Maggie."

Maggie looked intently at Sr. Charlotte and waited for her to go on.

"I went from fearing that God *might be* calling me to religious life to fearing that He *wouldn't* call me to religious life," she said with a laugh.

Maggie sighed and gently laughed. "I think I understand, Sr. Charlotte," the young aspirant said.

"Once there," the older Sister went on, "I knew where my heart's desire truly lay. I was able to let go of the dream of marriage and motherhood with a wonderful man, in order to embrace a new dream of a different kind of marriage and motherhood with *the perfect* man."

The smile on Sr. Charlotte's face said it all. Her love for her spouse, Jesus Christ, had filled her life with joys that were beyond her wildest dreams. "I could never have seen what joy was before me, Maggie, until I fully accepted God's will for my life. But I have never looked back . . . it was worth all the sacrifice and everything I left behind."

Maggie was speechless. What a privilege it was to have Sr. Charlotte speak so openly and candidly with her.

"You see, Maggie, what makes the sacrifice of entering religious life so great is that you are giving up something as good and beautiful as marriage and motherhood. But the joy that God has in store for you is definitely proportionate to the sacrifice you make. He will not disappoint you—if you follow His will for your life."

"I believe you," Maggie said in a quiet voice.

"So, upon reflection," Sr. Charlotte went on, "I officially remove my original 'romantic' bias," she said, making quotation marks with her fingers. "Both vocations, marriage and religious life, carry the potential for dynamic, exciting, God-glorifying romance. And I don't want to influence you either way, Maggie. You have to discern that for yourself."

Maggie nodded and smiled. Somehow the task of discernment did not seem so overwhelming anymore. She realized it was a win-win situation. Whichever vocation was hers, it would be a source of tremendous joy and blessing in her life—and she could trust God in that. "Thank you, Sr. Charlotte. I can't believe that I didn't want to come to speak with you in the first place—I was so scared to share this with you. Now I realize how silly I was," she confessed. "You've really helped me. Thank you."

Sr. Charlotte's smile spread across her whole face. Her eyes danced with delight. "I think you have a wonderful adventure ahead of you, Maggie. And I'll be praying for you every day for this intention."

"Thank you," Maggie repeated. She felt so humbled by the affection Sr. Charlotte lavished upon her.

"One more thing, though," Sr. Charlotte began rather firmly, with a finger raised in the air. "I strongly advise you *not* to discuss this with Charles just yet. As soon as you open that up you'll be bombarded with all kinds of emotions—both of you—that are only going to make your discernment process more difficult. And those feelings can begin to grow at an unnatural pace, just because you are exposing yourselves emotionally to each other. You have to be careful to guard yourself emotionally in a relationship with a man," Sr. Charlotte warned. "There is such a thing as 'emotional chastity'. Do you understand what I mean by that?"

"Emotional chastity?" Maggie repeated. "I think so."

"What I mean is that so often young couples will lay bare all their feelings for each other early in a relationship. But feelings can be fleeting and, once they've been shared, it's hard to take them back. And if the feelings pass—as they often do—then often what is left behind is hurt and rejection for one or the other or both people involved," she explained.

"I agree," Maggie stated. "I'm not ready to discuss this with Charles at all. For all I know, he maybe had no feelings for me whatsoever. This could all be in my head—conjured up by some crazy dream."

"I don't think that dream was crazy at all," Sr. Charlotte stated. She stood up, walked over to the window, and looked out into the night, enjoying the way the street lights were shimmering on the softly falling snow. "I think that dream was a real gift from God, presenting to you a vision of something that you have never really considered before now, Maggie."

"It sure did that," Maggie agreed, reflecting on the dream momentarily. There was something about it that had been so compelling and vivid that she could still recall every last detail of it, as if she had just wakened from it. "And I agree that I shouldn't talk to Charles about this."

"Good," stated Sr. Charlotte. "If God is calling you two together, you'll have plenty of time to sort this all out. Hastiness will only complicate your feelings and your ability to discern."

"I'll pray about it," Maggie promised, "just like you suggested—I'll ask God to let my desire for religious life either grow or diminish, according to His will for me."

"Good. And since you won't be seeing Charles for a while, that'll help," Sr. Charlotte added with encouragement.

"Actually . . ." Maggie began, biting her bottom lip in a nervous manner. "Did you forget that my family and I are going to spend the day tomorrow at your family farm with Charles?"

Sr. Charlotte's eyes opened wide. "That's right. I had forgotten."

"Can I still go?" Maggie asked, cautiously. She did not want to appear overly enthusiastic for the day, nor did she want to be denied the chance to go.

"Of course you can," the Director said. "It'll be a good test for you. But go with an open mind, Maggie. Don't go there looking for romance," she warned. "And don't go there hiding from it, either," she added with a smile breaking across her face. "Just see where Jesus leads your heart as you spend time with Charles and your family. I think it's a wonderful opportunity for discernment without your needing to reveal anything to anyone else, other than your parents and me for now."

Maggie thanked Sr. Charlotte. It was such a relief to have discussed this with such a wise woman. The aspirant now had a whole new perspective, with a sense of healthy boundaries to protect her tender heart. She gave Sr. Charlotte a hug and left to go up to her room.

As Maggie reached the top of the third floor, she ran into Kyra in the hallway. "Hey, kiddo," Maggie said with a big smile. "How's it going?"

Kyra looked at Maggie and smiled. "Fine, thanks. How about you?"

"I'm doing great," Maggie answered. Looking at her companion, Maggie sensed a distance between them. She knew that her over-attentiveness to the renovation project had prevented them from spending time together. Up until then, they had been growing in friendship quite nicely. Maggie had come to appreciate just how much she could learn from Kyra's gentle spirit and quiet personality. At the same time, Maggie had really enjoyed seeing this new friend come out of her timid shell and begin to shine in community life.

"Hey," Maggie stated with enthusiasm. "It's only just after nine o'clock. How would you like to stay up and play cards together tonight?"

"I'd love to," Kyra said with a warm smile. "Are you sure you're up to it? You've been working so hard on the renovations around here; I wouldn't be surprised if you were too tired to stay up late."

"Are you kidding?" Maggie blurted out with exuberance. "I used to stay up and party with my family all the time. I can be a real night owl when I want to be," she boasted. "Look, let's both get our pj's on, and then we'll have a pyjama party in my room."

"Sounds great." Kyra ran off to her room, as Maggie turned to her bedroom to get ready.

Maggie closed the door behind her. She went and knelt on the floor by her bed, and looked up at her pictures of Mary and Jesus. *Okay, Mother Mary and Jesus, my dear Lord, I'm asking you both, now—let my desire for religious life either grow or diminish. I'm laying it all down before You, Lord—my feelings for Charles and my new-found desire for marriage and motherhood, and I'm asking You to resurrect in me only the feelings You desire for me to have, so that I can discern Your holy will for my life. Amen.*

She sighed deeply, having said her prayer of surrender.

Pushing herself up from beside the bed, she rubbed her hands together. "Okay, Maggie, let's get at it," she said aloud with a clap. She got herself ready for bed and grabbed the deck of cards out of her drawer. Throwing a wink toward her pictures of Jesus and Mary, she sat and waited on her bed for her guest to arrive.

She was looking forward to having some good sisterly fun with Kyra. It just felt like the "old" Maggie was back in business.

Chapter 46

As the Collins family's Catholic Cadillac pulled away from St. James Church that Sunday morning, the fifteen-seater van was loaded down with two parents, seven children, bags of snowsuits, extra mittens, toques, and scarves, a cooler full of food for the road, a box filled with pies for dessert, and a few toboggans and sleds to add to the fun of the day. The air was filled with the noise of enthusiastic children, the chatter of adults, and the steady beat of Christian music pumped out in stereo. Judy Collins sat in the second seat passing out sandwiches to children behind her and to her husband and Maggie sitting in the two front seats.

"Did we pray grace, yet?" a little voice called out from the back.

Judy was not quite sure if it had been Aaron's or Zack's voice. "Not yet," she called back.

"Let's just do it now, so the kids can begin eating," said John from the front of the van, in his booming fatherly voice. "In the name of the Father . . ." he called out.

As he continued with the sign of the cross, silence ensued in the vehicle. He had learned over the years that the most effective way to quiet down a Catholic crowd was to begin making the sign of the cross. Maggie leaned forward and turned off the music, and everyone joined in saying grace. Once the prayers were completed, including asking for Our Lady's protection over their travels that day, the noise level resumed, the music went back on, and seven hungry children and their parents dove into the meal for their family road trip.

"How long until we get there?" called out Zack from the back of the vehicle.

"As long as it takes," called back his father from the front, looking at the child through the rear-view mirror.

Maggie turned around and looked at Zack. "About half-an-hour," she told him.

He looked at his watch. It was twelve-forty-nine. He nodded as he made quick calculations in his mind. "ETA, one-nineteen," he announced.

"What's an 'eatie-A'?" asked Jessie, turning around to look at her older brother from the middle seat of the van.

"Estimated Time of Ar-ri-val?" he returned, sarcastically punctuating each word.

"Curb the attitude there, boy," called out John from the front, "or you'll be doing extra time in the van while we're all out skidooing."

Zack made a face at Jessie, as she stuck her little nose up at him.

"Enough, you two," Judy said, reaching out to the four-year-old beside her and tapping her on the nose.

"Hey, that would be nineteen-nineteen Zulu," announced Isaac, who was seated next to Zack in the back seat.

"What's 'zoo-loo'?" asked Jessie, turning the other way to see Isaac.

"Well, officially it's called Coordinated Universal Time or UTC, but it refers to the 'clock' at Greenwich, England, which is used as the standard time reference for international communications such as military, that means the army, or aviation, that means flying airplanes, et cetera . . . things that cross the time zones. You see the world is divided into basically twenty-four time zones and to make communications easier, a letter of the alphabet was assigned to each time zone. Greenwich Time was designated by the letter Z, which is pronounced in the phonetic alphabet as 'Zulu'. When we calculate our time here in Saskatchewan, we're at UTC minus six hours. So one-nineteen, which is actually thirteen-nineteen in the twenty-four hour military format, works out to nineteen-nineteen Zulu." Isaac spoke slowly and deliberately, looking at Jessie the whole time, nodding and smiling as he answered her question.

The little girl looked intently back at her brother. Though totally confused by his explanation, she did not feel upset. Isaac never spoke down to her. He spoke to her just as he spoke to anyone else, giving her credit to be able to reason beyond her few tender years.

When he was done, Jessie looked up at her mother beside her and asked, "What does that mean, Mommy?"

Judy laughed. "I'm not sure, sweetheart, but maybe someday you and I'll figure it out together."

Jessie shrugged her shoulders and turned back to her sandwich, offering a bite to her doll. "It's made of Zulu," she told the doll. "It tastes really good if you ever go in the army on an airplane."

Amie picked up the doll beside Jessie and answered in a teeny-tiny voice, "I love Zulu sandwiches. They come from England and my brother calls them the Greenwich Sandwich."

Jessie nodded enthusiastically as she pretended to feed her baby.

Judy shook her head and laughed.

"Let's pray our rosary as we drive," called out John from the front of the van. He reached over and turned off the music.

Unfazed by the few groans and moans that came up from the backseat, John took down the rosary hanging from the rearview mirror and began. The activity level gradually subsided in the big van as kids made themselves comfortable for the next twenty minutes or so that would be spent saying the rosary together. Maggie called out the glorious mysteries with a quick reflection before each decade. After she announced the mystery, she designated one of her younger siblings to lead.

Jessie led the first mystery with her little voice calling out a mumbled stream of prayer. The boys in the back snickered at Jessie's creative pronunciations in the Our Father and Hail Mary. Judy looked back at her boys with that certain look that said, "Enough!" without words. They stopped.

As the family finished the rosary, Zack looked at his watch. "Nineteen-fifteen Zulu," he called out. "Four more minutes to arrival. Prepare for landing. Everyone fasten their seat belts."

"Faster than that," Maggie called back to him. "That's his farm right there." She pointed out the front right side of the vehicle, and everyone craned their necks to get a glimpse of their destination.

The energy level rose exponentially, as kids began fidgeting and wiggling around, getting ready to disembark in just a matter of moments.

✟   ✟   ✟

Charles was there to greet the Collins family as they poured out of the van into his yard. The young man stood there with his big smile, showing off all his white polished teeth, as the children jumped around with eager anticipation of the day. His dog, Kaiser, bounced around in all the excitement. Charles called out to the tricoloured shepherd-collie. The dog came back and stood at his heel, wagging its tail and whining.

Maggie stepped out of the front of the van and greeted Charles.

"My favourite side-kick," he called out to the young lady. "Long time no see."

"Thanks for having us Charles," Maggie returned. "Hey, Kaiser," she called the dog over and crouched down to pet him. "You're sure you're up to this?" she asked, looking back up at Charles.

"Been looking forward to it for days!"

"We sure got a nice day for it," she stated, standing up again and holding out her hands as she looked around. "First mild day we've had in a week's time."

"God is good," he told her.

"All the time," she agreed, with a friendly smile.

"Hello, Mr. Collins," Charles said, greeting Maggie's father as he stepped around the front of the van.

Charles extended his gloved hand, and John took it in a manly handshake. "Good to see you again, Charles. It's been a few years now. But you haven't changed much in that time. Nice pup you've got there," he said looking down at the dog, obediently waiting at his master's heel.

Charles looked down and patted the dog's head. "Yeah, Kaiser's a good dog, Mr. Collins. And gentle as can be around children. I made sure of that, what with having seventeen nieces and nephews coming around here on a regular basis."

"I can see that. Oh, and before I forget," the older man added, "I insist on you calling me John. Hearing you call me Mister makes me feel old."

"Fine, John," the young man said. "Welcome, Mrs. Collins," he turned to greet Maggie's mother as she stepped forward to join the conversation.

"You're not calling me Missus anymore, either, Charles," she corrected him. "I'm younger than my husband and don't want to be made to feel any older than I am."

Charles smiled and laughed. "Judy?" he asked.

"Yes," she said shaking his hand. She paused and put her other hand over his and held on a moment as she looked around to take in the farmyard. "You have a beautiful spot here, Charles. I forgot how lovely it was. Haven't been here in years."

"Thanks, Judy," Charles replied. "It's home. And I love it."

"Hey, you kids," called out John. "Come help carry in these bags before you disappear and get lost."

The boys who had been standing on the barnyard fence came running back to the vehicle. John walked around the van, opened the back doors, and began passing things to be carried into the house.

"Follow me, troops," Charles called out. "You can bring your stuff into the side porch, and if you're up to it, we can get bundled up to go skidooing right away."

A general cheer of excitement rose up from the kids.

"Hi, Charles, I'm Maggie's sister, Amie," said the nineteen-year-old, diverting the leader of the pack as he began walking to the house.

"And I'm Katie," added the younger sister. They had been standing off to the side waiting for an opportunity to be introduced.

"Sorry, girls," Maggie apologized. "I forgot you hadn't met Charles yet. Charles, these are my awesome sisters, Amie and Katie," she repeated their names, pointing to each. "But then again, they just told you that."

Katie rolled her eyes at Maggie and whispered under her breath, "Thanks, Maggie."

Charles just laughed.

"And Joanie and Brandon wanted to come today, as well," Maggie went on, "but they had company and couldn't get away. And somewhere around here is . . ." Maggie looked around. "There she is. Jessie, come here and say 'hi' to my friend, Charles."

Jessie came running up and jumped into Maggie's arms.

"Are those your horses?" Jessie asked.

"They sure are," Charles said. "Would you like to go for a ride on one?"

Jessie's eyes grew big. She smiled and nodded, looking back at Maggie.

"Sounds like fun," said Maggie. "I hope we all get to ride."

"Three horses," Charles said. "I think we can manage to get everyone on for at least a little ride. Have you ever ridden before?" he asked Maggie.

"Out at my uncle's acreage, just a few times. I'm not great at it, but I love it."

"Me, too," said Amie.

"You three girls should go out yourselves for a little ride, later," he told them. "There's no nicer way to spend time together than that."

Katie jumped in to accept before either of her sisters could decline the offer. "That'll be awesome, Charles."

He smiled at the girls. Just then a commotion on the doorstep caught his attention. "Excuse me, ladies." He ran to get in front of the boys standing at the top step, waiting to be let into the house. "Sorry about that, guys," he called out. "I got a little distracted." Charles opened the door and motioned for the boys to head in. "You know out here in the country we don't knock or ring doorbells, we just walk on in and announce our presence."

The boys dropped their bags on the floor.

"So, let me take a stab at this. Maggie told me all your names before. I'm guessing you're Isaac," Charles said, pointing to the oldest, dark-haired boy.

Isaac nodded.

"And you must be Zack," Charles said, pointing to the red-headed boy.

Zack nodded and said 'hi'.

"And you must be Aaron," he added, pointing to the youngest boy with a mess of blond hair which was standing up on end due to static from having just pulled off his toque.

"And you must be Charles," Aaron returned.

Charles laughed. "Guilty as charged. Look, does anyone need anything before we head out? The bathroom's there." He pointed to a door off to the side of the porch. "I can get you a drink of something. Is anyone thirsty?" he asked as the family all pushed their way into the now crowded porch area.

Judy stepped past her children, slipped off her boots, and entered the kitchen behind Charles. "Where can we put these?" she asked. Maggie followed her in with the box of pies.

"Just there on the counter," he said. "Looks great. I'm hungry already."

"It smells wonderful in here," Judy commented.

"Got some stew slow cooking in the oven," he told her.

"Well, I'll keep an eye on that for you while you're out entertaining the troops this afternoon. What else can I do for you in here?" she asked.

"It's all ready to go once we're all done playing outside. And I don't think you should spend the afternoon in the house when you could be on a snowmobile with your husband," he informed her.

"Oh," Judy responded. "I never thought of me going out to play."

"Come on, sweetheart," John called out. "We're going to be a couple of kids today."

Maggie laughed and pulled her mom back toward the porch. "Yeah, Mom. You have to have some fun here, too."

Judy complied, and they all began bundling up to go out. Amid the laughter and commotion, Maggie called out above the noise, "Well, this is certainly a first for me. I've never tried to fit a skirt into these ski pants before, but, by George . . ." She wiggled and wobbled about trying to push the length of long skirt down each leg.

"That's got to be uncomfortable," stated Amie, twisting her face as she watched Maggie struggle and half fall over.

"You're so crazy, Maggie," Katie said, pushing her older sister back up. "Not even I would have attempted a skirt today."

"I'm determined," she said. "It's just a small sacrifice that I make for religious life—but I'm counting on the grace to be worth it." She wiggled around some more and finally zipped closed the ski pants.

"You are a prize," Charles said with a chuckle, as Maggie held up her arms victoriously at the end of her battle to get dressed.

"One-of-a-kind," she returned to him. "Maggie all the way." She lightly patted his shoulder as she walked past him to go out the door.

He smiled watching her walk out into the fresh, country, winter air. Her arms were stretched wide open as she took a deep breath. Kaiser came up to the young girl, and she reached down to pat his head.

"You've got a little corner of heaven here, Charles," she called up to him from the bottom of the step.

"I sure do," he answered, still smiling at the young woman from the doorway.

One by one the rest of the family moved out of the porch, all bundled and ready to go. Charles waited until the last one was out—which naturally was Judy, as she had spent all her time helping little ones find what they needed. He had given her a snowmobile suit, mitts, and a toque to wear, as she had not come prepared for outdoor play. There were always extra outdoor clothes for guests on the farm for just such occasions. He walked with her down the porch steps and led them all down the side path to the Quonset where four skidoos were lined up and ready to go.

It was an afternoon of fun, from the word go. The weather was perfect for snowmobiling. Not too cold, to make it miserable, but not too mild to cause the snow to melt. Each driver was given instructions on how to handle the skidoo and then they loaded everyone on: two or three on a machine, until they all fit.

Charles led them down a path through the trees in the yard and out into an open quarter section alongside the farmyard, with some nice rolling hills. They raced around and chased around, going up and over the gentle prairie slopes. Kaiser bounded around the field, skillfully avoiding being run over. From time to time they would stop and change drivers and reload the skidoos. After a while, Charles and John drove back two of the skidoos to hook up a couple of large, inflated inner tubes from tractor tires. When they got back to the open field everyone, including Judy, took a turn being pulled around behind the snowmobiles.

After almost two hours of fun, they decided to go back to the house for a pit stop. Charles had hot chocolate ready to go. All it needed was a few minutes of heating on the stove. Kids piled into the house to get warmed up. Toques, scarves, mitts, boots, and coats were scattered all over the porch. John called back Isaac and Zack to reorganize the mess that had been left behind. The boys marched from the living room to the porch to do as they were told.

There was a beautiful, old, dark walnut table at the far end of the open kitchen-dining room. One by one the kids found a place to sit around it, while hot chocolate was served out to them. Charles had a big bowl of popcorn—made, buttered, and ready to serve. He placed it in the middle of the table, and the children dove in like a pack of hungry coyotes.

Charles, Maggie, Amie, Katie, and their parents stood around the kitchen, leaning against the counters, visiting. They had their own smaller bowl of popcorn to share while they enjoyed their hot chocolate.

"You sure know how to host a big family," John said to Charles.

"I've got a bit of experience with big crowds," the young man replied. "This is the gathering spot for my family. And since I'm single, it just seems natural for me to do the hosting, since everyone else is so busy with their kids."

"You're a good man, Charles," Judy said, taking a sip from her cup.

"Agh," he brushed off the compliment, waving a hand in the air, "it gives me something to do with all my spare time."

"Do you get lonely out here?" asked Katie. "I'm not sure if I could live in the country. It's beautiful and all, but I think I'm more of a city girl."

"I love the quiet and the solitude," he said. "Gives me lots of time to pray and just enjoy all my many blessings."

"Don't you ever plan to get married?" Katie inquired. "It seems like such a shame to not have a family to share all this with."

"I find it easier to be satisfied with life than to spend my time worrying about what I don't have. And God gives me lots of opportunity to share my blessings with other folks . . . like you," he said, motioning with his free hand around the room.

"That's all you needed," Maggie said, "was to adopt another family."

"Love it," he told her. "You folks are welcome to come out anytime. You don't need an invitation around here."

"I'm just wondering when we're going to get on those horses," Amie said, looking out the kitchen window at the barnyard. "What are their names?"

"The grey one is Pete. Right?" Maggie asked, turning to Charles from the window.

He stepped up beside her. "You remembered."

"Uh-huh," she said. "And the sorrel is Sally. Right?"

"Two for two."

"And the bay with the beautiful, long, black mane and tail is Moses. Right?" she said turning straight toward Charles with a big smile.

"Those are my babies," he announced, looking at the proud girl.

"Are they gentle?" Judy asked, stepping over to look out the window with the rest.

"I've raised them all from foals," Charles said. "They're as gentle as horses can be. Being single has given me lots of time to baby them. And I ride them often. We still round up cattle on horseback around this farm. I don't mind having quads and dirt bikes to play on, but when it comes to farming, I'm a bit old-fashioned."

"I'd love to come out for round-up," Maggie said. "That sounds like a hoot."

"It is. I'll let you know when we're ready. It won't be for a little while, though," he said with a chuckle.

"Can we all come?" asked Katie.

"Why don't we all just move in?" asked John, with mild sarcasm.

"I already told you, my door's always open around here. You just make yourselves at home," replied Charles.

"So, when are we going riding?" Amie asked again, not afraid of appearing overly anxious. "I love riding, and I just want to get out there."

"Let's not hold the lady up," Charles said, patting Amie gently on the back. "You any good at saddling a horse?"

"Not without instruction," she answered. "But I can certainly help."

Charles and the three older sisters got dressed up first to go out to the barnyard and saddle up the horses. The younger children were held back to give the older ones a few minutes lead, before they were let loose to go.

Each of the children had a chance to ride around the barnyard. Charles rode beside them on Moses and gave the little ones instruction on how to steer a horse, neck-reining western-style. The barnyard was big enough for them to trot and even get a few moments of a lope, before the horse would have to break gait to make the tight turns at the ends of the yard.

Judy, John, and the older girls stood at the fence watching and talking as the little ones took their turns. Kaiser sat quietly at Maggie's feet, staying out of the way of the riders. Finally Charles invited the three older girls to take the horses out of the barnyard and go out to the field where they had been snowmobiling. "Just head out through the trees on the same path we took before," he said, handing the reins to Maggie.

"Are you sure?" she asked, hesitantly, looking at Moses. "They won't run away with us in the open field?"

"I guarantee your safety. Moses knows he has to answer to me if he gets out of line." Charles looked the horse in the eye and patted its neck affectionately. "And Kaiser will go along to keep you all safe from coyotes," he said, with a teasing smile.

Maggie smirked at the young man. "I'm not so easily scared." She mounted the horse. "Well, if he bucks me off, at least I've got all that skirt under these ski pants for extra padding," she announced, bouncing up and down a bit to test out her theory.

Charles laughed. "One-of-a-kind," he said, looking up at Maggie now seated upon Moses. "You girls have fun. I'm going to take the little ones to play in the hay bales out behind the barn, and then we'll go in and get supper ready for when you get back. Take your time. There's no rush. Sundays were made for just this kind of thing."

The three sisters rode off, down the path to the open field. They were all a little nervous at first, not having ridden a horse for a long time. But the nervousness disappeared and their confidence grew as they felt the gentleness of the animals beneath them. Charles was right—there was no nicer way to spend a Sunday afternoon.

When the girls got back to the barn, they unsaddled their horses and led them into their stalls—each marked with a wood-burned name plate above the stall gate. Charles had shown the girls where to hang the saddles, blankets, and bridles. Each horse had hay, oats, and fresh water waiting in its stall. The girls quickly brushed down their horses as the hungry animals ate from the bounty left for them by their attentive owner.

"I could definitely get used to farm life," announced Maggie, as she ran the brush over Moses's back.

"That'd be kind of hard for you to do as a Sister of the Immaculate Conception," Katie stated. "Unless of course . . ." she began, but stopped herself.

"Unless of course, what?" Maggie asked.

"Unless of course, you . . . ditch the Sisters and marry Charles," Katie said with a laugh. The idea of Maggie leaving religious life was completely absurd to her. "But of course, that would never happen. At least you'll be able to come out here often, though, since Charles is Sr. Charlotte's brother. You've got an in."

"I'm just glad our ballroom dance class was cancelled this Sunday so we could come along and take advantage of your great connections, Maggie," Amie added.

Maggie laughed with her sisters. They really had no idea just how much the prospect of marrying Charles and spending the rest of her life on this farm appealed to her. She could feel her insides tighten as she brought her dream to mind. Hiding behind Moses, she closed her eyes and worked hard to hold back the flood of emotions that were filling her at the moment. She leaned her head into the nape of the horse's neck. It was warm and she could feel both the strength and gentleness of the animal at the same time. She breathed deeply; she loved the smell of a horse.

Okay, Jesus. I wanted to be able to lay all this down and forget about it. But today, all I want is my dream—Charles, this farm, those children . . . this horse. Just don't let me give myself away. These feelings are bigger than I can handle, so You're going to have to help me keep my cool.

She took another deep breath, smelling Moses. She gave the horse a hug and figured that that was as close as she should get for now, to hugging Charles.

"You coming in?" Amie called out to Maggie. "Or you gonna stand there and hug a horse all day?"

"I'm coming," she said, leaving the stall. She set the brush down in a box with the other brushes and currycombs as she walked out of the barn. Kaiser followed at her heels. She pulled the door closed behind her and caught up to her sisters, who were half-way across the barnyard.

Charles looked out the window and watched as Maggie closed the barn door. That was a sight he could easily get used to seeing: Maggie in his yard, every day. Even Kaiser seemed to have adopted her as his own. She fit in perfectly, as did her family. But she was off-limits for now—and quite likely forever—and so he reminded himself that he would do better to count his blessings than to worry over the things he did not and could not have.

"Here they come," he announced, as the girls walked through and closed the barnyard gate.

Supper was ready and waiting when the three girls got in from the barn. The little children were called in from the living room where they had been playing cards, waiting on the big girls.

Following grace, which Charles had asked John to lead, the food was served out from the counter in buffet style. Charles had set up a smaller table for the four younger children in the hall between the dining and the living rooms. Everyone else sat around the old kitchen table to eat. The randomness of conversation over the meal was in typical Collins family style. Charles enjoyed every moment of it.

Maggie sat beside the young host, offering to get up and help him serve, as needed. John and Judy sat at either end of the table, observing the young couple, who were not really a "couple", but certainly made a very natural looking couple just the same. John and Judy exchanged looks often. They were both confused. Certainly they could see why Maggie was struggling over Charles. There was no way of knowing what God could possibly have in store for these two. Time would tell.

Everyone helped with clean-up, in spite of Charles protesting. Maggie convinced him finally by saying, "We won't come back if you don't let us help, Charles. It's your choice."

"You win," he told her. "But let the record state—I gave in under duress."

The girl flashed him a big Maggie smile, satisfied in her victory.

Charles found some after-dinner, post-dessert treats for the little ones.

"Please, stop spoiling my children," Judy insisted, smiling at Charles. "I'll never be able to live with them after this."

"Oh, Lent starts in a few days," he told her. "They're just helping me clear out my cupboards before it begins."

Judy raised a brow at the generous young man.

"Come on, Mom," Zack pleaded. "We'll brush our teeth when we get home, and we won't get hyper, I promise."

"Now there's a promise I doubt you can keep," she said, looking down at her almost-always hyper nine-year-old. "Fine. But that's it, Charles, or we're going to end up eating you out of house and home."

"Oh, I'm not worried about that, but fair enough, I'll stop after this." The young man began doling out candies to the little ones.

"Hey, I've got a great idea," called out Aaron, waiting for his turn to get candies from Charles. "Maggie, why don't *you* marry Charles so we can come out here all the time?"

Silence fell over the room. The girls at the sink stopped doing dishes. Maggie turned abruptly to look at Aaron. She wanted to scold him, but could not find the words. John raised his eyebrows and looked at his wife, anticipating the potential fall-out of such a statement. Judy smiled nervously back at her husband, wondering how she could smooth over the tension of the moment.

Charles looked down at the boy and patted him on the head with a little chuckle. "Did you forget that your sister, Maggie, is going to soon become 'Sister Maggie'? And religious Sisters don't get married, Aaron," Charles explained. "My oldest sister, Sr. Charlotte, became a religious Sister, too. And it's really cool to have a religious Sister in your family, 'cause then you always have someone praying for you who's very close to Jesus. When Maggie becomes a Sister, she'll be married to Jesus. And I could never be a match for a husband like that," he said with a laugh.

Everyone around the room listened as Charles talked to the young boy.

"So, I'm afraid your great idea just won't work out, Aaron. But I already told your folks—and now I'm telling you so that you can remind them—you're welcome to come out here anytime. And I hope you do."

"Cool," said Aaron with enthusiasm. He took the candies from Charles and ran back to the living room.

Charles looked up. Everyone around the room—who had been listening in on his conversation with Aaron—quickly turned their heads away, except Maggie. She looked Charles in the eye and mouthed the words "thank you" to him from across the room.

He nodded back to her, with great respect.

She turned back to drying dishes, hoping that someone would soon kick-start another conversation to release the tension of the moment.

"How about one last skidoo ride before you all leave?" Charles offered.

"Oh, I couldn't, myself, Charles," Judy said with a laugh. "But I'll help you get the little ones ready. They'd never forgive me if I said 'no'."

Following their last tour on the sleds, Judy sent the children directly into the vehicle for home-time. Jessie had to run in to go potty, so Maggie helped her. By the time they came back out, everyone was packed in and ready for the trip home.

Jessie stretched her arms up to Charles, who picked her up to say good-bye. She gave him a big kiss on the cheek and wrapped her arms around his neck in an affectionate hug. "I love you, Charles," she said in sweet, childish simplicity.

"I love you, too, Jessie," he replied. He carried her to the van side door and set her in the vehicle.

"Thank you," Maggie said to Charles, as she stood beside the open door, waiting to climb into the back seat of the van. "Bye-bye, Kaiser." She crouched down to pet the dog affectionately. She stood up again and looked Charles in the eye. "I can't tell you how much fun we all had. And I'm sure we'll take you up on that open-door policy around here."

Charles smiled and put his hand on the side of Maggie's shoulder. "You'd better. I don't mind the solitude around here for most of the time, but I sure do enjoy the company of good folks like your family."

She smiled. She wanted to say more. She wanted to thank Charles for being such a noble guardian of her heart. How could she ever confess to him what was really going on inside of her? She could not . . . and so she would not.

"We'll see you around, Charles," is all that came out.

He gave her shoulder a little squeeze and smiled warmly at the girl as she turned to get into the vehicle. "God bless you all," he called into the van.

Everyone called out their good-byes one more time, and Charles closed the door. He waved as the van pulled out of the yard. Crouching down to pet Kaiser, he watched until the tail-lights were out of sight.

Jesus, just let me say, You do pick beautiful brides for Yourself. She's a keeper. But if You do happen to decide that You could let her go to someone else, please keep me in mind. Otherwise, I'll be happy to go on as I was . . . as I still am.

He walked out to the barn to check on the horses and to turn off the light, with Kaiser trotting alongside him each step. "You like her, too, don't you, pup?" he asked, looking down at the faithful companion. "I don't think she's going to be for us, though," he warned the dog. "So don't get your hopes up. But if that changes at all, you'll be the first to know."

By the time Charles got back into the house and closed the door behind him, he realized that he was experiencing something new—for the first time in his life—loneliness.

Chapter 47

After her Sunday with Charles and the family, Maggie was one confused aspirant. There was no denying a certain chemistry between them. It felt completely natural for her to be in his home, on his farm, riding his horse, playing with his dog, standing by his side.

Her feelings for Charles by now seemed bigger than life. She knew in her head that she dare not allow those feelings to run away with her. Committing that concept to the heart was another matter. Her heart was ready to run away with her at any moment. She was grateful that she would not be seeing Charles again for a while. She needed time to let the excitement of the relationship settle so she could sort out what was from God and what was just fleeting emotion.

Lent seemed to provide the perfect opportunity for discernment for her. It was a chance to slow down, focus on her relationship with Christ, indulge in some extra prayer time, and offer up fasting and other sacrifices. She had always enjoyed Lent, even as a child. Though her siblings would often complain that Lent was too long and that they could not wait until it was over, Maggie always found that the spiritual exercises of this penitential season were invigorating. She eagerly entered into Lent this year with great expectations.

Amie was ready for Lent this year as well. With her newly-awakened awareness of religious life, she was hoping that Lent would be a great time for her to see if she was really up to the challenge of the call. She decided to devote herself to prayer, fasting, and spiritual renewal with greater effort than ever.

The nineteen-year-old wrote out a list of all the things she would give up: from chocolate and sweets—the regular Lenten fare—to no butter on her food, only water or milk to drink, and no fighting with her younger siblings—which she figured would be the biggest penance of all. She also decided that in addition to her daily rosary and Bible readings, she would try to make it to daily Mass throughout Lent and to commit herself to one hour of weekly adoration time. She looked over her list and decided that it was a good start. If she found it was not enough of a challenge she could always add on more, later.

When Ash Wednesday came, Amie not only abstained from meat and dairy, but she decided to fast on just bread and water for the day. It went so well she figured she would add the bread and water fast every Friday

in Lent to her new spiritual regime. She was ready to take on just about
any spiritual discipline.

Two weeks into Lent, Maggie was a wreck. Never before had she found
Lent to be so long and dragged out. She had no patience for her daily devotions.
She restlessly sat through her prayer time in chapel. She resented fasting and
having given up sweets and junk food. She attended her classes on campus
with great irritation. She exposed herself to her books, but made no real effort
to study. She had become impersonal and elusive with the Sisters.

Sister Charlotte observed all the changes in the young aspirant. She
wondered when or if Maggie would come and speak with her. The Director
of Novices had no intention of forcing the issue with the young girl. This
was a spiritual journey she would have to take on her own, in order to find
where the Lord was truly calling her.

Kyra noted the changes in her companion as well. She had no idea what
was going on with Maggie. She concluded that the pressures of school were
bringing her friend down. She made an effort to stay out of Maggie's way. Kyra
was comfortable enough with solitude—she had grown up with it. She simply
decided to spend more time in prayer and adoration. She was happy that Lent
was affording her more opportunities than usual for private reflection.

Maggie observed her companion peacefully moving through Lent. The
more she noticed Kyra settling into religious life, the more she felt herself
pulling away from it. Funny how she had first thought she would be the
one to keep Kyra going. As it turned out—Kyra was the one persevering
with real fortitude. *Still waters run deep,* Maggie thought to herself. *All
I've ever been is a turbulent stream of rushing waters. No wonder I'm not
really cut out for this life.*

She wanted to run away. She wanted to go off and marry Charles and
be over with it—get on with her new dream in life. It seemed that her time
of discernment was clearly pointing her in that new direction.

Amie's spiritual vigor quickly began to wear off. After two weeks of
dedicated devotions and penance, she was fatiguing from all the discipline that
was being required of her. She was finding school harder than ever. While
she was happy to share with Samantha about faith—she felt guilty that she
was struggling to keep up with her own Lenten plan. She kept up her façade
as much as possible so as not to discourage Samantha's genuine interest. On

the other hand, Amie had little patience for Krystal's agnostic views. She was quick to change the topic any time Krystal took a shot at religion.

Band practices were a real source of stress-release for Amie. Spending time with these friends and cousins who were so close to her made her feel like her old self again. She liked being her old self—plain and simple Amie. When she sat at the piano and played with the band, she could just lose herself in the music. It was spiritually renewing for her to let the words of the praise and worship songs wash over her soul.

Kyle noted the change in Amie and was concerned. One Sunday after Mass he noticed Amie still sitting in her pew long after everyone else had stepped out of the church. It was not like her to hold back from hanging out with their group of friends. As he was leaving the church, he decided to go sit beside her and see how she was doing. "You okay these days?"

Amie shrugged her shoulders. "Yeah. Why?"

"You just seem to be so distant and distracted whenever I see you lately—except at band. I just thought I'd ask if everything's fine."

Amie looked at Kyle. She smiled at the dark-haired, dark-eyed boy sitting beside her. Of all the guys in their group, he was her closest friend. He noticed things the other guys did not. She knew she could talk openly with him, though she always kept an emotional guard between herself and any of her guy friends. "I'm fine. It's just that lately I've been really trying to discern whether or not God might be calling me to religious life."

"Seriously?" he asked.

"Yeah," she replied, straightening up in the pew.

Kyle laughed. "You know, I went through that a few months ago, myself," he said, sitting up straight beside her.

"No kidding? So what did you come up with?"

"I don't think I'm cut out for religious life."

"Does that mean you think you're cut out for married life? *You?* Kyle, the just-leave-me-alone-in-my-singleness dude?" she teased, nudging him with her elbow.

Kyle laughed. "Well, there's always the single option as well," he reminded her. "But actually, yes, I do think I'm being called to married life. I just know I'm not ready for it yet."

"So, when did you figure all this out?" Amie questioned.

"I don't know. I guess around New Year's." Kyle leaned forward with his arms resting on his knees, his feet propped up on the kneeler in front of him.

"New Year's!" Amie threw out at him, giving him a little push on the shoulder. "That would explain why you were such a Mister *Grumpy-Pants* at the New Year's Eve party."

"I guess so," he said, allowing himself to be pushed forward by her gesture. He thought back to the night for a moment and wondered if Amie would be able to put it all together. The smile on her face told him that she really still had no clue as to his feelings for her. He was grateful for that. It was not the time . . . and for that matter, maybe the time would never come. With Amie thinking about religious life, maybe she was not the one for him after all. "Sorry I wasn't such good company that night."

"Ahhh," she scoffed at his apology. "What's to be sorry about? I'm just glad to know that I'm not the only one who gets irritable at the thought of religious life."

Kyle turned to lean on his arm so he could look straight back at Amie. She winked at him, and they had a good laugh together.

"So how did you know you weren't being called to religious life?" She propped her feet up on the pew and leaned forward, resting her arms on her knees, so he would not have to keep twisting his body to look back at her.

"I don't know. How does one ever really know? I prayed about it, and it just didn't feel natural for me. Maybe I didn't pray enough about it. Maybe something will change my mind later on. But in my heart, I just really feel that God is calling me to be a husband and father someday. And when I pray about that, it just feels right."

Amie smiled at her friend. "I think you'll make an amazing husband and father someday for some really blessed girl."

Kyle smiled and thanked Amie. "What about you? What's made you think about religious life all of a sudden? Aren't you the I-can't-wait-to-get-on-with-married-life girl?" He nudged her in the same fashion she had nudged him.

Amie laughed at Kyle's gentle mockery. "Yes, I am. But it just seemed to me, after Connor and I called off our courtship, that maybe I wasn't focusing enough on my relationship with Jesus. So, as I started spending more time in prayer, I started realizing how much I was falling in love with Jesus—in a whole new way. And that made me start to think about religious life."

"That's cool. So why has that made you so *irritable* now?" he asked, using her choice of words.

"I think I'm realizing that I've gone to one of my typical Amie-extremes. I figured I'd try to imitate religious life right now, during Lent. So, I went and made up a Lenten plan for myself that would be something like Maggie would have done. Boy, do I ever have a new-found respect for that girl. She always made it look so easy, but it is definitely way beyond my typical daily devotions and penances . . . and I'm beginning to feel overwhelmed with how much Lent there is to go." She laughed at herself. "Pretty pathetic, huh? Just goes to show what kind of religious Sister I'd make."

"Well, it could be that there's more to religious life than just penance and prayer," Kyle suggested. "And you're not exactly living in a religious community to support your efforts," he reminded the girl. "So don't be so hard on yourself."

"And Maggie is just Maggie," Amie added. "She's so lucky; she knows *exactly* what God is calling her to. And you know Maggie, there's no wavering for her. She's full speed ahead with her vocation—without ever looking back." Amie shook her head and sighed. "I couldn't possibly begin to be as holy as she is."

"I don't know," Kyle encouraged the girl. "You and Maggie are different people. God calls everyone to holiness, but He has a different plan for each of us to be able to achieve it. You'll figure out what vocation He's calling you to, in due course. But in the meantime, just be you. You're an awesome girl, Amie. You've got a strong faith and a real gift for sharing it. Your outgoing personality makes it fun for anyone to be with you . . . and that attracts others to Christ. So I think you just need to work on being Amie—not Maggie—and let God work with the gifts and talents He's given you."

Amie looked down at her folded hands as Kyle was talking. As he finished, she lifted her eyes in a sideways glance to meet his. "Thanks, Kyle," she said in a soft voice.

"It's true, Amie. Look at your music and how you've used it to glorify God. And not only that, look how music ministers to you. You're a different girl when you get on that keyboard. All the worries of the world seem to melt away when you begin to play . . . not just for you, but for everyone listening." Kyle watched and waited for Amie to respond.

She lifted her head to meet him eye to eye. "How come you can see me so clearly? Why can't I see myself the way you see me?"

"It's just an outsider's point-of-view," he told her. "You probably see me better than I see myself, as well."

"True," she agreed. "But you're not just an outsider, Kyle, you're a good friend. And I really appreciate you taking time for me. I feel better." She sat up straight in the pew again. "I think I'm going to tone down some of my Lenten resolutions. Maybe that way I'll be a little more charitable with the people around me, instead of being so focused on spiritual exercises that are making me impossible to live with."

"I wouldn't say you've been impossible. Just a Miss *Grumpy-Pants*," he teased, as he stood up from the pew where they were sitting. "You want to go get something to drink downstairs?"

"Sounds good. I haven't had anything but milk or water all Lent and I'm dying for some juice." Amie stood up beside her friend. They left the pew, genuflected before the Tabernacle at the front of the church, and headed down to the church hall.

Their friends were standing around, as usual on a Sunday after Mass, talking. Amie and Kyle got themselves some juice and joined in with the group as they made plans for the day. Daniel Schultz had invited everyone to come over to his house for board games and supper. Amie and Katie made sure it was fine with their folks and then caught a ride with Kyle.

Amie was relieved to spend a day as *Amie* again. She was not quite sure if anyone else had noticed a difference, but every now and then Kyle would smile at her in a way that said, "Welcome back."

✟   ✟   ✟

By the Fourth Sunday in Lent, Maggie knew she needed help. No consolation was coming to her. Her heart was still in turmoil—torn between two loves. Though she knew Sr. Charlotte and her parents were praying for her, she realized now that she needed more than just prayers. It was time again for some spiritual direction and guidance. That Sunday after Mass she approached Fr. Steve to see if he had time to meet with her. As always, Fr. Steve made time.

Maggie arrived at the rectory that afternoon at four o'clock. Fr. Steve welcomed her with a hug. They were good friends. Fr. Steve had been like a big brother to all the Collins children, as they had become his surrogate family during his seminary years away from home.

"Tea sound good to you? Already got the kettle plugged in," Fr. Steve offered.

"Sounds lovely. You still remember how to serve tea?" Maggie questioned the young cleric.

"With crumpets—Collins-style," he said over his shoulder as he reached up into the cupboard to pull down a bag of chocolate chip cookies. He turned around to show them to the girl, with a big smile on his face. "These stay buried deep in the cupboard, so they don't tempt me all week during Lent. But Sundays, we get off."

He got out a plate and put some cookies on it. He pulled out two packages of tea and held them up for Maggie to choose. She pointed to the Apple Cinnamon.

"I should have guessed," he said. "You were always the spicy-tea type, weren't you? It goes with your spicy character."

"Thanks," she said, with a smirk. "But I'm not feeling so spicy these days."

"So, what's up with our Maggie?" Fr. Steve asked, leaning against the counter as he waited for the water to boil.

Maggie sat at the table, leaning on her elbow, with her face propped up by her hand. She shrugged and looked back at the young priest. She cast her eyes down at the black and white checkered floor. "I don't even know where to begin," she mumbled. "It's all so unbelievable and definitely unpredictable. . . . Say?" She suddenly perked up. "How about you try to guess what's wrong with me—test out your prophetic gifts?"

Fr. Steve raised his eyebrows and peered down at the girl through narrowed eyes. "Nice try, kiddo. You didn't come out this afternoon to test me for my prophetic gifts. If you had, I would have told you not to bother coming—'cause I don't have any."

"That's not true," Maggie disagreed. "You've always been very intuitive. I bet you if you just thought about it for a moment, you'd figure me out."

"They don't exactly train us in the seminary to play three guesses during spiritual direction." He looked at the young girl seated at his kitchen table. Her eyes were looking at him playfully, and he realized that for Maggie he could bend the rules a bit. "Fine. I'll take three guesses, but then you talk. Deal?"

"Deal," she said, sitting up, ready for the game.

"You've suddenly felt called to become an astronaut," he stated, holding up finger number one.

Maggie rolled her eyes. "Funny, Fr. Steve."

"Two," he said, holding up his second finger. "You've just discovered that you're really a princess from some obscure foreign country, and someone has come to inform you that you need to come and take your place on the throne."

Maggie rolled her eyes even bigger than before. "Fr. Steve, you have no intention of taking this seriously, do you?"

"Three," he went on, holding up his third and final finger. "You've suddenly fallen in love with some amazing man, and you no longer feel called to religious life."

Maggie's eyes opened wide and she stared at Fr. Steve, speechlessly.

Fr. Steve let his hand drop in front of him. The water began boiling. He turned around to unplug the kettle. With his back to Maggie he pursed his lips and shifted his eyes. *Oops! I think I hit home.* He picked up the kettle and poured the water into the teapot. When he was done, he turned around again to face Maggie. She was still staring at him in disbelief.

"I told you you were intuitive," she said, a little smile beginning to form at the corners of her mouth.

"Maggie, I thought I was being completely ridiculous," he told her. He brought the teapot over to the table, set it beside the plate of cookies, and went back to get the cups and saucers from the counter.

"And here I thought this was all so unpredictable. I guess I was wrong."

"No," he disagreed. "You were right. Who would have ever guessed that our Maggie, 'give me religious life or bust', would ever have diverted off course." Fr. Steve sat down at the table kitty-corner from the girl. "I guess God just likes to keep us on our toes."

"I guess," Maggie returned.

"I mean, when I was just about your age, I would never have guessed God was calling me to become a priest," he pointed out to her. "But He did, and I'm glad that He didn't just leave me headed down my own self-absorbed course in life."

"I'm glad of that, too," Maggie said, watching Fr. Steve pour out the tea.

"Not that I'm saying you've been self-absorbed, Maggie," Fr. Steve corrected himself.

She laughed. "Well, to be honest, lately I've felt really self-absorbed."

Fr. Steve picked up his cup of tea, pinkie up, and lifted the cup toward his young friend. "See, I haven't forgotten how to drink tea with a Collins girl."

Maggie laughed and picked up her own teacup, pinkie up, lifting her cup toward the priest. "To the good ol' days," she toasted. "When life seemed so simple and clear."

"To the present moment," he returned, "where the adventure of life is played out."

They both took a sip of their tea and put their cups down.

"So, Miss Maggie," he went on, "I'm still waiting for some details of what's going on with you. And just tell it as it is—Maggie Collins-adventure style."

Maggie smiled. She was much more relaxed now. Fr. Steve knew her well. He was not here to judge her or look down on her as some pathetic little schoolgirl who did not know her own heart. He was here to help direct her, like a safari guide on a wild adventure.

She opened up and told Fr. Steve about her relationship with Charles, from their work together at the Sisters' house, to her dream, to her day spent with him and her family on the farm. She told him how her time of "discerning" during Lent had just turned out to be a time of spiritual torment to her soul. She had no peace. "I feel like I don't even know who I am anymore," she concluded. "I'm not a suitable bride for either Charles or Christ, these days."

Fr. Steve listened and smiled, as he drank tea and ate "crumpets". He laughed when Maggie got to the crumpet part of the story. This was definitely a Maggie-style adventure.

"Maggie, I think you are going to make a beautiful bride for either Charles or Christ, or whomever He calls you to marry," Fr. Steve returned. "I think the problem is that you've always had such a high standard for yourself, spiritually, that you don't really know how to deal with the confusion that sometimes comes with discernment. But if the answers were given to you—plain as day—there'd be no discernment involved, now would there?"

Maggie shrugged her shoulders and gave a little laugh. "I guess not."

"I know for some," he went on to say, "that's just what happens to them. They get such a clear calling right off the bat that there's no mistaking it. But for most . . . we struggle with temptations, our human frailty, our desires, our past hopes and dreams . . . just like you're doing right now. Welcome to the world, Maggie," he said with a smile.

"Thanks," she said, shaking her head. "So you think that this whole business of me going crazy over the course of Lent is just part of the discernment process?"

"Sure it is," Fr. Steve acknowledged. "There are two paths at war inside of you right now, Maggie." Fr. Steve put up his fists, like a boxer sparring. "It's not a choice between good and bad . . . it's a choice between one good versus another good. That's what's making it so hard. If it were good versus evil, you'd clearly know the path to take. But you're the one creating the war, Maggie, not God. You see, the Lord has simply brought you to a fork in the road. And you just never anticipated the path to not be clearly marked out."

Maggie huffed, blowing her bangs up off her forehead. "No kidding."

"You want God to put up road signs. That's normal, but it's also not likely going to happen, Maggie. Jesus is inviting you to choose. And the signs He gives you won't be written out in big bold letters on sign posts, they'll be written in your heart—the fruit of the Spirit, which is love . . . joy . . . peace," he spoke each word slowly, letting Maggie absorb the meaning of each virtue. He then went on, "Patience, kindness, goodness, faithfulness, gentleness, self-control," quoting with his typical Fr. Steve grasp of Scripture, a broad smile lighting up his face. "Galatians five, twenty-two to twenty-three," he added with a wink. "It took me a while to get those memorized, and in order, but they come in handy at times."

Maggie smiled back. He was a good man and a very good priest. She understood what he was saying to her and she nodded slowly.

"You see, Maggie, once you find those virtues living in your heart, you'll know you're going down the right path. The trick is, sometimes you just have to choose the path in faith and hope—because it might take a while for you to know if those virtues really have taken seed in your heart. So, what I suggest that you do for the rest of Lent is really allow yourself to choose one path over the other and test it out. I don't mean leave the Sisters' house and start dating Charles."

Maggie laughed.

"I mean, choose one of the paths and allow your heart to sit in that decision for a while. Forget about the other for a time. You'll begin to see that either Jesus allows that love and joy and peace to begin to live in your heart, or He doesn't. Then test out the other path for a while. Let the first one go. Let you heart sit in that new direction and see whether you discover love, joy, and peace there. Surely Jesus doesn't intend for you to follow both paths. So if you're earnestly seeking His will, in prayer, He's going to make the path that He wants you to take open up to you. And then you'll know, because the footprints of His Spirit will be there, written in your heart. You'll know. Trust me." Fr. Steve sat with his hands folded and resting on the table. He looked at Maggie and she lifted her eyes to look back at him.

She smiled, her lips closed, her head gently moving forward and back. "I think I know what you mean, Fr. Steve. I've just been pushing my heart down both paths with such force, no wonder I feel like I'm going to explode. I can't handle the pressure. I haven't stopped long enough to just really assess either path on its own merits, and then weigh it out against the desires of my heart. I keep letting all these new and *big* emotions block my ability to go any deeper inside of myself." Her eyes widened on the word "big", and she made a gesture with her arms to match her expression.

Fr. Steve laughed and nodded. "That's the problem with trying to base major life decisions solely on emotions. While they can be helpful, they can also block us from going deeper—from discerning the real meaning and purpose of our lives. That's why God has given you an intellect and a will—to rule over your emotions and your instincts. It sets us apart from all the animals in creation and allows for us to exercise our free will. God won't push Himself on anyone. He won't force His will on us at all. We have to embrace it ourselves, whole-heartedly. That's the gift of His unconditional love for us. And that's what allows us to experience true love, joy, and peace in our lives . . . because it all comes to us freely. We just have to surrender ourselves to His will—once we discover what that is—and the rest will follow."

"Thank you, Fr. Steve," Maggie said, tapping her fingers on the table. "I feel like I can go and face this all again—without being so overwhelmed. It seems so much more manageable now, when you just take it one step at a time."

"And it takes time," he added. "You can't expect to make a life-changing decision overnight. You have to just relax and trust that if God is calling you to something, He's not going to take it away from you because you took too long to decide. He's patient—He's got all the time in the world."

Maggie laughed. "I guess. When you put it in those terms, I can slow down a bit and be more patient with myself."

"Good," Fr. Steve said, smacking his hands on the table. "So, why don't we say a prayer together before you go?"

"Sounds good," Maggie agreed.

Fr. Steve began with the sign of the cross, and Maggie followed, bowing her head in prayer.

"Heavenly Father, we thank You for the struggles and confusion that have come into Maggie's life at this time, because we know that through these difficulties she has the opportunity to come to know You and love You and serve You with greater vitality than ever before. We thank You and praise You for Your loving care of Your daughter.

"We know that You are calling her to a great mission in life—to love. Though how she is being called to fulfill that mission has not yet been fully revealed, we trust that You have a plan for her—a perfect plan for her—and that You have given her the earnest desire to seek to fulfill Your holy will.

"Please open the door to the path which You are calling Maggie to walk down, and let the other door close. Please give her peace during this time of discernment. Please fill her with joy for the journey—for this time, now, is also part of the journey that You are calling her on in her life.

"We praise You, and we bless You, and we thank You for Your loving care and protection for us all.

"And may the blessing of God, the Almighty Father, descend upon you, Maggie, and remain with you forever, in the name of the Father and of the Son and of the Holy Spirit. Amen."

"Amen," Maggie said. She had made the sign of the cross as Fr. Steve blessed her. Raising her head and opening her eyes to look up at the young priest, a smile began to emerge again upon her face. "Thanks, Fr. Steve."

"My pleasure and my joy, Maggie," he replied.

"Well," Maggie said, smacking her hands down on the table top. She stood up, with renewed energy and vigor. There was a twinkle in her eye. "You know what I think, Fr. Steve? I think you should work on that gift of prophecy."

"Who'd've thunk?" he said, with a chuckle. "The Lord moves in mysterious ways, and when dealing with Maggie—expect the unexpected. That's all I can say," he concluded, standing up and stretching.

They walked together to the front door of the rectory. Maggie put on her winter jacket.

"You want a ride home?" Fr. Steve offered.

"Nah. It's a beautiful day out there—maybe one of the last days of winter before this snow begins to melt away. I think I'll enjoy a good stroll home." She tipped her head, respectfully to the priest. "Thanks again, Fr. Steve," she added with a big smile. She reached up and gave him a hug. "I'm so glad we have you in our family. I feel very spoiled to be able to come to a priest who knows me and my family so well. I think every family should adopt a priest."

"I think every family should produce a priest," he corrected her, with a raised finger. "Then the rest of us would have more time for just this kind of thing."

"Good point," she agreed. "We're working on those boys. Personally, I have high hopes for Zack, since I can't imagine him ever being the kind of guy that any girl could ever stand to live with."

Fr. Steve laughed, picturing the rugged, red-headed little boy. "You just might have a point there, Maggie. Maybe God's given you your own gift of prophecy."

"Well, don't bet any money on it," she warned. "This is Maggie you're dealing with." She pointed at herself and made a comical Maggie-expression.

Fr. Steve laughed and waved to her, as she walked out the door and down the front steps of his house. She waved back, a big smile illuminating her face.

As Maggie strolled down the street on that bright winter's day, she knew the weight on her heart had lifted. Once again she could trust that God was not trying to mess with her fragile little mind. He was blessing her with this time of confusion. It was an adventure—a once-in-a-lifetime adventure of discerning and choosing. She thanked the Lord for the gift of this present trial in her life.

She pictured Jesus standing in a forest at a fork in the road, patiently waiting for her to choose a path. Both paths were brightly lit, beautifully lined with trees and flowers, invitingly laid out before her. She stepped onto the path of religious life and took a deep breath.

Okay, Maggie-girl, she said to herself, *we're going exploring. There's a wonderful adventure ahead.* She looked back at Jesus, in her mind. *You don't mind if I just explore this path for a while before I make up my mind, do You?*

In her mind's eye, Jesus smiled at her and extended an inviting hand down that path.

Thanks, the young girl said. *I'll be back to check out the other path, soon.*

Chapter 48

Joanie and Brandon entered into the forty days of preparation for Easter with real joy. This would be their first Lent and Easter as a married couple, also marking the anniversary of Brandon's entry into the Church the year before. They were excited that both Brandon's step-father, Dan, and Mark would be received into the Church at Easter. It seemed that much was going on around them pointing to the new life that was so evident in the Church.

Joanie was blossoming in her pregnancy, excited as she began to feel the baby kicking inside of her more and more. New life was indeed the theme of her Lenten journey, and she fully embraced the new role with which she had been gifted in motherhood. She began preparing their little apartment for the baby. With over fifteen weeks left to go, Brandon felt it was excessive—but he did not dare stand in the way of a nesting mother.

She had Brandon help her rearrange the bedroom furniture, making room for the baby's crib which she quickly made up, with little stuffed animals lining the end of the crib and a musical mobile hanging above it. They bought a new dresser for the baby and in no time she had it all arranged with newborn diapers, white and yellow baby clothes, bibs, blankets, and colourful toys. After several days of shopping and trying out various models, the young mother-to-be found a glider rocker that fit her just right. They brought it home and set it up in their room on her side of the bed. Joanie kept a quilt on the chair that Grandma Collins had made and given her as a little girl. Whenever she got the chance she would wrap herself in her blanket, sit in her rocker, and sing lullabies to her unborn child.

She read books on parenting and listened to tapes on the subject. She did pre-natal exercises and, together, she and Brandon did a prenatal class. Joanie was not missing out on one moment's opportunity to prepare for her life-long dream of motherhood. The more excited she got about it, the longer it seemed to take.

Brandon watched his wife with great delight. He marveled at how motherhood was transforming Joanie from a wife to an almost-obsessive mother. As for himself, he steadily moved along, excited about the baby, but able to keep it all in perspective. There were months yet until the little one's arrival. Brandon focused more on the spiritual journey of Lent and kept Joanie tuned in to their devotional commitments. He prided himself in his ability to keep some sense of balance in their home—with such a highly emotionally-charged woman.

✞   ✞   ✞

Brandon came home one night from R.C.I.A. class all charged up himself. As he entered their apartment he called out for his bride. He was in the mood for talking. Mark's upcoming entry into the Church was bringing back memories of the year before when he had been preparing to become Catholic. The whole process of walking through the R.C.I.A. program with Mark was like an opportunity for Brandon to recommit to his own Baptismal promises and to deepen his own faith convictions.

They were very blessed to have their R.C.I.A. program being led by such a solid group of Catholics—with Fr. Steve so intensely involved. Fr. Steve never compromised on the Church's teachings. "Tell the truth, the whole truth, and nothing but the truth," was his attitude; yet he always delivered it with such charity. That's what Brandon had come to appreciate so much about his cleric friend, and it was one of the things that had attracted him to become Catholic in the first place.

Spending an evening with Mark, Fr. Steve, and the other folks involved with the R.C.I.A. program at St. James, inspired Brandon. He wanted to shout from the mountaintops.

He called out again for Joanie as he hung up his winter coat and gloves in the front closet.

Joanie called out from the bedroom. "Hi, honey. Come see what I've done." Her voice was filled with self-satisfaction.

"Whatchy'a up to?" he asked, coming into the room.

There on the bed beside Joanie was their large suitcase, packed almost to overflowing. At the head of their bed was the baby's car seat with a colourful cover fitted in place.

"I've got my suitcase all ready to go to the hospital whenever we need it," she proudly stated. "Look." She pointed out the various things she had in it, including a small CD player with a stack of CDs beside it—for good music to listen to during labour. There were also diapers, baby clothes, and blankets. There were even books and framed photos, and of course Joanie had not forgotten clothes for herself and all her toiletries.

Brandon watched as she pointed things out. She picked up a little newborn diaper and said in an itty-bitty voice, "Isn't it cute? It's so ti-ny."

Brandon laughed at his wife.

"And over here's the car seat from Mark and Justine that you tried to take me out with," she said, walking over to it. She lifted the little cover off the seat; it, too, was filled with blankets.

"Don't you think you're a little ahead of yourself?" he asked. "You still have over two months to go before your due date . . . and at that you could go overdue?"

Joanie grimaced at her husband. "The prenatal instructor told us to be packed and ready, so we don't get caught by surprise."

"Well, there you go," he said with a chuckle. He walked over and took his wife in his arms. "No one can accuse you of not being organized, dear."

Joanie gave her husband a little shot in the ribs. "You're making fun of me, *dear.*"

"No, I'm not. I think you're wonderful, and I'm glad you're excited about having this baby. It'd be terrible if you had no enthusiasm for motherhood."

Joanie gave him a little squeeze. "Here, help me zip this up and tuck it into the front closet."

Brandon did as he was told, and they got things put away.

"So how was R.C.I.A.?" Joanie asked.

"Excellent," Brandon enthused. "It makes me want to become Catholic all over again."

Joanie laughed. "I'm glad it's not pushing you out the backdoor. How are Mark and Justine?"

"Great," Brandon answered as they walked to the kitchen for a bedtime snack. "Justine loves her new job. She's just on fire for bringing the message of chastity to young people. Mark said she's like a new woman. She's not worried about the whole fertility thing for now. They're still charting, and she'll get in with the ob-gyn next month, so she's excited about that."

"I'm so happy for them," Joanie said. "They really found a way to make good come out of the struggles, didn't they?"

"They did," Brandon agreed. "And Mark is totally pumped about Easter. He reminds me of myself, a year ago. I just can't believe a whole year's gone by since I became Catholic, and we got engaged. Life sure does fly by when you're having fun," he said, slipping his arm around his wife from behind.

"Can you still reach all the way around me?" she asked, looking down at his hands folded over her rounded tummy.

"Yup, with plenty of room to spare," he answered, leaning forward to kiss her on the cheek.

Joanie turned her head and returned his kiss. As she did, he skillfully turned her in his arms until they were face to face, still kissing.

"Mmm," she whispered. "Maybe we don't need a bedtime snack tonight, after all."

"You know I was all excited to come home tonight and talk to you about R.C.I.A. We had discussed the Church's teachings on marriage. But from this perspective, I think I'd rather just go put it into practice with you," he said with a smile.

All at once he bent down and swept Joanie off her feet.

"Hey!" she called out. "What're you doing? You're going to hurt your back, Brandon."

"Nah," he said. "I'm just getting into shape in case you suddenly go into labour, and I have to carry you and that monster suitcase and car seat all at once."

"Put me down, you goof," she called out, as he moved to go out of the kitchen.

"Nope. But since my hands are full, do you mind turning out the light?" He paused and waited for her to flick off the switch. He kicked open the swinging door between the kitchen and living room and carried his bride off to their sanctuary of marital love.

It was not just the intellectual truth of the Church's teachings that made it so appealing to Brandon, but the freedom and joy they had brought into his life as he lived it out day by day with his beautiful bride.

Chapter 49

"Girls' night out, tonight, honey," Joanie reminded Brandon as they drove home from work Tuesday afternoon. "I'm picking up my sisters at six, and we're meeting Annie and Jocelyn at a restaurant for supper. So you're on your own tonight. Can you handle it?"

"I managed to feed myself and stay alive for a few years before we married," he replied, as he turned the corner to their street. "I think I can remember how to fix a meal for myself."

"Tonight's your Bible study with Mike, anyway," Joanie mentioned. "So, at least you won't have to sit around an empty apartment, pining for your wife."

"I think I can handle it," he said, throwing her a sideways glance. "Where're you going to eat?"

"Amie's got this little restaurant she's totally hooked on, now. Country Kitchen . . . Café?" she said, trying to remember the name. "Anyway, she made reservations for us and knows how to get there."

"This is Amie we're talking about," Brandon cautioned. "Make sure you've got the directions good and set before you take off."

Joanie playfully smacked Brandon's arm just before they got out of the SUV. "Come on. Amie's not that bad with directions."

"All I'm saying is Amie isn't always the most careful about paying attention to her whereabouts. She's usually too busy enjoying the company around her to bother to care where she is," he commented with a laugh, as they headed up the walk to their apartment building. "Don't get me wrong. I love Amie, dearly, but I wouldn't trust her to find her way out of an elevator some days."

Joanie laughed. It was true. Amie was always depending on others to do the driving and navigating.

"Now if it were Katie, that'd be another story," Brandon noted, as Joanie walked passed him through the door. "That girl's got her head on straight."

"She sure does," Joanie agreed. "She reminds me of me at that age. She knows exactly what she wants out of life and how she plans to get it. There's no messing with her."

"And so did you succeed?" Brandon asked as they walked up the stairs to their third floor apartment.

Joanie walked in front of him, holding the rail, no longer paying attention to their conversation. "I can't believe I'm almost out of breath on these stairs. I'm so out of shape."

"You're pregnant, dear," he reminded her. "Now, I've never been pregnant, but it wouldn't surprise me if it took your breath away."

She heaved a deep breath as they reached the top of the steps. "What'd you ask me?"

"Did I ask you something?" he questioned, waiting as she caught her breath again before they walked down the hall to their apartment.

"Yeah," she insisted, trying to replay the conversation in her head. "Something about succeeding?"

"Oh, yeah. Did you succeed in getting what you wanted out of life?"

Joanie raised a finger in the air. "Ahhh, yes. Did I succeed?" She pondered a moment. "Let's see, I've got me a great husband and a baby that simply takes my breath away. I think I'm right on course."

"That's good. . . . See, that's the difference between us, dear. You got what you wanted in life, but I never wanted any of this for myself." He jumped to get out of the way of Joanie's arm swinging out to hit him. "But I'm sure glad God doesn't always give us what we *want* . . . instead He gave me a change of heart and then He granted me my heart's desires—which I certainly never deserved." He held the door open for Joanie to walk into their apartment.

"Well, just don't take it for granted," she warned. She kicked off her winter walking boots, went straight into their bedroom, and crawled onto the bed.

"You gonna take off your jacket?" Brandon asked, standing in the doorway of the bedroom.

"Just wake me up at five-forty and roll me out the door," she answered. "I'm exhausted."

Brandon laughed and closed the door to the bedroom. He looked at his watch. She had only twenty minutes to nap.

After Joanie left for her girls' night out, Brandon went to the kitchen to fix himself some supper. He fried a few eggs, made some toast, and poured a tall glass of milk. It was simple bachelor's fare for the evening, but more than sufficient.

It was only six o'clock. He and Mike usually connected around seven for their Bible study. With nothing else to do for the hour, Brandon decided to call Mike earlier.

Four rings and then the answering machine kicked in; Mike was not home. Disappointed, Brandon decided to sit and read for a while and try again later.

He had just settled nicely into a book when the buzzer for his apartment sounded. He got up to answer it and, to his total shock, it was Mike.

As Mike came into the apartment, Brandon stood dumbfounded. They gave each other a hug in greeting, and Brandon took Mike's coat to hang it up.

"What in the world are you doing here?" Brandon asked.

"I took a few days off work and decided to come to Saskatoon for a little get-away. I thought I'd phone and warn you, but since I knew you'd be home tonight for our Bible study, I decided the surprise would be better."

"Where's Ashleen?" Brandon asked.

"*That's* why I decided to take a few days off," Mike explained, taking a seat on the couch.

"Oh," Brandon said with understanding. "So what's up?"

"Well, I broke up with Ashleen on the weekend," Mike began. "I guess I'm just feeling a little restless . . . but I'm okay. I just needed to be around the old gang—get in touch with my roots again."

"What happened? Oh, can I get you something to drink?" he asked, interrupting himself on his way to sit down on the loveseat across from his friend.

"No, I'm fine for now," Mike said, putting up his hands. "Maybe later."

"Let's have it, then," Brandon prompted his guest. "What went down with Ashleen?"

Mike shrugged and held up his hands, thinking of where to begin. "You know, Brandon, I thought at first things were going to work out with her. When we re-started our relationship as a courtship, she was fairly game to go. She seemed genuinely interested in learning about Christianity and the Church. She willingly came and met with your mom and Dan every other week. It was fun. Your mom's an awesome lady, and Dan's a great guy."

Brandon nodded in agreement. "They're a pretty cool couple."

"It'll be great to see Dan coming into the Church this Easter. He's so excited. It's too bad you won't be able to be there as well," Mike commented.

"I've got to be here for Mark," Brandon replied. "I guess, though, it's a pretty good problem to have—too many friends becoming Catholic all at once, and I can't be there for them all."

Mike laughed. "Only you, buddy, could have problems like that."

"I don't know," Brandon disagreed. "All I know is that when I converted and started to live my faith, it wasn't just like throwing a pebble into a pond—it was like dropping a boulder into a pool of water. There weren't just ripples, there were outright waves. My whole world turned upside down, and my friends and family couldn't escape the splash."

"And it's a good thing," Mike said. He tapped his fingers on the arm of the leather couch, his restlessness apparent.

"So," Brandon brought him back on topic, "what happened with Ashleen?"

"I guess I'm not that good at dropping boulders," Mike commented. "Or she's just really good at avoiding getting wet."

Brandon chuckled.

Mike went on. "It's like I was saying, we were getting out and doing things together—more than just bar-hopping. There happens to be a Young Catholic Adults group there at St. Philomena's, and we were getting involved with that. It's not quite the same as C.C.E. back here, but it was fun. We'd play volleyball and basketball at a gym; get together for movie nights . . . just stuff like that. Not too heavy in faith—more like a social outlet for young Catholic adults to meet each other and hang out. At first Ashleen seemed to really be enjoying it all."

"And then?" Brandon asked.

"The whole thing about a physical relationship just kept coming up, over and over again," Mike said. "She was never really big on letting it drop in the first place, but I think she was just hoping I'd eventually wear down and give in to it again. When that didn't happen, she just started making more comments, then she started trying to seduce me back into her arms. . . . Let me tell you, when a woman wants to use her feminine ways on a man, it takes everything a guy has in him to say 'no.'"

Brandon laughed. "Tell me about it."

"But I resisted. And the more I resisted her come-ons, the more she resented us going out and doing other things together. Every time we'd get together to go out it was a battle. At first she was upset about having to go for suppers at your parents' place, though she'd end up coming anyway. Then she out and out refused going to the parish functions with the Y.C.A. group. It just got so that every night was a fight with her," Mike explained.

"Makes it hard to pursue a relationship with someone when all you do is fight," Brandon said.

"I keep wondering," Mike went on, "is it wrong for me to give up on her like this? I feel sorry for her. For Ashleen, the only way she knows how to be in a relationship with a guy is if she's sleeping with him. And, of course, she couldn't get that from me. So she figures I didn't care about her. And no matter how hard I tried to show her—in big and little ways—that I cared, and no matter how much I treated her with respect, she just couldn't get it. She was always turning the tables on me. If I really loved her, I'd show it. But I *was* showing her real love—she just can't tell the difference between the real thing and the counterfeit."

"The world thinks sex is love and love is sex," Brandon commented. "And there's a multi-billion dollar industry out there shoving that lie down our throats."

"But it's so empty and shallow," Mike complained. "And the more I tried to make Ashleen see that, the harder her heart became. She just closed off entirely to what I was trying to tell her."

"She's been hurt," Brandon said. "A girl can't go through life handing herself over for one guy after another to use for their pleasure and not end up broken and hurt. I know . . . I used lots of women in my life. I cared nothing for them—but I made sure they felt special for the one night I was with them. It's just a total abuse of them—emotionally, physically, spiritually. Eventually a person just has to let their instinctive desire for real love die; otherwise, they'd go crazy."

"I guess," Mike agreed. "I just don't know why I couldn't make Ashleen see that there's a better way. She kept saying to me that I just wanted to have it all my way. She'd call me a control freak and say that I was preventing her from being able to show me that she loved me in the only way she knew how. But I don't think I was being a control freak, just because I wouldn't go to bed with her."

"No," Brandon affirmed his friend. "She's just lost in the darkness of the world—truth becomes lies and lies become truth, and very few people know how to distinguish between the two anymore."

"But you'd think that if you brought the light of Christ in, that it would penetrate the darkness and expose the lies," Mike said. "So why didn't it? Am I a failure?"

"Mike, conversion is a gift from God," Brandon explained. "You can't force Ashleen to see the truth or to accept it. She has to be open to that grace. Maybe the time just wasn't right. I'm sure you've planted seeds of truth there . . . and they'll probably grow in time. But maybe God was protecting you and Ashleen because He isn't calling you to be together. Maybe there's someone else out there for you, Mike, and your work with Ashleen is done."

"But I feel like I'm running out on her . . . leaving her in the darkness. I know where she'll end up," Mike said. "She'll be back at a bar before the week's out, catching up on all the lost time she spent with me. She'll be sleeping with whoever's willing to have sex with her. And with a beautiful girl like Ashleen, she's not going to be at a loss for takers."

"Takers—and that's it," Brandon said. "Guys—and girls—hanging out at bars just waiting to take what they can get. But love's not about taking, it's about giving. And I'm not sure how God broke through this sinner's heart to make me see the difference—but He did." Brandon's eyes looked into the distance as he reflected on his radical conversion. "It was pure grace, Mike, and nothing else. I did nothing to merit it. Joanie threw the hook and I bit . . . and it sunk deep . . . and the more I resisted it, the more it hurt. I could have ignored it and kept going. Somehow, though, God just wouldn't let me. It was my time, and He reeled me in."

"Your conversion just made it seem so easy. I figured that all I had to do was show Ashleen the truth, and she'd want to accept it," Mike said. "I never expected that she'd reject it."

"Well, Mike, she's bit the hook," Brandon said. "God can let her run with an awful lot of line before He ever reels her in. But He will, someday, when it's her time."

"I guess," Mike said. "I just wish it could have been with me."

"That's just pride, Mike," Brandon pointed out. "We don't always get to reap what we sow."

"But what if Ashleen and I were married, and she suddenly lost her faith? Wouldn't it be wrong for me to walk out on her then?" Mike questioned. "Don't I have some obligation to her?"

"Mike, you were *courting*. You weren't married to her," Brandon reminded him. "There's a big difference. If you had been married, then no, of course you shouldn't walk out. You'd have made a vow to her—through sickness and in health, 'til death do you part. But you can't carry that weight of commitment into every relationship, Mike. There's a danger in spending your life trying to convert another person. Conversion is God's business—not ours. We're called to evangelize, to bring the light of truth into the world around us. What God does with that is up to Him. You can't burden yourself to think that you're responsible for Ashleen's salvation. That's Christ's job . . . and He's taking care of it in His own way.

"Be careful, Mike," Brandon went on to warn his friend. "Don't go saddling yourself to someone with whom you don't share faith, just because you feel sorry for her. You'd just be asking for a life of heartache. Marriage is hard enough on its own. I can't imagine what it would be like to be married to someone who didn't share the same faith and values that I now have. How would we decide on anything? How would we face adversities together? How would we be able to support each other, to love and to forgive each other on the little day to day things, let alone the big things?"

Mike sat silently, nodding in agreement with everything Brandon was saying. If he had not believed that in the first place, he would not have come to the conclusion of breaking up with Ashleen. He knew what Brandon was saying was true. He just wished there had been an easier way.

"And you know what?" Brandon asked, changing his tone.

"Hmm?" Mike replied.

"When God reveals to you His perfect plan for your life—with that perfect woman for you—you'll be so glad that things didn't work out with Ashleen the way *you* planned them. Just trust," Brandon added with great simplicity.

Mike heaved a sigh and nodded pensively. "I guess time heals all pain," he finally said.

"You'll be fine," Brandon assured his friend. "And so will Ashleen. You've done your part. Just pray for her and move on, Mike. God can handle it . . . He's a big boy."

Mike laughed. "You think?" he questioned in humour.

"Oh, yeah," Brandon said with a nod.

"Well, I think I'm ready for that drink."

"What'll you have?" Brandon asked, getting up.

"Just water," Mike said with a laugh. "It's still Lent, and I gave up booze and pop."

"I've got juice," Brandon offered.

"Water'll do just fine," Mike said, following Brandon to the kitchen.

"Have you eaten?"

"Not yet."

"Well, step up to the counter, my friend. *Brandon's Smorgasbord* is open for business." Brandon grabbed a chef's apron out of a drawer, for better effect.

Mike laughed and ordered up some eggs and toast, at the chef's recommendation. The two men continued visiting as Mike ate. Brandon then informed Mike that he was not off the hook for Bible study. He went and got out his Bible, opened it to where they had left off in *Paul's Letter to the Romans*, and they got down to work.

Chapter 50

Joanie picked up Amie and Katie shortly after six. From there they went to get Maggie, who was waiting on the doorstep of the Sisters' stately house, ready to go. The fun of getting together with her sisters had revived Joanie's energy. The vehicle was buzzing with their constant chatter.

"Okay," Joanie called out, before putting the Pathfinder into gear. "Where are we going, Amie?"

"*The Country Corner Café,*" she called out. "Don't worry, Joanie. I know how to get there. Just go down College Drive to Central Avenue."

"You're sure?" Joanie verified.

"Trust me, Joanie, I've been there before," she assured her.

"I checked with Mom before we left," Katie told Joanie. "That's how to get there."

"Okay," Joanie said, pulling out onto the street.

Amie turned around from the front passenger seat and raised her eyebrows at Katie seated behind Joanie. Katie smiled back at her sister. "I just wanted to be on the safe side."

The four girls met up with their cousins at the quaint little restaurant and were seated at a cozy booth. They were all impressed with Amie's recommendation as they took in the beautiful décor of the little café.

"Wait 'til you taste their food," Amie told them. "You can thank Kyle, later. He's the one who told Connor about this place—which is where we came when he asked me to court."

"Oh?" Joanie questioned her younger sister. "Fond memories of this place?"

"Not really," Amie confessed. "I was so awkward about that whole relationship that . . . well, I just look back at it and shake my head. I can't believe I was such an airhead."

"I can," stated Maggie. "Love can make you pretty silly."

"What would *you* know about it?" Amie blurted out. "You've never been in love or silly. Well, I mean in *that* way in love or silly. You're just a goof most of the time, Maggie, but definitely not an airhead like me."

Maggie shrugged her shoulders. She could certainly comment on the topic, but had no intention of opening up that whole can of worms.

"Anyway, who's talking about love?" Amie went on. "I was so *not* attracted to Connor in that way. I mean, I like him and all, but not in *that* way. I still don't know why he ever asked me—and even worse—why I ever said 'yes'."

"Well, I still think it's a shame," said Ann. "What a waste of a perfectly good guy."

Katie and Jocelyn, who were sitting beside each other on one side of the booth, both turned and looked at Ann.

Amie suddenly pieced it all together. "Oh, my gosh, Annie. *You* like Connor."

Jocelyn smiled as she sat and played with her long dark curls. She knew her sister was attracted to Connor, but she wanted to see if her sister would actually admit to it publicly.

Ann looked over at Amie as if to say, "Sometimes, girl, you are *so* slow."

Amie caught the look and then realized she probably should not have said anything. "Oops, sorry, Annie. I just . . . I just never realized . . . I should have put it together long ago. Oh . . ." she paused, looking very contrite. "I'm really sorry, Annie. You should have said something long ago."

"How could I?" Ann asked. "You were courting with him."

"We broke up a long time ago. And even before that—you should have said something to me . . . before I started courting him. I would have told him he's got the wrong girl."

"I don't want him, unless he wants me," protested the red-head. "And he hasn't exactly come around since you broke up," she pointed out.

"No, he's been really busy," Amie said. "I think he's just throwing himself into his school work for now. But . . . oh my goodness, would you two ever make the perfect couple. And you would *so* love his family, and they would just love you, Annie."

Ann smiled, rather weakly, at Amie. She tucked her short hair in behind her ears. "Well, I'm not in any hurry. I still have a couple years left in nursing, so I can't say that I'm entirely ready for romance, myself. If Connor ever notices that I exist, we'll go from there."

"He knows you exist," Amie insisted. "Just you wait and see."

"Don't you go doing any match-making on my part," Ann warned her cousin, shaking a finger at her from across the table. "I'm telling you, I'm quite happy to be single and carefree while I still have so much schooling ahead. Don't you go stirring up trouble for me, Amie Collins."

Amie put up her hands. "I promise I won't say or do anything."

"Fine," Ann said.

"Well, now that we've got that settled," Jocelyn piped in, "maybe we should look at our menus. Apparently they've got really good food here."

Everyone started to laugh. They opened their menus, just as the waiter came around. He looked to be in his early twenties, a clean-cut young man. "Welcome to *The Country Corner Café*," he said, looking around the table. "Wow, did I ever get lucky tonight—six beautiful women all at the same table. Girls' night out?"

"Yup," stated Maggie.

"Good guess," commented Amie.

"My name's Brad, and I'll be your waiter for the evening," he told them.

"Hi, Brad," they greeted him, pretty much in unison.

"Hey, you're good! One would think you had actually rehearsed that," he commented with a little laugh. "So, are you ladies ready to order?"

"Not at all," Maggie replied.

"Can I get you anything to drink?"

"Just water—a nice big jug of it for us to share," Maggie stated.

"Sure thing. One jug of water coming up," he said, putting his order pad in the pocket of his waiter's apron.

"That boy's going to get a good tip tonight," Amie observed as he walked away.

"As long as he doesn't get too fresh," Katie commented. "I don't mind flattery—just as long as a guy doesn't think it's going to get him anywhere."

Joanie pointed to her little sister and said, "You keep thinking that way, girl, and you'll be just fine."

Katie laughed. She sat tall and elegantly at the table, playing with her shoulder-length, straight dark hair. Her stunning blue eyes shone out against her fair complexion. She was a pretty girl who had attracted a lot of male attention over the years, but she did her best to remain impervious to it. In her group of friends, the guys treated her like a friend—with a great deal of respect. She was grateful that their church youth group had offered her the opportunity to get to know some really decent guys without the pressures of a dating mentality.

Going out into the world was different. She could not stand being reduced to just a good-looking girl. She had character, personality, talent, intelligence, morals, and integrity. It was a complete turn-off to her when strangers would try to pick her up. How could a guy think she would want anything to do with him just because he told her she was pretty? How lame and shallow was that? It certainly spoke volumes to her of the guy's character.

It was all irrelevant to her anyway. Katie had no intention of taking up any romantic pursuits at her age. She was sixteen and completely not ready or interested in dating. She had no use for a series of casual relationships over the next few years of her life. She fully intended to wait until she was old enough and ready for marriage before she would even consider seeing a guy. And then, at that, it would be courtship and marriage. In the meantime she was following in her older sisters' footsteps and saving herself—entirely—for marriage . . . that included her first kiss. *The winner takes all*, was her determined attitude.

Jocelyn and Katie had been such close cousins their whole lives that they shared the same views on the matter. They were a great support for each other. It was not easy to hold a counter-cultural attitude like that. The pressures were great to enter the dating scene—as soon as they stepped beyond their close circle of friends. But one good friend to support makes all the difference in the world.

"Don't worry, Joanie," Katie replied. "Jocelyn and I are sticking together on this."

"That's right," Jocelyn said, holding up her arms to show off her muscles. "Catholic girls stand strong on the *Rock*."

"You tell 'em sister," Katie said, showing off her muscles in solidarity.

Their older sisters laughed at the two teen-age girls, displaying their rock-solid strength of character, as Brad, the waiter, stepped up to the table behind the two girls' backs.

"I can see that you are not ladies to be messed with," he said, as he walked around to the side where Katie and Jocelyn could see him.

The girls started and looked up at the young waiter smiling at them. They both smiled awkwardly as they quickly lowered their arms.

"You definitely don't want to mess with those girls," Maggie confirmed to the waiter with a little nod.

"Well, I promise to behave," he replied with a friendly smile. "I'll just pour water here and allow you ladies some more time to look over your menus."

Katie and Jocelyn exchanged a timid look with each other as Brad came around to serve them. When the young man finally left the table they all burst out laughing.

"You certainly got your message across," Maggie told the two girls. "I don't think Brad will be getting fresh with anyone here tonight."

As the girls turned to look over their menus, Joanie addressed the group, "Order whatever you want, ladies, I'm treating tonight. Call it a pre-motherhood celebration. I still have money to spend on my friends . . . right now." She was the only one of them working—with a dual income at that. Since all the rest were students, no one objected to her generosity.

Once they had ordered and were waiting for their food, Joanie inquired, "So what's new with everyone lately? Let's catch up with each other."

"Well," Amie spoke up, "I've concluded that I am not being called to religious life."

A few titters and giggles from the group of girls later, Maggie asked, quite sincerely, "Did you actually think that maybe you were, Amie?"

Amie rolled her eyes. "Why does everyone react to me that way? *Yessss*," she held onto the word, "I *actually was* thinking about it for a while. Obviously I could have saved myself a whole lot of heartache and discernment and just asked everyone else if they thought I had a calling."

"It's just that you've always been so keen on marriage, Amie, it's hard for any of us to picture you in religious life," Ann explained. "But I think it was very noble of you to even take time to consider it." Ann looked at her friend and cousin with encouragement.

Amie chuckled. "I guess it wasn't very realistic to think that I might have a calling there . . ."

"I don't know," Joanie cut in. "I remember taking time when I was your age to really contemplate religious life."

"You?" Maggie inquired. "Why don't *I* remember that?"

"Well, it only lasted about two weeks," Joanie admitted, to the girls giggles. "It was more of a passing phase than anything. But I just remember thinking that I couldn't push ahead into marriage without ever letting myself really consider my options."

"So you don't think I was being ridiculous?" Amie asked her oldest sister.

"Not at all," she said.

"Neither do I," said Maggie. "I think it's good to consider all your options before you make any life-long decisions."

"That, coming from the girl who would never even think of anything but religious life," Amie said, pointing sideways with her thumb at Maggie, sitting beside her.

"Even I've been challenged this year, while living at the Sisters' house, to search out what God is really calling me to," she admitted.

"You?" Ann questioned. "Now *that* I find hard to believe. You're totally cut out for religious life, Maggie. I've never known anyone else so suited to be a Nun."

"Actually," Maggie corrected her, "the Sisters of the Immaculate Conception are not *Nuns*," she told her cousin. "I know everyone confuses the titles all the time—Sister and Nun. But a Nun is a Sister who lives in a cloistered monastery. They have little or no contact with the outside world—like the Carmelites. But a religious Sister, which is what I'm considering for myself, is part of an apostolic order that lives in community in consecrated religious life, but works out in the world."

"I never knew the difference," Ann said. "So, maybe I was wrong— maybe you're not suited to be a *Nun* after all. But I definitely see you as a *religious* Sister."

The group of girls giggled over Ann's self-correction.

"Well, we all know what *you're* considering for yourself," Maggie returned to her red-headed cousin. "We just have to pray that Connor wakes up one of these days and opens his eyes."

Ann shook her head. "I don't know. There are an awful lot of fish out there in the sea. I'm not pegging my hopes on just one of them."

"You know," Jocelyn piped in, "I know this is a completely random thought, but . . . do you know who I think would make *the perfect* couple?"

"Who?" Joanie asked.

"Amie and Kyle," Jocelyn said, nodding to herself.

"Shut-up!" Amie called with an outburst of laughter. "That's worse than me and Connor," she said, her face all scrunched up. "At least Connor was in the running. Kyle's like a brother to me. It'd be like me going out with Ben or someone like that."

"I don't know," Joanie teased her younger sister. "Ben *is* our cousin; Kyle's not."

"Yeah, but . . . *Kyle!* What would ever possess you to say that?" Amie asked Jocelyn.

"I don't know," the sixteen-year-old shrugged. "It's just that you and Kyle are so perfectly suited to each other. You're like . . ." she waved her hands around trying to come up with the right words. "You're like . . . you know. When we play music in the band—you and Kyle are the heart and soul of *New Spring* now. When you two are in sync with each other, the whole band sticks together. If you and Kyle are at odds at all, band practice totally sucks. It's just like a mom and dad in a family—when they're together, the family's together. When they're at odds, so are the kids."

Amie stared with total disbelief at her cousin, sitting around the corner of the booth from her.

"You know," piped in Katie. "Jocelyn's got a point, Amie. You should be more open to Kyle. Who knows, maybe *he's* the right one for you." Katie started laughing. She knew that Amie had absolutely zero romantic interest in Kyle. Still, she could see that the two went together like the treble and bass staves of a musical score. One just made the other more complete.

"Stranger things have happened," Joanie agreed. "I married Brandon— and that was a complete metaphysical impossibility two years ago." She looked at Amie. "The Lord moves in mysterious ways . . . marrying your friend does not really require a huge leap of faith."

"I'm still not sure why we're even talking about this!" Amie said in exasperation, holding her hands out in the air. She looked over again at Jocelyn and pointed a finger at the younger cousin. "This was all *your* crazy idea. Next time, keep your *randomnicity* to yourself."

Jocelyn giggled and returned an apologetic look at Amie. "Sorry, it was just something that struck me one night at band practice."

Amie smiled at the young girl and chuckled. "Oh, I forgive you. But please, don't ever breathe a word of this conversation to Kyle. I'd die if he ever thought we actually talked about this. Kyle has no more interest in me than I do in him—and I'd hate to ruin a perfectly good friendship."

"Fair enough," stated Ann. "And since our waiter's on his way over here with our dinners, it looks like you've been saved by the 'Brad', Amie."

"Thank goodness," Amie replied. "That last conversation just about made me lose my appetite. I might just go back to considering religious life all over again."

The girls were all laughing as Brad showed up with their meals. "No one can accuse you ladies of being dull. I rarely have the pleasure of serving such a happy group."

He served out their meals—getting every last detail of each order in place. They were all impressed and told him so. They waited for him to walk away and then initiated saying grace by making the sign of the cross.

As the group of girls bowed their heads and prayed together, an older man and woman sitting across the restaurant from them turned and watched. The gentleman, in his late sixties, winked at his wife.

The girls thoroughly enjoyed their meal together. The food was absolutely delicious and the company, even better. When Brad came around to see if they wanted dessert, no one had room to even consider it.

"No desserts tonight, anyway," Maggie said to the young waiter. "It's Lent, and we all gave up sweets for Lent."

"So, what's Lent?" Brad asked, with curiosity.

"You know, the forty days before Easter," Maggie explained.

"Isn't Easter in like a couple of weeks?" he asked.

"Yeah," Maggie said. "But for forty days before Easter, Catholics observe a time of penance and sacrifice—like giving up sweets and things—to help develop our self-discipline and to grow spiritually."

"Cool," the young man said with a nod. "So, you're all Catholic?"

"Yup," Maggie answered—the self-appointed spokesperson for the group.

"And are you all related?" he inquired.

"Sisters and cousins," Maggie stated.

"I have to admit, I've never seen a happier group at this restaurant," Brad said, as he walked around picking up the empty plates. "And I would never have thought it was because you were all so religious—but obviously you've got something going there."

"In spades," Maggie agreed.

"Well, I'll be right back with your bill, ladies," Brad said, excusing himself.

"Okay," Katie said, watching Brad walk away. "Go ahead and tip him well, girls. Not only did he not get fresh with any of us, but now that he knows we're all Catholic, we want to be sure to give him a really good impression."

Everyone laughed.

"Here," Jocelyn said, getting the momentum going. She threw a toonie out on the table.

One by one, they each dug into their purses until they had come up with more than fifteen dollars for a tip. Since Joanie was paying for the meal, they were all feeling extra generous.

As the girls got up to leave the restaurant, the older man and woman who had been watching them waved them over to their table. "We just wanted to tell you how refreshing it was to see such a lovely and happy bunch of girls," the woman began.

"We noticed you praying before your meal," the man added.

"And we think it's beautiful. You just keep it up. The world needs more young people like you," the woman told them. She held on to Katie's hand, who was the nearest one to her. Katie smiled at the woman and thanked her.

The girls left *The Country Corner Café* on a real high. An evening like that was nothing but pure blessing.

"I really think you should reconsider the Kyle-thing," Ann told Amie. "Any guy who can recommend a restaurant like that, has got to be worth marrying."

"If you want him," Amie replied, "you can have him."

"What's she going to do with two husbands?" Maggie asked. "I don't think Annie can keep up with all your leftovers."

The girls had one last good laugh and parted ways. Joanie dropped Amie and Katie off first and then took Maggie home.

Chapter 51

"Okay, out with it girl," Joanie said, as she pulled away from their parents' house.

"Out with what?" Maggie asked, taking off her toque. It was getting warm in the vehicle.

"You've been dropping mysterious one-liners all night long. There's something going on in your life. So, fess up!" Joanie insisted, pointing a scolding finger at Maggie between shifting gears. "If I didn't know any better, I'd say there was a man . . . and I'm starting to think that I'm right about that. In fact, I'd be so bold as to guess who."

"What makes you so confident that there's a guy?" Maggie asked, in a feeble cover-up attempt.

"Love can make you pretty silly," Joanie quoted Maggie, with an impressive impersonation of her younger sister. "Um, let's see . . . oh, yes—I think it's good to consider all your options before you make any life-long decisions. . . . Even I've been challenged to search out what God is really calling me to." Joanie looked over at the girl in the passenger seat. "I've known you your whole life Maggie, and that's just not Maggie-talk. Sorry."

Maggie played with the tassels on the end of her scarf as Joanie spoke. "Busted," she said in a quiet voice.

"I'd say. So, out with it, girl," Joanie prompted her sister.

Maggie shared with Joanie the tale of how romance and marriage had become not just a part of her vocabulary but an integral part of her entire discernment process. Joanie listened with interest. She felt for Maggie, yet at the same time she just knew that this was exactly what Maggie needed to experience in order to become the best religious Sister she could possibly be . . . or wife and mother, if that be the case. She was being forced by circumstances to really choose—not just fall into a religious vocation without really weighing out all the options, the pros and cons, the rewards and losses.

By the time Maggie was done telling her story, they were already parked in front of the Sisters' house.

"Do you want to come in?" Maggie asked.

"No. Let's just talk in the car," Joanie suggested. "Besides, this baby's kicking up a real storm here right now, and I'd hate to have to move."

"Ohhhhhhh," Maggie cooed. "Can I feel it, Joanie?"

"Sure," Joanie said. She opened up her jacket and placed Maggie's hand over her tummy where the best kicks were coming.

Maggie waited a moment, her eyes moving back and forth as she anticipated the baby's movement. Suddenly there was a small pressure that moved quickly from one edge of the palm of her hand to the other.

"Agh!" she screamed, jumping back. "Joanie, there's a baby in there—a real, live, kicking one!"

Joanie laughed at Maggie's reaction. "Come on, Maggie. You remember what it was like when Mom would let us feel the baby kick when she was pregnant."

"I know," Maggie said. "But somehow this is different. This is *you!* Which means, it could be me, too, someday. Do you mind if I feel it again?"

"Go ahead," Joanie said. "You got baby all excited with your screaming."

Maggie placed her hand back gently on her sister's tummy. There were a few quick kicks right away. Maggie did not jump back this time. "Ahhh," she said in a soft voice. "It's so cute. . . . What's it like to have another human being living inside of you, Joanie?"

"Beyond-words-amazing," Joanie responded. Maggie had pulled her hand away, and Joanie rested her hands on her tummy, perceiving each little movement of the precious life hidden within her. "It's like nothing I can explain to you, Maggie. One day you start to feel these little movements. At first you're not even sure if that was really the baby or just gas or something. Then all of a sudden something moves inside of you, and you just know—it's the baby. A life—completely separate from you, yet completely dependent on you—and you just fall in love like you've never loved before. I can't explain how it happens—but it just does."

Maggie listened to Joanie with wonder and awe. "You know, Joanie, if I do choose religious life—I'll never know what you're talking about. I'll never get the chance to feel that life moving around inside of me. And for the first time in my life, I'm trying to decide—am I willing to give that up or not?"

"I can't imagine how hard it would be to give it up," Joanie admitted. "But I just know it's a special calling to religious life, and I'm convinced that the joy the Lord has in store for you—if that's what He's calling you to—will be far greater than the sacrifices you'll have to make. I've just known too many religious Sisters . . . and Nuns," she added, for clarification of the distinction, "who have radiated such tremendous joy, that I have to believe they've been more than compensated for their losses."

"I know," Maggie agreed. "And I know that once I finally do choose . . . once I really give myself over to one or the other calling . . . Jesus will give me the grace to live it out."

"And you know marriage isn't easy," Joanie added. "Not that Brandon and I are having marital difficulties or anything. But there's a lot of give and take, in big things and in little things. And I just look at Mom and Dad and how they scrimped and saved and struggled daily—from finances, to dealing with sick children, to having to discipline us when we were out of line, to working long hard hours to meet the needs of everyone. I can still picture Mom, burned out at the end of the day—making supper with all kinds of commotion around her, everybody wanting her attention at the same time. I'm sure there were times she wondered why she hadn't chosen religious life—cloistered religious life, at that."

Maggie laughed and agreed. It had not always been easy for their parents. A mother sacrifices daily for her family. Perhaps there was more for Maggie to consider. Maybe all she had been looking at were the rewards of married life—what about the struggles?

"The thing is," Joanie went on, "I don't think it's enough to choose one vocation over another because you want to avoid the negatives of one, or benefit from the rewards of another. You choose a vocation because you believe God is calling you to it. And when you allow His voice to be loud enough within you—when you shut out the world around you long enough to find Him—you'll know."

Maggie nodded. The world had seemed awfully noisy around her lately. And with final exams around the corner—she was really having a hard time focusing in prayer.

"I just remember you telling me once, Maggie, how you longed to be with Jesus just as I longed to be with Brandon . . . one day we would both be married, just in different ways." As Joanie spoke, Maggie closed her eyes—remembering kneeling by her bed in their room back home, talking to Joanie after having prayed together a chaplet of Divine Mercy. She could still remember how the afternoon light was coming into the bedroom.

Joanie went on, "The love that shone in your eyes at that moment, Maggie, was like nothing I've ever seen on you before or since. You were one hundred percent sure that Jesus was calling you to be His bride, and you were just waiting—with bated breath—to be joined to Him."

A tear rolled down Maggie's cheek as she listened to her sister. It had been so long since she had felt that love burning inside of her for Jesus. But as Joanie spoke, Maggie felt an old flame rekindle within her heart. It was as though the flame of that love was alive inside of her—like the baby kicking within Joanie's womb—wanting her to notice it was there, calling out for her to nurture it . . . to give it birth.

Maggie opened her eyes and looked at Joanie. Joanie looked back at her sister. They knew each other and loved each other with a bond like neither had ever shared with any other person. They were more than sisters; they were best of friends. Maggie reached over and gave Joanie a hug. She held on tightly. She cried . . . and Joanie cried with her.

After a few minutes, Maggie pulled away, wiping her eyes. Joanie reached into her pocket and pulled out a tissue for both her sister and herself.

"Thanks," Maggie said, wiping her eyes and nose. "Not just for the Kleenex," she added, holding up the moistened tissue. "Thanks for talking to me . . . for making me talk to you. You reminded me of things that I had just forgotten about myself. Why I came to be here in the first place. Who I am—Maggie Collins."

"You, Maggie Collins, are one of the most amazing, beautiful people I have ever known," Joanie said, placing her hand on her sister's cheek. "And if you end up deciding to stay with religious life, I want you to know that I have every intention of sharing my baby with you. There's no way I would let my children grow up without knowing Auntie Maggie. I know it's not the same as motherhood. But . . ." she hesitated, not knowing what to say.

"But Jesus will take care of that," Maggie finished for her sister. "I've just seen too many sisters completely fulfilled in their vocation not to believe that."

"Exactly," Joanie agreed.

"And I feel it," Maggie said, her voice filled with amazement. She held her hands over her chest. "It's like a baby moving inside of me . . . and up until now I haven't been sure if that was really the baby kicking or just gas."

Joanie burst out laughing. "Oh, Maggie, you are a prize, aren't you?"

"It's true, though," Maggie insisted. "It was just like for the first time tonight, when you were talking . . . I felt it kick in a way that was undeniably a life within me. Somehow I've managed to ignore that life for the past few months. But it feels so real to me again, Joanie, I could just cry . . . all over again."

Joanie smiled and pulled Maggie in for another hug. "Well, kiddo," the older sister said. "I will keep praying for you—in a very special way. And I expect you to let me know what's going on. No more making me play detective with you. I didn't put up with living with you—sharing a bedroom together—for twenty-one years to be left out in the dark now."

"I'll keep better in touch with you," Maggie promised. "But it goes both ways there, little mama. You don't leave me out of the picture, either."

Joanie nodded. "Deal."

The two sisters hugged each other one last time. Maggie said good-night and left.

As the young aspirant walked up the front steps of the Sisters' house that cold, wintry night, she experienced something for the first time. Maggie *knew* she was coming home.

She stepped inside, waved to Joanie, closed the door, and locked it. The house was quiet and dark. Maggie took off her outside clothes and hung them in the front closet. She was going to head up for bed, but all at once she felt the pull of the chapel. She quietly stepped into the darkened room.

The only light to disperse the darkness came from the little, red candle flickering beside the Tabernacle. How Maggie loved the look of that light. She genuflected and then knelt in one of the pews to pray.

All at once the floodgates opened, and Jesus' love came pouring into her heart. She could feel her Lover calling to her, singing to her, courting her in the very depths of her soul. His voice was gentle. His song was beautiful. His love was tender.

Maggie closed her eyes and abandoned herself once again to the Lover of her soul.

Chapter 52

"Would you get the door there, Brandon?" Joanie called out from the bedroom. "I just buzzed someone up, but I've gotta go change into something more presentable."

"Who's here?" he asked, stepping out of the kitchen where he had been doing some baking. It was two o'clock on a Saturday afternoon, and they had not been expecting anyone. "Hey, Joanie?" he called out. There was no answer. She was in their bathroom en suite with the door closed.

Brandon walked to the door of their apartment and waited for the knock. When it finally came, he opened the door to a man and woman standing in the hall, smiling at him.

"Mom, Dan!" he exclaimed. "What the heck are you doing here in Saskatoon?"

"Happy birthday, Brandon," Caroline said, reaching out to embrace her son.

Brandon pulled his mom into a warm hug. Still in shock that she and Dan had come to surprise him on his birthday, he held on tightly for a few moments. "Mom, it's so good to see you. Come in. Come in, Dan," Brandon said, motioning for them to enter the apartment.

"Surprise," Joanie said softly over Brandon's shoulder, as he stepped back to make room for their guests coming through the door.

Brandon turned to his wife. "You knew about this?"

"Mm-hmm. Why do you think I was too sick to go out for lunch with you on your birthday, dear?" She snuck her arm around his waist and gave him a little squeeze. "By the way, happy birthday, honey," she added, reaching up to kiss him on the cheek.

Brandon laughed. "Not that I was feeling sorry for myself or anything, but it was starting to feel like everyone had forgotten me," he confessed. "When Joanie suggested I go bake a cake for my birthday so we could eat it later, I was beginning to wonder—what was the point?"

"So, did you get it baked?" Joanie asked.

"It's already out of the oven," he told her.

"Then our plan should be right on schedule," she said to her in-laws. "Come in and sit down. We'll have something to drink before we go out."

"What plan?" Brandon asked.

"We're taking you two out for supper," Caroline informed her son. "Then we'll come home and see just how good a birthday cake you can bake, dear."

"Will you stay the weekend?" he asked.

"We have to be back to Calgary tomorrow for noon Mass," Dan said. "It's Palm Sunday, and I have to be there since I'm in the R.C.I.A. program."

"The one-week count-down is on," Brandon said to Dan. "How are you feeling?"

"Terribly excited," Dan said.

Brandon laughed; he had never known Dan to be anything but happy about life. "Well, I can relate to that. I'm just sorry that I won't be there to celebrate with you both next Sunday."

"We certainly understand," Dan told the young man. "Which is partly why we came this weekend to celebrate with you. But we'll have to be on the road early tomorrow morning."

"Well then, let's get this show on the road. What can I get for you two to drink?" Brandon asked.

"I'd love a coffee," Caroline told her son.

"I can do better than that, Mom," the young man replied. "I'll make you both lattes. How does that sound?"

"He makes great lattes," Joanie informed their guests.

"Sounds great," Caroline said.

The two couples went into the kitchen to visit while Brandon set to work at creating the specialty coffees. "Sorry about the dishes in the sink," he apologized. "I wasn't expecting company."

"I'll do them up quickly," Joanie offered.

"You just sit down, there," Brandon told his wife. "You've all stepped into *Brandon's Café*. I can handle it. I'm a big boy now."

"I should say," Caroline said with a laugh. "And you were a big boy twenty-eight years ago, as well."

"How much did Brandon weigh?" Joanie asked her mother-in-law.

"Nine pounds, three ounces," Caroline told the expectant mother.

"Ouch," Joanie said, with a wince. "And you're so small."

"They don't call it labour for nothing," Caroline said with a laugh. "But it was worth it all—for the end result." She smiled looking over at her son, busily preparing their drinks. He turned and smiled back over his shoulder at his mom.

"I was kind of holding out for a seven-and-a-half pounder, myself," Joanie said, halfheartedly.

"Good luck," Caroline said to her, with a sympathetic smile.

Joanie looked down at her rounded tummy under her maternity top. "You be good to mommy," she said, talking to the unseen child.

Everyone laughed.

"Come, sit by me," Caroline said to Joanie, motioning for the young mother to take the stool beside her.

Joanie went and sat beside Caroline, across the little island from Dan. Together the two couples caught up with each other. They enjoyed wonderful lattes, courtesy of *Brandon's Café,* while Brandon iced and decorated his own cake. Though his wife and mother had both offered to finish the job, he stubbornly insisted that he would do it.

"You made me do this much of the work—I may as well get credit for all of it."

Finally, at about four-thirty they took their little party out for supper. When they returned to their apartment later that evening, Brandon was greeted with the screams and enthusiasm of a houseful of children. Joanie's family had come in and decorated the place for a birthday party for Brandon.

They sang "Happy Birthday" to the birthday boy, and Brandon cut the cake.

"Glad to see that you haven't lost your touch in the kitchen," John remarked, as he took a taste of the chocolate cake. "Though I'd question a wife who makes her husband bake his own birthday cake—especially the first year that they're married."

Joanie threw a pouty look at her father. "I would have made it for him, if I hadn't needed to use it as a distraction for his surprise," she said in her own defence.

Brandon put his hand on his wife's shoulder. "I'm sure she would have. That nap she took while I was in the kitchen was probably just part of the diversion as well."

Joanie's pout got bigger. "Well, next year I'll make you the biggest birthday cake you've ever seen. And I won't let you help me—even if you beg."

Brandon leaned over and kissed his wife. "Thanks for the surprise, sweetheart."

"I've got a birthday gift for you, too, dear." Joanie slipped into their bedroom and came back with a large, wrapped box to present to her husband. "And no comments from you," she said, pointing to her father.

Brandon opened the package, and everyone burst out laughing. Joanie had bought him a food processor.

"Really," she told everyone, "Brandon *loves* working in the kitchen." She looked around the room, trying to convince them all of her sincerity of purpose. "*Fine,* next year you're getting a Sawzall, Brandon," Joanie said, pointing at her husband.

"That would be to cut that birthday cake she plans to make for you," called out Isaac, as he rolled off the couch in laughter. Everyone joined in with the jocularity of the moment.

"I give up," said Joanie with a laugh. She threw her hands up in the air.

Brandon stood up and grabbed his wife's hands in his own. Pulling her in toward him, he gave her a big kiss. "Thank you, sweetheart. It was a wonderful birthday. The kind that makes me glad I'm a married man."

✞   ✞   ✞

"You ready to go, yet, Justine?" called out Mark from the living room of their new house. He walked to the base of the stairs and waited for a reply. After a moment of waiting, he walked up the stairs to look for his wife. "I still don't know why I let her talk me into a two-storey house with our bedroom-bathroom tucked away in the corner of the upstairs," he muttered to himself en route.

The neatly furnished home had been purchased by the young couple back in February. It was not a large house; Justine figured they could get by with a smaller home for some time at the rate that their family planning was going. But it was brand new, built in a newly developing area of the city. They had had fun picking out a floor plan and making decisions together about the exterior and interior finishing.

Justine's classy touch showed through in all the little details of setting up the home. It was simple, but tasteful, and each room had its own theme for colour with matching décor. What Mark appreciated most was how his wife, in the year-and-a-half since she had reclaimed her Catholic faith, had managed to find so many religious articles with which to decorate their home. There were pictures of Jesus, Mary, and the saints in every room, along with a crucifix over every doorway. There were statues and rosaries and all kinds of treasures to be found in every corner of their little home.

As Mark walked down the hall to their bedroom, a smile replaced the frown on his face. How could he be even remotely impatient or frustrated with his wife after just having walked past all those saints and reminders to call him to holiness? He laughed as he stepped into their bedroom and called out one more time to his bride, "Are you ready to go yet, honey?"

"Just about," she answered, stepping out of their bathroom in her new spring outfit: elegant as the woman wearing it, the soft pink dress, under a light-weight white sweater, moved gracefully with her. Her head was tilted to one side, as she finished putting on her earrings. A smile appeared on her face, beholding her husband in his suit.

"Are you all ready for tonight?" she asked.

"Most definitely." He stepped up to his wife and took her in his arms. "After tonight, dear, you're going to be married to a Catholic. Do you have any thoughts on the matter?"

"Just that it's about time," she said with a giggle.

He kissed her and, as she returned his kiss, suddenly he was no longer in a hurry to get going. Justine slipped her arms around her husband's shoulders and neck, losing herself in his affection. All at once, she stepped back. "Mark, we don't have time for this. You're going to be late."

He laughed and took her by the hand to leave the room. "Look when she finally realizes that we have to get going."

"No, just wait," she said, pulling her hand away. "I have a couple more things to do before we go. Just run out and start the car. I'll be right down. I promise."

Mark raised his eyebrows at his wife, but knew better than to argue. She had already disappeared back into their bathroom. "Don't take long, Justine," he called out as he left to go get the car started.

Justine stepped into the garage five minutes later, and got into the car. "Ready to go, sir," she announced.

Mark put the car in reverse and backed out of the garage. "Good thing we only live ten minutes from the church," he told her.

"Oh, we'll still be early," she dismissed his comment. "Are you excited?"

"Yup," he answered, nonchalantly.

"Are you nervous?"

"Nope," he replied.

Justine smiled, looking over at her husband. She ran her fingers through his wavy, light-brown hair. He had changed a lot over the past year-and-a-half. He had gone from being a boy who was all about having fun, to a responsible, rock-solid man of faith. Somehow through the interior transformation, he had gone from boyishly cute to irresistibly handsome. He was a man—and the only man for her.

Justine pulled down the passenger mirror to check over her quick make-up job.

"You're beautiful, dear," Mark said, without looking over at her.

"How would you know? You didn't even look at me."

"You can't help but be beautiful. Make-up can't add a thing to your beauty."

Justine smiled. She pushed up the mirror and took his hand. "I'll take your word on that."

"Do you want to pray together?" he asked.

"Sure," she answered, somewhat surprised.

Mark began, "Thank You, Jesus, for tonight. Thank You for my beautiful bride, who has loved me and encouraged me and brought me to this place. Thank You for every gift You've blessed us with. Thank You for bringing me tonight to the gates of Your Kingdom here on earth. And thank You for allowing me to enter into those gates—with praise and thanksgiving—as I come into the Catholic Church.

"Never let me forget the price You paid to allow me to become an heir to Your kingdom. Never let me forget the privilege that will be mine to receive You—body, blood, soul and divinity, in the Holy Eucharist. May Your life within us spill out of our love and our marriage, bringing other souls to You, through the joy we have received in our salvation. Amen."

"Amen," Justine echoed. Her eyes were closed, as she allowed the words of her husband's prayer to wash over her. Yes, indeed, he had truly become a man. "Thank You, Lord," she added to his prayer.

✞   ✞   ✞

The celebration of the Easter Vigil was beautiful. Words could not describe the joy that Mark experienced as he professed his faith and was received into full communion with Holy Mother Church. But Brandon understood. He had stood in that place one year earlier. Having walked step by step with his best friend through this spiritual journey, Brandon had relived every moment of his own joy at becoming Catholic and receiving Christ in the Eucharist.

"So now, we party," Mark announced, as they gathered around with family and friends at the end of the celebration.

Justine stood with her arm around her husband, beaming as she did on their wedding day. "Is everyone coming over?" she asked, looking around the group.

Mark's parents and hers were there, along with his brother, her sister, and their families. Joanie and Brandon stood off to the side, allowing the family time to congratulate Mark and visit together.

"I want some pictures taken here, first," Mark told Justine. "But then we'll head straight over to the house."

Justine gave a set of house keys to her mom and dad, and asked if they would go ahead and let in the others. They were happy to do that, and their family members got on their way.

Brandon and Joanie stuck around with Mark and Justine at the church. They took pictures with Fr. Steve, who also promised to come later and join their party for a little while.

When the two couples pulled up to the house, the party was already in full swing. Justine had left platters of food and a jug of punch in the fridge. Glasses and plates had been set out on the counter for serving.

Mark and Justine came into the house through the garage. As Mark entered the front foyer of their little home, something new immediately caught his eye. There, on a marble stand in the corner, stood a two-foot statue of the Holy Family, with a couple of Easter lilies on either side of it in full bloom. It was breathtaking. He stepped up to examine every detail of the hand-painted alabaster piece.

"Don't ask how much it cost," Justine said, standing behind her husband.

"Justine," he said. "This is incredible. Where did you get it?"

"I ordered it through the Catholic bookstore downtown. It finally arrived on Wednesday. I was getting so nervous that it wouldn't be here in time. . . . It's in honour of you coming into the Church, dear." She stepped up beside her husband and put her arm around his waist. "I pray that the Lord will bless us to become a holy family, too, someday." Tears were in her eyes, and her voice faltered.

Mark's eyes welled up with tears as well. He wrapped his arms around his beautiful bride and kissed her tenderly on the top of her head. "He will, dear . . . in His time and in His own way . . . He will."

Joanie and Brandon stood back and watched. Joanie reached up and wiped the tears from her eyes. *Please, Lord, bless them, soon,* she prayed.

Justine turned around to their friends and started laughing at herself, wiping away her tears.

"It's beautiful, Justine. May all our homes become like theirs," Brandon whispered.

Justine smiled. "Come on, we've got a party waiting for us." She took her husband by the hand and led him to the family room where everyone was visiting.

When Fr. Steve arrived, later on, Justine and Mark had him bless their new statue. He had already come to do a home blessing just a month earlier.

"We should be good and blessed here," Mark commented, upon conclusion of Fr. Steve's prayers. "So we'll have no excuses not to be good Catholics." They all laughed.

As the last of the other guests left, at about two in the morning, Mark turned to Brandon and said, "Ready for phase three of the party?"

"What's phase three?" Justine inquired.

"Phase one was at the church—that was the most important one. Phase two was with our families. And now, phase three," Mark explained, rubbing his hands together. He disappeared into the garage and returned momentarily with a platter of raw steaks.

"What are you doing, dear?" Justine asked, in utter confusion.

"Barbecuing these steaks," Mark announced. "Did you bring the other stuff, Brandon?"

"Yup," Brandon replied.

"What other stuff?" Joanie asked, as her husband stepped outside. After a few moments he came back in with a cooler and an overnight bag.

"We're having a sleep-over, dear," he announced. "Mark and I decided a week or so ago that we needed to mark this night in an extra special way. Hope you girls don't mind."

Justine and Joanie looked at each other and started laughing. "Let phase three begin," Justine announced.

"Are you okay to keep partying, dear?" Brandon asked. "You girls can go to bed anytime you like—or stay up as late as you want with us. We brought plenty of food," he said, pointing to the cooler.

Joanie took a peek inside. There were salads, desserts, and munchies, all neatly packed.

"Where'd you get this stuff?" she asked.

"Oh, I picked it up this afternoon at one of those specialty food stores," Brandon said. "Mark and I wanted to keep this all a surprise."

"The barbecue is moved around to the back and all ready to go," Mark informed them. "I haven't had any meat to eat all Lent, so let's not waste any more time." The two men had both agreed to give up meat as their extra Lenten sacrifice this year. It was a long forty days. The fast was now over, and it was time to feast. "Let's get this party under way."

"You know what I like about being Catholic?" Brandon asked, putting on his jacket as they headed to the back patio doors to start cooking the meat. Answering his own question, he went on, "There are more feast days on our calendar than fasting days. But you appreciate feasting so much more, if you've taken the time to fast."

They all laughed. With renewed energy, the two couples began "phase three" of their Easter celebrations.

Chapter 53

Maggie walked up the front steps of the Sisters' house, following her last final exam—her very last final exam. With that exam was the completion of her four years of studying. She would have her convocation the following month from university, and thus become a certified teacher. Her steps were light and happy, to match her mood. Life was good.

It was a beautiful day in late April. The sun was shining. Most of the snow had melted away and patches of green grass were appearing on every lawn. The cars made slushy sounds as they drove through the last remains of snow on the edges of the roads, where the snow had been piled throughout the winter. Maggie loved that sound. Each time she heard it, she would close her eyes and take delight. It was a hope-filled sound, announcing that spring was really on its way.

She opened the front door to the convent and stepped inside. "Hi, honey, I'm home," she announced, walking into the front porch. It was her typical greeting, when she thought no one was around. It was the middle of the afternoon, and all the Sisters were usually out at this time of day. Those who were at home were not hanging around the front foyer to hear her. Maggie imagined Jesus, in the Tabernacle in the chapel, calling back to her, "Hi, honey, I'm waiting for you."

She was laughing to herself for her goofiness as she went to open the door from the front porch into the house. She almost fell through, as the latch turned by itself beneath her hand, and the door pulled itself opened. She tripped into the house and was caught in the arms of a man, standing there by the door. Stunned and startled, she looked up.

"Charles!" she nearly screamed. "What are you doing here? Oh!" She straightened herself up and paused for a moment, wondering if he had heard her call out when she had come in.

Charles stood there laughing. "Maggie, you haven't changed a bit in the two months since I last saw you," he exclaimed.

"Oh, Charles," Maggie said, shaking her head and laughing at herself as she stood back up. "I'm not sure if I'm glad it was you or not—seeing me at my 'Maggie best'." She looked at his smiling face and decided she was glad. "It's so good to see you, again." She stepped forward and greeted him with a big hug. It was a friendly hug—chaste and warm with sisterly affection. She had missed her friend.

Charles hugged her back. He had never before hugged Maggie. They had only ever shaken hands. Then it struck him, there was something different about her. Maggie was completely comfortable and casual with him—like a friend, like a sister. The last few times he had seen her, she had not been like this with him. She had been guarded and careful. He knew in his heart that whatever had happened between them during the wintertime was now in the past.

"It's good to see you again, Maggie," Charles returned, with sincere affection.

"What are you doing here?" she asked again, looking around.

"I just came over to check on that leaky drainpipe—the one out in the back over the walkway. I thought I might try to get it fixed for you ladies before the spring rains hit. I just stepped in the house to make a few phone calls for parts, and I was on my way."

"You're such a gem, Charles. What would we do without you?" she asked. "Come," she said, taking him by the arm. "You're not leaving. I just got here. And it's time for crumpets and tea."

Charles looked at the girl, unsure as to whether or not he should take her up on the offer.

"Oh, please, Charles," Maggie begged. "I want to visit with you. I've missed your company."

Charles nodded and took off his spring jacket, hanging it up in the front closet. "So what's new with Maggie?" he asked, following her into the kitchen.

"Everything," she announced. "I just finished school today. Wrote the last exam of my life—I hope." She brought the teapot over to the island where Charles was seated and dropped in a bag of Apple Spice tea.

"So *that's* where you were. I figured I had missed you altogether, when you weren't here. I thought coming on a Thursday was a safe day to be able to catch you," Charles confessed.

"Normally, it would have been. But not today. Thank goodness, though, I got home just in time."

"Yes, I heard you calling when you came in," he said with a chuckle.

"Oh," Maggie murmured, shrugging with embarrassment. She brought over the teacups and looked at Charles, timidly. "I was hoping you hadn't heard that."

"Actually," Charles replied, "you caught me completely by surprise. I was kind of getting my hopes up for a moment, thinking I was the only guy here for you to call out to. Then I thought to myself," he raised his finger in the air and shook it, "wait a minute there, Charles, this is *Maggie* . . . and I suddenly remembered I *wasn't* the only man in the house. Then I knew who you were talking to—the God-Man, of course."

Maggie looked at Charles with wonder, as she slowly shook her head back and forth. "Charles, you *are* a gem. How is it that you got to know me so well in less than two weeks' time?"

He shrugged his shoulders. "I don't know, Maggie. But I'm awfully grateful to God that I did," he said, most sincerely. "Your friendship is pure gift in my life, and I thank God for you each time I think of you."

Maggie sighed. "I thank God for you, too, Charles. I learned a great deal during our time together. I've never known another man like you. I don't know if I ever will. But you worked your way into my heart in a category that belongs to you alone now—a brother and a friend and . . . well, just a 'Charles' category." She laughed, wondering if she made any sense at all.

Charles bowed his head, accepting the compliment. "I think I found a place for that 'Maggie' category in my heart, as well. You're a special girl, Maggie. I know that Jesus has taken for Himself a rare and beautiful bride. And I'm happy and honoured to know you as a friend and a brother."

Maggie stood at the island, looking at Charles. The teakettle began to boil on the stove. Before she stepped over to turn it off, she walked around the island where Charles was sitting and gave him another hug. "Thank you," she whispered. There was a tear in her eye.

"Thank *you*," he returned, softly.

Maggie went to the stove to get the teakettle. She breathed deeply, and with great self-control, held back her emotions. She turned back to the island, with a big smile on her face, as she filled the teapot with the hot water.

There was silence between the two for a few moments. Without having said anything to each other, they had said it all. They would never bring up the topic of romance between them openly. It was now a mute point.

After her talk that night with Joanie, Maggie had given her heart back to Jesus, her first love, with complete abandonment. She had not even stepped back to look at the path of married life. There had been so much peace and joy in her as she began to re-explore the path of religious life that she had all but forgotten about the other.

Not having seen Charles in two months had helped her to really sift through her emotions and examine the desires of her heart. Time had healed the pain and the confusion that had once clouded this relationship. She was completely free, now, to love Charles as a brother in Christ. And she knew in her heart that he had been able to let her go as well, to be his sister in Christ.

Maggie poured out their tea and sat down. Charles looked around the island. "What, no crumpets?" he asked.

"Oh!" Maggie exclaimed. She jumped up and ran to the pantry. The light came on, making the stained glass window sparkle. Maggie peeked back out through the door and said, "We all still love the job you did here, sir." She ducked her head back inside.

Charles laughed and waited for the girl to emerge from the pantry.

Emerge she did—victoriously—with a package of oatmeal chocolate chip cookies. "These are really my favourite crumpets," she told him.

"Mine, too," he said.

"Great," Maggie responded. She got down a plate and filled it with cookies.

Together they dunked their crumpets, sipped tea—pinkies up—and enjoyed an afternoon of visiting and laughs. There was a peaceful, comfortable feeling between the two friends. Having placed each other in their own special categories in their hearts, they were able to be together without any pressures or expectations. Maggie knew that with an honourable man like Charles, her heart was safe. And she promised herself to take extra care in guarding his heart, as well.

Before they knew it, over an hour had passed. Charles looked at his watch. He had to get going if he wanted to catch the hardware store before it closed. "I'll be back tomorrow," he informed her, "to fix that old drainpipe."

"I'll be here," Maggie told him, walking with him to the door. "If you still need an assistant, I'd be more than happy to give you a hand."

"I was hoping you would," he confided to the girl. "So, I'll see you then," he said, as he slipped his jacket back on at the front entry.

"Sounds great. God bless you, Charles," she called out behind him, as he went down the front steps.

"God bless you, too, Maggie," he said, pausing in his step to look at the girl standing in the doorway.

She waved good-bye, and he returned the gesture with a smile. Maggie stood and watched as Charles got into his truck. Funny, she had not even noticed it parked out front when she had come home that day—her mind had obviously been pre-occupied. She waved one last time to the young man. As the old pickup truck pulled ahead down the street, it ploughed right through a half-melted pile of snow. The slushy sound rang back to Maggie's ears. She closed her eyes and took delight. Springtime was on its way.

✟   ✟   ✟

Charles turned off the radio in his truck so he could have a talk with Jesus.

I guess that's it, Lord—my final answer with Maggie. I'm okay with it, because I know it's Your will for both Maggie and me. I'd be lying if I didn't say I was disappointed. But You know what, Lord? I'm not upset at all. In fact, I want to thank You for the gift You gave me in Maggie. You opened my eyes, through that special girl, to the possibilities of marriage and family life. You revealed to me what kind of woman I would want to marry someday, if that were Your will for me. But somehow, I don't think there's another Maggie out there. Which makes me realize that maybe, just maybe, You won't ever be calling me to marriage. And I'm all right with that, too, Lord.

You've given me so much in my singleness. At one point I was afraid that loneliness was going to take a hold in my heart, if I wasn't going to be able to have Maggie for a wife. Now, I know for certain that she won't ever be my wife—and yet I don't feel lonely. I feel honoured to be her friend. I cherish that girl, like no other. Somehow, just knowing that there is a special bond between us—that will only ever be friendship—is enough for me. No, I'm not lonely at all, Lord. I'm so rich in Your love, that it would be nothing but selfishness on my part to sink into loneliness now.

So, I just want to say thank You, Jesus, for allowing me to have learned what I came to learn through Maggie. Thank You that she will always be a special part of my life, as long as she's with the Sisters of the Immaculate Conception. Thank You for giving me the peace of mind, and the absolute joy, to be able to love that girl as my sister, in You. Keep me faithful, and keep our friendship pure and true, Lord. Don't allow my heart to stray.

Take my life, Lord, such as it is, and use it for Your glory. I give myself over to You completely, Jesus. Be it done unto me, according to Your word. Amen.

Charles drove on in the silence of his heart. He was fine. He was more than fine. He was a very blessed man—rich in the love of the Lord.

After a few minutes, Charles found himself chuckling. His chuckles soon turned into laughter. Before he knew it, his entire being was being flooded with a joy that surpassed all his understanding. "Praise You, Jesus!" he called out, as he drove toward the hardware store.

He turned on the radio, and one of his all-time favourite praise songs was playing. "Thank You, Jesus!" he exclaimed, for He knew that the Lord had given him that song at that moment, because He loved him and cared for him as only the God-Man can.

Charles joined in with the praises of the song playing and moved onward to what he felt was somehow going to be a brand new life in Christ.

✝   ✝   ✝

Maggie stopped in the chapel after Charles left. She dipped her fingers in the holy water font and made the sign of the cross as she genuflected toward the Tabernacle, before kneeling in one of the pews. "Hi, honey, I'm home," she whispered out loud, with a little giggle.

Maggie closed her eyes and began to pray. In her mind's eye she came back to that little spot in the forest, where the fork in the road had been. There she saw Jesus, standing and waiting for her.

I'm sorry it took me so long to come back here, she told Him.

I wasn't worried about you, He replied.

I sort of got lost, exploring down that path, she said, pointing down the path of religious life.

I know. I saw you. I was with you the whole time, He said.

I know You were; I could feel Your presence. Thank You. She hesitated a moment as she looked down the path of married life. *Do You mind if I don't even bother checking out that path?*

You're free, Maggie, He told her, *to do as you please.*

I just don't feel like I need to go back and check it out, now that I feel so much at peace down the path of religious life. I have so much joy again, and my heart is so filled with love—with Your love. I'm not worried about missing out on anything anymore. When I think about that dream, she told Jesus, *I don't get upset at all. It's like the colours have all faded now.*

That dream was never intended to hurt you, Maggie, Jesus told her. *It was intended to open your eyes.*

It did that, she said with a laugh. *And I think I understand what You mean. I needed to learn lessons, like how to guard my heart, and to recognize the beauty of the vocation of marriage.*

Jesus stood there, listening attentively and smiling, as Maggie spoke to Him.

I also needed to learn that emotions are fleeting. I'm so glad that You protected Charles and me from ever openly sharing our feelings. I know he was attracted to me. I think he realizes I was attracted to him. But now that those feelings have passed, I am so glad that we don't have to carry the emotional baggage in our relationship of having revealed ourselves to each other in that way. Charles and I are going to be friends for a very long time. After all, this old house breaks down a lot, she stated with a laugh. *I'm just glad that we can move on in friendship—a sister and a brother in You, Lord—without any strings attached.*

I'm glad, too, Jesus told the girl. *That way, you'll be free to love me completely. And as my bride, I want all your love, Maggie, so that as you empty yourself in me, I can pour my love into you and fill you completely with my joy.*

That's what I want, Jesus. My whole heart is longing for You, like a dry, desert plain. I'm ready, Lord, to make my decision for religious life, she professed to Him.

I know you are, Maggie. I want you to go talk to Sr. Charlotte. She's expecting you.

There's just one thing I didn't understand about that dream, Lord. Why was I so cold, sitting on the steps of the Sisters' house? If You were calling me to religious life, why was I left out in the cold?

Maggie, my dear, you were cold, because you were still choosing to be on the outside. You had not yet allowed your heart to come home to the Sisters of the Immaculate Conception.

Maggie's eyes widened with realization. *I remember when I did finally do that, Lord—the night I felt You leap within the womb of my heart. That was the night I knew Your love was alive in me. That was the night I heard You sing to me and court me as Your very own beloved.*

Oh, my Maggie, Jesus replied, *remain in my love and You will never be left out in the cold again. I promise that the flame of our love will continue to grow in Your heart. My love is an all-consuming fire that has the power to transform you and to perfect you in love. Live in my love, and my joy will remain in you, forever.*

In her mind's eye, Maggie reached out and hugged the Lord, like she had never hugged another man before in her life. Chastely and full of affection, she held onto Love itself. After a few moments, she stepped back and looked at the fork in the road again, for one last time.

May I go back down this path for good now? she asked Jesus.

He reached out His arm in invitation to her. *I'll be walking with you, Maggie. You need not come back to this place again. You're ready to move on, not just to explore, but to live out fully the adventure, day by day, that I have in store for us together down that path.*

Maggie took one step forward and then another. Before she knew it, she was running. The path was beautiful. It was brightly lit and filled with flowers and the sound of birds singing in the trees.

Suddenly she found herself on the doorstep of the Sisters' house, like she had been in her dream. She picked herself up off the step. She was not at all cold, but as she stepped inside and called out, *Hi, honey, I'm home,* a warmth flooded her being.

Then she heard His voice call back to her, *I'm so glad you're home, dear. I've been waiting for you.*

Chapter 54

The middle of May rolled around, and with it spring had finally come to Saskatchewan. The days were growing longer; the weather was warmer; flowers were blooming; trees were beginning to bud out their full array of greenery; and spring showers had washed away the dirty look of the long winter's leftovers.

New Spring had a number of weddings booked over the next few months, and the band was kept busy practising for them. The one wedding for which they would not be playing as a group was David and Leanne's; too many of the band members were involved with that wedding. The young couple had set their wedding date for the first weekend of August. Each band practice Leanne would bring new things to show to the other girls, as she and David solidified their plans.

"I love the colour you've picked," said Jocelyn, admiring the fabric swatches that Leanne had brought one evening. They were all sitting around after band practice at the Bander's.

"What do you even call that colour?" Amie asked.

"I'd say it looks like azure," Katie commented, taking the piece of material in hand.

"I'm impressed," Leanne remarked to the just-turned seventeen-year-old artist.

Katie smiled humbly. "That's just my thing. I love sewing and design, and anything to do with art."

"Hey! Would you be interested in designing and sewing dresses for my bridesmaids?" Leanne asked. Then, with hesitation, she added, "That is if you think you have time. There're only three of them. But I'm having the hardest time finding anything modest for them to wear. It's awful trying to find dresses with enough material to cover a girl appropriately. And the patterns aren't much better. But if I could find someone who could adapt a pattern—I found one with a really great skirt on it."

Katie's eyes grew bright with excitement. "I'd love to do that for you, Leanne. And you won't have to pay me anything. It's just an honour to do it for you."

"No way!" Leanne replied, quite emphatically. "If you don't let me pay you, then I won't let you do it," the young bride-to-be informed the aspiring seamstress. "I mean it, Katie. I'd have to pay someone. And for the price you pay for the dresses in stores—that are missing half the material . . . well, I'd rather pay you."

"I agree," piped in David, stepping up beside his fiancée. "I don't know much about colours and fabric swatches, but I do know this, Katie Collins, you're not donating all that time without getting paid."

Katie smiled at the young couple, standing side by side, facing her. David stood several inches taller than Leanne. His dark eyes just seemed to match well with her green eyes. Her dark, straight hair complemented his light, wavy hair. They looked nothing alike—but they looked good together. They stood smiling at Katie, waiting for her to answer. "Oh, fine," she said with resignation. "You can pay me—but not a lot. I'm still an amateur, you know."

"Amateur-nothing!" Amie called out. "Katie does incredible work. She sews just about everything she wears."

"Are you serious?" Leanne inquired of the teenager.

"Yeah," Katie answered. "Like I said, it's just my thing."

"She'll do a great job," Jocelyn added, nodding to Leanne. "You'll be really happy."

"I'm already happy about it," Leanne replied. "I had all but given up on the possibility of having modest yet fashionable dresses for my wedding party."

"What did you do for your wedding gown?" Ann inquired, stepping into the conversation.

"I actually found a few sites on-line with modest wedding dresses," she told the girls. "They do have bridesmaid dresses there as well, but the colours were very limited. And even if I had found what I wanted, I just couldn't justify paying those prices for a bridesmaid's dress, by the time it comes in and still has to be custom fit by a local seamstress."

"Uh-huh," accused Katie.

"But I'm paying *you*," Leanne insisted.

Katie shook her head in defeat. "So what's your dress like?"

"Oh, it's beautiful!" Leanne exclaimed. "I'll show it to you when we get together to look at bridesmaids' dresses. I couldn't believe how many options I had, once I went on-line. The local stores just don't get it, when it comes to modesty, I'm afraid."

"That's for sure," Katie agreed.

"So is Katie going to sew up our tuxes?" Kyle asked, rubbing his hands together, feigning girlish delight as he stepped into the conversation now, too.

David chuckled at his brother. "No need, Kyle. We're renting. But it wouldn't matter; they put twice the material into men's clothing, for a fraction of the price of the women's."

"Yeah!" Amie stated with indignation. "What gives with that? Man! You guys've always got it so easy compared to us girls . . . in just about everything—dressing, child-bearing, you name it." She stood with her hands on her hips, prepared to argue her point.

"I'm not complaining about being a guy," Kyle admitted to the girl standing beside him.

"Nor am I," Daniel said, putting in his two cents' worth.

"Well," Amie added, thoughtfully, taking her hands from her hips. "I guess the advantage of being a girl is that we do have it hard, naturally—which just gives us lots that we can offer up in sacrifice."

"True," agreed Ann. "And, it's probably harder than a girl realizes to be a really great guy, self-sacrificing and all—especially in this day and age."

"You can't even begin to imagine what an effort it is for us guys," said David. "Everywhere we turn we're surrounded by immodesty and impurity. It's on the magazine racks in the grocery stores, on the billboards as you drive down the street, in every movie and TV show you want to watch . . . and there are an awful lot of girls and women out there who don't make any attempt to dress modestly."

"True," Amie said. "And then there's the fact that the world just accepts that 'boys will be boys' and does nothing to encourage them to ever mature to be *real* men . . . which makes me appreciate all the more the effort that you guys make in order to be real men of integrity. So, I withdraw my original opinion—I'd just as soon be a girl than a guy."

"I think the good Lord knows what He's doing when He makes us each who we are," said David. "There's no easy riding for a Christian—man or woman. I mean think about the pressure on a guy when St. Paul tells us that we have to lay down our lives for our wives, just like Christ did for His Bride, the Church. That's no small order."

"And just think, David," Kyle said, punching his brother on the shoulder, "you'll be getting your big chance to lay down your life in just a few months from now."

"And what about you?" Leanne asked the younger brother.

"Me?" Kyle responded. "I'm still waiting for the right time and the right girl."

"I hope she's a patient one," Amie threw in, "since Kyle's sense of timing, I'm sure, won't involve any hastiness."

Kyle looked at Amie beside him and chuckled. "Haste makes waste," he reminded the young lady. "But I'm sure it'll all be worth the wait."

Jocelyn caught Amie's eye from across the circle of friends. Just the look told Amie she was still thinking about her random comment from the girls' night out at the restaurant. Amie stared down her cousin with a look that said, "Don't you *dare* say a thing!"

Jocelyn just started giggling. Katie caught on and she, too, began laughing. Suddenly Ann was in on the joke. Amie stood there awkwardly, hoping against hope that no one would say a thing.

"So, what's so funny?" Kyle asked, looking around at the girls laughing.

"Just an 'insider'," Amie informed him, her teeth clenched as she smiled at her sister and two cousins.

"Why aren't you laughing?" he asked.

"'Cause it's *not* funny," she said, staring down the three girls. She looked up at Kyle beside her and smiled sweetly. He was a good friend, and she wanted to keep it that way. "What d'you say we go make some refreshments for this crew?"

"Fine with me," he said. "Lead the way."

Amie began to walk upstairs with Kyle right behind her. A sudden outburst of laughter followed them from the three giggly girls.

"Please, ignore them," Amie called over her shoulder to Kyle.

Kyle looked back at the three girls, bent over in laughter. "I'm not even going to ask."

✝   ✝   ✝

Kyle's light was still on in his bedroom when David got in that night from driving Leanne home after band practice.

David tapped lightly on the open door to his brother's room. "Mind if I come in for a visit?"

"Not at all," Kyle said. "I was just studying for an exam coming up next week. Sit down. Something on your mind?"

"No," David said, pulling up the old wooden chair from the corner of the room and turning it around to sit on it backwards. He crossed his arms over the back of the chair and leaned his chin down on his arms as he looked around.

The bedroom was just like everything else in the Bander's home—simple and neat, in a quaint country fashion. There was a twin bed in a wooden frame, with a handmade quilt on top. The curtains were homemade, with a plaid print. There was an old wooden chest of drawers and a matching night table. The door to the little walk-in closet was open, where Kyle kept his books and things neatly stacked. A few pictures up on the walls of family, friends, and the saints, attested to Kyle's uncomplicated personality. And a large crucifix hung on the wall at the head of Kyle's bed.

After a few moments, David looked back at his brother who was sitting patiently on the bed, waiting for David to tell him why he had come in to see him. "I just wanted to tell you how much I've enjoyed growing up with you, Kyle."

Kyle chuckled. "The pleasure's been all mine. What's made you suddenly so nostalgic?"

"Ahhh, I just got thinking about old times together as I drove home tonight. In two-and-a-half months I'll be married and moving out. Life will never be the same again."

"Life's never the same from one day to the next," Kyle observed. "But I know what you mean. It'll be lonely around here once you're gone."

"Not that we ever see each other much anymore, anyway . . . apart from band," David commented.

"Thank goodness we joined up with *New Spring*," Kyle said. "We've had a lot of fun with that over the years."

"We sure have," David said. "And it's kept me on the straight and narrow, having had a group of friends like that to stick close to all these years."

"We've been blessed," Kyle agreed.

David remained leaning over the back of the chair, his eyes fixed in the distance. "I had a lot of fun growing up here on the acreage with you. I know there were times when I probably wasn't the best of big brothers . . ."

"I wouldn't say that," Kyle disagreed. "I was a little pest at times, always bugging you to play with me."

"Remember how we used to climb the trees lining the driveway?" David asked.

Kyle laughed. "When I was little I thought you were just like Superman, able to jump from tree to tree. Then I got older and taller and discovered it wasn't that impressive anymore—once I knew how to do it."

"Guess I lost my cape, once you learned how to do everything I could do."

"David, you still have a cape as far as I'm concerned," Kyle told his brother.

David lifted his head and chuckled. "I had fun building machines with you in Dad's shop," he reminisced.

"Yeah, we made some pretty cool things together," Kyle said. "I remember jumping off the school bus at the end of each day and heading straight for Dad's shop."

"We must have spent a good quarter of our lives out there with Dad," David said. "I'm glad Mom refused to let us sit around the house watching TV and playing video games, although all our friends at school thought we were so out of it 'cause we never knew the latest on any of the shows."

"That never bothered me," Kyle said. "I appreciated being different. Once they had all figured out that we weren't the same as everyone else, they stopped expecting us to be the same. It kind of gave us the freedom to do as we pleased. They didn't bother trying to peer pressure us—they knew it wouldn't work."

"I remember the guys in my grade constantly bugging me about you," David told his brother. "They couldn't believe that I'd rather spend time playing with you at home, than going out with them. I didn't care. So many of those kids just couldn't stand their own brothers or sisters. I never got that. What a waste for them. I could have spent all those years hanging out with those guys and ignoring you. And where would that leave me today? I've hardly seen any of my high school friends in five years' time now. But you, on the other hand," he said, motioning toward his brother, "you're still my best man!"

Kyle nodded. "I feel the same way, David."

"I'll remember that, if you ever decide to get married there, bro."

"In time," Kyle said, "God-willing."

"You still got anyone special in mind?" David asked with a smile, holding up two fingers in the air—the pledge of secrecy between them.

Kyle looked at his brother and smiled. David had known for years about his feelings for Amie, but he had never told anyone. Sworn to secrecy as kids, David was a man of his word.

"There are only four people on the face of this planet, apart from me, who know how I feel about Amie," Kyle said.

"Mom, Dad, me . . . and who?" David asked.

"Fr. Steve," Kyle said. "The two of us had a really good talk about things at Christmastime . . ."

". . . during Amie and Connor's courtship. I was impressed with just how cool you were about things," the older brother remarked.

"Maybe . . . on the outside," Kyle commented.

"I wondered if you had given up on her."

"My feelings haven't changed," Kyle confessed. "But she doesn't know anything—and that's the way I intend to keep it for now. I've got a month before I finish classes and then final exams. I'm too busy to deal with the emotional commitments of a courtship—especially with a girl like Amie. I've got my work cut out to make her see me as anything but a brother. And I'm not quite sure how I'm going to bridge that gap. But I'm sure it'll take a bit of emotional energy—which I just don't have to give right now."

"Yeah," David laughed. "You've got your work cut out for you. Amie's a wonderful girl—but set in her ways. I don't envy you."

"Thanks," Kyle said, with a chuckle. "Plus, I've been sending out job applications and resumes all over the place for the past few weeks. I want to know that I have something in place, before I go off courting a girl. You remember Proverbs, twenty-four, 'Get everything ready for you in the field; and after that build your house.'"

"Not that Dad would let us forget that one," David commented.

"He was big on making us into men," Kyle laughed. "But I agree with it. I wouldn't want to take myself a wife, if we can't be ready to begin a family. That means I've got to be able to provide, so she could stay at home. So, it could be a while, yet."

"Well, I'll keep praying for you that something comes around, sooner than later," David said.

Kyle lifted his hands upward. "It's all in God's hands . . . His timing. I'm a patient man."

"You are," David said. "And I guess I should let you get back to your studying. I don't want to compromise your chances at getting your fields in order."

"Thanks," Kyle said, with a laugh. He looked down at his books laid out in front of him on his bed. "Now I'm supposed to get my mind back into all this? I've got a better plan. Why don't we go play some cards?"

"It's a school night for you and a work night for me," David observed. He looked over at Kyle's alarm clock. "And it's already eleven-thirty."

"Agh," Kyle waved his hand, brushing away common sense. "It's almost the weekend. We can sleep in on Saturday. Let's go have some fun."

David stood up from the chair and in one smooth motion turned it around and set it back in the corner. "Come on," he agreed. "Life's too short to pass by an opportunity like this."

Chapter 55

Joanie worked at the television station right up until two weeks before her due date. She was ready to be finished. It was demanding work, with long, hard hours each day. The further she got along in her pregnancy, the longer and harder the hours seemed to be. Even still, as she packed up her little cubicle, that second last Friday of May, Joanie was filled with emotions. She knew—although she had not officially resigned from her job—that she would not be coming back. This was the end of her career as a journalist.

Over lunch their co-workers at the station threw the parents-to-be a baby shower. Shelly Lesichyn, Joanie's senior producer, had bought the expectant mother a basketful of bubble baths, scented beads, lotions, creams, candles, and things, with the instructions, "Go home and spoil yourself for the next few weeks."

Paul Petros, the cameraman with whom Joanie had worked the most, gave her and Brandon a gift certificate for a restaurant in town. "You two be sure to get out and leave that baby with a sitter," he told them. "My wife, Camille, and I would be happy to oblige you in that department."

"Thanks, Paul," Joanie said, giving her dear friend a hug.

"I'm going to miss you, kiddo," he replied, while returning the hug.

"Don't you go making me cry," she scolded him. "Not that that's hard to do these days."

"I'm just impressed that you never broke down in front of the camera on a shoot," he teased, with a laugh.

"This woman's got true grit," Brandon said, putting his arm around Joanie's shoulder.

As Joanie sat and opened the other gifts, a young woman stepped into the staff lounge, carrying a nine-month-old baby. Brandon looked up at the blond-haired lady, with a big smile on his face. The woman held her finger over her lips, motioning for him to not say a word as she passed her sleeping baby to Shelly. Everyone watched, with Joanie oblivious to what was happening behind her back.

Standing right behind the expectant mother, the young woman said, "Don't pay any attention to Brandon . . . he's just a commercial producer here at the station."

Joanie's eyes opened wide and she screamed as she jumped out of the chair to turn around to greet her friend. "Tessa!" She grasped her friend in a big hug. It had been months since she had seen Tessa, her first friend at the station, now a stay-at-home mom. Tessa had been a secretary at CNB, and the first person to know of Joanie and Brandon's budding romance . . . which now seemed a lifetime ago.

"I couldn't miss your going-away party," Tessa told her friend, while still hugging her.

"Where's Sarah?" Joanie asked, wiping the tears from her eyes.

"Right here," announced Shelly, proudly rocking the sleeping baby back and forth.

"Oh," Joanie said, with a sigh. "Come. Sit down beside me, Tessa."

Tessa took her place beside Joanie, as Brandon brought her a piece of cake.

"So, what's with the 'pay no attention to Brandon' thing?" Paul asked Tessa.

"I think that was the very first thing I ever said to Joanie, sitting here in the staff lounge—right under that dragon palm," Tessa said, pointing to the large plant in the corner.

"She obviously doesn't listen well," Paul chided.

"Thank goodness for that," Brandon said with a smile. He sat on the arm of Joanie's chair and put his hand on her shoulder.

"I don't know," Paul said to Tessa, "I think we did a pretty good job, in the end, of match-making these two, don't you?"

Tessa laughed.

"Just don't start messing with *my* life," called out Taylor, a sound technician from the station. He was lying on the couch across the room, his boyish immaturity shining through underneath his wild, bleached, spiked hair.

"I think we'll all leave you safely alone, Taylor. It's enough to have one of you in this world—let alone marry you off to start reproducing yourself," said Shelly.

Everyone had a good laugh, including Taylor.

The lunch hour passed by all-too-quickly. People headed back to work, saying good-bye to Joanie on their way out. Tessa and Brandon helped pack up the gifts, and Brandon carried them down to their vehicle.

Tessa walked Joanie to her cubicle in the newsroom. "How did it feel for you to leave a career behind?" Joanie asked her friend.

"It was hard and not hard," Tessa said, holding Sarah on her hip as she walked. "I miss the fun of working here. I loved the contact with other adults—especially you."

Joanie smiled at her friend and patted Tessa on the back. "Me, too."

"And," Tessa went on, "it always felt good to tell people that I worked for Canadian Broadcasting Network. But," she looked down at her little girl cooing away in her arms, "once I laid eyes on Sarah, I didn't want to ever be apart from her. Some days are long. Some days I wish I could get out and have a little more adult contact. But I could never give up this time in Sarah's life. I get to be there to watch her first everything . . . and I can't imagine how hard it would be to have to pick her up from a daycare and have some babysitter tell me she sat up or she crawled for the first time—and I wasn't there to see it. It's all those little rewards of motherhood, Joanie, that make it worth the sacrifice. I can go back and be a secretary again somewhere, someday. But I can only raise my children once."

"I needed to hear that today," Joanie told Tessa. "I agree with everything you're telling me. But somehow, today, as I'm packing up to leave it all behind, I feel . . ." she fumbled to find the right word.

"Like you're losing part of your identity?" Tessa filled in for her.

"Yeah," Joanie said.

"Believe me," Tessa told her, "you are about to acquire a new, all-encompassing identity that is going to transform you completely, Joanie. And as you lose yourself, somewhat, in motherhood, you're also going to discover the best that there is within you. And someday, if you still want all this again," Tessa motioned around with her free hand, "it'll be here for you, if you need it. God knows what we all need, and He supplies for every last detail."

"I know," Joanie said. "Thank you, Tessa, for coming today. I think we'll be able to stay better in touch, now that I'm going to be at home with this little one, too." She placed her hands over her tummy, gently holding them over her precious, hidden treasure.

✟   ✟   ✟

Joanie adapted quickly to being at home. It was fun to watch Brandon go off to work each day without her. It reminded her of playing house as a little girl, imitating her parents. She had waited her whole life to finally be at the point where she was playing house for real with her own husband and baby.

On the days when she needed the vehicle for appointments or running errands, she would drive him to work and drop him off. They quickly realized that a second vehicle would be in order. They had a few weeks before the baby would be born to do some car shopping.

On a couple of days, Joanie stopped in at her parents' home. Walking into the action of the home-schooling day brought back many fond memories for Joanie. Her mother welcomed Joanie's visits—as she quickly put Joanie to work helping the little ones with their school work. Joanie loved it. It had been a while since she had been fully involved with the little kids.

"Sound out the word," Joanie encouraged seven-year-old Aaron.

"I can't, Joanie. I *hate* reading," complained the little boy.

"Hate's a strong word, Aaron. I know it's hard, but you have to learn how to read. Wouldn't it be terrible if Brandon couldn't read, or Daddy couldn't read? They wouldn't be able to have jobs. Don't you want to be able to be like them someday?"

"I don't want to work," Aaron informed his sister. "Zack and Isaac and me are going to build a big house in the country and drive quads and ride horses and shoot guns. Pow! Pow! Pow-pow-pow!" The little boy pulled his hand up and took aim around the room with his imaginary gun.

Joanie laughed and rubbed Aaron's already messed up head of hair. "Well, you need to learn how to read so you can . . . so you can . . ." On the spot, Joanie could not think of anything that would appeal to this little boy's world-view in order to make reading seem attractive to him. "You just need to . . . because Mommy said so, and that's good enough."

Judy laughed from across the room as she made lunch. Joanie looked up at her mother from the dining room table. "Do you think I'll ever be able to do this, Mom?"

"Joanie, I don't know too many mothers who are 'qualified' and able to home-school," she told the girl. "We do it because we feel called to it—or we don't, because we don't feel called. One way or another, it's like the saying goes—God does not call the qualified, He qualifies the called."

"I hope you're right," Joanie said. Turning back to Aaron she decided to give it one last shot. "Look, buddy, you read to the bottom of this page, and I'll let you go play for a few minutes before lunch."

"What's for lunch?" the little boy asked.

"Egg salad sandwiches," his mother replied.

"Ah, man, that stuff is hypertrocious!" he complained.

"What's this *hypertrocious?*" Joanie asked, laughing at the obviously homemade word.

"That's Aaron's new word," Zack informed his oldest sister, as he sat doing his work on the other side of the table. "It means gross," he explained.

"Hypertrocious?" Joanie repeated the word.

"Yup," agreed Jessie, on the other side of Joanie. "It means gross."

"Cool word, Aaron, but egg salad sandwiches are hardly hypertrocious," Joanie stated. "Besides, Mom makes the best egg salad sandwiches."

"Thanks, Joanie," Judy called out. "But don't worry, Aaron. I know you don't like eggs, so I made you a peanut butter and bologna sandwich."

"Peanut butter and bologna?" questioned Joanie. "Now *that's* hypertrocious!"

"Tell me about it," agreed Judy. "But it's his latest thing."

"Yup," agreed Jessie. "It's his latest thing. But I think it's hypertrocious, too." The four-year-old wrapped her tongue around the big, new word.

Joanie laughed. "I'm done, Aaron. You go play, and we'll read this after lunch," she told him.

Aaron jumped up from the table and ran off, before Joanie could change her mind. Zack joined him, before he could get hooked into helping with lunch. Joanie looked down at Jessie, who had been colouring a picture beside her. "Do you want to run off and play for a while, too?" she asked the little girl.

"I want to stay with you, Joanie," Jessie answered, without looking up from her colouring.

Judy smiled. "You've been missed around here," she told her eldest daughter.

"I've missed being here," she told her mom.

"Well, once that little grandchild of mine is born, I hope you intend to come around often," Judy said.

Joanie got up and began to clear the kids' books off the table for lunch. "I just hope you don't get sick of me. Now that I'm home from work—I think I'll be coming 'round here lots."

"I'm looking forward to it. And who knows . . . ?" Judy added with a little laugh. "Maybe you and I'll get the chance to home-school our kids together."

"Oh my gosh," Joanie replied. "I never thought of that. But it's true. By the time I'm ready to start teaching my kids, Jessie will only be in . . . grade four." She quickly did the calculation in her head.

"Part of the joy of having a large family, Joanie. The fun just never ends," Judy stated with a laugh. "Come on. Help me get this stuff on the table, and we'll call in the kids for lunch."

Chapter 56

A week had gone by since Joanie had finished work. Brandon came home that Friday night to find his wife happily working away in the kitchen. "That's what I like to see," he said, walking up behind his wife at the stove. "My wife—barefoot, pregnant, and in the kitchen."

"Looks good on me, doesn't it?" she asked, lifting her right foot into the air. "If only they weren't beginning to look like little sausages," she commented, looking down at her foot.

"They look beautiful, just like the rest of you," he told her, kissing her on the neck.

"Cut it out, Brandon," she scolded, ducking away. "That tickles."

He snuck his hands around her and placed them on her tummy. Giving it a few taps he said, "Hi, baby, Daddy's home."

Joanie looked down at his hands on her tummy. "Can you feel baby kicking? He—or she—must be happy to hear your voice."

Brandon held his hands there and waited. He started to chuckle as the baby began moving and Joanie's entire tummy seemed to do the wave.

"Now you've got him good and excited," she said.

"Him?" Brandon questioned.

"Or her," she replied.

"So, what about names for this little bundle," he asked, getting himself a drink of water.

"Well, so far you haven't agreed to any names I've come up with," Joanie complained. "And I've had some good ones."

"I love all the names you've suggested," Brandon stated. "Here, do you want some water?" he offered her his glass.

"Thanks," she said, taking it.

He got himself another glass and went to sit down on the kitchen stool. "If you love them all, how come you can't agree to any?"

"Because I need to see the baby first."

Joanie was not sure if she was satisfied with his answer or not. "So, why do you even want to talk about names?" she asked, somewhat frustrated with her husband.

"Because I want to know what our options are." He took a sip of his water and put down his glass. Suddenly he realized that he was watching his almost-nine-month pregnant wife working away at making supper, while he was just sitting back, relaxing. "Here," he said, getting up, "you sit down, and I'll finish making supper." He walked over and ushered Joanie to the stool.

She laughed and complied. "I won't argue with you. I'm exhausted. And I really didn't even do anything today."

"What d'you have cooking here, anyway?" he asked, looking at the pot of vegetables simmering together.

"Some recipe I found in some health cookbook," Joanie said. "I don't know . . . looks disgusting to me, personally."

Brandon laughed. "I'd say it's fairly hypertrocious," he agreed, "to borrow Aaron's expression."

"For a kid who can't read, he sure can make up great words," Joanie commented.

"Look," Brandon said, turning off the element on the stove and removing the pot. "Let's just let this experiment die, and I'll take you out for supper tonight."

"Oh, praise be to Jesus," Joanie replied. "I was hoping my knight in shining armour would come home and rescue me from my own lousy cooking."

Brandon laughed. "You're a good cook, Joanie. Just stay away from those health cookbooks with ingredients we can't even pronounce."

Joanie laughed and agreed with Brandon's advice.

✟   ✟   ✟

After a very satisfying supper in a not-so-quiet restaurant, Brandon suggested to Joanie that they go test-drive some more cars.

"That sounds like fun," Joanie said. "I'm in."

They drove down to a dealership and looked around the used car lot. Joanie insisted on a used car. She had no intention of breaking the bank over a second vehicle. Brandon insisted it had to be foreign. "I'm just not big on domestic cars, dear."

Joanie laughed. "You might have to change your mind in a few years from now, honey. If we end up with that large family you always talk about—I don't think your foreign makes produce eight, ten, and twelve passenger vehicles."

"Good point," he said. "But by then I'm sure life will have softened my personality and made me less set in my ways."

After test driving three cars, they were both leaning toward a two-year-old Honda Civic that had low mileage. It was a four-door, which Joanie wanted, for getting in and out with a baby. It was fairly loaded and in great condition. Joanie especially liked it being red, with charcoal interior.

"You always did look good in red," Brandon told her, agreeing with her choice of vehicle.

Having made their final decision, they were walking across the parking lot to the dealership office when suddenly Joanie stopped.

"What's wrong?" Brandon asked, looking at his wife, bent over in her tracks.

"I think we should go home," she informed her husband.

"Are you okay?"

"I think my water just broke," she told him.

Brandon looked down.

"Skirts hide a lot," she said. "Let's go."

"Should we go home or to the hospital?" he asked.

"I don't know. I'm not really having any contractions yet. Oh!"

"That, I take, was a contraction?"

"I-I-I think so," she hesitated. "I don't know. I've never done this before."

"Okay, honey," he said, walking her back to their vehicle. He opened the door and helped her in.

Getting in on his side, he asked again, "Hospital or home?"

"Home," she said. "I want my suitcase."

Brandon laughed. "Ah, yes, the fifty-pound suitcase."

Joanie smacked him with a backhand. "No comments from the peanut gallery," she said, with her head bent over. She was breathing heavily.

"You having another contraction?" he asked.

"I think so. I don't know. It doesn't hurt that much, but it does hurt a bit."

Brandon quickly drove them home, ran in, grabbed the suitcase, and came back down to the vehicle. He threw it into the back of the SUV and jumped into the driver's seat.

"Ready?"

Joanie made a sort of groaning noise.

"I'll take that as a yes." He put the vehicle into gear and took off.

"What are you doing?" Joanie shouted out, as Brandon ran a red light.

"I've always wanted to do that—just like in the movies. I just wish a cop would pull me over so I could prove my wife is really going to have a baby."

"Brandon, you're crazy," she said, half-laughing, half-grunting.

By the time they got to the hospital, Joanie was in quite a bit of discomfort. They took her up quickly to the Ante Partum unit of the Labour and Delivery ward. Once Joanie was set up in a room, Brandon ran back down and filled in the forms and moved their car.

When he got back up on the ward the nurse informed him that Joanie was only about three centimetres dilated. "She's definitely in labour, but this is her first baby, and it could take a while. It could also go very quickly. We just don't know," the nurse added with a smile.

They set Joanie up with a fetal monitor and told her once they could see that the baby was happy with the contractions, she could get up and walk around. The nurse placed Brandon's hand on Joanie's tummy during a contraction. "Feel that," she said. It was hard. "It's going to get a lot harder than that." She pointed to the print out on the monitor. "When Joanie's in heavy labour, that'll shoot up to here." She indicated on the paper just how high up the intensity of the contractions would get.

Brandon raised his eyebrows and looked at his wife.

"You'll be great," the nurse told Joanie. "I'll be back in a little while."

Joanie and Brandon were left alone in their room, with the echoing sound of the baby's heartbeat from the monitor.

"Well, I guess we're really here, honey," Brandon said. "Who'd have thought this morning that we'd be having a baby tonight?" His face was beaming. The whole concept of fatherhood was beginning to set in.

Joanie laughed a little and then told Brandon, "You'd better phone my mom and dad, and your mom . . . and dad, and let them all know what we're up to."

Brandon made the calls and Joanie lay on the bed, with straps around her tummy, listening to the musical sound of her baby's heart. She closed her eyes and prayed quietly as she waited for Brandon to finish making his calls.

"Everyone's praying for you, honey . . . even my Dad, if you can imagine!" he said with a laugh.

"Really?" Joanie was impressed.

"What some girls won't go through to get a guy to pray," he said, winking at his wife.

She smiled back, but a contraction interrupted her expression and prevented her from answering.

"Well, there's hope for him yet," Brandon concluded, once he could see that Joanie was relaxed again. "Anyway, I guess we should be praying, too." He reached into his pocket and pulled out his rosary.

"Oh, wait, Brandon," Joanie said. "Open my suitcase and get a few things out for me, first."

Brandon chuckled as Joanie directed him to take out framed pictures of the Sacred Heart of Jesus, the Immaculate Heart of Mary and their wedding, her rosary, and some holy water. "You come prepared, don't you?"

They decided to pray the joyful mysteries. Joanie told Brandon she intended to offer up her labour pain for Mark and Justine and for his father's conversion, so they united their prayers in the rosary for those intentions, along with a safe and healthy delivery of their baby.

The nurse popped in a couple of times to check on them. She motioned for them to go on—she did not want to interrupt. By the time they were done the rosary the nurse told Joanie she could get up and walk around, if she felt up to it. "Walking will help your labour along."

Joanie got on her hospital robe, and she and Brandon hit the hallways of the maternity ward. After an hour of walking, contractions were no closer together, nor had they really increased in intensity. They walked back to their room, and Joanie lay down on the bed. It was ten-fifteen. She felt discouraged that things were taking so long.

Brandon reminded her, "You're a whole week early, Joanie."

"Please don't tell me I'm going to be at this for a whole week," she said in exasperation.

Brandon laughed. He walked around to the head of the bed and told Joanie to lean forward. "I'll rub your back for you, honey."

"Can you put on my music for me, too?" she asked.

"Sure. I'd hate to think I carried all that stuff in here, and then we never used it."

"Brandon, I'm warning you," she said with a laugh, followed quickly by a groan.

He kissed her on the cheek and went to pull out the suitcase to set up the CD player. Once the praise music started, Joanie felt herself relax. That was exactly what she needed to take her mind off things. Brandon took his place again at the head of the bed, so he could rub her back.

They sang together with the music. They praised God. They talked and laughed. They waited and they prayed. Every time the nurse came in she would smile. "With music like that playing, I just want to stay in here with you and join in the singing."

"Are you a Christian?" Joanie asked.

"I sure am," the woman answered. "And I love that music."

Joanie was grateful that the Lord had sent them such a wonderful nurse.

By midnight, Joanie was getting tired. Labour seemed to have slowed down. The nurse suggested that if Joanie could get any sleep at all, she should try. Brandon set himself up in the vinyl recliner in the corner. It was not terribly comfortable, but he figured he was likely more comfortable than his wife, and he could put up with it without complaining.

Joanie did fall asleep. At two a.m. she woke up, her contractions had suddenly come back in full force. The nurse came in to check on her. "Good girl," she announced. "You're already seven centimetres dilated. We can take you over to Labour and Delivery."

They got everything together and pushed Joanie on her bed down the hall to the neighbouring ward. As they entered the ward they could hear the intermittent screams of a woman down the hall. Joanie looked wide-eyed at Brandon. The nurse leaned down and whispered to Joanie, "Don't let that bother you. Some women are just louder than others. You relax and you'll do fine. And, I won't be your nurse anymore—I have to get back to Ante Partum—but I want you to know I'll be praying for you that everything goes well."

Joanie took the nurse's hand and held it through a contraction. She smiled as the lovely woman left. A new nurse was setting things up in the room. She introduced herself to Joanie. She was an older nurse who had worked Labour and Delivery for over twenty years. Joanie felt comfortable knowing that she was in well-experienced hands.

The doctor had left an order for Joanie to get an epidural, if she wanted. The labour pains had greatly increased, and Joanie opted for the pain relief. Within half-an-hour the anesthesiologist was there, and he got Joanie all set up. By that point in time she was really glad she had made the decision. The sudden break from pain was remarkable. Joanie relaxed. She could feel every contraction tighten—but the pain was gone. All at once, the labour seemed like fun.

After an hour of heavy contractions, Joanie was becoming more and more uncomfortable. The nurse checked her—she was ten centimetres dilated and fully effaced. "We're on, honey," she said.

The doctor was called, and the nurse quickly began to get things set up. Joanie had a hard time concentrating on everything going on around her. She closed her eyes and breathed through each contraction. Brandon stood at her side, rubbing her back, and praying silently.

Every now and then Joanie would get annoyed with his touch and move away. Brandon would stop. Within a few moments, she would tap his hand for him to begin again. She did not use any words. She was concentrating on everything going on inside her body. Though the epidural had cut the pain, the discomfort of labour was increasing with each contraction.

"I have to push," she called out.

The nurse ran out to call the obstetrical resident from down the hall. She returned quickly and began talking to Joanie in a soothing voice. "You're doing great, honey," she said. "The doctor's going to check you one more time, and we'll see where your baby's at." She placed the monitor over Joanie's tummy, and the sound of the baby's heartbeat immediately filled the room. The nurse held it there for a few moments. "Your baby's just fine," she assured the labouring mother.

Just as the resident finished checking Joanie, her family doctor stepped into the room. "I see we have quite a party going on in here," she said in a spunky tone of voice.

Joanie looked up and smiled at Dr. Wilson. "I'm glad to see you."

"I'm surprised to see you," Dr. Wilson answered with a big smile. "I would never have guessed at your last appointment that you were going to go early. But we're all here, so let's party."

Joanie laughed until the next contraction cut her off. "I wanna push," she said again.

The resident informed Dr. Wilson of Joanie's status. "Well, let's see what happens when you do, Joanie," Dr. Wilson replied.

"Just stick your chin deep into your chest, honey, and push hard all the way through the next contraction, okay?" instructed the nurse.

"Take a deep breath and go," called out Dr. Wilson.

Joanie breathed deeply and began to push.

"Push, push, push, push, push," the nurse repeated in a hushed tone, in Joanie's ear.

"Quick, take another breath and keeping pushing," called out Dr. Wilson.

Joanie did as she was told and kept pushing.

"And again," called out the physician.

Joanie breathed in quickly one more time and continued pushing until the end of the contraction.

"That was good," said Dr. Wilson. "You can relax now, Joanie."

Joanie leaned back on the bed and closed her eyes.

Turning to the nurse, Dr. Wilson said, "I could feel the baby's head moving forward all the way through that. We'll have this little one joining our party in no time."

Joanie held onto Brandon's arm, and when it came time to push again, she used it to brace herself. Brandon remained quiet, praying silently for his wife and child. Meanwhile, he was blown away by the strength and force of Joanie's grip.

During the fifth large contraction, Dr. Wilson called out, "Hold on, Joanie, stop pushing."

Joanie almost screamed out. "I can't! I wanna push."

"Baby's head is out," the nurse told her. "Dr. Wilson's just making sure the neck is clear and everything's good before you keep pushing, honey."

Joanie breathed deeply, shuddering with the energy of holding back from pushing.

"We're all good," Dr. Wilson announced. "Let's meet this little one."

Joanie felt the next contraction come on, and she began to push, but before she was done there was a great commotion at the end of the bed. She was confused and looked up. There stood Dr. Wilson holding a little baby and laughing. "It's a girl," she announced.

Joanie's eyes welled up with tears. The pain was gone, and it was over. Her ears suddenly tuned in to the sounds of her baby's cries. It was the most beautiful sound she had ever heard.

She had a baby. A baby girl! "Oh, praise be to Jesus," she said through her tears. "Thank you, Lord!"

Brandon held onto Joanie's hand. "A girl," he said. Tears were running down his cheeks. "A girl," he repeated. "Thank you, Lord," he whispered under his breath.

"With lungs like that, this girl's going to be a singer," commented Dr. Wilson.

"Just like her mommy," Brandon agreed.

The little baby's cries continued to fill the room with the sweet sound of new life.

"Come here, Daddy," Dr. Wilson said. "Do you want to cut the cord?"

Brandon stepped forward and took the instrument from the doctor and cut where she showed him. The nurse then quickly wiped down and wrapped the little girl in a blanket and brought her up to her mother. "You want to meet your little girl?" she asked Joanie.

Joanie took her baby in her arms and pulled the blanket back from around her little girl's face. She had a headful of thick, dark hair. "She's beautiful," Joanie said. "She's amazing."

Brandon stood at the bedside, looking on at his wife and child. More tears filled his eyes. He leaned forward and kissed the little girl on her forehead. Then he kissed her mommy on the top of her head and whispered, "Thank you, for bringing our daughter into the world."

Joanie looked up at Brandon. She had almost forgotten he was there. She smiled at him and asked if he wanted to hold their daughter. Brandon looked at the nurse. She nodded, and Brandon took the little bundle in his arms.

All at once, fatherhood was upon him. "I'm a dad," he said, with a big smile on his face. He looked down at his little girl. Her eyes were wide open and her little mouth was opening and closing. "You just made me a dad," he whispered to her. "Thank you. I love you. I love you so much . . . I'd give my life for you, little girl . . . my little girl."

Joanie smiled as she watched Brandon and their baby bond in that incredible moment. She put her hand up and held Brandon's arm. He looked back down at his wife. "You make beautiful babies," he told her.

The nurse stepped over and took the bundle from Daddy's arms. "I'll go get this little angel weighed and measured, and then I'll bring her back for you to nurse if you want," she said to Joanie.

"Oh, yes," Joanie said. "I'd like that."

"We're not quite done here," said Dr. Wilson. "There's a placenta that's just about ready to come."

By the time Dr. Wilson had finished up with Joanie, the nurse was back with their baby. "Nine pounds, one ounce," she announced. "That's one healthy little girl."

"Good job, Joanie," Dr. Wilson said. "And to think she's a week early!"

"And she's tall, too," said the nurse. "Twenty-one and a half inches long."

"I wonder where she gets that from?" asked the doctor, looking over at Brandon.

"Maybe," he said. "But the good looks she gets from her mother."

Dr. Wilson smiled.

The nurse passed the baby, all cleaned and bundled up, to Joanie. The new mother took the little one to her breast and with just the slightest coaxing, the baby latched on. Joanie started a little, and the nurse chuckled.

"You weren't expecting her to know what to do, were you?" she asked.

"No," Joanie answered in amazement. She looked down and watched her little girl moving her mouth and sucking.

"God knows how to design things well, doesn't He?" the nurse commented.

Joanie looked up at the nurse; she, too, was a woman of faith. Joanie was so grateful to have been surrounded by these faith-filled women throughout her journey into motherhood that night.

"So, did anyone notice what time our little guest of honour arrived at this party?" Dr. Wilson asked.

"Three-forty-six a.m.," Brandon announced. "May thirtieth."

"May thirtieth?" Joanie asked.

"Yeah, honey, it's after midnight."

Joanie started laughing. "I guess God does know what He's doing. Today's the feast of St. Joan of Arc—my patron saint."

They all laughed in amazement.

"Do you have a name for this little girl?" asked Dr. Wilson.

Joanie looked at Brandon. "Not just yet."

"Well, I'll leave you two alone for a bit. I've got some forms to fill out at the nursing station, but I'll check back in on you all before I leave. Congratulations, Joanie and Brandon. You have a beautiful little girl." Dr. Wilson left the birthing room, and Joanie and Brandon were now alone with the newest member of their family.

"So, do we have a name for her, dear?" Joanie asked, looking up at her husband.

"Mary Grace," he said, softly, gazing at their little baby who had fallen asleep at her mother's breast.

"Mary Grace?" Joanie repeated.

"Uh-huh," he replied. "Because Mary brought me to her Son. And it was His amazing grace that saved a wretch like me."

Joanie smiled through tears, looking up at Brandon whose eyes were still fixed on their little girl. "Mary Grace," she repeated, nodding. How could she argue with those reasons? "Can we call her Gracie?"

"Absolutely," Brandon answered. "Hello, Gracie," he whispered to the little one asleep. "This is your daddy, and I just wanted to tell you how happy I am to meet you."

Joanie leaned forward and kissed Brandon's cheek. He turned to his wife and kissed her tenderly on the lips. "Thank you," he said to his wife, "for sacrificing yourself to bring our Mary Grace into the world."

Joanie reached up with her hand and placed it on Brandon's cheek. "Thank *you* . . . for cooperating with God so that I could become a mom. I couldn't have done it without you," she added, with a little giggle. She handed Gracie over to her daddy and said, "Why don't you go cuddle up with her in that chair while she's sleeping."

Brandon took his daughter in his arms once again and sat in the big vinyl chair in the corner of the room. As he held her gently in his arms, he sang for her one of the songs he had written, which all at once seemed to make a perfect lullaby for his little Mary Grace.

Chapter 57

"How's the new grandpa doing?" Kevin Bander asked John Collins, Sunday after Mass. He patted John on the back and offered him a handshake in congratulations.

"Great!" John replied with enthusiasm. "A little older and a little wiser than the last time you saw me, Kevin. Just a few new grey hairs this morning," John said, pulling at the hair around his temple.

"I have to say, you're hiding your age well," Kevin added with a laugh. "I hardly noticed those."

John chuckled, rubbing his hands together. "Yup, it's a wonderful feeling to be a grandpa. But to tell you the truth, the most fun is watching Brandon become a dad. Takes me back twenty-odd years and makes me remember all over again what it felt like to hold Joanie in my arms for the first time."

"It's an amazing feeling, isn't it, when you hold that baby for the first time?" Kevin agreed.

"You know, a woman spends nine months bonding with that child and then gracefully steps into her role as a mother. But it just doesn't really hit a man until he's face to face with that little miracle. Then all at once, BANG, fatherhood is upon you," John commented.

"It's an overnight transformation," Kevin recalled. "Suddenly there's a new life depending on you."

"Brandon's hilarious to watch. He holds that baby every chance he gets. Sits and sings to her for hours. He coos away and makes faces at her . . . makes you wonder how this tiny little person, who can't even say a word, can turn a grown man into an absolute fool," John said with a chuckle. "Oh, and this was the best. . . . We were all standing around the hospital room visiting, when Brandon takes Gracie to go change her diaper. Joanie asked him what he was doing—the baby wasn't wet or dirty or anything. Brandon said he was just so excited to change his baby's diaper that he couldn't wait until she actually needed a change. He was just getting practised up!" John could not help but laugh. "That boy maybe doesn't realize it yet, but he's gonna get a lot of practice changing dirty diapers over the years."

Kevin chuckled along with John.

"Ah, but I guess I was the very same way when Joanie was born—not that I remember going and looking for diapers to change. But I was darn excited to be a dad. And Gracie looks just like Joanie did as a baby. It's completely *déjà vu*," the new grandpa remarked.

"It must be quite a feeling," Kevin said.

"You should be getting your shot at it soon enough," John remarked. "Just two more months to David and Leanne's wedding. We could very well be standing here having this same conversation in reverse in a year from now."

"I never thought of it, but you're right," Kevin replied. "So do you have to do something to acquire that wisdom of age, or does it just come to you?" he asked the "experienced" grandfather.

"It'll happen all on its own," John advised. "And as quickly as it comes, your wife will come along and remind you that it's just an illusion and that you're really just the same old fool you were before that baby elevated you a generation."

Kevin laughed. "I guess nothing in life comes that easy, does it?"

"Only pride," John answered with a chuckle.

✞　　　✞　　　✞

Amie and Katie gathered with their group of friends following Mass as usual. The excitement of the newest addition to their family was plainly evident.

"You should see that little baby," Amie told their friends. "She's *so* beautiful."

"And you thought Joanie and Brandon would make ugly babies?" questioned Daniel Schultz.

"Of course not," exclaimed Amie, backhanding her friend on the shoulder. "I've never seen an ugly baby," she remarked, emphatically.

"Exactly," said the guitar player, pointing a finger at the new auntie, his brown eyes proudly making his point.

"But Gracie is *so* cute." Amie cooed as she spoke. "She has the cutest little feet and toes. And her fingers are so long and tiny all at the same time,"

"And Brandon's *so* cute," Katie added in. "That man was born to be a daddy."

"I bet," replied Kyle.

"He's so in love with that little girl. He can't take his eyes off her," Katie remarked.

"That's how it should be," Kyle stated with a smile.

"Don't tell me this is making you think about fatherhood and marriage?" Amie threw out, in her typical pick-on-Kyle fashion.

"Hey, I've never been opposed to the idea. . . . Why can't I get you to understand this concept of waiting?" he asked, his hands held up in exasperation.

Amie giggled. "I'm just bugging you, Kyle, 'cause you're so much fun to bug. I think all you guys will make amazing dads someday."

"So do I," commented Samantha. She and Krystal were now Sunday regulars at St. James parish. Krystal was still just coming out for the company. She had no strong convictions about faith, but she loved the atmosphere and fellowship in this rare gem of a parish. Samantha was now totally committed to becoming Catholic and was planning on joining the R.C.I.A. that fall. Amie had agreed to be her sponsor.

Samantha looked up at Josh Forsythe, standing next to her. He smiled down at the dark-haired girl, who stood a whole foot shorter than he. Reaching over, he took her hand in his.

"What gives with this?" asked Amie, noticing the public display of affection. Everyone knew that Samantha and Josh had feelings for each other, but they had never made an official statement of it.

Samantha started giggling. She pulled Josh's hand up in front of her and held on to it with both hands. Looking up at the tall man, she waited for him to answer the question. All eyes were on the young couple.

"Samantha has agreed to court with me," Josh announced, to the squeals and delight of all the girls in the circle, except Krystal.

After the excitement of the moment wore off, Amie turned to Krystal and asked, "Aren't you happy for them?"

"Of course I am," Krystal stated, as if it should be obvious. "Sam's my best friend. It's just old news to me, now."

Samantha laughed and looked at Amie. "We told Krystal last night when Josh brought me home."

"True," Krystal commented, "it only became official last night. But I would've had to have been blind to not have seen this one coming. You should see this girl—she's almost impossible to live with. I tell you, if that's what falling in love does to a girl, I'm okay to wait for a while."

Everyone laughed at Krystal's remarks. She was one tough cookie: there to have a good time, but not quite ready to give herself over to any cause—not even romance, in spite of all her big talk.

"But I'm afraid it's going to have to be a long distance courtship for this Jolly Green Giant and Little Green Sprout," Josh said with humour, as he put his hand around Samantha's shoulder.

She laughed, looking up at him and nudging her shoulder into his rib cage. Everyone laughed in amusement.

"I'm moving back home this week," he went on to explain. "I had my convocation last Friday, and I'm finished here in the city. My dad needs help back on the farm, and I'll be there full-time from now on."

"That's sad," said Ann Ledoux. "You two finally begin a romance, and Josh is gone." Her voice was sympathetic, as she looked at Samantha.

"It'll be fine," said Samantha, the smile on her face undiminished. "It's only an hour-and-a-half drive. And having Josh gone will be less distracting for me while I finish up my course at Stettler."

"I'll be around enough," Josh said, looking at the girl beside him, with a twinkle in his eye. "In fact," he added, turning to Kyle, "I was wondering if I could stay at your place when I come to town to visit? I won't have my own place here anymore, and I certainly wouldn't stay at Sam's and Krystal's. I wouldn't want to give rise to scandal," he added with a little laugh.

"What could *possibly* be scandalous with you two?" Krystal questioned in full exasperation. "You've got more don'ts than do's on that list of guidelines you showed me last night," she said, with much sarcasm. "You're not kissing, you're not spending time alone together . . . what's the difference between now and before you started courting?" Her eyebrows were lifted as she stared down the couple, standing across the circle of friends from her.

Josh and Samantha laughed. Other friends quickly joined in on the laughter as well. They all understood. The concept of courting was not foreign to any of them. But they all found Krystal's take on the situation to be very amusing.

"You can stay at my place any time you want," Kyle told his friend, still chuckling over Krystal's remarks.

"And that goes for me, too," Daniel offered. "We're right here in town. My folks won't mind at all. And you won't have as far to drive as you would out at the Bander's," he pointed out.

"Thanks, guys," Josh responded, with a nod. "I didn't think it'd be a big deal for you. I figured you'd all be supporters of the cause."

"And I think it's wonderful that you two are taking this courtship thing so seriously," Katie observed. "I never saw a happier couple than Joanie and Brandon. And they didn't kiss until the altar," she told Krystal.

Krystal looked at the seventeen-year-old girl: sweet, but obviously totally naïve. "What would be the point of waiting to kiss? What if you get to the altar, say all your 'I do's', and then discover that the guy kisses like a wet fish?" she asked, looking at Samantha, in challenge of this ridiculous concept.

"I'll take my chances, Krystal," Samantha replied, shaking her head, a little too embarrassed to look up at Josh after Krystal's wet-fish comment.

"Don't worry, Sam," Josh said, patting her on the shoulder, "I'll work on my fish lips between now and then." He turned to Krystal, making fish lips.

Krystal burst out laughing at the tall, lanky, farm boy. "You'll certainly have enough time on your hands out there on the farm, Josh. And besides, you needed to find somethin' to do to keep yourself busy *and* thinking about Sam, all at the same time."

Everyone laughed.

"Well, that's wonderful news," Amie jumped back into the conversation. "I think we should celebrate. Why don't we get together for a big brunch today and then play some ultimate Frisbee or something?"

There was a general, enthusiastic, consensus among the group of friends. Kyle offered his place, knowing that his parents would not mind at all. Everyone agreed to go home, get changed, and meet out at the Bander's for one o'clock.

"You two ladies need a ride?" he offered to Amie and Katie.

"We first have to go home and get changed," Katie replied.

"That's no problem," he said, sticking to his offer. He was used to chauffeuring the girls around. It was never a big deal.

"That'd be great," Amie answered. "Mom and Dad left the Toyota with Maggie for a few days so she can get back and forth to the hospital to see Joanie and Gracie whenever she wants."

"Oh, she's *so* cute," Katie cooed, at the sound of her little niece's name.

"Well, if you two aunties want to go now, I'll drive you by your place and wait for you to get ready."

The girls spoke with their folks, made plans, and took off with Kyle for the day. Amie got into the front seat and Katie in the back of Kyle's little Ford Escort, with him holding the doors open for them both.

"How'd you learn to be such a gentleman?" Katie inquired of their older friend, as he got into the driver's seat.

"My dad taught us. Made us practise on our mom," he said with a laugh.

"Well, don't ever stop," she said.

Kyle laughed and winked at her, as he turned around to back the vehicle out of the church parking lot.

"What an exciting weekend!" Amie said, full of enthusiasm. She held her hands together, turning half-way around in her seat to see both Kyle and Katie as she spoke. "First Joanie and Brandon have their baby. Then Sam and Josh start a courtship."

Kyle nodded as he drove. Katie smiled at her sister.

"It just makes me want to go out and fall in love and get married," Amie stated, in complete Amie-style.

Kyle laughed and shook his head.

Katie turned to Kyle and asked, "Do you think this girl is ever going to settle down and get her head out of the clouds?"

"As much as I hope she does," Kyle told the younger sister in the backseat, "I hope Amie never stops being Amie."

He smiled at the girl in the passenger seat of his car. Amie shook her head and laughed at her friend who was driving. "Scary a thought as that may be, Kyle, you'll probably get your wish," she told him.

✝   ✝   ✝

Maggie tapped on the hospital room door. She waited for a response before entering.

"I'm here," Joanie called out in a hushed voice from behind the curtain.

Maggie stepped around to find her sister, cuddled up beside a little bundle on her bed.

"Auntie Maggie's here to see you, Gracie," Joanie said. She turned her eyes from her baby to her sister and smiled. "Nice to see you, Maggie."

"Can I hold her?" Maggie asked.

"Absolutely," Joanie said, sitting up so that she could rewrap Gracie properly before handing her over to the auntie.

"You're good at that," Maggie said. "I feel like I'm all thumbs when I go to hold her."

"Oh, Maggie, you held her yesterday, and you were just fine. And it hasn't been that long since you held a baby everyday," Joanie said. "Why are you so nervous?"

"It was always different with the little kids. They were my siblings. I don't know . . . it's not like Mom and Dad would have appreciated me dropping them, either. I think I'm getting old or something," Maggie confessed.

Joanie chuckled. "You are such a Maggie."

Maggie began to relax with the little bundle in her arms, as she bounced gently back and forth. "It's all coming back to me."

Joanie shook her head. "Pull up a chair and stay awhile," she told her sister, pointing to the chair beside the window.

Maggie sat down, without interrupting her rocking motion.

"So, how's Auntie Maggie these days?"

"Wonderful," Maggie said, smiling down at the baby. She continued to talk in a whisper, telling Mary Grace her good news. "It's official. I spoke with Sr. Charlotte last week, and I'll be beginning my novitiate with the Sisters of the Immaculate Conception starting Monday."

"Oh, Maggie, I'm so happy for you," Joanie said, a big smile coming over her face. "Are you completely at peace with this now?"

"Completely," Maggie replied, looking eye to eye with her sister. "Jesus and I have had a few really good heart-to-hearts in prayer. I just want to move on with religious life in the biggest way. And as for Charles and me, we've . . ." she stumbled, not knowing how to explain it. "Well, we just understand each other," she said with real serenity. "Whatever feelings were there before are past. He's completely supportive of my call to religious life and so respectful of me. And I'm just so glad to be able to still be his friend and to have everything comfortable between us. He's a wonderful man. But in the end, I couldn't help but choose my first love."

Joanie smiled. She knew Maggie was where she belonged—beaming like any girl in love would.

Maggie went on, "Once I had made that final choice for Jesus, all those feelings for Charles seemed to fade away. I'm so glad I never told him outright how I had felt. Some things are just better left unsaid. I don't think I could have handled it if he had told me exactly how he felt," she admitted. "I'm glad he's such an honourable man. And you know what, Joanie?"

Joanie shook her head, waiting for Maggie to go on.

"I learned a big lesson about guarding my heart. I am going to be so careful about how I interact with guys from now on," Maggie stated.

"We all have to be," Joanie agreed. "No person is beyond being tempted. And we can't take our vocations for granted. We have to work at them—keep the love alive and keep the fire burning—even when the feelings aren't so strong."

Maggie nodded and looked back down at Mary Grace. She gently kissed the child on the forehead.

"I wonder what kind of plan God has for her?" Maggie mused.

Joanie smiled and watched the auntie and baby have a quiet moment. A knock on the door announced Daddy's arrival back on the scene.

Brandon came around the curtain and saw Maggie. "Hey, Auntie Maggie?" His voice revealed his surprise to see her.

"You *can't* have her back," Maggie said, with a smile at her brother-in-law.

Brandon laughed. "Enjoy," he told her. He stepped over and gave his wife a kiss. "How're you doing?"

"Excellent," she answered.

"Here." He snuck a box of chocolates out from inside his jacket. "I brought you some contraband," he told her, taking off the jean jacket and hanging it on the back of a chair.

"Oh, thank you," Joanie said, opening up the box. "I can't believe how much I'm craving chocolate these days. Here, Maggie, have some with me."

"That's for you," Maggie said.

"Maggie . . . passing up chocolate?" Joanie questioned. "That's just not right. Here, take some or I'll be insulted." Joanie pushed the box toward her sister.

Brandon picked it up and passed it along for Maggie to take some.

"Thanks," she said, giving in to her love for chocolate. As she reached over to take a few from the box, her eyes caught sight of Brandon's arm, covered with bruises. "What in the world happened to your arm, Brandon?"

Brandon laughed, looking down at the purple marks on this left arm. "That, Maggie, is what your sister did to me during labour."

"You're kidding?" the girl exclaimed. She turned to her sister, sitting on the bed eating chocolates.

Joanie smiled back at Maggie, and shrugged her shoulders meekly.

"Never under estimate the strength of a woman fighting for the life of her child," Brandon advised Maggie.

"I had no idea I was holding on that tightly," Joanie said. "Why didn't you say something to me?"

Brandon looked at his wife, with one eyebrow raised in question. "You think I would have dared to interrupt you at that point in time, dear? It was a small sacrifice to pay, compared to what you were going through."

"No kidding," Maggie agreed. "I think Brandon got the better part of the deal, bruises and all."

Brandon chuckled and nodded. "No arguments there."

"So, any thoughts on fatherhood?" Maggie asked the new dad.

"I'm overwhelmed by how thrilled and terrified I am all at the same time," he told his sister-in-law.

"Really?" she asked, in surprise. "What would terrify you?"

"Jerks like I once was," he confessed. He looked down at the baby in Maggie's arms. "I can't imagine what I would do to any guy who came around and tried to do with my daughter the stuff I used to do with other men's daughters." He looked over at Joanie.

She smiled at him. She was not uncomfortable talking about Brandon's past, as long as he kept out the details—which he always did. He told her it was enough to try to block out all the memories, without giving them wings to fly freely by discussing them.

"No," Brandon said. "I am just so committed to raising Gracie to know and love Our Lord, to understand and live out purity, and to follow in the footsteps of her mother."

"Good for you," Maggie said.

"And it just makes me aware of the awesome responsibility I've been given," he said. "I hold her and realize—I'm completely unworthy to be her father. Then I remember, she's got a bigger and better Father than I. She's just on loan. It humbles a man, for sure."

"I can't imagine a better choice of parents for God to have loaned her to," Maggie said, with a big smile. She stood up and brought the baby to her daddy.

Brandon took his baby in his arms and kissed her tenderly on the cheek. Gracie turned her face toward her daddy. "I think someone's hungry," he said to Joanie.

Joanie laughed. "Of course she is. It's only been an hour since she last ate."

Mary Grace started moving around in her father's arms. Gradually one eye opened, and then the other. Brandon looked down into the eyes of his little girl. "I love you, Gracie," he whispered. "I promise to take care of you and protect you your whole life long."

Gracie stretched her face forward with her eyes open, looking toward her daddy's voice.

He pulled her up close to his face and kissed her forehead again. "And that's a promise I won't ever break."

Chapter 58

Brandon came to the hospital to pick up Joanie and baby Mary Grace on the Monday. Joanie had signed all the discharge papers with the nurse. She had dressed Gracie up in a little pink sleeper in which to take her home and was sitting in the chair waiting for Brandon to come get them.

He arrived all smiles, like a little boy who was all excited to go out and play. He kissed his wife and took the baby from her. He then kissed his daughter and put her into the car seat, fastening up her seat belt. "You got that suitcase all packed and ready?" Brandon asked his wife.

"It's ready to go," Joanie replied. "I just wish I were," she muttered.

"Hey?" he questioned. "What's wrong? I thought you were all ready to go? I mean, you were excited about it this morning when I talked to you. What gives?"

Joanie's eyes filled with tears and she closed them.

"Hey, honey," Brandon said, putting the car seat down on the bed with Gracie in it. He walked over to his wife, pulled her up from the chair and took her in his arms. "What's happening?"

"I'm just scared. I'm not sure if I can handle being a mom all on my own. It just feels like too big a responsibility all of a sudden." She kept her head on Brandon's chest as tears flowed down her face. "I need a Kleenex," she told him, with a giggle. "I'm messing up your jean jacket."

Brandon chuckled. "Don't worry about that." He reached over to the side table and took a tissue for his wife. He passed it to her and let her wipe her nose. "I've got the next three weeks off work. I'll be there to help you—make sure you get plenty of rest. You're going to be great; you're just feeling a little overwhelmed at the moment. Wait 'til we get outside and you get some fresh air. It's a beautiful day to be bringing our Gracie home."

He moved his head down and turned it to the side in an attempt to catch Joanie's eyes with his. "I can't imagine anyone better prepared for motherhood than you, Joanie. You helped your mother raise seven other children. This is going to be a walk in the park for you."

Joanie gave him half-a-smile. "This feeling of total inadequacy just came over me so suddenly. I can't believe how quickly I can go from ecstatic to depressed. The nurses warned me about day three. I guess this must be what they mean when they talk about baby blues." She laughed at herself. "I hope I can get a grip, or you'll be taking care of more than just a baby when we get home."

Brandon laughed and took his wife back in his arms, holding her gently one last time before they left. "I'll baby you both . . . quite happily. What else am I going to do for the next three weeks? Come on." He stepped over to the bed to pick up the big suitcase. With his other hand he picked up the car seat.

"Let me help," Joanie offered, reaching toward the baby.

"Sure," he said. "Jump on the car seat with Gracie to help balance it out with this suitcase for weight."

Joanie smacked Brandon on the chest, and he laughed.

"I'm okay. You just relax and carry those flowers." He motioned with his head toward the few bouquets of flowers that Joanie had already arranged and packaged to take home.

"Oh my goodness, I just about forgot my flowers." She ran back to the windowsill to get them.

The new little family made their way out of the hospital. As Joanie stepped outside, she took a deep breath. It had rained that morning and there was still a wonderful smell in the air—springtime. Brandon told her to wait at the bench with their stuff, and he would go pull up the vehicle.

Joanie sat with the car seat on her lap. Mary Grace was asleep. Joanie stared at her daughter and prayed in silence.

Oh, Mary, Mother of God and mother of us all, teach me to be a good mom for Mary Grace. Help me when I feel overwhelmed. Let me love her as you loved your baby, Jesus.

Thank You, sweet Jesus, for the gift of motherhood You've given me through this precious child. Keep her safe and healthy. Guide me to direct her on the path of righteousness, so that she will live her life in purity and holiness, for Your name's sake. Amen.

Joanie sighed and looked up from the car seat. It was a beautiful day. In fact, it was a perfect day: blue skies with white puffy clouds that created lovely shapes.

Out of the corner of her eye she saw Brandon step out of a vehicle. Confused, she turned her attention fully toward her husband. Her eyes grew big.

"How's this for a welcome home gift?" he asked her, standing beside their new—used—red, Honda Civic.

"Brandon! When did you pick it up? I had forgotten all about it."

"I went and signed the papers on Saturday, got it all licensed in your name and ready to go," he said proudly, as he stepped up to kiss his wife, still sitting on the bench holding the baby.

She smiled as she looked over at her new red car: the first car she had ever owned, herself. "Thank you, sweetheart. This is a wonderful surprise."

Brandon picked up the suitcase and heaved it into the trunk of the little car. "It fits," he announced with amazement.

Joanie shook her head at him. "Funny," she retorted. She stood up and walked toward the vehicle with Mary Grace. Brandon came forward and opened the passenger side back door. He took the car seat from his wife and set the baby inside the car. Joanie went to get the flowers and walked around to the driver's side.

"You want to drive it home?" he asked, somewhat surprised.

"No, silly, I want to sit with Gracie in the back," she answered, getting into the driver's backseat door.

Brandon laughed. "I guess I get to be chauffeur." He helped Joanie get in with all the flowers and then closed the door for her. Hopping into the driver's seat he turned to look at his wife in the rear-view mirror. "We're going home, thanks be to God, with a beautiful, healthy, baby girl."

Joanie smiled back at him through the mirror. "Amen," she said.

"And by the way, you really do look good in red." He waggled his eyebrows at his wife, looking at her through the rear-view mirror.

Joanie giggled. She was feeling better. Life was going to be okay. It was going to be better than okay. Life was absolutely full of promise and excitement. She breathed in deeply, looking over at their baby. The adventure of parenthood was about to really begin.

✟   ✟   ✟

Two weeks after Mary Grace was born, her parents brought her to St. James parish to be baptized into the body of Christ. It was an exciting day for the whole family. Proud grandparents were all in attendance, including James Vaughn, and Great-grandma and grandpa Ledoux. Justine and Mark, the godparents, were thrilled to stand up for their friends and share in the new life—the spiritual rebirth—of this little child. Aunties and uncles, as young as four and seven years old, buzzed around in excitement, before Mass began. Judy wondered if she would ever get the little ones to sit still throughout the Mass.

Fr. Steve warmly welcomed the congregation, including all their guests, to St. James parish, to the celebration of the Holy Sacrifice of the Mass, and to the baptism of the soon-to-be newest member of their congregation.

During his homily, Fr. Steve spoke about the wonderful gift of baptism. "How appropriate it is that we should celebrate this great sacrament in the context of the Mass, for indeed, the Eucharist is the source and summit of our faith. And today that faith is being passed on to Mary Grace.

"Joanie and Brandon, as you take this precious child home today, I want to remind you of this important truth. No matter what you do for her as parents in the natural realm—as you feed her and clothe her, teach her to walk and talk, give her opportunities to learn, study music, play sports, travel the world, and experience life—none of that will amount to anything at all if you fail in this task—to raise her as a child of God, to know, love, and serve the Lord in this life so that she might be happy with Him for all eternity.

"In Romans eight we read, 'We are children of God, and if children, then heirs, heirs of God and fellow heirs with Christ.' As she enters today into the waters of baptism, Mary Grace is entering into a share of Christ's life as an adopted daughter of God. She is destined for eternity—to share in the very life and love of the blessed Trinity. This is her heritage—and ours—as children of God.'

"Teach her this truth. Walk with her in this truth. And grow with her in this truth. There is no greater gift that you can give her. There is no higher purpose than this to which you have both been called as parents."

Fr. Steve challenged the entire congregation to reflect on their own baptismal promises and to recommit themselves to the life of faith that had been given to each of them in the waters of baptism.

After completing the opening rites of the ceremony, Fr. Steve invited the parents and godparents to bring forward Mary Grace for baptism. They approached the font, with Brandon carrying his daughter in his arms. Joanie stood by her husband, holding onto his arm as she gazed at her little baby girl.

This new life had come into being because of Brandon and Joanie's love for each other, because of the openness to life that they embraced in their marriage, and because God had called this little soul, from the beginning of time, to fulfill a very special purpose in creation. Her journey in faith was now about to begin.

Fr. Steve reached down into the baptismal font. Three times he scooped water into his hand, and poured it over the infant's head, as he said the words over Mary Grace of Christ's great commission for His Church. "Mary Grace, I baptize you in the name of the Father, and of the Son, and of the Holy Spirit."

✟   ✟   ✟

There was a wonderful celebration following Gracie's baptism, with family and friends sharing in a potluck meal down in the parish hall. Though still tired as a new mom, Joanie was thrilled to be out. The previous two weeks, adjusting to motherhood, had been rewarding but challenging.

"You remind me of your mother," Grandma Ledoux said to Joanie, as she took her turn to sit down and visit with the new mom.

"I bet *your* mother said the same thing to my mom when she started out, as well," Joanie returned, with a smile.

"Probably," agreed Grandma, remembering her own mother. "I can't tell you what a blessing it is for me to see the family growing into the next generation. Each child is such a gift and such a sign of hope." She reached down and touched Mary Grace on the forehead.

"Here," Joanie said, passing the sleeping baby to her great-grandmother.

Grandma Ledoux gently took the child in her arms and kissed her on the forehead. "Mmm," she said, breathing in the smell of chrism on Gracie. "I've always said that this must be what heaven smells like." She closed her eyes and breathed in the sweet perfume of the holy oil again.

Joanie smiled and put her head on her grandma's shoulder. "I love you, Grandma," she said quietly.

Grandma Ledoux smiled and turned to kiss Joanie on the head. "I love you, too, sweetheart," she whispered back to her granddaughter.

"I hope I can be as good a mother and grandmother as you've been," Joanie said, gazing at her baby, held so lovingly in the wrinkled hands of experience.

"You will be a wonderful mother, Joanie. You already are," her grandma assured her. "It doesn't take a university degree to become a mother. It just takes love, a little common sense . . . and a whole lot of prayer."

Joanie chuckled.

"I think you and Brandon will do just fine raising up a family of God-fearing children. And they're going to make a difference in the world. Every life does. But when a child grows up to be a responsible, strong, Christian adult—they change the world around them for the better." Grandma Ledoux gazed at the baby in her arms. "I know moms don't get a lot of worldly recognition—especially in our society. But I don't think there's anything more noble that you could do with your life, dear. I know that being a research-reporter on the local news each evening is probably much more glamorous."

Joanie shrugged her shoulders and smiled at her grandma.

"And if you ever were to become a famous singer someday—and you have the talent for it, my dear—just think of the prestige that would come from everyone knowing your name."

Joanie sat and listened without comment, her head resting again on her grandma's shoulder.

"But I'll guarantee you this much—there won't ever be a fan who loves you and admires you more than this little child will. You don't even have to sing in tune. You just have to love her."

Joanie sat up and nodded. She could not think of anything to say to add to what her grandmother was telling her, so she simply cherished the moment of being able to sit back and receive the wisdom of age, delivered with such love.

"I know it's hard at times to spend day after day doing the same old thing—changing diapers, preparing meals, cleaning a house, disciplining children. At times it can feel like you're stuck in some sort of time machine where every day just repeats itself over and over again, and you can't seem to move on to something new and more exciting."

Joanie laughed. It had only been two weeks since Gracie was born, and already the new mom had a sense of what her grandmother was saying.

"But it's the faithfulness to your daily duty," Grandma went on, "that is shaping you in holiness, my dear. Whatever you find yourself called to, moment by moment, in all the tedious, repetitive acts of motherhood, is exactly what God has called you to do. And He's pouring out His grace into your life and on your family as you respond faithfully to the call of the moment. Never underestimate the power of obedience to God's will. I once heard a very wise woman say, 'I'm changing the world, one diaper at a time.'"

Joanie laughed.

"That's the call of motherhood, Joanie, and it's more important than you'll ever realize here on earth. We won't ever see, until we get to heaven, what a difference we've made here during our lifetime. You won't win prizes or awards—though I hope and pray you get your fair share of dandelion bouquets. . . . But the heavenly rewards await us all on the other side." Grandma Ledoux turned and looked Joanie in the eye.

Joanie's eyes had tears in them, as she was painfully aware that Grandma Ledoux was approaching ever nearer to that heavenly reward. She prayed that the Lord would bless them with many more years with her beloved grandparents.

"Oh, now look what I've done," said the grandma with a laugh. "I should know better than to talk like that to a new mom—too many hormones to deal with."

Joanie laughed and wiped her eyes. She gave her grandma a kiss on the cheek and said, "Thank you, Grandma. I'd rather have a good cry with you than anyone else right now. And believe me—I've done my share of crying these past few weeks."

"Well, don't you worry about that," Grandma Ledoux advised. "That'll pass by soon enough. You'll start to get more sleep, and you'll start to feel like yourself all over again. And then, just wait for the adventure of motherhood to kick in," she said with a twinkle in her eye.

"I love you so much, Grandma," Joanie said, putting her arm over her grandma's shoulder and giving it a little squeeze.

"And I do, you," replied the white and curly haired woman.

Just then Grandpa Ledoux stepped forward and asked for his turn to hold his newest great-grandchild. As he took the baby in his arms he looked up at Joanie and said, "My goodness, you make beautiful babies. I sure hope you and Brandon intend to have a whole lot more."

"Oh, we do, Grandpa," Joanie answered. "Don't worry."

"I can't hope and pray for a better blessing in your life than having children . . . as many as the Lord sees fit to send. I know some people can't have big families—just doesn't work out for them. What counts is being open to life, Joanie," he told her. "Never limit the Lord's ability to work through your marriage to bring new life into the world. When you get to be my age, you'll understand why it's worth more than all the diamonds and treasures of the world."

"I have an idea already," Joanie told him. "But I imagine I'll only appreciate it all the more as the years pass by."

"Well, I hope you don't mind me walking off with this little angel," he said, "but I've got some showing off to do."

Joanie and Grandma Ledoux laughed as they watched the proud great-grandfather stroll around the hall, bragging about the newest member of his family.

Chapter 59

Amie, Katie, and their friends helped with clean-up in the kitchen after the potluck brunch. It had become tradition for the dads to round up the teenagers before they could slip away and put them to work. "What difference does it make what you're doing?" John Collins reminded them. "As long as you're all together, you'll be having fun. Besides, you all have the advantage of youth. You can get these dishes done in no time and still have plenty of energy to spare." The group of friends never complained. They got down to business, got the job done—with a few tea towel fights—and then made plans for the rest of their day together.

"Everyone's welcome to come out to my place and play football," Kyle offered. "We can have a campfire tonight and roast hotdogs for supper."

"Oh, I'm so glad campfire season's back," Amie said. "It's the best part of summer."

"Be sure to bring along some guitars," Kyle told Daniel and Caleb.

They agreed to meet at four o'clock at the Bander's, and everyone parted ways. Amie went back upstairs to the church to gather up the music from choir that morning. The group had left everything lying around to go down for the Baptism lunch. Kyle walked up with her to give his friend a hand.

"I wanted to ask you about something, Amie," he began, while collecting the loose sheet music lying around.

Amie looked at Kyle curiously. He almost appeared awkward—which was totally out of character for him. "What's up?" she asked, as she stopped organizing the music into her folder. She sat at the piano bench and waited for Kyle to go on with what he had to say.

Kyle took a quick breath and sat down on the choir chair nearest the piano bench. Looking intently at Amie he forced himself past his fear. "I was just wondering if you wouldn't mind being my escort . . . for my grad dance at the Tech School."

"Kyle!" Amie exclaimed, shaking her head. "You're such a goof!" she scolded. "Jeepers, you made it seem like there was something really awful you had to talk about."

Kyle shrugged his shoulders. "Sorry."

"And you make me so mad, too," she went on. "Why in the world would you ask *me,* of all people? Honestly, Kyle. I could come up with some great dates for you for your grad."

"I don't want some *great dates,*" he returned. "I'd rather go with you . . . as you are my friend, aren't you?"

"I'm not talking about strangers, Kyle," she informed him. "You'd be surprised how many girls have crushes on you—girls that you and I both know."

"I don't want to know," he told her. "I'm not interested."

"What's holding you back now?" Amie asked. "You're graduating from school, you'll be getting a job soon . . . isn't that what you were waiting for?"

"Yes," he agreed. "Nothing's holding me back. I just wanted to go with you. It's a dance, and since we took ballroom dance together, I figured you'd have a lot of fun."

"Well, thanks for thinking about me," Amie replied. She looked at him, weighing out the invitation. "It probably will be a lot of fun," she admitted. "Fine. I'll go with you. When is it?"

"A week from Friday."

"A week from Friday?" she yelled out. Then, remembering they were in the church, she began to whisper. "Kyle, why did you wait 'til now to ask?"

"I don't know," he replied, startled by her reaction.

"Well, maybe I have a life, too," she scolded, still in a hushed tone. "You don't just go asking a girl to your grad without giving her time to get ready for it."

"What's to get ready?" he asked, thoroughly confused.

"It's a grad," she pointed out. "I need something formal to wear." She grabbed at her skirt and stared intently at the boy across from her.

"Wear the one you wore at New Year's, that was nice," he suggested.

"Oh," she grumbled. "You are such a guy!"

"What?" he asked, raising his hands.

"That was a *winter* outfit," she explained. "It's summertime now, if you hadn't noticed."

"What you're wearing now looks great," he offered as a second suggestion.

"Kyle," she scolded again. "This is *not* a formal outfit. You just don't get it, do you?"

He shook his head and smiled apologetically. "I don't care what you wear, Amie. I just want to go with you and have fun dancing together."

Amie grunted under her breath. "I'll come up with something better than this," she assured him. "I'm not going to have all your friends at Tech School think you can't come up with a real date—even though you can't . . . or simply won't!"

Kyle laughed and stood up to gather in the rest of the music lying out on the music stands. "By the way . . . thanks."

"You're welcome," she said, still in a disgruntled tone.

Kyle passed her a handful of music, and she quickly sorted it into her choir folder. He smiled at his friend; she laughed and smiled back at him.

"Do you and Katie want a ride out to my place?" he offered.

"That would be lovely, sir," Amie replied, doing her best to restore peace to their relationship.

They got up to leave the church, genuflecting on their way out.

Thank You, Jesus, Kyle offered quickly in prayer, looking up at the life-size crucifix at the front of the church. *That went about as well as I could have expected it to go.*

✤   ✤   ✤

Amie and Katie caught a ride back home that night with Ann and Jocelyn. It was late when they got in, but their parents were still up, talking in the kitchen. The two sisters chattered away to their parents about their day and evening as they looked around the kitchen for a bedtime snack.

"Sounds like you all had fun," said Judy. "Ah, to be young and free again."

"I didn't think you had it so rough," John commented to his wife.

"Not rough—but not free," she stated.

"Well, I'll just have to work on freeing you up a little more, dear. Don't worry, summer holidays are just around the corner." He stood up and stretched. "But I'd better get to bed or I'll never finish off this school year in one piece. I've got a busy week ahead with testing and evaluations and then report cards . . . just one of the many joys of teaching."

Judy smiled at her husband. "I'll be up right away, dear."

"Hey, Amie," John turned to his daughter, before leaving the room. "You going with Kyle to that grad next Friday?"

Amie threw a surprised look at her father. "How'd you know about it?"

"Antennae," he told her, motioning above his head. "Remember?"

"Seriously, dad," she said. "I never said anything about it yet to anyone."

"Not even me," Katie protested. "What're you talking about?"

John laughed. "It's a father's responsibility to know."

Judy looked at John curiously.

"Dad, how'd you know?" Amie persisted.

"Kyle came and asked me last week if he could take you," John confessed. "Seems he has a better sense of protocol than you—I notice you didn't bother to check it out with us before you said 'yes'."

"Well, I didn't think it'd matter with Kyle," Amie explained. "Why wouldn't you say 'yes' to me going? And it's not like it's a real date or anything . . . this is Kyle we're talking about."

Judy laughed and shook her head. She walked over and gave both Katie and Amie a kiss good-night, before she headed up to bed. "Be sure to mark it on the calendar, Amie. Okay?"

"Fine, Mom," Amie replied as her parents left the room.

"So, what's this about Kyle's grad?" Katie questioned, pouring herself a glass of milk. "You want some?" she asked, holding the jug out toward her sister.

"No, thanks," Amie replied. "Oh, Kyle asked me to his grad for Tech School," she explained. "I could come up with all kinds of nice girls for him to take—but he's just so shy about girls. He'd rather take me, 'cause there's no romantic pressure there at all. Now I just have to figure out what to wear to it." She opened the fridge door and stared inside, trying to decide what she wanted to eat. After a few moments she noticed a platter of cold hamburgers, left-over from supper. "Looks like Dad barbecued tonight," she commented, taking out the mayonnaise to spread on a burger. "I love cold burgers. You want one, too?"

"Sure," replied the younger sister. "So, what do you have in mind to wear?"

"I have no idea," Amie replied. "I don't have any formal stuff for this time of year." She spread mayonnaise onto two burgers and handed one to Katie. Taking a bite, Amie nodded her head—that's the taste she was going for. "Do you have anything I can borrow?" she asked, still chewing her mouthful of burger.

"No," Katie replied. "But I've got some great material that I could make into something for you. You remember that light-blue chiffon I bought on sale a few weeks ago? It's got a soft floral pattern in it," she described.

"Don't you want that for yourself?"

"Nah. I just bought it 'cause I couldn't resist—it was such a good price and such pretty material. The colour'll look great on you. I could make it into a nice sundress. And you could wear that little white bolero you have over it. It'll look really classy, Amie," the young fashion designer assured her.

"Sounds nice," Amie agreed. "We can look at it tomorrow after school. But I'd better head up to sleep, or I'll never get out of bed in the morning."

"That's one thing I still enjoy about home-schooling," Katie said, wiping up the counter and putting their dishes in the sink. "I can sleep in when I need to . . . and I'm sure tomorrow will be one of those days." She turned off the light switch as they left the kitchen, eating their cold burgers.

Amie checked to make sure the back door was locked and followed her sister up to their bedroom. It had been a great day, but she was good and tired. Nothing would have kept her awake. As soon as she hit the pillow, she was out.

✛ ✛ ✛

The next morning as Amie was getting ready for school, she started thinking about what her father had said the night before. Kyle did seem to have the right protocol in mind—for going out on a *date* with Amie. *This is not a date, though,* she told herself as she diffused her hair with the blow dryer. *I guess Kyle's just covering his bases. He's got a lot of respect for Dad and Mom and their views on courtship. I can't fault him for that. Still . . . he asked Dad last week and never bothered mentioning a thing to me until yesterday. Honestly, that guy's going to drive me nuts.*

She pulled up her hair with pins, allowing the long curls to hang loosely around her shoulders. Quickly doing her make-up, Amie ran down to get a bite to eat before she caught her bus to Stettler College.

Sitting on the bus, Amie reached into her purse for some lip gloss. Noticing her prayer card of St. Mary Magdalene, Amie took it out and smiled. She had carried it with her every day to class since Kyle had given it to her last fall. She stared at the card for a moment—thinking about the person who had given it to her. It was a typical Kyle-thing to do—totally thoughtful and completely unexpected.

Amie smiled, thinking about her friend. As much as he frustrated her at times, she could not think of a guy with whom she was better friends. He knew her so well. She placed the prayer card back in her purse and looked out the window as the bus crossed the river to go downtown.

Suddenly Amie's eyes grew wide. She quickly opened her purse and took the prayer card out once again. Staring at it in disbelief, a sickening thought came over her. *Oh, no,* she thought to herself. *Please tell me I'm wrong,* she said, as if to St. Mary Magdalene herself. Amie shook her head, refusing to accept the idea that was quickly taking form in her mind. *No!* It was impossible. Amie hung her head down, still looking at the card, feeling somewhat defeated. It *was* possible! Kyle just might have feelings for her. Kyle was asking her to his graduation, not because he was too shy to go with another girl, but because *Amie* was the girl with whom he wanted to go!

Huffing to herself, Amie put the prayer card back in her purse. She was angry, but she was not sure at whom she was angrier—Kyle or herself? *How long?* she wondered, trying frantically in her mind to think of a time or an event that she could recall that would have triggered Kyle to have become interested in her in that way. True, she had had a crush on him when she was about fifteen years old. But that was so long ago. All she remembered about that was how he had avoided her—like the plague. Surely he would not have avoided her like that had he been attracted to her. She suffered a moment's embarrassment, remembering what a fool she had made of herself around him. The crush lasted for several months and then passed, as most schoolgirl crushes do.

And this will, too, she told herself. *Kyle's just feeling attracted to me because he's finally free in his own mind to court a girl, and he has no idea where to start. That makes sense. We're such good friends, after all. But I'm really going to have to put the kibosh on this quickly, before it gets out of hand. I'll talk to him Thursday at band practice. I don't mind going to the dance with him—but we're definitely going to clear the air on this beforehand. . . . Wait, band practice is cancelled this week because of Kyle's finals,* she grimaced. *Fine—it can wait until Sunday, but then I'm definitely not letting it go on any longer.*

The bus arrived at the city transit stop down the block from her school. Amie was glad someone else was getting off there and had pulled the cord; she had been too absorbed in thought to have noticed where she was. She got off the bus and walked up slowly to the Stettler College building. Her mind was preoccupied by thoughts of her relationship with Kyle; she hoped that this would not ruin their friendship.

As the day unfolded Amie's thoughts kept returning to the issue of Kyle. She would oscillate between anger and sympathy toward her friend. It annoyed her to no end that she was having a hard time concentrating on her classes that morning. Thank goodness she was not out on the floor doing hair. She could only imagine what disasters she would have created with her mind so distracted. She was definitely going to have to set the record straight with Kyle if she was going to have any peace of mind.

"You okay today?" Samantha asked Amie at lunchtime. "You seem so quiet."

"I haven't seen you this quiet *ever*," agreed Krystal. "You got boy problems?" she teased, nudging her friend.

"Give me a break," Amie replied. "I think I'm just overtired from the weekend. It was a lot of work getting ready for Gracie's Baptism. You two should have been there—it was really nice. And then we all got together for football and a campfire last night. You missed out on a great time."

"A girl's gotta get home sometime," Krystal said. "My mom puts a lot of pressure on me to come home at least once a month. I always hate missing out on what's happening back here, though, so don't rub it in."

"Sorry," Amie replied. "How was your weekend?" she asked, turning to Samantha.

"Awesome," Samantha replied. "Josh came and picked me up, and we drove home to visit my folks. They just love him. He fits in totally with my family, and my younger brother thinks he's the best thing since sliced bread."

"That's great," Amie said with a smile. "I think it's really important for a boyfriend to get along with a girl's family—or vice versa. It takes so much pressure off a relationship when that support is there."

"You bet it does," Samantha agreed. "And it helps when best friends are supportive, too" she said, throwing a look at Krystal.

"What?" Krystal asked, defensively. "I'm supportive of you and Josh. I've never said anything against it."

"No," Samantha agreed. "But you sure get frustrated with me when I talk about it."

"No, I don't. I'm just jealous . . . and you know it. That doesn't mean I don't think he's a great guy and all. I don't even want a boyfriend right now, myself," Krystal told her friends. "I just wish I had as much a sense of direction in my life as you two have. On one hand, I'd love to find a great guy, settle down, and get married. On the other hand, I don't want to tie myself down to that kind of responsibility yet. And . . . I don't know," she added, trying to think through her feelings. "I just see how you both have such strong religious convictions, and I don't have that at all. And I keep wondering how that would change me if I did. I feel afraid of losing myself if I were to *'give my life over to Christ,'"* she said, accentuating the popular phrase.

Amie laughed and shook her head at her friend. "Krystal, I hope you realize that we think you're a wonderful person, just the way you are. It'd be a lie for me to say that I didn't care about you finding Christ. But it's gotta come from the heart. You'll know when it feels right. And then you won't be losing yourself at all."

"You won't," agreed Samantha. "You'll feel like you've found a part of you that you never knew had been missing."

Krystal looked over at her best friend and roommate. "Well, I'm just glad you two don't put pressure on me. It's bad enough that I'm putting pressure on myself."

"Just relax," Amie told her. "And in the meantime, you and I can be old spinsters together. At the rate I'm going . . . I won't be finding me a man any too soon, either."

Krystal laughed and hunched herself over, pretending to knit.

"What a girl you are!" Amie said with a laugh, giving Krystal a gentle push on the shoulder.

She was glad to have her friends to take her mind off the Kyle-situation. *Somehow,* she assured herself, *it's going to work out all right. . . . I just know You won't let me lose that friendship over something so silly, Lord. And in the meantime, help me to feel less frustrated so I can go easy on Kyle when I do finally talk to him about it.*

Chapter 60

The week continued with Amie experiencing waves of anxiety over Kyle. She went back and forth between thinking she was just imagining the situation to being totally convinced that it was real. He had feelings for her and perhaps more than just a passing phase.

As she reflected on her last conversation with Kyle when he had asked her to his graduation, she recalled his awkwardness. Definitely that was a bad sign. And the fact that he had said, "Nothing was holding him back from pursuing a relationship with a girl—he just wanted to go with *her*," made Amie convinced that he was covertly admitting to her that she *was* more than just a friend—or a grad date—to him.

As Sunday approached, Amie felt sick about the whole thing. She had no idea how she was going to tactfully bring this up with Kyle. He was too good a friend for her to risk ruining their relationship. She would have to be sensitive, in a way that did not make too big a deal about the whole thing. *Just treat it lightly,* she told herself. *That way he'll be able to save face, and we'll be able to go on as friends.*

✝   ✝   ✝

Sunday following Mass, Amie waited to get a moment alone with Kyle. Their group of friends gathered around as usual, carrying on their regular tone of conversation—joking and teasing. Amie stood back quietly, watching Kyle intently every chance she could get, without him noticing. He smiled at her a few times, but there was an awkwardness behind the smile that left Amie very disconcerted.

Finally the group was breaking up for the day. There had been no plans in place to get together. The Collins family was getting together with the Ledoux families that afternoon out at their Uncle Jack and Auntie Karen's acreage. Her family would be leaving soon, and Amie was getting nervous that she was going to run out of time to talk with Kyle.

As Kyle said good-bye and was heading out to his vehicle, Amie quickly ran up to him and asked if they could talk.

"Sure," he said. "What about?"

"I'd like to talk to you alone, if you don't mind. I'll just walk you out to your car," she suggested.

They went up the stairs and out the front door of the church. Kyle pointed to the parking lot where his black Escort was parked. "So what's up, Amie?" he asked, cautiously.

Amie still was not sure how to approach the topic. She walked beside her friend silently. She wanted to wait until they were far enough away from anyone else overhearing their conversation.

Kyle waited for the girl to say something...anything...even a comment on the weather. But she said nothing until they reached his vehicle.

Kyle stopped and looked at the girl now standing before him, as he leaned against his car. She had a serious look in her eyes, and he became very nervous over what was coming next. He was not at all anxious to prompt her; he just waited for her to begin—when she was good and ready.

Taking a deep breath, Amie began. "Kyle, why did you ask me to your grad?"

"Because I needed an escort," he answered, carefully.

"Yes, but why did you ask *me?*" she reiterated the question with emphasis.

"Because you're my friend, and you like to dance?" he answered—questioning if he had got it right.

"Kyle," Amie scolded. "You know what I'm getting at—so don't make me come out and say it."

"Amie," Kyle said, looking straight at the girl, "I have no idea what you're getting at. I don't know what you want me to say to you."

"Kyle, you asked me to your grad because you like me, don't you?" she accused.

"Of course I like you, Amie," he replied, very collected in his thoughts. "We've been friends for years."

"Kyle," Amie said, clenching her teeth. "That's not what I mean and you know it. You *like me*, like me . . . don't you?"

Kyle closed his eyes momentarily. He had no idea how to deal with this situation. This was not exactly how he had pictured confessing his feeling to Amie—though he had long-anticipated her negative response. He opened his eyes again and looked at the girl. There was fire in her eyes.

"Admit it, Kyle," she said. "I'm not stupid. I think I've figured this out accurately, but I want to hear it from your lips."

"All right," he replied, defensively. "I like you, Amie. What do you want me to say?"

"You have feelings for me—more than a friend. Don't you?"

"Yes, as a matter of fact I do," he answered.

"Ohhhh," Amie growled, making a fist with her right hand. "I could just pound you," she said, shaking the fist now at the young man. "How could you go and do this? You know this is going to totally ruin our friendship, don't you? We'll never be able to be the same again, now that you've gone and got feelings for me! What were you thinking? Why would you do this to us?"

Kyle stood back and accepted the full force of Amie's venting. He made no effort to reply.

"Say something," she demanded. By now she was shaking two fists at his chest.

Kyle reached up and grabbed her hands, looking Amie in the eye. "I'm sorry," he said. "I'm not trying to ruin anything. And I never made any mention of my feelings for you for a reason—namely that I knew you'd want to kill me if I did."

Amie stared back at him, as he held onto her hands.

"All I did was ask you to my grad dance. I wasn't putting any pressure on you for anything more than that. If it upsets you this much, you don't need to feel obligated to come with me," he told her, gently bringing her hands down between them and letting go.

"Ah, Kyle," Amie said, softening her manner. "Of course I'm still going to go with you to your grad. What kind of friend do you think I am? I'm just so upset over figuring this out. I don't know how to deal with this at all. I love you too much as a friend to want to hurt you—but I don't have feelings for you, Kyle . . . not in that way. And how am I supposed to be around you, knowing how you feel about me?"

"Just be you, Amie. I'm not asking for anything from you. I want to be your friend, just like we've been for years. I've got three exams coming up this week and a graduation on Friday. I'm not looking for a girlfriend at the moment. My plate is plenty full," he assured her. "And I would never have asked you if it hadn't been that I'm graduating on Friday. But I can go alone. I don't need to take anyone with me. I just thought it'd be fun. I wasn't expecting you to go *figure everything out,* just because I asked you to come out with me to a dance."

Amie sighed and looked at Kyle, putting her hand on his shoulder. "I'll come with you, Kyle. I'm not going to leave you high-and-dry without an escort for your grad. Katie's making me a dress to wear and everything. I'm not about to back out now. I just wish I could do something to take away your feelings for me. I know I'm just going to end up hurting you and feeling awful—and we'll never enjoy the same friendship together again because of it."

"Let's just take this one step at a time, Amie," Kyle said, taking her hand in his again. "It's one dance, that's all. After that we can just go back to being friends, the way we've always been. And," he put up his other hand to stop her from objecting, "if we can't be friends, then we'll deal with it at that time. Okay?"

"Fine," she muttered, looking down at the ground. "But I just know what's going to happen, and I can't say that I'm happy about it at all."

Kyle chuckled and leaned forward to catch her eye with his. "Thank you."

Amie looked back up at the young man—one of her oldest and dearest friends. "You're welcome," she replied. "I've gotta get going. My family's going to be wondering where I am."

"Actually, I think they've found you," Kyle said, motioning with his head over Amie's shoulder.

She turned around to see her younger siblings running toward the family van parked across the lot from Kyle's vehicle.

He gave her hand a squeeze and let go of it. She forced a smile to offer to her friend. She felt like crying. Somehow it just felt like life had changed, beyond her control. She turned and walked away slowly, catching up to her family as they loaded into the van to head out to the farm for the day.

Through the window of the van, Amie watched Kyle as he started up his vehicle and pulled out of the parking lot. Tears filled her eyes; she kept her head turned away from her family members who were buzzing all around her. She wanted to scream at them all to shut up. As much as she loved her Uncle Jack and Auntie Karen—and all her Ledoux cousins—it was going to be a long day, surrounded by all this excitement and happiness.

This was a big burden on her heart, and she knew she could not share it with anyone—at least not yet—not her mother or father, not Ann or Katie . . . no one. She felt very alone as she watched Kyle drive up the street from the church and out of sight.

I guess I can tell You, Jesus, how I'm feeling . . . really lousy. I feel like I just lost my best friend.

✠   ✠   ✠

Amie did her best to perk up once she got out to the farm. The family started up a game of baseball, and Amie decided that if she just joined in on the fun she would have an easier time hiding her emotions from everyone. Ann asked her a few times what was bothering her, and Amie successfully averted the conversation each time. She had too much respect for Kyle to reveal this situation to anyone, even Ann. She just kept hoping that it would indeed pass, and Kyle would come to his senses. As long as she kept it all to herself there seemed to be room in her heart to hope that things could get back to normal.

That night when their family got home, Amie went up to her room to go to bed early. Her mother questioned her daughter's unusual behaviour, but accepted Amie's explanation that she was just not feeling well.

Amie sat in her pyjamas, staring at the dresser mirror right across from her bed. She did not even recognize herself. It seemed like a different person altogether looking back at her. Her zip was gone. She had never felt this bad about any relationship—not even when she broke up with Connor. Actually, she had felt so relieved about that, she found herself flying high for days. Now she felt like she could barely pick up her feet to walk.

She lay back on the bed and thought about Kyle and all their years as friends. After a few minutes she rolled onto her side, curled up into a little ball, pulled up her covers, and cried herself to sleep.

✝   ✝   ✝

Kyle found his way to the Catholic chapel on campus Sunday night. He knew it would be open, and he knew he needed time before the Blessed Sacrament to pray. There were a few students still around following Sunday evening Mass, quietly whispering, but they did not disturb the young man at all. He was deep in conversation with Jesus.

Okay, Lord, all the cards are on the table now. I didn't want it to go this way—but I can't change it now. Tell me what You want me to do. Show me what You expect from me. I'm so confused and . . . afraid. I don't want to lose Amie—but then again, I've never had her for anything more than a friend. But I don't want to lose that either.

Kyle sat quietly for a long time, listening in the silence of his heart. He knew that the time had come—one way or another he and Amie would never share the same friendship again. She was right when she had said that. Did that mean they could now make room in their relationship to become more than just friends? Maybe it simply meant that it was time for them to back off their friendship, so that they could each be free to be open to someone else. Kyle knew that to be true for himself. Until he could let go of Amie and step back from their friendship, he would never be able to let another woman into his heart. But it had never occurred to him that perhaps their friendship was blocking Amie's ability to be open to another man.

God, I don't know what You are calling either Amie or me to do with our lives. But I'm willing to be open to Your will. At least I'm wanting to be willing to be open to Your will. . . . You might have to actually help me be fully sincere in that. It's not that I don't want to accept Your will.

*And it's not that I don't trust You. It's just I have a lot of dying to myself
to do in order to fully accept whatever You show me to be Your will in this
relationship. So, I'm giving You permission to transform my heart, Lord.
Even if that requires open-heart surgery! Just help me be man enough to
accept whatever Your will is for my life and for Amie's.*

Again Kyle sat in silence. For almost an hour he sat and prayed. There
were no more words to his prayer. It was simply an offering up of his life
to his Creator. He knew that if he did all the talking, he would never hear
what God was trying to tell him. He was not at all sure—even with being
quiet—that the message was coming through. Still, he tried his best to
remove all the obstacles in his mind and in his heart so that Jesus could
speak to him and guide him on the path he should go.

Finally, Kyle stood up and left the chapel. The little red light flickering
by the Tabernacle assured him, as he genuflected, that Christ was truly
present there. There had been no major revelation to the young man that
night, but he felt better knowing that the Lord had heard his prayer and
that somehow He would make everything work for the good. If nothing
else, Kyle felt the peace inside himself that can only come by surrendering
oneself entirely to the will of the Father . . . whatever that might be.

✟   ✟   ✟

By Monday morning, Amie really did feel sick. She came down for
breakfast in her pyjamas and after a few minutes decided she was going
back to bed. Judy walked up to her daughter and placed her hand on Amie's
forehead to check for a fever.

"I'm fine, Mom," Amie insisted. "I just need to go back to bed and sleep
for a while. I'll call in sick to the college, but I don't think it'll be a big deal.
I've never missed a day of class before. But I feel way too dizzy and nauseated
to go in today."

"Well, get some sleep, sweetheart," her mother said. "I'll keep the
children as quiet as possible."

"Thanks, Mom."

Amie picked up the phone book to get the number for Stettler College
and made her call. The head instructor, Sherry, wished Amie well and told
her not to worry—she could get notes the next day to catch up.

Amie went back to bed. She slept until one-thirty that afternoon. When
she woke up, she was feeling better. She stayed in bed, contemplating life.
After a while she got up, took her photo album off the shelf and began
leafing through it, looking for pictures of her with Kyle over the years.

They had been so young when they met; the pictures dated back a long time. Amie could almost measure her lifetime by her friendship with this boy.

There was Kyle's birthday party when he turned eight—just weeks after they had met. It was the first time she had been to the Bander's acreage, and she had fallen in love with the place immediately. The children had spent the day climbing trees, and there was a picture of six of them hanging upside down from the branches of one of the Bander's big poplar trees that lined their driveway.

There was the time their families had gone fishing together, when she was just seven years old. Amie had caught her first fish that day. Kyle had helped her reel it in.

There was a parish picnic when she and Kyle had won the three-legged race together. They had beat Maggie and David, who had tripped just a few feet before the finish line. Amie laughed at the picture, remembering how she and Kyle had been the same height for so long.

There were youth group pictures of all sorts of events—from pool parties in the summer to skiing and snowboarding trips in the winter. Amie's first time snowboarding had been two winter's earlier. Kyle had taught her the basics, from getting off the chair lift to snow ploughing and turning. He had stuck with her the whole day; impressed with her ability to catch on so quickly, he had even begun teaching her how to carve. After a day of snowboarding, she swore she would never ski again; it had been so much fun—bruises and all.

There were pictures from band gigs and band parties over the years. How she loved making music with Kyle. She could not imagine what their band would have been like without that talented drummer. He quietly sat back at most practices, patiently waiting for everyone else to decide what they were going to do next. He always came in on time. His sense of rhythm was unmatched by any drummer she had ever heard—even professionals. Kyle just had that sensitive touch that made the music flow.

Amie lay on her side, turning page after page in the album. Kyle had been there for so much of her life. He was a good friend. He was so patient with her: sensitive to others—but no push-over himself. He had a strong faith, and Amie had always admired Kyle's determination and sense of integrity. He was a hard-working man. He had not wasted his life playing, but he knew how to enjoy himself when it was time for play. He had goals and dreams, and he did what he needed to do to achieve them. He was not at all afraid to make sacrifices. He was a gentleman at all times. She had never heard him say an unkind word about anyone—ever. He had a way of making Amie feel better whenever something was bothering her. Just a word or two from him seemed to repair any of her bad moods over the years.

She laughed to herself, looking at the pictures. She was so fond of Kyle. She appreciated him so much—for who he was, for everything about it him. She shook her head thinking of all the times she had teased him about not having a girlfriend. How could she have ever guessed that their relationship would come to this?

As she got near the end of the album, there was a picture of her and Kyle that had been taken at Joanie and Brandon's wedding. They had been dancing together and, when Maggie stepped up to take the picture, Amie moved in cheek-to-cheek with Kyle in fun. Amie slipped the picture out of the album and closed the book. Lying back on the bed she stared at it for a long time.

It was a good picture of both of them. Objectively speaking, Amie could see that they did look good together as a couple. There was just that energy between them that made them look so natural together.

She sighed. There *was* a good energy between them. She had never felt the same way for any other guy as she did for Kyle. True, it had always been just as friends for her, but as she stared at that picture she wondered if her feelings did not go deeper for Kyle than what she had realized.

She could not begin to imagine life without him. Technically speaking that probably was not a good position to be in, were she called to marry some other guy. Really, it was time for her childhood friendship with Kyle to go through transition. Either they would have to back off their friendship to make room for someone else in each of their lives, or . . .

Amie stared at the picture. "Or . . ." she whispered. "Oh . . . oh my goodness," she said, sitting up suddenly. She held up the picture in front of her in both hands. "Oh my goodness!"

She frantically went back over her thoughts of the past half-hour, since she had woken up. She had shared with Kyle so much of her life that he had become an inseparable part of her past—he was part of who she was and who she had become as a woman. She had described in Kyle everything she had ever wanted for herself in a husband. He was the unspoken standard by which she had measured every guy she had ever known. He was perfect—not that any person really is—but he was perfect for *her*.

"Oh, dear Jesus," she whispered. "I feel like you've just lifted a veil from my eyes. I feel like I'm seeing Kyle for the first time in my life . . . really seeing him."

She covered her mouth and continued to stare at the picture. The feelings welling up inside her heart were bigger than she could contain. She had never—ever—felt this way about any guy before in her life.

"How could this be?" she asked aloud, shaking her head back and forth. Turning to sit on the edge of her bed, Amie looked into the dresser mirror. Suddenly, as a smile lit up across her face, she saw a woman looking back at her whom she had never known. She was vibrant and full of life; her eyes, filled with hope and promise. She was radiant—simply glowing. . . . She was in love!

Amie stood up and walked toward the mirror for a closer look. She looked back down at the picture in her hand. At the sight of Kyle, smiling back up at her, Amie's eyes filled with tears. "Oh, sweet Jesus, I think I'm in love. No," she corrected herself, "I *know* I'm in love. It's Kyle. I'm in love with Kyle," she said—listening carefully to her voice as the unimaginable words took form.

She wanted to skip around the room and dance. She was so full of energy she hardly knew what to do with herself. Tucking the picture under her pillow, Amie quickly got dressed and ran downstairs.

Kids were playing out in the backyard—she could hear them through the open window above the kitchen sink. She looked outside and smiled at what a beautiful sight it was to see them at play. She poured herself a glass of water and looked around the room. The dishes had not been done since lunch, so Amie set to work doing them.

Her mom walked into the room just as Amie was finishing the clean-up. "How're you feeling, sweetheart?"

"Wonderful, Mom! Amazingly fine!" Amie said, as she gave her mom a kiss on the cheek and left to go play the piano.

Judy threw a curious look in the direction of her daughter. She shook her head and laughed. There was undoubtedly a good explanation for such a response—but she figured she would piece it all together in good time. As the old Heintzman piano began to ring out, under the delicate touch of the young pianist, Judy smiled. "Well, whatever You're doing in that girl, Lord, keep it up."

Chapter 61

Amie was in seventh heaven for the next few days. Krystal and Samantha pressed her to find out what was going on in their friend's life, but Amie insisted that she was just happy to be alive, enjoying being an auntie, and excited that summertime was finally here. Suspicious though they were, they realized that they were not going to get anything more out of Amie than that. Amie had not once mentioned Kyle's name—fearful that she would give herself away. She did not even mention to them about his graduation on Friday.

Wednesday evening presented a welcome opportunity for Amie, as she would be getting together with Joanie, Maggie, Katie, and of course, baby Gracie. The four sisters tried to find a night together at least once a month, just so they could stay closely in touch with one another. They were meeting at Joanie and Brandon's place; Brandon would be taking out Isaac, Zack, Aaron, and Jessie for supper and a show.

The three sisters arrived at Joanie's, and they ordered in Chinese food for supper. As they sat around Joanie's living room, taking turns holding Gracie while waiting for the food to arrive, Amie decided that now was as good a time as ever for her to spill the beans.

"So . . . I have something to tell you three—and Gracie, too—but you have to keep it a secret for now," Amie began, "even you, little Gracie," she said in a teeny-tiny voice to the little baby in Maggie's arms whose eyes were wide open and looking around.

"What's up?" Maggie asked.

"Well," Amie began. Not knowing where to go from there, she hesitated a moment, looking around at her three sisters. She closed her eyes, and a big smile came across her face as she forced herself to say the words she had not yet dared to confess to anyone else. "I think I've found Mr. Right."

Joanie and Maggie looked curiously at Amie. They could definitely see that Amie had a seriousness about her that overshadowed her typical flightiness. Everyone waited for Amie to go on.

Finally Amie asked, "What do you all think about me . . . and Kyle?" She nervously tucked her hands under her legs while awaiting the response of her sisters.

"Yes!" called out Katie, pulling down her right fist beside her. "I was hoping you would someday come to your senses, girl!"

Amie looked at Katie, completely dumbfounded.

"I've been waiting for a long time for you to figure out that Kyle is totally the perfect guy for you!" Katie exclaimed. "Ever since Jocelyn mentioned it that night at *The Country Corner Café,* I've been watching the two of you together—at band practices and when we all get together to do things. I am convinced that there is not a better match in the world for you, Amie, than Kyle. And I was beginning to worry that you might miss the boat and end up with some loser, with Kyle sitting there right before your eyes."

"I agree," Maggie said. "You two *are* perfect for each other. It always amazed me how Kyle could be so completely patient with you—when you would drive the rest of us all nuts with your silliness."

"Thanks, Maggie," Amie said, looking somewhat defensive. "This coming from you—the total goofball of the family!"

"You know what I mean," insisted Maggie. "I may be goofy—but you're just . . . you're just Amie. And we all love you. I don't know another girl happier to be alive than you. And it's just so easy to be happy when you're around—as long as you're in a good mood that is," she added.

Amie rolled her eyes as Joanie and Katie laughed in agreement.

"But you also know that you can try *everyone's* patience," Maggie continued. "Everyone's that is, but Kyle's."

"I know what you're saying," Amie agreed with a little laugh. "I always said I'd need a patient man."

"And I don't know any guy more patient than Kyle," Katie stated.

"He's a wonderful guy," Joanie said with a little laugh. "I'm just so stunned to think about it. I guess I've been out of the loop for too long . . . too preoccupied with my own life now. It never once occurred to me—other than that girls' night out—that you and Kyle might end up together. But it makes perfect sense, now that I think about it, Amie."

Amie had a far-away look in her eyes. She was thinking about Kyle and how her feelings for him had transformed so suddenly. "You know, I haven't said a word about this yet to Kyle," she informed her sisters. "I know he's interested in me—I figured that out last week. Oh, and I was *so awful* to him on Sunday when I last talked to him." Amie covered her mouth with her hand and shook her head shamefully. Suddenly a look of fear came into her eyes. "What if he's changed his mind since then? What if my volatile ways have finally caught up with me, and Kyle's lost all interest?"

Katie, Maggie, and Joanie all started laughing at Amie. It was a typical Amie-extreme—from "I'm in love with Kyle" to "what if Kyle no longer loves me?"

"Oh, Amie," Katie assured her older sister. "Kyle is as faithful as the day is long. It'd take a lot more than that from you to scare him off. And besides, I've finally finished your dress for his grad on Friday—and you're going to wear it there, if it's the last thing you do!"

"Hey, how'd it turn out?" Joanie asked.

"Great! Do you want to see it?" Amie offered. "We brought it along so I could show you both."

Amie went into Joanie and Brandon's bedroom to get changed. She strolled out of the room a few minutes later wearing the three-quarter length, light-blue chiffon dress and white bolero. She had white, low-heeled sling-backs on her feet, setting off the outfit with a very classy look.

Joanie and Maggie applauded the model and the fashion designer. "Katie, you do such beautiful work," Joanie enthused. "You can design my wardrobe for me, anytime!"

"I'd say the same," said Maggie, "but I'm afraid my wardrobe is just too plain and limited these days."

"Tell us about your life, Maggie," Amie said, now seated elegantly in her formal attire, her ankles crossed gracefully off to one side.

Maggie chuckled at the sight of her sister. "Amie, you make such a princess . . . and I'm really happy that you've finally found prince charming."

Amie smiled, but did not say a thing in response. She preferred to bask silently in her newly discovered feelings of romance.

"What's new with me?" Maggie reiterated the question. "I've begun my novitiate now with the Sisters, and I'm loving it. I have to admit, Amie, I've been feeling every bit as much in love with my Prince Charming as you seem to be with yours."

"That's so cool," Amie said. "Isn't love wonderful?"

"It is," Maggie agreed.

"I wouldn't know," Katie jumped in. "And listening to you both talk about it is starting to make me feel very impatient about life."

"Don't worry, Katie," Joanie told her. "You'll get your chance, yet."

"I know," Katie said. "I guess I'm not really that impatient. It's just all this talk about romance is making me feel left out of the excitement. But I'm in no hurry. At seventeen years old, what would I do with a boyfriend anyway? It would just be an exercise in total frustration, I'm sure, to have to wait several years trying to keep a romantic interest alive and at bay—all at the same time. I'm just as happy that the Lord hasn't put Mr. Right along my path. Or if he has, I'm glad I can't recognize him."

"That was me," Amie said with a laugh. "I lived with a total veil over my eyes, when it came to Kyle. I can't imagine how frustrating it would have been for me to have been attracted to Kyle all these years and to have to have waited on those feelings."

"Remember when you had that silly crush on him years ago?" Maggie asked, with a laugh.

"*Yes,*" Amie said, very embarrassed. "I'm so glad I got over that when I did. Those feelings were *nothing* compared to the feelings I have for Kyle now. It was just a silly, schoolgirl infatuation. I don't know how Kyle ever put up with me at that time."

"He's a patient man," Joanie reminded Amie. "A virtue we could all stand to practise a little more, I'm sure."

"Tell me about it," Amie replied. "It's only been two days, now, since I discovered these feelings for Kyle—and I can hardly contain myself."

"Well, I'm working on patience," Katie announced. "It's not easy to sit back and watch the three of you move ahead with life, leaving me behind. But I'm sure God has a perfect plan for me—and I have no intention of compromising it, no matter how attractive it seems to be in love."

"Good for you, Katie," Joanie said, getting up to answer the buzzer. "And in the meantime, how about a little Chinese food to fill the hole?"

"Sounds perfect," said Katie.

"Amie's probably too 'in-love' to be hungry anyway—so there should be plenty for the rest of us," Maggie threw in.

"Don't count on it," Amie retorted. "My appetite is fully intact these days. I guess falling in love with one of your best friends is not quite as traumatic as falling in love with a stranger. I'm sleeping like a baby and eating just fine. I've never felt better in my life."

Chapter 62

Thursday before band practice, Amie dropped Katie off at Annie and Jocelyn's so that she could head out a half-hour earlier to the Bander's. She needed to talk to Kyle—alone—and was suddenly very nervous about the whole thing. She skipped supper altogether that night.

Kyle greeted Amie at the back door when she arrived—no one ever used their front door. He was surprised to see her driving up their road early for practice and even more surprised that she had come alone. He invited her to come in; the family was just finishing up supper.

"Hey, Amie," Kathy called out. "Come have a piece of apple pie."

"You'll never taste better apple pie anywhere else," Kyle told her.

Amie smiled as she walked into the kitchen beside the young man.

"It's true," agreed David. "Mom makes the best apple pie."

Kathy smiled at her sons. "My greatest fans," she told Amie.

Amie smiled back at the gracious woman. She had always had a real affection for Mrs. Bander.

"Pull up a chair," Kevin offered, motioning with his fork for Kyle to bring over the chair from the corner of the room for their guest.

"No, thank you," Amie said. "The pie looks great—maybe I'll have some later. I was just hoping to have a chance to talk with Kyle before band practice, actually."

"No problem," Kyle said. "You want to go downstairs?"

"Could we go for a walk?" Amie asked quietly. "It's beautiful outside."

"It is," agreed Kathy. "Summer days don't come nicer than this—not too hot, no mosquitoes. It's just a perfect evening out there, isn't it?"

"It is," Amie said, turning to Kyle's mom and smiling.

"Come on," Kyle said, taking Amie by the elbow and walking with her to their back door.

They headed up the walk and then down the side path that led to the dugout through the trees.

"So what's on your mind?" Kyle asked, doing his best not to betray his total curiosity at this sudden and unexpected visit.

"I just wanted to apologize to you, Kyle, for my awful behaviour on Sunday." Amie looked over at the young man walking beside her.

He looked at her and shrugged his shoulders slightly. "I don't think you need to apologize. You were just being honest with me."

"No. I was very overwhelmed about everything and out-of-control with my emotions," she confessed. "But I was more than rude to you and ... well, I really over-reacted to the situation, Kyle. I'm sorry if I hurt your feelings at all."

"You didn't, Amie."

"Kyle . . ." Amie paused, searching for the words to express what she was feeling inside.

"Uh-huh?" He patiently waited for her to continue.

"I was wrong about . . . about my feelings for you," she said, nervously wringing her hands together.

By this time they had arrived at the dugout and had stopped walking. Amie looked around. It was a beautiful spot—a little man-made pond surrounded by a grove of poplars. There was a campfire pit off to the side of the path where they had enjoyed many a sing-song and party over the years. In the summer, they fished from the stocked pickerel and swam in the little pool. There was even a rope for swinging into the pond—which was the most fun of all. In the wintertime this little haven was the spot for skating parties and bonfires. The trees kept it well protected from the cold winter winds, with Christmas lights strung all the way around, creating a cozy, inviting atmosphere for friends to gather.

Kyle quietly waited as Amie looked around, apparently lost in thought. He was not anxious to press the point—having no idea where this conversation was headed.

Finally Amie looked up at him. Putting her hands on his shoulders, she said, "Look at me, Kyle. Do you see anything different about me?"

Kyle stared into the girl's bright blue eyes. This was just about more than he could handle. What was Amie getting at? He had no idea how to respond—as his heart pounded painfully within him.

"Anything?" she asked again.

"What am I looking for, Amie?" he asked, almost exasperated.

She smiled up at him. The moment was so emotionally charged, she could not contain all her feelings. Her eyes welled with tears, and she closed them, embarrassed that she wanted to cry.

"Amie," Kyle whispered to the girl. "I'm totally confused right now. I wish you would just tell me what's going on."

"Kyle," she said, now smiling, but her eyes were cast down to the ground. "I've just discovered—after all these years—how much you mean to me. And all of a sudden . . . I guess it happened on Monday . . . I realized that I really *do* have feelings for you—much deeper than friendship, Kyle." She looked up timidly to meet him eye to eye.

Kyle hesitated a moment and then began to laugh. Amie laughed along with him. He pulled her into his arms and held her gently. She wrapped her arms around him and held on. As they stood there, safely in each other's embrace, Amie knew that her heart had finally found a place to call home.

Kyle did not dare say a thing—lest the magic of the moment would pass and he would discover it was all a dream. He held the girl in his arms as tenderly as he could—the girl with the long, blond curls and the bright blue eyes and an infectious joy for living who had stolen his heart so many years ago. At long last, she had found her way into his arms.

Amie stepped back and looked up again at Kyle, laughing with apologetic eyes. "I'm sorry it took me so long to discover those feelings."

"I'm not sorry at all, Amie," Kyle said. "I could never have handled your affection for me and have kept my head on my shoulders all these years. I'm glad you were blind to me . . . but I'm also glad the blinders are gone."

"So am I," she said softly. Suddenly Amie became aware of the time—the other band members would soon be arriving. "Can I still have that piece of apple pie?" she asked. "I'm starving."

Kyle laughed and, taking Amie by the hand, led her back up the path toward the house. Amie smiled, looking down at her hand in his. What an incredible feeling it was to be holding hands with the man of her dreams. He let go of her hand as they came around to the front walk so that no one would be able to see them from the house or the road.

They walked into the kitchen, which was now cleaned up since supper, with no one left around. Amie sat at the table, and Kyle got her a piece of apple pie. "You want some milk or juice with that?" he asked.

"Milk would be great," she replied.

Kyle came and sat with her as she ate.

"Your mom does make the best apple pies," she agreed.

Kyle nodded his head and smiled.

"So, do you have a grad ceremony tomorrow during the day?" she asked.

"I do."

"Can I come to it?"

"It's in the afternoon—which means you'd have to miss classes," he warned.

"I want to be there, Kyle. Would you pick me up to go?"

"Of course I would. Can you be ready by one?"

"Rings on my fingers and bells on my toes," she replied.

"That sounds like some outfit that Katie made for you," he said with a laugh.

Amie giggled. "I'm saving *that* outfit for the dance. Will there be a chance to come home and change in between?"

"Yeah. The ceremonies are at one-thirty, and the supper's not until six. So I can take you home to get changed and then we'll head back out for the evening," he suggested.

"Great." She nodded, taking the last mouthful of pie.

Just then band members began pulling into the yard. Kyle took Amie's dishes over to the sink, and together they went down to the band room to get set up for practice.

The young couple kept a discreet cover over their relationship. No one at practice would have suspected a thing.

On the way home that night, Katie made the observation that the music had sounded particularly good that evening. "Just feels like the band is in total sync all of a sudden. Things must have gone well between you and Kyle, Amie."

"Perfectly . . . and beyond my wildest dreams."

Chapter 63

Kyle came to pick Amie up for the graduation exercises the next day. She was ready to go in a pink skirt and white, short-sleeve top. She had on a matching pink necklace and dangling earrings. Her hair was done up with ringlets hanging all around her neck and over her shoulders.

"You look great," Kyle said as he opened the door for Amie to get into the vehicle. "As good as a real date . . . my friends at Tech School should never suspect that I couldn't do this on my own."

Amie laughed and waited for Kyle to walk around and sit in on the driver's side. "You look good, too, Kyle, in your suit," she said. "Almost good enough for me to consider a real date."

He smiled at the pretty girl beside him, put the vehicle into gear, and drove away. Glancing at Amie from the corner of his eye, he could see she was looking at him and smiling. He reached over and took her hand in his.

She gave his hand a little squeeze and kept smiling. Here she was sitting in the same vehicle in which she had sat a thousand times; the only difference was now she was sitting beside the man who had won her heart. It was hard to get used to these new feelings and even harder to find a way to verbalize them. Amie looked down at their hands and then back up at Kyle. He knew her so well that there really was no need at all for words.

Amie sat with the Banders during the ceremony. Kyle had not bothered to mention to her that he had been voted class valedictorian. Amie was so proud of him as she listened to his address, delivered with such eloquence. He challenged his classmates to always strive to reach beyond themselves and to use their time and talents for good—to make a difference in the world. The greatest rewards would come to them, proportionate to the degree to which they would be willing to sacrifice themselves for others.

Amie could not take her eyes off the young man on the stage. How was it possible that she could have gone so many years without seeing Kyle the way she now saw him? It blew her mind away. *Thank you, Lord, for opening my eyes. I don't feel like I deserve Kyle at all—but now that I've found him, I'm not about to let him go.*

Following the ceremonies, they gathered for pictures. Along with the plaque for valedictorian, Kyle had received an award in the area of computer programming. Kevin Bander was bursting with pride for his son as he boasted of the young man's accomplishments.

"Not only does he take two awards away with him from Tech School, but he's sitting on three job offers before he ever graduated," the proud father told Amie, standing next to him.

Kyle threw a look at his father, and Amie's eyes quickly picked up on the strained expression of the son.

"All you have to decide now, Kyle, is if it'll be Toronto, Calgary or Vancouver?" Kevin went on.

Amie's heart sank within her. Kyle looked at the girl, not knowing what to say. Turning back to his father, he said, "I haven't decided on whether or not I'll take any of them yet, Dad. It's a little premature to talk about it."

"Well, you'll have to decide soon enough," Kevin responded. "Job offers like that don't come around every day."

Kathy, picking up on the reaction of the young lady in their group, added, "No need to talk about all that right now, Kevin. Let's just celebrate the day and enjoy our time together."

All at once Kevin tuned into the insensitivity of his boasting. He had no idea that Amie and Kyle were anything more than friends. The look between the young couple told the father that things had changed somewhere along the line. He must have blinked. *Father's should be careful about that blinking business*, he reminded himself.

"Congratulations, brother," David jumped into the conversation. "I'm glad I took the afternoon off work to be here with you. Wouldn't have wanted to miss this for the world."

"Me neither," Amie said softly. "I'm proud of you."

Kyle smiled at the young lady. Looking at his watch, he announced that he and Amie should get going. He promised his folks that they would stop by the acreage before going on to the supper and dance so that they could take more pictures together. The small group walked out to the parking lot together and parted ways.

✝ ✝ ✝

"You never mentioned anything to me about job offers," Amie said quietly as they drove.

"I'm sorry about that, Amie. Dad spoke out of turn. I haven't accepted anything yet, least of all out of town," he told her.

"I feel like I found you and lost you all in one week," Amie said. "I can't believe how life can turn on a dime."

"Amie, I'm not making any decisions about any of that right now," he promised. "I have other applications out, too, some for around Saskatoon. Can we just forget about all that for today and deal with it later?"

They were at a red light, and Kyle was looking over at Amie trying to catch her eye with his. She finally looked up at him. "I'd like to forget about it completely, not just for today," she said with a smile.

"Good. Then consider it forgotten. I've waited a lot of years to finally go out with you, and I'm not spoiling our time together worrying about something that may never happen."

"Agreed," she said, perking up.

The young couple arrived at Amie's house. Kyle visited with John and Judy in the kitchen, while waiting for Amie to get changed for the evening. Kyle's back was to the doorway, when suddenly the change of expression on John's face told Kyle that Amie had just entered the room.

Kyle turned to see the beautiful young lady enter, looking like a princess. The young man was speechless. Amie had always been a pretty girl—but dressed in her formal attire, she was breathtaking.

"Amie, you look lovely," said her mother, trying to fill-in for Kyle's apparent awkwardness.

"I'm sure you'll be the prettiest girl at the party," stated her proud father. "Which means I'm expecting you to be on your guard for her, Kyle."

Kyle turned to Amie's father. "I won't let anything happen to her, sir."

"Come on," Amie said, grabbing Kyle by the hand and leading him to the living room. "I want to get a few pictures before we leave."

Kyle followed Amie, and together they posed while John took a few pictures. "I have to admit, you two look way too good together," John said, as he put the camera back in its case. "Kyle, I expect Amie home at a decent hour."

"The dance goes until midnight and then we're expected to stay and help clean up," he said.

"Have her home by one," John instructed the young man.

"I will, sir."

"Well, we'd better get going; we still have a stop to make at your place, Kyle," Amie said.

John and Judy stood in the front porch and watched as the young couple left. "So, what do you make of it?" John asked his wife, motioning his head toward the couple who had just driven away.

"Oh, I think Amie's caught this time—hook, line and sinker," Judy said, her eyes still following the black Escort up the street. "Did you see the way she took him by the hand?"

John looked at his wife and waited for her to continue.

"They've held hands before," Judy concluded.

"How could you tell that?" John asked.

"It was the look in Amie's eyes. She was neither holding his hand as a friend, nor was she holding it timidly. She was completely comfortable with Kyle," Judy observed. "I expect we'll be hearing more from her about it in the very near future. It's just not like Amie to hold off talking to me about her feelings in these matters."

"Feeling left out?" John asked.

"A little," Judy admitted. "But it's all beginning to make sense now— when I think about how she's been acting these past few weeks. Her mood swings last week and then the way she's been floating around the house the past few days like she's walking on sunshine. Yup. Amie's in love."

"What do you think about the two of them together?" John questioned.

"I can't think of a better match for Amie than Kyle. Can you?"

"No," John said, shaking his head with a laugh. "No, I can't."

✝　　　　✝　　　　✝

Kyle and Amie stayed for an hour at the Banders' acreage, taking pictures out by the trees and pond, and visiting with his folks before they left for the supper and dance.

"I love your mom and dad," said Amie as they drove away.

"That's good," Kyle said. "'Cause they love you, too."

"Really?" she asked, almost shyly. "What have they said about me?"

"You have to remember, they've known for a long time how I felt about you. If they hadn't approved of you long ago—I don't think we'd be here today."

"When you say 'a long time ago', Kyle, just how long do you mean?"

"I'm not sure I'm prepared to answer that question, yet, Amie."

"That bad?" she questioned.

"All depends on how you look at it," he answered. "But what do you say we get through tonight before we worry about the past or the future?"

"Deal," she answered, reaching into her purse. "I have something for you, Kyle." She took out a small, bulky envelope and passed it to him.

He glanced at the girl. "Can I wait until I stop the car to open it?"

"Why not just pull off to the side and open it now," she suggested.

"Fine." Kyle pulled onto the nearest approach off the highway into town and put the vehicle into park. He opened the envelope and found a prayer card and medal of St. Joseph.

"I didn't wrap it fancy," Amie explained, "'cause there's not much room in this little purse. I actually have the box for the medal at home—I'll give it to you some other time. It's been blessed . . . by Fr. Steve—the medal, that is, not the box. And it's sterling silver."

"It's great," he said with a smile. He pulled the chain over his neck and tucked the medal into his shirt. "It means a lot to me, Amie. Thank you."

"St. Joseph *is* the model of virtues for men. And . . . well, I think you're a very virtuous man, Kyle," she said quite simply.

Kyle smiled. "You didn't need to give me anything, Amie. But I'm really glad you did. Thanks."

She reached over and put her hand on his arm. Kyle put the car into gear, and they continued en route to the graduation celebration. Amie slipped her hand down and held onto Kyle's, without saying a word. It was amazing to him how natural it felt to have Amie beside him, holding his hand, when just a week before he barely would have hoped that this could be possible.

The young couple walked into the supper side by side, but not holding hands. There still was a certain level of secrecy to their relationship. There was no official courtship as of yet, and though they had not discussed the issue between them, Kyle knew that Amie would not be comfortable being introduced as anything other than a friend.

The supper was exceptional, and Amie really enjoyed meeting Kyle's friends from school. They were a nice a group of young men and women—mostly in their early to mid-twenties, though some were older. Many of them were there with a girlfriend or boyfriend; a few were even married and had children. Some of the girls had asked Amie how long she and Kyle had been seeing each other. Amie explained that they were just friends, which won her a few shocked looks.

After a few speeches and some more ceremony, the dinner was finished. There was a short break while tables were cleared and then the dance began. Amie had been waiting all night to finally have the chance to dance with Kyle. Kyle felt like he had waited a lifetime.

It was fun, and though they danced with others from Kyle's group of friends, the young couple had the rare pleasure of being able to dance alone with each other for most of the evening. Having taken ballroom dance together certainly added to the fun of it all, but the way the two friends moved so smoothly together on the dance floor went beyond dance-training. They had a manner of communicating with each other through the look in their eyes and the touch of their hands that gave the impression of a couple who had been together for many years. Nothing could have felt more natural to either of them than being together.

There was an awkward moment between them when the first slow dance played. They looked at each other. In the past, they knew to keep a good and safe distance from each other—as did all their friends. But tonight,

Amie just wanted Kyle to take her in his arms and hold her close to his heart. He began the dance, keeping his distance. After a few moments Amie stepped into his embrace, laid her head on his shoulder, and closed her eyes. Kyle smiled and pulled their hands in closely against his chest. He wanted Amie in his arms more than anything, and what made it all the better was that the feeling was obviously mutual.

Kyle helped with clean up for a little while at the end of the dance, but since many of the others seemed content to just hang around visiting, Kyle offered the excuse that he had to get Amie home, and they left. He was not at all interested in hanging around just to hang around.

"I had a wonderful time tonight," Amie told Kyle as they walked to the car.

"So did I," he replied, reaching out and taking her hand in his.

When they got to the vehicle, Amie stood in front of the door, preventing Kyle from opening it for her as usual. He looked at her curiously and stepped back; they were still holding hands.

Amie pulled on his hand slightly and said, "Go talk to my father tomorrow . . . please."

Kyle began to laugh, shaking his head in disbelief.

"Don't laugh at me, Kyle," she scolded.

"I'm not laughing at *you*. But just think about the last time we were standing beside my car, talking."

Amie rolled her eyes. "Don't remind me."

"That wasn't even a week ago, Amie. And you were ready to pound the living daylights out of me."

Amie reached up and put her hand on the back of her neck. "I'm sorry, Kyle."

He laughed and pulled the girl into his arms for a hug. "I'm not. I can't imagine a happier man than I am on the face of this planet tonight, Amie."

She rested her head on his shoulder and kept her eyes closed, breathing in deeply. "Did I ever mention to you how much I like your cologne?" she murmured.

"No, as a matter of fact, you didn't."

"Please, Kyle, go talk to my father," she whispered. "I don't think I can keep my feelings for you to myself for much longer. I know you probably think that's fairly shallow, considering you waited longer than you care to reveal. But I'm ready to burst at my emotional seams here."

Kyle laughed, stepping back from the girl. He held her by the shoulders and looked her straight in the eyes. "Amie, are you sure you really want this now . . . or do you want some time to let those feelings all settle down?"

"Kyle, I want you to ask me, before I end up asking you," she said, staring intently at the young man.

"Fair enough," he said. He reached around and opened the door for the young lady.

She stepped out of the way of the open door, but before getting into the vehicle, she reached up and put her arms around Kyle's neck and gave him another big hug. Kyle held her firmly, yet tenderly, in his arms. After a moment, she pulled away and stepped into the car. Kyle closed the door and walked around to his side.

Amie was home twenty minutes early. There were no lights on in the house—just the porch light.

"It's probably best I show your dad I can get you home in good time, if I want him to say 'yes' to me tomorrow," Kyle stated.

"Call in the morning?" Amie asked. "If I have to wait all day—I think I'll die."

Kyle laughed. He picked up Amie's hand and kissed it gently.

"I'll take that as a yes," she said.

Kyle walked her to the porch door, and Amie went inside. She waited until he drove away before going into the house. As she locked the door behind her, she turned her heart to the Lord. *The only good thing about tonight coming to an end, Jesus, is that tomorrow promises to be even better. I can't begin to thank You enough.*

Chapter 64

"You got home in good time last night," John commented, as Amie came into the kitchen that Saturday morning. "But I didn't expect to see you up so early, Scuttle-Butt. It's only seven o'clock."

"I couldn't sleep very well . . . and I heard you up, and I wanted to talk to you, Daddy," she said, sitting at the end of the big oak table, kitty-corner from him.

"What's on your mind, sweetheart?"

"Kyle's going to call you today, Daddy."

"Is he?"

"Daddy, please say 'yes' to him," she pleaded.

"Well, that depends on what he's calling me about, Amie. If he's interested in borrowing a tool from my shop—I may say 'yes', as long as I don't need it to finish the job I'm working on."

Amie hit her father on the shoulder. He pulled away and laughed at his little girl.

"You know full well what I'm talking about, Dad," she said, giving him a shake.

"I might have an idea, Amie. But I have a question for you, first."

"What is it?"

"I've seen you excited about guys in the past, and it hasn't always gone the way you thought or hoped it would," he reminded the young lady. "So what makes you so sure that this time is going to be any different?"

"'Cause this is *Kyle*, Dad," she said, half-whining. "I admit that these feelings I have for him are fairly new, but my love for Kyle goes back so far I can hardly think of a time when I didn't love him . . . as a friend and a brother. That same love—that's always been there—has just . . . changed. It happened so naturally, that I can't imagine now going on through life without him, Daddy."

"Amie, a courtship is a time for discernment—it's not a given that you're going to get married, just because you begin to court. I'm a little concerned that you're going into this with the conclusion already set in your mind. That can blind-side you, sweetheart," the father warned.

"I know it can, and I promise I'll try to keep a level head about things," she said, pulling now on her father's hand. "Just give me a chance with him."

"If I give Kyle permission to court with you, sweetheart," John began, very soberly this time, "I expect you to establish some good, strong, healthy boundaries to your relationship. And I expect you to spend time with his parents and with us, discussing your relationship openly."

"Of course, Dad," she responded, somewhat defensively.

"Well, so far it seems that you've taken off—charting your own course in this relationship, Amie. You haven't breathed a word about your feelings for Kyle to either your mother or me," he stated.

"It just all happened so fast, Dad," she apologized. "I came to you this morning. I wasn't planning on sneaking around behind your backs or anything."

John laughed. "I know . . . I know how life can sometimes sneak up on a person, Amie. That's why I want you and Kyle to do your best to keep your relationship in good control."

"Okay, Daddy," she answered. "So, when he calls to come over—you'll say 'yes'?"

"Depends on what he asks, Scuttle-Butt. I already told you that."

Amie smacked her father playfully on the shoulder again. "I'll take that as a yes, Dad. And you'd better not blow this for me," she said, shaking a finger in warning at him.

John laughed, reaching forward to pull his daughter toward him so he could kiss her on the forehead. "Relax. I love you, dear. Why don't you get yourself some breakfast and come sit and eat with me?"

"Thanks, no, Dad. I couldn't possibly eat a thing!"

✟   ✟   ✟

The day seemed to drag on forever for Amie. She anxiously jumped to the phone each time it rang. Judy laughed and said nothing. Amie had spoken with her mother that morning and had brought her up to speed with what was going on in her life. It felt like all the pieces were now in place—all that was left was to wait until it could become official.

"Do you think it's possible for a guy to be *too* patient?" Amie asked her mother, as the young lady paced back and forth through the kitchen.

Judy laughed. "I think it's possible for a patient man to drive an impatient woman crazy." She walked to the fridge and took out some sandwich meat and other fixings for lunch.

"Why's it taking so long?" Amie looked at the clock, it was already after eleven. "The morning's almost all gone. . . . Something's gone wrong. What if he's changed his mind, Mom?" Amie's eyes had widened with fear.

"Amie, relax," Judy said, placing bread out on the counter for sandwiches. "Nothing's gone wrong. Just let life happen at its own pace. Why don't you go pray a rosary or take a shower or something?"

"I've done that already . . . I know, I'll go play the piano."

"Sure," her mother called out after her. "You've only played it for three hours already this morning," she muttered to herself while spreading mayonnaise on the bread.

Amie had just sat down to play when the phone rang again. She ran to the kitchen and picked it up. At last, it was him.

"Hey, Amie, how are you today?" Kyle asked.

"Just about to have a nervous breakdown," she stated. "Where *are* you? Are you planning to come over?"

Kyle laughed. "I am. That is, if your father has time to meet with me."

"He's in the shop. I'll run him the phone," Amie said, already out the back door. "And please don't make me wait until after lunch—I can't eat or sleep or anything."

Kyle laughed. "I'm sorry if I've caused your present state of distress. I've been helping my dad out in the shop since early this morning . . . and the day just slipped away. I really did mean to call sooner."

"Did you talk to your dad about things?" she asked, pausing outside the garage door.

"I did," he answered.

"And?" she prompted him.

"Nothing's changed," he said, "if that's what you mean."

"Sorry, if I sound like an idiot," she said meekly.

"You don't," he assured the girl. "But I wish you'd relax. I'm not going anywhere, Amie."

"I know you're not," she said with a smile.

"So, can I talk to your Dad, yet?"

"Here he is." She stepped into the garage and ran the phone to her father. Holding her hand over the mouthpiece she whispered, "*Be good,*" with great emphasis on each word.

John took the phone and motioned for Amie to leave, which she did. After a few moments he stepped out of the garage and passed the phone to his daughter.

"That was fast," she said, almost in shock.

"Kyle'll be here in about fifteen minutes," her father informed her. "I told him to come straight out to the shop."

"Promise you'll be good, Dad," Amie pleaded.

John looked at his daughter and smiled, not bothering to respond. He stepped into the garage and went back to work.

Amie went back into the house. Fifteen minutes seemed like an eternity. One of her concertos was at least fifteen minutes long. That was the ticket. The young pianist went back to the piano and began to play some more.

As the concerto was nearing the end, Amie heard Kyle's car door close.

She jumped to look out the front window. He headed straight through the side gate to the backyard. Not sure what to do next, she ran upstairs to her bedroom. Maybe if she just changed her outfit and redid her hair she would feel better. At least it would help the time to pass.

✝   ✝   ✝

"Come on in, Kyle," John said to the young man, as Kyle entered the garage through the open door. "Come see what I'm working on here."

Kyle stepped forward.

"It's a cradle for Gracie," John said. "Hopefully I'll have it done before she outgrows it. School got too busy on me, and I just couldn't get it finished before she was born."

"It's great," Kyle said. "I'm sure Joanie and Brandon'll love it."

"So, you want to talk to me about Amie, do you?" John opened the conversation. He set aside his tools and invited Kyle to lean against the workbench opposite of where John was standing. "I figure we'd best not beat around the bush since Amie's going crazy with impatience inside the house."

Kyle laughed. "I should have been more considerate and have come by earlier. I wasn't expecting her to be quite this anxious."

John shook his head and laughed. "Let me tell you something about Amie, Kyle. The girl has passion—passion for life, for love, for family, for God, for music. . . . If something means anything to her, it means *everything* to her. And right now, Amie is very passionate about her relationship with you."

Kyle smiled and looked down at the floor. He had not thought about it in those terms before. Looking John eye to eye again, he stated, "I want you to know, Mr. Collins, that my intentions for Amie are completely honourable. I want to court your daughter, and by that I mean to do things right. I wouldn't dream of taking advantage of her in any way."

"I know you wouldn't, Kyle. But I just think it's fair to warn you that you're going to have your hands full keeping her enthusiasm for you from getting out of hand. And you'd better be prepared to have strong boundaries and guidelines to keep yourselves from . . . well, to stay on track. I know you're both all for purity—but it's not enough to want to stay pure. You're going to find that it's a lot harder to live it out once you're in a relationship with a girl that you're really attracted to."

Kyle nodded his head. "I can see that, sir."

"I have a great deal of respect for you, Kyle, and for your family. I can't think of a finer young man to court Amie. But I just want to emphasize to you both that I want it done right—in a way that will leave neither of you with regrets." John crossed his arms and looked across at the young man.

"I'm completely committed to doing this right, Mr. Collins. I've waited quite a few years to be ready in my life to come and ask you if I can court Amie. I didn't wait this long and come this far just to throw all my principles out the window. I know it'll be a challenge to keep our relationship pure—both physically and emotionally. But I'm prepared to sacrifice whatever it takes to achieve that goal, sir." Kyle looked Amie's father directly in the eye as he spoke. He had respect for this man, and he had every intention of proving himself to Amie's father.

"I believe you, Kyle. And I trust, you," he added. "And I'm happy to give you permission to court Amie . . . as long as she's interested," he said with a laugh.

Kyle laughed and shook his head.

"So I suggest you take her out, ask her in your own way, and then I want the two of you to sit down and really discuss how you plan to do this. And then I'd like it if we could get together—maybe tomorrow—and talk about things. It'd be nice to have your parents over again."

"Sounds good," Kyle agreed.

"It takes more than a guy and girl to court, Kyle. It's a team effort. And if you allow your parents and us to work with you, I think you'll discover that the benefits to your relationship—however it turns out—will be worth all the extra effort involved."

"I'm all for it, Mr. Collins," Kyle replied. "And thank you for giving me this chance with Amie."

"You're welcome, son. . . . Just one more thing, Kyle."

"What's that, sir?"

"Please, call me John. I know I was your teacher back in high school, and it's probably more comfortable for you to call me 'sir' or 'Mr. Collins'. But I think it's time you realize that I now see you as a man—and a very honourable man at that, Kyle." John reached forward, extending his hand to the young man.

Kyle took his hand and returned a solid, manly handshake. "Thank you . . . John," he said. "I sure hope to live up to your confidence in me."

"I'm sure you will. . . . I have no worries. So, where does that leave us? I think it would be wise for me to let you go into that house and rescue Amie right about now," John suggested, walking toward the door with his hand on Kyle's shoulder. "I think we've tested her patience far enough for one morning."

Kyle laughed and headed up the walk. Amie stepped outside, before he reached the back door. She looked over Kyle's shoulder at her father coming up the walk behind him.

John nodded to his daughter as he approached the young couple. "I'm going in for lunch. I'll let your mother know you'll be out for the afternoon," he said, leaning forward and kissing Amie's cheek.

She reached up and gave her dad a big hug. "Thank you, Daddy," she whispered in his ear.

He patted her on the back and continued on his way, waving back to Kyle.

"So, would you like to go for lunch?" the young man asked.

"I'm not leaving this yard until we get this matter settled," she told him.

"Well," Kyle paused, "you might give a guy a chance to ask you in his own way, Amie."

"Fine. Go ahead and ask in your own way."

He shook his head and laughed. Taking her hands into his, he asked, "Amie Collins, would you consider courting with me, so that together we can discern whether or not God is calling us to marriage?"

"Yes!" she screamed, throwing her arms around his neck. "I thought you'd never ask," she laughed, as he lifted her up off the ground.

"Looks like you're not the only one who was waiting for me to pop the question," he said, setting Amie down.

She turned around and looked at the house where five of her siblings were waving at the young couple. Jessie started knocking on the window as Amie and Kyle waved back at the crew. Katie raised her hands together in victory, and Kyle laughed.

"Apparently she's been on your side for a while," Amie informed him. "I guess the whole world could see it coming, but me." She waved to her siblings and then took Kyle by the hand and led him around to the side gate.

Kyle stopped by the side of the house, with Amie in the lead still holding his hand. "You know what?"

"What?" she asked, turning around to look at him.

"You led me through that gate fourteen years ago, and I followed behind you knowing that once I got to the other side I'd have to let go of your hand—'cause I was afraid David and the other kids would tease me."

"You remember holding my hand *fourteen years ago?*" Amie asked incredulously.

"It was the first day we met . . . and the day you stole my heart," he confessed.

"Kyle!" Amie exclaimed. "Are you telling me that you've had these feelings for me for fourteen years?"

"I am," he admitted, still holding her hand.

She stepped up closer to him, taking his other hand in hers. "I can't believe that I could have been so slow to have missed out on fourteen years of you liking me in that way."

"I was a pretty shy kid, Amie. I would never have admitted to a soul how I felt about you back then. And by the time I was old enough to not be so shy, I realized that the best chance I'd ever have at winning your heart someday would be to stay friends with you—and just friends. So, I made up my mind that I wouldn't let my feelings for you ever step in the way of our friendship . . . until the time was right in our lives."

"Kyle, you are *amazing!* I couldn't even survive the morning—waiting for you to call to speak with my father—I was going completely nuts in there," she stated.

"Aren't you glad I kept it to myself all these years?"

"Thank you, Kyle. God knew you were exactly what I needed in a man . . . even if I couldn't see it."

"So, anyway," Kyle said, changing sides on the path with Amie. "I was okay being led around by you for fourteen years, never letting anyone see how much I wanted to hold your hand. But today . . . that all changes. I'm leading you through that gate—and I'm not letting go of your hand. I don't care who sees it. I want the whole world to know that I'm in love with Amie Collins, and she's my girl."

Kyle began to walk toward the gate, but Amie yanked his arm to stop him. He turned around and looked at her curiously.

"Not so fast there, Mister," she said. "You can lead me out that gate, and wherever you want to take me—I'll follow you. But I have one thing to say to you first that I've been dying to say for what seems like forever . . . though it's actually only been five days."

Kyle laughed and waited for Amie to finish, his smile entreating her to go on.

"I love you, Kyle Bander. And though I never saw it coming, and I spent all those years distracted, I want you to know something—I've never said 'I love you' to any other guy. And I hope and pray that God is going to allow us to stay together forever, 'cause there's no other guy I'd rather be with than you." Amie stepped forward and then stopped herself, waiting to let Kyle take the lead.

He laughed and pulled her toward him, and she threw her arms around his neck. "I love you," she whispered, softly in his ear.

"I love you," he whispered back. After a few moments he laughed a little. Stepping back again, he looked into her eyes and asked, "So, will you follow me this time?"

"Kyle, I'm right behind you, all the way."

As they turned to walk through the side gate, holding hands, Kyle looked at the pretty young woman with golden curls. He just knew that life would never be the same again.

଼ଓ

For I know the plans I have for you, says the Lord,
plans for welfare and not for evil,
to give you a future and a hope.

Jeremiah 29:11

ଌ

Special Thanks

To all those who have supported our family's efforts at One Way Publishing House through your prayers, encouragement, financial assistance, time, talents, and enthusiasm for this work . . . to all who have believed in the importance of this ministry of promoting purity, faith, hope, and love through Catholic fiction . . . to all the readers of *Arms of Love* who have waited so long for this sequel to finally make it to print, thank you! This book, *Surrender*, is a tribute to all you have done to help us trust in God's providence and to respond to His call for our family. It has been a spiritual journey like none other in our lives!

Thank you to all our friends at Our Lady of Lourdes Parish, and to the Catholic Home-Schooling Community in and around Saskatoon, and to those friends who have come into our lives through this ministry. You have demonstrated to me in profound ways that the Catholic culture is alive and well in our world. Your lives are beautiful testimonies of the hope to which I have been called to bear witness in my writing.

Special Acknowledgements . . .

Jim Marcoux, my husband, thank you for pushing me along at times when I needed pushing, and waiting patiently for me when I could no longer push on. This book would not have come into being without the help, love, support, and advice you gave me along the way.

Hannah, Rebekah, and Mikaelah Marcoux, you walked with me step by step through the entire process of writing and editing this book. Your special insights helped make this novel what it is today. Your enthusiasm, support, and encouragement got me through all the trials and challenges and helped me to stay focused as to what God was calling me to do in this work! It was a special privilege to have shared in this work so closely with you, my daughters.

Dan Brulé, thank you for believing so much in this work that you dedicated months of your life to helping our family build a ministry. I have learned so much from you by your witness and example of Christian living. You have become like a son and a brother to us, and we will always treasure the gift of the time you dedicated to our family and to this mission.

Eva Marcoux, you have generously dedicated your time and support to our family to allow us to dedicate our family to a full-time ministry. We could not have done this without you! The time you have shared with us will forever be a treasured memory and a great heirloom for our children.

Gay Couture and Lil Schroeder, thank you for taking time to edit and advise me in this work. Once again, I could not have done this without all the time and effort you so generously gave. And thank you, Mom, for the beautiful painting for the cover.

Fran Butek, Carolyn LeBlanc, Andréa Ledding, Claude Mireau, Monique Niemaszyk, thank you for taking time to help us through the editing and proofreading stages, and for all the support you have given to this work from the beginning.

Morgan Anding, Jacob Butek, Joseph and David Couture, April and Danielle Mireau, Daniel and Maria Zimmer, Matthew LeBlanc, Lynne Niemaszyk, and Kelly Redl, thank you for taking time to read *Surrender* in manuscript. The insights and feedback from your youthful perspectives were a great help to me.

Sr. Chantelle Bonk and all the Sisters of the Presentation of Mary, you have given a profound witness to me of the beauty of religious life. Thank you for sharing your stories with me and for allowing me to turn to you for advice and special insights.

Myles and Loren MacLennan, thank you for believing in the value of this work and for all the support you have given to allow us to continue to dedicate our lives to building the Kingdom in this way.

Mark and Léa Mallett, thank you for the way you have witnessed to us in your lives dedicated to building the Kingdom of God here on earth. Your ministry, friendship, and support have blessed us over and over again!

Shawna Kunz, it is a privilege to be able to work with you, a talented graphic designer and a beautiful Christian woman. Blessings on your beautiful family!

Stephanie Wood, thank you for your encouragement and enthusiasm for this work, and for all you do through your ministry, *NextWave Faithful*. Your life is a beautiful witness to Christian purity.

Ken Yasinski, thank you for *Face to Face Ministries* which has blessed our family many times over. You are an inspiration to many!

Del and Anne Marie Arens, Michael and Colleen Arsenault, Kevin and Annette Bentler, John and Elaine Boskill, Kevin and Fran Butek, Rick and Donna Dupuis, Mike and Theresa Fitzgerald, Willy and Chris Gaudet, Don and Gayle Jean, Gerald and Sandra Jean, Gerry and Kathy Katrick, David and Terrie Kostur, Kevin and Debbie Kowalski, André and Carolyn LeBlanc, Jeanne Manson, Irene Michaud, Claude and Annette Mireau, Gerald and Denise Monpetit, Loring and Angie Neufeldt, Mark and Monique Niemaszyk, Joseph and Virginia Onyilagha, Gary and MaryEllen Redl, Brian and Bobbi Sosic, Tim and Paulette Wilson, Mel and Cheryl Zimmer, and many others—too many to name—thank you for the numerous ways in which you and your families have encouraged and supported our family in the work we are now doing through this ministry.

Sr. Loretta McDonnell of the Sisters of St. Joseph, Sr. Juliana Heisler of the Sisters of Sion, and Srs. Georgina, Marie, and Delores of Les Filles de la Providence, thank you for being such wonderful examples in my life of the beauty of religious life and for supporting this ministry and sustaining it in your prayers.

To my brothers and sisters, Mary Couture, Gerry and Janet Couture, Louise and Bernie Smyth, James and Elizabeth Couture, Ed and Jackie Couture, and Albert Couture, thank you again for all the support you have given to this work in countless ways. You and your families are all a great source of blessing and inspiration in my life.

To my husband's family, Heather Marcoux, Val Marcoux, Sharon and Brian Harvey, Gerard Marcoux, Rob and Deb Marcoux, and all your children ... and now grandchildren, thank you for the many blessings you have brought into our lives.

Special Dedication:

Again, I pay special honour to the memory of two of the biggest heroes in my life: my dad, Gerald Couture, and my father-in-law, Vernon Marcoux. I thank God each day for blessing me to have been formed and nurtured in your love! Pray for us, as we pray for you!

From the bottom of my heart:

To my husband and best friend, Jim, thank you for giving up so much to dedicate your life to this ministry. Thank you for sharing with me in this vision. It has not been easy, but there is no one else with whom I would rather walk this path. Your love supports me daily and gives me a reason to continue following this call. Thank you for helping me in becoming the woman God created me to be and for loving me when I so often fall short of the call. I love you and cherish the gift you are to me.

To our children, the living sign of our love and the blessing of God in our marriage covenant, Hannah, Rebekah, Mikaelah, Jacinta, Matthew, Gemma, Benjamin, and Jacob, you have sacrificed so much to allow our family to work full-time in this ministry. May those sacrifices bear much fruit in the lives of all those who read these books. You continue to be my greatest inspiration for writing! I love you beyond what words could ever express and draw strength from your love for me each day!

To our three babies who have gone to be with the Lord, James, Thérèse, and Jude, thank you for your prayers for us from heaven. Thank you for reminding us that we are only here for a short time . . . we all belong to Him and our hearts will find rest in Him alone. We look forward to getting to know each of you in eternity. Please continue to pray us along our journey to join you forever with Him!

ᘓ

To Jesus Christ,
may all glory and honour be Yours
as we surrender our lives each day
to You and to Your Holy Will!

ᘔ

We pray for our readers daily. Thank you to all our readers who hold
Carmen, her family, and this ministry in your prayers.

Back Row: Carmen holding Gemma, Matthew, James holding Benjamin
Front Row: Mikaelah, Rebekah holding Jacob, Jacinta, Hannah

Carmen Marcoux

. . . is a prairie girl, born and raised in Saskatoon, Canada, the sixth child from a family of seven. She received her B.Ed. from the University of Saskatchewan. Carmen and her husband, Jim, have eight children whom they home-school. They are actively involved in their parish community at Our Lady of Lourdes where Carmen has a particular interest in youth and music ministries.

Surrender is Carmen's second novel, a sequel to *Arms of Love*. This story has been growing in Carmen's heart since before *Arms of Love* ever went to print. Over four years of ministry have gone into fully shaping this story. There yet remain stories unwritten that will hopefully someday become a part of this series. It has been a great privilege for Carmen to see how the Holy Spirit has used these works to inspire readers of all ages in purity, faith, hope, and love.

Carmen's family began and continues this ministry because they were inspired by Pope John Paul II's call to the New Evangelization. Fiction has proven itself to be a wonderful means to evangelize. As stated in Carmen's biography from *Arms of Love:* There are all too many examples of lifestyles that go against Gospel values and the Church's teachings. There is a need to have heroes in our lives, fictional and real, who model what it means to be fully Christian in this day and age. Many people are out there trying to live according to God's laws. They are as real as you, and they are transforming our society—one heart at a time.

We would love to hear from you. Please e-mail us at:
readerfeedback@courtshipnow.com

Since *Arms of Love* first came to print in 2002
Carmen has begun speaking at rallies and conferences promoting

Purity, Chastity & Courtship

"The most beautiful thing I have experienced, since beginning this ministry, is seeing the enthusiasm with which young people are embracing the message of purity. It is an honour to be a 'herald of hope' in our world. I thank God for having blessed me with this opportunity to proclaim His Good News to a world that is dying to hear it."

~ *Carmen Marcoux (April 2004)* ~

Carmen is available for a limited number of speaking engagements each year.

To book Carmen to come speak at an event or to purchase copies of her talks, call 1-800-705-7396.

Also available is Carmen's brochure ***"Twenty Tips for Christian Courtship".***

Have Carmen's novels, Arms of Love and Surrender, made a difference in your life?

We are a family of ten. We have dedicated our livelihood to working towards building a Civilization of Love through Catholic fiction. Through this work thousands of lives have been touched and changed: young and old, men and women alike! In order to continue bringing this much-needed message of purity, faith, hope, and love to our world we need your support, both in prayer and financially.

If *Arms of Love* or *Surrender* have made a difference in your life, please consider making a donation to help this ministry continue. We can not do it alone! This is a full-time ministry; however, we do not have charitable status and thus are not able to provide you with a tax receipt. We pray that God will bless you abundantly for your generosity!

To make a donation
Please visit our website **www.courtshipnow.com**
Or call us at **1-800-705-7396.**

Or send it to us by mail to:
**One Way Publishing House
Site 500 Box 17 RR5
Saskatoon, SK. CANADA
S7K 3J8**

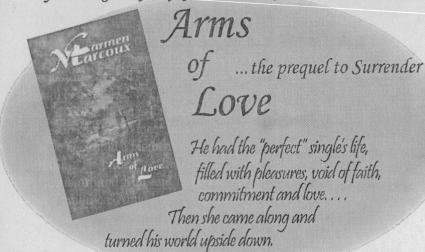